THE
COLUMBIA COMPANION
TO THE
TWENTIETH-CENTURY
AMERICAN SHORT STORY

THE
COLUMBIA COMPANION
TO THE
TWENTIETH-CENTURY
AMERICAN SHORT STORY

Blanche H. Gelfant, Editor
Lawrence Graver, Assistant Editor

columbia university press
new york

Columbia University Press
Publishers Since 1893
New York   Chichester, West Sussex
Copyright © 2000 Columbia University Press
All rights reserved

Library of Congress Cataloging-in-Publication Data
The Columbia companion to the twentieth-
century American short story / Blanche H.
Gelfant, editor.

   p. cm.
  Includes bibliographical references and
index.
   ISBN 0−231−11098−7 (cloth : alk.
paper)
     1. Short stories, American—
Dictionaries.   2. American fiction—20th
century—Dictionaries.   3. Short stories,
American—Bio-bibliography—Dictionaries.
4. American fiction—20th century—Bio-
bibliography—Dictionaries.   5. Authors,
American—20th century—Biography—
Dictionaries.   I. Title: Columbia
companion to the 20th century American
short story.   II. Gelfant, Blanche H.,
1922−

PS374.S5 C57 2001
831'.010905—dc21   00−031610
Casebound editions of Columbia University
Press books are printed on permanent and
durable acid-free paper.

Designed by Chang Jae Lee

Printed in the United States of America
c 10 9 8 7 6 5 4 3 2 1

CONTENTS

PART II. *Individual Writers
and Their Work*

CONTRIBUTORS

Kerry Ahearn
Oregon State University

Dale M. Bauer
University of Kentucky

Jonathan Baumbach
Brooklyn College

Robert Bell
Williams College

Lauren Berlant
University of Chicago

Erik Bledsoe
University of Tennessee

Kasia Boddy
University College, London

Jane Bradley
University of Toledo

Leonor Briscoe
Burke, Virginia

Suzanne Hunter Brown
Dartmouth College

Emily Budick
Hebrew University of Jerusalem

John Burt
Brandeis University

Robert Caserio
Temple University

Maria Elena Cepeda
University of Michigan

Nancy Cook
University of Rhode Island

Robert Corber
Trinity College

John Crawford
University of New Mexico

Elizabeth Cummins
University of Missouri

Morris Dickstein
City University of New York

Arthur Edelstein
Radcliffe Institute for Advanced Study

Stephen E. Fix
Williams College

Edward Foster
Stevens Institute of Technology

Robert Fox
Columbus, Ohio

Rhonda Frederick
Boston College

Andrew Furman
Florida Atlantic University

Fred Gardaphe
State University of New York at Stony Brook

Blanche H. Gelfant
Hanover, New Hampshire

Melody Graulich
Utah State University

Lawrence Graver
Williams College

Joan Wylie Hall
University of Mississippi

James Hannah
Texas A&M University

Donna Akiba Sullivan Harper
Decatur, Georgia

Tobey Herzog
Wabash College

Eric Heyne
University of Alaska, Fairbanks

Allen Hibbard
Middle Tennessee State University

Molly Hite
Cornell University

Greg Johnson
Kennesaw State University

Carla Kaplan
University of Southern California

Alice Kessler-Harris
Columbia University

Michelle Latiolais
University of California, Irvine

Luis Leal
University of California, Santa Barbara

Shirley Geok-lin Lim
University of California, Santa Barbara

Amy Ling
University of Wisconsin

Glen Love
University of Oregon

Wendy Martin
Claremont Graduate University

Peter Mascuch
University of New Hampshire

Charlotte S. McClure
Atlanta, Georgia

Lee Mitchell
Princeton University

David Mogen
Colorado State University

John Murphy
Brigham Young University

James Nagel
University of Georgia

Jay Parini
Middlebury College

Richard Pearce
Wheaton College

Sanford Pinsker
Franklin and Marshall University

Donald Pizer
Tulane University

Horace Porter
University of Iowa

Ruth Prigozy
Hofstra University

Janet R. Raiffa
New York, New York

Josna Rege
Dartmouth College

Russell Reising
University of Toledo

Gary Richards
University of New Orleans

Julie Rivkin
Connecticut College

Deborah Rosenfelt
University of Maryland

James Ruppert
University of Alaska, Fairbanks

Roshni Rustomji-Kerns
Stanford University

Elaine Safer
University of Delaware

Ramon Saldívar
Stanford University

Geoffrey Sanborn
Williams College

Gary Scharnhorst
University of New Mexico

John Seelye
University of Florida

Sofia Shafquat
Encinitas, California

Mark Shechner
State University of New York at Buffalo

Karen Shepard
Williams College

Ben Siegel
California State Polytechnic University

David L. Smith
Williams College

Larry Smith
Firelands College of Bowling Green State
  University

Werner Sollors
Harvard University

Silvia Spitta
Dartmouth College

Phillip Stambovsky
New Haven, Connecticut

David Stouck
Simon Fraser University

Rodger L. Tarr
Illinois State University

James Warren
Columbia University Press

Dennis Washburn
Dartmouth College

Barry Weller
University of Utah

Max Westbrook
University of Texas, Austin

Kenny Williams
Duke University

Mary Ann Wilson
University of Louisiana at Lafayette

Norma C. Wilson
University of South Dakota

Mary Ann Wimsatt
University of South Carolina

Dede Yow
Kennesaw State University

Zhou Xiaojing
State University of New York at Buffalo

THE
COLUMBIA COMPANION
TO THE
TWENTIETH-CENTURY
AMERICAN SHORT STORY

INTRODUCTION

A story can . . . open us up,
by cut or caress, to a new truth.
—Andre Dubus—

Designated a *companion* to the twentieth-century American short story, this collection of essays is both an accessory to the stories and writers it presents and a guide. As accessory or aide, it accompanies the stories, providing information about their writers' lives and literary achievements. As a guide, it points out literary paths taken by American writers whose works are admired throughout the world. By necessity, it has left many roads untraveled. Readers may wish that the *Columbia Companion* could have pursued these paths, some of them paved recently by best-selling young storytellers such as Nathan Englander and Melissa Bank, whose work appeared after this book went to press, as did the prize-winning stories of Barbara Mujica and Judy Doenges. Their absence and that of certain older, established writers argues for a sequel to *The Columbia Companion to the Twentieth-Century American Short Story,* a project perhaps for the twenty-first century.

Each of the essays is self-contained and can be read singly or in any sequence. However, if read chronologically, according to the writers' dates, the collected essays trace a history of the short story's development from the beginning of the century to the present, from Jack London and O. Henry to Andre Dubus, Joy Williams, Tobias Wolff, Deborah Eisenberg, David Leavitt, Lydia Davis, Nicholasa Mohr, Américo Paredes, and a dazzling diversity of others. Two sets of essays suggest this diversity: thematic essays that group together stories sharing a particular motif, cultural identity, or literary practice; and biographical essays, the body of the book, that focus on individual writers and their work. Writers mentioned in the thematic essays—Langston Hughes, Bernard Malamud, or Sandra Cisneros, for instance—may reappear in a biographical essay. Thus they are both contextualized and particularized, placed within a literary group and presented as unique artists.

All of the essays are designed to inform—to tell of a treasury of stories that evoke the multifariousness of American life by their variety and, by their brevity, suggest the fragmentation of the modern experiences they mirror. Offering practical criticism rather than theory, the *Columbia Companion* suggests ways of reading for understanding and pleasure. Thus it bypasses the vexed questions argued by short story theorists, the most argued of which is the most fundamental—that of definition. What, in essence, is the short story as a literary genre? What element distinguishes it from other narrative forms? Is it brevity (an arguable relative term), or any of the particular features favored by particular theorists, notably, unity of impression (posited by Edgar Allan Poe and now disputed); closure (absent in open-ended stories); dramatic conflict (missing in plotless stories); metaphysical substructures (underlying apparently realistic stories); or a "lonely voice" (heard by the Irish writer Frank O'Connor)? Is it appropriate, aesthetically and politically valid, to designate stories as American? What makes a story *American*? A sense of place, evoked by the writer's national origin or the story's

physical setting or locale; a sense of history, conveyed by a story's social themes or by a language and style traceable, through their colloquial intonations, to the oral traditions of American tall tales (and of storytelling generally)? Or is a story American because it dramatizes some aspect of a hypostasized American character?

American, short, story—these designating terms have become increasingly contentious, debated as literary and political issues. But central as terminological questions may be to critical theory, they are for the most part peripheral to the *Columbia Companion*'s essays, which assume that the texts they discuss are short stories, commonly regarded as such and quickly distinguished from anecdotes, sketches, fables, myths, parables, or any other short prose narrative. Readers at all levels of sophistication readily recognize a story and respond to it accordingly, though the genre is unnervingly fickle in its form. For American stories (like those of all lands) are realistic, romantic, modernistic, minimalistic, fantastical, mundane, parodic, gothic, comic, tragic, satirical, grotesque. They have a plasticity and thematic span that make reading them a wondrous surprise. By focusing on the act of reading, the *Columbia Companion* hopes to evoke expectations of the unexpected, of surprises that may be mixed with pleasure, poignancy, and the enrichment or loss that comes with wisdom.

For some readers, the essays will be introductory, a handbook that, like a good companion, guides them to a protean literary genre possessed with the power to enlarge their social and aesthetic vision. For literary critics (as opposed to general readers), the collection is a reference to consult, one that can remind them of stories they may have forgotten and acquaint them with new and boldly harrowing tales of contemporary life. The modernity of these tales—their mixed modes and sadly savvy sense of alienation—filiates from great twentieth-century storytellers to whom many American writers declare themselves indebted. Among the European masters frequently cited are Chekhov and Joyce; among South Americans, the exponent of magical realism, García Márquez. At the same time, modern writers acknowledge the influence of nineteenth-century storytellers who brought to American fiction the landscape and language of a new nation that was discovering, in Poe, Hawthorne, Melville, and James, its own ghosts, and in Mark Twain and Bret Harte, its own humor and colloquialisms. These and other writers—Irving, Crane, Chesnutt, Freeman, Jewett—are discussed in an introductory essay that gives a synoptic account of nineteenth-century American stories.

The essays that follow this account show how stories can be mixed and matched, commonly by class (working-class stories), gender (gay and lesbian stories), and ethnicity (African American, Asian American, Native American, Latino/a stories). Four essays suggest other ways of categorizing stories. Two deal with dire motifs: "The Ecological Short Story" with an imperiled environment, and "American Short Stories of the Holocaust" with the traumatizing memories of characters living in America. A third essay discusses short story sequences, collections of linked stories that can be read independently and as part of a continuous narrative, such famous works as *Winesburg, Ohio, In Our Time,* and, in recent times, John Updike's *Olinger Stories* and Gloria Naylor's *The Women of Brewster Place.* Last, a resourceful essay describes a wide range of stories critics consider American though they are written in languages other than English. Ways of grouping stories are indeed illimitable, as anthologists of short stories have discovered. Their collections display the virtuosity of story writers who can dramatize what seems the same human relationship or the same locale in strikingly different ways.

These differences emerge in the essays on individual writers, which by their number (a hundred and thirteen) turn the *Columbia Companion* into an elaborate do-it-yourself kit packed with literary material that can be ingeniously combined. A reader interested in regionalism, a subject critics are now rethinking, will find, for instance, a variety of writers focused on the American West, among them such well-known figures as Willa Cather, John Steinbeck, Walter Van Tilburg Clark, Thomas McGuane, and Wallace Stegner. The South has long been renowned for its storytellers, a large and multifarious group of writers who have influenced each other and the world's vision of the South as a place distinctive in its history, manners, and speech, and yet undeniably American in ways that sometimes seem ineffable. Like many of the writers in this volume, certain southern storytellers are famous throughout the world for novels—notably, of course, William Faulkner. The world-famous southern playwright Tennessee Williams has also written remarkable short stories, which an essay brings to the reader's attention.

Other essays throughout the book alert readers to themes being explored by contemporary women writers, such as the relationship between a mother and daughter, which in Lorrie Moore's stories is fixed by prescripted roles that neither character can escape.

Like the thematically determined essays, each of the hundred and more essays on individual story writers is distinctive, shaped in form and content by the critic who wrote it. However, all contain a brief biographical sketch, an overview of the writer's career and major motifs, an analysis of some representative stories, and a selected bibliography. Essay writers followed the general guidelines they were given in their own ways, some telling more, others less, about a writer's life. Each determined which stories and how many to choose for an exemplary reading. All present their material in clear, accessible language, though their voices vary. I am gratefully aware that the contributors have made this collection possible. They were generous with their time and literary insights, gracious in their response to editorial suggestions. As critics, writers, and professors, they were busy and committed, and yet they would willingly revamp a completed essay to include a writer's newly published, and often most acclaimed, book of stories. Their advice helped shape the *Columbia Companion* as they suggested story writers who should be noted and recommended colleagues who could, and did, write essays that enhance the collection. Unfortunately, and perhaps inevitably, two contributors found they could not complete the essays they had been promising, and so the book lacks entries for Alice Walker, Toni Cade

Bambara, and Isaac Bashevis Singer. I regret these omissions (as well as others) caused by the wayward circumstances that will beset any project.

As the *Columbia Companion*'s literary editor, I have been a kind of accessory after the fact, someone who helped bring to realization a project conceived by the executive editor for reference books of Columbia University Press, James Warren. In an unexpected telephone call, he asked me to serve as literary editor of the *Columbia Companion,* and so began a long and close relationship based on a shared desire to do well by the book. I am grateful to James Warren for all kinds of support along the way, and particularly for heeding my plea for help after I had been working long and relentlessly as sole editor. No one could have given help more graciously than Lawrence Graver, who agreed to edit a number of essays and did so with a good cheer that I found wonderfully infectious. He and I worked together on several pieces, and perhaps compulsively, I added my editorial two cents to comments he made on the essays he reviewed. Professor Graver also contributed splendid critiques of Raymond Carver, Stanley Elkin, and John Updike.

In the early stages of planning, as I was reading hundreds and hundreds of short stories—a happy windfall of this project—I had help in assembling the table of contents from friends and colleagues. One of the most steadfast of friends, the young writer Michael Lowenthal, sent long lists of authors to consider, starring those he thought must be in the volume (as they are) and suggesting topics for the introductory thematic essays. Two contributors, Werner Sollors and Amy Ling, were helpful consultants early on; they also sent lists of writers and recommended critics whom I might contact. Unhappily, Professor Ling did not live to see this publication or to receive her readers' thanks for the critiques of Asian American literature that are her scholarly legacy.

I will not attempt to name the contributors who became e-mail pals over the past years. Their airborne friendship was an unexpected reward of editing, a task I had long bypassed in favor of teaching and writing. Over the years, I found myself writing about various American storytellers whose work enthralled and sometimes dismayed me (all of them are in this volume), and my impulse to tell of stories I love is still strong. It is a common impulse, expressed in an often-heard imperative: "You must read this story." Perhaps sharing a story means sharing a newly perceived truth, as the writer Andre Dubus observed. A "story can . . . open us up, by cut or caress, to a new truth," Dubus wrote in an essay on Hemingway's famous story "In Our Time" (*Meditations*). The caress of a story, I believe, is experienced as aesthetic pleasure, the sheer delight evoked in a reader by an indelible work of art. A lifelong appreciation of the story's art as well as of its truths has guided me as literary editor of *The Columbia Companion to the Twentieth-Century American Short Story,* a book indebted to many people and dedicated to many—teachers, students, literary critics, theorists, and the reader at large, who, like me, like most of us, loves a good story.

Blanche H. Gelfant

SELECTED BIBLIOGRAPHY

Allen, Walter. *The Short Story in English.* New York: Oxford University Press, 1981.

Dubus, Andre. "A Hemingway Story." *Meditations From a Moveable Chair.* New York: Alfred A. Knopf, 1998.

Litz, A. Walton, ed. *Major American Short Stories.* Third edition. New York: Oxford University Press, 1994.

Lohafer, Susan, and Jo Ellyn Clarey, eds. *Short Story Theory at a Crossroads.* Baton Rouge: Louisiana University Press, 1989.

Magill, Frank N., ed. *Critical Survey of Short Fiction.* Englewood Cliffs, N.J.: Salem Press, 1981.

May, Charles E., ed. *Short Story Theories.* Athens: Ohio University Press, 1976.

O'Connor, Frank. *The Lonely Voice: A Study of the Short Story.* Cleveland: World Publishing, 1963.

Peden, William. *The American Short Story: Front Line in the National Defense of Literature.* Boston: Houghton Mifflin, 1964.

Williford, Lex, and Michael Martoni, eds. *The Scribner Anthology of Contemporary Short Fiction.* New York: Simon & Schuster, 1999.

PART I

Thematic Essays

THE AMERICAN
SHORT STORY CYCLE

The short story cycle is one of the most important forms of fiction in twentieth-century American literature. Although it has gone largely unrecognized as a genre distinct from the more highly organized "novel" and from the loose "collection" of stories, it has played an important role in literary history. A form centuries older than the novel, collections of unrelated narratives reach back to antiquity, to the Greek "cyclic" poets whose verse supplemented Homer's epics of the Trojan war, and to such landmark literary achievements as *The Odyssey,* Boccaccio's *Decameron,* Chaucer's *Canterbury Tales,* and John Gower's *Confessio Amantis.* Many of the significant medieval plays were produced in dramatic "cycles," each work serving as an independent entity while at the same time gaining in significance from the matrix of relationships with the dramas on either side of it. With the historical development of the concept of "fiction" and the ensuing establishment of periodical literature, the tradition of short stories produced in collections of linked episodes ultimately evolved. The convention of the form was that each element be sufficiently complete for independent publication and yet serve as part of a volume unified by a continuing setting, or ongoing characters, or developing themes, or coalescent patterns of imagery. In English literature, James Joyce's *Dubliners* has served as an archetype of the genre, a role fulfilled in the United States by Sherwood Anderson's *Winesburg, Ohio.*

In American literature, the genre emerged in the early nineteenth century in the form of related sketches and tales, beginning with Washington Irving's *Sketch Book* in 1820, unified by setting and regional character types. Nathaniel Hawthorne gave the form greater sophistication in his "Legends of the Province House," published as part of *Twice-Told Tales* (1851), as did Herman Melville in the *Piazza Tales* (1856). As brief fiction evolved into the more realistic "story" after the Civil War, the genre became increasingly popular, finding expression by writers of both genders and a broad spectrum of ethnic groups. Harriet Beecher Stowe dealt with "Downeast" characters and speech in *Sam Lawson's Oldtown Fireside Stories* (1871), and George Washington Cable depicted the South in *Old Creole Days* (1879), as did Kate Chopin in *Bayou Folk* (1894). Hamlin Garland dealt with economic and social injustice in the upper Midwest in his *Main Travelled Roads* (1891), one of the landmarks of American naturalism, and Margaret Deland explored themes of small town life in Pennsylvania in *Old Chester Tales* (1898). By the turn of the century, nearly a hundred volumes of interrelated short stories had been published in America, and the form was yet to find its most significant expression.

The short story cycle in twentieth-century American literature is decidedly a multiethnic tradition, perhaps because the brief narrative has its origins in the oral tradition and descends through cultures in every part of the world, uniting them in a legacy of universal storytelling. The evolution of the form would naturally take place with the telling of tales related to those told before, perhaps by other speakers. The formal "novel," as an extended narrative with a dominant protagonist and a central plot that extends from beginning to end, is not as universal an expression as is a series of stories linked to each other with continuing elements, whether ongoing characters, places, or situations. As the tradition evolved, often the stories would be told by a community of tellers weaving a pattern of related episodes involving a group of actors, each a brief tale having its own resolution. Scores of volumes of narrative cycles appeared in each decade of the new century, some of them containing individual stories that are among the best ever published in English, among them William Faulkner's "The Bear," which appeared as part of *Go Down, Moses*.

In the early decades of the century, for example, Susie King Taylor's *Reminiscences of My Life: A Black Woman's Civil War Memories* (1902) contributed an African American perspective on the most momentous event of the previous century. In *Friendship Village* (1908), Zona Gale perpetuated the emphasis on regional depictions, using her native Wisconsin. Sui Sin Far's *Mrs. Spring Fragrance* (1912), assembled from stories she had begun publishing in the 1890s, was the first important Asian American work of fiction. In a series of episodes linked by continuing characters and themes, and set in either San Francisco or Seattle, she was able to explore the complex psychology of cultural dualism and the process of social assimilation for Chinese immigrants. Zitkala-Sa served something of the same function in her *American Indian Stories* (1921), writing out of her Lakota background.

From this period, however, it is Sherwood Anderson's *Winesburg, Ohio* (1919) that attracted sustained attention and recognition. This volume of twenty-five stories, all set in a mythical midwestern town, further developed the traditional theme of the "village virus," depicting submerged lives, sexual frustration, and thwarted hopes and aspirations. Unified by a continuing narrative voice, by the setting, and by coalescent motifs, these stories also feature a dominant central character, George Willard, whose quest for self-realization and maturity creates a primary line of development for the volume, a strategy used successfully in such volumes as Ernest Hemingway's *In Our Time* (1925), John Steinbeck's *The Red Pony* (1937), and William Faulkner's *Go Down, Moses* (1942). Hemingway used not only the continuing character of Nick Adams, who progresses from adolescence to adulthood in the course of thirty-two narrative units, but also the unifying motif of the desire for "peace in our time" in a world of violence, war, cruelty, and disillusionment. Steinbeck used a similar technique to trace the development of a young boy, Jody, growing up on a ranch in California and learning about the realities of life and death. Faulkner's volume is unified by family relationships, the central characters all being descendants of Carothers McCaslin. As the title would indicate, a continuing theme is the fate of African American characters in the period after the Civil War. In "The Bear," a young white boy, Ike McCaslin, grows to moral maturity under the guidance of an older man of color, and, in the end, Ike relinquishes an inheritance of wealth built in an era of slavery, severing his ties to a legacy of cruelty and injustice.

In the period between the two wars, the short story cycle gained increased visibility and stature. John Steinbeck's *The Pastures of Heaven* (1932) is a key book, portraying the plight of families living in a mythical valley in California while developing the naturalistic themes that would inform his greatest work, *The Grapes of Wrath*. Steinbeck used a similar organizational strategy for his stories about an Italian neighborhood in Monterey in *Tortilla Flat* (1935). This period produced many important volumes of interrelated stories, among them Mourning Dove's *Coyote Stories* (1933), Caroline Gordon's *Aleck Maury, Sportsman* (1934), Zora Neale Hurston's *Mules and Men* (1935), and Djuna Barnes's *Nightwood* (1936), illustrating the cross-cultural appeal of the genre. Richard Wright's *Uncle Tom's Children* (1938), unified by themes of white oppression of black families, and William Faulkner's *The Unvanquished* (1938), held together by a continuing protagonist, Bayard Sartoris, were indicative of the range of the genre.

The next two decades brought the further enrichment of the tradition in the appearance of such volumes as Erskine Caldwell's *Georgia Boy* (1943), Edmund Wilson's *Memoirs of Hecate County* (1959), and, most notably, Eudora Welty's *The Golden Apples* (1947), a brilliant series of stories set around Morgana, Mississippi, in the period from 1900 to roughly 1940. As the title would suggest, all of the stories in some way relate to the themes of longing and searching in W. B. Yeats's celebrated poem "The Song of Wandering Aengus." Peter Taylor's *The Widows of Thornton* (1954) featured eight stories and one play dealing with family relations in a small southern town. In *Brown Girl, Brownstones* (1959), Paula Marshall presented a sequence of remarkable stories set in Brooklyn about an immigrant family from Barbados.

In *Going to Meet the Man* (1965), James Baldwin presented eight stories featuring progressively older black men in the midst of dramatic social transitions. Writing in a more metafictional mode, John Barth offered fourteen stories about the process of composition in *Lost in the Funhouse* (1968). Maxine Hong Kingston's *The Woman Warrior* (1976), a widely celebrated book most often regarded as a "novel," is, in fact, five long narratives based on Chinese mythology. That year, in *Speedboat*, Renata Adler told several stories about a journalist in New York, a book that, rather ironically, won the Ernest Hemingway Award for the best first "novel" of the year. Russell Banks's *Trailerpark* (1981) was tightly unified in that it presented thirteen stories about people living in mobile homes in New Hampshire, many of whom interact in the course of this book.

In the last two decades of the twentieth century, the short story cycle has become an even more prominent genre, with much of the very best fiction produced in America, written from a variety of ethnic perspectives, appearing in that form. The number of minority writers choosing to write story cycles rather than novels might suggest that such authors live in an environment in which the tradition of the "story," with its long history deriving from the oral tradition, is a more familiar and natural expressive form than the "novel," decidedly a written medium of European origin. In a contemporary world charac-

terized by progressive fragmentation and alienation, an episodic mode better reflects the psychic nature of modern life than would the extended flow of experience represented in long fiction. It would seem also that the changing nature of the literary market, with publishing houses eager for blockbuster novels, makes it easier for writers to establish themselves by writing stories for magazines and assembling them later to form cycles. Whatever the reason, the cycle has become increasingly vibrant in recent years as a fiction mode for writers of all ethnic traditions.

For example, Gloria Naylor won the American Book Award for *The Women of Brewster Place* (1982), a volume of seven stories set in an African American community. Louise Erdrich, writing from a Native American perspective, won the National Book Award in 1984 for *Love Medicine*. The *New York Times* called it one of the eleven best books of the year and, within a remarkably short period, it was in print in ten languages. This series of fourteen stories told the complex multigenerational story of three families living in what remains of their traditional culture while trying to find their place in white society. Sandra Cisneros used the form for her portrayal of Latino society in Chicago in *The House on Mango Street* (1984), which won the Before Columbus American Book Award for 1985. In a series of forty-four compressed vignettes, Cisneros sketched the life of Esperanza Cordero, a young Mexican American girl whose family has recently moved into a disappointing new house in a rough neighborhood. Jamaica Kincaid's *Annie John* (1985) is a classic cycle comprising eight stories, all previously published in *The New Yorker,* recording a young girl's painful but exciting development from age ten to seventeen, tracing her fight for independence from her mother and her quest to find a place in the world for herself, which prompts her to leave home forever.

In *Seventeen Syllables* (1985), Hisaye Yamamoto used the form to tell stories about Japanese American experience, particularly that in the internment camps during World War II. Louise Erdrich again used the genre in *The Beet Queen* (1986), forging an overarching narrative out of independent stories about a Native American family. In *The Last of the Menu Girls* (1986), Denise Chavez linked together seven stories of Chicano life centered on the maturation of a young woman, Rocio. Perhaps the most celebrated story cycle in the last decade is Amy Tan's *The Joy Luck Club* (1989), a best-seller in hardcover and paperback that was quickly made into a major motion picture. In a highly structured group of sixteen stories, divided precisely into four groups of four, with alternating sets of tales told by mothers and daughters, Tan traces the immigration of four Chinese women into the United States and their attempt to inspire their daughters to sustain an interest in their native culture.

But it is not only minority writers who have found the cycle format an appropriate medium. John Updike, for example, has published several volumes of interrelated stories, beginning with *Olinger Stories* (1964), works that trace the development of a local country boy. *Too Far to Go: The Maple Stories* (1979) records the

marriage, separation, and divorce of a suburban couple. The three volumes of stories about Henry Bech, *Bech: A Book* (1970), *Bech Is Back* (1982), and *Bech at Bay: A Quasi Novel* (1998), focus on conflicts in the life of a cosmopolitan urban writer. Harriet Doerr's *Stones for Ibarra* (1984) is a stunning portrayal of life in a Mexican village as seen from the perspective of an American couple that has come to manage a silver mine. Told with sympathy and yet ironic humor, these stories constitute an ongoing narrative while at the same time resolving a central conflict in each episode. One of the finest books in recent decades, Susan Minot's *Monkeys* (1986) is a remarkable collection of nine minimalist stories depicting salient episodes in the lives of the Vincent family, particularly that of young Sophie. The cultural conflict in this volume is not interracial but that of social class: "Mum" derives from an inner-city Irish Catholic family, while "Dad" is from an established Yankee tradition with long ties to Harvard.

Tim O'Brien used the tradition of the story cycle for *The Things They Carried* (1990), a searing portrayal of the moral and psychological burdens carried by young men in the military during the Vietnam War. *How the Garcia Girls Lost Their Accents* (1991) is a series of fifteen stories by Julia Alvarez about the life of a family from the Dominican Republic just before and after their immigration to the United States. Of particular emphasis are the theme of cultural duality and the process of social assimilation. Whitney Otto used the form for more "homely" matters in *How to Make an American Quilt* (1991), a series of seven stories about the members of a California quilting circle. Robert Olen Butler's *A Good Scent from a Strange Mountain* (1992) to some extent balances O'Brien's portrait of Americans in Southeast Asia by depicting the lives of Vietnamese in America after the conclusion of the war.

There are scores of other examples of the genre in modern American literature, but even these few examples demonstrate how important the short story cycle has become in contemporary fiction. It is a convention that needs to be recognized and understood not simply as ancillary to the more significant "novel" but as integral to literary history, with an ancient origin and a set of narrative and structural principles quite distinct from other fictional modes. That for the last century many of the most important works of this kind were written by authors from differing ethnic backgrounds suggests that despite its ancient history, the story sequence offers not only a rich literary legacy but also a vital technique for the exploration and depiction of the complex interactions of gender, ethnicity, and individual identity. It is an important genre, and it deserves to be defined and studied in terms of its vital and continuing contribution to twentieth-century American fiction.

James Nagel

SELECTED BIBLIOGRAPHY

Alvarez, Julia. *How the Garcia Girls Lost Their Accents.* Chapel Hill, N.C.: Algonquin Books, 1991.

Butler, Robert Olen. *A Good Scent from a Strange Mountain.* New York: Henry Holt, 1992.

Cisneros, Sandra. *The House on Mango Street.* New York: Alfred A. Knopf, 1994.

Crane, Stephen. *Whilomville Stories.* New York: Harper, 1900.

Dunbar-Nelson, Alice. *The Goodness of St. Rocque and Other Stories.* New York: Dodd, Mead, 1899.

Erdrich, Louise. *Love Medicine.* New York: Holt, Rinehart and Winston, 1984.

Garland, Hamlin. *Main-Travelled Roads.* Boston: Arena, 1891.

Hemingway, Ernest. *In Our Time.* New York: Scribners, 1925.

Ingram, Forrest L. *Representative Short Story Cycles of the Twentieth Century.* The Hague: Mouton, 1971.

Kennedy, J. Gerald. *Modern American Short Story Sequences.* New York: Cambridge University Press, 1995.

Kincaid, Jamaica. *Annie John.* New York: Farrar, Straus & Giroux, 1985.

Mann, Susan Garland. *The Short Story Cycle: A Genre Companion and Reference Guide.* Westport, Conn.: Greenwood, 1989.

Steinbeck, John. *The Pastures of Heaven.* New York: Viking, 1932.

THE AMERICAN SHORT STORY, 1807–1900

It is customary to suggest that the short story in America has its start in certain tales by Washington Irving, most famously "Rip Van Winkle" and "The Legend of Sleepy Hollow," published in *The Sketch Book* in 1820, stories with plots borrowed from German folktales but that became so thoroughly Americanized as to be thought of as native to our soil. However, a much earlier Irving story, "The Little Man in Black," has had an enduring influence. Included among the *Salmagundi* sketches in 1807, it established the "Mysterious Stranger" convention often associated with Mark Twain (because of the title of his never completed novel), a convention that continues to appear in the modern period, as Robert Penn Warren attests in an essay on his own "Blackberry Winter."

Even the stories of the man awakened to post–Revolutionary War America and the Yankee schoolteacher driven from a sleepy Hudson Valley town retain the essential frame of the "mysterious stranger" convention—which is that of the advent of an unknown and often unwelcome person who threatens the peace of a closed community. Exploiting the tension produced by the opposition of a minority to the wishes of the majority (early detected by de Tocqueville), the convention was particularly relevant to the United States during the rise of the short story, which occurred as that country made its slow and at times painful transition from federalism to Jeffersonian republicanism to Jacksonian democracy.

"Rip Van Winkle" was a parable apt in other ways to the United States in the 1820s, whose citizens at once took advantage of improvements in technology and yet expressed a deep uneasiness over the swiftness of the changes that inventions effected. Indeed, the short story itself, along with the steam-propelled riverboat and cotton gin (both of the last associated with the epochal year 1807, as were Irving's *Salmagundi* stories), was an American invention. The story's brevity was suited to a reader perpetually short of time, who desired the speed of communications and production that characterized the inventions of Fulton and Whitney.

Washington Irving, at least in his short fiction, was no friend to technological innovation. His sketches of life in the England of the 1820s seldom reflect the labor unrest of the day; instead, they create an antiquarian utopia into which the authorial persona, Geoffrey Crayon, retreats, finding a kind of sanctuary of Merry Olde England in the home of the eccentric master of Bracebridge Hall, modeled on Sir Walter Scott's Abbotsford. Nor were Irving's two chief heirs of the short story genre, Nathaniel Hawthorne and Edgar Allan Poe, particularly friendly to the age of improvements heralded by President John Quincy Adams and celebrated by the chief orator of the day, Daniel Webster. Though an active Democratic Party worker, Hawthorne at the start of his career avoided the present for the past, and sought to establish himself as a writer of what we now call gothic fiction. In imitation of European writers, he availed himself of the past as a zone sufficiently

unfamiliar as to permit a certain license with the observable facts of life—identified by him with the notion of "romance."

Hawthorne is supposed to have rifled the chronicles of the American colonial archives in quest of these materials, but by the early 1830s, when his stories first appeared, a number of writers had already established that period as a rich field for romantic fiction. Nonetheless, in the short story, Hawthorne's genius was unrivaled, and like Irving he wrote fables, such as "The Minister's Black Veil," "Young Goodman Brown," and "The Ambitious Guest," which through their popularity became virtual folktales. Also like Irving, he repeatedly returned to the theme of social alienation, which, in a Puritan setting—as in "The Gentle Boy"—took on the hard edge of persecution.

In contrast to Hawthorne, Poe did not evoke a historical setting for his stories, but despite his southern heritage, which was associated with the ongoing dispute over slavery, escaped the present controversy by inventing his own midregions of the imagination. His was a vaguely located but undoubtedly European scene, explicitly so in "The Pit and the Pendulum" and "The Cask of Amontillado," undeniably so in "The Fall of the House of Usher." Both writers were exotic in their geographies, but Hawthorne is commonly not thought of as such, perhaps because of his insistence on the historical validity of his often overwrought colonial scene. Certainly his insistence on deriving a moral lesson from his parables separates him in all respects from Poe, who is the most amoral of nineteenth-century writers, not only in America but in Europe as well, before the advent of the 1890s.

Of the two, it was Poe who continued to command a popular (as opposed to schoolroom) audience well into the twentieth century, this despite the attempts of his contemporaries to discount his work because of his personal life, the alcoholism and perhaps even opium addiction that resulted in his inability to hold the editorial positions that sustained him and his strange family, and that led to his early death. Hawthorne's personal and domestic life, by contrast, were solidly middle-class (following a youthful reclusive period associated with his literary apprenticeship), but his short fiction, being so morally constricted as to amount to virtual allegories, had greater difficulty in making the transition to the modern period. It is *The Scarlet Letter,* originally conceived as a short story, by which he is best known.

By 1853, Poe was dead and Hawthorne had turned from the short story set in the distant past to the novel with a modern setting, providing an opening that Herman Melville filled with a sudden explosion of talent. Famous today for his novelistic masterpiece, *Moby-Dick,* which failed to find a popular audience in his lifetime, Melville in the early 1850s reacted to that failure by seeking a wider readership and increased income. This effort first resulted in the misbegotten romance, *Pierre,* but then, unpredictably for an author who seemed perpetually to let his fictions run away with him, in a series of short stories that demonstrated an instant mastery of the highly compressed and stringent form. The first published was perhaps the greatest, "Bartleby, the Scrivener," yet another exercise in the mysterious stranger genre that tran-

scended the convention, so far ahead of the author's own times that it disappeared for a century, until it was resurrected late in the Melville revival. A contemporary witness has testified that in the Greenwich Village of the 1940s and 1950s, everyone had read and was talking about Melville's "Bartleby," shadows of which may be detected in the fiction of Saul Bellow from that time.

Of equal power was Melville's longer and less concentrated tale, "Benito Cereno," which also had to wait a century for recognition, a story that challenged both Hawthorne and Poe at their own gothic game and created a parable strongly anchored in the antislavery debate of the 1850s. So relevant did that story remain for people aroused by the civil rights struggle a century later that Robert Lowell dramatized it as part of his sequence *Old Glory.* "Bartleby," which appeals to modern writers because of its surreal qualities, also calls to mind the Transcendental revolt against materialism. Irving's pseudo folk-fables set in the Hudson Valley also reflected political concerns of his own day, "Sleepy Hollow," especially, with its Yankee-Yorker conflict.

Irving's influence was everywhere in the 1850s, from Melville's powerful parables to the dreamy romanticism of the sketches in Donald G. Mitchell's ("Ik. Marvell") *Reveries of a Bachelor* (1850), a favorite book of the young Emily Dickinson, to the pleasant purlieus of George W. Curtis's New York in *Prue and I* (1856). This last was a collection of connected sketches that notably featured a lassitudinous, even diaphanous young clerk who is advertised as Bartleby's friend, a connection that shows the great distance between the imaginations of these two contemporaries, Melville a contributor to, and Curtis a founding editor of, *Putnam's Magazine,* the most influential and well-paying periodical of its day.

From its inception, the American short story was connected to the rise of periodical literature in the United States, starting with the coterie journal *Salmagundi* and then expanding with much wider-circulating magazines, from *Harper's* to *Godey's* to *Graham's,* and including dozens of short-lived publications, many of which lasted a year or so before disappearing into debt. Poe, associated with both *Graham's* and the *Southern Literary Messenger,* spent his last years attempting to launch a magazine of his own, which undoubtedly would have suffered the fate of so many of his heroes (and himself)—a premature demise.

An alternative venue for the short story was the gift book, an annual collection of poetry and prose dressed out with engravings produced in time for the Christmas market in which a number of tales by Hawthorne and Poe first appeared. Unlike the magazines, the gift book was destined as a permanent fixture in the parlor, being relatively expensive and bound in gilt-embossed cloth or leather. Magazines were considered as ephemeral as the soft-paper wrappers in which they first appeared, although large numbers of the most popular survive in bound sets, confirming the hesitancy of Americans to dispose of something once they have bought it.

Short stories in periodicals in America seem to have been primarily written for readers on the run, so to speak, contrasting with the three-decker novels then in vogue, most of which were imported from

Great Britain, where the short story did not flourish until much later in the century, and then as an art form rather than as an item intended for popular consumption. In America, the production of short fiction from the 1830s on was vast, resulting in a kind of literary iceberg, the tip of which is represented by the work of Hawthorne, Poe, and Melville, while the bulk has remained below the surface. Even Longfellow early on tried his hand at short fiction, before settling for what proved to be for him the more profitable trade of poetry. Still, it was Longfellow's narrative poems that were the most successful, and *Evangeline* was derived from an anecdote first suggested to Hawthorne as the basis of a short story. The young Walt Whitman also ground out short fiction for the magazines, but he too opted for the long, if non-narrative, poem.

By the 1860s, a newer generation of writers began to appear, most of whose work is little known today. Edward Everett Hale, for example, wrote a considerable number of stories, but he is remembered solely for "The Man Without a Country," a patriotic tale inspired by the Civil War. It would be the local-color writers identified with the post–Civil War period who were to dominate the genre. Harriet Beecher Stowe, associated with the great novel in protest of slavery that brought her sudden fame in 1852, had begun her literary career ten years earlier with a collection of short pieces entitled *The Mayflower; or, Sketches of Scenes and Characters Among the Descendents of the Pilgrims* (1843). In *Sam Lawson's Oldtown Fireside Stories* (1872), Stowe produced a volume of New England tales that in terms of priority, if not actual influence, laid the foundation for much fiction about her native region that appeared subsequently.

Perhaps the most imitated short-story writer of the post–Civil War generation was Bret Harte, a New Yorker who followed the Gold Rush belatedly to California, where he became an editor and a positive influence on the emerging career of Mark Twain. Harte's tales with a Western setting, first collected in *The Luck of the Roaring Camp* (1870), would resonate down through the last third of the century and remain popular until his death. His mixture of rustic dialect, humorous situations, and sentimental conclusions managed to convince readers that such places as Angel's Camp actually existed, though they were for the most part an imaginative compound distilled from Dickens.

Harte too was indebted to Irving, his "Spanish" stories having been inspired by the older writer's tales of "Dutch" coloration, while his "The Right Eye of the Commander" resonates with Irving's conventions, including the mysterious stranger device. It is, however, Harte's sentimental stories of the Gold Rush frontier, like "The Luck of the Roaring Camp," in which the presence of the infant reformed a mining town, that made Harte famous. These stories are distinguished also by the original creation of an enduring American mythic type, the noble gambler, though the famous John Oakhurst, who figures memorably in Harte's "The Outcasts of Poker Flat," has in his personal sacrifice all the markings of Dickens's Sidney Carton.

If Harte was an innovator in the local-color convention, it must be allowed that his California (like Irving's Hudson Valley, Hawthorne's colonial Massachusetts, and Poe's mid-region of weird) was largely a territory of the postromantic imagination, a geographic anachronism validated by the grotesque stories of Ambrose Bierce. An Ohio-born journalist and Civil War veteran who migrated to California, Bierce inherited Poe's dark mantle, writing sardonic ghost tales with western settings and, most famously, surreal stories inspired by his wartime experience, such as "An Occurrence at Owl-Creek Bridge," notable for a trick ending that still brings readers up with a literal snap. Like Harte a voluminous but uneven writer, Bierce is best represented by his collection *Stories of Soldiers and Civilians* (1891).

Both Bierce and Harte were only superficially realistic in their fiction, while the regionalists associated with New England were most in tune with the emerging tradition of the 1870s and '80s. Realism as an ideology was chiefly associated in American literature with William Dean Howells and Mark Twain, neither of whom excelled in the art of the short story. George Washington Cable was famous in his day for his Creole tales, which drew upon the New Orleans backdrop and rendered skillfully the Cajun dialect, but for most American readers, his setting, like Harte's, was exotic.

Sarah Orne Jewett and Mary Wilkens Freeman made regionalism a serious dimension of literary realism, their stories of New England accurately and at times painfully rendering the minutiae of a region in decline. Jewett's "A White Heron," collected in a volume of stories of that title in 1886, is a masterpiece of the genre, a powerful fable playing off the attraction felt by a young girl for a handsome young hunter against the larger love she feels for the natural world. Freeman, in the story that gave its title to her *A New England Nun* (1891), frames a similar tension between the quiet life enjoyed by a spinster and its sudden and violent disruption by the return of the man to whom, during an absence of many years, she had been engaged. Of the two, however, Jewett's comparative genius must be emphasized. In *The Country of the Pointed Firs* (1896), Jewett wove together connected sketches that, by emphasizing a scene dominated by elderly or middle-aged folks, living in a seaport that had long since lost its economic basis in shipping, was ironically a shroud for the region she celebrated. Acknowledging the primacy of New England should not mean neglecting the work of Mary Noailles Murfree, who under the pen name Charles Egbert Craddock wrote dialect stories set in her native Tennessee mountains in the 1880s and 1890s, which lend a southern balance to the scales.

Women writers had long held considerable power in American literature, starting with Catharine Sedgwick and Lydia Maria Child in the 1820s. Sarah Josepha Hale had served as the influential editor of *Godey's Lady's Book,* a periodical that featured female authors, and Elizabeth Oakes Smith was a prolific writer of magazine fiction and a pioneer in the dime novel. The Warner sisters, Anna and Susan, emerged in the 1850s, as did Harriet Beecher Stowe. However, most of the significant women writers before the Civil War worked in the novel, not the short story; they were the "scribbling women"

of Hawthorne's notorious lament. Only in the forty years following Hawthorne's death did women become skilled in the shorter forms, at the same time as the best-known male writers (Howells and Twain, for instance) largely abandoned stories for novel-length prose. Rebecca Harding Davis's "Life in the Iron Mills" (1861), the savage social realism of which anticipates the naturalist writers of a later generation, and Charlotte Perkins Gilman's psychological study, "The Yellow Wallpaper" (1892), provide brackets that suggest both the range and supremacy of women writers during the last half of the nineteenth century.

A notable male story writer of the time was Henry James, whose masterful development as a novelist is matched, if not challenged, by his skill with short fiction. An expatriate for much of his creative life, strongly influenced by continental models, James wrote chiefly of transatlantic matters and used European settings in both his long and short fiction. Where his contemporaries in New England were skillful in working up portraits in which miniature touches made definitive outlines, James was less interested in physical detail than in psychological portraiture. "The Beast in the Jungle" is a study of a man so tormented by the fear of the consequences of action that he suffers a terrible fate because of his inaction, the unsuspected "beast" he has so long feared. Drawing on his own experience, James devoted many of his stories to the lives of artists and writers, as in "The Figure in the Carpet," stories with a complex weave and often tragic conclusions.

Though James looked to Hawthorne as

his American predecessor, he subsumed Hawthorne's gothicism and fantasy to a kind of inward grotesqueness, the impulses that led many of his characters into renunciatory and self-destructive gestures, as if possessed by Poe's Imp of the Perverse. Like other realists of his time, James was not interested in historical settings, though his European stories have qualities that would seem exotic to many American readers. A sojourner and a writer, James had access to areas forbidden to casual visitors and tourists in the Old World; his stories are a sequence of privileged penetralia into not only the places but also the psyches of the wealthy and gifted.

Though indebted to European models, James's stories were not influenced by contemporary political or ideological concerns, for his Old World, like Irving's, is a sanctuary and retreat. Yet even as James was creating his own intensely private world, American writers were developing a social conscience, perhaps most acutely expressed in the short story form by Howells's disciple, Hamlin Garland. Certainly a lesser artist than Henry James, Garland wrote stories redeemed by their honesty of vision, derived from the sad fate of his own parents, who were lured into the West with promises of a comfortable living from farming and then broken on the great wheel that was the remorseless cycle of climate and market demand. He thereby brought an angry edge to regionalism in his stories of life in the newly settled prairie states, writing of the injustices suffered by farmers who were caught up in the "lion's paw" of economic forces, chiefly symbolized by the railroads, which mercilessly changed their rates to reflect market needs, heedless of the effects on a people whose margin of profit was at best small and always at risk.

In 1899 there appeared Charles Chesnutt's *The Conjure Woman,* an effort by an African American to portray the details of lives of his enslaved brethren in the South before the Civil War, short stories rendered in dialect used for colorful but not comic effects. This was followed that same year by *The Wife of His Youth,* the title story of which told of the psychological conflict felt by a man of African descent who is married to a former slave but in love with a black woman of a much higher class and far greater refinement. Both collections helped to move African Americans out of the minstrel-show stereotype in which they were kept by white writers, even in the sympathetic stories told by Joel Chandler Harris through his popular mouthpiece, appearing in *Uncle Remus: His Songs and Sayings* in 1880 and continuing in other collections for the next twenty-five years.

Though intended for children, Harris's animal fables captured the adult imagination as well, and were derived from the folktales the author gathered from the black people he knew in his home state of Georgia. Less known are Harris's contributions to local color, like *Free Joe, and Other Georgian Sketches* (1887), in which he collected stories derived from material provided by his native region, giving friendly treatment to impoverished aristocrats, poor whites, and former slaves alike. Harris must be given credit for his personal qualities of tolerance, but the South in the 1880s was hardly a place in which such toleration was the rule, the end of Reconstruction being marked by an often violent bigotry that would have to wait for a much later generation of southern short story writers to record.

Hamlin Garland, like Rebecca Harding Davis, may be accounted a primitive naturalist, writing not so much from the European example set by Zola but out of personal experience, which validated the kinds of social injustice that Chesnutt had experienced and Harris mostly ignored. In contrast, the later group of naturalists, college-educated writers like Frank Norris and Stephen Crane, were more responsive to European ideological currents. Children of comfortable middle-class backgrounds, they were forced to search out materials which they could turn into fiction responsive to the new ideologies. Norris is not well known as a writer of short stories, though he did turn out several hilarious examples under the influence of Kipling's *Soldiers Three* (1883). Crane was a genius in the genre; his "The Blue Hotel" and "The Open Boat" are unchallenged masterpieces. "The Open Boat" was inspired by Crane's experience as a castaway from a sunken freighter carrying guns to insurrectionists in Cuba, while "The Blue Hotel," though colored by the author's relatively brief experience in the West, was a highly charged imaginative tale, expressionistic in its use of setting and heightened character.

Crane wrote also of the cowboy, who had emerged in the 1880s as a unique figure in the American landscape. The cowboy's most famous celebrant in the short story was Owen Wister, whose material somewhat transcended his art. Readers who form an opinion of Wister's fictional skills on the basis of his best-selling *The Virginian* (1902), with its romantic story and sentimental conclusion, need to consult his short stories, written during the previous decade (and often illustrated by Frederic Remington), which are unsentimental and save for a wry revision of chivalry are without romantic elements. The cowboys and cavalrymen he celebrates in collection such as *Red Men and White* (1896) are courageous exemplars of American manhood, indebted to Bret Harte but also influenced by Kipling. Wister's stories also exhibit a certain quiet humor and a practical realism despite the dangerous milieu they depict. Wister knew both Henry James and Howells, and the antisentimentalism that was part of the realist's code informs his short stories throughout; it was only in his first attempt at a novel that Wister gave way to sentimental necessity in order to attract the female readership needed to influence sales.

Jack London was another naturalist writer who emerged at the turn of the century. Unlike Norris and Crane, he lived the materials of his fiction, though like many of his contemporaries he could not escape the influence of Kipling, whose "code" he translated from the jungles of India to the wasteland of the Yukon. London would become famous with the publication of *The Call of the Wild* (1903), a novel virtually contemporaneous with *The Virginian,* but a book written as it were in another dimension, the outlines of which were drawn in the short stories published in the closing years of the decade and gathered as *The Son of the Wolf* in 1900.

Another vivid contrast to the gritty realism of Crane and London is provided by the short stories of Richard Harding Davis, a writer virtually lost to us today, but who during the early 1890s was widely popular for his journalism, travel writing, and fiction about life in New York City. The most if not always the best of these center on a dashing young dude named Courtlandt Van Bibber. As drawn by Davis's friend Charles Dana Gibson, Van Bibber is customarily dressed in a top hat, evening clothes, and a cape, but he often interrupts his sybaritic and privileged existence to effect a rescue or to change the direction of a troubled life. Indebted to Bret Harte's noble gamblers, Van Bibber is the romantic antithesis of London's rough-hewn dwellers in the forbidding wilderness of the Far North, and an eastern counterpart to Wister's chivalric Virginian. Early in the 1890s Davis also wrote a number of stories with sympathetic portrayals of lower-class characters who share the same chivalric qualities of his high-born hero, like "A Leander of the East River," who look forward to O. Henry's good-hearted rascals, much as Davis's use of surprise endings and sentimental closures presages the genre O. Henry would make famous. Very popular in his day, Davis is a writer who deserves more attention as a transitional figure and an innovator than he has hitherto been given.

To end this survey with Kate Chopin seems inevitable, for her career, accomplishments, and literary reception provide a natural bridge between the nineteenth- and twentieth-century American short story. Born Katherine O'Flaherty in St. Louis in 1851, she married Oscar Chopin and moved with him to Louisiana. After his death, she began to write profession-ally. Her first novel, *At Fault* (1890), was followed by two collections of stories, *Bayou Folk* (1894) and *A Night in Acadie* (1897), which established her reputation. In 1899, her masterpiece, *The Awakening*—a novel about the turbulent sexual discoveries of a married woman—shocked reviewers and readers, virtually silencing Chopin for the last five years of her life. In one sense, many of her short stories about French Creole Louisiana look back to the local colorists (Stowe, Cable, Murfee) and the regionalists (Jewett, Freeman); but in other ways, her most original work looks forward to the fiction of such iconoclastic twentieth-century writers as Joyce, Hemingway, Anderson, and Hurston. Brief, unvarnished, and exceptionally provocative, Chopin's stories challenge the comfortable assumptions of bourgeois society. "Désirée's Baby" is a shockingly ironic exposure of the tragic results of racism; "The Storm" tells of a married woman's afternoon of lovemaking with a former suitor; and "The Story of an Hour" is a brief sketch about a middle-aged wife who experiences an exhilarating release when she hears that her husband has died, an intense thrill of regained freedom that ends with a heart attack when the report proves untrue. A more positive yet unconventional view of marriage is put forward in "Athénaïse," about a discontented young bride who leaves her husband and has a brief, platonic relationship with another man, until the discovery that she is pregnant by her husband acts as a sudden and transformational epiphany that sends her happily back into his arms. These daring explorations of the consequences of gender, race, and class constrictions, with their vivid surfaces and insinuating depths, are now recognized as among the most prescient in late nineteenth-century literature.

John Seelye

SELECTED BIBLIOGRAPHY

Beer, Janet. *Kate Chopin, Edith Wharton and Charlotte Perkins Gillman: Studies in Short Fiction.* New York: St. Martin's Press, 1997.

Charters, Ann. *The American Short Story and Its Writer.* Boston: Bedford/St. Martin's Press, 1999.

Crowley, J. Donald, ed. *The American Short Story: 1850–1900.* Boston: Twayne, 1984.

Curnett, Kirk. *Wise Economies: Brevity and Storytelling in American Short Stories.* Moscow: University of Idaho Press, 1997.

Current-Garcia, Eugene. *The American Short Story: Before 1850.* Boston: Twayne, 1985.

Donovan, Josephine. *New England Local Color Literature: A Woman's Tradition.* New York: Ungar, 1983.

Fusco, Richard. *Maupassant and the American Short Story: The Influence of Form at the Turn of the Century.* University Park: Pennsylvania State University Press, 1994.

Levy, Andrew. *The Culture and Commerce of the American Short Story.* New York: Cambridge University Press, 1993.

May, Charles E., ed. *The New Short Story Theories.* Athens: Ohio University Press, 1994.

May, Charles E., ed. *Short Story Theories.* Athens: Ohio University Press, 1976.

Pattee, Fred Lewis. *The Development of the American Short Story: A Sketch.* New York: Harper, 1923.

Tallack, Douglas. *The Nineteenth-Century Short Story: Language, Form and Ideology.* London: Routledge, 1993.

THE AFRICAN AMERICAN

SHORT STORY

Like African American writing in general, African American short stories emerged as a genre in the context of slavery and the struggle against it. Only in the North, where slavery was illegal, could African Americans publish any writing at all, and even there, powerful pressures of moral imperative, commercial opportunity, and social obligation motivated black authors such as Maria Stewart, William Wells Brown, Martin R. Delany, Frederick Douglass, and Harriet Jacobs to invest their public voices in the abolitionist effort. Ironically, these imperatives worked against the development of short stories as a preferred genre for African American authors, and to this day, very few of them have been known primarily as short story writers.

Almost without exception, the intent of African American authors was to agitate, provoke, and persuade, not to entertain. The genres best suited to these objectives are oratory, autobiographical narrative, and the essay. Not surprisingly, the expressive energies of the antebellum black authors were most often manifested in these forms.

Among the short stories of this period, "The Heroic Slave" rises as boldly above its coevals as does its author, Frederick Douglass, above his own contemporaries. Some critics classify it as a novella, but in either case, it deserves an honored place in this history. It was published in March 1853, and it is an imaginative retelling of the story of Madison Washington, who led a successful revolt on the ship *Creole* in 1841. The story exemplifies Douglass's belief in the necessity for slaves to rise and fight for their own freedom.

Not until the emergence of Charles Waddell Chesnutt was there a true African American master of the short story form. The publication of his story, "The Goophered Grapevine," in the August 1887 issue of *Atlantic Monthly* catapulted Chesnutt into literary celebrity. By the time his collection *The Conjure Woman* was published by Houghton Mifflin in March 1899, Chesnutt had developed a broad and enthusiastic following for his dialect tales. Many of Chesnutt's readers were unaware of his racial identification. With his fair skin, blue eyes, and red hair, Chesnutt certainly appeared white. Other European Americans were writing Negro dialect tales at the time, and Chesnutt could easily have chosen his place among them. Instead, he became a strong race man, deeply committed to social issues affecting black people, which became increasingly apparent in his fiction. In the autumn of 1899 he published *The Wife of His Youth and Other Stories of the Color Line,* a work that explored the moral and social dilemmas of race. Though William Dean Howells and a few other critics praised these stories, most critics found them too honest about topics that were considered provocative, such as miscegenation and racist mob violence. Celebrated as a dialect writer, Chesnutt found himself controversial and increasingly marginalized as a serious writer on social conflicts associated with race.

At the turn of the century, W. E. B. Du Bois emerged as the preeminent African American intellectual. In addition to his works of social science and political commentary, Du Bois also occasionally wrote fiction. His best-known short story, "Of the Coming of John," appeared in *The Souls of Black Folks* (1903). This poignant tale chronicles the tragic results of the inherent clash between a culture of white supremacy and the transgressive aspirations of a young black man, inspired by a liberal arts education to pursue Du Boisian ideals of manly candor. Ironically, John's advent terminates in a heroic swan song. Du Bois used this short story to explore the limitations of his own social doctrine.

As the editor of *Crisis* (1910–1934), Du Bois occasionally published his own fictional pieces. More important, he published the work of many other black writers, and *Crisis* became an important outlet and inspiration for writers of the Harlem Renaissance. As the organ of the National Association for the Advancement of Colored People (NAACP), *Crisis* was the most important and widely disseminated of all African American periodicals. Thus, it provided national visibility to black writers. During the 1920s *Opportunity,* the National Urban League magazine, edited by Charles S. Johnson, played a similar role. In addition, the annual *Opportunity* literary awards focused attention on distinguished emerging writers. Unlike literary magazines, these journals were published monthly, year after year, and their mass membership base guaranteed their broad national distribution. Thus, they played a special role in black literary history.

Anthologies have also been very important, especially as definitive expressions of particular literary moments. Most famously, *The New Negro* (1925), edited by Alain Locke, articulated what remains the predominant conception of the "The Harlem Renaissance," a rubric for the flowering of African American writing during the 1920s. Locke asserts in his introductory essay: "with this renewed self-respect and self-dependence, the life of the Negro community is bound to enter a new dynamic phase." For Locke, the flowering of the arts represented this broader social vitality. "The Harlem Renaissance" is a misnomer, since several of the most important writers associated with it were not in Harlem for most of the 1920s (Claude McKay and Langston Hughes, for example), some such as Jean Toomer kept their distance, and others such as Zora Neale Hurston did their major work after the 1920s. Still, Locke's conception of a distinctively new literature, embodying racial pride and emphasizing themes derived from an honest reappraisal of black history and culture, including the African heritage, remains useful as a generalization about the period. Sixteen years later Sterling Brown and Ulysses Lee published *The Negro Caravan* (1941), the most important African American anthology of the Depression era. Neither is primarily a fiction anthology, but both offer valuable collections of short fiction, incorporating works by writers who continue to command our attention and by others who were well respected when the anthologies appeared but whose reputations have subsequently faded.

Jean Toomer's *Cane* (1923) is arguably the most important collection of African American short fiction ever published. A loosely integrated collection of stories, sketches, and poems, *Cane* is based on Toomer's experiences on an excursion he took through the Deep South with his novelist friend Waldo Frank in 1920. Frank's novel *Holiday* also derived from this trip. Much of *Cane* is written in an expressionist mode, calculated to evoke sensory and emotional responses to situations and not merely to describe characters, settings, and actions. Toomer represents the literary avant-garde of his day, and some of his formal experiments appear gratuitous, but more often in *Cane* they work brilliantly. For instance, "Karintha" uses a combination of poetry and prose to evoke the convergence of natural beauty and sexual passion around the figure of a young woman. It begins:

Her skin is like dusk on the eastern
   horizon,
O cant you see it, O cant you see it,
Her skin is like dusk on the eastern
   horizon,
. . . When the sun goes down.

Despite its lovely language, this story is tragic, describing the fate of a prematurely seductive girl ruined by undisciplined passion. "Blood-Burning Moon," using an incantatory rhythm, dramatizes the delirious ritual violence of a lynching. These short stories might easily be described as prose poems. Some stories, such as "Bona and Paul," are written in a conventional narrative style. "Kabnis," the long concluding work, is an avant-garde literary experiment, an odd hybrid of fictional and dramatic conventions. The critical reader can follow Toomer's shifts among prose narrative, interior monologue, dramatic dialogue, and poetic invocation. "Kabnis" is a fascinating example of the search for effective formal innovations, but most critics regard it as not wholly successful. *Cane* is a daring and visionary work that departs sharply from the dialect tales and reformist dramatizations of social problems that had preoccupied earlier black writers. It embodies a combination of the writer as not just a responsible citizen, an entertainer, or a credit to his race but a serious artist. It is the first work of an African American author to be admired more for its formal innovations than for its content, and for these reasons, despite its flaws, most critics regard it as a classic.

In addition to his poetry, Langston Hughes wrote many fine short stories. His first collection, *The Ways of White Folks* (1938), is a volume of sharply crafted and mostly ironic stories about racial attitudes, accommodations, and conflicts. Hughes's most important and memorable fiction, however, is his series of narratives based on a character named Jessie B. Semple. The "Simple stories" began in 1943 as a weekly feature in the *Chicago Defender,* a newspaper with a national circulation among all classes of black people, especially in the South, and continued for the next two decades. "Simple" was an immediate hit, and these weekly stories were read, often aloud, in homes, schools, barber and beauty shops, and bars across black America. Embraced as a black everyman, Jessie B. Semple is an opinionated working-class guy who frequents his local bar and declares his views on women, politics, white people, and life. Hughes developed a small cast of characters around Semple—bartender, wife, girlfriend, and landlady—and he established a comic paradigm that has in subsequent years been frequently appropriated by television situation comedies such as *Cheers.*

The Simple stories are a rare accomplishment in American literary history. Many of the episodes, jokes, and even characters have passed over into the oral folklore of African Americans and continue to be retold by people who are unaware that Langston Hughes wrote them.

Zora Neale Hurston is usually listed as a Harlem Renaissance writer, but she wrote most of her fiction during the Great Depression. She did not publish a volume of stories during her lifetime, but her stories have been collected in *The Selected Short Stories of Zora Neale Hurston.* Most of her stories are apprentice work, preliminary studies and sketches of characters and episodes that she developed more fully later in her novels. They are valuable, nonetheless, for what they reveal about Hurston's development as a writer. Furthermore, her best stories, such as "Spunk" and "Sweat," are humorous and entertaining tales of rural Southern life, and they merit attention on their own.

By contrast, Richard Wright thought that literature should instruct, not entertain. In fact, Wright and Hurston clashed over the appropriateness of depicting African American folk life. Wright, who believed that literature should be used as a weapon, argued that amusing stories of folk life allow racists to be entertained by the oppression of black people. His first volume of short stories, *Uncle Tom's Children* (1938), was a classic in the genre known as "protest fiction." Written in a naturalistic mode, these tales of black oppression depict men and women trapped and destroyed by forces beyond their control. Wright's subsequent volume of short stories, *Eight Men* (1961), represents a broader range of thematic concerns. Unlike the unremittingly grim stories of *Uncle Tom's Children,* the stories in *Eight Men* are sometimes humorous (as in "Man of All Work"), and they are written in several different styles. These stories provide insight into how hard Wright worked to continue developing and extending his literary craft.

During the 1950s some monumental works of African American literature were published, but it was a lean time for short stories. Several writers produced a few excellent stories during this period (for example, Ralph Ellison and Paula Marshall), but they all invested most of their energies in other genres. Ellison's stories were collected in *Flying Home and Other Stories* (1996), and Marshall's are represented by *Soul Clap Hands and Sing* (1961) and *Reena and Other Stories* (1983). James Baldwin's stories, eventually collected in *Going to Meet the Man* (1965), represent this period. The most famous of these is "Sonny's Blues," the most frequently taught and anthologized of Baldwin's works. It explores the vexed relationship between two brothers, one a teacher and the other a jazz musician who has struggled with drug addiction and spent time in prison. In coming to understand his brother's relationship to music, the protagonist also comes to understand the importance of music in African American life: "Sonny's fingers filled the air with life, his life. But that life contained so many others. . . . He really began with the spare flat statement of the opening phrase of the song. Then he began to make it his. . . . I seemed to hear with what burning he had made it his, with what burning we had yet to make it ours. . . . He

could help us be free if we would listen, that he would never be free until we did."

Baldwin's stories represent primarily black New Yorkers, struggling with the existential burdens of race, family, and love. Baldwin's writing was sometimes undisciplined in his longer works. His stories, therefore, reflect more favorably upon skills as a literary craftsman. Nevertheless, Baldwin's literary reputation rests upon his full-length works, not his stories.

Ernest Gaines too has been primarily a novelist, but his *Bloodline* (1968) is a thematically integrated collection, a major literary accomplishment in the tradition of *Cane* and *Uncle Tom's Children.* In *Bloodline,* explicitly in the title story, Gaines takes up the challenge posed by William Faulkner's powerful representation of the South. Writing as a black southerner, Gaines attempts to render black Louisiana folk with the complex sense of history and social conventions that Faulkner attributes to the white people of his fictional Yoknapatawpha County. The collection opens with "The Sky is Gray," a story about the dignity and stubborn pride of a poor young black woman who perseveres through adverse conditions to teach her young son how to be a man. The civil rights movement, with all its cultural and social entailments, forms the basis for Gaines's fiction. In *Bloodline* and in his novels, Gaines examines the intricate tensions between stable community and individual freedom.

Amiri Baraka is best known for his poems and plays. In the mid-1960s, however, when he was still known as LeRoi Jones, he published two remarkable works of fiction: *Tales* (1967) and a novel, *The System of Dante's Hell* (1965). *Tales* is a collection of poetic and autobiographical stories, notable for their expressionistic style and their emotional candor and intensity. These stories are primarily concerned to dramatize particular existential moments, especially moments of crisis or revelation. The poetic quality of these tales is apparent in the following passage from "Words":

> Magic and ghosts are a dialogue . . . invisible and sound vibrations, humming in emptyness . . . images collide in emptyness, and we build our emotions into blank invisible structures which never exist, and are not there, and are illusion and pain and madness. Dead whiteness.
>
> We turn white when we are afraid. We are going to try to be happy.

Baraka eschews conventional plot and character development, concentrating instead on emotional effect. These are avant-garde stories. As such, *Tales* represents a significant departure in African American writing. It is the first collection of African American short fiction since *Cane* to adopt a forthrightly experimental style throughout.

During the period of the mid-1960s through the mid-1970s, generally known as the Black Arts Movement, there was a significant upsurge of African American literary activity. Though this period is usually described as featuring primarily poetry and drama, it includes a remarkable amount of fiction in both conventional and experimental styles. The fiction of this era has been relatively neglected by scholars, though there is a substantial amount of it,

representing many styles and perspectives, and written in many cases by authors who continue to receive critical attention for their subsequent work as poets or novelists. One can only speculate about the reasons for this neglect. A major factor many be the general perception of the 1960s as an era of oral and polemical expression. We give far more attention to African American speeches of that era than to its fiction. Poetry, drama, and polemical essays also have a great advantage in this era that we understand as a culture of public rhetorical expression. It may be, in other words, that we are predisposed not to notice the fiction of this period.

Ironically, much of the short fiction was published in periodicals that are readily available to researchers. Even high-profile literary/intellectual journals such as *Atlantic Monthly* and *Harper's* began to publish works by African Americans with some frequency. More important, a number of African American venues became available. Under the editorship of Hoyt Fuller, *Negro Digest* (renamed *Black World*) developed into an important monthly platform for black writers. In the 1970s a number of high-quality journals, representing a broad spectrum of literary and political values, were publishing fiction and other work by African American writers: *The Black Scholar, Black American Literature Forum, The Yardbird Reader, Obsidian,* and *Callaloo,* to name the most prominent. Despite the odd scholarly silence on the subject, this is arguably the richest, most diverse period ever for African American short fiction, comprising a wide spectrum of literary sensibilities and approaches.

At one end of the spectrum are the avant-garde works of writers associated with bohemia, represented by Greenwich Village in the East and the San Francisco/ Berkeley enclave in the West. Amiri Baraka, during his early days as LeRoi Jones, was a Village writer, and Samuel R. Delaney, best known for his works of heroic fantasy and science fiction, also deserves mention in this bohemian context. Ishmael Reed began his career in New York's UMBRA Writers' Workshop, alongside several other notables such as Eugene B. Redmond, David Henderson, and Henry Dumas, but he and Al Young are primarily known as Bay area writers with iconoclastic, satirical styles. Clarence Major was long associated with the Fiction Collective, a midwestern guild of experimental writers. Though they differ from each other, all of these writers are literary innovators in some sense, and aside from Reed's novels, critics have given little attention to their fiction, some of which is dazzling.

At the other end of the spectrum, many writers of this period worked in conventional realist styles, obvious examples including Toni Cade Bambara (*Gorilla, My Love*, 1972), Alice Walker (*In Love and Trouble*, 1974), and John Edgar Wideman (*Damballah*, 1981). Bambara specialized in capturing the fast-paced vernacular language of urban black people, and many stories in *Gorilla, My Love* skillfully depict the voices of children. This passage from "Raymond's Run" is representative:

If anybody has anything to say to Raymond . . . they have to come by me. And I don't play the dozens. . . . I much rather just knock you down and take my chances even if I am a little girl with skinny arms and squeaky voice,

which is how I got the name Squeaky. And if things get too rough, I run. . . . I'm the fastest thing on two feet.

A remarkable variety of writers worked in the wide realm of avant-garde formal experimentation and conventional realism. Henry Dumas, for example, who died a tragic and senseless death when he was shot by a policeman for no apparent reason as he stood waiting on a New York subway platform, was greatly admired by other writers, including Toni Morrison, for his deft combination of realistic, vernacular language and compelling symbolism. His fiction was first collected in *Ark of Bones and Other Stories* (1974) and later in *Goodbye, Sweetwater: New and Selected Stories* (1988). Gayl Jones, from the publication of her first novel, has been regarded as a provocative and compelling writer. Her works explore the depths of psychological trauma, focusing on sexuality and the conflicts between men and women. Toni Morrison edited Jones's first two novels, *Corregidora* and *Eva's Man,* and her collection of stories *White Rat* (1977). Finally, writing in a style reminiscent of Ralph Ellison, James Alan McPherson published *Hue and Cry* (1970) and the Pulitzer Prize-winning *Elbow Room* (1978), an entire collection of stories that is remarkable for its technical virtuosity. Critics have especially admired McPherson for his skill in rendering a wide variety of social perspectives and verbal styles.

The 1980s was, by contrast to the 1970s, a period of relative drought for African American writing. Though a few writers such as Alice Walker, Gloria Naylor, and Toni Morrison enjoyed great success, the prominence and diversity of published African American voices diminished, and many established writers had difficulty finding publishers. Two notable collections from this era that announced the emergence of major new voices were Gloria Naylor's *The Women of Brewster Place* (1982) and Jamaica Kincaid's *At the Bottom of the River* (1983). The situation was so bad that Terry McMillan felt obliged to publish an anthology of contemporary African American fiction to address the dearth. Called *Breaking Ice* (1990), it included short stories and novel excerpts by both established and emerging writers, including Naylor, McMillan, John Wideman, Charles Johnson, Randall Kenan, and Angela Jackson. It was hailed as the first anthology of black writing to be published in over a decade. Many writers and critics believed that in the distinctly conservative political climate of the 1980s, there was a backlash among publishers against African American writers. Whether this was true or not, much less work by black writers was being published. *Breaking Ice* was a very inclusive collection that represented the diversity of African American fiction writing at that time. McMillan explains her intentions in the introduction:

> Our visions, voices, outlooks, and even our experiences have changed and/or grown in myriad ways over the last two decades. Much of our work is more intimate, personal, reflects a diversity of styles and approaches to storytelling, and it was this new energy that I hoped to acquire for this anthology. This is exactly what I got . . . . Some of [our stories] are warmhearted, some zingy, some have a sting, and a bite, some

> will break your heart, or cause you to laugh out loud. . . . You may very well see yourself, a member of your family, a loved one, or a friend on these pages, and that is one thing good fiction should do.

This introduction in effect announces the advent of a new cultural epoch, one in which black writers have effectively rebelled against the traditional dogma that blackness must entail some specific and limited range of styles. The anthology received a great deal of attention from reviewers and media commentators.

Breaking Ice had the salutary effect of goading publishers. Several of them reissued works by African Americans that had fallen out of print, and some offered contracts to established writers who had gone unpublished in recent years. Nonetheless, the 1990s has mostly continued the trend of the 1980s, bringing success to a few major novelists but offering few exciting new voices. Indeed, the only collection of stories by a black writer who emerged in the 1990s that seems clearly to have earned a long-term audience is *Krik? Krak!* (1995) by Edwidge Danticat. Like Jamaica Kincaid, Danticat is a Caribbean immigrant. Her stories in this collection deal with Haiti under the Duvalier regime, and they are especially memorable for their crisp and original, yet idiomatic, language. Her title refers to a vernacular convention in Haiti. *Krik?* means, in effect, are you ready to hear a story? *Krak!* is the affirmative response. Her opening story, "Children of the Sea," depicts boat people fleeing Haiti, and it is told in the voices of two lovers, one on the island and the other in a makeshift boat, addressing thoughts to each other. This final monologue conveys the magic of Danticat's prose:

> All I hear from the radio is more killing in port-au-prince. the pigs are refusing to let up. . . . I am writing to you from the bottom of the banyan tree, manman says that banyan trees are holy and sometimes if we call the gods from beneath them, they will hear our voices clearer. . . . last night on the radio, I heard that another boat sank off the coast of the bahamas. I can't think about you being in there in the waves. my hair shivers. from here, I cannot even see the sea. behind these mountains are more mountains and more black butterflies still and a sea that is endless like my love for you.

Edwidge Danticat is clearly a major literary voice of the next generation.

Few African American writers have adopted the short story as their primary genre. It remains, rather, a form that novelists and poets use from time to time. There is no distinctively African American style or tradition of the short story. It would be accurate to say that black writers have worked in virtually all of the modes practiced by other writers and have produced distinguished work in all of these modes. They have brought African American perspectives and cultural traditions to bear upon their short fiction, and some of the most important works of African American writing are short stories. Taken as a whole, African American short stories effectively represent the larger traditions of African American literature in all of its diversity. Thus, the study of them can be a very effective introduction to this literature. It may seem odd, then, that James Alan McPherson is the only major black writer of recent decades who has devoted his creative energies exclusively to story writing. Still, as Jamaica Kincaid and Edwidge Danticat have recently shown, the short story remains a powerfully effective literary mode.

David Lionel Smith

SELECTED BIBLIOGRAPHY

Bone, Robert. *Down Home: Origin of the Afro-American Short Story.* New York: Columbia University Press, 1988.

Karrer, Wolfgang, and Barbara Puschlmann-Nolenz, eds. *The African American Short Story, 1970 to 1990: A Collection of Critical Essays.* Trier: Wissenschaftlicher Verlag Trier, 1993.

McMillan, Terry, ed. *Breaking Ice: An Anthology of Contemporary African American Fiction.* New York: Penguin Books, 1990.

Naylor, Gloria, ed. *Children of the Night: The Best Short Stories by Black Writers, 1967 to the Present.* New York: Little, Brown, 1995.

THE ASIAN AMERICAN
SHORT STORY

Geographically, the border of Asia begins west of the Ural Mountains and includes all the countries of the so-called Middle East, East Asia, South Asia, and Southeast Asia. Theoretically, the term *Asian American* includes Americans whose ancestry is from any of the countries in this entire continent. But in practice, when Asian American studies began after the Third World Student Strike at San Francisco State University in 1969, the focus was on Americans of East Asian descent. Kai-yu Hsu's introduction to the first literary anthology, *Asian American Authors* (1972), defined Asian American as Americans of Chinese, Japanese, and Korean lineage, limiting the group to one race (Mongolian) and one cultural heritage (Confucian and Buddhist). Frank Chin and the other editors of *AIIIEEEEE!* (1974) chose a political definition, excluding those whom they felt were overly assimilated and including only writers with an "authentic Asian American sensibility," but they did not define their terms. Elaine Kim, in the first book-length scholarly study, *Asian American Literature: An Introduction to the Writings and Their Social Context* (1982), defined her subject as literature written by Americans of Asian descent living in the United States about the experience of living there. But this definition leaves out Asian Americans who choose to write about their Asian experience, such as Richard Kim and Shirley Lim. Inclusive and yet not so large as to be meaningless, the operative Asian Pacific American "borders" extend as far west as Pakistan and as far east as the coast of California, including Hawaiians and other South Sea Islanders, Eurasians, and Amerasians of mixed races, whatever their subject matter, wherever they choose to set their stories.

Each Asian group in the United States has had a distinctive history and yet, despite the diversity of race, language, religion and cultural background, all share the experience of exclusion as a nonwhite, foreign element, regardless of the length of time the group or individual has been in the United States. Thus, Asian American short stories by first-generation immigrants often deal with themes of displacement, dislocation, exile, and nostalgia for the country of origin. The second-generation writers are more concerned with sorting out identity issues and family and personal relationships, confronting racism, and asserting a place for themselves in the United States. The third generation is often curious about the customs and cultural specificities of Old World grandparents or the experiences about which the first and second generations have been silent, such as the incarceration of Japanese Americans during World War II. Thus, Asian American short story writers may be grouped by generation and subject matter, or by national origin and chronology. I have chosen to use a combination of chronology and national origin. Furthermore, because the subject is so vast, I have for the most part focused on writers who have published a collection of short stories, deciding, perhaps somewhat arbitrarily, that an entire collection attests to a writer's greater significance than any single story.

The earliest short story writers were two Eurasian sisters, Edith Maud Eaton and Winifred Eaton. Born to an English father and a Chinese mother, the sisters began publishing short stories at the end of the nineteenth century. Despite the virulent sinophobia of the period, Edith, the elder sister, chose a Chinese pseudonym, Sui Sin Far (Narcissus), and wrote stories protesting the mistreatment of the Chinese in Canada and the United States. Her collected stories, *Mrs. Spring Fragrance,* were first published in 1912 and reprinted in 1995. They are admired today for their progressive stance in advocating the rights of Chinese immigrants and single working women. The younger sister, Winifred, using a Japanese-sounding pen name, Onoto Watanna, published seventeen novels, and hundreds of stories in the popular magazines of the period. Economically motivated, Winifred created best-selling romances linking Japanese or Japanese Eurasian heroines with Caucasian men. From 1926 to 1931, she wrote screenplays for Hollywood, but her short stories remain to be collected in a single volume.

Japanese Americans have produced a number of remarkable short story writers. During the late 1930s, Toshio Mori first began writing spare vignettes of Japanese American life in the farms and small towns of California. Both *Yokohama, California,* Mori's first collection, and *The Chauvinist and Other Stories,* his second, are distinguished by subtle portrayals of characters that tremble on the fine line between fools and heroes ("The Japanese Hamlet," "Say It With Flowers," "The Seventh Street Philosopher"), exemplifying what writer Hisaye Yamamoto has called "the bulldog tenacity of the human spirit."

Hisaye Yamamoto, herself an extraordinary writer, presents the woman's perspective in her collection *Seventeen Syllables and Other Stories*. Master of indirection and understatement, Yamamoto employs unreliable narrators in "Seventeen Syllables" and "Yoneko's Earthquake," young girls who tell a story from their limited perspective, but the reader understands that another tale is all the while emerging in spite of them. Wakako Yamauchi is best known for her plays, but she is also a masterful short story writer. Her themes— love unconsummated, opportunities missed, songs of longing and resignation, of repression and self-denial and its psychic cost, of despair and the renewal of hope—are handled with consummate skill, with poignancy and wistfulness. In "The Coward," for example, a woman does not succumb to an affair. "Shirley Temple, Hotchacha" most explicitly deals with the trauma of World War II for both Japanese and Japanese Americans. In *The Loom and Other Stories*, R. A. Sasaki explores the beauty that is discernible only when one looks "real close." In the title story, "The Loom," grown daughters finally recognized their mother's strength when reviewing the hardships of her life. In Sasaki's humorous "American Fish," which has been made into a short film, two women shopping at a fish market speak warmly as if they know each other well, yet neither is able to call up the other's name or any details of the other's life. Their exterior friendliness contrasts with their interior confusion and creates a tension leading to a humorous denouement.

Filipino American short story writers include Carlos Bulosan, N. V. M. Gonzales, Bienvenido Santos, Marianne Villanueva, Peter Bacho, and M. Evelina Galang. In the comic title story of Bulosan's *The Laughter of My Father* (1944), a man is suspected of dishonoring a bride. In "The Romance of Magno Rubio," a short, ugly Filipino falls in love with a beautiful, tall American woman, and in "Silence," Bulosan evokes a lonely Filipino man's fantasy as he gazes with love and longing from his window at an American college coed and changes the color of his curtains to match her clothes. N. V. M. Gonzales began writing stories in English in the 1930s; his first collection, *Seven Hills Away,* was published in 1947, followed by *Children of the Ash-Covered Loam* (1954), *Look, Stranger, on This Island Now* (1963), *Mindoro and Beyond: Twenty-One Stories* (1979), and the retrospective volume *The Bread of Salt and Other Stories* (1993). Although most of his stories are set in the Philippines, he has chosen to write in English, for as he explains in his preface to *The Bread of Salt,* "An alien language does not fail if it is employed in honest service to the scene, in evocation of the landscape, and in celebration of the people one has known from birth." Like Gonzales's, Marianne Villanueva's stories record the daily lives and struggles of the people of the islands that she knew. Most of her stories are realistically detailed; however, "The Special Research Project" is an imaginative, very pointed anti-Marcos allegory, which was published in the Philippines just before the dictator's fall from power. Bienvenido N. Santos's *Scent of Apples: A Collection of Stories* evokes the nostalgia for the homeland experienced by Filipino students and professors, barbers and cooks, clerks and aging Pinoys living in exile in the United

States. Santos conveys with great sensitivity the gentleness, resiliency, and tragedies of the "old-timers" making do in a world far from home. Peter Bacho's collection *Dark Blue Suit and Other Stories* also employs nostalgia in re-creating the masculine world of Filipino cannery workers, boxers, and labor organizers of an earlier generation in Seattle. In the last story of the collection, "A Family Gathering," a young man returns to Seattle to visit his beloved father and Uncle Kiko at their gravesites, conversing with them and reliving memories with sadness and deep love. M. Evelina Galang's *Her Wild American Self* explores the struggle between Old World Catholic mores and American freedom from a young feminine perspective. Both "The Look-Alike Women" and "Filming Sausage" expose the stereotype of the exotic, docile Asian beauty and the constrictive effect of this stereotype on the daily lives of women of Asian ancestry living in the West.

After the early work of Sui Sin Far at the beginning of the twentieth century, the next notable Chinese American short story collections did not appear until the latter two decades of the century with Frank Chin's *The Chinaman Pacific & Frisco R.R. Co.* (1988) and David Wong Louie's *Pangs of Love* (1991). Chin, primarily known as a playwright, dazzles readers with his verbal pyrotechnics and saddens readers with his intense love/hate reaction to the Chinese American identity. The afterword to his collection is an unsympathetic parody of Maxine Hong Kingston's *The Woman Warrior*. In David Wong Louie's stories, marked by sophistication and humor, the anguish of ethnicity and identity is replaced by other,

more generalized concerns: finding love in spite of a domineering mother's interference, keeping ties to one's child after a divorce, caring for an aged father. In *American Visa,* newly arrived writer Wang Ping recounts stories of China's Cultural Revolution and of the experience of the recent immigrant to New York in tones irreverent and unsentimental. Amy Tan's popular *The Joy Luck Club* and Sigrid Nuñez's *A Feather on the Breath of God* may both be classified as short story cycles, an intermediary genre between fragmented novels and connected short stories. In Tan's book, four sets of Chinese immigrant mothers and their Americanized daughters take turns telling their individual stories of love and betrayal, of war and peace, of personal victories and defeats, set in both China and the United States. In 1995, under the directorship of Wayne Wang, *The Joy Luck Club* was made into a full-length feature film, the first since *Flower Drum Song* in the 1950s to have an all-Asian cast. Sigrid Nuñez, who is part Chinese, part Spanish, and part German, divides her volume into three sections: "Chang," the father's between-world story of his birth in Panama, his education there, and his immigration to the United States; the story of the mother, Christa, who was born and reared in Nazi Germany, marries on a whim, and finds herself unhappy: "I thought I had died and gone to hell. . . . But it was only Brooklyn"; and the narrator's story, "A Feather on the Breath of God," about the daughter who studies ballet, starves herself to be as light as a feather, and falls in love with one of her ESL students, a married Ukrainian taxi driver. Nuñez writes simply but evocatively.

Hawaiian writers from a variety of

Asian, native islander, and haole (white) backgrounds have published their work in *Bamboo Ridge,* which in 1986 collected an anthology of poetry and prose, *The Best of Bamboo Ridge.* The most notable fiction writers in this anthology are Darrell H. Y. Lum, Rodney Morales, and Sylvia Watanabe. In a bold move to break new ground and perhaps influenced by Mark Twain's *The Adventures of Huckleberry Finn* and the young African American narrators of Toni Cade Bambara's short stories, Darrell H. Y. Lum published a collection of short stories in 1990, written entirely in pidgin English, entitled *Pass On, No Pass Back!* With its cartoon cover and cartoons interspersed with stories whose narrators sound to the uninitiated like illiterates and fools, Lum's collection democratizes literature and demonstrates that pidgin can be as expressive and capable of portraying depth of character and emotion as standard English and that pidgin-speaking adolescents are as morally complex as the rest of us. Sylvia Watanabe has coedited a collection of Asian American women's fiction, *Home to Stay,* including the work of many well-known writers, like Maxine Hong Kingston, Gish Jen, Cecilia Manguerra Brainard, Meena Alexander, Fae Myenne Ng, and Jessica Hagedorn. In Watanabe's own collection of stories *Talking to the Dead,* Hawaii, far from being a profit-making tourists' paradise, is alive with a host of quirky but sensitively portrayed characters: a senile Laundry Burglar, an old woman called Aunty Talking to the Dead who knows the power of herbs and how to lay out a body, and a young woman whose life's goal is to be a female Japanese American impersonator of Fred Astaire.

South Asian writers of short fiction are numerous and many have been collected in recent anthologies: *Our Feet Walk the Sky, Living in America: Poetry and Fiction by South Asian American Writers,* and *Contours of the Heart: South Asians Map North America.* To date, only Bharati Mukherjee, Chitra Divakaruni, and Tashira Naqvi have published collections of short stories. Although primarily a novelist, Mukherjee has published one volume, *The Middleman and Other Stories,* which won the National Book Critics Circle Award. In sure tones and varying narrative voices, Mukherjee presents a diverse array of recent immigrant and multicultural experiences at moments of intense feeling. The title story is narrated from the perspective of a man, an Iraqi Jew from "Smyrna, Aleppo, Baghdad—and now Flushing, Queens" attempting to do business "deep in Mayan country," and sexually attracted to the mistress of a jungle drug lord. In "Jasmine," which grew into a novel with the same title, a young Indian woman comes to "Detroit [and later Ann Arbor] from Port-of-Spain, Trinidad by way of Canada" and works as an au pair for an American couple. The narrator in "The Management of Grief" is an Indian woman just informed about the death of her husband and two sons in an airline crash over Ireland. Mukherjee records the effect of rapid crossings of cultural and geographical boundaries, accompanied by both excitement and a disquieting sense of dislocation. *Arranged Marriage,* Chitra Divakaruni's moving and often ironic collection of stories, focuses on South Asian women's experiences, beginning in India with "The Bats," a story of a battered wife as narrated through the eyes of her young, uncomprehending daughter, and ending with "Meeting Mrinal," in which a South

Asian American woman whose husband has just left her tries to put up a good front before a visiting childhood friend, a career woman; each woman believes the other has led the ideal life. In "Clothes" and "Silver Pavements, Golden Roofs," Divakaruni shows how violence and racism in the United States shatter the recent immigrant's American dreams. In "The Ultrasound" and "Doors" Divakaruni contrasts Indian mores with American customs, showing how significant these divergences can be in the lives of those caught between two worlds. In "The Ultrasound," a South Asian woman living in the United States and her cousin living in India both become pregnant at the same time. When the ultrasound shows the Indian cousin's baby to be a girl, her parents-in-law, with whom she lives, want her to abort because the first child of their distinguished family must be a son. In "Doors" a young Indian man comes to visit with his newly married cousin and prepares to stay for a year, sleeping in the young couple's dining room, while the young Americanized wife is appalled. Tahira Naqvi, originally from Pakistan, who is now teaching at Western Connecticut State University, published a collection, *Attar of Roses and Other Stories from Pakistan*. Acerbic, humorous, nostalgic, her stories remember and re-create life in Pakistan, giving informative and entertaining glimpses into family relationships, marriage, rites of passage, gender roles and limitations, and a yearning for the unattainable.

Other notable story collections set in Asian countries, written by Americans of Asian ancestry, include the work of Richard Kim and Shirley Geok-lin Lim. Richard Kim, who was born in Korea and who has been a U.S. resident since 1955, when he came for graduate studies, is the author of a number of critically acclaimed novels. The largely autobiographical short stories collected in *Lost Names* record his boyhood experiences of the cruelty of Japanese colonial rule in Korea. The son of a well-known dissenter, Kim was particularly targeted by Japanese officials, who were trying desperately to maintain control of Korea in the last days of World War II. In the memorable story "An Empire for Rubber Balls," all the Korean schoolchildren are required to contribute and collect rubber balls for the war effort. When Kim punctures the balls, thinking thereby to get more into each sack, he is brutally beaten by school officials who interpret his action as a comment on the failing strength of the Japanese empire. In *Two Dreams,* Shirley Lim collects some stories previously published and adds a few new ones set in the United States. Most of the stories in her collection take place in Malaysia and are redolent with the sights, smells, and sounds of the tropics and peopled with Chinese Malays, rich and poor, those struggling for survival and others, like Mr. Tang, pampered by two households with two wives and two sets of children.

The newest Asian group to immigrate to the United States, Southeast Asians from Vietnam, Laos, and Cambodia, including the Hmong, are only just beginning to produce literature. Poet Barbara Tran has edited an anthology of Vietnamese American literature that is scheduled to be published by the Asian American Writer's Workshop in New York, but as yet, no collection of short stories from this group has appeared. Arriving in the wake of the Vietnam War, most Southeast Asians have had first to master the English language, adapt to new customs, and attend to the demands of making a living before they can devote time and energy to writing stories.

In conclusion, the short story as a genre—a form that can be completed without a lengthy investment of time; that permits a narrow focus on one theme, character, or mood; and that is flexible and accessible in magazines as well as books—is thriving among Asian Pacific Americans. The stories of those who have immigrated as adults, like Gonzalez, Wang, Naqvi, Kim, and Lim, will naturally be focused on experiences from their countries of origin. For readers of English, such stories provide the pleasure of a window onto lives in Asian countries without the pain of having to master different Asian languages. The stories of American-born Asian Americans, on the other hand, which focus on the experience of Asians in the United States, offer the dominant reader insight into how this nation of immigrants has received immigrants from the East, often providing important lessons from history on what to avoid repeating. For Asian American readers, these stories preserve memory, provide models to emulate, give spiritual sustenance, and embody communal identity.

Amy Ling

SELECTED BIBLIOGRAPHY

Short Story Collections

Bacho, Peter. *Dark Blue Suit*. Seattle: University of Washington Press, 1997.

Chin, Frank. *The Chinaman Pacific & Frisco R.R. Co.* Minneapolis: Coffee House Press, 1988.

Chock, Eric, and Darrell H. Y. Lum, eds. *The Best of Bamboo Ridge*. Honolulu: Bamboo Ridge Press, 1986.

Divakaruni, Chitra Banerjee. *Arranged Marriage*. New York: Anchor Books, 1995.

Far, Sui Sin. *Mrs. Spring Fragrance and Other Writings*. Urbana: University of Illinois Press, 1995.

Galang, M. Evelina. *Her Wild American Self.* Minneapolis: Coffee House Press, 1996.

Gonzalez, N. V. M. *The Bread of Salt and Other Stories*. Seattle: University of Washington Press, 1993.

Kim, Richard. *Lost Names*. Seoul: Si-Sa-Yong-O-Sa Publishers, 1970.

Lim, Shirley. *Two Dreams: New and Selected Stories*. New York: Feminist Press, 1997.

Louie, David Wong. *Pangs of Love*. New York: Alfred Knopf, 1991.

Lum, Darrell H. Y. *Pass On, No Pass Back!* Honolulu: Bamboo Ridge Press, 1990.

Maira, Sunaina, and Rajini Srikanth, eds. *Contours of the Heart: South Asians Map North America*. New York: The Asian American Writers' Workshop, 1996.

Mori, Toshio. *The Chauvinist and Other Stories*. Los Angeles: Asian American Studies Center, UCLA, 1979.

Mori, Toshio. *Yokohama, California*. Seattle: University of Washington Press, 1985.

Mukherjee, Bharati. *The Middleman and Other Stories*. New York: Ballantine, 1988.

Naqvi, Tahira. *Attar of Roses and Other Stories of Pakistan*. Boulder: Lynne Rienner Publishers, 1997.

Nuñez, Sigrid. *A Feather on the Breath of God*. New York: HarperCollins, 1995.

Rustomji-Kerns, Roshni, ed. *Living in Amer-*

ica: Poetry and Fiction by South Asian American Writers. Boulder: Westview Press, 1995.

Santos, Bienvenido N. Scent of Apples. Seattle: University of Washington Press, 1979.

Sasaki, R. A. The Loom and Other Stories. St. Paul: Graywolf Press, 1991.

Tan, Amy. The Joy Luck Club. New York: Putnam, 1989.

Villaneuva, Marianne. Ginseng and Other Tales from Manila. Corvallis, Ore.: Calyx, 1991.

Wang, Ping. American Visa. Minneapolis: Coffee House Press, 1994.

Watanabe, Sylvia. Talking to the Dead. New York: Doubleday, 1992.

Watanabe, Sylvia, and Carol Bruchac, eds. Home to Stay: Asian American Women's Fiction. Greenfield Center, Vt.: Greenfield Review Press, 1990.

Women of South Asian Descent Collective, eds. Our Feet Walk the Sky. San Francisco: Aunt Lute Books, 1993.

Yamamoto, Hisaye. 17 Syllables and Other Stories. Latham, N.Y.: Kitchen Table / Women of Color Press, 1988.

Yamauchi, Wakako. Songs My Mother Taught Me. New York: Feminist Press, 1994.

Yep, Laurence, ed. American Dragons. New York: HarperCollins, 1993.

Critical Works

Kim, Elaine. Asian American Literature: An Introduction to the Writings and Their Social Context. Philadelphia: Temple University Press, 1982.

Ling, Amy. Between Worlds: Women Writers of Chinese Ancestry. New York: Pergamon, 1990.

Lim, Shirley, and Amy Ling, eds. Reading the Literatures of Asian America. Philadelphia: Temple University Press.

THE CHICANO-LATINO
SHORT STORY

Chicano-Latino short story writers have been at the forefront of a cultural renaissance that has reshaped the landscape of late twentieth-century American fiction. To best understand this emergence of Chicano-Latino short fiction as an important part of American literature, it is necessary to see its source not in recent immigrant experiences alone but rather in historical plots that were formed as early as the first decades of the nineteenth century. In relation to history, the distinguishing feature of Chicano-Latino short fiction is its recurrent attempt to situate us in the aftermath of the historical scenario emerging from the settlement of the American West and Southwest. It takes its tonal key from the pathos of bitter defeat after the events of 1848 and the subsequent struggle to retain an ethnically homogeneous and culturally autonomous nationalist identity within an alien political sphere. In the writings of both men and women, this concern for political and social history structures and transforms aesthetics into social action.

There is no more apt place to begin to address the themes of identity and the forms of critique that Chicano-Latino fiction typically take than in the works of Américo Paredes (1915–1999). Scholar, folklorist, and creative writer, Paredes stands with Ernesto Galarza, Jovita Gonzalez, and George I. Sanchez as one of a handful of intellectuals who served as the originators of Chicano cultural studies. In the short story "The Gringo" (1952–53), from *The Hammon and the Beans and Other Stories* (1994), Paredes exemplifies the process of historical remembrance that is characteristic of his scholarship and his creative writings. "The Gringo" is a vignette of historical romance set in the opening days of the U.S.-Mexican War. Ygnacio, the titular "gringo," is a fair-skinned, blue-eyed Texas Mexican boy caught in the midst of those events. His story is part of the narrative of nineteenth-century American national formation as Paredes situates us within the developing discourses of nation, region, and political allegiance. Having been wounded by real "gringos" in an ambush in the disputed borderlands between the United States and Mexico, his father and brothers killed while he is spared when mistaken for an Anglo because of his blue eyes and fair skin, "the Gringo" is nursed back to health by the daughter of one of his assailants. This minor firefight represents the first shots of resistance to the enactment of the grand design that John L. O'Sullivan termed Manifest Destiny in 1844 and signaled U.S. goals for a continental nation with hemispheric and global imperial ambitions.

When Ygnacio regains consciousness and attempts to talk, the American woman warns him not to speak, as she has already seen beyond his blue eyes and fair complexion to the truth of his ethnic identity. She understands fully that a lynching will follow if her father discovers the truth as well. Appropriately named Prudence, the woman tends Ygnacio's wounds, teaches him some English, and even convinces her father that the boy is "white" and can perhaps be taught to be "a real Christian." Paredes is clearly interested in the dynam-

ics of American ethnophobia, as Ygnacio's culture and language, not his skin color, are the sources of the Americans' enmity. Like other minority intellectuals at mid-century, Paredes understood that racism is motivated at times by racial and ethnic phenotypes that are never absolutely clear and distinct. At other times it is based on sociocultural factors that try the boundary between what is acquired and what is essential in a person's identity. On the border, racism was but a form of prejudice pitting one culture against another, differences of religion, class, language, and other cultural gestures being others. The indeterminacy of racist attitudes aside, however, Paredes shows that such distinctions are made and acted upon. Thus, at first hint that a romantic attachment between Prudence and Ygnacio might be forming, the Mexican "Gringo" quickly becomes in her father's eyes just another "greaser," fair skin or no. With Prudence's help, Ygnacio manages to escape toward the Rio Grande into Mexico.

At the border on the Mexican side, in identifiably American attire, "the Gringo's" identity is mistaken once again. This time, however, he is taken for an American. At issue now is the recognition by Mexican nationals of Ygnacio's subtle transculturation as a Mexican American "gringo." Through his contact with Americans, attenuated as it has been, Ygnacio is now different, no longer purely Mexican but something else. For Paredes, that this play of misperceptions occurs at the border between the two nations is crucial. Before the coming of the Americans, the Rio Grande was a unifying focus of regional life. Now it becomes a symbol of separation between what was and what is, dividing once homogeneous Mexican space into an overdetermined site of conflicting national and racial identities. In the representational space of the border, the complexity of dress style, speech gestures, cultural habits, and skin color overlap to construct a doubly ambiguous identity for this sign of contradiction, the Mexican Gringo.

At story's end, helping set an ambush for a patrolling U.S. cavalry unit, Ygnacio is goaded by his suspicious comrades to prove his Mexican identity. When the American patrol stops short of the ambush, Ygnacio rides impetuously toward their position, hailing the Americans, attempting to lure them into the trap, only to be given away by his Spanish inflected, newly acquired English: "Thees way, boyss!" It is May 8, 1846, at Palo Alto, Texas, site of the first major encounter between American and Mexican armed forces during the U.S.-Mexican War. Ygnacio unsheathes his machete and charges an American cavalry officer who calmly awaits him with drawn pistol. The technology and symbolism of weaponry is significant. After 1838, when Samuel Colt produced his first revolvers, the balance of power shifted remarkably on the Great Plains away from mounted Mexican and Indian lancers toward rapid-firing Anglo gunmen. The man with a pistol in his hand, symbolic and real instrument of power, comes hereafter to dominate in the popular imagination as the active subject of history. Facing the weaponry of the new American technology of war armed only with the machete, "the Gringo" rides headlong into history as "the guns of Palo Alto went off inside his head." In the last

few moments of his life, Ygnacio dares to stand against the massively unstoppable force of American historical destiny. While only a minor skirmish, the action is a prelude to the seizure of the northern Mexican territories of the present American West and Southwest. In the various thematic strands combined at story's end, Paredes articulates the grand disjunctures between the socio-spatial levels and social practices of race, nationalism, gender roles, and the developing implications of U.S. expansionism.

Paredes's short story describes a paradigmatic situation. While the experience of military and cultural defeat is an aspect of the past, the sense of loss and of existing at the margins, "in between" two worlds resulting from that defeat remains very much part of the present. This mixture of bitter pathos and heroic struggle constitutes both the thematic integrity of the literature and its difference from writings describing other U.S. Latino, Asian American, Native American, and African American experiences. The struggle to retain vestiges of cultural autonomy in the midst of assimilation is the very substance of some of the classical instances of Chicano-Latino fiction.

Paredes's short story collection offers one account of the lingering division of worlds in the Southwest. Such writers as Tomás Rivera in *And the Earth Did Not Part* (1971), Rolando Hinojosa in *Estampas del Valle / The Valley* (1973), and Jovita Gonzalez in *Caballero* (1996) also describe the historical period of the late-nineteenth to mid-twentieth century. Rivera's stories are of special importance, however, because of their artistic qualities. They are taut in form and lean in language, their vocabulary and syntax rigorously controlled and held consciously within the cognitive sphere of the 1940s Chicano migrant farm worker. As in William Faulkner's or Juan Rulfo's best short fiction, Rivera's language is not expository even while it documents the reality of a region's daily life. The complex narrative of subjective impressions lacks chronological presentation, traditional compositional development, and linear plot progression. Instead of linear narrative, the fourteen stories of *And the Earth Did Not Part* follow a stream-of-consciousness thread relating the seasonal events of an allegorical year in the life of an unnamed child. The narrative voice is not even present as a protagonist but serves as a chronotopic point around which the collective subjective experiences of Rivera's characters coalesce. Only in the very last piece of the collection, where we find a child reminiscing about the events that have formed the substance of the previous stories, do we begin to sense a coherent consciousness governing the narrative.

Why turn to narrative experimentation to represent the reality of mid-century farm laborers' lives? Rivera's implicit response is that unity, coherence, and causality associated with realistic plot lines and narrative modes may be inadequate for articulating the story of the fragmenting effects of modern and emerging postmodern life. Written at the height of the politicization of the Chicano labor struggles and the formation of the United Farm Workers union in the late 1960s, Rivera's stories are charged with a political urgency to counteract the reality of economic exploitation and social injustice. The twelve core stories of Rivera's collection function aesthetically and ideologically as memorials to and reconstitution of the forgotten history of the struggle for social justice.

Attempting to recover that lost history, the interior monologues of Rivera's stories portray a community's will to survive and flourish. In each of the stories, we see glimpses of a world of class and racial oppression: the death of a child, shot to death when he pauses from his work in a sun-baked field to steal a drink of water; a mother anxiously praying for her son who is fighting in Korea; another child's first shocking encounter with abusive adult sexuality; an agoraphobic woman painfully venturing out into the marketplace; a truckload of migrant farm workers speeding northward through the midwestern night toward endless agricultural fields. Like Paredes's stories, Rivera's are socially symbolic acts of resistance, attempting to chronicle a community's will to survive in the midst of wrenching social dislocation. Rivera does not offer stories so much of personal discovery as of collective redemption. Together, the writings of Paredes and Rivera serve as narrative sites of struggle for the privilege of representation, showing how a subaltern population might gain an autonomous identity in the realm of cultural production by writing its own history and establishing its own collective unity. This concern with nation building and the retention of cultural identity represents one more salient feature of Chicano short fiction.

Principal in the exploration of radically

new forms of personal and communal identity has been a whole new generation of writers, born in the Cold War era and coming to maturity during the Vietnam War and the civil rights struggle. These include Alberto Ríos, Dagoberto Gilb, Sandra Cisneros, Helena Maria Viramontes, and Denise Chavez, to name just a few. In each of their story collections, Ríos's *The Iguana Killer: Twelve Stories of the Heart* (1984), Gilb's *Winners on the Pass Line and Other Stories* (1985), Cisneros's *Woman Hollering Creek* (1991), Viramontes's *The Moths and Other Stories* (1985), and Chavez's *The Last of the Menu Girls* (1986), the predominant theme is a search for authenticity of social and gender identity in the midst of postmodern chaos. The salient form is a critique of the dominant forces of tradition that seek to bind while they define.

In each of these works we find characters seeking psychological coherence, rational congruence, and epistemological mediation in the course of decidedly fractured life events. And these personal, internal conflicts hint at four other kinds of conflict that are also at play in the complexity of identity of Chicana and Chicano fiction of the post–World War II era. The identity of the legal subject, sanctioned in its individuality by the state apparatus; the identity of the economic subject, reified into a singularly commodifiable object in the labor marketplace; the gendered subject and the racialized subject, constructed by both biological and sociocultural discursive forces, are additional versions of the problematic self vitally present in Chicano-Latino short fiction of the last decades of the century. Contemporary Chicano-Latino short fiction has thus been predominantly concerned with sorting out the intertwined complexities of identity in late twentieth-century society. This sorting out has included a difficult but necessary critique of traditional religious, political, sexual, and cultural mores. Like the writers of the earlier generation, this postmodern group also seeks to portray the struggle to resist being swallowed by the master social and cultural forms and narratives. Unlike some of the former group, however, Ríos, Cisneros, Viramontes, Gilb, and others like them include the restrictive practices of traditional Latino culture as part of their critique.

Alberto Ríos and Dagoberto Gilb exemplify the pattern of this recent fiction. Ríos's young boy protagonists struggling toward a resilient manhood not tainted by restrictive codes of macho masculine conduct and Gilb's hard-edged working class men and women gambling for an even break while yearning for coherence in their lives offer snapshots of life in the postmodern barrio on the borders of the new urban centers of Los Angeles, Phoenix, Tucson, El Paso, and Houston. In Ríos's "The Iguana Killer," for instance, an eight-year-old Mexican boy receives a baseball bat from his grandmother, who lives in the United States. Having never seen a baseball bat in his rural Mexican fishing village, the boy takes it to be a perfect weapon for hunting and killing iguanas for food. In the end, however, the boy lovingly transforms the weapon into a tool to create a beautiful tortoiseshell cradle for a neighbor's newborn child. He shapes the violence implied by the club into a source of nurture. With the sensibility of a poet, Ríos here realistically depicts the nature of play and everyday life for a child who seeks to understand and express alternate ways of being masculine. Similarly, the conflicted winners and losers of Gilb's "Winners on the Pass Line" are psychologically real types struggling to shape themselves. In parallel narratives, Ray Muñoz, a construction worker with whom fortune has played haphazardly in Houston, and Sylvia Molina, a lonely housewife from El Paso yearning for authenticity, cross paths at the gaming tables in Las Vegas. Each wants vaguely something other than what they have in their mundane lives. Brought together entirely by the chance throw of the dice, they find that each other's presence helps them renew a sense of self beyond the mundane. In the process, they also win mutual recognition as lonely, desiring, and vital human beings, even if only momentarily on the pass line.

Interrogations of gender formation and elaborations of feminist positioning are evident from the beginning of the history of Chicano-Latino short fiction. However, the writers who come to prominence after 1975 in the post–Chicano movement and postnationalist era make the construction of gender and sexuality central features of their analysis. Like Cisneros's heroines "hollering" their defiance against patriarchal constraint, Helena Maria Viramontes's and Denise Chavez's characters develop resistance strategies that work in the face of domination not just by the ruling class and dominant race but also by the stifling gender prejudices and sexual proscriptions of the Latino community itself.

All the while continuing the critique of American economic and social structures that serve to diminish and control all waywardness of spirit, their analyses also pose crucial questions about constraints on female sexuality and the creation of gender inequalities within Mexican and Chicano culture.

Sandra Cisneros's *Woman Hollering Creek and Other Stories* (1991) offers an excellent opportunity to see how the concern for political and social history and the themes of identity and the forms of critique that Chicano fiction typically takes can be articulated with a critique of gender ideologies and traditional gender roles. In stories that address the changing nature of the Chicano-Latino community, Cisneros shows that the constraining manipulation of identity for purposes of control is sometimes effected not just by the alien outsider but also by one's own loving family and life companions. In the title story of the collection, Cisneros examines how written and televised myths, romances, popular legends, and even conventional wisdom compel us to assume socially prescribed roles. She also shows what it might take to overcome the power of such interpellations. If the social order functions as a way of sustaining and reinforcing itself, and if through the social order human subjects are called into being as subjects, how can authentic resistance to that order be formulated? Are there means and occasions whereby individuals and groups in opposition are able to challenge effectively and perhaps even transform the hierarchical nature of the social order? Because people are called into being as citizen-subjects of racialized and gendered forms and must ineluctably act from within the order that structures them, the question for these Chicano-Latino writers becomes, then, how authentic insurgency might really arise and what guise it might take. These are the issues that Cisneros deals with throughout "Woman Hollering Creek." In particular, Cisneros shows how tales of Chicano-Latino male dominance and female submission might still be transformed into stories about strong women who, in solidarity with one another, might reconfigure the sorrowful laments of other weeping women into battle cries of resistance.

Viramontes too, in the title story to *The Moths and Other Stories,* seeks to know whether there are means and occasions generated within the prevailing mores and patterns of contemporary society whereby individuals and groups in opposition to those prevailing patterns might be able to challenge effectively and perhaps even transform the seemingly natural social order. The difficulty of finding those means and occasions are compounded for Viramontes, as for Cisneros, by the fact that the limitations her female protagonists feel so acutely are forced upon them by their own families and their own culture. At the same time, variations on the customs of traditional culture do offer a residual possibility of hope. In "The Moths," the adolescent protagonist mourns the death of her grandmother, the only person who has understood her, and longs for the comfort and feeling of safety associated with the grandmother. Unlike the cold emptiness created by church ceremonies or the overt indoctrination to the role of woman pushed upon her by her father,

mother, and sisters, her grandmother provided a sanctuary for her difference as a rebellious tomboy. Now, with the grandmother's death, the young girl experiences a reconciliation of the conflicts occasioned by generational, gender, and sexual constrictions. Confronting the harsh reality of the physical corruption of a diseased body, the mourning young girl finds rebirth for the grandmother and herself by ritually bathing and cleansing the body, rocking it gently like a baby, and weeping over it as symbolic moths emerge from the grandmother's mouth. The protagonist's acceptance of death is thus linked in this final poetic image with the acceptance of other forms of difference.

When read in their historical context, the stories written by both pre– and post–World War II authors emphasize that the space we inhabit and the time within which we write are not marginal matters in relation to the question of political change. Rather, they are the very terms through which the issue of social marginality might best be understood. The collective histories spoken by the characters of Chicano-Latino authors are like morality tales that pluralize the meaning of American political and social life, that violate the taboos erected by uncritical classist, racist, and sexist ruling orders, that politicize the word and proclaim its transforming potential. The promise of that potential transformation is for the disruption of too easy answers to the question: who is an American? In answering that question, Américo Paredes, Tomás Rivera, Sandra Cisneros, Maria Helena Viramontes, Alberto Ríos, Dagoberto Gilb, and many other Chicano-Latino writers participate in the ongoing revision of the history of North American short narrative fiction.

Ramón Saldívar

SELECTED BIBLIOGRAPHY

Short Story Collections

Chavez, Denise. *The Last of the Menu Girls.* Houston: Arte Público Press, 1986.

Cisneros, Sandra. *Woman Hollering Creek and Other Stories.* New York: Vintage Books, 1991.

Gilb, Dagoberto. *Winners on the Passline and Other Stories.* El Paso: Cinco Puntos Press, 1985.

Gonzalez, Jovita. *Caballero.* College Station: Texas A & M Press, 1996.

Hinojosa, Rolando. *Estampas del Valle / The Valley.* Tempe, Ariz.: Bilingual Press. 1973/1983.

Paredes, Américo. *The Hammon and the Beans and Other Stories.* Houston: Arte Público Press, 1994.

Ríos, Alberto. *The Iguana Killer: Twelve Stories of the Heart.* Tucson, Ariz., and Lewiston, Ida.: Blue Moon Press and Confluence Press, 1984.

Rivera, Tomás. *And the Earth Did Not Part.* Houston: Arte Público Press, 1971.

Viramontes, Helena Maria. *The Moths and Other Stories.* Houston: Arte Público Press, 1985.

Critical Studies

Calderón, Hector, and José David Saldívar, eds. *Criticism in the Borderlands: Studies in Chicano Literature, Culture, and Ideology.* Durham, N.C.: Duke University Press, 1991.

Herrera-Sobek, María, and Helena María Viramontes, eds. *Chicana Creativity & Criticism: New Frontiers in American Literature.* Albuquerque: University of New Mexico Press, 1996.

Saldívar, Ramón. *Chicano Narrative: The Dialectics of Difference.* Madison: University of Wisconsin Press, 1990.

THE ECOLOGICAL

SHORT STORY

Ecology has become a fashionable word in recent times, its scientific meaning—the study of the interrelationships between organisms and their environment—suggesting important new ways of approaching literature, including the short story. The term *ecocriticism* refers to a critical perspective that pays close attention to the relationship between literature and the natural world. Traditional literary criticism, powerfully influenced by a pastoral tradition more than two thousand years old, generally regards the natural world as simple and subservient to a complex human culture. The usual assumption of literary criticism is that the only really interesting and significant relationships are those between human beings. "These stories have trees in them," wrote an editor in rejecting the manuscript of Norman Maclean's *A River Runs Though It*. An ecocritical approach to literature takes nature as seriously as traditional criticism takes society or culture.

Another way of saying this is that ecocriticism assumes a perspective of scientific awareness, changing our way of thinking, as W. H. Auden describes it, so that the nonhuman universe becomes even more mysterious to us than our own. Ernst Haeckel, who coined the word *ecology* in 1866, was a biologist and a follower of Darwin. The work of nature writers, many of whom were trained in sciences like biology and anthropology, has been instrumental in raising the general level of ecological awareness and understanding in the nineteenth and twentieth centuries. Although they are not primarily story writers themselves, naturalists like Henry David Thoreau, John Muir, Loren Eiseley, Edward O. Wilson, Ann Zwinger, and many others have given us work rich in narratives that link their scientific understanding to shared human experience. In short, literature is about interrelationships, and ecological awareness expands our sense of interrelationships to encompass nonhuman as well as human contexts. Not only is the nonhuman universe more mysterious than our own, as Auden says, but it is also inseparably a part of our own, and its mysteries increasingly challenge our artists and writers.

A growing awareness of the nonhuman has been pressed upon us by such ominous threats as pollution of the earth's air, ground, and water, as well as runaway population growth, global climate changes, desertification, the destruction of remaining native forests, and the rapid extinction of plant and animal species. These concerns—quite literally vital matters—have become part of the underlying assumptions of our lives, part of the ecology of being human. Thus it is not surprising to find ecological themes and ideas appearing increasingly in the short fiction of the twentieth century.

This ecological presence may be found most often clustered around three central ideas: a sense of a degraded environment, a sharpened awareness of geographic place, and an examination of animal lives. Underlying these three topics is not only a general acknowledgment of the legitimacy of what modern science has told us, but also a correlative resistance to it, a questioning of the nature of nature, as is

suggested by portrayals of ecological unease in R. H. W. Dillard's "The Bog," from his collection *Omniphobia*, and in the title story of J. F. Powers's *Look How the Fish Live*.

THE BLIGHTED ENVIRONMENT

One can find early visions of the rape of the fair country and other manifestations of the poisoned earth in the English and American romantics, among them Wordsworth, Thoreau, and Melville, and continuing in the unsettling depictions of machine civilization in American writers such as Sherwood Anderson, Willa Cather, the Southern Agrarians, and John Steinbeck. As Leo Marx has made clear, the threatening machine in the pastoral garden serves as a representative emblem for much postromantic American fiction. What is apparent now is how powerfully the sense of a degraded natural world has grown in the latter half of the twentieth century. During the Cold War, popular novels such as Nevil Shute's *On the Beach* and films such as *Dr. Strangelove* thrust before the public the real possibility of worldwide nuclear destruction. Rachel Carson's *Silent Spring* and Paul Ehrlich's *The Population Bomb* brought corresponding biological imperatives into common consciousness, and thus inevitably into artistic expression.

The field of science fiction, or futuristic fiction, offers the largest number of stories dealing with environmental destruction. Stephen Vincent Benét may have originated the surge of postcatastrophe short fiction with his fine story "By the Waters of Babylon," published in 1932 in his collection *Thirteen O'Clock*. In this story, a civilization that perhaps consumed itself in its own technology was destroyed by fire from the sky and a poisonous mist. More recent typical examples may be found in the work of such science fiction writers as Isaac Asimov, Ursula Le Guin, Kate Wilhelm, Robert Silverberg, and Kurt Vonnegut (especially the title story in *Welcome to the Monkey House*). Silverberg's anthology *The Infinite Web* reveals an array of eco-science fiction possibilities, from the futuristic formula-western of Arthur C. Clarke's "The Deep Range" (sea-ranching on plankton farms, and whale herds cowboyed by friendly porpoises) to Silverberg's "The Wind and the Rain," wherein the work of repairing the earthly ravages of "the ancients" (that is, us) has begun.

Other story writers approach the blighted environment realistically, or, in some cases, through a kind of magical realism. The latter category describes such stories as Barry Lopez's "Benjamin Claire, North Dakota Tradesman, Writes the President of the United States," in which a man levitates a warship to protest the nation's ruinous environmental policies; and Neal Morgan's "Joe Willie's Problem," wherein the title character's mere presence is sufficient to destroy machinery. A memorable example of realism twisting into a nightmarish Armageddon is Rick DeMarinis's "Weeds," in his *Under the Wheat*, in which indiscriminate aerial spraying of weed killer on the narrator's family farm kills or sickens people and animals. Eventually, the environmental poisoning is linked to human figures, including a ragged and filthy tramp who carries seeds that, when sown, produce a crop of obliterating weeds resistant to all con-

trol. As the story ends, the ripe pods of the weeds split and spill their destructive seeds into the wind and across the land, an ominous metaphor for the consequences of a heedless assault against nature.

T. Coraghessan Boyle's "Top of the Food Chain" (*Harper's,* April 1993) details another string of unanticipated outrages in the chemical warfare game, this time in third-world Borneo. The story unrolls as the direct testimony of a chemical industry spokesman before a Senate investigating committee. His monologue, a triumph of industry evasion and excuses, would be comical if its record of destruction were not so appalling, a version of *Silent Spring* in fast-forward. Other noteworthy stories of environmental degradation include Joanne Greenberg's "The Supremacy of the Hunza," William Eastlake's "The Death of the Sun," Julie Hayden's "In the Words of," Ron Tanner's "Garbage," Rudolfo Anaya's "Devil Deer," and Thom Jones's "I Want to Live!" Jones has said that his story is based on the death of his mother-in-law from cancer and on the daily wash of bad news about the carcinogens that surround us—a remark that reveals clearly how environmental conditions may serve as fictional genesis.

THE IMPORTANCE OF PLACE

As human beings, we are creatures for whom geography, territory, the ecology of place, has been basic to our evolutionary development. Nowadays, when much of the American population is casually migratory, and a change of place involves little more than plugging the old appliances into different outlets and learning the way to the nearest shopping center, place may seem less important. But to geographers, phenomenologists, anthropologists, and many of our thinkers and writers, a sense of where one is, a conscious appropriation of a piece of the earth, is important to the fullness of our lives.

Great American short fiction, from Washington Irving's Hudson River Valley tales to the present, has always been deeply imbued with a distinctive sense of the American land. In recent decades Wallace Stegner, Gary Snyder, and Wendell Berry stand out as eloquent and perceptive advocates of knowing one's geographic place. Stegner's entire record as a writer has been a testament to the shaping power of the western landscape. Snyder believes that we in North America have yet to discover where we are, that we live on the land like an army of foreign occupation, and he has given over his life and work to accomplishing a true inhabitation. Berry too has spent a lifetime understanding the patch of Kentucky geography that is his blood's country, as is seen in a story like "The Boundary," in his The Wild Birds, in which the knowledge that comes from living, working, enjoying, and suffering on a particular piece of the earth, in all seasons and over a long time, is memorably rendered.

Place-centered stories may be defined as stories in which place becomes, in effect, the central character, a supportive or adversarial presence. For the first half of this century, mention should be made of the Mojave Desert narratives of Mary Austin's The Land of Little Rain; the Mesa Verde cliff dwellings of Willa Cather's "Tom Outland's Story" in The Professor's House; and

H. L. Davis's Northwest end of the road, "The Homestead Orchard," in his Team Bells Woke Me. Further examples include Walter Van Tilburg Clark's story of the timeless circle of life, "The Indian Well," in his The Watchful Gods; Eudora Welty's title story in A Curtain of Green; and John Steinbeck's "Flight," in his The Long Valley, wherein a boy's doomed attempt to flee from a murder he has committed is figured in the increasingly arid and alien country through which he passes. More recently, the shadowy but compelling forest of Flannery O'Connor's "A View of the Woods," in her Everything That Rises Must Converge, serves as an emblem of the powerful presence of the unique and the ungovernable in life. One also notes the profound presence of the Montana mountains and streams of Norman Maclean's A River Runs Through It, the careful integration of setting and life in the Southwest Indian reservation of Leslie Silko's "Lullaby" (Storyteller), and the Anasazi country of Russell Martin's "Cliff Dwellers" in his Writers of the Purple Sage. All of these ecologically conscious stories return us to a world that encloses and antedates our culture and social presence, and that powerfully evokes the wisdom of such places and the human need to reconnect with them.

The encounters with place are not always beneficent, however. Depicting the modern Americans' alienation from place, Baine Kerr dramatizes an urbanite's unsettling confrontation with a primal landscape in "Rider." Edward Allen, in "River of Toys," seems to find, in urban creeks lined with trash and asphalt parking lots, places all his own, because no one else wants them. In John Edgar Wideman's "what he saw," from his all stories *are true,* a black American narrator ponders racial and cultural connection to what might be his own ancestral hellish home place as he and a group of journalists tour a violence-ravaged South African squatter camp. Here, as well as elsewhere, environmental degradation falls most heavily upon the poor and the powerless.

ANIMAL LIVES

A shape that increasingly haunts the writer's imagination is the animal. As Paul Shepard writes, "This creative perception of animals is still in us, a perennial satisfaction and pleasure, one of the oldest human vocations." In American short fiction, John Muir's incomparable "Stickeen" and Jack London's dog stories, written around the turn of the nineteenth century, marked the beginnings of a large popular readership for stories in which animal lives seemed to challenge traditional humanistic assumptions of otherness. Such stories offer a much deeper and more thoughtful penetration into the animal mind and spirit. Fascination with animal presences continues to emerge in American short fiction in the first half of the twentieth century in such classics as the title story from Sherwood Anderson's *Death in the Woods*, William Faulkner's "The Bear," and Vardis Fisher's "The Scarecrow."

Some memorable contemporary animal-centered stories are Peter Matthiessen's "The Wolves of Aquila," from his *The River Styx and Other Stories*; the title story of William Kittredge's *We Are Not in This Together*; Barry Lopez's *Lessons from the Wolverine*; and Rick Bass's "The Myth of Bears" in his *The Sky, the Stars, the Wil-*

derness. Bass prefaces his Alaska story of a man and his wife, both more animal-like than human, with a passage from Alaskan poet and former trapper John Haines, who questions whether we can ever fully know the animal mind, saying that "the life of the animal remains other and beyond, never completely yielding all that it is."

Animal subjects are not limited to the wild. Urbanites and suburbanites ponder their relationships to the lives of various animals in fine stories like John Updike's "The Man Who Loved Extinct Mammals," M. Pabst Battin's "Terminal Procedure," Wright Morris's "Fellow-Creatures," Maxine Kumin's "The Match," and Frederick Busch's "One More Wave of Fear." Scott Bradfield's "The Parakeet and the Cat," like Bernard Malamud's "The Jewbird," revives the animal fable, as do several stories that center on a growing awareness of the possibilities of animal-human communication, such as Joyce Renwick's "The Dolphin Story," Ursula Le Guin's fictions in her *Buffalo Gals and Other Animal Presences*, and John Randolph's tour de force, "The Dolphin Papers." In all of these stories, animal presences do more than meet a part of a writer's responsibility, which, as Camus and Matthiessen remind us, is to speak for those who cannot speak for themselves. They foster an enlightened awareness, taking us to the antecedents and borders of our species and involving readers in the ecological fascination with such edges.

A more extensive ecocritical reading of a classic short story might be instructive at this point. Ernest Hemingway's works reveal a deep interest in ethology, one that, if closely attended to, can revivify some characteristic interpretations. For example, his "The Short Happy Life of Francis Macomber" is commonly read as a story about what constitutes manliness. But it speaks to a new generation of readers with new meanings. To begin with, it seems impossible to read the story today without thinking of the decimation of African wildlife. With that in mind, one notes that the human interactions in the story—characterized by pettiness, jealousy, cruelty, fear, and bravado—are mutedly set against the purity and nobility of the hunted animals. "What is this joy? That no animal / falters, but knows what it must do," as Denise Levertov's poem expresses it. Hemingway twice takes us into the mind of the wounded lion to reveal this absolute guilelessness and purity of purpose. After the first such revelation, the next sentence tells us that Macomber gave no thought to how the lion felt, but the more aware Wilson later reminds his client of the animal's suffering. The following pages develop the byplay between Macomber's selfish ignorance and Wilson's awareness, though they convey also that any level of human awareness is unmatched by the inenarrable purposefulness of the lion, who knows only its suffering and what it must do. Wilson, who understands something of the wounded animal's feelings, says only "'Hell of a fine lion,'" a characteristic Hemingway retreat from language, down below the word-surface, where the real meanings are.

Current-day environmental concerns were not unanticipated by Hemingway, and even the most admirable of his hunters are party to the destruction of that which they most love. In "The Short Happy Life" the characters emerge in a kind of circle of moral awareness and responsibility that includes even the hunted, and that, once noticed, enriches the story for today's reader. That same reader would find a contrasting response to a contemporary Africa in naturalist Terry Tempest Williams's story "In the Country of Grasses," from her *An Unspoken Hunger*. Williams's narrator travels in lion country, but listens to the Maasai guides and elders instead of a white hunter and his clients, watches rather than shoots, and finds strength in a handful of grass.

If the twenty-first century becomes, as it is being called, the century of the environment, then the questions and issues raised in the works surveyed here can be expected to occupy our writers increasingly in the territory ahead.

Glen A. Love

SELECTED BIBLIOGRAPHY

Many of the stories cited in the essay, as well as other works of ecologically inspired fiction, can be found in the annual *Pushcart Prize* and *Best American Short Stories* volumes from 1973 to the present.

Glotfelty, Cheryll, and Harold Fromm, eds. *The Ecocriticism Reader*. Athens: University of Georgia Press, 1996.

Halpern, Daniel, ed. *On Nature*. San Francisco: North Point Press, 1987.

Marx, Leo. *The Machine in the Garden*. New York: Oxford University Press, 1964.

Shepard, Paul. *The Others: How Animals Made Us Human*. Washington, D.C.: Island Press, 1996.

LESBIAN AND GAY
SHORT STORIES

The Stonewall riots of 1969 radically transformed the conditions under which lesbian and gay writers wrote. Precipitated by what began as a "routine" police raid on the Stonewall Inn, a gay bar in Greenwich Village frequented by Puerto Ricans and African Americans, many of whom were drag queens, the riots radicalized lesbians and gays by demonstrating the importance of openly resisting the homophobia of American society. In the wake of the riots, lesbians and gays were significantly less willing to treat their sexuality as a shameful secret and aggressively asserted their right to participate in the lesbian and gay subcultures without fear of reprisal.

With the opening up of the closet, new forms of lesbian and gay literary expression emerged. Writers who openly explored lesbian and gay themes no longer faced ostracism by critics. In the 1950s, when writers with established reputations such as Gore Vidal and James Baldwin had published novels that centered on gay experience, they were accused of squandering their literary talent. The opening up of the closet also created a new type of reader who was eager for fiction that explored lesbian and gay life from an anti-homophobic perspective. This reader sustained the publication of new lesbian and gay magazines such as *Christopher Street* and *On Our Backs,* which were radically different from lesbian and gay magazines published before Stonewall. Publishing short fiction written by and for lesbians and gays, these magazines actively promoted the controversial ethics of pleasure pioneered by the gay liberation movement, but they were not pornographic. More important, the political mobilization of lesbians and gays enabled writers to imagine alternative forms of lesbian and gay life. Before Stonewall, fictions such as Vidal's *The City and the Pillar* (1948) and Baldwin's *Giovanni's Room* (1956) usually ended tragically with the hero or heroine committing suicide or abandoning the lesbian or gay subculture. Written primarily for heterosexuals, this fiction was a poorly disguised plea for tolerance.

This is not to disparage the literary achievements of pre-Stonewall writers. Perhaps the most significant of these writers was Tennessee Williams, whose collections of short stories *One Arm* (1948) and *Hard Candy* (1954) were remarkably bold and unapologetic in their treatment of homosexuality. Williams's skillful manipulation of point of view in such stories as "Hard Candy" worked to expose the hypocrisy of the social and literary conventions that required writers to approach homosexuality discreetly so as to avoid offending heterosexual readers. The recovery and reevaluation of the fiction of pre-Stonewall writers like Williams has been a central project of lesbian and gay studies, and a canon of lesbian and gay short story writers has begun to take shape, as evidenced by the anthologies of Edmund White and David Leavitt, which include many of the same writers. In addition to Tennessee Williams, this canon also includes writers who did not identify themselves as lesbian or gay, indeed who

might not have known that such terms existed or, if they did, might have strenuously objected to having them ascribed to their sexuality. Such stories as Henry James's "The Beast in the Jungle" (1903) and Willa Cather's "Paul's Case" (1905) now appear regularly on the syllabuses of courses in lesbian and gay literature.

Locating James and Cather in a tradition of lesbian and gay writers promises to complicate our understanding not only of their work but also of American literary history. It raises an issue of definition or labeling not faced by scholars of African American literature or the literatures of other minoritized groups. How does the critic justify labeling writers such as James and Cather with the recently invented categories *lesbian* and *gay*? After all, James and Cather belonged to a society and culture that were radically different from the ones to which post-Stonewall writers belong. Because of the stigma attached to homosexuality, pre-Stonewall writers, especially those writing in the early part of the twentieth century, were forced to translate their experience into heterosexual terms or to encode it in ways that rendered it ambiguous. Even Tennessee Williams was considerably less explicit about homosexuality in his plays, which had a larger audience than his short stories. Thus, recovering the homosexual meaning of the work of earlier writers often entails reading autobiographically or between the lines, strategies fraught with peril. To avoid distorting their work, it is important to resist the temptation to approach pre-Stonewall writers from a post-Stonewall perspective.

But even if scholars are careful to distinguish between pre- and post-Stonewall writers and to take into account the shifting construction of homosexuality, which makes the project of identifying a continuous lesbian and gay literary tradition a vexing one, there are other issues that need to be addressed. A key issue is how to define lesbian and gay short stories— as stories written by lesbian and gay writers specifically for lesbian and gay readers; or stories written by lesbian and gay writers, including ones that do not address lesbian and gay themes; or stories with lesbian and gay themes, even ones written by heterosexuals.

For historical reasons, it makes sense to consider only stories written by and for lesbians and gays. Storytelling has played a crucial role in what is arguably the most significant development in post-Stonewall lesbian and gay life, the emergence of an imagined community to which the mass of lesbians and gays feel politically and culturally attached. In the wake of the Stonewall riots, telling family, friends, and colleagues the story of how one came to recognize that one is lesbian or gay operated as a powerful political act, shifting the authority to define homosexuality from the dominant culture to lesbians and gays themselves. A variation of the coming-of-age story, the coming-out story transforms homosexuality from a shameful secret that one should keep hidden into an integral part, or property, of one's selfhood. A classic example is Edmund White's autobiographical novel *A Boy's Own Story* (1982), in which the narrator describes coming of age as a homosexual in the Midwest of the 1950s. Lesbians and gays emerge from such stories as bearers

of rights who should be allowed to participate in the nation's political and cultural life without having to make their homosexuality invisible. For this reason, the public avowal of homosexuality in the form of a coming-out story is wholly consistent with the liberal individualism underpinning American national identity, which may explain why it has been so successful in mobilizing support for gay rights among heterosexuals. But even more important, this form of storytelling has been crucial to promoting a sense of community among lesbians and gays. It allows the storyteller not only to locate his or her personal history in a larger collective history but also to impart valuable knowledge to the listener about how to negotiate the homophobic structure of American society.

Lesbian and gay short stories have performed similar political and cultural work, not only contributing to the project of eroding the cultural authority of homophobic narratives of homosexuality but also enabling readers to imagine that they are deeply connected to other lesbians and gays through a shared experience. Not surprisingly, one of the most common and enduring themes of lesbian and gay short stories has been the difficult passage from homosexual desire to a lesbian or gay identity. It is central to the stories of such important writers as Lev Raphael and Jane Rule. But the ability of the short stories to perform this work has been contingent upon the sexual identity of their writers. Regardless of their content, stories written by heterosexual writers such as A. M. Homes and Ann Beattie have been unable to create the same sense of community among lesbians and gays as those written by lesbian and gay writers. This does not mean that heterosexual writers are incapable of creating believable lesbian and gay characters or of writing compellingly about lesbian and gay life. But their relation to the dominant culture is different from that of lesbian and gay writers, and thus they cannot write about lesbians and gays with the same cultural authority.

Despite their desire to transform the reader's sense of identity, lesbian and gay writers have tended to avoid engaging in technical experimentation, although this is less true of lesbian writers such as Michelle Cliff and Kathy Acker than of gay writers such as Edmund White and David Leavitt. Despite their explicit treatment of homosexuality, lesbian and gay short stories are fairly traditional in their structure and style. For example, the stories of White and Leavitt, two of the best-known gay writers, all have a beginning, middle, and end; maintain a consistent point of view; are realistic; focus on a protagonist who must overcome a set of obstacles; and are organized teleologically. Lesbian and gay writers have also tended to share one of the central goals of the gay rights movement, that of making available to lesbians and gays a form of selfhood usually reserved in American society for white, middle-class, heterosexual men (although again this is less true of lesbian writers). Many lesbian and gay stories center on a protagonist who struggles to achieve a coherent, fully integrated sense of self, an achievement made difficult by his or her homosexuality. Thus in Lev Raphael's classic coming-out stories "Another Life" and "Welcome to Beth Homo," the protagonists are initially unable to come to terms with their homosexuality because of their orthodox Jewish backgrounds, but they ultimately learn how. It is precisely because their formal properties are so conventional that lesbian and gay short stories have been able to fulfill the storytelling needs of lesbians and gays. For those properties render the stories accessible to their lesbian and gay readers, which in turn ensures that they help those readers to make sense of their own experience.

Despite their many similarities, however, there are significant differences between lesbian and gay short stories that linking them obscures. The storytelling needs of lesbians and gays have not always coincided. Indeed, stories by feminist writers such as Tillie Olsen, Margaret Atwood, and Alice Walker that center on women's struggle to overcome patriarchal oppression have been as important to lesbians as stories about coming out. Because they are women, lesbians have faced greater obstacles in creating a distinct subcultural identity than have gays. Until recently, their economic opportunities have been considerably more circumscribed than those of gays. Consequently, they have lacked the financial resources necessary for sustaining a subculture centered on their political and sexual needs. Their attempts to fulfill those needs have also been hampered by an oppressive sexual ideology that places women in a passive position in relation to desire, if it even acknowledges that they have desire. From the perspective of this ideology, sex between women, indeed any sex that does not involve penile penetration, is all but inconceivable. In light of these obstacles, it is hardly surprising that the women's movement has had as profound an influence on lesbians as the Stonewall riots. Indeed, in the wake of the riots, lesbians vigorously debated whether their needs and interests were better served by feminism or by gay liberation.

The influence of feminism on the lesbian subculture accounts for what is perhaps the most significant difference between lesbian and gay writers. Gay writers have tended to generalize the experience of white, middle-class, urban gays. They have treated other forms of gay culture (working-class, Latino, African American, rural) as marginal, if they have even acknowledged their existence. By contrast, lesbian writers have tended to explore a wider range of experience. Their short stories usually center on characters that must overcome multiple forms of oppression. The autobiographical stories in Dorothy Allison's *Trash* (1988), which received the prestigious Lambda Literary Award for Lesbian Fiction, exemplify the differences between lesbian and gay writers. An unidentified narrator reconstructs her traumatic experiences growing up poor and lesbian in rural South Carolina. She must struggle not only with being "white trash," but also with a misogynistic stepfather who physically abuses her. Deeply influenced by feminism, the stories avoid reducing the narrator's experiences to a single form of oppression, whether homophobia, sexism, or classism. Consequently, they are able to shed considerable light on the tangled relations among class, gender, and sexuality in American society.

The differences between lesbian and gay short stories can also be traced to the AIDS epidemic. The most serious crisis facing gays since the McCarthyite purges of the 1950s, when thousands lost their jobs because homosexuality was thought to threaten national security, AIDS has undermined many of the social and political gains made by gays since Stonewall. As potential carriers of HIV, the virus that causes AIDS, gays have reemerged as the "enemy within": they supposedly threaten to contaminate the nation as a whole. The lesions caused by Kaposi's sarcoma and the gaunt physical appearance that, thanks to the dominant media's sensationalistic coverage of the epidemic, have become telltale signs of HIV infection are thought to inscribe gay identity directly on the body. These symptoms have emerged as signs of gay men's inner corruption, bodily evidence of their "perverted" sexuality. In other words, the epidemic has reversed one of the gay rights movement's most important achievements, the medical profession's declassification of homosexuality as a disease.

Some of the most significant stories about AIDS deal with this aspect of the epidemic, tracing the transformation of the gay male body from a site of pleasure and desire into one of danger and disease. In Andrew Holleran's "Sunday Morning: Key West," AIDS has displaced sexuality as the basis of gay identity. The protagonist Roger returns after several years to Key West, the site where in his late teens he had his first sexual encounters. But the beaches have lost their erotic allure, and he spends most of his vacation looking through his friend Lee's old scrapbooks of Fire Island and reminiscing with him about the friends and lovers they have lost to AIDS. "The *Times* as It Knows Us," one of the stories in Allen Barnett's *The Body and Its Dangers* (1990), an important collection of stories about AIDS, explores the tensions the epidemic causes in a group of gays who have made a tradition of spending weekends together at Fire Island. The men who are still healthy unconsciously resent those who are not because they remind them of the profound changes that have occurred in the resort community's culture of cruising, changes that prevent them from experiencing their sexuality without guilt or anxiety.

Some writers have taken a different approach to the epidemic, minimizing its impact on gay sexual practices and emphasizing instead the cultural and affectional ties that have been essential to combating the epidemic. In the title story of David Leavitt's acclaimed collection *A Place I've Never Been* (1990), the self-centered Nathan does not adequately appreciate the heterosexual narrator Celia, his closest friend since college. He is so consumed by his anxieties about AIDS that he fails to notice her own loneliness and frustration. The growing lack of connection between these two friends, who once shared the most intimate details of their lives, seems both regrettable and unnecessary. For it is a sign that they have allowed their different needs and desires to come between them. In Rebecca Brown's deeply moving "A Good Man," one of the few stories about AIDS written by a lesbian, the normally taciturn lesbian narrator struggles to put into words her love and admiration for Jim, a friend who

helped her to come out and who is dying from AIDS. Unlike her, Jim is an accomplished storyteller who entertains his friends with campy stories about everything from old Hollywood movies to his increasingly lengthy stays in the hospital. When he eventually dies, he seems to bequeath to the narrator his gift for narrative. By memorializing her dead friend's storytelling, the newly eloquent narrator testifies to the importance of camp as a narrative mode.

In addition to the AIDS crisis, another recurrent theme in lesbian and gay short stories has been the intersection of homosexuality with race and ethnicity. Stories concerning the divided loyalties and conflicting demands experienced by lesbians and gays of color have reinforced the need for lesbians and gays to develop an understanding of identity that is more complex than the one embedded in the coming-out story. Lesbians of color have made the most important contributions here. In such groundbreaking books of feminist theory as *This Bridge Called My Back* (1981), writers such as Gloria Anzaldúa, Audre Lorde, and Cherríe Moraga have insisted on the multiplicity of all identities. The characters in their stories feel as out of place in the lesbian subculture as in their own racial or ethnic communities. In Lorde's autobiographical story "Tar Beach," for example, the narrator Audre recalls in lyric detail her passionate affair with an older black woman. The intensity of the women's passion for each other reflects their ability to share the psychological costs of having to struggle constantly against racism. Audre's previous lovers, who were all white, accused her of exaggerating the problem of racism in the lesbian subculture. By treating the goal of achieving a fully integrated self as not only impossible but also undesirable, stories like Lorde's expose the limitations of both the women's and the gay liberation movements. Neither movement has adequately considered the importance of race and ethnicity as determinants of identity; both have generalized the experiences of middle-class whites. Thus stories by lesbians of color have enabled their readers to imagine that they are part of a more expansive community than the one projected by the coming-out story. Their short stories have underscored the need for minoritized groups in general to develop forms of solidarity not patterned on kinship structures or grounded in monolithic, homogeneous communities, forms of solidarity that inevitably lead to the exclusion of people who are or seem different.

The desire to complicate the humanistic conception of selfhood affirmed by the coming-out story underlies another significant difference between lesbian and gay writers. Lesbian writers have been more willing than have gay writers to experiment with structure, point of view, and style. Lorde's autobiographical stories blur the distinction between fiction and nonfiction, creating a hybrid form she called "biomythography." Cherrie Moraga's story "La Offrenda" interweaves prose and poetry, some of which is written in Spanish. Michelle Cliff's dreamlike "Screen Memory" alternates scenes of the protagonist's childhood in the Caribbean with a strict but caring grandmother with scenes of her struggles as a black actress

in a racist Hollywood. Kathy Acker's "The Language of the Body" also eschews linear narrative: the unidentified narrator shifts from a disjointed account of her marriage to a "journal" in which she records her experiences masturbating to her fantasies about attending a drag ball dressed as Patti Page. These formal strategies seem intended to unsettle the reader's sense of identity: they place him or her in a position similar to the one occupied by the characters. The characters' experience is so fragmented that it prevents them from achieving a coherent, stable identity. Thus, the technical experimentation in which lesbian writers have engaged moves lesbian and gay storytelling significantly beyond its original function of affirming a unitary lesbian and gay identity. In complicating the coming-out story, lesbian writers have reinforced the need for lesbians and gays to develop complex understandings of identity as multiple and never fully achieved. It is precisely because lesbian and gay short stories address such issues of identity and identification that they are so important.

Robert J. Corber

SELECTED BIBLIOGRAPHY

Allison, Dorothy. *Trash*. Ithaca, N.Y.: Firebrand, 1988.

Anzaldúa, Gloria, and Cherrie Moraga, eds. *This Bridge Called My Back: Writings by Radical Women of Color*. New York: Kitchen Table, 1983.

Barnett, Allen. *The Body and Its Dangers*. New York: St. Martin's, 1991.

Holoch, Naomi, and Joan Nestle, eds.

Women on Women 2: An Anthology of Lesbian Short Fiction. New York: Penguin, 1993.

Leavitt, David. *A Place I've Never Been.* New York: Penguin, 1990.

Leavitt, David, and Mark Mitchell, eds. *The Penguin Book of Gay Short Fiction.* New York: Penguin, 1994.

McKinley, Catherine E., and L. Joyce DeLaney, eds. *Afrekete: An Anthology of Black Lesbian Writing.* New York: Doubleday, 1995.

Osborne, Karen Lee, and William J. Spurlin, eds. *Reclaiming the Heartland: Lesbian and Gay Voices from the Midwest.* Minneapolis: University of Minnesota Press, 1996.

Reynolds, Margaret, ed. *The Penguin Book of Lesbian Short Stories.* New York: Penguin, 1994.

White, Edmund, ed. *The Faber Book of Gay Short Fiction.* London: Faber and Faber, 1991.

THE NATIVE AMERICAN

SHORT STORY

Throughout the twentieth century, the voices of Native Americans have provided an essential American "Other" by which white America's image becomes defined. From the early years of the century, when Indians were still portrayed as ignorant savages, cordoned off in reservations and destined to cultural and physical death by assimilation, up to the late twentieth century, when New Age pilgrims sought out Natives for romantic ecological insights, white Americans long believed that whatever "We" are, the Indian was always something "Other." This popular essentialization has sparked both interest and lack of interest in Native peoples and cultures. In this cultural context, Native American short fiction writers have emerged as significant literary figures who have, over the century, assumed their own innovative positions as storytellers and witnesses for their people.

Early twentieth-century writers such as Gertrude Bonnin and D'Arcy Mc-Nickle, influenced by realism, naturalism, and regionalism, created works in keeping with non-Native literary expectations while chipping away at stereotypical images of Indians. After a dry spell of the 1930s and 1940s, the Native American Renaissance propelled Native writers into a wide reading audience composed of Native and non-Native readers. When their voices were finally heard, some were angry, some were confused, some were nostalgic, and some were the voices of dreamers. As the twentieth century closed,

Native writers had positioned themselves in the forefront of American writers because their visions unveil a world that is unified as a reality composed of mythic verities, spiritual mystery, and human sensibility. Much of this work is grounded in the experiences of Native communities. The stories grow out of place and the writer's ties to an animate, powerful landscape that includes human, animal, and spiritual presences. As contemporary writers such as N. Scott Momaday, Leslie Silko, Gerald Vizenor, Louise Erdrich, Simon Ortiz, Sherman Alexie, Thomas King, and others seek identity, connection, continuance, survival, and autonomy, they create stories that draw from the oral tradition, from the Native communities they know, from a historical vision, and from their understanding of Western literature.

During the first quarter of the century, many literary magazines were aggressively pursuing regionalist stories. *Harper's, Atlantic Monthly, Century,* and *Saturday Review of Literature,* to name but a few, wanted to counter European influences with authentic American fiction. The search for community amid a growing impersonal society, the belief in the importance of the land as the country urbanized, and an idealization of the uniqueness of American life formed the ground of many popular literary assumptions. Some of this popular interest manifested itself in the movement toward preservation of wilderness and the creation of national parks. At the same time, many early modernists were exploring the connections between the primitive and the modern. Together these trends created an audience for Native American short stories.

During the late nineteenth century, Indian schools and mission schools had begun to produce literate graduates who could write poetry and fiction. One of the most popular writers of the time was Charles Eastman (1858–1939). Raised in a traditional Santee Sioux environment, Eastman graduated from Boston University in 1890 to become one of the first Native American physicians. He was also the author of nine books and numerous articles, a popular speaker, and a noted progressive champion of Native peoples. Eastman published two books of short stories, *Red Hunters and the Animal People* (1904) and *Old Indian Days* (1907), and one book of fictionalized Sioux folktales, *Wigwam Evenings* (1909). Influenced by the popularity of Indian stories aimed at a juvenile market, Eastman wrote *Red Hunters and the Animal People*. This book of animal stories aimed at children presented clear-cut morals reflecting the virtues of a good hunter. Because Eastman, like other Native writers of the day, Luther Standing Bear and Pauline Johnson for instance, was writing for non-Native audiences, he presented Native men and women as conforming to some aspects of popular stereotypes, especially the virtuous and courageous characters of his adult fiction, such as *Old Indian Days*. The brave warriors and modest girls served as models for young readers partly because of their closeness to the natural world. Within this framework, Eastman and others tried to broaden public good will toward Native peoples by representing Indians as honorable people, with intelligence, humanity, and virtue. As such, they were entitled to the reader's respect and help and not to be subjected to brutalities like the

Wounded Knee Massacre and the confiscation of the Black Hills.

During the first two decades of this century, E. Pauline Johnson (1861–1913) was well known throughout Canada, Great Britain, and the United States. Born on the Six Nations Reserve in Ontario, she was noted as a poet and short story writer, but her real celebrity came as the result of her extensive stage performances of her own work. Many of her short stories published in *Boys World* and *Mother's Magazine,* such as "Red Girl's Reasoning" and "As It Was in the Beginning," portrayed the values, virtues, and tragedy surrounding Native women in a melodramatic manner that met contemporary expectations.

The subject of Indian women was explored also by Gertrude Bonnin (1876–1938), who was born on the Sioux reservation and wrote under the pen name Zitkala Sa (Red Bird). Her stories and essays appeared in *Harper's* and *Atlantic Monthly*, and gained her some public notice. She was a noted progressive and member of the Society for the American Indian whose autobiographical writings and essays argued for a reevaluation and appreciation of Native American identity. In her short fiction, some of which was collected in *American Indian Stories* (1921), she tried to reach beyond stereotypes, drawing psychologically rich portraits of Native women acting with courage and merging traditional and contemporary influences.

One noteworthy Native writer who has received little attention is John M. Oskison (1874–1947). Born in the Indian Territory, he received a bachelor's degree from Stanford and worked for a while as an editor on the *New York Evening Post* and *Collier's Weekly*. Though known for his novels, Oskison published stories in *Collier's, Century,* and other magazines between 1900 and 1925. Among his most memorable stories are "Walla-Tenaka-Creek" and "The Singing Bird." Most of his stories are set in the rugged frontier environment of Oklahoma. With his emphasis on the characters' relationships to the land and their struggles with social expectations, Oskison's short fiction typifies the regionalist's assumption that cultures respond to the region's spirit.

In the years between 1930 and the mid-1960s, little short fiction by Native Americans was published. The Depression and World War II had much to do with this decline, as did a lack of interest in Native writers within the literary world. However, this period of Native American literary history is marked by two major writers: John Joseph Matthews (1894–1979) and D'Arcy McNickle (1904–1977). Matthews's national reputation came from his novels and his historical books on the Osage Indian experience. Born on the Osage reservation in Oklahoma, Matthews eventually earned a degree from Oxford, worked in Europe for a number of years, and then returned to Oklahoma and became involved with tribal government. Between 1929 and 1933 he published nine short stories, including "Hunger on the Prairie" in *Sooner Magazine,* an alumni magazine of the University of Oklahoma. These adventure sketches juxtapose learned philosophical ruminations about man, nature, and the outdoors with Indian dialect and the exhilaration of the hunt.

D'Arcy McNickle was born near the Flathead Reservation and was adopted into that tribe. After college studies at the

University of Montana and Oxford, he stayed in Europe until his return to New York in the mid-1920s. McNickle tried to survive as a professional writer but was unable to sell his short fiction or novels. In 1935, he did sell a story to *Esquire,* but he turned most of his attention to novels and to his employment with the Bureau of Indian Affairs. For the next thirty-five years, he published novels and ethnohistorical books while working as an Indian rights activist. His short fiction was set both in New York and on Indian reservations in the West. Most of these stories were written in the late 1920s and the 1930s but were not published until recently in a collection entitled *The Hawk and Other Stories.* In this volume, McNickle contrasts the values associated with the land and the community to modern materialist society. Often, as in "Hard Riding," cross-cultural misunderstanding causes distress because characters will not examine their cultural assumptions. With their greater concern for the ties between literature and tribal communities, their increasing abilities to blend Native and non-Native epistemologies, and their penetrating historical analysis, the works of both Matthews and McNickle form a bridge that leads to 1968 and the Native American Renaissance.

With publication of N. Scott Momaday's *House Made of Dawn* in 1968 and its subsequent Pulitzer Prize, the landscape of Native American literature changed. Not only was there increased public interest in writing by Native Americans, but also Native writers felt inspired and encouraged. Suddenly it seemed possible that they could be successful with their writing and still remain true to their unique experience. Momaday himself has written little short fiction. What little he has done consists of rewriting traditional oral narratives and expanding observations and remembrances, some of which have been collected in *In the Presence of the Sun* (1992) and *Man Made of Words* (1997).

Throughout the late 1960s and 1970s, many small presses and magazines began to promote Native writers and the expression of a Native voice. A few national publishers even began to seek out Native writers. Harper & Row became the best known with the series of publications it started in the early 1970s. Without a climate like this, the publication of *The Man to Send Rain Clouds: Contemporary Stories by American Indians* in 1974 would not have been possible. Edited by Kenneth Rosen, the book brought together the short fiction of seven unknown Southwestern Indian writers, propelling the work of Leslie Silko and Simon Ortiz to national attention. Silko and Ortiz created rich stories layered with myth, witchcraft, and spirituality. Their narrative stances articulated a Native worldview, one critical of non-Native ignorance and cultural assumptions and centered on the intelligence of a Native perspective. Rather than dwell on historical oppression, their stories, such as "The Man to Send Rain Clouds" and "The San Francisco Indians," reinforced a belief in the continuance and continuity of Native cultures and values. Both Silko and Ortiz deliberately incorporated oral narratives as subject matter and oral storytelling techniques into their fiction. Both wanted their narrative standpoints to represent authentically Native perception because, for the first time, Native fiction writers recognized the existence of a Native literary audience. From this point on, Native writers needed to address two sets of narrative expectations, and much contemporary short fiction is grounded in that need. Ortiz's volume of short fiction *Howbah Indians* (1978) was followed by *Fightin': New and Collected Stories* (1983). Silko's use of myth and oral tradition was emphasized in her 1981 volume *Storyteller,* which included a number of her popular short stories, such as "Storyteller" and "Yellow Woman." Many of the noteworthy elements of her short fiction, such as the use of oral narrative and the evocation of mythic reality, can be found in her highly acclaimed novel *Ceremony* (1977).

In 1983, Ortiz edited one of the best collections of contemporary Native American short fiction, *Earth Power Coming.* In it, Ortiz brought together the fiction of Silko and Louise Erdrich with that of many other writers previously noted for their poetry, for example, Maurice Kenny, Paula Gunn Allen, Carter Revard, Ralph Salisbury, and Linda Hogan. Striking stories by Anna Walters, Elizabeth Cook-Lynn, and Peter Blue Cloud combined with work from less well-known writers to create a powerful anthology, one still used in many classrooms today.

In 1978, both Peter Blue Cloud and Gerald Vizenor published their first collections of short stories. Blue Cloud took for his inspiration the Coyote tales common among many western tribes to create the stories in *Back Then Tomorrow.* In his retellings, he fictionalizes and restructures the tales so they read like short fiction. He also takes the Native trickster and places him in contemporary situations to give a material presence to Native mythic reality. This volume was expanded and revised in 1982 and published as *Elderberry Flute Song.*

Vizenor's fiction also explores the trickster, but it is the urban, compassionate trickster that fascinates him. Vizenor uses myth to blur the lines between fact and fiction and to force readers to reject simplistic and stereotyped views of Native American experience. For him the oral tradition is a liberating realm of imagination that enhances the calcified arena of realistic prose. His 1978 book of stories, *Wordarrows: Indians and Whites in the New Fur Trade,* centers on urban Indian experience in Minneapolis, while *Earthdivers* (1981) broadens the geographic focus and furthers his development of the compassionate, urban trickster by embedding him in a satiric narrative structure. *Trickster of Liberty* (1988) weaves nine loosely related trickster narratives into what might be called a novel. *Landfill Meditation* (1991) continues his fabulist, postmodern experimentation with narrative structure, character development, word play, and representation.

Louise Erdrich published her award-winning book *Love Medicine* in 1984 to great critical success. After winning a number of fiction prizes, Erdrich expanded and interwove her short stories into a novel that consists not so much of chapters as of a complex design of braided family and historical narratives. The stories center on a fictional Chippewa reservation in North Dakota and generations of close and distant relatives. Using this reservation and these families as a focus, Erdrich has completed a quartet of books: *Love Medicine, The Beet Queen* (1986), *Tracks* (1988), and *The Bingo Palace* (1993). Many of her published short stories are chapters from these books. Erdrich's fiction is noted for its striking symbolic episodes, its use of oral tradition, its unique characterization, and its humor.

Anna Lee Walters's short story collection *The Sun Is Not Merciful* (1985) includes her much-anthologized story "The Warriors" and won an American Book Award in 1986. Walters's short fiction, grounded in the landscapes of New Mexico and Oklahoma, shows great sensitivity to character, culture, and the influence of oral tradition. In this book, Walters creates vivid portrayals from her Oklahoma past of characters who struggle with cultural and personal forces that would limit their potential. They seek a harmonious balance between these forces, the needs of others, and their own desires. Walters sees this harmony as an extension of Native tradition into a tenuous future, but one that will exist as long as it is built on the strength of the community and kinship.

Throughout the late 1980s and 1990s, Joseph Bruchac has continued to publish collections of short stories such as *Turtle Meat* (1992) and retellings of traditional Abenaki and Iroquois tales, as in *The Faithful Hunter* (1988). In his role as publisher and editor, Bruchac has made a lasting contribution to the development of Native American literature.

In 1990, Elizabeth Cook-Lynn published *The Power of Horses*, containing thirteen short stories and featuring two well-respected stories, "The Power of Horses" and "A Good Chance." Set in the Dakota hills over many years, her stories draw readers into a specific landscape inhabited by a wide spectrum of Native people, young and old, male and female, traditional and progressive. Cook-Lynn's work expresses a strong appreciation of the history and politics of cross-cultural interaction. Her characters battle social transformations to retain and reimagine cultural values, and to maintain the slender threads that tie them back to oral traditions and ancestral wisdom. Cook-Lynn's sense of social responsibility and her political/historical inquiry provide the focus for much of her work as a writer, professor, editor, essayist, and activist.

As the 1980s ended and the 1990s began, publishers became attentive to New Age thinking and to the curricular movements in American education. The general interest in multicultural voices encouraged the publication of a surprising number of anthologies of Native American short stories and oral tales. In 1989, Paula Allen combined traditional tales and contemporary stories in her anthology *Spider Woman's Granddaughters*. Both *The Lightning Within*, edited by Alan Velie, and *Talking Leaves*, edited by Craig Lesley, were published in 1991. These collections were followed by two anthologies edited by Clifford Trafzer: *Earth Song, Sky Spirit* in 1993 and *Blue Dawn, Red Earth* in 1996. Paula Allen has continued on the tack with *Song of the Turtle* in 1996. These anthologies and other publications introduced a number of promising short story writers while publishing the work of more established writers, most of whom had not published short story collections. Notable among the many stories were new writings by Paula Allen, Maurice Kenny, Ralph Salisbury, Robert Conley, Mary Tall-Mountain, Diane Glancy, Greg Sarris, Beth Brandt, Gloria Bird, Linda Hogan, and Tom King.

As the century closed, Tom King had become an influential short story writer with many anthologized stories, most of which are collected in *One Good Story, That One* (1993). His writing is distinguished by his use of contemporary characters designed to burst stereotypes with humor, playful satire, and frequent references to popular culture. Sherman Alexie's collection of short fiction *The Lone Ranger and Tonto Fistfight in Heaven* (1993) established him as an important young fiction writer whose work presents contemporary Native experience, complete with pain, anger, and grim humor.

The literary history of Native American short fiction suggests that Native writers will continue to focus on destroying stereotypes, and on forging connections with oral traditions and cultural heritage. Contemporary writers such as Silko, Ortiz, Hogan, and Allen are guided by their need to bolster communities and strengthen cultural continuance. Traditional narratives and mythic perception will remain the unyielding foundations for future stories as Native American short story writing enters its most fertile era yet.

James Ruppert

SELECTED BIBLIOGRAPHY

Alexie, Sherman. *The Lone Ranger and Tonto Fistfight in Heaven.* New York: Atlantic Monthly Press, 1993.

Allen, Paula Gunn, ed. *Song of the Turtle: American Indian Literature, 1974–1994.* New York: Ballantine, 1996.

Allen, Paula Gunn, ed. *Spiderwoman's Granddaughters: Traditional Tales and Contemporary Writing by Native American Women.* New York: Fawcett Columbine, 1989.

Blue Cloud, Peter. *Elderberry Flute Song: Contemporary Coyote Tales.* Trumansburg, N.Y.: Crossing Press, 1982.

Bonnin, Gertrude (Zitkala Sa). *American Indian Stories.* Lincoln: University of Nebraska Press, 1985.

Bruchac, Joseph. *The Faithful Hunter: Abenaki Stories.* Greenfield Center, Vt.: Greenfield Review Press, 1988.

Bruchac, Joseph. *Turtle Meat and Other Stories.* Duluth: Holy Cow Press, 1992.

Cook-Lynn, Elizabeth. *The Power of Horses and Other Stories.* New York: Arcade, 1990.

Eastman, Charles. *Old Indian Days.* New York: McClure, 1907.

Eastman, Charles. *Red Hunters and the Animal People.* New York: AMS, 1976.

Eastman, Charles. *Wigwam Evenings; Sioux Folktales Retold by Charles A. Eastman (Ohiyesa) and Elaine Goodale Eastman.* Boston: Little, Brown, 1909.

Erdrich, Louise. *Love Medicine.* New York: Holt, 1984.

Johnson, E. Pauline. *The Shagganappi.* Toronto: William Briggs, 1913.

Johnson, E. Pauline. *The Moccasin Maker.* Toronto: William Briggs, 1913.

Lesley, Craig, ed. *Talking Leaves: Contemporary Native American Short Stories.* New York: Dell, 1991.

King, Thomas. *One Good Story, That One: Stories.* Toronto: Harper Perennial, 1993.

McNickle, D'Arcy. *The Hawk Is Hungry and Other Stories.* Tucson: University of Arizona Press, 1992.

Momaday, N. Scott. *House Made of Dawn.* New York: Harper & Row, 1968.

Momaday, N. Scott. *In the Presence of the Sun: Stories and Poems, 1961–1991.* New York: St. Martin's Press, 1992.

Momaday, N. Scott. *The Man Made of Words: Essays, Stories, Passages.* New York: St. Martin's Press, 1997.

Ortiz, Simon, ed. *Earth Power Coming: Short Fiction in Native American Literature.* Tsaile, Ariz.: Navajo Community College Press, 1983.

Ortiz, Simon. *Fightin': New and Collected Stories.* Chicago: Thunder's Mouth Press, 1983.

Peyer, Bernd, ed. *The Singing Spirit: Early Short Stories by North American Indians.* Tucson: University of Arizona Press, 1989.

Rosen, Kenneth, ed. *The Man to Send Rain Clouds: Contemporary Stories by American Indians.* New York: Viking 1974.

Trafzer, Clifford, ed. *Blue Dawn, Red Earth: New Native American Storytellers.* New York: Anchor Doubleday, 1996.

Trafzer, Clifford, ed. *Earth Song, Sky Spirit: Short Stories of the Contemporary Native American Experience.* New York: Anchor Doubleday, 1993.

Velie, Alan, ed. *The Lightening Within: An Anthology of Contemporary American Indian Fiction.* Lincoln: University of Nebraska Press, 1991.

Vizenor, Gerald. *Landfill Meditation.* Middletown, Conn.: Wesleyan University Press, 1991.

Walters, Anna Lee. *The Sun Is Not Merciful.* Ithaca, N.Y.: Firebrand Books, 1985.

NON-ENGLISH AMERICAN SHORT STORIES

What are non-English American stories, and why should they be included in this book? Although earlier literary histories of the United States routinely covered works in American Indian, colonial, and immigrant tongues, "American literature" has now become synonymous with English-language literature written in the United States. This is a great loss, for American literature in Yiddish, Polish, Swedish, Welsh, Norwegian, Portuguese, Spanish, Chinese, and German—the list goes on and on—offers fascinating insights into American ethnic diversity in formally accomplished and thematically provocative works. This is particularly true for twentieth-century short fiction: one only has to think of Vladimir Nabokov's Russian stories or of Isaac Bashevis Singer's Yiddish tales and imagine what readers would be missing if such works had never been made accessible in English versions or were not considered part of American literature (but were also outside the purview of other national literatures). This is the limbo in which non-English short fiction finds itself, even though its linguistic difference might constitute a particular invitation to readers interested in other areas of ethnic, gender, and cultural difference in multicultural America. How many Nabokovs and Singers are still waiting to be discovered? To be translated into English? Or to be presented to readers in bilingual editions?

No one quite knows how many short

stories were written or published in the United States in the twentieth century in languages other than English, but it is probably safe to say a great number, at least hundreds and perhaps thousands of them. Electronic library catalogues have made it much easier than it used to be to do bibliographic research that can provide access to little-studied areas of knowledge. In Harvard University's Library system alone, a database search produced a list of more than 120,000 imprints published in the United States in scores of languages other than English. These include works in many American Indian languages, as well as in virtually every tongue spoken in the United States, but they cover titles in all genres and periods, and I know of no method to limit findings to non-English short fiction of the twentieth century. The list of only those multilingual American newspapers that were under the surveillance of the U.S. Postmaster in 1917 includes over two thousand titles of periodicals in languages ranging from Ruthenian to Syrian, Bohemian to Ladino, and Tagalog-Visayan to Rumanian, as well as many bi- and tri-column formats such as Polish-Latin, Danish-Norwegian-Swedish, or German-Hungarian; many of these periodicals probably published numerous short stories (or such related genres as tales, novellas, feuilleton stories, sketches, or vignettes). However, until a research team goes through the vaults of the National Archives, it is impossible to know just how many pieces of short fiction are buried there. Given this state of affairs, the following pages resemble more the tentative forays of a blindfolded man than the expert coverage given to other areas of modern American short fiction. Per-

haps this necessarily unrepresentative survey will convince readers that more investigations and translations of non-English literature of the United States are desirable. This essay is indebted to the specialists in different language groups who recommended the best published short stories of the century.

Shortly before the turn of the century, Abraham Cahan (1860–1951)—working with the encouragement of Lincoln Steffens and William Dean Howells—began to develop a particular form of short fiction in which Jewishness, immigration, cosmopolitanism, assimilation, and labor were successfully fictionalized. Cahan's formal choices—to represent the immigrants' English as dialect writing full of malapropisms and Yiddishisms, and their Yiddish as somewhat more idiomatic English (though also with some language interference)—and his love-and-marriage (and divorce) plots have remained popular, not only with later ethnic writers who read him, like James T. Farrell, but also with general audiences who were given movie versions many decades after Cahan published his most famous tales, *Yekl: A Tale of the New York Ghetto* (1896) and "The Imported Bridegroom" (1898). *Yekl* was particularly influential as a novella that contrasts the protagonist Yekl, an Americanized Russian Jewish immigrant, with his wife Gitl, who arrives in America two years after him and embarrasses him by her old-country ways, which, however, yield to a healthier mode of transplantation, combining tradition with New World impulses.

What has remained little known is that Cahan wrote and published Yiddish versions that differed from those he presented to English-speaking readers. Even Cahan's most famous tale is a case in point. Originally serialized under the title "Yankel der Yankee" (and under the author's pseudonym "Socius"), the Yiddish *Yekl* differed not only in the name of its protagonist (the English "Yekl" was not actually a Jewish name) but also in its strategy of cultural mediation and its form of narration. Cahan's Yiddish-language tales include omniscient socialist narrators instead of English-language happy endings; more social criticism, more profanities in characters' dialogues, and more sexual frankness than those "same" tales would contain in English. His double stories are suggestive of the kinds of worlds that non-English short fiction opens to American literature.

Helena Staś's Polish-American story "Marzenie czy rzeczywistość: obrazek polsko-amerykański" (Dream or Reality: A Polish-American Picture, 1907) follows Wanda, the rebellious, idealistic, and stubborn heroine, from Poland to America, when her impoverished-gentry parents emigrate in order to separate her from her Russian lover. "Are you so emancipated that religious and national feelings have died in you?" Wanda's scandalized father asks her. "I don't acknowledge national or religious feelings," Wanda answers. "Not one nation and creed, but all humanity should be our motto." "Renouncing national or religious feeling is the same as renouncing family feeling," old Kęszycki objects. "Oh, this world is so backwards," insists Wanda. "I want to belong to the universal, to move freely, to be a child of the whole world, and to love everyone equally."

But Wanda's idealism leads to rootlessness. When she abandons her parents aboard ship and returns to her village, she discovers not only that the Russian has betrayed her but also that without her family she has no place in the community. So she goes to America after all, tries in vain to find her parents, makes two unhappy marriages, contributes to the suicide of her teenage son, and is finally pursued by the police as an anarchist before she stumbles back into the family and the national fold. Staś's remarkable story ends with a visualization of this prodigal daughter's new worldview. An embroidered canvas over her bed depicts the Polish eagle held by Prussia, Russia, and Austria-Hungary, the three powers that had partitioned Poland. Hope comes from overseas, however, as a Polish army is shown in America, ready to fight for the violated Motherland. Staś's family drama of betrayal and reconciliation turns emigration into a source of solving the Polish national tragedy of partition.

Carl Wilhelm Andeer, born in Sweden in 1870, emigrated in 1891 and served as a minister in Swedish-American churches in Iowa, Massachusetts, North Dakota, and Minnesota. Among his stories that he published in the Augustana Synod publication *Ungdomsvännen* (Friend of Youth), is the 1904 tale "Svensk-amerikanen" (The Swedish-American), which dramatizes class differences and hypocrisies. Returning to Sweden for a visit, the second-generation Professor Arvid Norén of North America appears like a miracle in a world of hypocrites who believe that all Swedish emigrants are drunk farmhands or bragging servant girls. Norén claims his position as an American to question "Swedish class distinctions and Swedish self-importance" and frankly criticizes the anti-American hypocrites in town in a comedy of manners style that is characteristic of much of the story. Only at the end comes the revelation that Norén is in love with Anna, the daughter of the baron on whose estate Norén's father had been a poor farmer. Just as Norén exhorts his beloved to accept that this match can never be, the old Baron Sjärnfält, who had overheard the sad conversation, gives his consent and blessing: "Children—God bless you! I can gladly leave my child in such hands, even if his father was my father's servant." The surprise happy ending reveals that there is change in the Old World as well as in the New, and the truly educated emigrant is portrayed as the equal to the old aristocrat, for both are superior to the prejudiced crowd.

In an effort to enrich the Welsh language with stories that delve into life's mysteries, Dafydd Rhys Williams published a collection of stories, *Llyfr y Dyn Pren ac Eraill* (The Book of the Wooden Man and Others), in Utica, New York, in 1909. Williams's book is a collection of morality tales—temperance stories, a story against smoking, and the story of a gossip—that are distinguished by their fantastic plots. In one case, Williams was inspired by the popular German writer Rudolph Baumbach's story "Nicotiana," yet he insisted that his own treatment was fresh, colored by Welsh and American characteristics. Thus, young Hugh is spooked out of a bad habit by the appearance of a demon "seated on a great roll of tobacco. His face resembled the one that appears on bundles of Franklin Tobacco, with his hair like American 'fine cut,' his teeth like Scranton stove coal, and his veins like the fine tobacco of the Old Country."

Though it does not thematize biculturalism as a marriage plot, the story's demon points in the direction of assimilation, while the influences Williams acknowledged are of a bicontinental cast: the Welsh folktale (Twm Shon Cati), the European short story, the heroic narrative (Homer and Ovid), and the literary productions of Americans such as Nathaniel Hawthorne and William Cullen Bryant.

Leon Kobrin (1872–1946) came to America from Russia in 1892, and, after some early writing in Russian, he was so prolific that by 1910 his collected American short stories in Yiddish added up to more than nine hundred pages. His sketch-like stories, often told in the first person singular, portray greenhorns and Old-World radicals in their new environments, or focus on chance encounters of strangers. In "Di shprakh fun elnt" (The Language of Misery, translated under the title "A Common Language"), the greenhorn narrator has found a job as a night watchman but is worried about the dangers of his work: "With an old-country thief I would have flown out there like a bomb. With an American, however—who knows what kind of cutthroat was out there in the dark?" Yet he rises to the occasion soon and beats burglars to a retreat—even though he is bruised. A week later his heroic mood changes when he finds that the burglars he beats up turn out to be an Italian immigrant in his forties and his five- or six-year-old daughter. A bond of empathy soon links the watchman and the burglars, even though they have no language in common: "We talked in sign language, with our hands, with gestures. But we understood each other." The narrator lets the burglars go and gives them kindling wood—an act of kindness for which he is fired. Later he sees the "Italian friend," who offers him a banana. The story ends with the sentences: "I told him about *my* calamity in my language, and he told me again about *his* troubles in his language, and again we both understood each other. We understood each other very well indeed." The solidarity that connects the poor and separates them from the world of hypocritical employers (embodied here by the boss's wife) bridges national and linguistic boundaries in Kobrin's tale.

Ole Amundsen Buslett's Norwegian-language tale "Veien til Golden Gate" (The Road to the Golden Gate, 1915) is an allegorical expression of the cultural program of pluralism; the story thematized and offered support for the continued use of languages other than English in the feverish climate of World War I. A kind of pilgrim's progress in immigrant America, the story depicts Haakon's road to the Golden Gate, beginning with the landing at Castle Garden, even though his mother Kristiane's path begins in Norway. Buslett's warnings against going too far, too fast on that road had been traditional in American conservative thought from colonial times on, and his negative portrait of the restless Aasmund Skaaning, always on the move farther west with his ax on his shoulder, is a version of Ishmael Bush in James Fenimore Cooper's *The Prairie*. A long dialogue between Kristiane and Skaaning's daughter Rosalita reviews the issues of ethnic identity and assimilation. Buslett allegorized assimilation as the mad rush into a "Yankee Slough" in which all would become alike (and ultimately go under), whereas the Norwegians who do

not sell their birthright also retain their know-how and are able to build safe roads across that slough of Americanization. Despite its opposition to assimilation, "The Road to the Golden Gate" represents American pluralism rather than Norwegian nationalism; it is telling that the road back to the old country is explicitly dismissed as "the road of nostalgia." The story ends as Rosalita declares her love for Haakon, leaving the reader with the prospect of a couple that has just the right degree of ethnic loyalty, sharing neither Rosalita's father's shallow Americanism nor Haakon's mother's Old-World orientation.

Dorthea Dahl's "Kopper-kjelen" (The Copper Kettle) was published in the Chicago Norwegian-language literary journal *Norden* (1930). Born in Norway, Dahl came to South Dakota with her parents at the age of two, and lived in Moscow, Idaho, for most of her life. The story presents a Norwegian immigrant couple, Trond Jevnaker (the center of consciousness in this third-person narrative) and his wife Gjertrud, who had come to America before Trond, is better assimilated and more fluent in English than her husband, and even asks him to Americanize her name as "Gørti"—which he refuses indignantly. (Dahl's story thus inverts the gender pattern of Cahan's story, in which Gitl emigrates after her husband Yekl, so that for Cahan the woman seems less hasty in assimilation than the man does.) Dahl's Gjertrud is the type described by Lawrence Rosenwald as the "language traitor" who rushes into (incomplete) Anglicization and is embarrassed by her husband's old-country ways. The pivot of the story is an old kettle that had belonged to

Trond's grandfather in Norway and that Gjertrud was planning to discard—when an American lady, Margery Green, who comes to the Jevnakers for a cure in the country air, sees the kettle and expresses her wish to buy it as an antique. Though neither Trond nor Gjertrud knows what she means by "*æntik*" their reactions differ: Gjertrud wants to sell the kettle now, but Trond talks back to her for once: "You've had contempt for the copper kettle all these years, just as you've had contempt for me and all that's been mine. I won't sell it. It will be my wedding gift to Miss Green. For once I'll decide what is to be done around here." Strangely, this changes Gjertrud's relationship to Trond, and she not only asks him for copper polish but offers him coffee and cookies and even promises to abandon one of her American improvement schemes, the "skrinport-sen" (screen porch), for a while. The eyes of the American native had seen the value of the Norwegian heirloom that the too speedily assimilated immigrant woman had regarded only as a source of embarrassment.

The Portuguese-language short story "Gente da Terceira Classe" (Steerage, 1938) is representative of José Rodrigues Miguéis's oeuvre. Born in Lisbon in 1901, Miguéis died in Manhattan in 1980, after having spent the last forty-three years of his life in New York, where he had gone into political exile. University-trained and a translator of F. Scott Fitzgerald, Erskine Caldwell, and Carson McCullers into Portuguese, he wrote numerous American short stories in his native language. The story "Steerage," formally cast in the manner of a log, is set in the melting-pot world

of an ocean liner returning from South America to Portugal via Madeira and Southampton. Among the third-class passengers of the title are return emigrants whose hopes of a successful return to their homelands have been dashed, as well as new emigrants setting out for the New World. These different "currents" meet, and the narrator's dining table is a world in miniature: "At meals, at my table, eat Poles, Portuguese, some lower-class Englishmen (Irish surely), an incommunicative German couple, a large Syrian clan returning from the north of Brazil with jaundiced children, and others of the same breed." Ethnic types described include an Irish emigrant, a Madeiran woman, a Polish woman returning from Argentina and her Jewish companion, both trying to pass for French, a poor Turk (or maybe a Lebanese) woman, and assimilated Luso-Americans. The somewhat snobbish and misanthropic narrator uses descriptions as if they were weapons against "Aryanist" waiters and loud crowds; he swallows bad coffee (and is surprised since the ship started from Brazil) and tea, and mulls over the signs of class and ethnic discrimination, *For Spanish and Portuguese people only.* "Looking at these people, I sometimes wonder, in anguish, if the people exist, if they actually exist." Assimilation has brought out the worst in them, as the narrator finds them idolizing material things and abandoning spiritual values. Still, he wonders at the end whether the voyage has created a bond of sympathy among these heterogeneous and largely unsympathetically drawn passengers.

Occasionally, non-English stories were published in bilingual format. Sabine R.

Ulibarrí's *Mi abuela fumaba puros / My Grandma Smoked Cigars / y otros cuentos de Tierra Amarilla /and Other Stories of Tierra Amarilla* (1977) is an example of a genuinely bilingual short story collection published with a Spanish and an English title; and the ten-story collection matches a Spanish text on the left with an English version on the right page, though neither language is defined as "original" or "translation" in this New Mexican work. The collection also alternates from a folk voice (in "El Negro Aguilar," a near mythic tale of a black cowboy-hero) to a focus on education (in "Elacio era Elacio / Elacio Was Elacio"), and a meditative tone (in "Se fue por clavos / He Went for Nails," the tale of a man who goes to fetch nails and returns four years later).

Chinese-language writers in the United States have sometimes looked at Jewish Americans as a model for an ethnic integration that retains a strong sense of special cultural identity despite full Americanization. Zhang Xiguo's short story "Ge Li" (Circumcision, 1971) is a case in point: the protagonist Song Daduan is a Chinese immigrant who chairs a political science department in a large university and has kept a low ethnic profile, but is reethnicized when he is present at a bris—and suddenly begins to think more about his childhood in China and his own Chineseness.

Class differences among Chinese Americans are the themes of stories about the "downtown Chinese," for example "Duo Tai" (Abortion, 1979) by Yi Li (Pan Xiumei), an immigrant from Hong Kong. The understated and sketchlike story focuses on Mrs. Luo, who needs an abortion but is afraid that this could become public knowledge, is scared to ask her husband (who opposes abortion) for the money, and instead decides to earn the money by doing additional piecework. The conversation of the women in the San Francisco sweatshop—euphemistically called "Harmony Garment Shop"—focuses on issues of birth control and work and reveals the women's and mothers' desperate situation, between the "white devil doctor" who cuts the wombs "of folks who don't understand English" and the tough employer Mrs. Zhou who ignores Mrs. Luo's obvious predicament and cruelly gives her a firm deadline for the completion of the additional garment pieces: "'Bring them back at eight tomorrow morning,' Mrs. Zhou's pale face was expressionless. Mrs. Luo thought she looked as if her soul had been stolen by the devil, just as the folktale said. Her eyes had no life, causing Mrs. Luo to think of that of a dead fish." The hell of Chinese immigrant women laborers in San Francisco has its white American and its Chinese American devils.

At first glance, this survey suggests only a shared condition in these short stories: it is their non-Englishness, which also accounts for the fact that these stories are so little known. Yet there are also some shared features. Thematically, many tales could be classified as love stories and other tales of migration, assimilation, transplantation, pluralism, or nationalism; others emphasize class (Andeer, Kobrin, or Yi Li) or suggest the possibility of empathy across ethnic and linguistic boundaries (Buslett or Zhang Xiguo). What many of the American short stories in languages other than English have in common for-

mally is that they inscribe an English linguistic presence in the texts or otherwise
thematize English in a way that English
original stories or English translations (in
which English is the medium of communication) cannot adequately replicate.
"Yankee" is a charged term in Cahan's and
Buslett's stories; Kobrin inserts English
phrases such as "business was booming"
and "business was rotten" (in the story
"Actors"—in which these phrases furthermore mark whether the theater cash-
ier speaks English or Yiddish); Yi Li startlingly puts the English word "cancer" into
the Chinese text. Dahl spices up his Norwegian with "Hadjudusør" (how do you
do, sir), "spærrummet" (spare room),
"nervøsbreikdaun," and some complete
sentences in English in order to suggest
the different speed of assimilation that
separates Trond and Gjertrud. Miguéis's
"Gente da Terceira Classe" includes many
English words, entire sentences in English
and French (suggesting also the importance of "third" languages in such mixed-
language locations), and such "Portingles"
terms as *cracas* (crackers), *dolas* (dollars),
bossa (boss), and *racatias* (racketeers) that
are representative of the employment of
mixed tongues in works in many other
languages in the United States.

Gert Niers is a contemporary German
American who writes "prose" (rather
than "short stories"), yet his minimalist
sketches and expanded aphorisms show
not only a modernist experimenter at
work but also a writer who, like his precursors, examines bilingual consciousness, now in the context of transnationalism. The following sketch from
"Entwirrungsversuche" (Attempts at dis-

entanglement, 1998) is representative,
and it is also an appropriate conclusion to
this first foray into the non-English short
story: "The wonderful privilege of turning
crazy in at least two countries. This handsome schizophrenia permits the immigrant to switch from one country—when
things get too unbearable—into another,
until that also becomes insufferable, and
he has released himself as temporarily
cured. Hence emerges a to and fro that
can be undertaken for years, and even for
a lifetime. Professionals at this game even
let themselves be reimbursed for damages
or sick pay—as cultural mediators, teachers of literature or other carriers of
infections." What Niers expresses hyperbolically, sarcastically, and through presumably hostile eyes actually points to the
great value of literature that crosses linguistic boundaries. Moving back and forth
from one code to another is precisely what
gives some of the best non-English stories
their particular qualities: an ironic sense
of freedom from linguistic constraints in
any language, a readiness to experiment
with the different meanings languages associate with the same sounds, and a willingness to make readers attentive to the
many voices of America.

Werner Sollors and the Longfellow Institute

SELECTED BIBLIOGRAPHY

Øverland, Orm. *The Western Home: A Literary History of Norwegian America*. Northfield, Minn.: Norwegian-American Historical Association, 1996.
Rosenfeld, Max, ed. *Pushcarts and Dreamers: Stories of Jewish Life in America*. South

Brunswick, N.J.: Thomas Yoseloff, 1967.

Shell, Marc, and Werner Sollors, eds. *The Multilingual Anthology of American Literature: A Reader of Original Texts with English Translations*. New York: New York University Press, 2000.

Sollors, Werner, ed. *Multilingual America: Transnationalism, Ethnicity, and the Languages of American Literature*. New York: New York University Press, 1998.

Yin, Xiao-huang. *Chinese American Literature Since the 1850s*. Carbondale: Southern Illinois University Press, 2000.

Zyla, Wolodymyr T., and Wendell M. Aycock, eds. *Ethnic Literature Since 1776: The Many Voices of America*. Lubbock: Texas Tech University Press, 1978.

THE AMERICAN
WORKING-CLASS
SHORT STORY

American working-class writing is about people and work—rural, industrial, and postindustrial. It includes the unemployed and goes beyond narrow socioeconomic definitions of income and family background. It offers a cultural appreciation of a majority of Americans who depend "for a living" on "wages" rather than "salaries," who are closely tied to the immigrant or migrant experiences, are often self-educated or first-generation high school or college graduates, and value a practical and functional use of skills including language, passing their history and values along through oral storytelling and direct speech and actions, and dealing with denial and anger as well as sacrifice, persistence, and cooperation. Working-class writing is a multicultural mix of the unemployed, the poor, the working poor, the working class with mid-range incomes, and the complex system of values they embrace.

As American cultural studies have shown, a person's class is largely self-defined, dependent most upon how that person perceives him- or herself, so that a nurse, a teacher, a college professor, an industrial worker advanced to foreman or supervisor with strong working-class values and outlooks can remain working class. In fact, much of contemporary working-class writing treats the conflicts of class identity, posing the question: Where do I belong? That one need not be born into a working-class family to write well of it is clear in the examples of Harriett Arnow's novel of a family's forced migration from Appalachia to Detroit factories in *The Doll Maker* (1954), in Muriel Rukeyser's impassioned proletarian poetry, and in Harvey Swados's gritty tales of the auto industry in *On the Line* (1957). Though working-class writing is as much a part of American literature as of American life, the term *working class* is often ambiguous, at times amorphous, and forever evolving within American culture. Each generation redefines it. Despite all false admonitions to vanish into middle class, the working class still strongly exists, though it has evolved, and so the relevance of such a literature to record and express these lives becomes more relevant today. It exists within the broad tradition of American literature, its poetry (Marge Piercy, Jim Daniels), its memoir, autobiography (Richard Rodriguez's *Hunger of Memory* [1982]), and its fictions (Russell Banks's novel *Continental Drift* [1985], Chris Offutt's short stories in *Kentucky Straight* [1992]).

In her helpful study "In the Skin of a Worker," Janet Zandy emphasizes the strategic elements in citing its action: "those external forces that shape a text as well as those internal elements, residual and emergent, that represent working-class lived experience." She asks, "What space is there for working-class voices, for descriptions of material conditions—the food, clothing, possessions, homes of working-class communities, and between workers and their employers/bosses?" Just as ethnic, racial, and working-class cultures have been exploited in film, so have they been in literature. What is authentic about the treatment becomes a central question, for as Zandy notes,

though working-class writing "may or may not have an overt political consciousness, it always has a consciousness of class—not in an abstracted academic way—but class as a set of lived human relationships shaped by economic forces and centered in shared materiality and relationship to work at particular historical moments. A working-class text invites, cajoles, even insists that the reader step into the skin of a worker." Zandy then enumerates some essential "elements" of a working-class text, and though a work need not contain all of them, they are the primary criteria that authenticate that literature: (1) The text centers on the lived experience of working-class people. The working life is given space and taken seriously by the author; (2) The text permits the working-class person to represent him- or herself, to speak, often as a narrator in short fiction; (3) Its consciousness is not wholly individual but collective in sensibility; there is a "we" as well as an "I"; (4) The working-class culture with its complex of values is revealed with respect, providing an opportunity for reader recognitions; (5) The texts "give language to human suffering and grief," validating the physical experience of working-class life, the physicality of suffering and its depth of feeling and thought; (6) The writings are concerned with cultural formation; and (7) "Many working-class texts are often intended 'to be of use,' to have agency in the world, and not to be mere decorations or aesthetic commodities." Writer Toni Cade Bambara helps to clarify this human engagement in her declaration, "Writing is one of the ways I participate in the struggle—one of the ways I help to keep vibrant and resilient that vision that has kept the Family going on. Through writing I attempt to celebrate a tradition of resistance, attempt to tap Black potential, and try to join the chorus of voices that argues that exploitation and misery are neither inevitable nor necessary. Writing is one of the ways I participate in the transformation." (8) Working-class texts often challenge the dominant assumptions about content and form. They are organic in form, finding their design in the sense of lived experience. Texts are conscious of class oppression; the writer witnesses what is at stake and takes sides. To this list we need to add (9), the factor of money and employment as an essential element and force in working-class fiction.

Most of the short story writers discussed in this essay are also novelists, and virtually all of them have been affected by the fiction that has come before. Certainly the fiction of the later 1800s led many writers to a wider view of subject matter and a more intimate point of view. American realists and regionalists of local color broke new ground, as in Hamlin Garland's stark prairie tales in *Main Travelled Roads* (1891), and Stephen Crane's revealing novella *Maggie, A Girl of the Streets* (1893), but so did the intimate portraits of humble people in Sarah Orne Jewett's *A White Heron and Other Stories* (1886) and *The Country of the Pointed Firs* (1896), and the strong woman imaged in Mary Wilkens Freeman's "The Revolt of Mother" from her *A New England Nun and Other Stories* (1891). It is also hard to underestimate the work of Mark Twain's *The Adventures of Huckleberry Finn* (1884) and Walt Whitman's *Leaves of Grass* (1855) for opening subject matter and creating texts committed to working people. But perhaps the earliest working-class fiction came from a woman, Rebecca Harding Davis, and her searing novel *Life in the Iron Mills*. Appearing first in *Atlantic Monthly* in 1861, the book reemerged in 1972 from Feminist Press, then with an introduction by Tillie Olsen and two short stories from Davis's short story collection *Silhouettes of American Life* (1892) in 1985. Here is writing that meets all the criteria for a working-class text suggested earlier: a text that views the working-class experience from the inside, is intimate with characters who raise their own voices, is conscious of a collective identity, reveals the working-class family and home life, validates their daily suffering and their life circumstances, a text that could be used to awaken social consciousness of class oppression, and that is daring in its bold originality. This end-of-the-century era of roughly 1890–1900 fostered the first period of working-class fiction; it was also a time of less reputable work such as the popular urban journalism of "slum stories," along with the ethnic and dialect tales of Finley Peter Dunne and Joel Chandler Harris.

Also of profound influence on twentieth century working-class stories is the fiction of the Russian authors Dostoevsky, Turgenev, Tolstoy, and particularly Anton Chekhov as a master short story writer. As their stories came into translation, American authors were astounded at the deep connections they felt. In his letters Sherwood Anderson would exclaim, "Until I found the Russian writers of prose, your Tolstoy, Dostoevski, Turgenev, Chekhov, I had never found a prose that satisfied me. . . . In your Russian writers one feels life everywhere, in every page." Two decades later, another American short story writer, James T. Farrell, would declare Chekhov as his model. "Chekhov raised the portrayal of banality to the level of world literature. . . . [He] encouraged the short story writers of these nations to revolt against the conventional plot story and to see a simple and realistic terms to make the story a form that more seriously reflects life. . . . Chekhov has not only influenced the form of the short story, but he has also influenced its content." American realists were moved by the intimacy of the narrative voice and egalitarian approach of these Russians, who present a nonjudgmental, subjective point of view, intimate and even loving with details, a perspective that welcomed these sons and daughters of the working class. They also taught a psychological realism, where each character had a story to tell and each was given respect and space to tell it. They broke the formulaic definition of the short story as having "a single or a unified impression" and thus freed working-class writers to treat their world and find their own form.

America entered the twentieth century in a wave of change, which its writers sought to record. In the first two decades, it would experience an industrial coming of age, a loss of American farm life for urban expansion, a flow of immigration, a rise of feminism, and its first world war. One of the great writers of these events was Theodore Dreiser (1871–1945), who captured with compassion the characters caught in this change. His novels *Sister Carrie* (1900) and *Jennie Gerhardt* (1911) brought the age of literary naturalism into the twentieth century, opening censored subject areas and documenting with realistic detail the darker sides of sociali-

zation, revealing a human urge for self-preservation as basic. What differed, however, from Dreiser's treatment and the naturalistic exaggeration of Frank Norris, in his popular novels *McTeague* (1899) and *The Octopus* (1901), was Dreiser's great compassion for his poor and working-class characters. In his novels and short fiction, Dreiser gives dignity to the human wreckage he portrays, capturing the flow of life with simple sincerity and a bold theme of brotherhood, approaches that shaped the working-class story. In "The Lost Phoebe," for example, he portrays a couple on their run-down farm and follows widower Henry's search for his lost love as he rambles the neighborhood. In "A Doer of the Word" humble Charlie Potter leads an exemplary life amidst the social struggles and advises charity, for "All the misery is the lack of sympathy one with another. When we get that straightened out we can work in peace." Though Dreiser's stories may seem to modern readers plodding and dense with detail, they are well-crafted portraits of American life, focused more for theme than the easy charm of popular fiction, and they take the reader inside the characters' experiences and points of view. Dreiser's fiction fits well the criteria for a working-class text.

Dreiser was carrying forward the realism-naturalism of the age from such writers as Jack London (1876–1916) whose stories appeared regularly in magazines ("To Build a Fire" in *Century,* 1908) and were collected in *Brown Wolf and Other Jack London Stories* (1920). London embraces both naturalism and its implicit determinist philosophy and a social realism that took him into the lives of American outcasts. Upton Sinclair (1878–1968), though primarily a novelist and the author of *The Jungle* (1906), *King Coal* (1917), and *Oil* (1927), took naturalism further into a socialist format, often using his short stories as political tracts but also revealing the hidden cruelty of a capitalistic society; he is an immediate precursor of the leftist writing of the 1930s.

Some short story writers in the Roaring Twenties, such as F. Scott Fitzgerald, Ernest Hemingway, and Ring Lardner, enhanced the American short story in its form and popularity, creating terse and poetic portraits of individuals. However, they were not concerned with working-class characters and themes or with portraying a collective sensibility. Nevertheless, there were writers of the 1920s who were; three in particular are Sherwood Anderson (1876–1941), Anzia Yezierska (1880–1970), and Margery Latimer (1899–1932). Anderson entered the lives of the Midwestern small town facing increased industrialization and dislocation of social values, first in his story sequence *Winesburg, Ohio* (1919) and again in his short story collections *The Triumph of the Egg* (1921) and *Horses and Men* (1923). *Winesburg, Ohio* is a masterful collection of interlocking short tales composed around a locale, and recurring characters, themes, and central point of view. The town's young reporter, George Willard, delivers but more often receives the stories of his working-class townspeople. Besides bringing an intimate perspective on the people of this town, Anderson developed a form to capture the fragmented feel of their lives. Refusing to falsify their experience by forcing them into slick plotted fictions, Anderson follows his Russian

mentors Chekhov and Turgenev, but also Theodore Dreiser and James Joyce, in particular Joyce's *Dubliners* (1914). Anderson brought two particular innovations to working-class short fiction. The first is the use of subnarrators through which the central character meets and yields to the tale-telling of another character, as in "A Man of Ideas," in which fast-talking Joe Welling puzzles George with his scheming, and "Respectability," in which Wash Williams confesses the betrayal of his wife. The book is full of humble characters, each of whom, like Chekhov's characters, has his or her story to tell. This nonjudgmental and egalitarian approach to character is an important development. In his later stories "I Want to Know Why," "The Man Who Became a Woman," and "I'm a Fool," Anderson's second innovation is with the form of the tales. Taking his lead from others, he sought a flat and organic form that reflected the patterns of his characters' lives. His characters and readers are given puzzling and partial epiphanies that draw them closer into the struggle to understand the lives, as in "I'm a Fool," in which the sympathetic boy-narrator cannot grasp the full significance of his own tale and so must curse himself as a fool. Unlike Sinclair Lewis, who uses distance to satirize midwestern life, Anderson collapses the aesthetic distance between his readers and his characters, forcing empathy, an essential working-class writing device.

Also from the 1920s is Margery Latimer, whose short life is marked by the fine work of *Nellie Bloom and Other Stories* (1929) and *Guardian Angel and Other Stories* (1929). Her work has been reissued by the Feminist Press in a combined collection (1989). Growing up in Portage, Wisconsin, Latimer came under the tutelage of playwright Zona Gale, who encouraged her social realism. Latimer pays homage to Gale in her declaration, "All my writing is like hers, to make our pain and our death articulate . . . illuminating" (*Guardian Angel*). Her refusal to accept the emptiness of literary naturalism is apparent in her impassioned approach: "There's only one possession that's worth having," she wrote, "and that is the capacity to feel that life is a privilege and that each person in it is unique and will never appear again." This romantic realism is much akin to Anderson's. Significantly, it does not reduce to sentimentalism, as is evident in her portrayal of a family worn down by change and the loss of an American Dream in "Marriage Eve." Though Latimer often deals with the middle class, she is a feminist writer creating empathy for working-class women as well.

Anzia Yezierska is perhaps best known for her immigrant novels set in New York's Lower East Side, *Salome of the Tenements* (1923), *Bread Givers: A Novel* (1925), and *All I Could Never Be* (1932), but her short fiction offers fine examples of working-class writing. It was first collected in the acclaimed *Hungry Hearts* (1920). A subsequent edition of stories has the equally revealing title, *How I Found America* (1991). Heavily autobiographical of her Jewish-American background, these stories are full of crowded street detail and reveal the real poverty and discrimination met by so many immigrants as they struggle for the American Dream, then and now, as in the disillusion and defiance of "America and I." Her women characters are resilient, and Yezierska herself be-

came the first Jewish American woman to receive recognition for her stories.

What emerges in the 1920s, then, is a characteristic working-class short story form, told in the first person by a working-class person struggling to tell his or her own story to express the life. Form and theme meet, giving space and respect to the tellers and allowing for a revelation of their culture, conflicts, and values. This first-person narrative form gained immense popularity in the 1930s and 1940s, as America listened closely to the tales of the downtrodden. In particular, we see it in the Federal Writers' Project during the Great Depression, in which ten thousand first-person narratives (interviews and oral histories) were collected and appeared in journals, eventually being published as *First Person America*. Oral histories of workers were also published, as in *Plain Folk: The Life Stories of Undistinguished Americans* and Studs Terkel's collections of American workers talking in *Hard Times* (1971) and again in *Working* (1974). During the leftist 1930s, the letter poem also evolved out of the labor movement's tradition of publishing the letters of workers. It was a small step for writers such as Mike Gold, Tillie Olsen, or Kenneth Patchen to digest the letters and transform them into art, much as the short story writers were doing. The genre allows the writer to enter the world, locate within a voice, and create an authentic empathy.

The 1930s saw some strong and varied writers of short fiction. Leftist fiction espousing socialist and communist views was published in such journals as *The New Masses, Liberator, Partisan Review, Dynamo, The Hammer, Anvil, Blast,* and the *Daily Worker*. Novelists such as Mike Gold, Jack

Conroy, Grace Lumpkin, Agnes Smedley, and Waldo Frank were reaching a larger audience. Among the short story writers were Tillie (Olsen) Lerner, who published an early segment from her *Yonnondio*, and the prolific Meridel Le Sueur. Le Sueur's early stories depicted the social struggle in urban and rural settings, as in "The Afternoon" (1928) and "Harvest" (1929), in which she portrays the travail of midwestern farm life—men and women laboring hard in the fields and seeking to survive together. Her stories have a sharp sense of nature, romance, and the struggles of good people. Her first collection of stories, *Salute to Spring*, was published in 1940, and after a period of being politically blacklisted in the 1940s and 1950s, she saw work issued in *Corn Village* (1970) and collected in *Harvest and Song for My Time* (1977) and expanded in *Ripening* (1982), a collection published by the Feminist Press, which rightly claims her as an early spokeswoman. Le Sueur's tales can be both lyrical and terse, moving the reader by feelings as much as thought.

As leftist organizations and publications came to the fore in the 1930s, they underwent change. The John Reed Clubs, which had been responsible for promoting proletarian culture, had been encouraging workers to write their lives, thus opening the doors to women and minorities. However, in 1936 the Communist Party replaced the John Reed Clubs with the League of American Writers, whose membership was made up of established liberal authors rather than left wing and working-class writers. Paula Rabinowitz described the effects: "What was gained in flattening out party line to attract a broader spectrum of intellectuals to the Left was lost in the dissipation of voices from among the young working-class writers who retracted into 'silences'" (*Writing Red*). In their recent anthology *Writing Red: An Anthology of American Women Writers, 1930–1940*, Rabinowitz and Charlotte Nekola reclaim some of these important women who "wrote in new forms that addressed class, gender, sexuality, and race as the complex background to the female experience in America." Besides more familiar voices of Le Sueur, Agnes Smedley, and Josephine Herbst, strong minority voices are Leane Zugsmith (*Home Is Where You Hang Your Childhood* [1937]), Ramone Lowe, Lucille Boehn, Morita Bonner, and Tess Slesinger (*Time: The Present* [1935]).

The 1930s was also a rich period of regional and ethnic writing that treated class. The South was being explored by William Faulkner (1897–1962) in his early stories *These Thirteen* (1931) and in his later *Collected Stories* (1948), which included "Barn Burning," his early portrayal of the southern "white trash" Snopes family. Erskine Caldwell (1903–1987) had already located his fiction in the southern poor in the story collections *American Earth* (1931) and *Jackpot* (1940). Both writers give an exaggerated, grotesque image of the working class. However, in "Saturday Afternoon" (1935) Caldwell writes a powerful antilynching story and moves from naturalism and comic caricatures to a realistic depiction of class and racial brutality. A rich addition to the literature of the working-class South came as well from the stories of Zora Neale Hurston (1903–1966), a pioneer African American author. Her *Eatonville Anthology* (1927) presents portraits of characters from her youth in Eatonville, Florida, and her *Mules and Men* (1935) reveals the colorful folk myths of her people. In "Spunk" she immerses us in the language, longing, and sometimes violence of that world.

William Saroyan became the spokesperson for the immigrant experience in his tales of his Armenian American family as they ventured West. In *The Daring Young Man on the Flying Trapeze* (1934) and *My Name Is Aram* (1940), he writes self-conscious narratives as writer, family, and community emerge, full of humorous idiosyncrasy and compassion. "The Daring Young Men on the Flying Trapeze" depicts the young writer's finding expression beyond his poverty; "Seventy Thousand Assyrians" shows him befriending an Iraqi barber whom he challenges with a continuing belief in brotherhood and hope. Saroyan is a romantic realist who portrays a revised American Dream of collective strength and individual genius.

Like many of these writers who existed outside of leftist politics, Chicagoan James T. Farrell (1904–1979) wrote a rich variety of stories treating the working-class world: the Catholic church and clergy, schools and universities, unions and laborers, ward and radical politics, street gangs, the often ignored poor of this country. In his critical writing, Farrell was outspoken in his opposition to forced models of the popular and the Leftist presses. His candid tales are austere and plain, unmarked by exaggeration or caricature. Significantly, Farrell views his working-class world from the inside, creating solid and memorable characters in their own language. While graphically depicting their crippling circumstances, he does so with compassion and is never mean-

spirited. His earliest collection *Calico Shoes and Other Stories* (1934) was followed by *Can All This Grandeur Perish? And Other Stories* (1937) and *$1,000 a Week and Other Stories* (1942). Many of these sketches and slice-of-life tales are character studies. "Studs" and "Jim O'Neill" contain the seeds for his two novel sequences about the Lonigan and the O'Neill-O'Flaherty families. Farrell's stories have the complexity of lived experience, evoking the chief elements of a working-class text and suggesting a brave empathy as a different kind of political act.

The 1940s continued with the broad thrust of working-class writing. John Fante (1909–1979) was publishing his Italian American tales of life in Boulder, Colorado, for his bricklaying family. The stories of *Dago Red* (1940) are rich in character and warm humor and were subsequently enlarged in *The Wine of Youth: Selected Stories* (1985). In autobiographical stories, such as "The Odyssey of a Wop" and "A Bricklayer in the Snow," he combines Saroyan's human spirit with the candidness of Farrell. John Steinbeck was doing the same in his long novel, *The Grapes of Wrath* (1939), but also in his tales of California working people in *The Long Valley* (1938).

Farrell's spirit was also finding a new spokesperson in Nelson Algren (1909–1981), who wrote gritty tales of Chicago's down-and-out. In *The Neon Wilderness* (1947) Algren's prostitutes, pimps, police, and convicts speak their lives bluntly, as in the monologue of a young thief in "A Lot You Got to Holler," who is explaining how he "gets by" in Chicago. Studs Terkel describes Algren's people as "clowns in a kind of circus, whiteface clowns, tragic clowns, that speak to you about what it means to be human" (*Neon Wilderness*). Algren lists his chief influences as the terse style of Ernest Hemingway and the philosophical outlook of existentialist Jean-Paul Sartre. Consequently, his stories are both lively and experimental in style, and much colder in tone and less empathetic than Farrell's.

Eudora Welty's stories in *Golden Apples* (1949) are brilliant and challenging in style and form, yet richly human in their depiction of southern characters. Her characters may be common, but they are richly complex—never ordinary. They lack both the grotesque exaggeration of southerners Caldwell and Faulkner and the colder tone of Flannery O'Connor.

In the 1950s and 1960s, leftist writing waned as it suffered the political repression of McCarthyism, Hollywood blacklisting, and Cold War fears. Still, strong stories treating contemporary working-class life survived in the work of Harvey Swados, Grace Paley, and Tillie Olsen. Although born into an upper middle-class family with a physician father, Swados had social concerns and a radical education that took him into the working-class life, where he would labor in the automotive plants of New Jersey. From this experience he learned "the pity and vanity of American life from the inside" (*On the Line* [1957]). Swados tells how he witnessed the decline of the American worker and the American Dream as the country moved from production to consumption as its chief concern. "Never mind the machinery, remember the men!" Swados shouts through his stories, which detail the growing alienation of modern work. His themes become those of solidarity and

fair play, unionism and an advocacy of humanizing the workplace. *On the Line* depicts the lives of auto workers given only first names to emphasize their collective nature. Orrin in the title story is a World War II veteran, honest and hard working, whose labor injuries move him up to the unhappy role of a boss. Buster of "Just One of the Boys" is another laborer moved up from years of spot-welding to the foreman's position and the impossible role of low management. These compassionate monologues of America's forgotten workers prove essential records of a workingman's way of life.

Grace Paley's *The Little Disturbances of Man* (1959) delivers delightful and full-voiced storytelling by colorful Jewish American, working-class characters. Pathos and humor are blended as her women characters speak their lives. A gem among the stories is "An Interest in Life," in which Virginia with survival wit confesses her husband's abandonment, then confides her struggles to get by with three children, until an old beau, John, reenters her life. Here self-revelation is made with great understanding and a bold spirit that refuses self-pity. Paley's later stories are collected in *Enormous Changes at the Last Minute* (1974) and *Later the Same Day* (1985).

In another vein, Tillie Olsen's *Tell Me a Riddle* (1961), collection of four stories, has become a classic of working-class literature. Less mirthful than Paley, Olsen knew the pains of poverty first-hand and delivered poignant and pointed tales of her characters and their struggles. Her nonfiction *Silences* (1978) helps to explain the brevity of her work, the forty-year trial to finish her novel *Yonnondio* (1974), and the oppressive atmosphere around women's lives and their art. *Tell Me a Riddle* opens with a working mother's monologue about her struggles with child-raising in "I Stand Here Ironing." "Hey Sailor, What Ship?" reveals the oppressive force of poverty and alcoholism in a family; "Oh, Yes" treats racism in America; and in "Tell Me a Riddle," early struggles are taken into old age as the aged and querulous couple try to make sense of their lives and love. Olsen has lived the struggle she portrays; her characters have authenticity as human beings.

Other books focusing on working-class culture include John Updike's early stories of life in coal-mining Pennsylvania from *Pigeon Feathers* (1962) and his novel trilogy launched with *Rabbit Run* (1960). Philip Roth's novella and New Jersey stories of working-class origins and class conflicts were published in *Goodbye, Columbus and Five Short Stories* (1959).

The 1970s and 1980s saw a host of new writers of the working class. Some, like John Sayles, held close to working-class roots and themes. The stories in his *The Anarchist's Convention and Other Stories* (1979) are all told in first-person monologues, the title story turning from satire to tribute for the aging radicals. "7–10 Split" is a characteristic piece, in which the workers from a nursing home gather for a bowling match. Their work and values are explicit; Sayles is one with working people. Tobias Wolff's *In the Garden of the North American Martyrs* (1981) and *The Barracks Thief and Selected Stories* (1984) portray working-class individuals in conflict with identity and class. Russell Banks began his working-class fiction with *The New World: Tales* (1978) and *Trailerpark* (1981). The latter is a kind of contemporary

Winesburg, Ohio, consisting of intertwining characters brought together in a Vermont trailer park. Many of these stories and those of *Success Stories* (1986) are closely autobiographical, depicting what Banks calls his own "scrabbleass" background. Banks has proven himself one of America's most successful writers of the working class, as seen in his acclaimed novels *Continental Drift* (1985) and *Affliction* (1989). Richard Ford should be added to this list for his compelling stories of the wild and run-down towns of Wyoming in *Rock Springs: Stories* (1983). In dynamic style he delivers closely wrought characters caught in America's postindustrial decline.

Many of these writers, whether in admiration or opposition, were affected by Raymond Carver's minimalist stories of working people. Carver became a major writer of the working class with his *What We Talk About When We Talk About Love* (1981) and *Fires* (1989). His stories are not only intimate with the working-class experience but also often grim and terse in their portrayal of lost values.

The 1980s also witnessed the development of a loose regional group of writers dealing with the history and hazards of life in Appalachia. Chief among them is Bobbie Ann Mason, whose *Shiloh and Other Stories* (1982) conveyed contemporary Appalachian life. Her title story portrays a young family caught in the displacement of joblessness and a growing feminism. Breece D'J Pancake's stunning work of Kentucky life appeared in the posthumous *The Stories of Breece D'J Pancake* (1983). A gifted young writer who took his own life, Pancake wrote stories that convey both the beauty and pain of Appalachian life. Other writers who capture the hardships and beauty of this world are Mike Henson, whose *A Small Room with Trouble on My Mind* (1983) uses an impressionistic style to capture his broken-hearted characters; Annabel Thomas, whose *The Phototropic Woman* portrays Appalachian women and won the 1981 Iowa Short Stories Award; and Robert Fox, whose *Destiny News* collection (1977) often rocks from social to magic realism. Poet and fiction writer Wendell Berry has also provided agrarian tales of families struggling to keep their Kentucky farms going in *Wild Birds and Other Stories* (1986).

In the late 1980s and following through the 1990s, America began to embrace in spirit its rich multicultural diversity. Not surprisingly, in stories of minority cultures is a wealth of writing on class. This multicultural wave gained critical and academic appreciation in a climate where feminism, minority programs, and cultural studies had established a footing. It was also pushed along by early and popular writers such as Alice Walker and Toni Morrison. Toni Cade Bambara's youthful stories of life in New York City and North Carolina first appeared in *Gorilla, My Love* (1972) and again in *The Sea Birds Are Still Alive* (1977). Her musical style, based on urban and African American speech, is dazzling in spirit, revealing themes of individualism within a community. "The Lesson," about a group of tough-talking schoolchildren taken for a Saturday field trip by an educated black neighbor woman, has become a classic.

Dorothy Allison, famed for her novel of family and abuse, *Bastard Out of Carolina* (1992), began as a short story writer with *Trash: Stories* (1988). Those unfamiliar with Allison's work often assume her themes are restricted to sexual abuse and lesbian lifestyles, but this misses the rich texture of family and working-class culture in all of her writing. Unabashedly, she delivers her world for what it is. Her characters are round, loving, and violent, bonded to family and alienated from much of the dominant culture. There is great commitment in her writing, as she tells in the book's preface: "The desire to live was desperate in my belly, and the stories I had hidden all those years were the blood and bone of it. To get it down, to tell it again, to make sense of something—by god just once—to be real in the world, without lies and evasions or sweet-talking nonsense" (*Trash*). "River of Names" recounts all the victims in her family; "The Meanest Woman Ever Left Tennessee" begins the women's story leading to her mother in "Mama," her aunts in "Gospel Song," and always to herself, as in "I'm Working on My Charm."

Mexican American culture has been shared and celebrated in the fine work of Sandra Cisneros through her novel *The House on Mango Street* (1989) and the short stories of *Woman Hollering Creek and Other Stories* (1991). In both books, Cisneros uses the intimate monologue voice of children and women who are usually trying to understand their world by telling of it. The stories are colored by rich ethnic detail and humor and reveal oppression from without and within a culture. In "Woman Hollering Creek," she shows how women become victims when they see themselves through macho eyes and how other women can help them rescue themselves. Cisneros deals with poverty, work, family, and cultural values, and she does so with great compassion.

The 1990s has also seen this flow of working-class, multicultural writing in many young writers. Sherman Alexie's *The Lone Ranger and Tonto Fistfight in Heaven* (1993) reveals life inside the Spokane reservation of his native Coeur d'Alene tribe. His comic-tragic tales combine social and magic realism in a way that Native American storytellers often do. Two fine writers of Appalachia are Chris Offutt and Barbara Kingsolver. Both use a contemporary Kentucky setting in their short stories to convey the rich bonding of family and the pressures of economic change and forced migration of the young. Offutt's two books of stories, *Kentucky Straight* (1992) and *Out of the Woods* (1999), weave family legend with the voices of youth, thereby creating haunting narratives and great empathy. In Kingsolver's novels and *Homeland and Other Stories* (1989), she brings together her two worlds: the working-class people of Kentucky and those of Arizona. Kingsolver had begun her serious writing with a nonfiction study of the mining strikes of Arizona entitled *Holding the Line: Women in the Great Arizona Mine Strike of 1983*. In interviewing and listening closely to stories and their telling, she was moved from objectivity to an impassioned advocacy. In her short story "Why I Am a Danger to the Public" she allows Vicki Morales, a striker, to tell her story of dealing with scabs and neighbor betrayal with vigor and an endearing resilience. "I was raised up to believe in God and the union, but listen, if it comes to pushing or shoving I know which one of the two is going to keep tires on my car."

In most ways, this last story is a perfect model of a working-class short story: intimate with the working experience, its work and culture; giving respect and space for the worker to speak her grief and joy within a collective sensibility; creating a form that exposes the effects of oppression and how character can be molded in resistance. It also relies on a vibrant intimacy of voice through an oral, first-person narration, includes memoir, and allows the life experience to find its own organic form. It is that deeply human story, an engaged working-class text.

Larry Smith

SELECTED BIBLIOGRAPHY

Bambara, Toni Cade. "What It Is I Think I'm Doing." *The Writer on Her Work.* New York: W. W. Norton, 1980.

Ann Banks, ed. *First Person America.* New York: Random House, 1981.

DeMott, Benjamin. ed. *Created Equal: Reading and Writing About Class in America.* New York: HarperCollins, 1996.

Dreiser, Theodore. *Best Selected Short Stories of Theodore Dreiser.* Cleveland: World, 1947.

Farrell, James T. *Chicago Stories.* Urbana: University of Illinois Press, 1998.

Howe, Florence, ed. *Women Working: An Anthology of Stories and Poems.* New York: Feminist Press, 1979.

Katzman, David, and William Tuttle Jr., eds. *Plain Folk: The Life Stories of Undistinguished Americans.* Chicago: University of Chicago Press, 1982.

Kingsolver, Barbara. *Homeland and Other Stories.* New York: Harper & Row, 1989.

Latimer, Margery. *Guardian Angel and Other Stories.* New York: Smith & Hass, 1929.

Le Sueur, Meridel. *Harvest Song: Collected Essays and Stories.* Albuquerque: West End Press, 1990.

Le Sueur, Meridel. *Ripening.* New York: Feminist Press, 1982.

Le Sueur, Meridel. *Salute to Spring.* New York: International Publishers, 1940.

Martz, Sandra, ed. *If I Had a Hammer, Women's Work: In Poetry, Fiction, and Photographs.* Watsonville, Calif.: Papier-Mache Press, 1990.

Nekola, Charlotte, and Paula Rabinowitz, eds. *Writing Red: An Anthology of American Women Writers, 1930–1940.* New York: Feminist Press, 1987.

Shevin, David, and Larry Smith, eds. *Getting By: Stories of Working Lives.* Huron, Oh.: Bottom Dog Press, 1996.

Shevin, David, Janet Zandy, and Larry Smith, eds. *Writing Work: Writers on Working-Class Writing.* Huron, Oh.: Bottom Dog Press, 1999.

Swados, Harvey. *On the Line.* Boston: Little, Brown, 1957.

Yezierska, Anzia. *Hungry Hearts.* Boston: Houghton Mifflin, 1920.

AMERICAN SHORT STORIES OF THE HOLOCAUST

In less than ten years, and primarily between 1941 and 1945, Adolf Hitler and the Nazis systematically murdered six million Jews in Europe, nearly 40 percent of the world Jewish population. It was not until the late 1950s that the word *Holocaust* became the standard term to refer to this annihilation of the Jews. In recent years, this powerful term has been appropriated to refer to various acts of inhumanity, including the middle passage and slavery in America, the near extirpation of the American Indians, and the slaughter of the Armenians by the Turks. For this reason, among others, many today prefer the Hebrew term *Shoah* (catastrophe) to refer to the Nazi genocide against the Jews, while several people use the two terms interchangeably.

While scholars and laypeople cannot quite agree upon what to call the atrocity in Europe, its role as an artistic subject for the Jewish American writer is even more hotly contested. Sanford Pinsker describes the moral quandary concerning such fiction when he notes that for many people, "Holocaust fiction is not only an oxymoron but a travesty—especially if attempted by Jewish-American writers who were not there and who could not possibly know." Indeed, until quite recently, Jewish American writers have proven especially reluctant to broach the European atrocity directly or indirectly in their work. Some twenty years after the liberation of the concentration camps, Robert Alter bemoaned the dearth of any

Jewish American imaginings of this twentieth-century Jewish experience: "With all the restless probing into the implications of the Holocaust that continues to go on in Jewish intellectual forums . . . it gives one pause to note how rarely American Jewish fiction has attempted to come to terms . . . with the European catastrophe."

Cognizant of the slippery moral terrain, Jewish American writers, if they dared to address the Holocaust at all, only did so allusively in the wake of the tragedy (Saul Bellow's *The Victim* [1947] and Bernard Malamud's *The Fixer* [1966] exemplify this approach). Still, Jewish American writers have in recent years produced a sizeable canon of Holocaust fiction—enough novels and short stories to merit book-length studies. Thus far, the novels have received most of the critical and popular attention. American works such as Edward Lewis Wallant's *The Pawnbroker* (1961), Richard Elman's *The 28th Day of Elul* (1967), Saul Bellow's *Mr. Sammler's Planet* (1970), Arthur A. Cohen's *In the Days of Simon Stern* (1972), and Leslie Epstein's *King of the Jews* (1979) routinely appear on Holocaust literature course syllabuses alongside works by European writers such as Primo Levi, Jerzy Kosinski, Elie Wiesel, and André Schwarz-Bart. But Jewish American stories of the Holocaust offer unique pedagogical opportunities as well, given their emotional intensity (facilitated, in part, by the economical genre itself) and the sheer range of post-Holocaust issues and concerns addressed.

Most Jewish American short story writers have chosen not to depict the Holocaust directly. Some evoke the Holocaust only allusively, albeit unmistakably, in their fiction. Many, perhaps most, have focused upon its aftermath, exploring the trauma that continues to plague Holocaust survivors after their "liberation," and their various strategies for coping in an unsympathetic or even downright hostile post-Holocaust world. Children of Holocaust survivors are just beginning to explore, through the short story, the unique burdens of the "second generation," to borrow from Alan L. Berger's lexicon. Finally, there are those Jewish American short story writers who have dared to imagine the unimaginable. That is, they have depicted the ghettos, the concentration camps, the gas chambers, the crematoria. The stories below, selected from an ever-growing field, embody this emotional intensity and thematic range.

Cynthia Ozick's "The Shawl," originally published in *The New Yorker* in 1981, represents one, if not the most, powerful direct treatment of the Holocaust, a story Ozick had withheld for several years. She remains ambivalent about having sent it to *The New Yorker* for publication. "I've accused myself for having done it," she said in a recent interview. "I wasn't there, and I pretended through imagination that I was." Some critics, as well, objected to Ozick's ground-breaking story. Susanne Klingenstein's initial response to "The Shawl" typifies this censure: "given the incredible nature of the Shoah (and the inevitable revisionism of historiography), I considered it unethical to make up fictions about the Shoah. For me 'Holocaust fiction' is an intolerable concept."

In "The Shawl," Ozick depicts the psychic terror that consumes Rosa in a concentration camp, where she endures not only her own starvation but the torment of watching her infant daughter, Magda, and her adolescent niece, Stella, wither away before her eyes. Ozick subtly explores the complex, distorted, and even ruthless relational dynamics fostered by conditions of such ineffable horror. Rosa, who struggles desperately to keep Magda alive, projects her fear and animus not so much upon her Nazi persecutors but upon Stella: "Rosa gave almost all her food to Magda, Stella gave nothing. . . . They were in a place without pity, all pity was annihilated in Rosa, she looked at Stella's bones without pity. She was sure that Stella was waiting for Magda to die so she could put her teeth into the little thighs."

In contrast to Ozick's direct approach in "The Shawl," allusive treatments of the Holocaust contain a haunting power all their own. The main characters in Bernard Malamud's "The Loan," first collected in *The Magic Barrel* (1958) and most recently collected in *The Complete Stories* (1997), are not Holocaust survivors but elderly Jewish Americans who emigrated before the war. The action takes place not in a concentration camp but in a postwar bakery in America, as Kobotsky enters the shop of his old friend Lieb to procure a loan, even though they have long been estranged over a dispute involving a previous loan that might or might not have been repaid. The plot, then, would seem to have little to do with the Holocaust and everything to do with money and the bitter feuds money engenders. Nevertheless, the Holocaust pervades "The Loan." Although none of the characters experienced the Holocaust directly, Malamud shows how the event forged their immigrant identities, dividing their lives into

two discrete periods: before and after the atrocity. For example, after impatiently listening to Kobotsky's *tsores* (troubles), Lieb's second wife, Bessie, must vent her own history of suffering rooted in the European anti-Semitism that culminated in the Holocaust: "how the Bolsheviki came, when she was a little girl, and dragged her darling father into the snowy fields without his shoes on. . . . How, when she was married a year, her husband, a sweet and gentle man, an educated accountant . . . died of typhus in an epidemic in Warsaw; and how she . . . later found sanctuary in the home of an older brother in Germany, who sacrificed his own chances to send her, before the war, to America, and . . . in all probability ended up with his wife and daughter and her two blessed children in Hitler's incinerators."

The Holocaust, then, dictates the course of Bessie Lieb's life. After the atrocity, she must seek out a second husband and a second life in America. Moreover, the Holocaust does not simply fade away into the past but haunts her psyche as she continues to mourn her dead. Malamud dramatizes hauntingly the *presence* of the Holocaust in these Jewish immigrants' lives as Bessie Lieb rushes to the bakery ovens toward the end of the story to discover a "cloud of smoke" billowing out at her; "the loaves in the trays were blackened bricks—charred corpses."

Like "The Loan," each of the stories in Melvin Jules Bukiet's award-winning first collection, *Stories of an Imaginary Childhood* (1992), might be considered an allusive treatment of the Holocaust. Through the perspective of an unnamed twelve-year-old narrator, Bukiet brings to life the Polish *shtetl,* Proszowice, the setting for each of the twelve interrelated stories. The year is 1928 and the rapidly approaching Holocaust thus looms throughout the collection for the perspicacious reader. Indeed, Bukiet quite intentionally elicits responses like the following from Lawrence L. Langer: "As a member of the post-Holocaust generation, I was unable to banish from consciousness the sense that I was reading about a doomed people."

The final story in the collection, "Torquemada," stands out as the collection's most provocative American story of the Holocaust. Psychologically wounded by an anti-Semitic assault, the adolescent narrator revisits, in a delirium, several especially virulent episodes of anti-Semitic persecution and occupies the persona of the persecutors, from the Egyptian Pharaoh, to "Nebuchadnezzar sacking Jerusalem," to a disciple of Mohammed vowing "eternal enmity" toward the Jews, to the Grand Inquisitor in Spain, Torquemada. The narrator's father ultimately draws his son out of his trance, comforting him, "We have each other and it's the twentieth century of civilized man. There, there. What harm could possibly come to us in 1928?" In these final lines of the collection, Bukiet alludes eerily to the imminent Holocaust, the horrific culmination of Jewish persecution in Europe that his narrator glimpses in a protracted moment of both disorientation and stark lucidity.

Several American writers have explored various Jewish American responses to the Holocaust. In Philip Roth's "Eli, the Fanatic," perhaps the most powerful story in his collection *Goodbye, Columbus* (1959), Roth scrutinizes the post-Holocaust mores of the Jews living in Woodenton, an affluent New York suburb. Woodenton's Jews live "in amity" with their gentile neighbors by eschewing their "extreme practices" (that is, by avoiding any outward display of their Judaism). Consequently, they perceive the newly established yeshiva in their town as a formidable threat to their upwardly mobile lives in bucolic Woodenton. Since a convenient zoning ordinance restricts boarding schools in residential areas, they leave it up to Eli Peck, the story's protagonist, to convince the yeshiva's principal to close the school. The assimilated Jews of Woodenton seem not to care that the yeshiva houses and supports eighteen young Holocaust survivors and their Hasidic teacher, also a survivor. The plot unfolds as the more sensitive Peck struggles to strike a balance between the apparent political exigencies and his moral responsibility, as a Jew and as a human being, toward the Holocaust survivors in his midst.

Hugh Nissenson also addresses the issue of the Jewish American response to the Holocaust in "The Law," first collected in *A Pile of Stones* (1965) and most recently collected in *The Elephant and My Jewish Problem: Selected Stories and Journals* (1988). Nissenson, however, concerns himself with more overtly theological matters in his story, which might be seen as a meditation upon the role of Holocaust remembrance and Jewish Law in an overwhelmingly secular, post-Holocaust America. Nissenson addresses these contentious issues through the narrative perspective of a thoroughly assimilated Jew who questions both whether his uncle should burden his son with the horrific stories of his experiences in the concentration camp and, given the boy's severe stammer, whether his uncle should even encourage him to recite the Torah portion at his Bar Mitzvah.

The narrator's uncle, Willi Levy, describes his epiphany at Bergen-Belsen, which explains his resolve: "The Commandments. All the Laws. . . . They were murdering, humiliating us because whether it was true or not we had come to—how shall I say it?—embody that very Law that bound them too—through Christianity, I mean. . . . " What the narrator's uncle cannot quite articulate is that in murdering the Jews, the Nazis sought to destroy the Laws of an ethical monotheism that bind Jews, Christians, and Muslims to a code of humane behavior. Hence, to ignore the Law after the Holocaust would be to complete the arc of the Nazis' sins. "I just feel," Willi explains, "that the least we can do is pass it on, the way we always have, from father to son. The Bar Mitzvah." The story draws to a close at the Bar Mitzvah service as Willi Levy's son arrives at his own decision concerning this crucial post-Holocaust issue.

Finally, two stories in Bukiet's second collection, *While the Messiah Tarries* (1995), deserve at least brief mention for the complex manner in which Bukiet engages increasingly vehement (and morally ambiguous) attempts to record, catalogue, and preserve survivor testimony and other audiovisual materials of the genocide. In "Himmler's Chickens," a nominally Jewish protagonist—who "took obscure pride in Barbra Streisand's career, and peppered his conversation with words like *hondle* and *shvartz*"—must decide what to do when a Nazi offers to sell him a home video of Heinrich Himmler madly executing chickens with a pistol. Should one pay a Nazi for such material? Preserve the film? Destroy it? These are the questions that Bukiet poses for his protagonist and for his readers. In "The Library of Moloch," Bukiet betrays his deep skepticism regarding the documentation and preservation of Holocaust survivor testimony. The story revolves around a fastidious librarian, Dr. Arthur Ricardo, who is obsessed with his project to "preserve their suffering, to remit immortality in return for the chronicle of their woe." Although driven by what he perceives as the ethical imperative of his work, an implacable Holocaust survivor whom Ricardo interviews for the project charges (convincingly?) that an insidious victim envy besmirches such American endeavors.

Heralding a new wave of Jewish American fiction, Nessa Rapoport recently observed that among other emergent voices from within the Jewish community, "we are only beginning to hear from: children and grandchildren of Holocaust survivors." As Rapoport suggests, children of survivors have begun to explore through fiction the specific burdens that the second generation faces. However, children of survivors are not the only Jewish American writers to take up this theme. For example, Rebecca Goldstein has written, perhaps, the most trenchant story that focuses upon the legacy of the Holocaust for the second generation in "The Legacy of Raizel Kaidish," collected in *Strange Attractors* (1993). The story begins as the narrator, a child of survivors, describes the heroics of her namesake, Raizel Kaidish. A prisoner at Buchenwald, Kaidish takes an enormous risk to save the life of her best friend, whose name has been put on the death list. Tragically, an informant foils the plan and the Nazis murder Kaidish and her friend in the gas chamber. "The informer," the narrator reveals, "was rewarded with Raizel's kitchen job." The narrator learns of the story through her mother, who was also an inmate at Buchenwald. Kaidish's act of courage serves as the foundation of the mother's anti-Positivist ethical theory (a theory that affirms the existence of moral obligations and inquires into their nature) that she relentlessly attempts to instill in her daughter. As the young Raizel reflects, "One of her central concerns was that I should come to know, without myself suffering, all that she had learned there." Raizel Kaidish's legacy, as one might expect, proves overwhelming for the narrator. Goldstein skillfully depicts her retreat into a pedantic, amoral philosophy, and fashions a chilling conclusion that forces the reader to reevaluate the contrasting post-Holocaust philosophies of mother and daughter.

The survivor mother in Jane Yolen's "Names," collected most recently in *Nice Jewish Girls: Growing Up in America* (edited by Marlene Adler Marks, 1996), also passes on the painful legacy of the Holocaust to her daughter. At the death camp, the mother learned a list of victims' names and continues to recite this list spontaneously in the present as a "living yahrzeit" (*yahrzeit* is the anniversary of a Jew's death, according to the Hebrew calendar, during which family members of the deceased recite the Mourner's Kaddish and light a twenty-four-hour yahrzeit candle). In doing so, she transfers the burden of remembrance onto her daughter: "Rachel knew that the names had been spoken at the moment of her birth: that her mother, legs spread, the waves of Rachel's passage rolling down her stomach, had breathed the names between spasms long before Rachel's own name had been pronounced." Yolen, like Goldstein, emphasizes that the legacy handed down from the survivor parent can exact a dangerous psychic toll upon the second-generation inheritor. In Rachel's case, her pathological identification with Holocaust victims leads to her self-starvation.

Lev Raphael, the son of Holocaust survivors, also grapples with the legacy of the Holocaust in his fiction, most notably in his award-winning collection of stories, *Dancing on Tisha B'Av* (1990). Raphael's evocative depiction of the psychic wounds that scar Holocaust survivors and their children, and his adroit exploration of the rifts between these generations, represents the greatest strength of his fiction. The protagonist of "Fresh Air," for example, reflects poignantly upon his particular tensions with his survivor parents: "So I was a child of necessity, of duty to the past, named not just for one lost relative but a whole family of cousins in Lublin: the Franks. Frank. My incongruously American first name was their memorial. Perhaps that explained my mother's distance, my father's rage—how could you be intimate or loving with a block of stone?" What makes Raphael's stories unique is that his protagonists must reckon not only with their identities as Jewish American children of Holocaust survivors but also with their homosexuality. In "The Life You Have," Raphael excoriates both Nazism and the homophobia of the mainstream Jewish American community, and enacts a controversial narrative leveling of these two versions of hatred.

Thane Rosenbaum, a child of survivors as well, also focuses upon the painful legacy passed down to the second generation in each of the stories of his award-winning debut collection, *Elijah Visible* (1996). Rosenbaum creates a single protagonist, Adam Posner, but varies the details surrounding Posner's identity from one story to the next to capture the fractured identity of the Holocaust survivor's child in America. Through the many Posners, Rosenbaum dramatizes the vicarious psychological immersion of the second generation in the European atrocity, their insatiable urge to reconstruct the experiences of their parents, and their ambivalence toward Judaism and its rituals given the silence of God during the atrocity.

In "Cattle Car Complex," for example, Posner is a high-powered attorney who suffers a psychological trauma after his elevator malfunctions and traps him inside. The claustrophobia of the elevator transports Posner to a Nazi cattle car in Holocaust Europe. "This is not life—being trapped in a box made for animals! . . . We can't breathe in here!" Posner cries at the understandably perplexed security guard. If "Cattle Car Complex" illustrates how Posner inherits a legacy of suffering from his parents, "The Pants in the Family" suggests that experience itself cannot be inherited. In this story, the mystery of his parents' experiences during the Holocaust burdens Posner, who struggles to glean all he can through his parents' silence: "It was always such an impene-

trable secret—my parents, speaking in code, changing the passwords repeatedly, keeping me off the scent." The silence of Rosenbaum's survivors contrasts interestingly with the survivors' constant telling of their Holocaust experiences in Goldstein's and Yolen's stories. Finally, in "Romancing the *Yahrzeit* Light," Rosenbaum engages the second generation's tortured relationship with Judaism as Posner, an artist in this story, attempts to honor the memory of his mother on the first anniversary of her death by seeking out a yahrzeit candle. Alienated from Judaism, he hopes that lighting the yahrzeit might help him "find his own way back, too." The story unfolds as secular distractions and religious doubts war against his impulse to commemorate his mother in a Judaically meaningful way.

All these stories—along with recent novels and novellas by Aryeh Lev Stollman, Joseph Skibell, Dani Shapiro, Harvey Grossinger, and Melvin Jules Bukiet—combine to suggest that American fiction of the Holocaust has now come to occupy an important place as a subgenre of Jewish American fiction. That Ted Solotaroff referred to the Holocaust as "the subject that doesn't go away" in his introduction to *The Schocken Book of Contemporary Jewish Fiction* (1992) illustrates just how far these stories have come since Robert Alter lamented the shortage of such work in 1966. By now, Jewish American writers have engaged this nearly insurmountable challenge to the literary imagination from manifold perspectives: from Bukiet's allusive treatment in "Torquemada" to Ozick's depiction of a death camp in "The Shawl," from Rosenbaum's explorations of the agonizing plight of the Holocaust survivors' child to Roth's scathing critique of a pocket of Jewish Americans either oblivious to the genocide or impervious to its lessons.

The European atrocity continues to inform the Jewish American experience, across the generations, in a variety of ways. Indeed, as Mark Krupnick recently suggested, it will be many years before we know the effect of the Holocaust on Jewish identity. In the meantime, Jewish American Holocaust stories will continue to offer a precious glimpse into the essential and evolving role that the Holocaust plays in forging the Jewish American ethos.

Andrew Furman

SELECTED BIBLIOGRAPHY

Berger, Alan L. *Children of Job: American Second-Generation Witnesses to the Holocaust.* Albany: State University of New York Press, 1997.

Bukiet, Melvin Jules. *Stories of an Imaginary Childhood.* Evanston, Ill.: Northwestern University Press, 1992.

Bukiet, Melvin Jules. *While the Messiah Tarries.* Syracuse, N.Y.: Syracuse University Press, 1997.

Dickstein, Morris. "Ghost Stories: The New Wave of Jewish Writing." *Tikkun* 12, no. 6 (November/December 1997): 33–36.

Goldstein, Rebecca. *Strange Attractors.* New York: Penguin, 1993.

Kremer, S. Lillian. "Post-alienation: Recent Directions in Jewish-American Literature." *Contemporary Literature* 34, no. 3 (fall 1993): 571–591.

Kremer, S. Lillian. *Women's Holocaust Writing: Memory and Imagination.* Lincoln: University of Nebraska Press, 1999.

Malamud, Bernard. *The Complete Stories.* New York: Farrar, Straus & Giroux, 1997.

Nissenson, Hugh. *The Elephant and My Jewish Problem: Selected Stories and Journals 1957–1987.* New York: Harper & Row, 1988.

Ozick, Cynthia. *The Shawl.* New York: Alfred A. Knopf, 1989.

Pinsker, Sanford. "Dares, Double-Dares, and the Jewish-American Writer." *Prairie Schooner* 71, no. 1 (spring 1997): 278–285.

Raphael, Lev. *Dancing on Tisha B'Av.* New York: St. Martin's Press, 1990.

Rosenbaum, Thane. *Elijah Visible.* New York: St. Martin's Press, 1996.

Roth, Philip. *Goodbye, Columbus and Five Short Stories.* Boston: Houghton Mifflin, 1959.

Solotaroff, Ted, and Nessa Rapoport, eds. *The Schocken Book of Contemporary Jewish Fiction.* New York: Schocken, 1992.

PART II

Individual Writers

and Their Work

ALICE ADAMS

(1926 – 1999)

Since *Beautiful Girl,* her first collection of short stories, appeared in 1979, Alice Adams has been considered one of America's most distinctive practitioners of the genre, noted for her wide range of characters, deft command of fictional technique, and compressed, graceful prose style. Many of her stories appeared in *The New Yorker,* and twenty-two were anthologized in the annual *Prize Stories: The O. Henry Awards,* whose editors gave her a Special Award for Continuing Achievement in 1982.

An only child, Adams was born in Fredericksburg, Virginia, in 1926. She spent her childhood in a large farmhouse near Chapel Hill, North Carolina (her father was a professor of Spanish); the house and its surrounding masses of flowers furnished the setting for some of Adams's fiction. Educated at Radcliffe, Adams spent most of her adult life in San Francisco and traveled extensively in Mexico and Europe. This geographical diversity is reflected in the extraordinary range of her stories: she writes equally well about southern families and West Coast eccentrics, academics and cleaning ladies, straight women and gay men. She also explored Henry James's "international theme" by portraying Americans in Europe and in Mexico. Her work is consistently impressive in the delicacy of its craft, the way in which her shimmering, finely wrought sentences—extending the tradition of Virginia Woolf and Katherine Mansfield—move through the minefields

of human interaction convincingly, expertly, and with a mix of irony and grace that is all her own.

Although she studied creative writing in college, Adams's literary career had a relatively late start. She married in 1946, had a son in 1951, and divorced in 1958; she worked at a series of part-time secretarial jobs while raising her son and trying to pursue her writing. Her first novel, *Careless Love,* appeared when she was forty, and she was fifty-three when she published her first book of stories. Her subsequent career, however, was a productive one. By 1999, the year she died, she had brought out ten novels, including the critically praised *Families and Survivors* (1975), *Second Chances* (1986), and *A Southern Exposure* (1995), as well as four additional volumes of stories: *To See You Again* (1982), *Return Trips* (1985), *After You've Gone* (1989), and *The Last Lovely City* (1999).

For all the variety of her work, there are recurring themes and situations throughout her five collections. Several of her best stories explore emotionally intense friendships between women. In "Roses, Rhododendron" (from *Beautiful Girl*), the narrator recalls her childhood best friend, whom the narrator meets shortly after she and her mother move from Boston to North Carolina; for the rest of the narrator's life, she associates her lost friend, Harriet, as well as the girl's southern home and its lush natural surroundings (drawn from Adams's memories of her childhood environment), with her own coming of age: "Harriet and I used to sit and exchange our stores of erroneous sexual information," she remarks, and she also remembers marveling over Harriet's house with its "bay window and a long side porch, below which the lawn sloped down to some flowering shrubs. There was a yellow rosebush, rhododendron, a plum tree, and beyond were woods—pines, and oak and cedar trees. The effect was rich and careless, generous and somewhat mysterious. I was deeply stirred." After college the girls lose touch, but as adults they exchange letters and affirm their undying bond. The narrator finds Harriet's letter "amazing": "It was enough to make me take a long look at my whole life, and to find some new colors there."

Despite Adams's interest in women's friendships, her stories about romantic love—usually involving romantic disaster—are even more numerous. In the title story of *Beautiful Girl,* a former beauty queen—a straight-A student, who had been an "infinitely promising, rarely lovely girl"—has become a miserable alcoholic. After surviving a divorce and, more recently, "an especially violent love affair," she has given up men in favor of drinking. Adams seems to ascribe the woman's unhappiness in part to her stereotypical role as a "beautiful girl" who has depended on her appearance and has never discovered any meaningful identity.

In Adams's more recent volumes, the typical character is an intelligent, career-minded woman whose personal history includes a series of failed relationships with men. Adams's heroines tend to hold feminist ideals—generally they are self-supporting, intellectually autonomous, and politically liberal—but fail to practice these ideals when choosing and relating to their male partners. In the title story of *After You've Gone,* a successful lawyer has been abandoned by her handsome lover (a charismatic poet whom she has supported financially) in favor of a younger woman. An epistolary narrative addressed to the poet but probably never mailed, "After You've Gone" is sarcastic and affectionate, embittered and fair-minded. But if the woman's recollections and present resolve to do better suggest her intelligence and renewed self-esteem (she has since become involved with another man—"a more known quality than you were," she tells her former lover), they also betray her lingering investment in the failed romance.

Although the majority of Adams's stories deal with women in relationships with either women or their romantic lovers, she occasionally focuses on male protagonists. Some are unavailable to women romantically because they are gay, while Adams presents others as charming but insensitive lovers who hurt the women in their lives. In "Molly's Dog" (*Return Trips*), an aging poet and her gay friend Sandy take a fateful trip together, and in "Snow" (*To See You Again*), a callous father spends an uncomfortable weekend of cross-country skiing with his lesbian daughter and her girlfriend. "At First Sight," also from *To See You Again,* deals with a young boy, Walker Conway, who becomes instantly infatuated with one of his mother's women friends. The son of wealthy but unaffectionate parents, Walker here begins a search for love that Adams traces deftly through his adolescence (when he is cursed, he feels, by "his unruly, brilliant mind" and "his ungainly body") and his young adulthood. The story closes with the kind of unexpected but appealing symmetry that marks many of Adams's carefully constructed narratives. By now,

Walker's mother has committed suicide and he has discovered his own homosexuality. He returns to the enormous house where he had lived with his parents as a child, and in the same room where he had become smitten with his mother's friend he again experiences love "at first sight," this time more appropriately toward a young man his own age.

Two of Adams's stories are worth examining in some detail, for they illustrate both her characteristic themes and her distinctive achievement as a prose stylist. In the superb "New Best Friends" (*Return Trips*), Adams explores the themes of both women's friendships and romantic love. Jonathan and Sarah Stein have moved from New York to the "mid-Southern" town of Hilton (a fictional university town not unlike Chapel Hill, and the setting Adams uses for many of her stories focused on southerners and academics). Sarah has become infatuated with Hattie McElroy, whom she calls her "new best friend." A gregarious, witty woman who owns a bookstore, Hattie helps to ease the loneliness that Jonathan and especially Sarah (who has no job to keep her occupied) feel in their new surroundings. Soon Hattie and her husband move away, however, and when they return for a visit Sarah learns painfully that Hattie's southern friendliness has been less than genuine. In the climactic scene, Sarah prepares a sumptuous dinner for the McElroys, but Hattie calls at the last minute and backs out in favor of an evening with her native Hilton friends. Sarah and her husband experience a renewed sense of isolation, feeling acutely their status as displaced northerners. As Jonathan remarks, "Friendships with outsiders don't really count? Does

that cut out all Yankees, really?" Near its conclusion, the story seems to acknowledge the perils of friendship but also to affirm the comforts of marriage: Sarah abruptly decides that her own husband will become her "new best friend."

This unexpected focus on the Steins' relationship is handled with the delicate ambiguity that is one of Adams's trademarks. The reader has learned already that the Steins' five-year marriage is based on intellectual talk; they enjoy "insights, analyses—and, from Sarah somewhat literary speculations." At several points during their marriage Sarah has developed intense, unrequited friendships with women that have all ended in disappointment. "New Best Friends," narrated from Jonathan's somewhat detached and skeptical viewpoint, ends with his realization that Sarah's sudden focus on him is potentially disruptive to their marriage: "as she looks at Jonathan, he recognizes some obscure and nameless danger in the enthusiastic glitter of her eyes." Adams leaves open the question of whether the Steins' relationship, newly freighted with Sarah's emotional need, will now become stronger or begin plummeting toward disaster.

More recently, in "Tide Pools" (*After You've Gone*), Adams movingly describes the reunion of Judith Mallory, a lonely, middle-aged professor, with her "closest early-childhood friend," Jennifer Cartwright. Like the narrator in "Roses, Rhododendron," the child Judith had not only loved her friend but had also coveted her friend's parents. Gradually Judith had learned that the stylish and glamorous Cartwrights' high-spirited charisma had related primarily to their alcoholism, a disease from which Judith's parents also suffered, leading to their premature deaths. Later in life, Jennifer becomes an alcoholic like her parents, whereas Judith remains abstemious but unhappily isolated.

When Judith and Jennifer reunite, however, Judith is assailed "by the sheer intensity of all that childhood emotion, my earliest passions and guilts and despairs." The girls' wading expeditions through tide pools off the Santa Barbara coast are at the center of Judith's fiercely nostalgic memories. Impulsively, Judith takes a leave of absence from her teaching job in Minnesota and returns to California, wanting to help her old friend recover from her alcoholism. Together again, the two women discuss their failed marriages and love affairs. Their reunion seems to have a positive effect on Judith. "I really feel better and better," she says, "and I think I have never been so happy in my life." However, instead of helping Jennifer to stop drinking, Judith has been joining her for glasses of wine in the evening: "Well, why not?" she thinks. "This is, after all, a sort of vacation for me." Because the story is told in first person, the reader is encouraged to see Judith as an increasingly unreliable narrator, one who has perhaps started down the path to alcoholism herself.

Adams concludes the story with her usual subtlety: although Judith insists that she is now happy, the reader is aware that Jennifer has refused to seek treatment and that the renewed friendship is likely to prove mutually destructive, each woman reinforcing the other's denial. At the same time, Judith has seemed, at least temporarily, to reenter the tide pools of her halcyon early days in California, escaping the loneliness and romantic misfortune that have marked her recent life. Like much of Adams's work, the story finally suggests the delicate symbiosis involved in close friendships and highlights the evanescent nature of human relationships generally. In the beautifully cadenced final paragraph, Judith has returned home from an evening of drinking wine with Jennifer and sits alone outside her apartment. A neighborhood cat appears on the scene as an emblem of the pleasant but fleeting connections that so often mark the lives of Adams's characters. Judith feels "the sudden warm brush of [the cat's] arching back against my leg. I reach to stroke him. He allows this, responding with a loud purr—and then, as suddenly as he appeared, with a quick leap out into the dark he is gone."

In Alice Adams's best work, such understated yet breathtaking moments are achieved with seemingly effortless skill. Adams's striking verbal economy, her instinctive sense of form, and her gift for delineating the complexities of human relationships all enabled her graceful mastery of the short story, the genre that best displays her unique and forceful talent.

Greg Johnson

SELECTED BIBLIOGRAPHY

Works by Alice Adams

Beautiful Girl. New York: Alfred A. Knopf, 1979.

To See You Again. New York: Alfred A. Knopf, 1982.

Return Trips. New York: Alfred A. Knopf, 1985.

After You've Gone. New York: Alfred A. Knopf, 1989.

The Last Lovely City. New York: Alfred A. Knopf, 1999.

Critical Studies

Goodwin, Stephen. "Alice Adams's San Francisco Chronicles." *Washington Post Book World,* May 9, 1982.

Lowry, Beverly. "Women Who Do Know Better." *New York Times Book Review,* September 1, 1985.

Phillips, Robert. "Missed Opportunities, Endless Possibilities." *Commonweal,* March 25, 1983.

SHERWOOD ANDERSON
(1876–1941)

Sherwood Anderson, the son of Irwin and Emma Anderson, was born in Camden, Ohio, on September 13, 1876. When he was fourteen he dropped out of school, worked as a stable boy, delivered newspapers, and took other available odd jobs. For midwesterners in the later years of the nineteenth century, "going to the city" meant going to Chicago in search of success; and so it was that with unrealistic hopes Sherwood Anderson made his first trip there in 1896. However, the only job he could get was in a warehouse, where he worked for several months.

In 1898, as a member of the Ohio National Guard, he was sent to Cuba to fight in the war against Spain. Returning to the United States in 1899, he spent a year at Wittenberg Academy in Springfield, Ohio. In 1900, he again moved to Chicago and worked as a writer of advertising copy. During this period, he wrote character sketches, many of which appeared in *Agricultural Advertising* and were supportive of the national business ethic, for Anderson was a disciple of a prevailing optimism that believed success to be available to all who worked for it.

Anderson married Cornelia Lane, the daughter of a well-known Toledo businessman, in 1904. They lived first in Chicago and then in Ohio. In 1906 he assumed the presidency of Cleveland's United Factories Company. The following year, the couple moved to Elyria, where Anderson was the president of a mail-order paint factory that became the Anderson Manufacturing Company. Between 1907 and 1911 they had three children: two sons and a daughter. Anderson had moved rapidly as a businessman, and it seemed that he had achieved that elusive American Dream for which he had long searched.

But in 1912 he suffered a strange illness. In a moment of alleged amnesia, he left not only his family but also his business. He was found wandering the streets of Cleveland and was briefly hospitalized. On his release, he once again returned to Chicago and advertising. The year was 1913, and he began a new life without his family. For many years he had been working on stories in his spare time, and he took these fragments to Chicago. While employed at the Long-Critchfield Advertising Agency, he continued to produce stories and soon became associated with the writers and artists of the Chicago Renaissance. In the early years of the twentieth century, this movement included Henry Blake Fuller, Robert Herrick, Theodore Dreiser, Floyd Dell (who became known as Anderson's "literary father"), Carl Sandburg, Vachel Lindsay, Harriet Monroe, and Edgar Lee Masters. They were so productive that H. L. Mencken, the well-known critic, could refer to Chicago as "the literary capital of the United States" because of the distinctive writing that seemed to come out of the city.

Much happened to Anderson in rapid succession. After divorcing Cornelia, he married Tennessee Mitchell, the one-time paramour of Edgar Lee Masters, who was a popular sculptor and part of the bohemian crowd of Chicago's art world. In the same year, 1916, *Windy McPherson's Son* was published. This first novel was quickly followed by a second, *Marching Men* (1917), which also portrayed the rite of passage of a young man as it traced the effects of Chicago on the protagonist. The next year, Anderson's book of verse, *Mid-American Chants,* appeared. It shows the unmistakable influences of both Walt Whitman and Carl Sandburg, but it also exhibits Anderson's ability to intensify language, a quality that was to serve him well in his short fiction.

Anderson's first three books demonstrated talent, but no one of them was extraordinary, despite some very positive reviews. *Winesburg, Ohio* (1919), however, is now accepted as a groundbreaking short-story cycle reflecting Anderson's interest in language and in the limited lives of the residents of small midwestern towns. These short stories were followed

quickly by the publication of *Poor White* (1920), another novel.

Anderson spent several months in Europe, where he met Gertrude Stein, and on his return to the United States lived briefly in Greenwich Village, at a time when New York was a flourishing artistic and literary center. Though he was publishing steadily, his personal life was in disarray. His second marriage, supposedly devoted to free love and openness, was stormy and ended in divorce, as did his subsequent marriage to Elizabeth Prall, a bookseller. Meanwhile, in 1921, his second collection of short stories, *The Triumph of the Egg,* was issued, and in 1923 *Horses and Men,* a third collection, appeared. The proceeds from the novel *Dark Laughter* (1925), one of his few best-sellers during his lifetime, gave him the resources to move to Virginia, where he became the owner/editor of two newspapers, *The Smyth County News* and *The Marion Democrat.* He also built Ripshin, his home for the remainder of his life; yet he continued to wander and to spend time in various places from New York to Corpus Christi. But he now thought of himself as a Virginian and married Eleanor Copenhaver of Virginia in 1933. From that time on, Anderson continued to publish a variety of works: critical and political essays, memoirs, newspaper columns, and fiction. He died on March 8, 1941, in the Panama Canal Zone, after becoming ill on a trip to South America with his wife.

Winesburg, Ohio, probably his best-known work, consists of twenty-one short stories and the longer "Godliness," which Anderson called "a tale in four parts." Some of the narratives had appeared earlier in *Masses, Seven Arts,* and other magazines of the period. The collected stories are loosely held together by repeated themes relating to alienation, isolation, and self-revelation. Moreover, all of them are bound by the setting and the presence of George Willard, a young man in Winesburg, who is often an observer in the tales dealing with the townspeople. As the stories progress, Willard appears to grow in understanding of both himself and those around him.

Winesburg, Ohio begins with a foreword known as "The Book of the Grotesque," which eventually elevates the figure of the grotesque to an important level of consciousness in American fiction. Anderson had experimented with this approach to character in the creation of Beaut McGregor in his early novel *Marching Men* (1917). In time, the grotesque seemed to focus not only on an exploration of truth but also on the presentation of character through a defining trait: few readers, for instance, can forget the hands of Wing Biddlebaum in the story "Hands."

The search for a workable truth leads the characters in *Winesburg, Ohio* to become grotesques. At the same time, the twisted lives Anderson describes are like the exemplum of the twisted apples of "Paper Pills." In this tale, the storyteller acknowledges that pickers reject warped apples because they are ugly and not suitable for the market; however, these are really the sweetest fruit, and, he notes, "Only the few know the sweetness of the twisted apples."

In *The Triumph of the Egg* (1921), Anderson abandons the unity of place and the interrelationships among characters that had proved so successful in *Winesburg,*

Ohio. Yet, a consistency of thought makes the collection an important work in the Anderson canon. In addition to the frequently anthologized "I Want to Know Why," "The Egg" exhibits both the simplicity and ambiguity of Anderson's attempt to come to terms with the meaning of life.

The general theme of *Horses and Men* (1923) is established through an introduction that, like "The Book of the Grotesque," gives elements of foreshadowing that help to determine the intention of the stories that follow. The lead story, "I'm a Fool," illustrates without moralizing the price of lying and the importance of truth. Many of the tales explore some overt or covert act of rebellion. In "The Triumph of a Modern," Anderson examines the revolt that marked the Chicago Renaissance. Some stories are located in a small-town setting and others in a city, but the problems of human deception and human isolation remain the same. These alternate settings occur throughout the collection with such tales as "Unused," "The Man Who Became a Woman," "A Chicago Hamlet," and "Milk Bottles." While a thread of despair seems apparent in these stories, which examine the ambiguities of life, the final story, "An Ohio Pagan," reintroduces the power of love as a mitigating force in human existence.

With few exceptions, the individual tales in *Winesburg, Ohio, The Triumph of the Egg, Horses and Men,* and *Death in the Woods* (1933) are concerned with the inner lives and outward manifestations of those hidden recesses of inarticulate loners who are representative of repressed people everywhere. They do not have the resources to subsist in an isolated environment. They are trapped, and Anderson views their imprisonment as an inevitable result of the barrenness of their lives. Some make futile attempts to escape, but like Rosalind Wescott in the final story of *The Triumph of the Egg,* they come "out of nowhere [and go] into nothing." Not only does "Out of Nowhere into Nothing" illustrate the extent to which Anderson could sometimes infuse his realism with vivid impressionistic images, but also it exemplifies the estrangement that occurs when traditional and mythic sources of continuity such as a workable religion, a caring family, or an inspirational commitment to something or somebody are missing.

That many of Anderson's characters are midwesterners lends an aura of regionalism to his stories, but the situations and responses of his "story people" transcend locale. Despite his obvious use of specific traits in order to individualize them, ultimately their similarities outweigh their differences. The fact that there are so many people like this in his universe tends to make that fictional world even more substantial.

For example, Anderson depicted a number of adolescent boys who, having passed the stage of childhood, have not yet reached the imagined independence of adulthood. They are puzzled by the dichotomy between what they think is true and what appears to be a surface truth. In his stories of adolescence, there is a pervasive sense of panic and a self-conscious fear of not appearing "grown up." Few of his young men have the faith or assurance of George Willard, who is willing to face the future, feeling that he has the inner resources to succeed or at least to survive. In "I'm a Fool," the fear

of possible ridicule from the girl the narrator wishes to impress leads to his admittedly stupid actions, although, like other Anderson characters, he has a longing for some ill-defined fulfillment. Here, as in "I Want to Know Why," the romantic view of life is juxtaposed with a recognition not only of what might be but also of what is.

"I Want to Know Why," "I'm a Fool," and "The Egg" observe young men who are on the threshold of knowledge. They raise some informed questions about life and the adult world. But in the process, Anderson redefines the nature of growing up as he also alters the death and resurrection theme. Small-town characters are reborn in an urban environment, where they discover more ordinary people crowded together with little sense of direction. When characters recognize the futility of their dreams, they are unable to articulate their discoveries. Partly because of this, Anderson—the storyteller—often intrudes to help them. As a result of this narrative point of view, many of Anderson's stories seem to have the aura of autobiography.

Generally stronger than his men, Anderson's pathetic women are singularly distinguished by their maternal roles even when they are not actually mothers. The "pedestal" effect perhaps dates his work and creates a certain chauvinistic air about much of it; but the fact that his female characters are customarily able to know truth and beauty intuitively does not alter the static quality of many of them. His creation of the mother figure is especially well done in the presentation of George Willard's mother in *Winesburg, Ohio* and the old woman in the title story of *Death in the Woods*. The latter illustrates not only a woman of strength and character but also the duality of life and death.

In the final analysis, Anderson's characters represent a series of conflicting emotions. A sense of determination and attempts toward self-direction are in absolute opposition to feelings of isolation and alienation. These feelings grow with the inability to communicate. The spirit of aloneness, when reinforced by portrayals of pitiful mothers and ineffectual fathers, can be alleviated through the death of the parents, which releases the character from any connection to the past. In the meantime, seldom do the searches of the characters end on a note of fulfillment; and Anderson's work—which seems to begin *in medias res*—generally stops with an unanswerable question.

During his career, Anderson created some memorable characters, although some might argue that Anderson's story people—when taken individually—are not particularly remarkable. As a group, however, they are distinguished by the persistency with which they endure their small struggles. As his characters occupy center stage, they display the extraordinary nature of ordinary lives, and readers are reminded that the material of literature as of life can be created out of the nonheroic. Despite their differences in subject matter and the various characters that appear in his short stories, Anderson's fiction continued from *Winesburg, Ohio* to repeat his concerns. His characters usually seem to be captured at a moment of some personal crisis that eventually leads to self-discovery. And this, in turn, leads them to an irrevocable truth that ultimately defines them.

Anderson's work appeared in an era that deified individualism at the same time that it expected the individual to conform to the demands of the group. Going counter to the American emphasis on success, Anderson—through his characters—suggests the narrative possibilities of failure. In a materialistic world governed by business entrepreneurs, his characters are often ill equipped to deal with American life as it is. In an earlier age, Emerson might preach the advantages of nonconformity, but such behavior—when moved from the philosophical to the actual—too frequently was associated with failure rather than with success. Moreover, Anderson's story people are not simply victims of their wishful thinking. Generally shaped by their unfulfilled longings and desires, many are so ordinary that they would escape notice except for their pathetic inability to communicate. However, despite all that they cannot say and do, his characters often have enough free will to avoid being caught in a trap of overwhelming powers. Moreover, he accepts their capacity to love as a humanizing force.

Anderson's prose style influenced his contemporaries, among them Hemingway, as well as later writers. He was committed to clarity and simplicity. He captured rhythms of midwestern speech, achieving power from its plainness and cadences. Sherwood Anderson's stories balance predictability with a sense of surprise, and create a world peopled with characters that seem familiar and real.

Kenny J. Williams

SELECTED BIBLIOGRAPHY

Works by Sherwood Anderson

Winesburg, Ohio. New York: B. W. Huebsch, 1919.

The Triumph of the Egg. New York: B. W. Huebsch, 1921.

Horses and Men. New York: B. W. Huebsch, 1923.

Death in the Woods and Other Stories. New York: Liveright, 1933.

Certain Things Last: The Selected Stories of Sherwood Anderson. New York: Four Walls Eight Windows, 1992.

Critical Studies

Anderson, David, ed. *Sherwood Anderson: Dimensions of His Literary Art.* East Lansing: Michigan State University Press, 1976.

Small, Judy Jo. *A Reader's Guide to the Short Stories of Sherwood Anderson.* New York: G. K. Hall, 1994.

Williams, Kenny J. *A Storyteller and a City: Sherwood Anderson's Chicago.* DeKalb: Northern Illinois University Press, 1988.

JAMES BALDWIN
(1924–1987)

The author and coauthor of twenty-two books, James Baldwin became famous after the publication of his controversial novel *Another Country* (1962) and his influential book-length essay *The Fire Next Time* (1963). His other works include several novels—*Go Tell It on the Mountain* (1953), *Giovanni's Room* (1956), *Tell Me How Long the Train's Been Gone* (1968), *If Beale Street Could Talk* (1974), and *Just Above My Head* (1979). His essay collections—*Notes of a Native Son* (1955), *Nobody Knows My Name* (1956), and *The Price of the Ticket* (1985)—are widely read. He also wrote two plays, *Blues for Mister Charlie* (1964) and *The Amen Corner* (1968). These works focus on Baldwin's central themes: African Americans fighting and yet adjusting to racial discrimination; artists struggling to express meaning and beauty; and gay men searching for love and respect.

The themes are directly connected to Baldwin's own life. The grandson of a slave and the stepson of a southern-born Harlem preacher, Baldwin was born in New York City on August 2, 1924. He grew up in Harlem and graduated from Dewitt Clinton High School. During his high school years he started writing while also struggling to understand his sexual identity. Reflecting on his youthful sexual "anguish" in "Here Be Dragons," he writes, "All of the American categories of male and female, straight or not, black or white, were shattered . . . very early in my life. Not without anguish certainly; but once you have discerned the meaning of a label . . . it does not have the power to define you to yourself." In 1948 he left New York City and sailed to Paris on a one-way ticket. As he explains in "Nobody Knows My Name": "I doubted my ability to survive the fury of the color problem here. . . . I wanted to prevent myself from becoming merely a Negro or merely a Negro writer." Baldwin returned to the United States for periods during the late

1950s and the early 1960s. He was a self-described "commuter" between the United States and Europe during the 1970s and 1980s. During this period he was a visiting professor at various universities, including Bowling Green State University in Ohio and the University of Massachusetts at Amherst. Baldwin died on December 1, 1987, at his home in St. Paul de Vence, France. A memorial service in his honor was held on December 8 at the Cathedral of the St. John the Divine in New York City.

Baldwin quickly became known as a brilliant essayist on racial matters in America during the late 1940s, when his first significant essay, "The Harlem Ghetto," was published in *Commentary* (1948), and he started publishing book reviews, essays, and occasional short stories in *The New Leader, The Nation,* and *Partisan Review.* In 1953 he published his first novel, *Go Tell It on the Mountain,* the story of John Grimes, a Harlem teenager, torn between his religious home and the beckoning lights of midtown Manhattan. Baldwin was a successful and much-honored writer. Throughout his career, he received various fellowships and awards, including a Eugene F. Saxton Memorial Trust Fellowship (1944–45), a Guggenheim Fellowship (1954), and a National Institute of Arts and Letters grant (1956). After the publication of *The Fire Next Time* (1963), he received the George Polk Memorial Award.

In 1965, Baldwin published *Going to Meet the Man,* his only collection of short stories. The eight pieces are diverse. The title story, "Going to Meet the Man," and "The Manchild" are set in the South and focus on lonely and troubled white men.

Jesse, the protagonist of "Going to Meet the Man," remains disturbed and sexually traumatized because his father once took him to watch the castration and lynching of a black man. He is also a violent bigot. Like *Go Tell It on the Mountain,* two stories, "The Rockpile" and "The Outing," feature black boys growing up in strictly religious Harlem households. The "outing" refers to a boat trip up the Hudson to the Bear Mountain area sponsored by Harlem's Mount of Olives Pentecostal Assembly. The story involves three adolescent boys, Johnnie, Roy, and David, and one girl, Sylvia. One of the boys, David, adores Sylvia. Baldwin adds a thematic twist as the story concludes. Johnnie struggles "to ignore the question which now screamed and screamed in his mind's bright haunted house." Johnnie discovers that he is as smitten by David as David is by Sylvia.

"Previous Condition," "Sonny's Blues," and "This Morning, This Evening, So Soon" depict African American artists and their struggles. "Previous Condition" (1948), Baldwin's first published short story, which appeared (like his first essay) in *Commentary,* demonstrates how Baldwin would in future stories and novels show the inextricable links between racial discrimination and artistic freedom. Peter, a black actor, wants to live downtown in Manhattan rather than in Harlem. After being rejected by various landlords and then abruptly evicted after Jules, a Jewish friend, secretly gets an apartment for him, Peter tells Jules he simply wants a place to sleep "without dragging it through the courts." And Baldwin shows how Peter, like most blacks, adjusts to the racial discrimination and violence he faces. Peter says: "Like a prizefighter learns to take a blow or a dancer learns to fall, I'd learned how to get by. . . . When I faced a policemen I acted like I didn't know a thing. . . . I took a couple of beatings but I stayed out of prison and I stayed off the chain gang."

Peter is also forced to learn to deal with the rage he has within. He tells his friend: "I'm worried about what's happening to me, to *me* inside!" But he does not allow his anger to cloud his vision as an artist. Although he is unemployed, he maintains his artistic principles. He refuses to play Bigger Thomas in a movie version of Richard Wright's *Native Son*: "Metro offered me a fortune to come to the coast and do the lead in *Native Son* but I turned it down. Type casting, you know, it's so difficult to find a decent part." Peter's principled objection to typecasting (or what Baldwin often refers to as categorization) mirrors Baldwin's own attempt to get beyond various prescribed racial and artistic boundary lines.

Baldwin explores another artist's struggle in "Sonny's Blues," his best-known and most frequently anthologized story. At the beginning of "Sonny's Blues," Sonny, a black heroin addict and jazz musician in New York City, is arrested on drug-related charges. His brother, the nameless narrator, is a high school algebra teacher who reads of the misfortune in the subway on his way to work: "I read it, and I couldn't believe it, and I read it again." To give us a sense of what led to the estrangement between the brothers, Baldwin uses flashback, a technique he frequently employs. In "Sonny's Blues," we are taken back several years before the narrator married and before his mother's death. The narrator's mother prophetically tells him: "You got to hold on to your brother . . . and don't let him fall, no matter what it looks like is happening to him and no matter how evil you gets with him." Her message becomes linked to the narrator's belated perception of Sonny's life, his blues.

The narrator does not understand the true meaning of his mother's words until the story's end. His reconciliation with Sonny highlights Baldwin's preoccupation with artists. Entering a club with his brother, Sonny is greeted warmly by his fellow musicians. The bandleader, Creole, says to the narrator: "You got a real musician in your family." Before long Creole leads Sonny to the piano and the band starts playing. As Sonny plays, the music inspires the narrator to reflect upon Sonny's life and his own. The narrator's reconciliation with his brother goes beyond mere fraternal loyalty. He experiences an epiphany. He now understands and accepts some of his own past experiences, including the death of his daughter and his estrangement from Sonny: "Sonny's fingers filled the air with life, his life. But that life contained so many others. . . . I saw my mother's face again, and felt, for the first time, how the stones of the road she had walked on must have bruised her feet."

"This Morning, This Evening, So Soon" represents Baldwin's international variation on "Previous Condition." Baldwin was deeply influenced by Henry James, and he sometimes, like James, places American characters in international settings, especially Paris and London, to test their reactions to other countries and cultures. "You are full of nightmares," Harriet, a beautiful Swedish woman, says to her black American husband at the beginning of "This Morning, This Evening, So Soon." Her husband (who is never named) has become a famous singer / actor in Paris. They have lived in Paris for twelve years and are the proud parents of a son who has never set foot in America. The husband is having nightmares because he is getting ready to return to the United States. Despite his freedom and success in Paris, he remains apprehensive about American racial prejudice and violence.

Baldwin complicates this simple plot line with various flashbacks. The narrative takes us back to the time one "tremendous April morning" in Paris when Harriet and her future husband fell in love on the Port Royal Bridge. The nameless narrator says: "During all the years of my life, until that moment, I had carried the menacing, the hostile, the killing world with me everywhere. . . . And for the first time in my life, I was free of it. . . . For the first time in my life I felt that no force jeopardized my right, my power, to possess and protect a woman; for the first time, the first time, felt that the woman was not, in her own eyes or in the eyes of the world, degraded by my presence." Nevertheless, the successful actor remains at the mercy of his nightmares. For instance, he is "surprised at" his own racially charged "vehemence" when he lashes out at Vidal, his French director, over the appropriate manner to play a scene. The story then is both a dramatization of the possibility of interracial union and a scathing critique of racial prejudice in the United States.

Although Baldwin published very few short stories after the 1960s, and most critics consider him a superior essayist and novelist, his best stories are unforgettable.

All his life, he had devoted himself to conveying in all his writing an international, transracial, and androgynous vision of human possibility—a vision as evident in the stories as it is in the essays and novels.

Horace Porter

SELECTED BIBLIOGRAPHY

Baldwin, James. *Going to Meet the Man.* New York: Dial Press, 1965.

Campbell, James. *Talking at the Gates: A Life of James Baldwin.* New York: Oxford University Press, 1991.

Harris, Trudier. *Black Women in the Fiction of James Baldwin.* Knoxville: University of Tennessee Press, 1985.

Leeming, David. *James Baldwin.* New York: Penguin, 1995.

Porter, Horace. *Stealing the Fire: The Art and Protest of James Baldwin.* Middletown, Conn.: Wesleyan University Press, 1989.

JOHN BARTH
(1930–)

Born in 1930, John Barth grew up on the Eastern Shore of Maryland, a circumstance, he suggests in his autobiographical essay "Some Reasons Why," that is one of the roots of his often unconventional writing style. "Your webfoot amphibious marsh-nurtured writer," he explains, "will likely by mere reflex regard many conventional boundaries as arbitrary, fluid, negotiable." Among other factors, he feels, is that he came into life with a twin sister with whom he shared a private language "before and beyond speech," a language, in that regard, like the music of the jazz groups with which he played to support himself in college and in his early teaching. Though he had studied at Juilliard, he was not long in deciding that his talent was insufficient to make a career of music. At Johns Hopkins University he conceived his enduring interest in tale cycles like *The Thousand and One Nights* and the Sanskrit *Ocean of Story* and discovered his vocation for writing.

To date, Barth has published nine novels that range in mode from the nihilistic— *The Floating Opera* and *End of the Road*— to the encyclopedic—*The Sot Weed Factor* and *Giles Goat-Boy*. Two of the novels were nominated for the National Book Award, which was given to Barth's collection of three novellas, *Chimera,* in 1973. He has published also two collections of essays, *The Friday Book* and *Further Fridays,* and two volumes of short fiction. He has taught at Pennsylvania State University, the State University of New York at Buffalo, and, since 1973, at Johns Hopkins University, where he is currently professor emeritus in the Writing Seminars.

Barth's first volume of short stories, published in 1968, was an interrelated series entitled *Lost in the Funhouse: Fiction for Print, Tape, Live Voice,* fourteen items initiated by a ten-word "Frame-Tale": "Once upon a time there was a story that began." A note instructs the reader to scissor out the "tale" and form it into a Möbius strip so that the words will go on ad infinitum: by implication, one is cued not to expect fictions that necessarily hew to literary conventions. Though "Ambrose His Mark" and "Water-Message" are conventional narratives, "Lost in the Funhouse" repeatedly breaks through its narrative with apparently extraneous pedagogies, questions, and self-criticisms; "Echo," "Menelaiad," and "Anonymiad" are radically transformed classical myths; and "Title" and "Life-Story" are fictionalized explorations of issues Barth has addressed in his essays. These tales show Barth moving toward the strategies implied in his well-known *Atlantic Monthly* essay of 1967, "The Literature of Exhaustion," in which he asserted "the used-upness of certain forms or the felt exhaustion of certain possibilities." He has explained in this piece and in his essay "The Literature of Replenishment" that he did not mean that literature was exhausted, but rather that the time had come to transcend the strategies of both premodern and modernist literature. This possibility he defines mainly by example, citing Gabriel García Márquez's brilliant novel *One Hundred Years of Solitude* for its sustained "synthesis of straightforwardness and artifice, realism and magic and myth, political passion and nonpolitical artistry, characterization and caricature."

"Night-Sea Journey," the first full tale in *Funhouse,* is told by a unique narrator that many early reviewers took to be a fish. He (it) is actually an articulate sperm cell struggling to swim in its specialized sea while voicing lamentations on the millions of others who perish in the attempt. Along the laborious way, a companion of this tale-bearer indulges in speculations that are cleverly conceived to have multiple references. When he theorizes about their "Maker," their "Father," he is not only engaging in a kind of theistic philosophy but is also addressing—especially in his more cynical conclusions—the perhaps frenzied act of coition indulged in by that as yet unknown father. Finally, the maker is, of course, Barth himself, who may be having a little joke at his own expense over the head, as it were, of the guileless narrator: "No less outrageous, and offensive to traditional opinion, were the fellow's speculations on the nature of our Maker: that He might well be no swimmer Himself at all, but some sort of monstrosity, perhaps even tailless." (Pun on tale?) Because the next tale in the series, "Ambrose His Mark," opens with reference to the birth of its title character, we may have come upon the identity of the father-figure discussed by those fluent spermatozoans, one Hector, father of Ambrose, though he himself doubts his paternity.

Ambrose, age thirteen, is the antiheroic hero of Barth's much anthologized tale, the title story, "Lost in the Funhouse," a labyrinth full of tripwires attached to apparently irrelevant instructions as well as of truncated sentences we fall off the ends of: "The smell of Uncle Karl's cigar reminded one of." Set in an amusement park during World War II, the main action takes place in a funhouse from which Ambrose is unable to find his way out. He is as lost in that place of puzzlement as he is in his own life: "Everybody else is in on some secret he doesn't know; they've forgotten to tell him." The tale too seems to be lost in the funhouse of its writing, thus inviting readers into an experience like that of Ambrose.

Via such stratagems, Barth takes up the postmodern gauntlet, putting his readers through a funhouse barrel roll, throwing them off balance by violating their expectations, forcing them to deal with the fact that fiction is artifice as well as art. His main tactic to this end is to break through the narrative repeatedly with textbookish directions on writing, directions, moreover, that are often violated in the very story that offers them: "Description of physical appearance and mannerisms is one of several methods of characterization used by writers of fiction." Discussion of writing techniques interjected within a fiction may seem only distantly relevant. As may the intensification of that practice—the criticism of its own procedures—into which the story slides as it goes along: "All the preceding except the last few sentences is exposition that should've been done earlier. . . . " But Barth surely does not expect those reflexive criticisms and discourses to be taken simply at face value. Rather they serve as a strategy, a demonstration of one of the ways Barth feels that fiction may be revitalized: by owning up to its irreality, to the fact that it is crafted, and despite that acknowledgment, stirring the reader to feel for the human plight it manifests.

If some of the acrobatics in this tale are excessive, on the whole "Funhouse" stands up remarkably well; no doubt that is why it has been much anthologized. It has passed the test of time. By the standards Barth summarizes in his preface to "The Literature of Exhaustion"—that "passion and virtuosity are what matter" in literature—"Funhouse" is a spirited performance. Though his involvements with Magda suggest that at thirteen Ambrose is still lacking in sexual passion, his anxieties and sympathies are fully ripened: "Nothing was what it looked like. Every instant, under the surface of the Atlantic Ocean, millions of living animals devoured one another. Pilots were falling in flames over Europe; women were being forcibly raped in the South Pacific." Ambrose's callow grandiloquence is touching as he fantasies dying of starvation in the funhouse while telling himself stories that "an exquisite young woman" on the other side of a partition transcribes, recognizing "that here was one of Western Culture's truly great imaginations, the eloquence of whose suffering would be an inspiration to unnumbered." Finally, in the light of his concluding decision to become a writer, and like Barth to "construct funhouses for others," the "digressions" on writing that have hovered in the context of his story seem pertinent.

In 1996 Barth published *On with the Story,* his second volume of short fiction, this time tied together by a series of brief interstory segments entitled "Pillow-Talk" in which a couple vacationing at a beach resort entertain themselves by telling each other these very stories. Essentially new to these tales is the use they make of various concepts of modern physics and astronomy—quantum mechanics, Heisenberg's indeterminacy principle, Planck's constant, the Arrow of Time—that are assimilated to the contingencies of the characters' lives. In "Ever After," for instance, a married couple who enjoy watching meteor showers, those apparently random celestial events, is subjected to the possibility of collision with quite other seemingly random phenomena: cancerous tumors, spotted-fever ticks, a serial rapist. In the title tale, the stalled economic status of its mid-life protagonist is set against the speed of the planet Earth

as it "careens through its solar orbit at a dizzying 66,662 miles per hour" and the Milky Way as it soars through space at nearly half a million miles per hour. Despite the stellar sophistication of these tales, they are not in need of commentary to the same extent as the first collection.

To read John Barth is to come into contact with a bold and agile mind, the mind of a writer who probably *would* be hampered by the methods he has called for fiction to terminate. He is a writer who demands ample elbow room, room to digress, to express his interests in writing, in science, in classics, in languages. Having seized the room he needs, he has created stories that are often dazzling in their methods and moving in their exploration of human themes, especially the theme of lostness in its various manifestations.

Arthur Edelstein

SELECTED BIBLIOGRAPHY

Works by John Barth

Lost in the Funhouse: Fiction for Print, Tape, Live Voice. New York: Doubleday, 1968.
The Friday Book: Essays and Other Nonfiction. Baltimore: Johns Hopkins University Press, 1984.
On with the Story. Boston: Little, Brown, 1996.

Critical Studies

Fogel, Stan, and Gordon Slethaug. *Understanding John Barth.* Columbia: University of South Carolina Press, 1990.
Harris, Charles B. *Passionate Virtuosity: The Fiction of John Barth.* Urbana and Chicago: University of Illinois Press, 1983.
Tobin, Patricia. *John Barth and the Anxiety of*

Continuance. Philadelphia: University of Pennsylvania Press, 1992.

DONALD BARTHELME
(1931 – 1989)

The first appearance of Donald Barthelme's short fictions challenged the conventions of narrative order, closure, and mimetic fidelity that had dominated the preceding generation of American storytelling. In their matter-of-fact way these stories presented readers and critics with a series of metaphysical and narratological perplexities—a provocation no less potent because the stories' narrative facts seem, at first, disarmingly familiar, even banal. "The Piano Player" begins simply: "Outside his window five-year-old Priscilla Hess, square and squat as a mailbox (red sweater, blue lumpy corduroy pants), looked around poignantly for someone to wipe her overflowing nose." However, as the title of Barthelme's first collection, *Come Back, Dr. Caligari,* promises, readers quickly found themselves in expressionist territory, and a simple opening sentence like "Hubert gave Charles and Irene a nice baby for Christmas" ("Will You Tell Me?") seemed—and seems—charged with an unsettling plurality of narrative possibilities. Barthelme's understated dislocations of everyday experience and his discovery of the absurd and arbitrary in the verbal formulas and codes of conduct that govern daily American life anticipated the fictional innovations of subsequent de-

cades. Jorge Luis Borges has been described as the kind of writer whom post-structuralist critics would have had to invent if he had not already existed; Donald Barthelme can be plausibly seen as his American counterpart. Surprisingly, however, American critics and theorists have preferred to borrow their paradigms of representation—and its subversion—from European and South American authors, perhaps because Barthelme's metaphysical musings are less explicit—and funnier—than those of Borges, Dino Buzzati, Raymond Queneau, and other writers who have made the short story a medium for disrupting our ordinary perceptions of "reality." Barthelme's work draws freely on cosmopolitan sources, including these writers, but his laconic brand of surrealism, as well as his appetite for both the junk food and the high art of American culture, mark him as unmistakably native.

Barthelme does not altogether discard the possibilities of plot, but his stories often seem deliberately to offer the least that will suffice to meet the reader's expectation of a shaping order, something that provides contingent closure to a series of events, images, and observed phenomena. "On the Deck," for example, describes the story's setting (in effect, its stage set), but suspends all action until the final paragraph—and then that action is merely an accidental collision of bodies, as though fiction were the medium through which "You" and "I," the reader and writer, could make random contact. Beginning with an "initial impulse," perhaps an anecdote or vignette, Barthelme's stories grow by what he himself described to Larry McCaffery as a process of "accretion," and the promptings of language itself, experienced as a source of power beyond the writer, provide the primary agency of this expansion. Moreover, their techniques of collage, both verbal and visual, in, for example, "At the Tolstoy Museum" and "The Flight of Pigeons from the Palace," often suggest an understanding of the story as *found* rather than made. Historical gossip, pop physics, and artistic credos (Paul Klee's, for example) mingle promiscuously with the more commonplace fictional materials of first-person introspection and domestic conflict, and empirically attested "facts" thus lose their real-world status—their nonfictionality—through absurdist juxtaposition. The reader learns, for example, that Tolstoy "first contracted gonorrhea in 1847. He was once bitten on the face by a bear. He became a vegetarian in 1885. To make himself interesting, he occasionally bowed backward" ("At the Tolstoy Museum").

The protagonist of "See the Moon" declares, "Fragments are the only forms I trust." Speaking to Jerome Klinkowitz, Barthelme disavowed this phrase as a statement of his own aesthetic, but some of his admirers have nevertheless identified the character's creed with the writer's practice. Barthelme not only anticipated the preoccupations of subsequent literary and cultural criticism, which would dub itself "postmodern," but influenced the proliferation of American short short stories— a form whose European precedents go back at least as far as Kleist—and he practiced "minimalism" before it received a name or became a catchword. Nevertheless, few of Barthelme's successors have matched the sustained seriousness or the

imaginative wildness of his condensations of fictional possibility.

Donald Barthelme was born in Philadelphia in 1931, and grew up in Houston, where his family moved in 1933. His journalistic career, begun in high school, continued at the University of Houston, where his writing expanded in the direction of parodies, satirical pieces, and reviews. From 1951 to 1953 he worked on military newspapers and was posted to Japan and Korea, among other places. After his stint in the army, he resumed employment with the *Houston Post* and other publications, where his writing increasingly focused on the fine arts. (His father's work as an innovative architect no doubt influenced this direction of his interests.) In 1961 he became the director of Houston's Contemporary Arts Museum. In the same year, the story "Me and Miss Mandible" (originally titled "The Darling Duckling at School"), published in *Contact,* signaled the new direction his career was about to take. He moved to New York in 1962 in order to edit the short-lived magazine *Location,* and the following year he published "L'Lapse" (described by Barthelme as "non-fiction") and "The Piano Player" in *The New Yorker,* where many of his subsequent stories initially appeared. In 1964, *Come Back, Dr. Caligari,* his first book-length collection of fiction, immediately consolidated his literary reputation; in all, he would publish seven collections of stories. While Barthelme classified *Guilty Pleasures* as a "non-fiction" gathering of parodies and occasional pieces, his untraditional practices make the distinction among genres difficult to maintain. Each of his compendia, *Sixty Sto-*

ries (1981) and *Forty Stories* (1987), included a handful of new stories and gave many of his early stories new currency. In addition, Barthelme published four novels: *Snow White* (1967), *The Dead Father* (1975), *Paradise* (1986), and *The King* (1990); a children's book; two dramatic adaptations of his work; and various non-fiction pieces. The posthumous collection *The Teachings of Don B.* (1992), with an introduction by Thomas Pynchon, brings together some of his stray writings in generically elusive categories. Barthelme married twice—the experience of divorce figures obliquely in his fiction—and his second marriage produced a daughter. In 1972 he did his first teaching at SUNY, Buffalo, and eventually, in 1981, he assumed a lifetime position in the creative writing program at the University of Houston. He died of cancer in 1989.

Despite the playfulness and the surprising fictional premises of Barthelme's stories, their most sustained mood is melancholy and a kind of inchoate longing. The period of Barthelme's greatest productivity coincided with the Cold War, and some of its atmosphere pervades his pages. Historical crisis is just offstage. "Robert Kennedy Saved from Drowning" (April 1968) reminds us of what Robert Kennedy was not saved from. Nevertheless, despite Barthelme's explicit recoil from the politics of the Nixon, Bush, and Reagan administrations, his gentle disillusionment with experience reaches beyond the political. His invention of the field of "lunar hostility studies" (in "See the Moon") suggests how diffuse its sources might be. The first story of *Sadness* (1972), his fourth collection, is entitled

"Critique de la Vie Quotidienne," and in "The Temptation of St. Anthony," in the same volume, the temptation is to accept "ordinary life." St. Anthony is harried to renounce "the higher orders of abstractions" by those who find his taste for the "ineffable" irritating and pretentious. Though Barthelme is too self-mocking to hint that he himself is the secular counterpart of a saint, his sympathy with St. Anthony's resistances seems clear. On the other hand, the gregarious Barthelme's worldly tastes included Dairy Queen, Tex-Mex food, and plenty of television. Thomas Pynchon comments that what prevented Barthelme from becoming a "world-class curmudgeon" was "the stubborn counter-rhythms of what kept on being a hopeful and unbitter heart"—which sounds like a rather saintlike attribute, after all.

Just as the title of "Robert Kennedy Saved from Drowning" recalls the Jean Renoir film *Boudu Sauvé des Eaux,* "The Indian Uprising," mingling reminiscences of John Ford westerns and *Death in Venice* with contemporary reports of urban warfare, testifies forcefully to the way in which the apprehension of history is filtered through inherited forms, even when Barthelme's persistent parody and fragmentation of nineteenth-century novels, fairy tales, and philosophy suggest that these forms survive primarily as cultural detritus. Nevertheless, these damaged inheritances represent one of the forms of plenitude for which Barthelme longs—a longing that Charles Baxter writes of as specifically religious. The past is a public, institutional space, a museum or abandoned palazzo, where, in "The Educational Experience," students wander among the exhibits (to the music of "Vivaldi's great work, *The Semesters*") to learn that "the world is everything was formerly the case . . . now it is time to get back on the bus." "At the Tolstoy Museum," whose holdings "consist principally of some thirty thousand pictures of Count Leo Tolstoy," "we sat and wept"; the architects in Barthelme's story observe that the entire building, viewed from the street, seems about to fall on you, and they relate this sensation to Tolstoy's moral authority.

If the past is a source of oppression, it is not because it is disciplinary or coercive, but rather because it is beautiful, eloquent, and distant. The nostalgia it inspires is for a world in which signs keep their promises and narratives have a knowable logic. By contrast, in "Me and Miss Mandible" (the earliest of Barthelme's stories to be collected in his first book), a failed insurance claims adjuster finds himself reassigned to an elementary school class of eleven-year-olds because he has misunderstood the mendacity and bad faith that compromise the signs of his society: "I myself, in my former existence, read the company motto ('Here to Help in Time of Need') as a description of the duty of the adjuster, drastically mislocating the company's deepest concerns. I believed that because I had obtained a wife who was made up of wife-signs (beauty, charm, softness, perfume, cookery) I had found love. . . . All of us, Miss Mandible, Sue Ann, myself, Brenda, Mr. Goodykind, still believe that the American flag betokens a kind of general righteousness." When the narrator, "officially a child," makes love to Miss Mandible in the cloakroom, this breach of hierarchy and trans-

gression against authority announces and initiates the saturnalia of signs to which Barthelme's subsequent fictions will inevitably be drawn.

Despite its forbidding dimensions, the past also represents a more secure collectivity than the present, in which collectivities must be improvised—not least of all by the tenuously poised fiction-making that Barthelme himself practices. Stories, as Barthelme presents them, are stationed at the intersection of public and private spaces. "The Balloon," for example, a "concrete particular" with the "free-hanging," "frivolous and gentle" properties of a fiction, seems to expand, impersonally, "northward all one night" until it reaches Central Park. There, the story's "I," suddenly explicitly announcing itself, arrests its motion, only to disappear for most of the story. While the "I" remains invisible, the balloon in effect replaces the weather of New York, as its citizens cautiously find it "interesting," debate its meanings but learn "not to insist on meanings," discover that it brings the city's architecture into new unities, and, strolling or bouncing on the balloon's pleasurably varied surfaces, explore its dimensions and pneumaticities. Whether hostile or receptive to this new phenomenon, they conclude that nothing can be done to remove or destroy it. Yet at the very moment that this undulant suspension seems to have imposed itself as a fact of life, the narrator speaks once again in the first person; he declares that the balloon is a "spontaneous autobiographical disclosure," emanating from unease and sexual deprivation; he announces its deflation, and the "depleted fabric" is trucked away to await renewed deployment at "some other time of unhappiness"—but an unhappiness, significantly, no longer marked as purely personal.

In such stories as "The Crisis" or "Departures" the narrative also switches, as though indifferently, between political and personal, cultural and bodily, moments of collapse and decision. The historical wears the guise of the personal and vice versa. In *The Dead Father* (a novel extracted in *Sixty Stories* and, like *Snow White,* close in spirit and technique to Barthelme's short stories), the ferociously mythological elaboration of the Father— or, in Lacanian terms, the *Nom du Père*— conveys the magnetism and terror of both domestic and political power.

The stories are projections of their author's desires, but whether the selves in which they traffic are aggrandizements or containments remains, like the indefinite contours and dimensions of the balloon, an elusive matter. In "A Few Moments of Sleeping and Waking," the protagonist Edward quotes Freud: when "only a strange person appears in the dream-content, I may safely assume that by means of identification my ego is concealed behind that person. I am permitted to supplement my ego." Concealment here seems a peculiar form of supplementation. The narrator of "Daumier" is even more explicit about the topic of "self-transplants," but he sees them as a means of restraining the "insatiable rapacity of the ego": whereas the self is a Messalina, a Bonaparte, a Billy the Kid, "the surrogate, the construct, is in principle satiable." The story goes careening through the history of the Jesuits, the Wild West, and the novels of Dumas, among other locales, and ends in a compromise: "The self cannot be escaped, but

can be, with ingenuity and hard work, distracted. There are always openings, if you can find them, there is always something to do." The upshot of all this travel across genres and eras, therefore, is historical as well as psychological optimism, and the narrator's interlocutor Amelia assures him, "We have all misunderstood Billy the Kid." In any case, Barthelme's fictional operations inescapably resemble Freudian dreamwork, in which, Pynchon says, "images from the public domain are said likewise to combine in unique, private, with luck spiritually useful, ways." Pynchon emphasizes Barthelme's rare ability to "smuggle [his] nocturnal contraband right on past the checkpoints of daylight 'reality,'" and he suggests the affinity of this fictional dreamwork to Barthelme's love of collage.

It is not the characters, however, that serve most notably as Barthelme's "surrogates" within the stories, but words, with their powerful reservoir of agency. Words are the "furiously busy" medium through which history enters fiction: they have, Barthelme declares in "Not-Knowing," "haloes, patinas, overhangs, echoes," and he goes on to explore the shared memories encoded in each of these metaphors. Barthelme's critics have often insisted that he wants to purge language from its contaminations by commerce, politics, and daily banality, but Barthelme asserts that the "trace elements of the world" it carries can also "be used in a positive sense." Art is "always a meditation upon," rather than a representation of, "external reality," Barthelme writes, claiming for it a modest, oblique and fundamentally meliorative efficacy. "The combinatorial agility of words, the exponential generation of meaning once they're allowed to go to bed together," enable the imagination of alternative realities and thus a productive "quarrel with the world." One may suspect that this defense of fiction is wishful, and question, for example, whether a story in which one lover discovers that another has become, or always has been, a lizard ("Rebecca") is really a speculation about how reality might be improved. On the other hand, there is no doubt that Barthelme saw imaginative license as a liberating weapon against the debasement—more specifically, the numbness—of "the way we live now." Although critics sometimes complained that his later collections of short fiction were self-repetitive, Barthelme maintained a remarkably high and consistent level of invention throughout his career. If the stories in *Overnight to Many Distant Cities* (1983) had less capacity to provoke and astonish than those of the 1960s and early 1970s, it may have been because the reaches of the psyche he had colonized had by the 1980s become recognizable territory, and his fictional world had installed itself as part of contemporary readers' shared perception of historical and personal absurdity. Just beneath the surface of serene bemusement or melancholy resignation, in Donald Barthelme's stories there is always, if we care to hear it, an incitement to rebellion.

Barry Weller

SELECTED BIBLIOGRAPHY

Works by Donald Barthelme

Come Back, Dr. Caligari. Boston: Little, Brown, 1964.

Unspeakable Practices, Unnatural Acts. New York: Farrar, Straus & Giroux, 1968.

City Life. New York: Farrar, Straus & Giroux, 1970.

Sadness. New York: Farrar, Straus & Giroux, 1972.

Guilty Pleasures. New York: Farrar, Straus & Giroux, 1974.

Amateurs. New York: Farrar, Straus & Giroux, 1976.

Great Days. New York: Farrar, Straus & Giroux, 1979.

Sixty Stories. New York: G. P. Putnam's Sons, 1982.

Overnight to Many Distant Cities. New York: G. P. Putnam's Sons, 1983.

"Not-Knowing." In Alan Weir and Don Hendrie, Jr., eds., *Voicelust,* pp. 37–50. Lincoln: University of Nebraska Press, 1985.

Forty Stories. New York: G. P. Putnam's Sons, 1987.

The Teachings of Don B. New York: Random House, 1992.

Critical Studies

Baxter, Charles. "The Donald Barthelme Blues." In *Burning Down the House,* pp. 197–218. St. Paul: Graywolf Press, 1997.

Klinkowitz, Jerome. "Donald Barthelme." In Joe David Bellamy, ed., *The New Fiction: Interviews with Innovative American Writers,* pp. 45–54. Urbana: University of Illinois Press, 1974.

McCaffery, Larry. "An Interview with Donald Barthelme." In Tom Le Clair and Larry McCaffery, eds., *Anything Can Happen: Interviews with Contemporary American Novelists,* pp. 32–44. Urbana: University of Illinois Press, 1983.

Molesworth, Charles. *Donald Barthelme's Fiction: The Ironist Saved from Drowning.* Columbia: University of Missouri Press, 1982.

RICK BASS
(1959–)

Rick Bass's best-known story might well be the one referred to during interviews and in *Fiber* (1998), the journey he narrates in *Winter: Notes from Montana* (1991) and retells in *The Book of Yaak* (1996). Leaving the South and an oil-industry job in his late twenties like the quest-hero of myth, drawn west, "as seems to be the genetic predisposition in our country's blood," traveling through New Mexico, Arizona, Colorado, Utah, Wyoming, Idaho, into Montana, he came, finally, "over a pass and a valley appeared beneath." He lives there still. Bass had first encountered Rocky Mountain life as a geology student at Utah State University in the late 1970s, before he thought of himself as a writer. Before his return to the West, Bass was, by his own description, an author only of unmarketable hunting and fishing stories. Since 1987, writing from the remoteness of Montana's Yaak Valley, Bass has transformed himself, producing twelve books, including four volumes of short fiction: *The Watch* (1989), *Platte River* (1994), *In the Loyal Mountains* (1995), and *The Sky, the Stars, the Wilderness* (1997). His stories have won inclusion in multiple volumes of *The Best American Short Stories, The Pushcart Prize, The O. Henry Awards,* and *New Stories from the South,* and he has received a General Electric Younger Writers Award and a PEN/Nelson Algren Special Citation.

As Bass's autobiographical quest narrative suggests, he considers his Montana valley symbolic. It opens north, away from its American neighbors. It is a purely natural place and its location on the margin has so far kept it safe from our material culture's exploitations. "I'm hiding up here—no question about it," Bass writes in *Winter,* and he describes the community members of Yaak as sharing that ironic trait: "We're all on the run from something, and it makes us feel safe, this isolation." From this life on the margins, Bass has drawn the two qualities for which his short stories have been most praised: the vernacular characters and the implicit or explicit appeal against American materialist culture's corrupt relationship with the natural world. "In cities I feel weak and wasted. . . . I like to be in nature," Bass has said, "and I figure when it's time to kick me out it will, and if it's time to tear me apart it will." He puts himself in the tradition of masculine pastoral stretching back to James Fenimore Cooper and Henry Thoreau, wherein nature's most interesting element is its power, its potential for physical and spiritual testing. *Winter* is his season, Flatiron Mountain his Snowdon, described in a spirit Wordsworth might not have recognized: "anyone in the valley who's ever been wild, who's ever been worth a damn, has hiked to the top of Flatiron."

This masculine vernacular is an especially strong feature in *The Watch* and *In the Loyal Mountains,* whether the stories are set in Houston, the Gulf Coast of Texas, Mississippi bayou country, or the Montana wilderness. All but two stories are narrated in the first person, a folksy male voice and nonreflective consciousness, with openings like, "It rains in Rodney in the winter. But we have history . . ." or "Kirby's faithful. He's loyal: Kirby has fidelity." The lack of a conceptual narrator is, in fact, the concept Bass favors. The nearly complete absence of dialogue hints at a narrative consciousness not attuned to the subtleties of individual human characters, and the stories' seemingly artless, meandering construction duplicates the spontaneity of each picaro's existence. As Andrew Ettin points out in *Literature and the Pastoral,* male characters can in such marginal situations express a wider range of emotions than society traditionally allows. The naiveté in Bass's narrators grants them an ironic freedom to amble, as in this paragraph from "Mississippi": "Owls. We got owls. At night they say whoo, and make you question your place in things, and even sometimes what is in you." Joseph Coates pointed out a major problem inherent in this reliance on the vernacular male; all thematic awareness must come from outside the words themselves. The stories in *The Watch,* Coates reflects, have "no more conceptual baggage than the values of a buddy movie." Yet it should also be pointed out that no concept will resolve Bass's major question about how humankind is to relate to the natural world. Bass's work in the South drilling wells as a petroleum geologist acquainted him well with the precise point where technological society punctures the natural world. As a fiction writer, he does not suggest that one must be simple to connect spontaneously with nature, but in *The Watch* and *In the Loyal Mountains* he chooses the superior position of dramatic irony and communicates over the heads of his characters. Bass has said that he tries to write positive essays, but in "fiction there's not that same pressure to celebrate the good." Western-epic expectations about proving or regenerating the self through encounters with nature usually seem irrelevant to the experiences of Bass's fictional male characters.

A good example of the benefits and possible liabilites of the vernacular narrator is "Choteau," from *The Watch.* The gullible speaker is a man who attributes his failures with women to the Yaak Valley itself, "rough country . . . beauty doesn't do well up here unless it's something permanent, like the mountains." He saves his admiration and his verbal riffs for his liege lord, the mock-heroic Galena Jim Ontz, forty with a bad heart, "a kid's grin," a son in prison, two girlfriends, "two of everything . . . the last tough man there is." An avalanche of ironic details proves Jim to be a failure as a husband, father, and friend, but much of the avalanche also detracts from the narrator's intelligence. He is sometimes a perfect vehicle of comic incomprehension, such as when he describes Jim's emptiness with a condescending remark about the townspeople, who "don't understand that [Jim is] still growing up, that he's just getting rid of things, and trying to keep other things out." Similarly, the apparent tall-tale climax of Galena Jim's bad ride on a moose leads without the narrator's comprehension to a reminder that the story concerns alchemy in reverse—a destructive prankster who once spread galena ore (lead) across the landscape. At the end, the narrator rushes the moose-gored Galena Jim along a galena-sparkled road, trying to understand why the man-boy looks "as if he had done something wrong, had made a mistake somewhere." This somewhere is, of course, the state prison where his son is held: Choteau. The narrator could not have chosen the story's title because he does not understand the implication of the word.

Since settling in the Yaak Valley, Bass and the artist/illustrator Elizabeth Hughes married, and they have two daughters. What he subsequently wrote of America in *The Book of Yaak* might also be called a self-assessment: "I can sense a turning-away from the idea, once pulsing in our own blood, that drifting or running is the answer." This is a very different pulsing from that of the solitude seeker writing five years before of Yaak: "still no sign of life, no people. It was as if they had all been massacred, I thought happily." Perhaps not coincidentally, two story collections from this period, *Platte River* and *The Sky, the Stars, the Wilderness,* also show fundamental changes. Bass begins to emphasize a self-consciously poetic style, longer narratives than before, and more sophisticated perspectives on human interaction, especially male-female relationships, and abandons the folkloric anecdote, the two-buddy configuration, and the vernacular first-person narrator. For example, the opening sentence of "The Sky, the Stars, the Wilderness," the only first-person narrative in these volumes, sounds more like a Sartoris and less like Sut Lovingood: "At first we explored the country with crude maps drawn by Grandfather on the back of paper bags, but

as we got older we used blank maps that we were supposed to fill in ourselves as we went into new places, the deep wild places that Grandfather knew about." These longer stories, though still communicating an edgy relationship between individuals and society, nevertheless emphasize human beings of mutual regard. Women, so often the disappearing enigmas in stories like "Fires," "Mississippi," and "The Watch," are still enigmatic and sometimes disappear, as in the buddy story "Platte River," but now tend to share equal billing with the men.

"The Myth of Bears" is a good example of a synthesis of wilderness and human relationships, not how they exist as opposites, but how they are inseparable in the metaphors commonly used to define and explain our interactions. Protagonists Trapper and Judith migrate north from cattle-ruined Arizona to a winter-dominated "Yukon"—a true place, Bass might say, found on no map—and, pressured there by cabin fever, find their love has become a savage symbiosis: he predator and she prey. The strange fairy-tale narrative, shifting from male to female consciousness, constitutes a meditation on the costs of getting close to wild nature, which the story implies is one's own nature. The myths of bears are really questions about humanity: are we essentially solitary, and is love merely the desire to possess (as suggested by Uncle Harm's tale of the Circe bear with a cave full of pigs) or to be pursued (Judith's pleasure knowing that her husband tracks her)? Is there some middle place, like the river barrier between them, where masculine and feminine can meet? Bass tempts a reader to look for answers in the neat dualities he seems to project on his characters, such as in the absolutist dialogue, the "shaking" and the "stronger part," he uses to characterize Trapper's mental processes: "For thirty miles slogging through snow he thinks of words like 'domination' and replays every day of their life together, putting the days together like tracks, but he's puzzled, can find no sign of error, no proof of her unhappiness with him." Likewise, Judith has two visions of freedom: the space between her and the North Pole, and the river she imagines can take her south. The story's climax is their encounter in that river, and there is no androgynous compromise. The water, Judith admits, would have drowned her; Trapper's desire for domination has no small part in her rescue. In the end, "they fall back into being as they were before," but in the story's last moment, when Judith asks for a statement of love, she performs the gesture that has been established as a symbol of domination: "'Say it,' she says, gripping his wrist."

This stasis is typical of Bass's fiction because it holds for the moment but makes no promises. His is a world where winter, a wall of mountains, or a swamp hideaway provides the precarious margin of safety. In *Platte River* and *The Sky, the Stars, the Wilderness*, Bass uses nature less for what Paul Fussell called "compensatory imagery" and more as a register of characters' psyches. Within the contradictions of nature as healer and destroyer, Bass's stories move intuitively rather than conceptually. They move as if to avoid their own ending, and Rick Bass has described part of his writing process as "looking for side cracks or seams, fissures . . . to keep

[the story] from all rushing down" and becoming "predictable."

Kerry Ahearn

SELECTED BIBLIOGRAPHY

Works by Rick Bass

The Watch. New York: W. W. Norton, 1989.
Platte River. Boston: Houghton Mifflin, 1994.
In the Loyal Mountains. Boston: Houghton Mifflin, 1995.
The Sky, the Stars, the Wilderness. Boston: Houghton Mifflin, 1997.

Critical Studies

Coates, Joseph. "A 'Natural' Writer Who Won't Grow Up." *Chicago Tribune Books*, December 11, 1988.
Lyons, Bonnie, and Bill Oliver. "Out of Boundaries." In *Conversations with Notable Writers*, pp. 72–84. Urbana: University of Illinois Press, 1998.
Terrell, Dixon. "*In the Loyal Mountains*." *Western American Literature* 25 (May 1995): 97–103.

RICHARD BAUSCH
(1945–)

Born in Fort Benning, Georgia, on April 18, 1945, Richard Bausch moved to Washington, D.C., at age three and then to the Maryland suburbs in 1950. Bausch, who now lives in Fauquier County, Virginia, has spent much of his life in the Southeast. Richard and twin brother Robert Bausch have the bizarre distinction of being the only identical twin novelists on the contemporary literary scene in the United States. Their togetherness extends back to 1965–69, when they both served in the United States Air Force. Following his stint, Bausch toured briefly as a guitar player in a rock band and, in 1969, married photographer Karen Miller, with whom he has five children. After receiving his master of fine arts degree from the University of Iowa Writers' Workshop in 1975, Bausch returned to Virginia, taking a job at his undergraduate alma mater, George Mason University, from which he had received his bachelor of arts degree in 1974 and where he currently teaches in the Creative Writing Program. His short fiction and novels have won numerous awards, including a Lila Wallace–Reader's Digest Writers' Award, the Award in Literature from the American Academy of Arts and Letters, and two National Magazine Awards; Bausch has also recently been inducted into the Fellowship of Southern Writers. The late Michael Dorris praised Bausch for bringing "to life characters and situations as vivid and compelling as any in contemporary literature," an endorsement that fully registers Bausch's particular focus in his short fiction—small collections of people experiencing life-bending moments amid fully realized, precisely documented environments. Described by the Los Angeles Times as "one of the best short-story writers working to-

day" and praised by The Detroit News for his "way of reaching into your body and gently holding your soul," Bausch continues to produce novels, novellas, and short stories of remarkable clarity and voice.

Although he may be better known for his many novels, short stories were among Bausch's earliest literary efforts and remain a deep passion. Converted to a world of words by praying the rosary with his Catholic family (he recalls his realization that "words counted"), Bausch believes short fiction to be a form of "profound recreation," whereas the novel is a form of "profound commitment and obsession." In fact, though, his stories glow with all the complexity of character and situation that we normally associate with novels. Revelatory at their most intense moments, they are nonetheless never merely epiphanic.

Bausch's stories often involve catching characters in impossibly strained situations. Characters or narrators often drop provocative, almost seductive, asides about a yet unstated pressure on the protagonists' lives. Always balancing, without necessarily juxtaposing, two lines of development, his short tales seem almost novelistically complex in their visions and gradual in their revelations and their resonances. In "The Great Tandolfo," a drunken young clown miserably destroys some little monster's birthday party because the woman for whom he has bought an enormous wedding cake (sweltering in the back seat of his little car) just notified him she was engaged. In "Evening," an aging man on a ladder touches up some house paint, and, as he waits for his wife to return with Chinese takeout food, his daughter is fighting (and sobbing) with her husband over the phone while his grand-daughter cavorts in the twilight glow of his suburban home.

Bausch's themes vary, but often return to the intergenerational baggage heaped upon families backward and forward through time, quite frequently in stresses passed down by virtue of hidden trauma and guilt. Sometimes he creates Poe-esque tales of anguish and self-deception in which the narrators cannot help revealing, all unconsciously, their horrible lives and thoughts, while in other stories he seems to revisit a Hawthornian moral tale of guilt, failed honesty, and lost illusions. Bausch grasps characters at the precise moment in which they are struggling to move, to break either out of an old life or into a new one. But these struggles often result in the realization that the very struggles that we imagine consuming our lives, perhaps even giving us meaning, are little more than lies generating the pain we inflict on those closest, and maybe even dearest, to us.

"The Person I Have Mostly Become" is one of Bausch's most chilling stories. An internal narrative of the barely suppressed rage and frustration of a divorced, single dad whose son prefers playing soldiers to watching baseball games on television or throwing the ball around with his father, "The Person I Have Mostly Become" grips the reader with moments of astonishing pain and stress. His mother, Ruth, who wants her handyman son to make some money amid a failing construction market, sets up an interview for him with a woman interested in extensive interior renovations. The unnamed narrator, hu-miliated by the realization of Ruth's demeaning role as the household's cleaning woman, can express only surliness during his brief and disastrous interview and tells Ruth comforting lies to cover up his self-destructive performance. This man's relationship with his son, Willy, however, provides a powerful undercurrent for all of his failings. Rage over Willy's leaving his baseball glove out for a neighbor's dog to chew up elicits the first clue to this man's dysfunction: "so I was giving him words about the baseball glove, wondering to myself if they called him sissy in school and wanting, even if I don't know exactly how to go about it, to at least be there for him—tending to him and giving a damn what happens to him—like my father never was, or did, for me." Almost as though aware of what he reveals, the narrator reflects that "sometimes it feels like you put so much into a child, into the raising of him, you live him so hard, there's not much left for liking him, particularly." Such heartbreaking asides punctuate the entire story. After realizing that Willy is "scared of the ball . . . no matter how easy I lobbed it," the narrator gives his son permission to go inside. The son offers to continue playing catch: "'That's all right,' I told him, and I patted his skinny shoulder. My boy. 'You go on in,' I said." Ruth's repeated remarks suggesting that Willy's behavior and attitudes resemble his own as a child do not enable this man to save himself or his son from the monster he has become.

Bausch writes about characters of different ages, situations, interests, and values. He convincingly depicts the doubts and anxieties of a young woman, recently married and not sure she has made the correct choice; the shock of an aging father getting a phone call from his young daughter, who announces that the man she is marrying is old enough to be her father; and the racing guilt of a man who has recently ended a protracted affair with a woman colleague, but whose discovery of a lost high-heeled shoe plunges him into a crisis and precipitates a dogging fear that his wife must actually have known all the while of the affair, though she gives no sense whatsoever within this narrative of any such awareness.

But Bausch often draws characters out of various doldrums and reintroduces them to a sense of wonder and togetherness in their lives. In "Consolation," a young widow, whose fireman husband was killed before their child could be born (in "The Fireman's Wife"), struggles to take her baby boy to meet his paternal grandparents for the first time. Accompanied by her soon-to-be divorced sister, she suffers at what strikes her as the distance and callousness of her in-laws, before the entire group swirls together (including her sister's estranged husband, who has come hoping to patch things up) in a reconciliation scene of great emotional depth and sensitivity. In "Weather," a middle-aged woman and her young and miserably married daughter brave tornadic assaults of weather and banal rudeness on their trip to a shopping mall to buy a rap recording, before finally being drawn into each other's gentle spheres by the mother's physical assault on a man who insults her beleaguered daughter. "The Natural Effects of Divorce" reunites a mother with her divorced son and his child for a nos-

talgic train ride. We learn of her own marriage in crisis, of the collapse of her son's marriage, and of the ways that the grandchild manages to negotiate his own painful state. Three generations wrestling with loneliness and the pains of separation and abandonment manage to forge a moment of understanding and recovery (strained to be sure) that has been orchestrated by the mother's persistence and optimism. "Luck" dramatizes a young man struggling with the predictably erratic and destructive alcoholic behavior of his painting-partner father. Embittered by his father's treatment of his mother and resigned to complete a job that his father has predictably run out on amid promises of merely getting some money for a family restaurant outing, the nineteen-year-old is interrupted by a surprise visit from their wealthy employer. Hearing of this man's own struggles and terrible relationship with his son propels him into a new, albeit painful, sense of appreciation for what he and his father do share.

Still other stories strand Bausch's readers in some inner circle of ambivalence and ambiguity. In "Old West," a work reminiscent of Stephen Crane, an aging protagonist comes to grips with the shattering of his illusions about the famous drifter, Shane, who in the misty streets of the narrator's imagination performed a heroic, guns-blazing cleanup of a mythical "valley" in the past. An aging and decrepit Shane, who has never even strayed very far into the sunset, returns, ratty and reticent, lonely and broke, to deconstruct the imaginative glorification that has sustained the narrator's life since he witnessed the gunfight during his childhood.

A final orgy of bloodshed leaves a pile of bodies, each one having a correlative in the narrator's organizing life-narrative, littering the story's conclusion. Shane, along with Bagley (the drunken, itinerant preacher Shane was pursuing as a bounty hunter and with whom the narrator's senile and trigger-happy mother seems amorously involved) and an "innocent" bar owner all die in the bright midday sun. As the narrator redefines his life, he finds a small truth that "means more to me than all my subsequent reading, all my late studies to puzzle out the nature of things . . . remember now, in great age, is that during the loudest and most terrifying part of the exchange of shots, when . . . I was most certain that I was going to be killed, I lay shivering in the knowledge, the discovery really, that the story I'd been telling all my life was in fact not true enough—was little more than a boy's exaggeration."

Bausch stories transcend their usually Virginian setting, and he is one of the most extraordinary writers of dialogue, clipped but never obviously stylized, and amazingly rooted in the time and character of each story. Yet he resists viewing his characters as being infused with any sociological or political significance and announces as much when he declares, "I have imagined them all," in the author's note prefacing *Rare and Endangered Species*. In his defense of his characters as "recognizable, complicated human beings" rather than as vulgar and monstrous representations of some, however, Bausch plays down the extent to which the recognizability and complexity of his expertly realized characters stem precisely from their being situated in stressful human situa-

tions that resonate with the fullness of their social, economic, familial, geographic, educational, and political contexts. While he may not want them limited, allegorized, or otherwise recast within some interpretive scheme, Richard Bausch's characters and his narrative scenarios, like those of most writers of important literature, have left the protection of his imagination. Once on the page and in circulation, they change and grow with the lives and priorities of his readers.

Russell Reising

SELECTED BIBLIOGRAPHY

Works by Richard Bausch

Spirits and Other Stories. New York: Simon & Schuster, 1987.

The Fireman's Wife and Other Stories. New York: W. W. Norton, 1990.

Rare & Endangered Species: A Novella and Stories. New York: Vintage, 1994.

The Selected Stories of Richard Bausch: An Original Collection. New York: Modern Library, 1996.

Someone to Watch Over Me. New York: HarperCollins, 1999.

Critical Studies

Brainard, Dulcy. "Richard Bausch." *Publisher's Weekly* 237 (1990): 425–426.

Kaston, Elizabeth. "The Author Giving Rise to Violence." *Washington Post*, March 2, 1992.

Lilly, Paul R., Jr. "Richard Bausch." *Dictionary of Literary Biography*. Detroit: Gale Research Group, 1993.

CHARLES BAXTER
(1947 –)

Charles Baxter was born in Minneapolis on May 13, 1947. He graduated from Macalester College in 1969, completed graduate work at the State University of New York at Buffalo in 1974, and went on to teach for several years at Wayne State University in Detroit. Married to Martha Anne Hauser, he has one son, Daniel John. He now teaches at the University of Michigan, where he directs the Master of Fine Arts Program in writing. He is the author of two novels, four books of short stories, a novella, a book of poetry, and a collection of essays on short fiction. Baxter has received grants from the National Endowment for the Arts, Guggenheim, and the Lila Wallace–Reader's Digest Foundation.

Writing of the Midwest, Charles Baxter has noted how the setting of his homeland shapes people—and his writing: "It's a nondescript landscape that has a tendency to turn people inward. . . . It's a sense of enclosure. There's no ocean to solve anything. No mountains. Just . . . gray. And perhaps it's not a coincidence that in the rural Midwest, there's an odd sense of privacy, of things unsaid." Understated, patient, much in the tradition of Chekhov, Baxter's narrative voice is tightly focused on details of objects and gestures that evoke the unsaid desires and disappointments of characters.

His first collection, *Harmony of the World,* establishes him as a writer concerned with the humorous, ironic, and often tragic disharmonies of domestic life. The title story begins, "In the small Ohio town where I grew up, many homes had parlors that contained pianos, sideboards, and sofa, heavy objects signifying gentility. These pianos were rarely tuned." Objects in Baxter's world are more than props; they have personality and often reverberate with their presence, evoking the inner reality of characters' lives. His characters, like the pianos, are plagued by discord. In their struggle to respond to an untrainable universe, his characters frequently misbehave with actions that only contribute to the cacophony of a world out of tune. Such disharmony is usually a primary discovery, but Baxter believes stories should do more than offer discreet epiphanies.

In *Through the Safety Net,* Baxter provides carefully arranged stories about lives becoming disarranged. Baxter's stories take off with sudden interruptions, a piece of news, a stranger who comes like a messenger from some other world, a harbinger of mystery and wonder. The protagonist of the title story receives a call from her psychic, who warns that her family is headed for a "Book of Job kind" of disaster. The psychic tells her, "I saw your whole life . . . the whole future just start to radiate with this ugly black flame . . . and then I saw you falling, like at the circus, down from the trapeze. Whoops . . . down through the safety net. Through the ground." Baxter's word "whoops" distances the calamity, rendering it almost trivial, but not.

In this bizarre story of psychic predictions, the characters are grounded in ordinary suburbia. Abruptly, the psychic's warnings plunge the protagonist into a surreal world of unnamable danger. She locks the door against darkness and wind. Suddenly the tree in her front yard, a water glass, a serrated knife for eating grapefruit all become ominous threats. The suburban world with its cars and house alarms offers no security. The protagonist is left with a sinister silence in her house while the natural world of calamity seems to push its way in.

Most of Baxter's stories occur in a home, ostensibly a place of safety, but the order of domestic architecture is quickly threatened by forces from outside, and occasionally from within. Domesticity is uncontrollable in Baxter's world, and therefore potentially dangerous. In "Surprised by Joy," young parents install child-safety gadgets and assume their daughter is safely alone in her room. But she chokes on a red ball and falls dead, silently waiting to be discovered. Her death haunts the parents with their inability to secure a small domain of safety. When the mother tries to comfort the father, he clings to his suffering with fury. She notes, "In the midst of the sunlight he was hugging his darkness." Such is the story of many of Baxter characters, haunted by loss, embracing darkness in suburban light. Disoriented, many choose to hang on to whatever can define them, even if that self-definition is one of extreme pain.

In Baxter's world, the mysterious and the ordinary are hopelessly and hopefully intertwined. "Gryphon" illustrates the way Baxter's stories move forward, intertwining external and internal plot, with random events shifting, sometimes shattering the protagonist's interior world. A schoolteacher develops a cough that starts small and quickly overwhelms

him. The narrator, a boy who, like most of Baxter's characters, has a habit of assessment, knows that the next day a substitute teacher will appear. Enter Miss Ferenczi with a purple purse and a checkerboard lunch box. She enthralls with implausible stories, including one about her visit to Egypt, where she saw a creature half-lion and half-bird called a gryphon. Doubting her credibility, the narrator looks up *gryphon* in the dictionary and is delighted to find the gryphon validated as a "fabulous beast." With one fact confirmed, he is vulnerable to the mind-expanding narratives of his new teacher.

At this point, Baxter allows the reader to see the boy's naiveté and to guess the boy is about to learn of something more complex than gryphons. This first-person narrative provides an ironic distance between what the protagonist observes and what the reader knows. Soon Miss Ferenczi crosses a line that jolts the plot forward. Using tarot cards, she predicts a boy's early death. She is promptly dismissed, and the students are forced back into ordinary education.

The plot has allowed the narrator to experience a process of imaginative vision; then almost immediately his expanded world is shut down to fit into a model of tightly structured categorization. The boy has gained a mysterious kind of knowledge, an education that cannot be charted on any test the school can provide. Finally, the reader shares the boy's delight at experiencing wonder and his sorrow at the constraints of the imagination. Externally, Baxter's characters struggle to adjust to discord, while internally, a note, off key, continues to twang.

Baxter presents a world where the ordinary is perched on a precarious place; domestic calm is vulnerable to sometimes wonderful and sometimes tragic cosmic twitches. Caught in chaos, Baxter's characters seek ways to connect with each other and to find some meaning in the muddle of their daily lives. But connections are hard to come by. In "Prowlers," a suburban minister struggles to write a sermon, which begins, "Fear not. . . . " But he's stuck. His wife has a phobic fear of prowlers. A visiting family friend, who happens to be the wife's ex-boyfriend, tries to comfort the minister with a suburban reality check: "Look at these houses you and your neighbors live in. Little rectangles of light. Nothing here but families and fireplaces and Duraflame logs and children of God. Not the sort of place where a married woman ought to worry about prowlers." Knowing that the friend and the minister's wife are still in love, the reader sees past the safe suburban facade. The wife articulates her fear of a thief seeking household goods, but the thief, we know, has already prowled within.

"The Disappeared" moves out of the midwestern household to tell the story of a foreigner's comic and pathetic desire for connection in the American world. A Swedish engineer on business visits Detroit, an unglamorous, industrial, dirty city churning out the machinery that keeps a country of dreams moving down hard highways. Anders wants nothing more than "to sleep with an American woman in an American bed." When he is immediately disoriented by the prevalent acrid smell of ash in the Detroit air, we receive the first of many clues that Anders is about to have a tour of a world far more complex

than the mapped streets of Detroit. When he finally meets his "American woman," she cryptically reveals that she is one of the "Last Ones," a member of The Church of the Millennium, which preaches "the Gospel of Last Things." After warning him that his soul is like shiny raw oyster while hers is "Plutonium," she leads him home and gives him a sexual experience that can only be described as psychedelic. His body seeming to explode with color and heat, he cannot identify the emotional response she has awakened. She coolly explains that "the word for something that opens your soul at once" is addiction. Unfazed by her cold emotional landscape, he pushes for a future. She refuses, stating that her faith stipulates that she make no plans. On their second date, she promptly, permanently disappears.

Like many of Baxter's characters, Anders has gone on a quest for a connection that catapults him into a surreal world of disorientation. His quest leaves him not only abandoned but also mugged, robbed, and waiting to get back to his home. But his experience in a dirty manufacturing town has exploded his interior world. Anders is to remain confused by a faithless American world, where events, even the most intimate ones, come, go, and leave the pilgrim alone, nostrils quivering with the pervasive, suspicious odor of fire and ash.

Baxter's characters change through strange encounters. His strangers are strange; in Baxter's world eccentricity is a relative term, and most often these strangers serve to awaken a strangeness already present in the protagonist's sensibility. There is a subtle and mysterious relation among all strangers.

Baxter takes his time in his stories, using sharp detail and crisp, sometimes surreal, dialogue to evoke intensely complex emotion. His characters are sincere and humble in their effort to understand a world that beguiles with its incongruities. They are startled by strangers and shaken by accidents as they look for connection and affection in a world unraveling, and the stories leave us, like many of his characters, simultaneously dazzled by wonder and baffled by loss. Any epiphany offers more confusion than enlightenment for the protagonist, and also withholds narrative closure from the reader. Like Flannery O'Connor, who believed that the best stories are hinged on mystery, Baxter refuses to make all the pieces of his story perfectly fit. His stories grow from incongruities and then rest on conclusions that are complex and mysterious. The familiar becomes at best strange, if not destroyed. There is no conclusive wisdom.

The narrator in "A Late Sunday Afternoon by the Huron" seems to speak for the writer when observing his world: "For an instant I glance at all the other people here and try to fix them in a scene of stationary, luminous repose, as if under glass, in which they would be given an instant of formal visual precision, without reference to who they are as people. . . . I cannot do it. These people keep moving out and away from the neat visual pattern I am hoping for." Baxter submits to mystery, the limitations on the intellect. His fiction begins with trying to explain an event and ends, as its characters do, lifting somewhere off the page, in an ineffable realm of wonder, the eternal and un-

charted space beyond the safety net of what they can only claim to know.

Jane Bradley

SELECTED BIBLIOGRAPHY

Works by Charles Baxter

Harmony of the World. Columbia: University of Missouri Press, 1984.
Through the Safety Net. New York: Viking, 1985.
A Relative Stranger. New York: W. W. Norton, 1990.

Critical Studies

Baxter, Charles. *Burning Down the House.* Saint Paul: Graywolf Press, 1997.
Caesar, Terry. "Charles Baxter." *Dictionary of Literary Biography.* Detroit: Gale Research, 1993.
Draper, James P. "Charles Baxter." *Contemporary Literary Criticism* 78 (1994):15–34.
Trosky, Susan. "Charles Baxter." *Contemporary Authors.* Detroit: Gale Research, 1994.

ANN BEATTIE
(1947–   )

Born in 1947 and raised in Washington, D.C., Ann Beattie attended local schools and graduated, in 1969, from

American University. She attended graduate school at the University of Connecticut and has taught at various universities, including Harvard and the University of Virginia. Married to the painter Lincoln Perry, she now divides her time between Key West and a house on the Maine coast.

Beattie emerged in the 1970s as a representative voice of her generation, those who like herself came of age in the 1960s—a period of acute social change and upheaval. Her fiction teems with characters from this period: pot-smoking, long-haired, laid-back, hip, and wry figures with names like Sam and Griffin, Mark and Milo, Amy and Louisa. As the 1960s slipped into the 1970s, disillusion on many levels set in. In the public realm, the political dreams of Beattie's generation were dashed as Richard Nixon took office and a long era of Republican dominance (broken only by Jimmy Carter's one-term presidency) began. In the private realm, a realization began to dawn: there is no free love.

Beattie's first book of stories, *Distortions,* appeared in 1976. It was published simultaneously with her first novel, *Chilly Scenes of Winter,* and the effect of this double publication was to make a crucial point: Ann Beattie was here. She was already known, in fact, to readers of *The New Yorker,* where her work often appeared. (Eight of the nineteen stories in her first collection were published there.) In the mid-1970s, postmodern writers such as Donald Barthelme, John Barth, and John Hawkes had been afforded a good deal of attention by serious critics; but this movement, if writers as different as these can be called a movement, was by now

exhausted. Beattie came along with a new kind of story, quickly branded "minimalist," a term previously used only in the world of art criticism.

The term *minimalist* was generally applied to the plastic arts to describe a kind of work that used small spaces as elements within a larger dynamic. Other writers associated with this approach to fiction are Raymond Carver, Mary Robison, Tobias Wolff, and Alice Munro. Proponents of minimalism focused on the concept of space, which they regarded as a "free" medium, unrelated to intention. Translating this concept to literature, critics pointed to the silences and absences in a story as the "free" element. The meaning of the story would thus reside in the margins, as in a Hemingway story (and Hemingway has often been cited as a source for Beattie's method). By the deft use of silences and absences, then, the minimalist writer intensifies what *is* said. Meaning is derived obliquely, but it gains force from this obliquity.

Distortions, which contains such important stories as "Dwarf House," "Wolf Dreams," "Vermont," "Marshall's Dog," and "Victor Blue," remains a seminal volume of the 1970s. This was a period, as Beattie once remarked, when people were "tremendously interested in either fancifying or romanticizing the 1960s." Her characters too seemed either to "fancify" or romanticize that period; indeed, many of them were living in a dream, imagining that the previous decade had been a great deal more interesting and "real" than the current one. A general malaise hung over these characters, as in "Dwarf House," the opening story in this collection, which begins with a question: "Are you happy?" Almost all of the stories that follow return to this question as Beattie ponders the distortions in perception that create frustration in the lives of her characters. Their quest for fulfillment is apparent in nearly every story in the collection.

One sees this quest in "Dwarf House," where James, a dwarf who lives by choice in a "dwarf house," is confronted by his brother, MacDonald, sent by his mother to get him out of this unseemly residence. James's deformity or "distortion" operates on many levels, physical and psychological. Not only is James unnaturally small, but he also is dwarfed by the world, which he seeks to escape in the company of other dwarves. The bizarre peer group might well be thought of as the company of generational friends that envelops many of Beattie's characters; within these self-selected communities, there is perhaps some security. The dwarves in "Dwarf House" are bound by their status as outsiders and freaks. Because they cannot find happiness in the world of "giants," they make their own happiness together.

Taking a leaf from Hemingway, Beattie relies heavily on dialogue, rarely using "he said" or "she said" to tag a line. (Another obvious influence on Beattie is Samuel Beckett, with his sly, indirect dialogues.) The dialogue is almost always spare and elliptical, so that the reader is left to fill in the silences, to read between the lines. The surface, as usual in Beattie, is witty; but what is not said is always more important than what is. Indeed, if these characters were talking in a movie, one could use subtitles (as in the famous scene in *Annie Hall* where Woody Allen visits his girlfriend's parents in the Midwest).

Thus, when James asks MacDonald if the place makes him lose his appetite, a reader might hear underneath something like this: "Given that your values are so different from mine, it is no wonder you find everything here disgusting. Even I disgust you, don't I? But you'll never tell the truth. Your sort of people never tells the truth."

Typically, Beattie's stories build to a moment of epiphany, often embodied in a totalizing image: a luminous moment that absorbs the previous tensions of the stories and pulls them through its crystal center, dispelling them. Thus, "Dwarf House" culminates in a memorable image of James's bride: "MacDonald sees that the bride is smiling beautifully—a smile no pills could produce—and that the sun is shining on her hair so that it sparkles. She looks small, and bright, and so lovely that MacDonald, on his knees to kiss her, doesn't want to get up." This amusing image—of MacDonald on his knees kissing the radiant tiny bride—helps to unify the story, tonally and symbolically.

The search for love dominates the stories in *Distortions*. Everywhere, Beattie's characters reach beyond the narrow circumference of bad marriages or failed love affairs, seeking relief. In "The Parking Lot," for example, Beattie examines the marriage of an unnamed woman to a man called Jim. (There are usually no last names in Beattie's stories, a trademark turn that reduces her characters to integers in a social equation the sum of which is always pain.) She finds her marriage symbolized by "a black and regular" parking lot, tedious and restricting—although, as ever, the reader has to infer this. The protagonist finally seeks an outlet with a man she once met in an elevator; after they meet in a parking lot, accidentally, they go to a motel for sex. But no satisfaction follows. Beattie's characters will rarely find it on these escapades.

Among the best stories in this collection is "Fancy Flights," in which Beattie's protagonist, Michael, escapes the tedium of everyday reality through smoking hashish. The story, which is extremely funny, begins in a typically droll manner, focusing on a growling, frightened dog, Silas—one of many dogs in this collection, many of whom are metonymically associated with their owners and embody their owners' moods. Michael, the owner, is a vivid character, alienated from the world he lives in, separated from his wife, Elsa, and from his small daughter. One suspects that his closest emotional connection is, indeed, to the dog, Silas. Symbolically, Michael is a house-sitter; he is unhoused, literally and metaphorically. He pays no rent and has no income except for a little money coming from his grandmother. Even when he is lured back into the nuclear family, he remains a figure of disconnection, alienated from the possibility of happiness. He is a perpetual child in need of parenting, hopelessly mired in private conflicts that seem beyond resolution. In a final, poignant scene, Michael becomes aware of the exact nature of his situation, feeling the full weight of his alienation and loneliness.

The brilliant, sad, elliptical writing found in *Distortions* continues in *Secrets and Surprises* (1978), a collection that contains some of Beattie's finest stories, such as "Friends," "Octascope," "The Lawn Party," "Secrets and Surprises," "Weekend," and "A Vintage Thunderbird." By now Beattie had perfected her cool, clear-eyed, reticent style, as in "The Lawn Party," where the narrator comments: "Banks is here. He is sitting next to me as it gets dark. I am watching Danielle out on the lawn. She has a red shawl that she winds around her shoulders. She looks tired and elegant. My father has been drinking all afternoon." The discontinuities among these sentences represent a mode of thinking as Beattie moves rapidly from one bright perception to the next.

Whereas the stories in *Distortions* center on the desire to escape a humdrum, harried world in which people are, as T. S. Eliot once said, "distracted from distraction by distraction," those in *Secrets and Surprises* revolve around relationships and their surpassing insufficiencies. This theme dominates "Friends," a story about a man called Perry, a vague-headed romantic who observes closely the misery of his friends' lives as he pursues Francie, an artist who has divorced her husband in part because he belittled her painting. Since Francie is not attracted romantically to Perry, the relationship is doomed, even though in the end she goes to live with him. The story is eloquently drawn and powerfully evocative. In a telling moment, Francie complains, "I don't know how to talk." She says she is "either alone and it's silent here all day, or my friends are around, and I really don't talk to them."

Throughout her career, Beattie has often focused on inarticulate or self-deluded characters, who are frequently her narrators as well. This technique has confused reviewers at times, who seem to take what is said by a character as something that is being said by Beattie, thus missing the irony that pervades her work.

Reading Beattie, one might well conclude that it is possible to choose one's family, but one cannot choose one's friends. In story after story, a central character gets stuck with acquaintances they can't seem to shake or are somehow afraid to shake. As in "Octascope," her characters will often reach out, hoping to find a sense of security in a precarious world. The narrator in this story is a woman who has been left by her previous boyfriend, a musician. He may or may not be the father of her child. When Nick comes along with a friend called Carlos, "a kind person who wanted a woman to live with him," the narrator moves in, "feeling like a prostitute." This feeling is aggravated by the lack of connection to Carlos, who spends all his time working on his marionettes, refusing to respond to his new lover's questions. A familiar pattern emerges here: the passive female who is driven into action by circumstances; hilariously, Beattie's narrator here types up lists of facts about Carlos, some real, others imagined.

"Octascope" ends with a totalizing image: the octascope, a kaleidoscope without the colored glass. As the narrator holds the scope to her eyes, she sees a "picture": "the fields, spread white with snow, the palest ripple of pink at the horizon—eight triangles of the same image." Almost magically, the octascope reveals the beauty and complexity of the world, which the narrator has thus far refused to see. The scope is, of course, a symbol for art itself. In Beattie's hands, it becomes luminous and beguiling. Her symbols, like all successfully employed symbols, isolate parts of the world while suggesting there is more.

Beattie's characters often express a ferocious longing for a past that may never have existed. Nick, in "A Vintage Thunderbird," dreams of that perfect moment when he and his former lover, Karen, drove her white Thunderbird through the Lincoln Tunnel, a colorful streamer of crepe flying from the antenna. In a subtly figurative sentence, Beattie writes of Nick: "Years later he had looked for the road they had been on that night, but he could never find it." This line could serve as an epigraph for the entire volume.

The characters who appear in *The Burning House* (1982) are a little older, perhaps, but no wiser, nor more likely to stumble upon happiness. Freud has suggested that the house is the symbol of the soul, and one senses in this intensely poetic, deeply felt volume that Beattie is watching her souls burn in self-pity, narcissism, pettiness, and willful misalliance. Her technique is often innovative, with stories, like Chinese boxes, often enveloping stories, as in "Learning to Fall." Beattie ends this story with the beautiful sentiment: "Aim for grace." Just previously, we have been told that "what will happen can't be stopped." Indeed, a certain fatalism is apparent everywhere in Beattie; wisdom is only a question of learning to deal, or dealing gracefully, artfully, with life's fierce blows.

The title story is easily among the finest Beattie has written, a rhetorical tour de force. It follows a form typical of her short fiction: a first-person narrator is surrounded by friends: Freddy Fox, Frank, J. D., and Tucker. The tale revolves around a weekend in the country at the house of the narrator, who believes she has "known everybody in the house for years," and yet that she knows them "all less and less" as the years roll by. In a poignant scene at the end, her husband tells her that her big mistake was to surround herself with men. "Let me tell you something," he says. "All men—if they're crazy, like Tucker, if they're gay as the Queen of the May, like Freddy Fox, even if they're just six years old—I'm going to tell you something about them. Men think they're Spider-Man and Buck Rogers and Superman." They all feel that they are "going to the stars."

In *Where You'll Find Me* (1986), her next collection, Beattie demonstrates increasing control over her material. Her characters express a new world-weariness and a deeper level of wisdom. A sense of loss pervades these stories, of having to accept life in a diminished world. The characters are almost all upper-middle class; they live well and have been well educated, but they are imbued with an intangible sense of loss. "In the White Night," a central story in this collection, focuses upon a middle-aged couple who lost their daughter from leukemia some years before.

The best stories in *Where You'll Find Me,* such as "The Working Girl," "In Amalfi," "Windy Day at the Reservoir," and the title story, show Beattie as chronicling her generation, again, but reaching for deeper meaning. One finds in Beattie's later stories an appreciation of that quality known in theological terms as *grace,* revealed in "the way people and things turned up when they were most needed and least expected," as in "Windy Day at the Reservoir." Grace is revealed in the glints of memory that soothe Jeanette, in "The Working Girl," after her husband has died, and in the gorgeous last long paragraph of "Imagine a Day at the End of Your Life," in which the narrator understands the con-

solations of the natural world as she sees "Flowers, in the distance. Or, in early evening, a sliver of moon."

Hemingway's influence becomes apparent in the story "Summer People," which takes its actual title from a Hemingway story about Nick Adams, who first makes love to his girlfriend, Kate, on a blanket in the woods in Michigan. In Beattie's story, Tom and Jo are in Vermont, and though he can't "imagine caring for anyone more than he cared for her," he wonders if this means he is still in love with her. The tale ends with a pool attendant making "an adjustment to the white metal pole that would hold an umbrella the next day," and Beattie seems to be inviting her characters to begin making adjustments too.

The need to make adjustments pervades Beattie's most recent work, such as "Park City," the title story of *Park City: New and Selected Stories* (1998). In this, the narrator is "stringing along to Utah" with her half-sister, Janet, and looking after Janet's small child, Nell. When she takes Nell on a ride on a chairlift, she is startled by the speed of the mechanism, and this nearly results in a terrible injury to the child as they get on the lift. She is told firmly at the end of the ride that "the one thing you've got to remember next time is to request a slow start." That is, one has to begin to take care of oneself in order to take care of other people: a lesson learned the hard way—here as elsewhere in *Park City.*

More so than in her previous work, the later stories may turn on actual events, as in "Second Questions," for instance, in which a young man dies of AIDS. These complex, edgy, often funny later stories show Beattie as a writer of compassion and deep artistic intelligence. Her surface style remains breezy, witty, and sharply imagistic; but the content deepens as her characters attempt to locate themselves in the universe (as in "Cosmos"), trying to determine what this peculiar thing, the cosmos, might even be as they deal with family secrets, with the tragedy of AIDS, with infidelities, pointless arguments, and unexplained desires that disrupt even good marriages. In all, Ann Beattie seems intent on providing an inner history of her generation, in both her shorter and longer fictions. She has remained, over several decades, a writer of unusual grace and style.

Jay Parini

SELECTED BIBLIOGRAPHY

Works by Ann Beattie

Distortions. New York: Doubleday, 1976.
Secrets and Surprises. New York: Random House, 1978.
The Burning House. New York: Random House, 1982.
Where You'll Find Me. New York: Simon & Schuster, 1986.
What Was Mine. New York: Random House, 1991.
Park City: New and Selected Stories. New York: Alfred A. Knopf, 1998.

Critical Studies

Murphy, Chistina. *Ann Beattie.* Boston: Twayne, 1986.

SAUL BELLOW
(1915–   )

Saul Bellow is one of the most renowned of contemporary American novelists. His intellectual and verbal brilliance, comic gifts, and imaginative craftsmanship have won him popular and critical acclaim, as well as the Nobel Prize for Literature in 1976. Born of Russian-Jewish parents in Lachine, Quebec, he was nine when his family moved to Chicago. Theirs was an Orthodox Jewish household in which English, French, Yiddish, and Hebrew were spoken or read. After two years at the University of Chicago, Bellow switched to Northwestern University, graduating in 1937 with honors in anthropology and sociology. He then entered the University of Wisconsin on a graduate scholarship, but he soon withdrew to write fiction. To support himself he took odd jobs and taught for four years at a Chicago teacher's college. Serving briefly in the Merchant Marine in World War II, he later worked on the editorial staff of the *Encyclopedia Britannica.* After that, he divided his professional life between writing and teaching, mainly at the University of Chicago and Boston University. Bellow has married five times and has four children.

Bellow's reputation has derived primarily from full-length novels and novellas, but he has always written memorable short fiction. Long or short, his narratives are essentially dramatic, depicting painful self-explorations that lead his protagonists to life-altering acts. His vibrant voice—

heard in internal monologues, dialogue, and discursive commentary—is self-reflexive and mocking, often echoing the ironic, chiding melody of ghetto speech. What it mocks is the inflated human Self—that is, the flamboyant speaker and his arguments and analyses, his lamentations and joys. Not surprisingly, Bellow's first published piece, "Two Morning Monologues" (1941), reveals the internal agonizing of an unemployed young man waiting and indeed wishing to be called up for military service, and then the inner musings of a compulsive horse player driven to assert his freedom and identity through gambling. Bellow developed this initial idea of the waiting draftee into the story "Notes for a Dangling Man" (1943) and then into his first novel, *Dangling Man* (1944). In its differing forms, this narrative introduces some of the key characters and themes to be found in Bellow's later work. His hero Joseph repeatedly asks, "How should a good man live, what ought he to do?" Either rephrased or implied, these moral questions echo throughout Bellow's fiction. Finally called up, Joseph concludes sadly that "I had not done well alone." So will think most of Bellow's later protagonists.

In 1949 Bellow published "Dora" and "A Sermon by Doctor Pep." The first, a variation of Freud's *Dora: An Analysis of a Case of Hysteria,* articulates an idea to be found in his mature work. Only by truly seeing and appreciating one another do people affirm their own value as human beings. Dora, a middle-aged seamstress, hears a frightening thud and finds that in the next apartment a man to whom she has never spoken has had a stroke. Shocked at how unattached he is, she dresses up daily to visit the comatose stranger in the hospital. Alone and lacking social or intellectual sophistication, Dora fashions a new code of values through her concern for her neighbor. In the second story, Dr. Pep, a street-corner philosopher, holds forth in Bughouse Square, near Chicago's Newberry Library. Mixing wisdom and foolishness, this self-styled "Professor of Energy" regales his listeners with theories on love and nature, nutrition and health, life and death. Like Bellow's later combination of con artists and "reality instructors," Dr. Pep is as much poet as charlatan.

In the early 1950s, Bellow published a number of short narratives, some of which he extracted from his breakthrough novel, *The Adventures of Augie March* (1953), or salvaged from works later discarded. In addition to these novelistic segments, he also wrote several independent short stories, the most notable of which is "Looking for Mr. Green," a tale set in Depression-era Chicago. George Grebe, a former classics fellow at the university, has been reduced to distributing welfare checks. Like the soon-to-appear Tommy Wilhelm of *Seize the Day,* Grebe experiences a day exhausting enough to try his soul. His mission is to deliver a check to an elusive, ultimately invisible Negro named Tulliver Green. Grebe wants to believe that his search enables him to reach out to his fellow man. However, as he wanders South Chicago's black ghetto, he grows aware of the distrust and hostility the very poor feel toward those who claim to have something to give them. Despite the humiliating and questionable circumstances under which he finally delivers the check,

Grebe is convinced that he has scored a small victory. But Bellow's conclusion is a darker one, underscoring not only modern man's inevitable loss of identity but also the transience and illusion at the core of his existence.

Hovering over the stories of the early 1950s are the characters and plot lines of *Augie March.* As he began to focus on *Seize the Day,* Bellow wove together in "A Father-to-Be" (1955) both Augie's wistful thoughts of fatherhood and Wilhelm's tangled feelings about money. Rogin is a young research chemist with heavy financial responsibilities and a dream of becoming rich by creating a synthetic albumen that would revolutionize the egg industry. Meanwhile, his beautiful, well-educated but unemployed fiancée Joan is spending his money freely. One day, on the subway, he finds himself next to a well-dressed passenger who resembles not only Joan's father, whom he detests, but also Joan herself. Forty years from now, he muses, a son of Joan's might look like this "fourth-rate man." But then he, Rogin, would be the father. Frightened and revolted, he considers extricating himself from their relationship and defeating fate. But Joan welcomes him warmly and insists on shampooing his wet hair. As Rogin feels her caressing fingers and the warm fluid, his anger disappears and he experiences a gush of love for her.

Bellow's next story, "The Gonzaga Manuscripts" (1954), involves another search with a provocative, problematic conclusion. Fashioned after Henry James's "The Aspern Papers," this tale follows a young scholar, Clarence Feiler, to Spain, where he seeks the unpublished poems of an obscure and dead poet. By reveal-ing Gonzaga's poems to the world, Feiler hopes to give shape to his own life. The failure of his search reveals the unreliability of human connection and suggests the ultimate death of high hopes for man generally held by poets, scholars, and lovers of literature.

In "Leaving the Yellow House" (1957), Bellow depicts a more sedentary quest for identity and meaning. Hattie Waggoner, a cheerful, tough-talking, solitary old woman, has to decide to whom to bequeath her precious yellow house. Stubbornly refusing several offers to sell, she finally wills the house to herself but realizes that her decision, like her life, requires further thought.

A decade passed before Bellow published his next story, "The Old System" (1967), in which he explores a favorite theme: the power of memory to alter character and enrich life. Here Dr. Samuel Braun, a distinguished geneticist who specializes in "the chemistry of heredity," recalls the life-long quarrel between two of his departed cousins. His recollections prompt him to reflect not only on the ethical and spiritual values of traditional Jewishness (the "old system") but also on that "crude circus" of Jewish feelings of love and connection he had rejected in his pursuit of science. Described by Bellow as one of his favorite stories, "The Old System" assesses the costs of assimilation and tracks the American-born narrator as he is revitalized by long-suppressed memories of his cantankerous relatives.

Although memory is also central to "Mosby's Memoirs" (1968), it fails to have the same salutary effect as in the previous story, for the remembering character here reacts very differently to his mental sifting of his past. While writing his memoirs, Willis Mosby, a former Princeton professor of political theory, realizes that he has made serious mistakes in his life, but he harbors neither regrets nor any sense of moral failure. Hoping to fashion his memories into an intellectual history of the modern age, he decides to leaven his somber observations with humor. He selects as his comic target a Jew suggestively named Hymen Lustgarten. A former Marxist striving to be a capitalist, Lustgarten is a political and social bumbler but also a warmhearted husband and father. "Jewish-Daddy-Lustgarten" is Mosby's disdainful mental description of him. The joke, however, is on Mosby. At the story's end, in a stone tomb, he has a frightening intimation of his own death and self-fashioned isolation.

In the highly praised "A Silver Dish" (1978), Bellow returns to a favorite theme: the tangled emotional bonds between fathers and sons. The recent death of his father leads Woody Selbst to ponder the role of the quixotic old man in his life. The latter had always caused difficulties for his family, once even stealing a silver dish and allowing his son to take the blame. Trying to puzzle out his own unflagging devotion to so unreliable a father, Woody grasps not only the true depth of their relationship but also the redemptive power of familial love.

Herschel (Harry) Shawmut, the narrator of "Him with His Foot in His Mouth" (1982) is another of Bellow's self-pitying and self-probing intellectuals. A former professor of music history and a renowned musicologist, Shawmut is in tax trouble with the U.S. government and is living in exile in Canada. Still, he feels that his life

and career have been blunted less by money than by the outrageous insults he cannot refrain from uttering. Indeed, the story itself is rough draft of a letter of apology intended for a retired college librarian whom Shawmut had insulted thirty-five years earlier, an offense he is convinced had ruined the harmless lady's life. When he "said things," he explains, he said them "for art's sake, ie. without perversity or malice." In effect, Shawmut is engaged in a favorite Bellow pastime: ruminating on the paradoxes of American moral and cultural values.

In "What Kind of Day Did You Have?" (1984), Bellow suggests why he was reprising themes and relationships from his own earlier fiction. The aging critic and social philosopher, Victor Wulpy, who has helped shape the standards of modern art, still has a powerful mind, but bodily ailments make him aware his time is limited. Bellow seems to be suggesting in this story that art offers modern man his best means of formulating responses to the transcendent. Like other Bellow protagonists, Wulpy argues for the existence of universal ideas that transcend the merely physical. But art is not life, and life is not always satisfying. The small plane carrying Victor and his pliant mistress Katrina is caught in a storm. With death seemingly imminent, Katrina pleads with Victor to say he loves her. He refuses, and the married Katrina receives little emotional payment for having risked life, limb, and reputation.

Also in 1984, Bellow published "Cousins," one of his most personal, deeply felt stories. Here he uses his narrator, Ijah Brodsky, to flesh out once more his concern for the diminishing of communal and personal ties and the consequent gap between public and private selves. Like his creator, Brodsky is dismayed at the steady erosion of moral and spiritual standards that Judeo-Christian humanism has provided. Ijah's own family has produced only one kindred spirit, Cousin Scholem Stavis, who has devoted his life to philosophy while driving a cab. Dying of cancer, Scholem wants to see his writings published, and Ijah agrees to raise the necessary funds. As the elderly cousins meet in Paris, Ijah suddenly feels robbed of his own strength. "He doesn't know his own weakness while he goes on observing others," Bellow has said of Ijah. "Maybe that is what happens to one." Seemingly, it may also happen to an elderly writer who has devoted his life to depicting human interconnections and now cannot help wondering about the fate awaiting *him* at corridor's end.

In his mid-seventies and early eighties, Bellow published three novellas, *The Theft* (1989), *The Bellarosa Connection* (1989), and *The Actual* (1997), and two notable short stories, "Something to Remember Me By" (1990) and "By the St. Lawrence" (*Esquire,* July 1995), which explore the commingling of sex and death, the therapeutic powers of memory, and the nature of family bonds. In "By the St. Lawrence," the elderly Robbie Rexler recalls a childhood and family that resemble those of Bellow himself, and also evokes in different ways the biographical details of his major fictional protagonists. A near-fatal illness having convinced him that his time is short, Rexler feels compelled to revisit his birthplace—Lachine, Quebec, near a canal tributary of the St. Lawrence River,

and Bellow's own birthplace. Walking and sitting by the canal, he recalls two different times there, both centered on images of dying and death: the body of a victim of a train accident and two cousins dying of cancer. At eighty, Bellow was still ruminating on the social and moral struggles of immigrant Jews and their children in the New World, a struggle that has always been the central story of his short and long fiction. A careful reading of the short stories reveals them to be not only extensions of Saul Bellow's novels but also an integral part of his searching, coherent narrative of twentieth-century American life.

Ben Siegel

SELECTED BIBLIOGRAPHY

Works by Saul Bellow

Mosby's Memoirs and Other Stories. New York: Viking, 1968.

Him with His Foot in His Mouth and Other Stories. New York: Harper & Row, 1984.

Something to Remember Me By: Three Tales. New York: Signet, 1991.

Critical Studies

Friedrich, Marianne M. *Character and Narration in the Short Fiction of Saul Bellow.* New York: Peter Lang, 1995.

Fuchs, Daniel. "Bellow's Short Stories." In *Saul Bellow: Vision and Revision,* pp. 280–304. Durham, N.C.: Duke University Press, 1984.

Stevick, Philip. "The Rhetoric of Bellow's Short Fiction." In Stanley Trachtenberg, ed., *Critical Essays on Saul Bellow,* pp. 73–82. New York: G. K. Hall, 1979.

GINA BERRIAULT
(1926–   )

Born in 1926 in Long Beach, California, Gina Berriault spent much of her childhood reading books in order to escape her poverty-stricken existence. Her father, a freelance writer, owned an old typewriter, and it was not long before Berriault began to strike its keys. Typing passages from the books of admired authors, Berriault dreamed of someday writing words as beautiful as the ones she copied. By the time she reached her teens, Berriault was writing her own stories and sending them to magazines, hoping that she would sell one and earn money to help her struggling family. Unlike her blind mother, who would wave her hands before her eyes so that she might see them produce the stories she heard from the radio, Berriault saw results from her efforts when she read notes of encouragement from editors who had received but did not publish her early work. Their interest reinforced her belief in herself, and she continued writing. Although she did not pursue a formal education after high school, Berriault exemplifies her own belief that if a person has a "true" compulsion to write, she will write regardless of academic training. And write she has. Berriault's four-decade career has pro-

duced one screenplay, four novels, and three volumes of short stories. A recent collection, *Women in Their Beds,* received the PEN/Faulkner and National Book Critics Circle Awards. Residing in California, Berriault is divorced and remains close with her one daughter, Julie Elena. She teaches creative writing classes at San Francisco University.

Readers of Gina Berriault's fiction are struck immediately by the wryly honed, economical prose that invokes new considerations from personal and social issues. Each of her novels expresses a steadfast dedication to ordinary folks in order to bring original insights to such vast issues as nuclear war (*The Descent*), suicide (*Conference of Victims*), dependence and incest (*The Son*), and, broadly, human relationships (*Lights of Earth*). However, it is for her short stories that Berriault has garnered the most attention and praise.

Long admired by her peers, Berriault's short stories have been anthologized, widely published in literary presses and journals, and included in three praiseworthy collections: *The Mistress and Other Stories* (1965), *The Infinite Passion of Expectation* (1982), and *Women in Their Beds* (1997). Offering intricate views into the lives of the still unknown, the unheralded members of the general population, Berriault's stories privilege the lives of those economically and socially impoverished. The feelings of hopelessness that mark Anton Chekhov's characters also pervade the lives that Gina Berriault has created, nurtured, and validated. *Women in Their Beds,* in particular, is a virtuoso performance, marked by a consistently discerning and always haunting prose.

If only her characters stood a chance of recovery, Berriault's fiction might not be deemed so dark, so bleak. In the title story from *Women in Their Beds,* Angela Anson, "odd-job actress, bold on stage but not as herself," takes on the role of a lifetime when she fakes credentials and lands herself a position as a social worker in the women's ward of a county hospital in San Francisco. Once inside, she is cautioned by one of her cohorts that she must take short breaths, that she was not hired for the role of Saint Teresa of Avila. Still, she lies awake at night trying to understand the lives of the women in her ward. Her efforts lead her to a Gypsy woman and her family's request for candles. Bringing what they wanted the day after their inquiry, too late to offer them any relief, Angela learns firsthand the brevity of a life when Nurse Nancy puts out her candle's flame "with a breath that failed to be strong and unwavering but did the job anyway." Taken back by her coworker's apparent lack of contrition, Angela allows herself to be led back into the corridors, where deep breaths are saved for one's last.

In "Soul and Money," readers witness another character who is interested in but not successful at "living a useful life." When Walter Stenstauffer, an aged and impotent husband, father, and Communist, reflects on another comrade grown old, readers are reminded of the women in their beds: "What they saw in their mirrors was not just themselves grown considerably older but an ideal world nowhere near accomplished in their lifetimes." The relationship between the elderly Communist and the God-fearing women is tenuously carried to fruition when the old man forces his own narrative

on a comrade he happens upon during an escape to the city that never sleeps, Las Vegas. He is able to validate his own worries of a paradise lost by reasoning that Jesus was "the greatest gambler. . . . Went around telling everybody how much his father loved him. Gambled on that and lost." Cast aside as crazy by his comrade, Walter is left alone with his thoughts and boards a plane back home, trying to think of a way to tell his own son about this new knowledge.

Such is the case in Gina Berriault's fictive world. Hers are not stories that one rushes to finish, although sometimes one wishes one could. Rather, Gina Berriault asks her readers to ponder carefully the personal and agonizing decay of her characters; daring them to think their lives are different, less mundane, more significant than those of the characters who muddle through her stories. In "Stolen Pleasures," for example, the protagonist, Delia, notices some old women sitting alone in a cafe. The narrator comments, "Nobody knew what pleasures life had stolen from them or what pleasures they'd stolen from life, if any," but Berriault's fiction implicates more than the characters Delia and her sister, Fleur. For readers are being asked if their lives are really different; and inevitably they come to share Delia's fear of ending up old and alone, sitting at a small table in an unremarkable cafe, or worse.

Throughout her stories of characters plagued by self-deceptions and silent aspirations, Berriault continually reinforces the notion that reading is a collaborative effort. An ordinary reader may not have the tendency toward preoccupation and self-destruction, as do so many of Berriault's characters, but she recognizes that possibility. Even in the somewhat predictable "Anna Lisa's Nose," the ultimate failure of the protagonist is not viewed harshly. Instead, Berriault urges her readers to continue, guiding them through a series of worlds, at once mysterious, horrid, and familiar.

It is perhaps ironic that a writer who takes as her subject the lives of people who live their lives without recognition has produced such a memorable collection—ironic, that is, until one experiences the unforgettable "The Diary of K.W." The story of a woman hungry for attention who eventually dies of starvation, this gem delivers a torturous and alienated account not soon forgotten. In a note to the young man who lives in the apartment above her, the old woman closes without revealing her name: "But I couldn't make myself sign my name. My name meant too much when I imagined it at the bottom of that note. It made me wonder too much who I was." Berriault shows who the woman is and how she came to be withered and old, someone who "can't look anybody in the eyes because she's ashamed of who she is and ashamed for them for not seeing her Soul instead of her." Moreover, as with most of these stories, Berriault's concise presentation of the only apparently commonplace leaves a reader feeling like both an eavesdropper and a conspirator.

The fiction of Gina Berriault is limited only by her reader's inability to transcend the seemingly ordinary. She may linger in a California landscape, but she and her characters dream of places far away. The recurring theme of failure is sometimes overwhelming, but Berriault presents these meditations with pen strokes both

memorable and breathtaking. It is to her credit that she presents such penetrating and tragic insights in so few pages.

Karla J. Murphy

SELECTED BIBLIOGRAPHY

Works by Gina Berriault

The Descent. New York: Atheneum, 1960.
Conference of Victims. New York: Atheneum, 1962.
The Mistress, and Other Stories. New York: Dutton, 1965.
The Son. New York: New American Library, 1966.
The Infinite Passage of Expectation: Twenty-Five Stories. San Francisco: North Point, 1982.
The Lights of Earth. San Francisco: North Point, 1984.
The Stone Boy. Los Angeles: Twentieth Century-Fox, 1984.
Women in Their Beds: New and Selected Stories. Washington, D.C.: Counterpoint, 1997.
Afterwards. Washington, D.C.: Counterpoint, 1998.

Critical Studies

Davenport, Guy. "The Blessed and the Forsaken." *Kenyon Review* 7/4 (fall 1985): 122–125.
Harshaw, Tobin. "Short Takes." *New York Times Book Review,* May 5, 1996.
Lyons, Bonnie, and Bill Oliver. "Gina Berriault: 'Don't I Know You?'" In *Passion and Craft: Conversations with Notable Writers,* pp. 60–71. Urbana: University of Illinois Press, 1998.
Matuz, Roger. "Gina Berriault: 1926– ."

Contemporary Literary Criticism. Detroit: Gale Research, 1992.

DORIS BETTS
(1932 –)

An award-winning educator, short story writer, and novelist, Doris Betts was born in 1932 in Statesville, North Carolina. Surrounded by an extended family in a working-class region, Betts read widely and found her vocation early in composing poetry and fiction. After two years at Woman's College of the University of North Carolina, she transferred to the University of North Carolina at Chapel Hill. In 1953 she won a short story prize from the *Mademoiselle* College Fiction Contest of 1953 that confirmed her literary ambition. She and her husband, Lowry Betts, a lawyer-judge, have three grown children and now live on a farm in Pittsboro, North Carolina, where they raise Arabian horses.

Teaching at the University of North Carolina at Chapel Hill since 1966, Betts is Alumni Distinguished Professor of English (1980) and has served two terms as Chairman of the Faculty. She has extended her award-winning teaching of creative writing into published discussion of the aesthetics of writing ("The Fingerprint of Style," 1985) and of the literary heritage of southern women writers. The recipient of a Guggenheim Fellowship (1988), a John Dos Passos Prize (1983), and a Medal of Merit in the Short Story Division from the American Academy of Arts and Letters (1989), Betts has written perceptively on southern writing in recently published reassessments in such books as *Southern Women Writers: The New Generation* (1990), *The Future South: A Historical Perspective for the Twenty-First Century* (1991), and *The Female Tradition in Southern Literature* (1983).

Betts has published three collections of short stories and six novels. Although Dorothy Scura calls Betts's natural forte the short story, she also remarks that in both the novels and short fiction, Betts consistently deals with the themes of time and mortality, the characterization of children and older people, relationships among family members and between races, and the possibilities of love and growing up. Writing short fiction has helped Betts to hone for the novel her characterization of working-class people and grotesque types, her fresh look at place, and her use of humor and depiction of various people trying to interact with each other. Having learned these skills from writing short stories, she has steadily developed what Scura calls "a more complex, layered and subtle style" of storytelling.

Betts's first collection of short stories, *The Gentle Insurrection and Other Stories* (1954) consists of twelve stories of characters who gently rebel against family ties that smother or fail to recognize the dignity of the individual. Lettie of the oxymoronic title story intends to leave her mother and brother to their sharecroppers' life. However, when her mother promises that eventually they will buy their own place, Lettie ignores her lover's whistle to come and join him, knowing she will never leave her family. In "The End of Henry Fribble," Lena Fribble risks the wrath of her demanding attorney husband but also succeeds because she finds happiness, sociability, and even a purpose to her life as she attends funerals. This collection won the publisher's Putnam Prize.

A novella, the title story in Betts's second volume of short fiction, *The Astronomer and Other Stories* (1966), is considered to be one of her masterpieces. Betts portrays Mr. Beam, an amateur astronomer late in life, as a complex character and complicates the plot of his lonely life since his wife's death twelve years before by his renting a room to an unmarried couple, Fred Ridge and pregnant Eva Sion. As a result of his new interest in astronomy, his homemade telescope, and his growing love of Eva, who helps him see the larger world of his neighbors via the telescope, Mr. Beam seems to connect the earthly and cosmic dimensions that his life had never held before. When Eva has an abortion and scolds herself for taking the life of an unborn child, Mr. Beam takes care of her and berates her for calling on God only when in trouble. Eva's return to her husband and children forces Mr. Beam to reexamine his own shortcomings in his pre-astronomer days for which he needs forgiveness: his neglect of his wife, his harshness with his sons, and his lack of belief in God. His insurrection against the earlier conformity in his life has opened up new worlds of learning, relationships with others, and a belief in what lies "beyond the stars."

In the nine stories of *Beasts of the Southern Wild* (1973), Betts culminates her art of depicting characters, even grotesque ones ("the beasts"), who seek meaningful identity and satisfying relationships with others in a "southern wild" that is softened with nature's beauty and sensitive to an individual's possible spiritual connection to the universe. In three stories—the title story, "Burning the Bed," and "Still Life with Fruit"—Alice Sink identifies the theme of "Woman at the Crossroads." The title story portrays Carol Walsh, a white, married high-school English teacher who tries to balance the reality of her white husband Rob's prejudices with her romantic fantasy of Sam Porter, a black revolutionist who encourages Carol to make choices at her crossroad and who fulfills his promise in her fantasy to kill the white husband who rapes her.

"The Ugliest Pilgrim" depicts Violet Karl's search for removal of a disfiguring facial scar through an appeal to a TV revivalist-healer and her finding love and relief from isolation in her mountain home in the friendship of two soldiers. This story inspired both film and musical-theater renditions of Violet's spiritual pilgrimage to Tulsa. Under the title "Violet," the story was adapted in film for the American Short Story Series, winning an Academy Award in 1982; in March 1997 the musical-theater version of *Violet* opened at the Playwrights Horizon Theater in New York to enthusiastic reviews.

Combining humor, satire, and the grotesque in moving lonely Violet from her mountain home by bus to sterile urban Tulsa, Betts makes the reader respond to Violet's writing in a notebook her quirky observations of people and places on her journey as well as her disillusionment with the indifference of the TV healer's assistant to her plea for a lesser affliction than the facial scar. Violet's faith, only slightly shaken, is rewarded when two soldiers, white-skinned, blue-eyed Monty and black Grady "Flick" Fliggins, who befriended her on the bus to Tulsa, meet her at Fort Smith, as they promised to do on her return trip. Flick has provided Violet with sensitive understanding of her search for physical beauty while Monty brags about his motorcycle exploits. Betts satirizes this stereotyping of white and black male traits, while at the end Violet recognizes that both young men, unlike the TV healer, have looked beyond her face. As Violet runs from them, she sees Monty "running as hard as he can and he's faster than me. And Oh! Praise God! He's catching me!"

The astronomer Mr. Beam, Carol Walsh, and Violet Karl exemplify Betts's literary response to what Lewis Simpson names "the self's difficult, maybe impossible, attempt to achieve a meaningful identity." Along with other southern short story writers such as Flannery O'Connor and Eudora Welty, Betts adds to her characters a sense of the self with a spiritual connection in the universe. Her short stories underwrite her vision of what the regionalism of southern literature always aspired to be—a local means to universal ends.

Charlotte S. McClure

SELECTED BIBLIOGRAPHY

Works by Doris Betts

The Gentle Insurrection and Other Stories. New York: G. P. Putnam's Sons, 1954.

The Astronomer and Other Stories. New York: Harper & Row, 1966.
Beasts of the Southern Wild and Other Stories. New York: Harper & Row, 1973.

Critical Studies

Barnes, Clive. "Musical 'Violet' Earns Bouquets." New York Post, March 12, 1997.
Evans, Elizabeth. Doris Betts. Boston: G. K. Hall, 1997.
Kimball, Sue Laslie, and Lynn Veach Sadler, eds. The "Home Truths" of Doris Betts. Fayetteville, N.C.: Methodist College Press, 1992.
Scura, Dorothy. "Doris Betts at Mid-Career: Her Voice and Her Art." In Tonette Bond Inge, ed., Southern Women Writers: The New Generation, pp. 161–178. Tuscaloosa: University of Alabama Press, 1990.
Simpson, Lewis P. "Introduction." 3 x 3: Masterpieces of the Southern Gothic. Atlanta: Peachtree Publishers, 1985.

PAUL BOWLES
(1910–1999)

Paul Bowles's short stories, which Gore Vidal has deemed "among the best ever written by an American," occupy a unique place in American literature. Their distinctly gothic flavor and their tautness suggest comparisons with the stories of Edgar Allan Poe, a connection Bowles himself invites in dedicating his first volume of stories to his mother, "who first read me the stories of Poe."

In the tradition of American expatriate writers such as Henry James, Gertrude Stein, Ernest Hemingway, Djuna Barnes, and James Baldwin, Bowles found life abroad more suitable to his disposition than life in the United States. Bowles was born in Jamaica, Long Island, on December 30, 1910, the only child of Rena and Claude Bowles. In his late teens he enrolled at the University of Virginia, conscious of the fact that Poe had studied there nearly a century earlier. He soon gave up his studies, however, and set sail for Europe, staying until his money ran out.

As a young man in his twenties and thirties, Bowles was known primarily as a composer. He received encouragement from Henry Cowell, Virgil Thomson, and Aaron Copland. It was Copland, in fact, who suggested that Bowles return with him to Paris and study music composition. From a young age Bowles had literary instincts as well. When just seventeen he had published poetry in *transition*. In Paris he looked up Gertrude Stein, who first suggested he go to Morocco, the country that became an important source of inspiration and his adopted home.

One of the distinguishing characteristics of Bowles's fiction is the use of foreign settings he came to know firsthand through his relentless travels. Three of his four novels (*The Sheltering Sky, Let It Come Down,* and *The Spider's House*) as well as the bulk of his stories are set in North Africa. His fourth novel, *Up Above the World,* and a number of stories are set in Latin America, where Bowles traveled with his wife Jane, also a very talented writer, during the 1930s and 1940s. Still other stories are set in Sri Lanka, where in the 1950s Bowles owned an island, and in Thailand, which he visited in 1966.

Many of Bowles's stories, not surprisingly, depict cross-cultural encounters that often involve American characters traveling through exotic, inhospitable landscapes. These narratives often transport characters across moral and social boundaries as well. His well-known story "Pages From Cold Point," for instance, features a father who goes with his son to a Caribbean island where the son apparently seduces him. In "The Echo," set in the jungles of Colombia, a teenage girl is forced to come to terms with her mother's affair with another woman. The threat of violence is often close to the surface in Bowles's stories, creating an ominous tone. At times, as in "Doña Faustina" and "Julian Vreden," violent crime becomes a central, absorbing preoccupation. Still other stories, such as "Señor Ong and Señor Ha" and the four stories in *A Hundred Camels in the Courtyard* (the "kif quartet"), explore altered states of consciousness produced by drugs. Stories such as "By the Water," "Allal" and "Kitty," in the tradition of Kafka's "The Metamorphosis," show transformations from human to animal. No matter what form the crossing takes, the Bowles story typically portrays a desire for human contact and communication, which usually ends in failure, often tragic.

A good many of these elements coalesce in "A Distant Episode," a story written in 1945, published in *Partisan Review* two years later, and selected for inclusion in *The Best American Short Stories of 1948.* This story and the even more gruesome "The Delicate Prey" are probably Bowles's two best-known, most anthologized stories. The story's general trajectory and concerns in some ways prefigure those Bowles develops in his first novel *The Sheltering Sky* (1949). An American linguistic anthropologist, referred to simply as "the Professor" in the story, sets out on a journey to Aïn Tadouirt (an imaginary place somewhere in the south of Morocco), expecting that his study of the language and culture of these tribes will be sufficient to sustain him in his work. The reader quickly perceives that the Professor is reading the signs very poorly. Soon the Professor is wholly on his own in a hostile world, with nothing to rely on and no one to whom he can turn for help. He is captured and beaten unconscious by members of the Reguibat tribe, whose fearful reputation for violence is legendary. The Professor wakes to the terrifying sight of a man clutching a knife in one hand and his tongue in the other. Dizzy and speechless, the tongueless Professor is put in a bag and carried away by camel, tin cans tied to his body. For a year or so he is used for entertainment before he finally escapes into the desert, where presumably he dies.

This resonant story is powerful because it registers so dramatically and forcefully the existential terror at the heart of all human experience. Step by step, Bowles skillfully and economically leads us away from the familiar into unfamiliar regions of horror. The story, like so much of Bowles's work, also inscribes essential tensions between East and West. The sharp irony at the story's center is that in the end speech and rationality do not offer what is necessary for survival. The story also urges us, implicitly, to consider what forces govern the movement of events.

The universe depicted in "A Distant Episode" is distinctly godless and Manichean. Things happen simply because they happen, not because of they are part of any divine scheme. This rather existential, even nihilistic, philosophy permeates Bowles's fiction.

"The Frozen Fields," written in the mid-1950s and published in *The Time of Friendship,* does not conform to the typical patterns of the Bowles story, in large measure because it is one of only a handful of stories set in the United States. Nonetheless, the story is an important one, shedding light on the creative process and relations between sons and fathers. In writing the story Bowles relied on his own childhood memories, particularly those of times he spent with his grandparents, August and Henrietta Winnewisser. The story is set at Christmas. At the story's opening, six-year-old Donald and his father are shown traveling by train to the grandparents' farm. When Donald begins to sketch out pictures with his fingernail through the frost on the train's window, his father yells at him to stop. The conflict between father and son escalates during the visit, heightened by the presence of Donald's Uncle Ivor and his companion Mr. Gordon. Apparently anxious about Mr. Gordon's interest in his son, Donald's father rather fiercely tries to make a man out of his son, at one point forcefully rubbing snow in his face. In his own imaginative world, Donald constructs a wolf, fantasizing that it breaks through the windowpane and seizes his father by the throat. In the final scene of the story, Donald imagines himself running with the wolf across the frozen fields.

Like many other Bowles stories, "The Frozen Fields" displays a profound sympathy for the child whose delicate world is always at the mercy of adults. Donald's struggle with his father, who seems bent on suppressing his artistic inclinations, resembles that of Stephen Dedalus in James Joyce's *Portrait of the Artist as a Young Man*. More autobiographical than most of Bowles's stories, "The Frozen Fields" displays connections between attitudes and feelings Bowles had toward his own father, childhood isolation, and the creative act.

"Here to Learn," the longest and most ambitious story in his collection *Midnight Mass* (1981), serves as one last example of Bowles's versatility and range. The story follows the course of a journey as is typical in the Bowles story, though this time the protagonist is a young Moroccan woman named Malika, and the journey is from East to West. Through a series of chance occurrences, Malika moves from one Western man to the next, from Morocco to Spain, to Paris, to Switzerland, and finally, in the tow of an American named Tex, to Los Angeles. There Tex dies unexpectedly, leaving Malika free with a comfortable fortune. She decides in the end to return for a visit to Morocco, where she finds her native village entirely changed and her mother dead.

The story covers much ground quickly. Though told in the third person, the action is filtered through Malika's consciousness, so the reader feels quite directly her reactions to her first exposure to Western culture. In composing the story Bowles doubtless relied on his knowledge of Moroccan culture and the experience he had

watching Moroccans encounter the West for the first time.

After the publication of his autobiography, *Without Stopping,* in 1972, Bowles lived a sedentary life in Tangier, venturing forth only on occasion for business or medical reasons to Paris, Atlanta, and New York. His fourth and last novel, *Up Above the World,* came out in 1966. While Bowles continued to write stories in the seventies and eighties, his production tapered off substantially. These later stories, particularly those collected in *Unwelcome Words,* are quite different from his early work in style and tone. Their sparse style likely is to some degree a consequence of the extensive efforts Bowles put into translating the work of Moroccan storytellers such as Mohammed Mrabet. Several stories take the form of dramatic monologue and rely on memories of earlier times. Taken together, they have a more settled feel to them and are clearly the work of a writer whose traveling days had ended.

At the end of his life, with more than sixty published stories to his name, Paul Bowles had earned an indisputable place among American short story writers. No other American writer had written so well about the attempt to know the other, which may well be but another form of coming to know the self.

Allen Hibbard

SELECTED BIBLIOGRAPHY

Works by Paul Bowles

The Delicate Prey and Other Stories. New York: Random House, 1950.

A Little Stone. London: John Lehmann, 1950.

The Hours After Noon. London: Heinemann, 1959.

A Hundred Camels in the Courtyard. San Francisco: City Lights, 1962.

The Time of Friendship. New York: Holt, Rinehart & Winston, 1967.

Pages from Cold Point and Other Stories. London: Peter Owen, 1968.

Three Tales. New York: Frank Hallman, 1975.

Things Gone and Things Still Here. Santa Barbara, Calif.: Black Sparrow Press, 1977.

Collected Stories, 1939–1976. Santa Barbara, Calif.: Black Sparrow Press, 1980.

Midnight Mass. Santa Barbara, Calif.: Black Sparrow Press, 1981.

Call at Corazón and Other Stories. London: Peter Owen, 1988.

A Distant Episode: The Selected Stories. New York: Ecco Press, 1988.

Unwelcome Words. Bolinas, Calif.: Tombouctou Books, 1988.

A Thousand Days for Mokhtar. London: Peter Owen, 1989.

Too Far from Home: Selected Writings of Paul Bowles. Edited by Daniel Halpern. New York: Ecco, 1993.

Critical Studies

Caponi, Gena Dagel. *Paul Bowles: Romantic Savage*. Carbondale: Southern Illinois University Press, 1994.

Hibbard, Allen. *Paul Bowles: A Study of the Short Fiction*. New York: Macmillan, 1993.

Patteson, Richard F. *A World Outside: The Fiction of Paul Bowles*. Austin: University of Texas Press, 1987.

Stewart, Lawrence D. *Paul Bowles: The Illumination of North Africa*. Carbondale: Southern Illinois University Press, 1974.

KAY BOYLE
(1902 – 1992)

Born on February 19, 1902, in St. Paul, Minnesota, Kay Boyle was the second of two daughters of Howard Peterson Boyle and Katherine Evans Boyle, for whom she was named. Until her death in 1992, her life encompassed the major events of the twentieth century, just as her writing chronicled her life in thinly veiled, acutely honest depictions of her signature autobiographical protagonist—the "American Girl."

After World War I the family moved to Cincinnati, Ohio, where Boyle worked as secretary in her father's business. She briefly attended the Cincinnati Conservatory of Music and the Ohio Mechanics Institute, where she met Richard Brault, a Frenchman whom she married in 1922. They moved to New York, where she worked with Lola Ridge on *Broom*, a small literary magazine publishing exciting new writers such as William Carlos Williams and Marianne Moore. In 1923, Boyle accompanied her husband to France. In later years she would point out heatedly that she was not one of the expatriate generation made famous by Ernest Hemingway; instead, she was a French resident and a French citizen by marriage. Nevertheless, in France Boyle began to move with the circle of avant-garde writers who populated Europe between the world wars, and to mature as a writer.

In 1925 Boyle met and fell in love with Ernest Walsh, the coeditor of *This Quarter*. Leaving Brault and their marriage, Boyle joined Walsh to lead a nomadic life through Europe, collecting and editing manuscripts for *This Quarter*. Walsh died in 1926, and five months later, in March 1927, their daughter Sharon was born. In 1930 Boyle married avant-garde writer Laurence Vail. Professionally, the 1930s were prolific years, Boyle publishing four novels, three short story collections, one book of poetry, two book-length translations, and numerous individual stories and essays. She was awarded a Guggenheim Fellowship in 1934 and an O'Henry Award for the year's best short story in 1935 for "The White Horses of Vienna," published in a collection of the same title. In 1940, she was awarded her second O'Henry Prize for "Defeat."

In 1941, Boyle married Joseph Franckenstein, who until his death in 1963 provided her with one of the few stable relationships of her life. During World II, she toured Europe as a correspondent for the *New York Times*, and at the invitation of the U.S. Army Boyle toured airbases in Europe and North Africa. She began to write commercial stories for various publications, such as the *Saturday Evening Post* and *Ladies Home Journal*.

In the early 1950s, both Boyle and Franckenstein came under the investigation of Joseph McCarthy's House Un-American Activities Committee. Although ultimately exonerated, Boyle found herself blacklisted as a writer, with the *Nation* being one of the few publications daring to carry her work. In 1962 Boyle accepted a teaching position at San Francisco State University, which she held until her retirement in 1979. Her writing interests shifted from short fiction to nonfiction as she published numerous essays and collections of essays during the ensuing decades. In 1973 she founded the San Francisco chapter of Amnesty International, which she supported until her death in 1992.

Boyle's writing always reflected the landscapes, personal situations, and political/historical contexts of her life. Her themes dealt with the ongoing search for connectedness in an impersonal world. In her earlier stories, such as "Wedding Day," "The First Lover," and "Artist Colony," she explored these themes within the context of individual characters. Her stories looked inward. In such later works as "Defeat," "The Canals of Mars," and "Lovers of Gain," she placed her characters in a particular place and time, thus adding a contextual complexity to the themes that had interested her from the beginning.

An early story, "Episode in the Life of an Ancestor," collected in *Wedding Day and Other Stories* (1930), pays homage to Boyle's grandmother, who in the 1850s left a loveless marriage in Kansas and took her two children, Boyle's mother and aunt, to Washington, where she forged a career in government service, a feat virtually unheard of for women of that time. Challenging the parameters of traditional narrative plot, the action of the story consists of the wild horseback ride across the Kansas plain of a young woman as she tries to decide whether to defy her father or not. In a foreshadowing and personalizing of time, Boyle calls this character "the grandmother," although she does not explain this reference to the reader. Instead of taking us into the mind of this character, Boyle creates an assemblage of perspectives voiced first by the young woman's father, who admits he cannot understand her and who holds values very different from hers; more unconventionally, by the horse as he gallops over the plain, instinctively responding with a kind of admiration to the strength of this young rider. The two perspectives balance each other and, taken together, provide a portrait of the young woman's nature. The story ends where a more conventional one would begin, as the daughter returns to confront the father in anger and in a spirit of resolve. Clearly the prelude to impending action, this scene ends the story. Boyle provides the reader with no information about the outcome of their meeting. There is no resolution to this story, nor in fact is there even a climactic scene, for that height of action will occur seconds after the story ends, and after the reader has been dismissed. With this story Boyle has experimented both with perspective by telling it from two radically different observers, neither of whom is capable of communicating his thoughts to the central character, and with narrative structure by virtually ignoring its conventions.

By the 1930s, as a more mature writer, Boyle begins to make more use of the settings of her stories, developing them far more fully than she did in her early work. She set "The White Horses of Vienna" in 1930s Austria, where she was living at the time. Filled with a subtle and inclusive irony, the story deals with an Austria caught between an ineffectual government under Engelbert Dollfuss and a takeover by the Nazis under Adolf Hitler. Boyle tells the story of this conflict in human terms, showing the effect of political turmoil on ordinary people. The protagonist, an Austrian doctor, injures his knee while lighting swastika fires in the mountains at night as a form of pro-Nazi protest. A young Jewish doctor, Dr. Heine, is sent to help him maintain his medical practice as he recovers. While the doctor's wife is rabidly anti-Semitic, her husband remains impartial. Yet, both the Austrian doctor and his wife respond positively to Dr. Heine as an individual, albeit she more grudgingly than he. As the story unfolds, the philosophical differences between the two doctors become apparent and critical to the outcome, not only of the story but of history as well. The Austrian doctor had been a Russian prisoner of war during World War I. He has seen political movements come and go, the issues of one day disappear in the flood of time. However, he allows himself to act politically in ways that contradict his own experience. This is true even of his relationship to the young doctor—the Austrian doctor likes the young man personally, but is part of an anti-Semitic political movement. On the other hand, the young Jewish doctor is virtually apolitical, and in this he serves as a counterpoint to the Austrian doctor. He sees people as human beings, and believing only in his own experiences, he ignores the possibilities of personal consequences in the political situation. He recognizes that a way of life—the aristocratic life of the Austrian nobility—is disappearing in the face of contemporary Europe, but sees no parallels to his own life.

The story ends the day after Dollfuss's assassination with the old doctor's being taken to prison for his pro-Nazi activities. Even at this point, Dr. Heine wants to help him and asks what he can do. The old doctor tells him to throw oranges and chocolates to his prison window, a final subtle irony, for in Austria during this period, such extravagances were not available. In this story, Boyle again works with the theme of lack of connectedness, for neither of the two men integrates personal and societal experience. Each denies one facet of life in favor of another; each remains blind to vitally important observations. In the Austrian doctor, she allows a basically good man to become involved with unspeakable evil; in Dr. Heine, she allows an intelligent man to ignore the warning signs all around him. Boyle expects her reader to know current history, to understand the tragic irony encompassed by this story.

Again, stylistically, Boyle redefines narrative. The story is told in three parts, presented chronologically, but in three kinds of narrative. The first deals with the personal responses of the three main characters to each other. Of the entire story, this section reads more conventionally. Boyle describes the setting and provides the details that make the characters live. The second section presents a philosophical discussion told in analogy through a puppet show and a fairy tale. Here the characters speak allegorically, and because they come from different perspectives, they misunderstand each other's meaning. Rather than hear what the other has said,

each interprets the other's story as a confirmation of his own beliefs. The third and final part offers the concrete results of the political situation: the beginning of life-changing events throughout the Austria of the story. As is typical for her, Boyle provides no resolution for this story. It simply ends. Instead of closure, the reader is left with the characters, to wonder at what will happen to them. At the time the story was written, there was no answer to that puzzle.

Throughout her life, Kay Boyle wrote about damaged relationships, people seeking connection in a world unresponsive to them, individuals caught in circumstances that demand strength and courage if there is to be hope. She based those themes unabashedly on her own life, and as a result, recorded for us the twentieth century in its folly and its promise.

Elizabeth Bell

SELECTED BIBLIOGRAPHY

Works by Kay Boyle

Short Stories. Paris: Black Sun Press, 1929.
Wedding Day and Other Stories. New York: Jonathan Cape & Harrison Smith, 1930.
The First Lover and Other Stories. New York: Harrison Smith & Robert Haas, 1933.
The White Horses of Vienna and Other Stories. New York: Harcourt, Brace, & Co., 1936.
Thirty Stories. New York: Simon & Schuster, 1946.
The Smoking Mountain: Stories of Postwar Germany. New York: McGraw-Hill, 1951.

Nothing Ever Breaks Except the Heart. Garden
   City, N.Y.: Doubleday, 1966.
Fifty Stories. Garden City, N.Y.: Doubleday,
   1980.
Life Being the Best and Other Stories. New York:
   New Directions, 1986.

Critical Studies

Bell, Elizabeth S. *Kay Boyle: A Study of the
   Short Fiction.* New York: Twayne, 1992.
Mellen, Joan. *Kay Boyle: Author of Herself.*
   New York: Farrar, Straus & Giroux,
   1994.
Spanier, Sandra Whipple. *Kay Boyle: Artist
   and Activist.* Carbondale: Southern Illi-
   nois University Press, 1986.

RAY BRADBURY
## (1920 – 	)

More than readers might expect,
given the eerie and otherworldly
settings in many of his stories, Ray Bradbury's biography is interwoven into his
fiction. Known primarily as a science fiction and fantasy writer, Bradbury nevertheless grounds even his most exotic
landscapes and characters in his own
experience, which helps to create the
atmosphere of poetic magic realism
generated in his best fiction. His most
fabulous creations often transform into
mythic images specific characters and
situations encountered in his own middle-
class American life, most notably in the
wide varieties of stories and books set in
different versions of "Green Town," based
on his childhood in Waukegan, Illinois.
Many of these stories transform both
mundane and bizarre experiences into
fantastic fiction: the local barber becomes
an alien vampire in "The Man Upstairs,"
and he himself is his model for the murderous infant in "The Small Assassin," just
as his own experience as a young man
traveling in Mexico informs his macabre
portrait of a woman descending into madness in "The Next in Line." As is most
evident in *Dandelion Wine,* a collection that
can be categorized both as fantasy and as
a kind of mythic autobiography, Bradbury's fiction weaves his life into his art.

Bradbury's life, as he has interpreted
it, is both magical and archetypally American. He was born in Waukegan on August
22, 1920, the younger of two sons of
Leonard Spaulding Bradbury and Esther
Marie Moberg Bradbury. In interviews
and autobiographical sketches his reminiscences about growing up in Waukegan
recount exuberant encounters with media: viewing Lon Chaney in his first encounter with film at the age of three; reading his first science fiction in *Amazing
Stories* at the age of eight; writing his first
science fiction novel (a sequel to Edgar
Rice Burroughs's *The Gods of Mars*) on
butcher paper at the age of eleven; attending the Century of Progress exhibit
at the Chicago World's Fair at thirteen.
After a year in Tucson, Arizona, his family
moved to Los Angeles in 1934, where
Bradbury found himself at the media center creating the worlds of enchantment
that had shaped his youth in the Midwest.
As an adolescent in Los Angeles he became
an enthusiastic fan; at age fourteen, he and
a friend became the first live audience for

the Burns and Allen radio show. In time he became a major media figure himself, as the science fiction and fantasy writer of his generation most successful at gaining a mainstream audience.

During his prolific career as a writer in Los Angeles, Bradbury has raised a family, garnered numerous awards recognizing his multifaceted accomplishments, and become America's most widely anthologized short story writer, a process that began dramatically in the late 1940s. In 1947 he married Marguerite McClure, and his short story "Homecoming" was selected as an O. Henry Prize story. In 1948, "Powerhouse" was selected by the O. Henry Awards, and "I See You Never" was selected for *Best American Short Stories 1948*. In 1949 he was voted the "Best Author of 1949" by the National Fantasy Fan Federation, and the first of his daughters was born. In 1950 he published his first novel, *The Martian Chronicles,* which was among the first science fiction works to reach a mainstream audience. In decades to come, he continued to garner awards and recognition, including the selection of "The Other Foot" for *Fifty Best American Short Stories: 1915–1965* in 1965, selection for the Science Fiction Hall of Fame by the Science Fiction Writers of America in 1976, and selection for the Valentine Davies Award by the Writers Guild of America for his work in film in 1984.

Bradbury began his career as a short story writer when the science fiction and fantasy magazines created the market in their fields, and while he has gone on to explore other major genres (such as novels, drama, poetry, and essays) he has consistently produced short stories throughout his career. Though he has written several successful novels—most notably *Fahrenheit 451* and *Something Wicked This Way Comes*—his style seems most attuned to the tighter focus of the short story, where his gift for lyricism and his striking imagery often create poetic intensity and vivid dramatic resolution. In two of his other most famous books, *The Martian Chronicles* and *Dandelion Wine,* he weaves short stories together to develop a larger narrative.

Once he discovered his distinctive style in the early 1940s, Bradbury quickly established a reputation as the preeminent stylist to emerge from the fantasy and science fiction magazines. "The Next in Line," one of his most sophisticated early gothic stories—actually more psychological horror than fantasy—illustrates how his gift for lyrical description can generate an eerie atmosphere of horror. The protagonist, an American woman mesmerized with obsessive dread by the sight of the Guanajuato mummies, helplessly identifies with what she imagines to be their endless silent screams. Bradbury's description reveals her inner feelings, dramatizes the central image that inspired the story (based on Bradbury's own experience in Mexico in 1945), and implies the psychological dynamics that ultimately cause the protagonist's death: "Marie's eyes slammed the furthest wall . . . swinging from horror to horror . . . staring with hypnotic fascination at paralyzed, loveless, fleshless loins, at men made into women by evaporation, at women made into dugged swine. The fearful ricochet of vision . . . ended finally . . . when vision crashed against the corridor ending with one last scream" (*The October Country*).

Though this description presents the

central image that establishes the story's atmosphere of soundless horror, it also establishes the underlying metaphor that expresses Marie's state of mind: to her the mummies are emblems of her own silent anguish, the quiet desperation of her poisonously polite, lethal relationship with her husband. The sexlessness of their "paralyzed, loveless, fleshless loins" parallels her own body image, for even before this encounter she has lain awake sleeplessly contemplating the fact that she is "past saving now" because she lacks the "warmth to bake away the aging moisture." The image of her vision "ricocheting" from "skull to skull" expresses her state of mind as it builds into a crescendo of horror. And by paralleling the feverish rhythm of her vision with the imagined "chant" of the "standing chorus," ending with "one last scream from all present," Bradbury dramatizes the special horror of his character's own agony and eventual death. Like the unburied dead, her inner scream is soundless, unrecognized by the outer world. With this vivid impression of the protagonist's reaction to the mummies, Bradbury focuses the energies and meanings of his plot.

"The Veldt," one of Bradbury's most vivid science fiction warning stories, provides an eloquent image of ultimately self-destructive overdependence on technology. The title itself expresses the theme, since the "veldt" refers to the savage center of an immaculate high-tech home of the future—the "nursery," where a technological toy designed to enhance children's playful fantasies destroys its owners. Rather than charming fairylands, the children use their new "virtual reality" machine to create the veldt, where blood-

thirsty lions ultimately feed on their parents. Here Bradbury dramatizes with chilling effect the potentially ironic impact of technology that fulfills his characters' deepest dreams, since the slaughter in the nursery emanates from the deprived hearts of two normal-appearing children who love their fabulous nursery more than their doting parents. Ultimately, their new toy becomes the instrument of their inner rage.

Bradbury creates a complex, disturbing image of the potential dangers posed by television, an entertainment medium whose impact was first being felt as he wrote the story (published in 1950). Characteristically his warning focuses not on the machine itself, but on its relationship to the disturbing psychology of a family that has unwittingly enslaved itself to virtual reality entertainment. Like many of Bradbury's most haunting fictions, the story begins by placing readers among familiar things and then menaces them in ways all the more horrifying for being disguised by comfortable appearances. As the father explains, their very dependence on their home creates alienation: with its marvelously intricate video and olfactory technology capable of transforming fantasy into reality, the nursery is the central symbol of an environment in which humanity has become addicted to machines. The helpless parents realize that the children's pathologically dependent relationship with the artificial world of the nursery carries to an extreme the family's ambivalent relationship with their home: "I feel I don't belong here. The house is wife and mother now and nursemaid" (The Illustrated Man).

Ultimately, "The Veldt" warns not

about the danger of technology itself, but about the consequences of substituting technological marvels for basic human relationships. The lethal nursery is only a sensitive piece of machinery, after all, which enhances the latently murderous dynamics of spoiled children and overly solicitous parents. The machine simply literalizes the underlying emotions of the family, creating real wilderness and lions to express the murderous rage behind the children's forced politeness and impatience. Though apparently the children murder to preserve their beloved machine after their father decides to shut it down, their deeper motivation stems from parental deprivation: they identify so fiercely with the nursery because the parents substituted it for themselves. In spoiling their children, the parents have actually deprived them of necessary human nurturing—just as the parents in turn realize that they secretly hate the efficient modern home that satisfies their every desire, yet leaves them feeling depersonalized and useless.

As is illustrated by essentially gothic tales like "The Next in Line" and "The Veldt," many of Bradbury's most memorable stories dramatize the dark side of human nature and the ominous potential of technological change. But, as he has stated vociferously throughout his career, Bradbury is at heart a fervent optimist about mankind and the future, and these underlying beliefs also find expression in his fiction. His dark stories warn of dangers that he believes we can survive, but his fiction presents visions of transformation and progress as well, as is most evident in the Mars stories he has written throughout his career. His deeply ironic space-colonization novel, *The Martian Chronicles,* concludes, in "The Million-Year Picnic," by depicting two American families beginning life anew after earth has been destroyed in nuclear war, accepting their new identity as "Martians" in a new "New World." In "Dark They Were, and Golden-Eyed," the protagonist lies in a Martian canal contemplating the physical and psychological transformation of human pioneers into Martians, in imagery that echoes Shakespeare's song of transformation from *The Tempest,* "Full Fathom Five Thy Father Lies": "Up there . . . a Martian river, all of us lying deep in it . . . in our summer boulder houses, like crayfish hidden, and the water washing away our old bodies and lengthening our bones—" (*A Medicine for Melancholy*).

Arguably the world's most widely read and popular short story writer, Bradbury has elicited passionate but often ambivalent critical response throughout his career, both within the genre magazines and later within mainstream and academic evaluations attempting to define his relationship to major traditions of American literature. Like subsequent writers such as Ursula K. Le Guin and Kurt Vonnegut, Bradbury successfully bridged the worlds of popular culture and serious literature. At least since the 1960s, when anthologies designed for classroom use began printing Bradbury's stories, critics have focused on the artistry of Bradbury's fiction, approaching it both through traditional methods of literary analysis and as provocative speculation about present and future problems. As Christopher Isherwood and other writers have perceived, Bradbury's best work is part of an American literary tradition that connects him to the contemporary idiom of major writers in his own era—such as Sherwood Anderson, John Steinbeck, and Ernest Hemingway—as well as to earlier mythopoeic writers like Edgar Allan Poe, Nathaniel Hawthorne, and Herman Melville.

Perhaps from this perspective we can appreciate the full range of Bradbury's contributions to the short story form. As a title bestowed upon him early in his career suggests, at his best the "Poet of the Pulps" demonstrated to a subsequent generation of New Wave writers the lyrical and mythic potential of science fiction and fantasy archetypes. Laced with irony and yet generating an authentic sense of wonder, Ray Bradbury's best stories continue to provide both popular entertainment and enduring eloquence.

David Mogen

SELECTED BIBLIOGRAPHY

Works by Ray Bradbury

Dark Carnival. Sauk City, Wisc.: Arkham House, 1947.

The Martian Chronicles. Garden City, N.Y.: Doubleday, 1950.

The Illustrated Man. Garden City, N.Y.: Doubleday, 1951.

The Golden Apples of the Sun. Garden City, N.Y.: Doubleday, 1953.

The October Country. New York: Ballantine, 1955.

A Medicine for Melancholy. Garden City, N.Y.: Doubleday, 1959.

R is for Rocket. Garden City, N.Y.: Doubleday, 1962.

S is for Space. Garden City, N.Y.: Doubleday, 1966.

The Machineries of Joy. New York: Simon & Schuster, 1964.

I Sing the Body Electric! New York: Alfred A. Knopf, 1969.

Long After Midnight. New York: Alfred A. Knopf, 1976.

The Stories of Ray Bradbury. New York: Alfred A. Knopf, 1980.

A Memory of Murder. New York: Dell, 1984.

The Toynbee Convector. New York: Alfred A. Knopf, 1988.

Quicker Than the Eye. New York: Avon, 1996.

Critical Studies

Greenberg, Martin Harry, and Joseph D. Olander, eds. *Ray Bradbury*. New York: Taplinger, 1980.

Johnson, Wayne L. *Ray Bradbury*. New York: Frederick Ungar, 1980.

Mogen, David. *Ray Bradbury*. Boston: G. K. Hall, 1986.

KATE BRAVERMAN
(1950–)

Kate Ellen Braverman was born on February 5, 1950, in Philadelphia, Pennsylvania, but soon moved to Los Angeles, where her father underwent treatment for cancer and her mother struggled to support the family. An only child, Braverman grew up coping with isolation and continual dread of disease and death, factors that later shaped her sensibility as a woman, an addict, and a writer. Braverman received a bachelor of arts degree in anthropology from the University of California, Berkeley, in 1971 and became an active member of the Los Angeles poetry scene. A single mother struggling to establish herself as a poet, she published two books of poetry with small presses. However, it was *Lithium for Medea*, a novel still considered a classic on cocaine addiction, that established her as a writer of national recognition. Unable to live from royalties, Braverman decided to become a teacher and received her masters of arts degree in English at Sonoma State University. After trying to publish her second novel, *Palm Latitudes,* for several years, she placed it with Simon & Schuster, and it was hailed as a "work of hallucinatory, poetic power" by the *New York Times*. She quickly published her highly acclaimed story collection, *Squandering the Blue*. Braverman briefly taught creative writing courses at UCLA and California State University. She now lives in Alfred, New York, with her daughter and husband.

Kate Braverman's literary territory is that of women controlled by destructive men, crippled by fears of cancer and abandonment, caught in depression, and addicted to any intense experience that distracts them from pain. Reluctant to discuss details of her own life, Braverman prefers to let her characters, plots, and themes offer glimpses of her story. Commenting on her impulse toward self-destruction, she states, "becoming a mother was the turning point. Then health and sanity began to have the allure that sickness had had. I used writing as a way back to sanity."

In *Squandering the Blue,* Braverman produces narratives of addiction through her interlocking stories of women struggling to attain self-identity, fulfillment, and ultimately transformation. She tells stories of women on the edge both psychologically and continentally. They have climbed out of a ravine of narcotic addiction and stand on the precipice of change struggling for balance. These alienated addicts are not stereotypical street crooks; they are smart, beautiful Beverly Hills women working to make a fresh life in the decayed and depraved tropical paradise of Los Angeles. Braverman's women wander the metropolis's streets and malls fully aware that they reside in the "city of the millennium," a city one character describes as "some sort of organic ruin, an accident of architecture and brutal necessity." Los Angeles is portrayed as a wasteland precariously perched on the edge of the continent where the American dream has been used, abused, and exhausted, only to be artificially revived by Hollywood hype and Colombian drugs.

Braverman's women speak from a place of alienation, anxiety, and despair. Her plots hinge on tiny movements toward mental health as she depicts the wrenching and sometimes mysterious process of growth. In the opening story, "Squandering the Blue," a woman recalls her mother, who emotionally abandoned her through an addiction to vodka and poetry and then finally deserted her by dying from cancer. The story establishes a theme of waste, a waste of the potential bond that could have occurred when mother and daughter lived in the tropical paradise of Hawaii, where the blue sky "was an intoxication." Instead of connecting with her daughter, the mother drank vodka and wrote poetry by "finding a vast and remote blue space within herself." Hawaii seems to be a paradise lost. Reflecting on the damage done, the narrator recalls being so enraged that she wished her mother would die from the vodka she craved, but now she "cannot say when shame and cruelty were transformed to love."

But in Braverman's world, peace of mind is precarious. Women suffer, recover, and often slip back to habits of despair. "Tall Tales from the Mekong Delta" dramatizes how a recovered addict, barely held in balance by daily AA meetings, visits to the shrink, and manicures, is toppled by a repulsive yet hypnotic drug dealer. A personification of the protagonist's old addiction, he is dressed like a degenerate. He is fat, with bad teeth and greasy hair, and yet is hypnotically appealing with his offer of a walk on the wild side with roses, Rolexes, and drugs. He expertly manipulates her away from her safe world and toward his dangerous world of drugs, sex, and money by leading her into small acts of acquiescence. When he asks for her watch, she instantly gives it and immediately loses track of time, observing, "the air felt humid, green, stalled." In his presence she slips into a psychotic sensibility, noting, "the palms were livid with green death," and, against her better judgment, she succumbs to his will. Reluctantly swimming in his pool, she notices, "The water felt strange and icy. . . . There were shadows on the far side of the pool. The shadows were hideous. There was nothing ambiguous about them. The water beneath the shadows looked remote and troubled and green. It looked contaminated. The more she swam, the more infected blue particles clustered on her skin." Braverman's vivid surreal images

exceed descriptive function and serve to articulate abstract states of mind. Once the protagonist says yes to the dealer, her compromised sensibility perceives the crisp green and clear blue colors of her controlled Beverly Hills life as polluted. The external landscape appears as polluted as her internal world. When he tells her to kiss him, she is quietly repulsed, but agrees, opening her mouth to him as an addict opens a vein to the obliterating rush of a drug. The sensation of kissing him is equivalent to a narcotic surge: "Outside, the Santa Ana winds were startling, howling as if from a mouth. The air smelled of scorched lemons and oranges, of something delirious and intoxicated. When she closed her eyes everything was blue."

Braverman's description of the sensual experience becomes a metaphor for the narcotic intoxication. The protagonist is submerged in a drugged spell, and yet a small fragment of her healthy self remains aware: "She felt like she was being electrocuted. . . . It occurred to her that it was a sensation so singular that she might come to enjoy it. There were small blue wounded sounds in the room now. She wondered if there were coming from her." Braverman evokes the addict's alienation from self. Having totally succumbed to the drug dealer's blue spell, the protagonist senses her spiritual wound but cannot connect enough to her own pain to take responsibility for it. Braverman illustrates how an addict's fragile boundaries can allow her to slip passively toward destruction.

In "Points of Decision," another addict wrestles freedom from a controlling man. Jessica Moore's husband humiliates her and yet keeps her controlled with money, premium cocaine, and annual trips to Hawaii. On her fortieth birthday, realizing she is running out of time to live her life, she determines to escape. Her inspiration comes in part from the personal supply of cocaine hidden in her compact, and in part from the simple life force of Hawaii's undefiled landscape. Recalling that in Los Angeles green is the color of decay, she observes that in Hawaii, green is the color of perennial growth and "the air seems charged, altered in a manner that makes her think of drugs or God." She connects with the undefiled potency of nature and draws strength. She kicks off her sandals and runs down the beach realizing that "running is like flying, you must divest yourself of everything but purpose." Jessica's moment of clarity springs from decisive action and leads to her transformation into a woman with purpose rather than need.

Throughout her stories of women succumbing to and recovering from compulsion, Braverman renders the addict's chronic need so vividly it becomes experiential. In "Touch of Autumn" Laurel Sloan, a teacher of poetry, walks the darkened campus and imagines that her life will always be like "these acres of agitated solitude . . . empty and repetitive with unanswered longings." She recalls the sensation of being drugged as one where she was "purified by intensity." She longs for a bottle of vodka: "With glass in hand, her entire molecular structure would alter, becoming defined and edged. She simultaneously craves and is repulsed by the old days of addiction where she never traveled without pain medications, tranquilizers, several joints, a chunk of black hash, a ball

of opium, paraphernalia, the minimal chemicals required to exist on this hostile planet."

Braverman's plots hinge on the conflict of women struggling to love a world that has hurt them, and exhausted by a sense that life is just a process of dying. Some women languish in a depression that slips toward psychosis, and some, drawing on a flickering faith, make a move toward life. In "Clairvoyant Ruins," the final story, Braverman completes the cycle of an addict struggling toward a connection that will redeem her from the temptation of the blue haze of drugs. In many ways, the final story inverts the plot of "Squandering the Blue" where a daughter reached through the past to connect with her dead mother. Here the daughter, now turned mother, reaches toward a future to connect with her very-much-alive daughter. Walking the streets of Los Angeles, Diane realizes that the depleted landscape offers more than signs of exhaustion. The sunset is unusually magnificent; it looks Hawaiian. There are white lights strung in dark palms. Diane discovers that the "ruins of civilization" can also harbor mysterious secrets of continuation.

At Christmas, a season that "always unhinges" Braverman's women with its ritual of artificial cheer, Diane is healthier than the numbed and alienated mother of other stories. Connected with her daughter, she occasionally bickers, but listens, advises. She realizes she is "learning how to be a mother" as she walks her daughter to the school where a Christmas pageant is to be performed. After sitting through her daughter's painfully bad violin performance, Diane applauds with the enthusiastic audience and is surprisingly uplifted. She notes, "It is the resonance rather than the production values. . . . The way our children stand before us, with wings, with ceremonial robes, reciting from Genesis. They bow. We applaud. The earth is renewed. . . . We have small hands. We applaud our mediocrity. We will celebrate anything."

Spontaneous love of her daughter's effort to perform with less than perfect skills jolts Diane into forgiveness of a flawed world. Walking toward home in the night, Diane and her daughter share a mystical vision of a "truth" in the darkness somewhere between a garbage dumpster and a tree. When at first her daughter cannot see "the truth" that Diane sees, Diane consciously chooses to tell her to look near the tree. Miraculously the daughter "sees," and they are joined in a healing glimpse of mystery. Astounded, Diane reflects, "If they hold hands they can see in the darkness without their eyes. There is no darkness." No longer requiring the crystalline white light of cocaine, the soothing blue illuminations of narcotics, Diane finds light in the human connection of love and makes the crucial shift from the addict's habit of seeing life as a process of dying. Life, her daughter shows her, is a process of living too, a fact that seems obvious to most of us. But caught in a pit of despair, blinded by a sense of futility, the addict often needs a reminder that life is a simultaneous process of growth and decay.

In her most recent collection, *Small Craft Warnings,* Braverman continues to tell stories of addictive women abandoned by mothers and haunted by death, but here her protagonists struggle up from despair to push through the curse of mortality, to looking for eternal connection with loved ones through a belief in the natural unity of all things. As the writer has matured, her protagonists have developed a spiritual vision that transcends individual feelings of betrayal and abandonment. In the title story, the protagonist, a girl routinely abandoned by her mother and left to the care of her grandmother, now faces the death of her grandmother, a woman who has steadily provided comfort as well as spiritual inspiration. The old woman seems to possess mystical powers of connecting with and taking pleasure in the things of this world. Unlike most women in Braverman's world, the grandmother loves life and sees her senses as means for expansion of the soul rather than avenues of self-destruction. She surrounds herself with scented candles, seeming to breathe "the creamy flames into her body."

Elderly and knowing that she is dying of heart failure, she refuses to waste into a rank pool of self-pity; she takes up sailing lessons, and on a final boating trip with her granddaughter, she dares to go out when red flags are up and to defy dangerous weather as she affirms her life and her right to pleasure. The protagonist, like most protagonists in Braverman's stories, is simultaneously fueled and crippled by grief; however, in this story as well as others in this latest collection, there is hope, beauty, and power in a recognition that the human spirit is eternally merged with nature and thus never truly abandons this world. The girl's last image of her grandmother alive is one of the old woman sailing forth into rough weather and yelling into the wind. The girl reflects: "Certainly she was talking about her heart and how it belonged to the sea and the wind and the fluid elements . . . the deceptive hazels and silvers in which we do not randomly drift. And of all that occurred to me then and later, this is the one truth of which I remain absolutely convinced." This affirmation of an eternal loving force is a new direction for Braverman. In stories haunted by death and alienation, she sometimes allows a moment's grace and peace through mother-daughter relationships, but this last collection is a spiritual breakthrough that reaches beyond human connections to affirm natural and supernatural powers that give lost and frail humans an enduring strength.

Often categorized in the tradition of William Burroughs and his tales of addiction, Braverman's stories are about a terrain that is more complex and relevant to a world of nonaddictive readers. In depicting the interior world of the addict, Braverman re-creates an emotional state that transcends the addict's simple need for a fix. Her evocations of anxiety, alienation, and despair are familiar to anyone who has lost faith and felt disengaged, worried, afraid. Braverman's stories illustrate that addicts are not freaks; they are human beings caught in universal emotional storms and struggling to make sound philosophical choices. The conflict of whether to run drugs or not becomes a metaphor for a philosophical choice: whether to perform actions of life-preservation or of self-destruction. Bolstered by the love of friends and daughters, Braverman's women learn to love and take care of themselves. They learn to value the everyday details of living such as getting a child to school, shopping for groceries—routines many readers take for granted. But for the addict, as well as for many nonaddictive personalities, the sense of wanting more from daily experience is a painful obsession, and the lesson to value the mundane routines of living is crucial for mental health. This is an essentially human lesson that Katherine Braverman's stories rehearse and that many of us, addictive or not, could benefit from learning again.

Jane Bradley

SELECTED BIBLIOGRAPHY

Works by Kate Braverman

Milk Run. (Poems.) Los Angeles: Momentum Press, 1977.

Lithium for Medea. (Fiction.) New York: Harper & Row, 1979.

Lullaby for Sinners. (Poems.) New York: Harper & Row. 1979.

Hurricane Warnings. (Poems.) Los Angeles: Illuminati Press, 1987.

Squandering the Blue. (Fiction.) New York: Ballantine/Fawcett Columbine, 1989.

Palm Latitudes. (Fiction.) New York: Ballantine/Fawcett Columbine, 1990.

Postcard from August. (Poems.) Los Angeles: Illuminati Press, 1990.

Wonders of the West. (Fiction.) New York: Ballantine/Fawcett Columbine. 1993.

Small Craft Warnings. (Fiction.) Reno: Nevada Humanities Committee, 1998.

Critical Studies

Lothyan, Kate. "The Poetry of Addiction: A Study of the Work of Kate Braverman." M.A. thesis, Sonoma State University, 1988.

See, Lisa. "Kate Braverman." *Publishers Weekly* 237 (1990): 42–43.

Matuz, Roger, ed. "Kate Braverman." *Contemporary Literary Criticism*. Detroit: Gale Research, 1992.

LARRY BROWN
(1951–)

The story of Larry Brown's becoming a writer weaves into his fiction in literal and metaphorical ways. He had a "late start," he states in an address by that title, but it is his early life that holds the "heart of the matter" of his fiction writing. As a boy he listened to his father's stories of combat in World War II, hearing "terrible, frightening things about the friends he had seen killed . . . the overwhelming amount of death he had seen on both sides." "I was exposed to these things early," Brown said, "and it instilled in me a strong belief in the resiliency of the human spirit."

That resilience is reflected in his growing up, living in a "series of rented houses in Memphis." The family started out farming: "My sister doesn't like for me to tell this—she seems ashamed of it somehow—but when I was born in 1951, my father was sharecropping on some land at Potlockney, in a small creek bottom . . . south of Tula where I ran a little country store for a couple of years." In 1972, after spending two years in the marines, Brown came back to Mississippi to live in Oxford, near Tula. He married, started his own

family, joined the Oxford Fire Department, and began what he calls his "apprenticeship period": "I had checked out books from the library by the armload—Flannery O'Connor, Raymond Carver, William Faulkner, Harry Crews, Cormac McCarthy. I found I wanted to write 'literature,' the kind of stories that I had read over and over again" (Ketchin 133–134). One night he sat down in his bedroom in front of his wife's old portable Smith-Corona electric typewriter and started to write.

Five novels and more than a hundred stories later, Larry Brown's first published story, one he said he had rather forget about, appeared in 1982 in a motorcycle magazine. Then in 1986 "Facing the Music" came out in the *Mississippi Review* and caught the attention of Shannon Ravenel, editor at Algonquin Books in Chapel Hill, who engineered the publication of Brown's first collection of ten stories, *Facing the Music* (1988). Greeted by critics as a fresh and honest voice, Brown immediately produced his first novel, *Dirty Work*. Although Brown was never in Vietnam, he had heard veterans telling stories in the North Carolina bars he went to in the service, and the voices of the two wounded veterans, one black and one white, rang as true as those in his stories. *Dirty Work* received the Mississippi Institute of Arts and Letters Award for fiction, and *USA Today* named it one of the best works of fiction in 1989. In 1990 *Big Bad Love,* a second collection of ten stories, was published. Brown's stories have appeared in anthologies as impressive as *Best American Short Stories 1989,* edited by Margaret Atwood and Shannon Ravenel, and in magazines such as *St. Andrews Review, Southern Exposure, Fiction International, Paris Review,* and *Chattahoochee Review.* His 1996 novel *Father and Son* mirrors once again Brown's belief that "any literature, if it's going to be any good, has to be about right and wrong, good and bad, good versus evil" (Ketchin 135).

Brown's fiction appeals to both a literary audience and a popular audience because most readers can recognize the purgatory where Brown's characters live. Lonely and often grieving, down but not out, they are, in his words, "proceeding out from calamity," trying to make sense of the suffering and at the same time, trying to find a way to numb the pain. "I try," Brown says, "to fix it where things are not hopeless for them, where they can make the decisions that will pull them out— although sometimes that's not possible" (LaRue 49). His characters struggle with fundamental issues—whether to be bad or good, whether to do the right thing or the wrong. They are "struggling to be good people. . . . They don't always do what's right, because they're imperfect like all of us. . . . I try to give my characters those human traits that we all recognize and all have and all feel" (Ketchin 136). How Brown creates his characters—through tough, vulgar language and simple, stark sentences—evokes the manner of Harry Crews and Raymond Carver. Brown's fiction radiates also with the magical realism of his fellow Mississippian, Lewis Nordan. The inevitable comparison is, of course, to Faulkner, since both claim Oxford, the same postage stamp of soil, but whereas Faulkner's Snopeses presage the amorality soon to predominate the Bible

Belt, Larry Brown's characters have within them a core of decency that runs often to compassion. The narrators in "Samaritans," "Leaving Town," "Big Bad Love" and "92 Days" grieve for broken babies, abandoned and abused puppies, and people for whom "bleak was a word they didn't understand since that was the world as they knew it" (*Big Bad Love*).

Brown's characters roam a stark landscape. They go from corner grocery stores to shanty bars in decrepit cars and trucks; ride for miles and miles on dirt roads; play out their most intimate moments by the glow of a television screen in small bedrooms and sleazy motel rooms. In a setting as exposed as Thomas Hardy's heath, these men and women reckon that circumstances, if they can, will work against them, and usually they are right. As the narrator in "Facing the Music" says, "You can be around the house all your life and think you're safe. But you're not. Something from outside or inside can reach out and get you." The something that has come into this house is the wife's mastectomy. The husband, who narrates the story, cannot bear to see his wife's body anymore, and she knows it. The nightly ritual of their struggle takes form within the narrative's syncopation. The narrator watches old movies and drinks whiskey; his wife fixes her face and puts on a pretty gown to entice him. On this night he identifies with Ray Milland's alcoholic character in *The Lost Weekend.* Like Ray, "he has responsibilities to people who love him and need him; he can't let them down. But he's scared to death. He doesn't know where to start." His thoughts shift among scenes, moving from the physical reality of his bedroom to Ray's alcoholic meandering, to the fantasy of the drunken lust he shared with a woman with breasts "like something you'd see in a movie." When his wife comes to their bed, he thinks: "I feel like shooting both of us because she's fixed her hair up nice and she's got on a new nightgown. . . . If I say the wrong thing, she'll take it the wrong way. She'll wind up crying in the bathroom." The story moves to resolution: her shoulders are "jerking under the little green gown"; in the movie "Ray's got the blind staggers. . . . He's on his way to the nuthouse." The ending is his last thought of their honeymoon, long ago "in that little room at Hattiesburg, when she bent her arms behind her back and slumped her shoulders forward, how the cups loosened and fell as the straps slid off her arms. I'm thinking that your first love is your best love, that you'll never find any better." They "reach to find each other in the darkness like people who are blind." Like the stories of Raymond Carver, Mary Hood, Mark Richard, and the most recent stories of Lee Smith, "Facing the Music" is resolved with sad endurance. Characteristically, even though Brown's stories close in physical darkness, he allows his characters a glimmer of light and, at the very least, of dim hope.

The characters in the title story of *Facing the Music* may be the lucky ones in Brown's fictional world because they do have each other. In contrast, the isolation of the characters in "Samaritans," a story in this same collection, forces the conclusion to an inevitable despairing end. The distance between the author and the narrator, and between the narrator and the reader, is minute, possibly nonexistent.

The reader sees Brown's typically self-conscious first-person narrator in the rare act of coming out from the darkness of his own thoughts to view the world from another perspective. He tries to be a good Samaritan, Brown says, to these "outcasts of society," people "who do nothing to help themselves." And while his attempt to help is futile, the point is "that it's a good thing to try" (Ketchin 129–130).

While Brown's fiction, certainly in theme and plot, has roots in the tradition of American naturalism and realism, his humor is unique. Plots turn on sexual peccadilloes: in "Wild Thing" a lovers lane is a dope drop checked regularly by police; in "Discipline" an author imprisoned for plagiarism is forced to copulate with repulsive women. In "Big Bad Love" a wife runs off with a man whose sexual organ is large enough to satisfy her, leaving Leroy, the narrator, in the dark on his porch, his dead dog still unburied. Typical of Brown's male characters, who are cuckolded by wives and mistresses, Leroy sports a wry, self-deprecating humor that blunts the edge of the familiar, weary pain: "My *dog* died. I went out there in the yard and looked at him and there he was, dead as a hammer. Boy I hated it. . . . Birds were singing, flowers were blooming. It was just wonderful. I hated for my old dog to be dead and miss all that, but I didn't know if dogs cared about stuff like that or not." True to macho form, his compassion is unstated, but he is open to understanding in a way that Harry Crews's comparable male characters never could be.

This unexpected tenderness surfaces in surprising places in "Waiting for the Ladies," a story Brown delights in reading to an audience. A flasher becomes the obsession of a character whose wife's infidelity lurks just outside his conscious recognition. The story opens: "My wife came home crying from the Dumpsters, said there was some pervert over there jerked down his pants and showed her his schlong. I asked her how long this particular pecker was." The narrator's ensuing search takes him on a chase, like Jason's chase in *The Sound and the Fury,* that shows reason run comically amok. In the end, however, Brown allows his buffoon characters dignity, giving them fragile faith that humans will endure and prevail. The closing scene of "Waiting for the Ladies" shows the narrator shifting to higher ground as he enters the flasher's home carrying his gun. The flasher and his mother are watching Johnny Carson saying goodnight: "His hair wasn't like what I'd imagined," the narrator says. "It was gray, but neatly combed, and his mother was sobbing silently on the couch and feeding a pillow into her mouth." The flasher asks him, "Are you fixing to kill us?" And here is where Brown amazes: "Their eyes got me. I sat down, asking first if I could. That's when I started telling both of them what my life then was like."

Situations, plot, and character in Larry Brown's fiction work together to tease readers out of complacency about how the world runs. The stories depict men and women and children who are not going to survive, and the ones who do render us speechless by their audacity and their courage. "I write," Larry Brown told an audience in 1989 in Chattanooga, "out of experience and imagination, toward blind faith and hope."

Dede Yow

SELECTED BIBLIOGRAPHY

Works by Larry Brown

Facing the Music. Chapel Hill, N.C.: Algonquin Books, 1988.
How I Became a Writer: A Late Start. Chapel Hill, N.C.: Algonquin Books, 1989.
Big Bad Love. Chapel Hill, N.C.: Algonquin Books, 1990.

Critical Studies

Farmer, Joy A. "The Sound and the Fury of Larry Brown's 'Waiting for the Ladies.'" *Studies in Short Fiction* 29, no. 3 (summer 1992): 315–322.
Ketchin, Susan. "Proceeding Out from Calamity: An Interview with Larry Brown." In Susan Ketchin, ed., *The Christ-Haunted Landscape: Faith and Doubt in Southern Fiction,* pp. 126–139. Jackson: University of Mississippi Press, 1994.
LaRue, Dorie. "Interview with Larry Brown: Breadloaf '92." *Chattahoochee Review* 13, no. 3 (1993): 39–56.
Richardson, Thomas J. "Larry Brown." In Joseph M. Flora and Robert Bain, eds., *Contemporary Fiction Writers of the South: A Bio-Biographical Sourcebook*, pp. 54–65. Westport, Conn.: Greenwood Press, 1993.

ERSKINE CALDWELL
(1903–1987)

Erskine Caldwell is primarily remembered, perhaps unjustly, as the author of novels and stories about southern poor whites and their lusty appetites. He came to national attention after a highly successful dramatic adaptation of his novel *Tobacco Road* (1932) opened on Broadway in 1933 (he did not write the adaptation). The play went on to become the longest-running in Broadway history at the time, closing in 1941, and Caldwell became one of the best-selling authors in American history, mostly through twenty-five-cent paperbacks featuring semiclad women on the covers.

Caldwell was born in Georgia to an Associate Reformed Presbyterian minister father and a schoolteacher mother. Because of his father's position, he traveled widely and lived throughout the South as a child. Reverend Caldwell was more concerned with social justice than theology, and from him the younger Caldwell gained a sensitivity to the plight of the poor that would be reflected in his writing. *Tobacco Road,* his first novel (two novellas and a story collection preceded it), tells the story of a family of degenerate sharecroppers in Georgia. *God's Little Acre,* Caldwell's biggest seller, followed it the next year. Over a long and productive career, Caldwell published more than two dozen novels, a dozen volumes of nonfiction, and more than 150 short stories in various collections. Once considered by critics to rank with Faulkner among southern writers (Faulkner ranked Caldwell one of the top five living authors in 1945), Caldwell's critical reputation declined rapidly in the 1950s, even as his sales figures continued to climb. Most of his best work was written during the 1930s and bears the mark of the Depression, and all of his short

stories of note were written before the end of World War II. Throughout the 1930s, Caldwell flirted with the Communist Party, as did many other writers, but he continually frustrated the party's desire for fiction that could be used unproblematically as propaganda, prompting one Marxist critic to comment that Caldwell needed to learn that the revolution begins above the belt, a criticism of the way Caldwell's characters are driven by sexual desires more often than by political ones.

Although he is best known for *Tobacco Road* and *God's Little Acre,* many critics consider Caldwell's talents as a writer of short fiction to exceed his skills as a novelist. Some of his stories are little more than anecdotes or extended jokes; however, at their best Caldwell's stories are carefully constructed and haunting. Common themes include racial and social oppression, the dehumanizing effects of poverty, the confrontation of sexuality by an innocent (or not so innocent) character, and regional customs (of both the South and New England, where he lived for several years as an adult), among others.

Like many writers of his generation, Caldwell honed his craft writing short stories for the "little magazines," the often experimental literary journals where writers such as Hemingway and Faulkner published before attracting the attention of major publishers. Because of Caldwell's overt social concerns, though, his formal experimentation is often overlooked. He once commented, "I did a lot of experimental writing. Of the 150 short stories I've written, I doubt if more than two or three are written in the same manner, style, background." Caldwell overstates the extent of his experimentation, but it should be remembered that he sought to do more than present a naturalistic vision of society. One of his most intriguing experiments is a series of three stories, originally published separately in little magazines, then gathered together as the third section of *American Earth* (1931), his first collection of stories, before finally being published as a single entity under the title *The Sacrilege of Alan Kent* (1936). The "story" consists of dozens of brief numbered segments (sometimes as short as a single sentence, other times a brief paragraph) that chronicle the life of Alan Kent from his birth to adulthood and his various quests to find meaning in his lonely life. The form echoes Kent's fragmented sense of self and life. Stylistically, the story is unlike anything else Caldwell ever wrote. Its vignettes read like Imagist prose: "Once the sun was so hot a bird came down and walked beside me in my shadow." "When the woman who told fortunes went crazy, we had to carry her into another tent and cut her throat there." Seeking to label the unusual piece, critics have called it a prose poem. As Guy Owen shows, the work anticipates many of the themes to which Caldwell would return in his later work, but it does so in a strangely successful form to which he would never return.

More typical of the experimentation Caldwell was attempting with his stories is his fascination with repetition. Perhaps no American writer other than Gertrude Stein has used repetition as an aesthetic device as well as Caldwell. As Scott MacDonald has shown, Caldwell uses repe-

tition in a variety of ways, among them, to create erotic excitement, for humorous effect, to maintain a deceptively simple narrative form, and to bring to the fore sublimated threats of violence, among other uses.

In "August Afternoon," Caldwell uses repetition to great effect, although the story is more of an anecdote than a fully developed plot. Vic Glover is awakened by his black helper, Hubert, who informs him that while he was napping a young man had arrived and begun flirting with Vic's young bride (she is fifteen; he is much older). Roused from his nap, Vic surveys the scene. His scantily clad wife sits on the porch "showing her pretty" while the virile intruder sits in the yard whittling a stick and watching her. As Hubert informs Vic, he is afraid something is going to happen when the man whittles the stick down to nothing. The repeated references to the shrinking stick, the intruder's nonchalant flipping of the knife, and Hubert's refrain of "we ain't aiming to have no trouble today, is we?" all combine to create a highly charged atmosphere of impending violence and sexuality. As the phallic stick is whittled down, Vic's impotence to stop the inevitable act of infidelity becomes apparent. Unable even to attempt preventing his wife from running off with the stranger for a very audible encounter across the field, Vic repeatedly threatens the scared Hubert should he slip off, an understated and effective statement about the relationship between racial oppression and sexuality. In frustration, Vic pounds the porch with a large metal stick, paralleling the beating with which he constantly threatens Hubert. The story ends with Vic lying down to return to his nap, content in his belief that his wife "acts that way because she ain't old enough yet to know who to fool with. She'll catch on in time."

One of Caldwell's most successful experiments is "Candy-Man Beechum," an attempt to capture the rhythm and feel of African American folk speech without resorting to the potentially racist implications of dialect represented by phonetic spelling. The simple plot involves a black man walking ten miles to see his "gal" after work on Saturday: "Make way for these flapping feet, boy, because I'm going for to see my gal. She's standing on the tips of her toes waiting for me now." In his single-minded quest Candy-Man takes on almost mythic, Paul Bunyan-like proportions as he strides along taking hills in a single bound and attracting followers in awe of his determination. Even when stopped by a white policeman who threatens to take him in as a potential troublemaker, Candy-Man refuses to have his spirit broken, even though it may cost him his life, as the ending of the story hints.

Perhaps Caldwell's best story is "Kneel to the Rising Sun" (1935). Lonnie, a white tenant farmer, comes to his landlord, Arch Gunnard, seeking more food for his starving family. Intimidated by Arch and unable to articulate his complaint about Arch's short-rationing, Lonnie can only watch as Arch cuts off the tail of Lonnie's hound dog, adding it to a trunk of such trophies. Lonnie wishes he could be more like Clem Henry, a fellow tenant farmer who, although he is black, stands up to Arch and demands food for his family when short-rationed. Arch's inhumane treatment of his tenants is emphasized when Lonnie's father, driven by hunger and hoping to sneak into the smokehouse one night, falls into Arch's pigpen, where the well-fed hogs eat him alive. When Lonnie is unable to confront Arch, Clem takes up the cause, implying that Arch bears some responsibility for the old man's death. When Arch physically assaults Clem, the tenant escapes to hide in the woods. Warned not to protect "the nigger," Lonnie reveals where Clem is hiding to the lynch mob Arch has assembled. He even joins the mob, becoming progressively animalistic, scrambling nearly on all fours ahead of the group like a hound on a hunt. Following a graphic lynching scene, the story ends with Lonnie stumbling back to his home and wife.

The story raises questions about the interplay of race and class and the difficulty of organized resistance. When Lonnie reveals Clem's location, he chooses race loyalty over class loyalty and friendship, bringing to the fore the problems leftist organizers faced in the Depression South. Although Caldwell's sympathies were certainly with the leftists who sometimes hailed his work in the 1930s, he often frustrated their desires for his work to contain hopeful messages about class action, and "Kneel to the Rising Sun" is no exception. After the lynching Clem seems on the verge of transformation as he kneels, faces the rising sun, and mutters to himself, trying "to say things he had never thought to say before." But when his wife, unaware of the evening's occurrences, asks him to speak to Arch about receiving more rations, Lonnie replies only, "I ain't hungry." It is unclear whether Clem's sacrifice will bring change, whether Lonnie's statement is indicative of a continued fear of confronting Arch, or whether it marks an essential change of perspective that may lead to resistance. More so than most Caldwell stories, "Kneel to the Rising Sun" is rich in symbolism, which, combined with its interesting political and social issues, makes it an ideal story for the classroom. There is the animal imagery that corresponds to the dehumanizing effects of poverty and racism. Clem is described at various times as being Christ-like (he is executed in a tree; the rising sun/son pun; his betrayal by Lonnie who promised him three times he would not reveal his location; his refusal to strike back when Arch hits him).

Brief mention should also be made of *Georgia Boy* (1943), a story cycle that some critics and sometimes Caldwell himself have called his best work. The fourteen stories are narrated by the young William Stroup and center mostly on the often comic, sometimes disturbing, shenanigans of his father, a vagabond prone to womanizing, thievery, drunkenness, and assorted schemes. Much of the power of the cycle comes from the tension between the innocent narrator's obvious admiration for his father and the reader's ability to recognize the negative implications of the father's actions. In *Georgia Boy,* as in many of his stories, Caldwell shifts rapidly from comedy to tragedy, leaving the reader uncertain of the proper response and questioning the relationship between the two. The stories show the influence of both Mark Twain's *Adventures of Huckleberry Finn* and Sherwood Anderson's *Winesburg, Ohio,* presenting an interesting portrait of childhood in a changing South.

Erskine Caldwell's writings fit well into several strands of the American short story. His work moves from the comic as it recalls at times the southwestern humorists of the nineteenth century, to displays of the grotesque commonly associated with southern writers, to social fiction, to the experimental. Caldwell's sparse prose at times belies the emotional impact his stories are capable of delivering. Particular scenes, such Lonnie's discovery of his father in the pigpen, linger with the reader long after the story is finished. He is particularly adept at combining comedy and tragedy in one short piece. His work is also revealing about the way writers in the 1930s attempted to integrate a political and social consciousness into an aesthetic founded on modernist conceptions of art. Though seldom anthologized in recent years, Caldwell deserves a large audience among readers today, who will rediscover the relevance and power of his stories.

Erik A. Bledsoe

SELECTED BIBLIOGRAPHY

Works by Erskine Caldwell

American Earth. New York: Scribner's, 1931.

We Are the Living: Brief Stories. New York: Viking, 1933.

Kneel to the Rising Sun and Other Stories. New York: Viking, 1933.

The Sacrilege of Alan Kent. Portland, Maine: Falmouth, 1936. Reprint, Athens: University of Georgia Press, 1995.

Southways. New York: Viking, 1938.

Jackpot: The Stories of Erskine Caldwell. New York: Duell, Sloan & Pearce, 1940.

Georgia Boy. New York: Duell, Sloan &

Pearce, 1943. Reprint, Athens: University of Georgia Press, 1995.

The Courting of Susie Brown. New York: Duell, Sloan & Pearce/Boston: Little, Brown, 1952.

The Complete Stories of Erskine Caldwell. New York: Duell, Sloan & Pearce/Boston: Little, Brown, 1953. Reprinted as *The Stories of Erskine Caldwell.* Athens: University of Georgia Press, 1996.

Gulf Coast Stories. Boston: Little, Brown, 1956.

Certain Women. Boston: Little, Brown, 1957.

When You Think of Me. Boston: Little, Brown, 1959.

Critical Studies

Cook, Sylvia Jenkins. *Erskine Caldwell and the Fiction of Poverty: The Flesh and the Spirit.* Baton Rouge: Louisiana State University Press, 1991.

Hoag, Ronald Wesley. "Canonize Caldwell's *Georgia Boy*: A Case for Resurrection." *Southern Quarterly* 27/3 (1989): 73–86. Reprinted in Edwin T. Arnold, ed., *Erskine Caldwell Reconsidered*, pp. 73–86. Jackson: University Press of Mississippi, 1990.

MacDonald, Scott. "Repetition as Technique in the Short Stories of Erskine Caldwell." *Studies in Short Fiction* 5 (1977): 213–225. Reprinted in Scott MacDonald, ed., *Critical Essays on Erskine Caldwell*, pp. 330–341. Boston: G. K. Hall, 1981.

Owen, Guy. "*The Sacrilege of Alan Kent* and the Apprenticeship of Erskine Caldwell." *Southern Literary Journal* 12 (1979): 36–46.

HORTENSE CALISHER
(1911–)

The author of more than two dozen novels and novellas, two autobiographical works, and four collections of short stories, Hortense Calisher was born and raised in New York. She grew up in Manhattan's Upper West Side with a younger brother in a uniquely mixed middle-class Jewish family. Her father, Joseph Calisher, was a small-scale manufacturer who had moved from his native Richmond, Virginia, in the 1880s. He was a generous, mild-mannered "Victorian" southerner and a great raconteur, but his temperament and milieu stood in sharpest contrast to those of his wife, a defensively exacting and emotionally withdrawn German émigré twenty-two years his junior. Amplifying the clash of cultural and subcultural worlds, numerous aunts and cousins of both clans were a constant presence in the Calisher household. The colorful and complex interplay among southern, Old World, New York, and Jewish norms, styles, and sensibilities would provide Calisher with everything from the peripheral ambience to the sharply defined focal issues of her best and most characteristic short fiction. Significantly, Calisher clustered as the centerpiece of the *Collected Stories* (1975) her semiautobiographical tales, which feature her fictional alter ego, Hester Elkin.

Graduating from Barnard (1932) with a bachelor of arts degree in English and a minor in philosophy, Calisher found work as an emergency relief investigator in Depression-stricken New York. In 1935, she married Heaton Heffelfinger, an engineer, and devoted herself over the next dozen years to raising a daughter (Bennet Hughes) and a son (Peter Heffelfinger) while continually struggling to reestablish her household as her husband followed work opportunities from one industrial city to another. ("The Rabbi's Daughter" is a short story that affectingly depicts how such dislocation challenges the strengths and hopes of an artistically talented young mother.) Although when she was professionally established Calisher traveled and taught widely, she remained a lifelong resident of New York and the Hudson Valley region north of the city, environments that provide the settings of the bulk of her fiction.

Calisher's writing career began in 1948 when at thirty-seven she placed "A Box of Ginger" with *The New Yorker*. Over the next half century, she published short fiction, essays, and reviews in *The Reporter, The New Yorker, Harper's, The Saturday Evening Post, American Scholar, Kenyon Review,* and in a variety of small literary periodicals. Her first book, *In the Absence of Angels* (1951), established her reputation as a significant figure in American letters. An impressive collection of fifteen tales, the volume includes "The Middle Drawer" (a 1949 O. Henry Prize winner and by any measure one of the author's finest stories), "A Box of Ginger," and the prominently anthologized "In Greenwich There Are Many Graveled Walks." During the 1950s, Calisher continued to produce short fiction of exemplary literary merit, with "A Christmas Carillon" and "What a Thing, to Keep a Wolf in a Cage" taking O. Henry

prizes in 1955 and 1958. In addition, she worked on a first novel, spent time in England on two Guggenheim fellowships (1952, 1955), traveled to Southeast Asia on a Department of State grant (1958), and taught briefly at Barnard (1956–57), Stanford (1958), and the University of Iowa (1957, 1959–60). Calisher divorced her first husband in the 1950s and in 1959 married the novelist Curtis Harnack, whom she met at Iowa. The decades since her fiftieth year have seen the publication of all of Calisher's novels, collected novellas, memoirs, and the balance of her short stories. (In 1964, "The Scream on Fifty-seventh Street," a Jamesian study of loneliness, was yet another O. Henry Prize winner.) In the 1960s and 1970s Calisher taught at a number of colleges and universities, and she received awards from the National Council of Arts (1967) and the American Academy of Arts and Letters (1967). More recently, Calisher was awarded honorary doctorates by Skidmore (1980), Grinnell (1986), and Hofstra (1988); won the Kafka Prize (1987); and served as president of American PEN (1986–87) and of the American Academy and Institute (1987–89).

As a novelist, Calisher exhibits a range that is surprising if, for some, disconcerting. Novels such as *False Entries* (1961) and *The New Yorkers* (1969), its "companion piece," subtly chronicle the reflective life and painful development of marginalized characters in evocatively observed historical and social, typically urban, contexts. On the other hand, Calisher ventures into extraterrestrial zones with space fantasies such as *Journal from Ellipsia* (1965) and *Mysteries of Motion* (1983) that iconoclastically examine the inner sense of what it is to be human. ("Heartburn," which oddly reverses a familiar fairy-tale motif, is an early Calisher fantasy fitted to the scale of the short story.) If the novels have received a mixed critical reception, the novellas—*Saratoga, Hot* (1985) and the exquisite *Age* (1987) among the most notable—have fared considerably better. Readers of Calisher savor her longer fictions for their figuratively rich and allusive linguistic texture, their social-historical realism, and for the author's virtually prismatic psychological and perceptual acumen in delineating character and situation.

Stylistically, Calisher's short stories tend to incorporate the strengths of her novels and novellas, concentrated in a tighter, more compellingly plotted form. Finely turned sentences like this one, from the title piece of *In the Absence of Angels*, suggest why critics remain divided over the readability of Calisher's work and why she is often classed as a writer's writer:

Mostly, they were pleasantly favored women who had never worked before marriage, or tended to conceal it if they had, whose minds were not so much stupid as unaroused—women at whom the menopause or the defection of growing children struck suddenly in the soft depths of their inarticulateness, leaving them distraught, melancholy, even deranged, to make the rounds of the doctors until age came blessedly, turning them leathery but safe.

While one critic finds this "lavish prose that tends toward surfeit" (Bruce Allen), another regards it as "humming elo-

quence" that evinces a "subtle knowingness," prose that is a "prism of sensibility" (Morris Dickstein). If most of Calisher's phrasing is not quite so complex, she regularly achieves the same effect with great economy, as in this ten-word sentence: "The nude walls poured from ceiling to floor, regarding her" ("The Gulf Between"). Though some readers object to her story lines as "often fragile, if nonexistent," Calisher has an aesthetic orientation that suggests an approach to her art which moots such criticism: "A story," she argues, "may float like an orb, spread like a fan or strike its parallel ceaselessly on the page—as long as its clues cohere. Language itself may *be* the idea" (Introduction to *Collected Stories*).

In Calisher's most memorable short stories—and it is likely that her reputation as a literary artist will rest principally on her accomplishment in this genre—language becomes a luminous instrument of insight and revelation. For instance, in "The Gulf Between," her story of dislocation and the attendant emergence of mature understanding in twelve-year-old Hester, Calisher sketches a vignette that depicts Hester's sense of the gulf between her parents: "On the one side stood her mother, the denying one, the unraveler of other people's facades, but resolute and forceful by her very lack of some dimension; on the other side stood her father, made weak by his awareness of others, carrying like a phylactery the burden of his kindliness. And flawed with their difference, she felt herself falling endlessly, soundlessly, in the gulf between." Throughout the story, Calisher deftly articulates Hester's formative experience of defining gulfs, gulfs that irremediably separate expectation from fact, ideals from realities, childhood from adulthood, and the living from the dying.

"The Middle Drawer," one of Calisher's strongest pieces, unforgettably traces Hester's painfully transcending the existential gulfs that have conditioned her sensibility. Now a mother herself, she sits on her recently deceased mother's bed and contemplates opening a locked bureau drawer of valuables and mementos. This act, she knows, would reveal "only the painful reiteration of her mother's personality and the power it had held over her own." Although the plot is parablelike in its simplicity and spareness, the narrative exposes the intense, complex, and painful relationship between Hester and her mother, different phases of which appear in other stories such as "The Coreopsis Kid," "Old Stock," and "The Gulf Between." The opening sentences of "The Middle Drawer" establish, compellingly and with Jamesian intricacy, the narrative and psychological frame of the story. They masterfully convey the sense of invading a forbidden zone and discovering a known tragic quantity of oneself linked inexorably with the dead: "The drawer was always kept locked. In a household where the tangled rubbish of existence had collected on surfaces like a scurf, which was forever being cleared away by her mother and the maid, then by her mother, and, finally, hardly at all, it had been a permanent cell—rather like, Hester thought wryly, the gene that is carried over from one generation to the other."

Hester, "facing the drawer," reflects on what she knew it to contain over the years and on the associations that items stored within it had with the sources and con-

sequences of her unmotherly mother's "deep burning rage against life." The theme of scarring as an inescapable emotional inheritance from mother to daughter informs much of Hester's revelatory reminiscing; and it reaches a climactic, symbolically pregnant expression as Hester recalls secretly viewing and tracing with her fingertips the scar, hidden from others like an item in the middle drawer, that a cancer operation left on her mother's chest. Hester's reaction had been typically complex: she stood "eye to eye" with her mother, "on equal ground at last." She felt "a hurt in her own breast that she did not recognize," realized at last that her mother was always vulnerable, "As we all are." She discovered, moreover, that "what she bequeathed me unwittingly, ironically, was fortitude—the fortitude of those who have had to live under the blow." The story ends as Hester "turned the key and opened the drawer."

The most accomplished of Calisher's short fiction that is not overtly autobiographical commonly explores the facets of loneliness, particularly the pathos of older people whose estrangement is desperate, if unacknowledged. "The Scream on Fifty-seventh Street," perhaps the best known of these, concerns a recently widowed woman living alone in a city apartment. The action focuses on her attempt to determine the source of a scream that she hears at night, a scream that turns out to be her own. "What a Thing, to Keep a Wolf in a Cage" is another such story, and one of several that Calisher sets in Europe. The protagonist is a female American professor on sabbatical in Rome, a widow who has left her two boys at a boarding school at home. Her profound loneliness comes dramatically to the fore when, observing an older, married actress pick up a younger man at a bar, she climactically realizes that her life alone as a mother and teacher leaves an essential part of her caged: "something rammed itself hard against her chest, inside. Not enough, it said, beating behind the mapped crease between the breasts. Not enough."

Hortense Calisher's best short stories are signal achievements. However, while they initially garnered their fair share of critical acclaim, they have elicited little in the way of detailed scholarly appreciation or popular esteem over the decades. This neglect is lamentable, inasmuch as Calisher's work in the genre frequently rises to a level of stylistic virtuosity, psychosocial acuity, and nuanced pathos that one typically encounters only in the most celebrated productions of the literary imagination.

Phillip Stambovsky

SELECTED BIBLIOGRAPHY

Works by Hortense Calisher

In the Absence of Angels: Stories. Boston: Little, Brown, 1951.
Tale for the Mirror: A Novella and Other Stories. Boston: Little, Brown, 1962.
Extreme Magic: A Novella and Other Stories. Boston: Little, Brown, 1963.
The Collected Stories of Hortense Calisher. New York: Arbor House, 1975.

Critical Studies

Murphy, Christina. "Hortense Calisher." In Frank N. Magill, ed., *Critical Survey of Short Fiction,* vol. 3, pp. 1034–1040. Englewood Cliffs, N.J.: Prentice-Hall, 1981.
Penden, William. *The American Short Story: Continuity and Change 1940–1975.* Boston: Houghton Mifflin, 1975.
Snodgrass, Kathleen. *The Fiction of Hortense Calisher.* Newark: University of Delaware Press, 1993.

TRUMAN CAPOTE
(1924–1984)

Truman Capote was born Truman Streckfus Persons on September 30, 1924, in New Orleans. His parents, Arch and Lillie Mae (Faulk) Persons, soon separated, and Truman was placed—or abandoned—in various relatives' households, including that of four unmarried Faulk cousins in small-town Monroeville, Alabama. (Like their neighbor Nelle Harper Lee, who would go on to write *To Kill a Mockingbird,* these cousins figure prominently in Capote's writing.) After her divorce Lillie Mae married a Cuban businessman, Joseph Garcia Capote, in 1932, and Truman, to his father's dismay, took Capote's name. In 1935 the boy moved to New York City to join the Capotes and, after an unhappy education and a stint as a clerk at *The New Yorker,* began to write seriously.

Capote first attracted professional attention in the 1940s with his short fiction, collected in *A Tree of Night and Other Stories* (1949), and his debut semiautobiographical novel, *Other Voices, Other Rooms* (1948), published by Random House with a scandalously provocative photograph of the impish young author on the dust jacket. His wistful second novel, *The Grass Harp* (1951), also draws upon memories of his bittersweet southern childhood but minimizes the homoeroticism of *Other Voices, Other Rooms*. Capote's subsequent longer fiction includes *Breakfast at Tiffany's* (1958), a novella about the spirited Holly Golightly, who, like Capote's mother, masks her rural past to thrive in uninhibited cosmopolitan circles; and *Answered Prayers* (1984), the long-germinating but unfinished roman à clef about the rich and famous. (When *Esquire* published sordid early chapters in the mid-1970s, a chorus of wealthy socialites whom Capote termed his "swans" felt he had betrayed their secrets, and the women largely ostracized their former confidant and darling.)

Capote's literary reputation rests equally—if not more so—on his nonfiction, which he also began writing in the 1940s. He brought early travel pieces together in *Local Color* (1950), while he collected biographical sketches depicting such notables as Marlon Brando, Isak Dinesen, Mae West, Pablo Picasso, Louis Armstrong, Humphrey Bogart, and Marilyn Monroe in *Observations* (1959) and *The Dogs Bark: Public People and Private Places* (1973). Capote's first extended work of reportage was *The Muses Are Heard* (1956), a comic account of a trip to Russia by an African American cast of *Porgy and Bess*. It also anticipates what many consider his masterpiece, *In Cold Blood* (1966), a self-proclaimed "nonfiction novel" detailing the brutal 1959 murder of a Kansas family by Dick Hickock and Perry Smith and their resulting imprisonment and execution. Like works by Norman Mailer and Tom Wolfe, *In Cold Blood* and *Handcarved Coffins* (1979), another ostensible true-crime account, were pivotal texts in the New Journalism, a more "literary" style of reporting freed from traditional objectivity. With less success Capote also experimented with stage adaptations of his fiction— *The Grass Harp* (1952) and *House of Flowers* (1954, revised 1968)—and with screenplays—*Beat the Devil* (1953) and *The Innocents* (1961).

Despite periodic returns to the South, Capote considered New York his home after relocating there as a boy; however, he often lived in Europe and North Africa for extended periods, typically traveling until the late 1960s with his longtime companion, Jack Dunphy. As Capote aged, he grew increasingly addicted to alcohol, drugs, and disastrous romantic and sexual liaisons, as he famously acknowledges in his self-interview "Nocturnal Turnings": "I'm an alcoholic. I'm a drug addict. I'm homosexual. I'm a genius. . . . But I shonuf ain't no saint yet." He nevertheless remained a prominent public figure until his overdose-induced death in California on August 25, 1984.

This drugged, bloated Capote stands in marked contrast to the captivating boy who burst onto the American literary scene when *Mademoiselle* published his short story "Miriam" in June 1945. The haunting tale charmed readers, and others quickly followed in the magazine: "Jug of Silver," "Children on Their Birthdays," "A Christmas Memory," and "House of Flowers." *Harper's Bazaar*, competing with *Mademoiselle* to publish quality fiction, retaliated with Capote's "Master Misery," "The

Headless Hawk," "A Tree of Night," and "A Diamond Guitar." Although their form and content vary, many of these early stories link Capote to writers of the mid-century southern gothic school, such as William Faulkner, Carson McCullers, Tennessee Williams, and Flannery O'Connor. Capote's gothic stories are unique, however, in that they are usually set in a nightmarish New York City rather than the rural South.

Also reminiscent of Nathaniel Hawthorne's fiction, these stories have a singular focus in which grotesque freaks or sinister outsiders, often variations of a mysterious "wizard man," invade the lives of unsuspecting everyday people and disrupt their sanity and sense of identity. "Miriam," for example, features the macabre, unblinking, and perhaps nonexistent title character who torments an unassuming widow, while "The Headless Hawk" chronicles a lonely art dealer's perverse fascination with a bizarre painter who is in turn haunted by the sinister Mr. Destronelli. Similarly, A. F. Revercomb so mesmerizes the protagonist of "Master Misery" that she sells him her dreams despite sensing that she is slowly bargaining away her soul. Showing McCullers's particular influence, "A Tree of Night" depicts a garish dwarf and her leering mute companion's terrifying symbolic violation of a young woman traveling with them on a train. But perhaps the most dismal is "Shut a Final Door," which recounts how the loveless Walter Ranney is terrorized by a stranger's persistent phone calls in retribution for his thoughtless cruelties. A bleak view of humanity emerges here, as in most of these stories, and Capote asserts that ultimately "all our acts are acts of fear."

In contrast to these gothic tales, "Jug of Silver," "Children on Their Birthdays," and "My Side of the Matter" are light stories set in the small-town South that anticipate The Grass Harp in temper and tone. The first culminates in a poor boy's elation when he successfully guesses the amount of money in a glass jar, while the second, despite beginning and ending with the protagonist's violent death, focuses on two teenage boys' humorous competition for the attention of the aloof Miss Lily Jane Bobbit, a forerunner of Holly Golightly. The most comic, however, is "My Side of the Matter." Plundering the early married life of Capote's parents and resembling Eudora Welty's "Why I Live at the P.O." in structure and effect, the story features an unreliable narrator who reveals his own foibles as he tells how he enters the chaotic household of his wife's extended family as a newlywed.

Later stories tend to defy these two neat categories. "House of Flowers" draws on Capote's 1948 visit to the Caribbean and adopts a fairy tale's simplified form and detached tone to relate the courtship and marriage of Royal Bonaparte and a beautiful Haitian prostitute, Ottilie. A male prison sets "A Diamond Guitar," in which Tico Feo, owner of the guitar, betrays an older fellow inmate's affections. With its action confined to a Queens cemetery, "Among the Paths to Eden" at first seems akin to the earlier gothic tales, but crippled Mary O'Meaghan's desperate attempts to catch a husband among visiting widowers are far more touching and less horrifying than the events of "Miriam" and "A Tree of Night." And the much later "Mojave," originally conceived as a fiction within the larger fiction of Answered Prayers, is like no other Capote short story. Published in *Esquire* in 1975 to significant acclaim, it recounts the dispiriting details of a promiscuous socialite marriage of appearances.

But of his shorter pieces, Capote is perhaps best remembered for his memoirs of childhood in Monroeville and elsewhere, writing that blurs the lines between fiction and nonfiction. "A Christmas Memory," first published in 1956 and later adapted to film, details his relationship with Sook Faulk, the gentle cousin who also bases *The Grass Harp*'s Dolly Talbo. Written in the present tense, the moving first-person narration recounts the duo's final Christmas together, ending with memories of Sook's death. Although less elegiac, "The Thanksgiving Visitor" and the stilted "One Christmas," Capote's last story, similarly focus on Sook's humane influence in a less than welcoming household and larger world, while "Dazzle" rehearses the author's childhood desire to be a girl. These accounts reveal an unabashedly nostalgic writer perhaps guilty of romanticizing the past.

As with these memoir-stories, many of Capote's other later short pieces seem neither traditional fiction nor purely nonfiction. Typical of the New Journalism, these works include the author as a character, whether central or virtually stripped of identity as he reports on the doings of others. Therefore, when form is considered, these supposedly nonfiction pieces are amazingly similar to several of the early short stories, as all of the works are detached first-person narratives relayed with an attention to clarity. Moreover, as critics have shown, Capote frequently alters factual reporting to enhance the artistry. That is, he often does not "tell truth" but rather "what ought to be truth," as Tennessee Williams's Blanche DuBois phrases it. Nevertheless, although Capote even referred to these works as short stories, Random House editors labeled them "essays" in the posthumous reader. These pieces, such as "Music for Chameleons," "A Lamp in the Window," and "A Day's Work," were first collected in *Music for Chameleons* (1980).

Although Capote considered himself unjustly slighted of major literary prizes, both "Miriam" and "Shut a Final Door" won O. Henry awards. Today his corpus of amazingly diverse texts, ranging from the maudlin to the macabre, continues to interest general readers and critics alike, particularly as emerging literary trends provide new contexts in which to examine these works. The early gothic stories, for instance, with their wedding of the supernatural and the psychological, seem all the more relevant in light of similar preoccupations in the works of later writers such as Gabriel Gárcia Márquez and Toni Morrison. And, as a stylist, Capote remains a model of precision and clarity, perhaps even justifying Norman Mailer's assessment in *Advertisements for Myself* that "word for word, rhythm upon rhythm," Truman Capote "is the most perfect writer of my generation."

Gary Richards

SELECTED BIBLIOGRAPHY

Works by Truman Capote

A Tree of Night and Other Stories. New York: Random House, 1949.

Breakfast at Tiffany's: A Short Novel and Three Stories. New York: Random House, 1958.

Selected Writings. New York: Random House, 1963.

The Thanksgiving Visitor. New York: Random House, 1968.

Music for Chameleons. New York: Random House, 1980.

One Christmas. New York: Random House, 1983.

Critical Studies

Clarke, Gerald. *Capote: A Biography.* New York: Simon & Schuster, 1988.

Garson, Helen S. *Truman Capote: A Study of the Short Fiction.* New York: Twayne, 1992.

Reed, Kenneth T. *Truman Capote.* Boston: Twayne, 1981.

RAYMOND CARVER
(1938 – 1988)

Raymond Carver was born in the logging town of Clatskanie, Oregon, on May 25, 1938, the first child of Ella Beatrice Casey, a waitress, and Cleve Raymond Carver, a sawmill worker. He grew up in Washington and California; at nineteen he married sixteen-year-old Maryann Burk, and they had two children before he was twenty-one. To support his family, Carver worked as a pharmacy deliveryman, janitor, salesman, mill hand, store clerk, and textbook editor. He attended Chico State College (where he studied writing with the novelist John Gardner) and then Humboldt State College, from which he graduated in 1963. During this period he was regularly writing poetry and short fiction. Soon afterward he published two small-press books of poems, and several of his stories were chosen for prestigious annual prize collections.

Despite these accomplishments, Carver's life in the late 1960s and early 1970s was peripatetic and bitterly frustrating. As he later said, "we were just looking for a place where I could write and my wife and two children could be happy. It didn't seem like too much to ask for. But we never found it." He worked continually at odd jobs, taught briefly at three University of California campuses and at the Iowa Writers' Workshop, filed twice for bankruptcy, drank heavily, was often hospitalized for acute alcoholism, and finally separated from his wife.

In 1976, however, his first story collection, *Will You Please Be Quiet, Please?*, published by McGraw Hill, received praise for illuminating the exposed lives of the working poor "without condescension or sentimentality," and the next year was nominated for a National Book Award. At this point, Carver entered what he often called "my second life." He stopped drinking, got divorced, married the poet Tess Gallagher, and settled into a steadfast career as a writer and teacher. In 1978 and 1980, he received fellowships from the Guggenheim Foundation and the National Endowment for the Arts, and with the 1981 publication of *What We Talk About When We Talk About Love,* he was recognized as one of the most innovative and influential of contemporary American short story writers. As Frank Kermode observed, "Carver's fiction is so spare in manner that it takes a time before one realizes how completely a whole culture and a whole moral condition is represented by even the most seemingly slight sketch. This second volume of stories is clearly the work of a full-grown master."

In 1983, with the support of a five-year Straus fellowship from the American Academy and Institute of Arts of Letters, Carver resigned from teaching and devoted himself full-time to writing. *Cathedral,* his third major collection of stories, was published in 1983. In the fall of 1987, Carver was diagnosed with lung cancer, and, following operations and chemotherapy, he died on August 2, 1988, at his home in Port Angeles, Washington. *Where I'm Calling From: New and Selected Stories* appeared to great acclaim three months before his death.

The stories in *Will You Please Be Quiet, Please?* are graphic yet skewed renderings of the small-town, working-class world of Carver's early manhood. Set in the Pacific Northwest and Northern California, they dramatize unexpected, often menacing moments in the lives of what an early reader called people on the outs—out of work, out of luck, out of sorts, out of touch— solitary men and women hemmed-in by unlikable, dead-end jobs and chronic insecurities about money, sex, and family obligation. To write about what he called "my people" (unexceptional laborers, salesmen, mechanics, waitresses, mailmen, clerks), Carver perfected an unadorned, uninflected prose: short, simple declarative sentences devoid of authorial commentary, lush detail, or metaphorical flourish—a language precisely calibrated to register dearth, drabness, futility, need.

Given their brevity and bone-dry style, stories such as "They're Not Your Husband," "What's in Alaska?" "Collectors," or "What Do You Do in San Francisco?" were quickly labeled "Mimimalist," "Dirty Realist," "K-Mart Fiction," and linked to work by an emerging group of contemporary writers (Ann Beattie, Richard Ford, Frederick Barthelme) who often represented the impoverishments and barely submerged violence of late twentieth-century American life by portraying laconic characters in a flat, unforthcoming style. The tags, however, are misleading, for Carver's chiseled prose has always been more resonant than these labels imply. As Ann Beattie herself noted, his matter-of-factness, his quiet observation "gains power as the events become increasingly odd and discomfiting." In 1998, a controversy erupted about the influence of Carver's editor, Gordon Lish, on the shaping of Carver's early style.

The early story, "Fat," for instance, begins with these simple yet disorientating words:

> I am sitting over coffee and cigarettes at my friend Rita's and I am telling her about it.
>
> Here is what I tell her.
>
> It is late of a slow Wednesday when Herb seats the fat man at my station.

In the six pages that follow, the waitress describes the night she served the fattest man she had ever laid eyes on, a huge, neatly dressed, uncommonly polite, puffing stranger who orders and eats a dozen courses, consuming at the same time basketsful of bread served with butter. Although Rudy, the cook, and the other restaurant workers snicker about "old-tub-of-guts" and "the fat man from the circus," the waitress admits from the start that she intuits something extraordinary going on. Stunned by the sight of his "long, thick, creamy fingers" and enormous appetite, she keeps registering her fascination with the uniqueness of the occasion, confessing, "I know now I was after something but I don't know what."

At the story's close, the waitress explains to Rita that after returning home with her boyfriend, Rudy, she felt preoccupied and estranged. In bed, when Rudy made love to her, she suddenly felt fat, "terrifically fat, so fat that Rudy is a tiny thing and hardly there at all."

> I feel depressed. But I won't go into it with her. I've already told her too much.
> She sits there waiting . . . .
> *Waiting for what?* I'd like to know.
> It is August.
> My life is going to change. I feel it.

By the end, a commonplace anecdote has turned into a haunting, disconcerting piece of self-exposure and only partially understood self-discovery. In the waitress's mind, the fat man has become an emblem of the abundance and promise that is absent from her life, but for which she intensely, inchoately yearns. She tells Rita the story because she senses its implications, but unable to express its full meaning, she feels balked, irritable, let

down. Nevertheless, she insists on asserting the prospect of her life's changing for the better. As Carver remarked to an interviewer: "She can't make sense out of the story herself, all of the feelings she's experienced, but she goes ahead and tells it anyway."

The compulsion to tell about an unsettling event one does not understand is the generative impulse behind many of Carver's best early stories, among them such monologues as "Nobody Said Anything," "So Much Water Close to Home," and "What We Talk About When We Talk About Love." Even some fine works not told in the first person have a similar structure. At the end of "Neighbors" and "Why Don't You Dance?" characters are baffled by the meaning of the bizarre incidents in which they have just participated, events that frighten them or elude their customary categories of understanding.

Unlike James Joyce's famous epiphanies in *Dubliners*, or the startling gestural moments in tales by Flannery O'Connor, the denouement in a Carver story is more like a confounding than a revelation. An unforeseen event intrudes into the daily routine of an ordinary person and brings with it a perplexed, shivery apprehension of more mysterious and alarming things than the character customarily perceives or feels, or has the language to express. But at the end of the story something happens, or the characters respond in such a way that, despite an awkwardness in the face of meaning, a previously unacknowledged possibility is disclosed—if not to the character, then to the reader. Part of the impact of stories like "Fat" comes from Carver's talent for locating reserves of resistance and dignity in lives that on the surface appear forlorn, even hopeless. As Michael Wood has shrewdly pointed out, Carver makes "audible the eloquence of the seemingly inarticulate. It's not that he lends speech to his characters or talks on their behalf. He hears what they are saying when the words run out."

Having perfected this kind of terse, reverberating cameo story in his first two major collections, Carver went on to create an even more remarkable kind of fiction in the last decade of his life. The cast of characters and the settings of most of his later stories remain the same, but the plain people are given more words, more evocative gestures, and a wider range of reactions to the adversities of their lives. Pluck, humor, magnanimity, and a savviness about their bleak condition lead more often than not to hard-won, delicately qualified affirmations.

At least six of the stories from the 1980s are likely to have enduring appeal: "Where I'm Calling From," "Feathers," "Cathedral," "A Small, Good Thing," "Elephant," and "Errand." Each is a singular achievement in its own right: "Errand" an exquisite evocation of the death of Anton Chekhov and a young bellman's instinctive tribute to the great writer; "Elephant," a comic fable about the enigmas of altruism and compassion; "A Small, Good Thing," a generous tale about grief and human connection in the face of the ambiguous malignity of fate: and "Feathers," a wickedly comic account of the energizing power of the grotesque.

Of this group, two stories may serve to illustrate some of the most memorable characteristics of Carver's mature fiction. The narrator of "Where I'm Calling From" is a recovering drunk swapping an-

ecdotes with a fellow named J. P. on the front porch of a detox center during the last days of December. In a voice grittily realistic but dryly funny, he casually describes the daily routine of blackouts, shakes and seizures (of looking up "at somebody's fingers in your mouth"); and yet he manages to spot lifelines that reconnect him to the world outside. Narrative is the form these connections continually take. He prods J. P. to keep talking about his infatuation with, courtship of, and marriage to a beguiling chimneysweep named Roxy, a story J. P. interrupts with a lyrical recollection of having fallen to the bottom of a dry well when he was twelve. As these riveting tales are told, the narrator's own stark history seeps through. Recently tossed out by his wife, he is now involved with a woman who has "a mouthy teenaged son," a worrisome Pap smear report, and her own drinking problem. With troubles shadowing his mind, he talks away the time with his friend. On New Year's Day, when Roxy comes to visit and demonstrates her love for J. P., the narrator asks for, and gets, a good luck kiss, and then inexplicably recalls a funny incident when he had appeared naked at his bedroom window early on a Sunday morning to confront his house-painting landlord, who grinned and prompted him to return to bed with his wife.

The sweet kiss and warm memory induce him to consider phoning his wife and girlfriend. He thinks warily about the mouthy kid and a desolate Jack London story he read in high school. "This guy in the Yukon is freezing. Imagine it—he's actually going to freeze to death if he can't get a fire going. . . . He gets his fire going, but then something happens to it. A branchful of snow drops on it. It goes out. Meanwhile, it's getting colder. Night is coming on." Reaching for coins in his pocket, he thinks of calling his wife first, resolving not to react if she lectures him. Maybe, though, he'll call his girlfriend first, hoping not to get the kid on the line. "'Hello, sugar,' I'll say when she answers. 'It's me.'"

The unmistakable Carver signature here is the somber yet slyly playful balance between the ominous and the comic, chill and warmth. Night *is* coming on; but the imperiled narrator gets his fire going by a homely assertion of intimacy—a gesture that reveals tenderness, vulnerability, and a last vestige of self-respect.

A similar poise and complexity is evident in "Cathedral," one of the most admired of all Carver's stories. Here another unnamed, "what's to say" kind-of-narrator begins telling us about an event he doesn't look forward to and doesn't understand: the upcoming visit to his house of Robert, a blind friend of his wife. As he explains the background of the friendship and his reluctance to meet the guest, the husband unwittingly betrays a great deal about his own sour and stunted nature: his jealousy, insecurity, suspicion, and self-imposed isolation. In the ten years that have passed since his wife worked for the blind man, they have exchanged audiotapes in which each has spoken intimately about their separate lives: she about a failed first marriage, a suicide attempt, occasional efforts to write poetry, a second husband; he about his brief happy marriage and the cancer that killed his wife. In recounting this history, the narrator obtusely expresses astonishment at

other people's efforts to give voice to inner feelings and cope with loss and grief.

When Robert arrives, the narrator's continued churlishness creates a zany, offbeat humor—breathtakingly cruel and exposing a man more handicapped than his guest. He suggests taking the blind man bowling and asks him which side of the train he sat on when he traveled up the scenic Hudson. As the evening goes on, the trio swaps stories, drinks too much, and engages hilariously in some "serious eating." As Robert becomes increasingly affable and responsive, the grudging husband begins to soften. He proposes that they smoke cannabis; afterward they settle in to watch TV. Frustrated by the absence of any show he likes, they stick with a program about the church in the Middle Ages. As pageants and processions pass, the husband tries unsuccessfully to describe to the blind man what a cathedral is, displaying in the stumbling effort his imaginative poverty and lack of faith. Unexpectedly, Robert suggests that together they draw a cathedral on heavy paper. As one hand guides another, a surprising intimacy and expansion occur. After urging the sighted man to keep his eyes closed, the blind man cries out, "I think you got it," and says, "Take a look. What do you think?" But the husband keeps his eyes shut and to the questions, "Well? Are you looking?" he tells us: "My eyes were still closed. I was in my house. I knew that. But I didn't feel like I was inside anything." And to Robert and us he says, "It's really something."

What is "really something" about the close of "Cathedral" is the way Carver sends us soaring at the same time that he keeps our feet firmly on the ground. One is thrilled that the men *do* achieve an intense moment of kinship and that the narrator should feel himself in a lofty place we assume he has rarely, if ever, occupied. It is lovely to imagine that they glimpse a private idea of God's house that exists only in *their* imaginations. But the reader suspects too that the miracle is likely to be transitory. Both men are high in ways that suggest the imminence of sleep and a return to normal life tomorrow. Yet with that image of joined hands trying to sketch a cathedral, Raymond Carver powerfully conveys the unspoken dreams and yearnings of two ordinary men, and convinces us, if only for a time, that something radiant has been found in everyday life.

Lawrence Graver

SELECTED BIBLIOGRAPHY

Works by Raymond Carver

Will You Please Be Quiet, Please? New York: McGraw Hill, 1976.

What We Talk About When We Talk About Love. New York: Atlantic Monthly Press, 1981.

Cathedral. New York: Atlantic Monthly Press, 1983.

Where I'm Calling From: New and Selected Stories. New York: Atlantic Monthly Press, 1988.

Critical Studies

Campbell, Ewing. *Raymond Carver: A Study of the Short Fiction.* New York: Twayne, 1992.

Gentry, Marshall Bruce, and William L. Stull. *Conversations with Raymond Carver.* Jackson: University of Mississippi Press, 1990.

Max, D. T. "The Carver Chronicles." *New York Times Magazine,* August 9, 1998.

Runyon, Randolph Paul. *Reading Raymond Carver.* Syracuse, N.Y.: Syracuse University Press, 1992.

Wood, Michael. "Stories Full of Edges and Silences." *New York Times Book Review,* April 26, 1981.

WILLA CATHER
(1873 – 1947)

Willa Cather, a novelist and short story writer famous for her portrayal of frontier settlers and artists, is one of the most accessible and at the same time sophisticated writers of the twentieth century. She was born on December 7, 1873, in Virginia, but when she was nine her family moved to Nebraska as pioneer homesteaders. In this prairie state, Scandinavians, Germans, and Bohemians who had recently immigrated outnumbered native-born Americans. After a year, Cather's father abandoned farming and moved the family to Red Cloud, where he became a mortgage and loan broker. In town Cather befriended immigrant girls who worked as servants, and she was exposed to European culture by a German music teacher and Jewish neighbors who encouraged her to use their library. She attended the local high school and then the University of Nebraska in Lincoln (1891–95), where she wrote columns and theatrical reviews for the *Nebraska State Journal* and published her first short stories about the harsh conditions of pioneer farming. After graduating in 1895, she worked as a newspaper writer, first in Pittsburgh from 1896 to 1901, then in New York with *McClure's Magazine* from 1906 to 1912. Her years as a reporter and editor were interrupted by five years of teaching high school in Pittsburgh, during which time she lived at the family home of Isabelle McClung, a beloved friend for whom she later said all her books were written.

Cather's first volumes of verse and fiction appeared while she was still teaching, but it was not until 1912 and the publication of her first novel, *Alexander's Bridge,* that she made the decision to devote all her time to writing. In 1913 she published *O Pioneers!* and continued thereafter to write such novels as *My Ántonia* (1918), *A Lost Lady* (1923), *The Professor's House* (1925), and *Death Comes for the Archbishop* (1927), novels for which she is justly famous. In 1922 *One of Ours,* a novel about World War I, was awarded the Pulitzer Prize. Other awards included the Prix Femina for *Shadows on the Rock* (1931) and medals from the National Institute of Arts and Letters. In 1936 she became the first woman to receive an honorary doctorate from Princeton University. Willa Cather never married, but lived in New York with a companion, Edith Lewis, for more than forty years. She traveled widely in Europe and within North America, to regions of the continent as disparate as the American Southwest and Quebec, drawing on these locales as sources for her fiction. But Nebraska remained the center of her creative life, and she returned there in memory to write "Old Mrs. Harris" (1932), a poignant autobiographical story in which she reimagined her childhood relations with family and neighbors. She died in New York on April 24, 1947.

Willa Cather published three collections of short stories—*The Troll Garden* (1905), *Youth and the Bright Medusa* (1920), and *Obscure Destinies* (1932)—but although she wrote at least sixty-four stories, beginning and ending her career with short fiction, when she prepared her work for Houghton Mifflin's Autographed Edition (1937–40) she chose only eleven of her stories to be reprinted. She regarded most of the early ones, about the bitter life on the Nebraska Divide, as apprenticeship pieces, though Cather scholars have found thematic and stylistic features in these stories that anticipate significant elements in her mature work. Some of the stories are conventional exercises in the kind of fiction that was selling in the magazines of the day, for example, Cather's attempt to write the kind of Oriental tale made fashionable by Bret Harte and Rudyard Kipling. Although she knew nothing firsthand about either Chinese immigrants or San Francisco, she wrote two stories on the subject, "A Son of the Celestial" (1893) and "The Conversion of Sum Loo" (1900), and made a half-Chinese a central, rather sinister character in "The Affair at Grover Station" (1900).

In 1905, *The Troll Garden* included three stories that she would continue to endorse: "Paul's Case," "A Wagner Matinee," and "The Sculptor's Funeral." All three juxtapose the cravings of the imagination against the crude realities of philistine America. "Paul's Case," one of Cather's best-known stories, dramatizes this opposition memorably. Paul is a motherless Pittsburgh schoolboy who detests his teachers and his life at home on respectable Cordelia Street; he spends as much time as possible at Pittsburgh's Carnegie Hall, where he works as an usher, and at the local theater where the lead actor enjoys his attentions. When Paul's father takes him out of school and sends him to work, he embezzles money from the company and takes a train to New York. There for eight glorious days he lives in a luxury hotel surrounded by all the splendid things he has desired during his short life. When he learns from the newspaper that his father is coming to take him home, he throws himself under the wheels of a train. The character of Paul was drawn from Cather's experience as a teacher in Pittsburgh, where she had observed in one of her classes a high-strung youth who was always impressing on his classmates that he had friends among members of the local theater company. The story is imbued with Cather's feelings for New York and the old Waldorf-Astoria Hotel when she made her first trips there.

"Paul's Case," subtitled "A Study in Temperament," is Willa Cather's portrait of the aesthete. Paul is not an aspiring artist—he does not try to sing, act, or paint; rather, he is intoxicated by the power of the arts to transform a drab and ordinary world into something beautiful and full of magic. Cather writes that "it was at the theatre and at Carnegie Hall that Paul really lived. . . . The moment the cracked orchestra beat out the overture from *Martha*, or jerked at the serenade from *Rigoletto*, all stupid and ugly things slid from him, and his senses were deliciously, yet delicately fired." Paul's "hys-

terically defiant manner" and his preference for artifice over nature have led critics to read him as a "study" of a young gay man, an interpretation for which Cather may have left some clues in Paul's physical behavior. When he is in New York he goes out on the town for a night with a freshman from Yale, but the escapade ends in a cool parting that underscores an important motif: that Paul exists alone in his state of enchantment, that he will never be understood, that no one will share his garden of earthly delights. Cather may have intended to portray a gay youth, a character of special contemporary interest, but the story has a timeless appeal as it describes the adolescent's lonely path and the plight of the misfit.

In middle age, at the height of her career, Cather wrote few stories, devoting most of her creative energy to novels. Nonetheless, "Coming, Aphrodite!," the lead story in *Youth and the Bright Medusa*, is a remarkable work of fiction. Set in New York, "Coming, Aphrodite!" is about a passionate love affair between two very different kinds of artists. Don Hedger is an avant-garde painter, living in a garret on Washington Square, who insists on following his own ideas, refusing easy commercial success. His reclusive existence is upset when Eden Bower, a young singer who is seeking fame and material success, rents the room next to his. An open knothole in the partition between Hedger's closet and her room allows him the voyeuristic pleasure of watching the beautiful young woman exercise nude in front of a long gilt mirror. As Hedger crouches in his dark closet watching Eden exercise, the physical sensations of his body and his art are suggestively joined when his "fingers curved as if he were holding a crayon; mentally he was doing the whole figure in a single running line, and the charcoal seemed to explode in his hand at the point where the energy of each gesture was discharged into the whirling disc of light, from a foot or shoulder, from the upthrust chin or the lifted breasts." Nowhere in her fiction was Cather ever as explicit in her portrayal of sexual passion. Indeed, the sexuality seemed so explicit that H. L. Mencken published a bowdlerized version of the story in *Smart Set* in 1920 that dressed the singer in a chiffon wrap and omitted references to her thighs and breasts. Cather shows Hedger and Eden becoming lovers, but she grounds the passion in primitive, mythic references. When Hedger sees Eden exercising in a shower of gold (like Danae being covered by Zeus) he thinks that "a vision out of Alexandria, out of the remote pagan past had bathed itself there in Helianthine fire," and that the girl "had no geographical associations: unless with Crete, or Alexandria, or Veronese's Venice. She was the immortal conception, the perennial theme."

Cather dramatizes the primitive, elemental nature of their sexual passion through one of her characteristic devices—the telling of a story within the larger story. This inner story, about a Mexican-Indian Rain Princess enamored of one of her father's captives, suggests that the bondage Hedger feels to the capricious Eden is linked to large and contending views of art. Eden's ambition for a musical career includes the desire to live in material comfort and be widely admired by the public, while Hedger is determined to experiment and find new

forms of artistic expression. Eden wants him to make money and meet successful, influential artists, but he resists and temporarily leaves her in order to regain the strength of his convictions. When he returns a few days later, she is gone, leaving him with his painting and "the loneliness of a whole lifetime."

The story ends with another of Cather's characteristic writing features, the creation of a temporal framework that puts the main action somewhere in the past. This distance in time has already been hinted at in the narrative with phrases such as "in those days" and references to hotels "long since passed away," but time present and the meaning of the story become clearly marked when Eden Bower returns to New York to star in *Aphrodite* and remembers her love affair with the painter eighteen years before. Here the gaze is now reversed; we see the story from the woman's point of view. Curious to know what happened to Hedger, Eden learns that he has become one of the first men among the moderns, not a commercial success, but an influential figure in the world of art. Eden herself is now starring in one of the popular operas of the day, Camille Erlanger's *Aphrodite*; her name is in lights, her face "hard and settled, like a plaster cast." "Coming, Aphrodite!," one of Cather's densest stories, contains several of the recurrent figures in Cather's fiction: the motherless male protagonist, the beautiful and desired woman figured as a modern-day Venus, and a story from the Mexican Southwest. It contains also Cather's pointed reflections on the nature of art and the artist. Cather saw art as an exacting taskmaster, a jealous god who required that the artist resist the temptation of companionship and continue to work alone. To appease that god, she developed a highly allusive poetics for her fiction, which she outlined in an essay, "The Novel Démeublé" (1922). There she writes: "Whatever is felt upon the page without being specifically named there— that, one might say, is created. It is the inexplicable presence of the thing not named, of the overtone divined by the ear but not heard by it . . . that gives high quality to the novel or the drama, as well as to poetry itself."

In *Obscure Destinies,* Cather realizes most fully in short form a prefigurative mode of communication, an art suggestive of music. "Neighbour Rosicky" from this collection is frequently anthologized, perhaps because it provides a coda or epilogue to *My Ántonia,* giving us a later picture of the Bohemian family that served as prototype for the novel. It is also written in Cather's favorite mode, the pastoral of happiness. In contrast to her artist stories, "Neighbour Rosicky," the story of a dying man who has lived his life fully and without regrets, celebrates family relationships rather than success and accomplishments. It celebrates also an immigrant farmer's life as a way of criticizing American values. The Rosickys have not been infected by the American urge to get ahead in the world; their happiness and well-being are measured by comparing them to the Marshalls, rich American neighbors with a big barn and expensive machinery, but a wife who is a dispirited and slovenly housekeeper.

At the center of the Rosickys' domestic happiness is the wife and mother Mary, who expresses her "affection" through the food she cooks and serves her family: cof-

fee cake, *kolache* with apricot stuffing, roast chicken, roast turkey, fresh homemade bread, prune tarts, apple cake, nut loaf, plum conserve, wild grape wine, and strong coffee with thick cream (for unlike the American farmers, the Rosickys refuse to sell their cream to the dairy agent). Nourishment is pivotal in the story and a recurrent motif for Rosicky. His most painful memory is of a Christmas in London when he was so hungry that he stole and ate half the roast goose belonging to his landlady and her family. But it carries a happy memory as well because that night, while wandering the city, he is befriended by a group of his fellow countrymen who take him to a restaurant, feed him desserts, and give him enough money to buy food and presents for his landlady's family—a big goose, pork pies, potatoes, onions, cakes, and oranges.

Food is a means of meeting and averting crisis. One Fourth of July, a hot wind burns up the crops, but Rosicky's reaction is to kill two chickens and have a picnic with a bottle of wild grape wine in the back orchard. The American neighbors spend the evening at the schoolhouse praying for rain, and Mary Rosicky reports that they grieved so much over their losses "they got poor digestion and couldn't relish what they did have." Food helps to bridge the two cultures within Rosicky's immediate family, particularly with the son's American wife, Polly. Ill at ease with her foreign in-laws, Polly feels drawn to old Rosicky by his stories of poor, hungry people in the cities in which he has lived, for the young wife has come from a poor family and knows what it means to go without.

This preoccupation with nourishment

informs the language of the story at a subliminal level, characteristic of Cather's allusive poetic style. Rosicky "*hungered*" to know that his sons would carry on the farm after he was gone; he doesn't want his boys to know the cruelty of city people who "live by *grinding* or cheating or *poisoning* their fellow men." "Poison" is part of the language of ingestion, and "grinding" connects through association and usage with grain, wheat, and bread. Similarly, the wind is "*bitter, biting,*" words that connect with taste and consumption, and the sky in spring is "dry as *bone*." This harsh language of hunger is mitigated by words of nourishing and contentment. Even if another bad year is coming and Rosicky himself must die, he is content to know he will remain in the country no farther away than the edge of his own hayfield, that he will be buried by "*fat* Mr. Haycock," and that his cattle will be in the cornfield nearby "eating fodder" as the winter comes on.

Looked at closely, "Neighbour Rosicky" is a story about starvation, poverty, and dying, and about tensions bound up with ethnicity and class. At the same time it is a pastoral of innocence, celebrating a life that seems "complete and beautiful," to cite the last words of the story. That so many contradictory aspects of living are contained within this straightforward tale told in a pellucid style is typical of Willa Cather's art of suggestion. In 1940 Wallace Stevens said of Willa Cather, whose popularity had waned, "We have nothing better than she is. She takes so much pains to conceal her sophistication that it is easy to miss her quality." Today Willa Cather is regarded as one of America's finest writers of fiction, one whose work, to paraphrase her words about her friend Sarah Orne Jewett, will surely have a long, long life, confronting serenely time and change.

David Stouck

SELECTED BIBLIOGRAPHY

Works by Willa Cather

Collected Short Fiction 1892–1912. Edited by Virginia Faulkner. Lincoln: University of Nebraska Press, 1965.
Obscure Destinies. New York: Vintage Books, 1974.
Youth and the Bright Medusa. New York: Vintage Books, 1975.
The Troll Garden. Edited by James Woodress. Lincoln: University of Nebraska Press, 1983.

Critical Studies

Arnold, Marilyn. *Willa Cather's Short Fiction.* Athens: Ohio University Press, 1984.
Gelfant, Blanche. "The Magical Art of Willa Cather's 'Old Mrs. Harris.'" *Willa Cather Pioneer Memorial Newsletter* XXXVIII (fall 1994): 37–38, 40, 42–44, 46, 48.
Gerber, Philip. *Willa Cather.* Revised edition. New York: Twayne, 1995.
Slote, Bernice. Introduction to *Uncle Valentine and Other Stories: Willa Cather's Uncollected Short Fiction 1915–1929.* Lincoln: University of Nebraska Press, 1973.

JOHN CHEEVER
(1912 − 1982)

Born in Quincy, Massachusetts to an old, well-established New England family, John Cheever wrote closely observed, evocative stories about upper middle-class and middle-class Protestants of the American Northeast. Almost all of his fiction is set in a social milieu fixed in its rituals, codes of behavior, and hierarchy of values. Cheever's characters understand themselves to be the inheritors of a particular cultural and historical tradition, with the responsibilities and privileges that tradition imposes. Although Cheever is often said to be the best short-story chronicler of the American WASP, the crucial historical events that shaped (and were shaped by) these modern descendants of the New England way of life—World War II, the atomic bomb and the Cold War, the radicalism of the 1960s—figure only in the background of his fiction. His enduring concern is not the human dramas surrounding those shaping events, but the moral choices and challenges that engage his characters as they go through their daily rituals and routines.

The experiences of these ordinary American Protestants seem genuine, and they are often both moving and comical. Cheever has an impeccable ear for dialogue, and his prose style, which is chaste and lyrical, is almost always perfectly in tune with the design of the story he tells. He captures all the details of cocktail parties, domestic quarrels, and family vacations on New England's islands, and he conjures up with great emotional force the experiences of people in the midst of spiritual and domestic disarray.

Cheever's literary career spans more than fifty years. His first story, published by Malcolm Cowley in the *New Republic* in October 1930, recounted Cheever's expulsion from Thayer Academy in Massachusetts at the age of seventeen, the end of Cheever's formal education. Cowley introduced the young writer to New York's literary society and helped him place stories in *The New Yorker*. After marrying Mary Winternitz in 1941, Cheever served four years in the U.S. Army. Following World War II, the couple lived in New York City, and then in the suburbs of Westchester, New York, until Cheever's death from cancer in 1982. In addition to publishing six collections of stories, he wrote four novels and a number of screenplays and television scripts. *The Stories of John Cheever* (1978), a compilation of his last five collections, won the Pulitzer Prize, the National Book Critics Circle Award, and the American Book Award for fiction. In the last few years of his life, Cheever was often interviewed by popular magazines and made frequent appearances on the talk-show circuit as a kind of wise elder statesman of American letters.

Cheever has often been called the quintessential *New Yorker* writer—a label he disliked, inasmuch as it was often uttered less to praise his work than to indicate its limitations in subject matter and theme. Leaving aside the question of limitations, the label is apt. He published 141 of his 180 stories in *The New Yorker*—making him (along with John O'Hara and John

Updike) one of the most frequent contributors of fiction in the magazine's long
history. Although he sometimes employed
experimental narrative technique and in-
jected fantasy and dreams into his stories—he once said he was interested in
the "unreal" and in reverie—he was essentially a realist writer of manners.

Cheever's stories, often critical of
contemporary American mores and values, usually assert that life offers many
possibilities and blessings. Despite confusion, humiliation, and suffering, life remains appetizing because of what the narrator in "Goodbye, My Brother" calls the
"harsh surface beauty of life . . . the obdurate truths before which fear and terror are powerless." Cheever does not
define those truths in any systematic fashion; nor does his fiction present a clearly
defined moral order or philosophical system. But such truths are made available
to his characters in ways that seem credible and often moving. They become real
to his characters through the vehicles of
love and nostalgic recollection of a traditional moral order of honesty and decorum. Cheever does not say explicitly
when or where such an order obtained,
but its existence for Cheever's characters—and for the author himself—expresses what Richard Locke has called "a
yearning for white, Episcopal Anglo-
Saxon, New England upper-class decency
[and] cultivation." Cheever himself was
distrustful of modern values, commenting in a 1976 interview that the "splen-
dors of the imagination have suffered in
the post-Freudian generation" and that
he found this development "an endless
source of anxiety."

As Cheever wrote in the preface to his
collected stories, "The constants that I
look for . . . are a love of light and a
determination to trace some moral chain
of being." This order figures in the makeup
of "Cheever country" at least as much as
the quaint New England village of St. Bo-
tolph's, or that placid kingdom of the New
York suburbs known as Shady Hill, the
scene of several of Cheever's masterfully
executed tales of disarray, longing, and
hope. It rests in the background, often
just out of the protagonist's reach until
the very end of the story. Then it is brought
forward dramatically by a mysterious in-
tercession—with no mention of God, but
with something like Christian grace—or
by the wrenching crisis of conscience the
story itself chronicles.

The corollary to Cheever's notion of
an abiding moral foundation for human
existence is that the grueling pace and
pressures of modern life often cause people to lose touch with that foundation.
Their struggles to understand their position and gain or regain balance and a
measure of happiness are the central concern of a number of his best stories.

In "Clancy in the Tower of Babel," a
story in *The Enormous Radio and Other Stories*
(1953), a bigoted New York apartment
building superintendent, baffled and
deeply incensed by a homosexual tenant's
bizarre lifestyle and suicide attempt,
"wonder[s] what sort of judgment he
should pass on the pervert," and he begins
to think of hurtful remarks to pass on to
the tenant when they next cross paths.
Clancy is brought to a more compassionate understanding of the tenant's plight
through sudden recognition of his own

love for family and the humility that love inspires. As the superintendent looks out his apartment window into the backyards of the tenements nearby, he is heartened by their symmetry, "as if it . . . conformed to something good in himself," and by gazing on his wife and the image of his son. To Clancy, his wife appeared "to be one of the glorious beauties of his day, but a stranger, he guessed, might notice the tear in her slip and that her body was bent and heavy. A picture of [his son] hung on the wall. Clancy was struck with the strength and intelligence of his son's face, but he guessed that a stranger might notice the boy's glasses and his bad complexion. And then, thinking . . . that this half blindness was all that he knew himself of mortal love, he decided not to say anything to Mr. Rowentree [the tenant]. They would pass in silence."

The moment of heightened moral consciousness that Clancy experiences is a common feature in the landscape of "Cheever country"—a fictional world invariably set in the present but bearing the imprint of the author's stern Puritan heritage. "Calvin," he wrote in the preface to *The Stories of John Cheever,* "seemed to abide in the barns of my childhood," and the reader senses the abiding presence of Calvinism's call to moral reflection and discernment in many of Cheever's short stories. In an interview, Cheever told Scott Donaldson that "the darkness—the capacity for darkness that was cherished in New England—certainly colored our lives."

Moral darkness figures in the makeup of a number of Cheever's most memorable characters, albeit in different forms.

And its presence in one character often elicits a forceful reaction in another character with strong inclinations toward the light and the good. In "Goodbye, My Brother," Lawrence's smallness, his inclination to judge the lives of his family harshly, brings unbearable tension—and ultimately violence—to what was to have been a relaxing seashore vacation. The New York businessman tailed and ultimately humiliated by his sexually exploited secretary as he leaves the office for the train station in "The Five Forty Eight" seems the essence of moral darkness. He has no conscience. The feelings of others matter to him not at all.

Cheever, however, rejects the New England Puritan's harsh distrust of nature and earthly beauty. Nature in his fiction is highly valued, often anticipating a mysterious intervention. His prose is sprinkled with sensuous images of land, light, clouds, and wind. When revelations of some import come to his characters they are often ushered in by abrupt changes in climate (as, for example, in "The Country Husband"), and the sea is an abiding and life-affirming presence in a number of stories, especially "The Seaside Houses" and "Goodbye, My Brother."

Nevertheless, Cheever has retained the Puritan belief that good and evil are in constant struggle in the human heart, and like Nathaniel Hawthorne, another New England writer often said to have influenced him, he is intensely interested in moral predicaments and choices. His stories can be read as chronicles of how the struggle between good and evil impulses unfolds in the lives of people of varied temperaments and weaknesses—usually, though not always, amid the complex so-cial rituals of upper middle-class Ameri-can Protestant society. Johnny Hake in "The Country Husband," Asa Bascomb in "The World of Apples," Mr. Bruce in "The Bus to St. James's"—all these Cheever creations are involved in prurient esca-pades or exploitative behavior, and it is Cheever's gift to chart with great preci-sion of language their experiences as they try to reconcile their actions and impulses with their consciences. In each of these stories, Cheever explores the tension be-tween what he once referred to as our erotic nature and our social nature.

The title story of Cheever's critically acclaimed third volume of stories, *The Housebreaker of Shady Hill,* explores a sub-urbanite's journey to "the moral bottom." A successful manufacturing executive is forced out of his job by the tyrannical head of the family business. Shady Hill is an expensive place to live, and Johnny Hake's wife enjoys spending money and likes to keep up appearances. With his checks about to bounce, Hake, too proud to bor-row, burglarizes a wealthy neighbor's home for cash and plans other illicit forays. A man of the world, an adulterer who nevertheless loves his children deeply and enjoys looking down his wife's dress when "she bends over to salt the steaks," Hake finds himself repulsed by his housebreak-ing, faced with the knowledge that he "had done something so reprehensible that it violated the tenets of every known reli-gion. . . . I had criminally entered the house of a friend and broken all the un-written laws that held the community to-gether. My conscience worked on my spir-its—like the hard beak of a carnivorous bird." His deep guilt begins to threaten

seriously his relationship with both his wife and his children.

Cheever's portrait of an apparently well-adjusted man on the verge of collapse is skillfully rendered with a light satiric but sympathetic touch. Hake's inner tur-moil contrasts dramatically with the tran-quility of life in Shady Hill, and the un-guent pleasures of the place, along with his recollection of deep love for his wife, begin to signal a strong desire on Hake's part to make amends. After a particularly harsh quarrel with his wife, Hake leaves, only to be brought back home for a night of sleep and reconciliation. But the allures of housebreaking remain. He makes an-other attempt at robbery, but before he can commit the crime, a mysterious rain shower brings grace and, ultimately, re-stores his broken connection to the com-munity: "the smell of [the rain] flying up to my nose . . . showed me the extent of my freedom from . . . the works of a thief." Hake returns the money he stole on his first housebreaking, gets his old job back, and finds himself wondering "how a world so dark could, in a few minutes, become so sweet."

Water figures as an agent of moral transformation and affirmation in several of Cheever's stories, including "The World of Apples," in which an old Amer-ican poet, Asa Bascomb, is demoralized by the promiscuity and shabbiness of a world that seems to have passed him by. What is worse, the pornographic tenden-cies of the day seem to have captured some part of his imagination. He finds himself writing dirty limericks and wondering what sort of evil force has overtaken him. "Back in the streets he wondered if there was a universality to the venereal dusk that had settled over his spirit. Had the world, as well as he, lost its way?" Bascomb goes on a pilgrimage to a small Catholic church and then to a waterfall he had not seen since his youth. He steps into the torrent, and, Cheever writes, "when he stepped away from the water he seemed at last to be himself." As in "The Housebreaker of Shady Hill," water brings grace, that mysterious force that Cheever's Puritan ancestors defined as beneficence shown by God to man.

In the much-anthologized "A Country Husband," also published in *The Housebreaker of Shady Hill,* Cheever takes a more critical view of the values and hollow rituals of the Shady Hill community than he does in the title story. Francis Weed, the protagonist, is frustrated and annoyed by his family's inability to commiserate with him over an emergency landing his plane had to make. Troubled by his family's apparent indifference and alienated from a community that believes "there was no danger or trouble in the world," Weed turns for solace to young Anne Murchison, a baby-sitter whose "image seemed to put him in a relationship to the world that was mysterious and enthralling." But like Johnny Hake, he comes to realize that giving in to his lust will bring only harm and further suffering, and the story ends with a dazzling array of comic images of the Shady Hill landscape as a place where life and love can thrive. In Cheever's classic concluding phrase, "it is a night where kings in golden suits ride elephants over the mountains."

Cheever's only story to have been made into a film, "The Swimmer," portrays a character bent on demonstrating athletic prowess and youthfulness. Neddy Merrill,

an apparently happy and prosperous resident of the New York suburbs, decides to travel the eight miles from a friend's house to his own by swimming all the backyard pools along the way. Neddy cuts quite a figure. His uncommon mode of travel "gave him the feeling that he was a pilgrim, an explorer, a man with a destiny, and he knew that he would find friends all along the way. " At first all goes well. He is welcomed warmly at the first few pools by his neighbors. As the narrative progresses, subtle signs of problems surface, soon followed by not so subtle ones: Neddy is jeered at from passing cars as he attempts to cross a highway and loses some of his confidence; a drained and deserted pool leaves him dispirited; he is called a gatecrasher at a party given by a hostess he recalls as unworthy of his social circle; and a former mistress rebuffs him as he approaches her pool. Neddy wonders, "Was his memory failing or was he so disciplined in the repression of unpleasant memories that he had damaged his sense of truth?" The swimmer does indeed reach his objective. Exhausted, crying, his spirit utterly broken, he finds the door of his old home locked, and the house empty of furniture or family.

Much of the power of "The Swimmer" comes from Cheever's subversion of the pilgrimage motif. Readers would expect Neddy to gain an education on his quest, and the education, even if it contains formidable obstacles, to offer lasting significance and meaning in his life. Instead, Neddy comes to possess only the desperate knowledge of his own humiliating downfall. The story is made all the more haunting by Cheever's implicitly raising the question of whether the events happened at all—for it is at least arguable that the events occurred only in Neddy Merrill's deluded mind. Moreover, the cause of Neddy's woes remains unknown, and could as easily be of his own making as not. Cheever's portrait of the pretentious and debauched pool owners adds to the bleak effect. This is hardly the life-sustaining social world of "The Housebreaker of Shady Hill" or "The Country Husband."

Another of Cheever's memorable explorers is Bertha, the wife of the sophisticated, gin-drinking narrator in "The Fourth Alarm," who gives up teaching sixth-grade social studies in the suburbs to perform in an avant-garde play in New York City. In addition to performing fully nude, Bertha must simulate sex twice during the performance, as well as join a "love pile" with members of the audience at the conclusion. The narrator finds his wife's participation in the performance, and the performance itself, disconcerting, to say the least. He wonders, as his wife prances about naked on the stage, if "nakedness . . . had annihilated her sense of nostalgia? Nostalgia . . . was one of her principal charms. It was her gift gracefully to carry the memory of some experience into another tense."

When the audience is asked to remove their clothes and join in the fun onstage, the narrator strips, but after a moment of humiliation, turns from the stage, gets dressed, and leaves, seeming "not to have exposed my inhibitions but to have hit on some marvelously practical and obdurate part of myself." Here Cheever directly asserts the value of the past, of nostalgia, for enlarging human experience. The narrator's act of defiance contrasts favor-

ably with the groupthink of the "liberated" cast and audience, which seems more inhibited and doctrinaire than does the narrator.

"The Fourth Alarm" is one of many Cheever stories that create an affinity between the narrator's voice and the writer's. The abiding authorial voice in Cheever's fiction—wry, sophisticated, wise, but never arid or dismissive of his character's weaknesses—somehow enriches the experience of the stories and the characters that people them. Readers come to trust Cheever's voice in his fiction, and to rely on its subtle clues to guide and enlarge their understanding of the stories' trajectory and texture.

Cheever's own participation in his fictional world is itself an affirmative act, and it may help explain why many stories resonate in the mind long after reading. Cheever himself is fully, passionately engaged in the domestic disruptions, sufferings, and nostalgic longings of his creations. As he once said: "I know of almost no pleasure greater in life than having a piece of fiction draw together disparate incidents so that they relate to one another and confirm that feeling that life itself is a creative process, that one thing is put purposefully upon another, that what is lost in one encounter is replenished in the next, and that we possess some power to make sense of what takes place." Even John Cheever's darkest stories reveal the pleasure that comes in knowing that "one thing is put purposefully upon another," and that we have the power to "make sense of what takes place" despite the formidable obstacles we encounter along the way.

James Warren

SELECTED BIBLIOGRAPHY

Works by John Cheever

The Way Some People Live: A Book of Stories. New York: Random House, 1943.

The Enormous Radio and Other Stories. New York: Funk & Wagnall, 1953.

The Housebreaker of Shady Hill and Other Stories. New York: Harper & Row, 1958.

Some People, Places, and Things That Will Not Appear in My Next Novel. New York: Harper & Row, 1961.

The Stories of John Cheever. New York: Alfred A. Knopf, 1978.

The World of Apples. New York: Alfred A. Knopf, 1978.

Critical Studies

Byrne, Michael D. *Dragons and Martinis: The Skewed Realism of John Cheever.* San Bernadino, Calif.: Borgo Press, 1993.

Donaldson, Scott, ed. *Conversations with John Cheever.* Jackson: University Press of Mississippi, 1987.

Locke, Richard. "Visions of Order and Domestic Disarray." *New York Times Book Review,* December 3, 1978.

Peden, William. *The American Short Story.* Boston: Houghton Mifflin, 1975.

Waldeland, Lynne. *John Cheever.* Boston: Twayne, 1979.

SANDRA CISNEROS

(1954–)

Born in Chicago in 1954, Sandra Cisneros has spent most of her life crossing borders. She lived in Chicago, the home of her Chicana mother, and visited the family home of her Mexican father. After graduating from Loyola University in Chicago in 1976, spending two years at the Iowa Writers' Workshop, and receiving a master of fine arts degree in 1978, she received grants, fellowships, and visiting appointments in Texas, California, and New York. She has lived in different parts of the country since becoming a more or less independent writer, and she continues to cross and recross geographic and cultural borders. At the Iowa Writers' Workshop, she began drawing on her experience of what Gloria Anzaldúa calls a "border woman," a woman who lives fully, thoughtfully, and creatively in the "borderlands": the "cultural, physical, spiritual, sexual, and linguistic spaces . . . where people of different cultures occupy the same territory, where under, lower, middle, and upper classes touch, where the space between two individuals shrinks with intimacy. . . . It's not a comfortable territory to live in, this place of contradictions."

In 1980 Cisneros published *Bad Boys,* a collection of poetry, as part of a series of Chicano/a chapbooks. In 1984 she received the Before Columbus American Book Award for *The House on Mango Street,* first published by Arte Público, one of the important small presses that helped develop the Chicano/a movement in the 1970s. In 1987 Third Woman published *My Wicked, Wicked Ways.* In 1991 she broke into the mainstream with *Woman Hollering Creek,* with endorsements by Ann Beattie, who said that "her stories about why we mythologize love are revelations," and the *Washington Post Book World,* which commented, "Sandra Cisneros knows both that the heart can be broken and that it can rise and soar like a bird. Whatever story she chooses to tell, we should be listening for a long time to come."

For a writer from a marginal subculture to be recognized and presented this way by the mainstream press was indeed a breakthrough. But there was also a price to be paid, for the recognition obscured just those storytelling skills that distinguish her revelations. Granted, the *Washington Post*'s Susan Wood and other mainstream press reviewers were sensitive to the distinctive Chicana subject matter and captured the fiery flavor of Cisneros's stories. But the trajectory of their reviews led away from this particularity and what distinguishes Cisneros's imagination and skill: the ability to tell heartbreaking yet at the same time inspiring stories that vivify myths of crossing borders or living in the borderlands. Cisneros extends the borderlands to include barrios all over the United States as well as "the physical, spiritual, sexual, and linguistic borders" that define Chicana/o culture. The stories and myths are of a culture that is both and neither Mexican and American, where the Mexican heritage includes both Indian and Spanish, and in which the Spanish heritage is strongly patriarchal. In a singular fashion, Cisneros has participated in the imaginative and historical recovery of stories and myths of strong border women. The skills of this remarkable Chicana writer involve the creative use of a trilingual heritage: standard Mexican Spanish, standard English, and Chicana/o Spanglish. She has developed an apparently simple and playful but nonetheless sophisticated border style by choosing which words of a Chi-

cana story to translate and how to translate them so that, while appealing to the English reader, they resonate for Mexican Americans and shift the margins to the center. She has also developed narrative techniques to tell border stories of marginal people who have not been the subjects of stories marketed by the mainstream presses and whose stories, therefore, require conventions that cross the borders of ethnicity, class, gender, and sexuality.

Cisneros has developed a style for telling what might be called a "found"—or, better, found again—story. It may be found again by being taken out of its familiar context—of physical setting, historical meaning, daily experience, or commonplace language, with its overlapping Anglo and Mexican frames of reference. Then it is literally revised or re-visioned, highlighted in ways that vivify or ironize different parts. For instance, when asked about incorporating Spanish into her stories, Cisneros answered that it changed the rhythm, especially when she translated them literally. "I love calling stories by Spanish expressions. I called this story 'Salvador Late or Early.' It's a nice title. It means sooner or later, *tarde o temprano,* which literally translates as late or early. All of a sudden something happens to the English, something really new is happening, a new spice is added to the English language."

Found-again stories are also contained in the letters left at the shrines of Chicano/a saints in her simple but sophisticated "Little Miracles, Kept Promises." Some of them highlight the everyday tragedies and resilience of ordinary people in the barrio: "Dear San Martín, Please send us clothes, furniture, shoes, dishes. We need anything that don't eat. Since the fire we have to start all over again." Some illuminate little miracles: Victor A. Lozano thanks Saint Sebastian, "who was persecuted with arrows and then survived," just as he was persecuted by his brother-in-law Ernie and his sister Alba and their kids. "Now my home sweet home is mine again, and my Dianita is *bien* lovey-dovey, and my kids have something to say to me besides who hit who." Victor maintains his independence, leaving "the little gold *milagrito*" he promised at the shrine. "And it ain't that cheap gold-plate shit either. So now that I paid you back we're even, right?" On the other hand, Cisneros distances herself from Victor by framing his thoughts, or artfully representing in letters designed for us to read what could be his speaking voice. She also ironizes his machismo: "Cause I don't like for no one to say Victor Lazano don't pay his debts. I pays cash on the line, bro. And Victor Lazano's words like his deeds is solid gold." In another letter she ironizes the ways these ordinary people have internalized institutions that keep them disempowered, in this case the suffering mother of the Church: "Virgencita de Guadalupe, I promise to walk to your shrine on my knees the very first day I get back, I swear, if you will only get the Tortilleria la Casa de la Masa to pay me the $253.72 they owe me for two weeks' work."

The same principle of found-again or revisioned stories can be applied to "My Lucy Friend Who Smells Like Corn": "like Frito Bandito chips, like tortillas, something like that warm smell of *nixtamal* or bread the way her head smells when she's leaning close to you"—commercial and homemade products serving as a Chicana madeleine. Or "Mexican Movies" and "Barbie-Q" that become touchstones of poor Chicana nostalgia. Or "Eleven" and "Mericans" that focus traumatic experiences of racism through the voices of innocent children. Or "One Holy Night" when a girl is "initiated beneath an ancient sky by a great and mighty heir—Chaq Uxmal Paloquin," who steals Abuelita's pushcart and turns out to be a thirty-seven-year-old man by the name of Chato (fat face), who has killed eleven young girls.

Another class of found-again stories is based on Chicana feminist revisions of history and myths, which are transformative. "Woman Hollering Creek" is the name of both the title story and the creek Cleófilas crosses from her father's home in Mexico to her abusive husband's home in Texas, and recrosses in her liberating return—even though it is to "the chores that never ended, six good-for-nothing brothers, and one old man's complaints." The creek is named La Gritona ("the howling woman") and recalls the patriarchal myth of La Llorona, who wails for the children she has killed or abandoned. It parallels the better-known myth of La Malinche, the Indian woman who is said to have betrayed her people by becoming Cortez's mistress and translator. As Jean Wyatt points out, the stories of La Llorona and La Malinche, along with the Virgin of Guadalupe, exercise great pressure on Chicana identity, but feminist historians have been revising them. Malinche is now seen as a figure of resistance, who maintained her identity as an Aztec and used her influence to save the lives of many Native Americans. One version of her story links her to La Llorona: she drowned a son rather than have Cortez take him back to Spain. There are versions of La Llorona as a mother who killed her children to spare them from the cruel world, or who was a single mother who died after becoming a prostitute to save her children from starving. In Cisneros's story, Cleófilas manages to escape from her husband with her children through the aid of Felice, who drives a pickup. "When they drove across the arroyo, the driver opened her mouth and let out a yell as loud as any mariachi. . . . Every time I cross that bridge I do that. . . . Makes you want to holler like Tarzan." Felice replaces the model of the women in the *telenovélas* that Cleófilas admired when she lived in Mexico, passive figures of romance who inspired her to see love as suffering. She also transfigures the wailing of Llorona to the hollering of Tarzan (crossing the borders of both nationality and gender). Although Cleófilas returns to her father's house, she is changed. In the end she tells the story to them and hears Felice laughing. "But it wasn't Felice laughing. It was gurgling out of her own throat, a long ribbon of laughter like water." Cleófilas's laughter unites her with Felice, the found-again Llorona, and, by implication, the revisioned Malinche, the strong woman of Mexican history.

Some of Cisneros's stories confirm the reality of border experience in ways that highlight the power cultural myths hold over ordinary people but are nonetheless liberating. In "The Marlboro Man" and "Remember the Alamo," machos turn out to be gay. "Eyes of Zapata" is told by Emiliano Zapata's Malinche mistress, who translates and re-visions her ambivalent story of the revolutionary hero. "Little Miracles, Kept Promises" ends with a young woman's letter to the Virgencita: "I have cut off my hair just like I promised I would and pinned my braid here by your statue. . . . My mother cried, did I tell you? All that beautiful hair."

She wants the Virgencita to be "barebreasted, snakes in your hands. I wanted you leaping somersaults on the backs of bulls. I wanted you swallowing raw hearts and rattling volcanic ash." That is, she wants the Indian god, on whose site the Virgen de Guadalupe appeared, who has always been part of the Mexican American Virgin Mary, and who has always had "one foot in this world and one foot in that." Now "no longer Mary the mild, but our mother Tonantzín. Your church at Tepeyac built on the site of her temple."

Sandra Cisneros has disturbed conservative Chicanos with stories like this, which express the anguish of domination, the triumph of little miracles in the borderland, as she finds again and revisions the border stories and myths that ground Chicana identity.

Richard Pearce

SELECTED BIBLIOGRAPHY

Works by Sandra Cisneros

The House on Mango Street. Houston: Arte Público Press, 1984.

My Wicked, Wicked Ways. Berkeley, Calif.: Third Woman, 1987.

Woman Hollering Creek. New York: Vintage, 1991.

Critical Studies

Anzaldúa, Gloria. *Borderlands/La Frontera: The New Mestiza.* San Francisco: Aunt Lute Press, 1987.

Jussawalla, Feroza, and Reed Dasenbrock. *Interviews with Writers of the Post-Colonial World.* Jackson: University Press of Mississippi, 1992.

Wyatt, Jean. "On Not Being La Malinche: Border Negotiations of Gender in Sandra Cisneros's 'Never Marry a Mexican' and 'Woman Hollering Creek.'" *Tulsa Studies in Women's Literature* 14 (fall 1995): 243–271.

WALTER VAN TILBURG

CLARK

(1909 – 1971)

Walter Van Tilburg Clark was dedicated to the American West, especially the mountains, hiking trails, cold lakes, and even the deserts of his beloved Nevada. He liked the people of the West and enjoyed western history written by those who had lived it. He was born, however, near East Orland, Maine. His mother was an accomplished musician who had graduated from Cornell. His father became head of the political science department at City College of New York. In 1917 Professor Clark moved the family to Reno, where he served as president of the University of Nevada from 1917 to 1938.

In Reno, young Walt came to love both nature and learning. He took B.A. and M.A. degrees at the University of Nevada and a second M.A. at the University of Vermont. Teaching in various high schools and colleges—but primarily at the University of Nevada—Clark developed his critical abilities and seemed to be working full time at both teaching and writing.

As he did, Clark developed a clear set of values: a strong belief that the survival of the human race depends on voluntary birth control and "the preservation and even, where possible, the restoration, of other forms of life and of all natural resources"; abhorrence of all prejudice; a conviction that "conceit, self-righteousness, and violence" are "self-destructive"; a fundamental preference for the unitive over the divisive; and the necessity of education, "mutual understanding, and tolerance" as the prerequisites of any progress toward the unitive and of survival.

Clark was well educated. It is thus surprising that he made his reputation with *The Ox-Bow Incident* (1940), one of the best cowboy novels yet written. *The City of Trembling Leaves* (1945), a somewhat autobiographical novel, received mixed reviews; but *The Track of the Cat* (1949), a successful combination of mythology and realism, added to his high standing in American letters. Both *The Ox-Bow Incident* and *The Track of the Cat* were made into excellent movies.

The Watchful Gods and Other Stories (1950) is a widely respected collection of his best short stories (half a dozen good ones have appeared only in magazines), but the variety of Clark's themes and styles eludes critical categories. "The Portable Phonograph," for example, is a classic in science fiction. Four survivors of an apocalyptic war gather in a dug-out cave to savor selections from their host, who has managed to save four books, a few records, and a portable phonograph. Clark knew both literature and music, and it is interesting to ask why the host chose each book and each record. When the evening is over, the host lies down to sleep, clutching a "piece of lead pipe" that is "comfortable." Thus an evening of high culture is sandwiched between apocalypse and a lead pipe.

"Hook," by contrast, is the story of a hawk named Hook. Obviously, Clark was taking a risk. Could he ascribe feelings such as "joy," "hope," "shame," and "anger" to a hawk and make his story convincing?

"Why Don't You Look Where You're Going?" is a simple story, apparently written to set up one good punch line, and yet a reader's chuckle, at the end, fades into reflections on the serious level of the story. An ocean liner, a "sainted leviathan," is so huge and self-sufficient that its passengers feel complacent. They have no control over this floating marvel of civilization and need none. Everything is being taken care of for them. When a lone sailor in a tiny craft is almost run over by the "leviathan," when the sailor angrily shouts the title question, the reader is invited to reflect on what Clark has said about modern civilization: where is it going, what is it doing to its "passengers," and what about the role of the one truly independent character in the story?

"The Anonymous" reads like an early version of 1990s multiculturalism. Again, the end of the story challenges the reader

to reflect on the whole story. Obviously, the chauffeur's remark—"a fellow's gotta live"—applies to Peter Carr, who is being molded into a fake Indian for display in fancy living rooms; but the remark also applies to the chauffeur himself, the narrator, and—with a slight adjustment—to other featured characters.

"The Fish Who Could Close His Eyes," a haunting puzzle no critic has yet resolved, is unlike any other story Clark has published. "The Buck in the Hills" is a tough-sensitivity story of the type associated with Ernest Hemingway.

"The Indian Well," however, features what is probably Clark's most basic theme: nature is a living organism, and human beings need to find their place in its ancient and ongoing story. Clark begins with a description of a desert well that is "in constant revolt" against the dominating sun. There are signs of "man's participation in the cycles of the well's resistance" and a description of the "busy day" when Jim Suttler arrives "to take his part in one cycle." A roadrunner is "stepping long and always about to sprint." Lizards stop to do "rapid push-ups, like men exercising on a floor." A rattler appears, a hawk, then swallows, insects, rabbits, two coyotes, a range cow with a calf, mice, and nine antelope. All are busy searching for food or drinking at the well. Clark then devotes two pages to recording inscriptions written on the wall of a tumbledown shack by the well, for the past is also a part of the current cycle. The plot is simple: a cougar kills Jenny, Suttler's beloved burro; Suttler waits a full year for the cougar to return; he kills it and undergoes an elaborate ritual of shaving, bathing, clog-dancing, hollering-singing, and doing what he can to honor the grave he has dug for Jenny. The reader's challenge is to track a revolving series of connections. The "canyon was alive," Clark writes. All nature—including "thinking cliffs . . . who could afford to wait"—is alive; and ritual is the language of the respect that is necessary to survival.

"The Watchful Gods," a novelette, concludes the volume. On his twelfth birthday, Buck is allowed to go hunting alone with a .22 rifle instead of a toy rifle. He kills a rabbit, but it turns out to be a baby rabbit he has cruelly marred with bad shooting. Searching for expiation, Buck buries the rabbit, but the nagging voice of reason forces him to admit that burying the rabbit will hide both his baby trophy and his bad shooting. "You aren't going home," the voice of reason says for the fourth time, and Buck wades out into the ocean.

Is Buck never going home as a child, or is he quite literally going into the ocean? Did Buck, perhaps like Clark, demand too much of himself? Did the writer's career as a teacher block his creativity, with the result that during his last twenty-one years he published only a couple of items of significance? Such questions—like Clark's daring combination of intuition, nature, reason, and realism—are complex and fascinating.

Max Westbrook

SELECTED BIBLIOGRAPHY

Clark, Walter Van Tilburg. *The Watchful Gods and Other Stories*. New York: Random House, 1950.
Laird, Charlton, ed. *Walter Van Tilburg Clark: Critiques*. Reno: University of Nevada Press, 1983.
Lee, L. L. *Walter Van Tilburg Clark*. Boise: Boise State College Press, 1973.
Westbrook, Max. *Walter Van Tilburg Clark*. New York: Twayne, 1969.

ELIZABETH COOK-LYNN
(1930–)

Dakotah Sioux author Elizabeth Cook-Lynn considers herself a storyteller in the tradition of the Dakotah culture, the *Dakotapi,* or eastern group of the larger nation that also includes the Lakotah and Nakotah literary traditions. Consequently, her fiction shares many qualities of the oral narratives told within America's First Nations. These narratives, forming the longest tradition of imaginative prose created in the Americas, often defy the categories of literary critics. Cook-Lynn has expressed frustration with the narrow focus on identity that monopolizes many critical commentaries. She feels that First Nations' literatures deserve the kind of serious attention from literary critics that they give to the indigenous literatures of Nigeria and other Third World nations. In her essay "The American Indian Fiction Writer: Cosmopolitanism, Nationalism, the Third World, and First Nation Sovereignty," Cook-Lynn challenges writers and critics to focus their attention on the "sovereign rights and obligations of the citizens of First Nations of America." In another essay, "The Radical Conscience in Native American Studies," she addresses Native scholars and writers, suggesting that they ask themselves, "is what I am teaching and writing and researching of value to the continuation of the Indian Nations of America?"

Born on November 17, 1930, at the government hospital in Fort Thompson, on the Crow Creek Sioux Reservation in South Dakota, Cook-Lynn grew up on the prairie near Crow Creek. Politics and writing were part of her family's life and heritage. Both her grandfather, Joe Bowed Head Irving, and her father, Jerome Irving, served on the Crow Creek Tribal Council. Elizabeth was named for her grandmother, Eliza Renville Irving, who had written bilingual articles for the early Christian newspapers published in the late 1800s by the Dakota Mission at Sisseton, South Dakota. This grandmother, who sometimes stayed with the family, lived only four miles away when Cook-Lynn was a child. Another formative influence was Gabriel Renville, an ancestor who died before she was born. Renville was instrumental in developing early Dakotah language dictionaries.

When she left the reservation to study at South Dakota State College (now university), Cook-Lynn took a history course on the westward movement in which there was no mention of the Indian nations. This inspired her to become a teacher and writer. She completed a bachelor of arts degree in English and journalism there in 1952. The following year, she married a fellow student, Melvin Traversie Cook of Eagle Butte, South Dakota, a marriage that ended in divorce in 1970. She worked as a journalist and taught at the secondary level before completing a

master's degree in educational psychology and counseling at the University of South Dakota in 1971. That year she began teaching English and Indian Studies at Eastern Washington University in Cheney while raising her four children from her first marriage. In 1975, she married Clyde Lynn, a Spokane Indian from Wellpinit, Washington. She was a National Endowment for the Humanities Fellow at Stanford University in 1976. Professor emeritus at Eastern Washington University since 1989, Cook-Lynn lives in Rapid City, South Dakota. She has served as writer in residence at Evergreen College, West Virginia University, and the Atlantic Center for the Arts. She has also been a visiting professor at the University of California, Davis.

Cook-Lynn's short stories were initially published in her mixed-genre collection, *Then Badger Said This* (1977). Her title refers to the badger's function in traditional Dakotah literature—to keep the plot moving. She told Joseph Bruchac in an interview published in 1987 that she intended the collection to be "the Sioux version of *The Way to Rainy Mountain*." James Ruppert has pointed out that N. Scott Momaday's and Cook-Lynn's "approach to history is . . . a highly oral process where the personal and the cultural merge." This is evident in Cook-Lynn's short, fictional vignette republished as "A Child's Story" in *The Power of Horses and Other Stories* (1990), a collection of fifteen short stories.

Cook-Lynn has explained that "A Child's Story" grew out of her grandson's naming ceremony. There had been a lot of conflict between the child's parents, and the two families held the ceremony so that both families could be involved in the boy's life. The story, told from the mother's consciousness, reveals her feelings of sadness, fascination, and fear as she sees the horseback father of her daughter "sweep the child from her arms and begin the ritualistic drama." The mother watches as they ride among other horsemen, who say in celebration "I am the elk," thus accentuating their potency as males. Later the father keeps repeating "This is my daughter," as he holds her "at arm's length toward the crowd" and the "faceless riders" affirmation is stated: "*Hechetu*" (It is well). Fearful for her child's safety, the mother rushes to grasp her daughter when the baby's father reaches down from his mount, allowing the child's feet to touch the ground. At the end of the ceremony, the mother finally comes to understand its meaning as an expression of "whatever is certain," a refrain repeated throughout the story. Her certainty, made apparent by the ritual, is the strong connection between her culture, her child, and their spiritual life. The story ends as she tells her child, "Listen! Listen!" As in most of her fiction, Cook-Lynn has placed a greater emphasis on character and theme than on plot in this story, and she has included Dakotah language, concepts, ceremony, culture, and myth.

The title story of the collection, "The Power of Horses," opens as a mother and daughter are preparing beets for canning. Looking out the window, they see the girl's father with a white man. The men have run horses into a corral, and the daughter asks her mother why her father is going to sell them. At first the mother says nothing, and the daughter notices that her own horse, whom she calls Shota, is in the pasture and not the corral. As they continue to prepare the beets, the mother says, "I used to have land, myself, daughter . . . and on it my grandfather had many horses. What happened to it was that some white men from Washington came and took it away from me when my grandfather died because, they said, they were going to breed game birds there; geese, I think." The mother goes on to tell her daughter about a special horse in her memory that resembled her daughter's Shota. Her story about the primordial horse is a story that her grandfather Bowed Head had told "when he wished to speak of those days when all creatures knew one another." In its retelling, the story of these primordial horses and their swift descendents is embedded within the mid-twentieth-century family experience of Dakotah people. The daughter is awakened early the following morning by her father, who asks her to ride with him to take the horses to the north pasture before the horse buyer returns. Despite the fact that the grass is short and it will be difficult to provide food for the horses, her father has decided to keep them. The story shows the important influence of both parents on this girl. As Paula Gunn Allen stated, "the centrality of the feminine power of universal being is crucial to" Cook-Lynn's fiction. Yet even more crucial to Cook-Lynn is the ancient concept of balance, which she referred to in the interview with Bruchac as "respect of gender."

Cook-Lynn's most overtly political short story, "A Good Chance," is set in the late 1970s at Fort Thompson on the Crow Creek Reservation and in the town of Chamberlain, South Dakota. The narrator of the story, who seems to be someone much like Cook-Lynn herself, is searching for a man named Magpie to tell him that he is being offered a scholarship to enter a writing program for Indians at a university in California. Her search leads her to two women who live in Fort Thompson; both love this man, and they tell her he is on parole, that he is content living among his people, and that he would never want to leave again. Magpie has been a member of the American Indian Movement and was arrested for being part of the 1975 riot at Custer Courthouse, which began over police abuse of Sarah Bad Heart Bull, whose son had been murdered.

In her two-day search for Magpie, the narrator and his mistress, Salina, go to Chamberlain, where Magpie is staying at a house by the bridge with his brother. When the women arrive, they learn that Magpie was arrested for breaking the conditions of his parole and that he has been shot and killed while in jail. The police had claimed they were afraid of him, but he wasn't armed. Thus, the title of this story is ironic. Magpie had anything but a "good chance" to make something of his life. "A Good Chance" grew out of the murders of two men Cook-Lynn knew. Sam Crow, a good friend of her father, was shot to death in a Chamberlain jail when Cook-Lynn was eleven. Melvin White Magpie, a member of AIM and a friend of Cook-Lynn, was stabbed to death in the Nebraska State Penitentiary. Cook-Lynn's story suggests that this kind of oppression is historical and ongoing: "I saw all sorts of murders and beatings and inappropriate actions against Indians," she has said.

Cook-Lynn's stories describe the results of the "violent diaspora and displacement" of the Dakotah, as Cook-Lynn called it, and of the destruction of their land over the course of a century. Yet, though her perspective is culturally specific, Cook-Lynn's emphasis on nature and on family is universal. Anyone can relate to the father's grief in her story "Loss of the Sky," when he loses his "middle son, the finest rider anywhere around," who died in France during World War I and whose bones "could not mingle with the bones of his grandfathers."

Realizing that most of her readers lack an understanding of the cultural background of her fiction, Cook-Lynn has written a number of commentaries on her work in a magazine she founded, *Wicazo Sa* [Red Pencil] *Review* and in a more recent magazine founded by Florestine Renville German, *ICKE WICASTA: The Common People Journal*. In "A Journey Into Sacred Myth," she explains the importance of two elements in her story "A Visit from the Reverend Tileston": the Sioux *Oyate* concept of themselves as "a spirit people called the star people" and the significance of the Sacred Dog, or *Shu(n)ka*. Initially published in Cook-Lynn's chapbook *Seek the House of Relatives* in 1983 and also included in *The Power of Horses*, "A Visit from Reverend Tileston," set in 1935, describes the intrusion of a white Christian minister and his sister missionaries on a Dakotah family living fifty miles away from the nearest town in a deep bend of the Missouri River. Two of the women in this family have "spent the afternoon picking wild plums and buffalo berries along the river." A loudspeaker blaring "On-ward Christian so-o-o-l-diers" announces the strangers' arrival. Clearly, the Dakotah family is not eager to welcome these intruders. But the Reverend and the two women push their way into the house and ask the Dakotah women to pray. The Reverend launches into a long prayer during which he scares the dog, which upsets two pails full of wild plums and berries gathered that hot afternoon. The Reverend's ironic last words, "Meditate, Mothers, on the Scriptures . . . for they are the food which sustains men during times of strife," are ignored. For the women are "engrossed in saving the berries." Clearly, these Dakotah people have their own spirituality embodied in the ancient stories the uncle tells of the star people and the blanket carriers still visible in the night sky. The Youngest Daughter knows this story, and as the Reverend leaves, she hopes that he also is aware of it. In her commentary on "A Visit from the Reverend Tileston," Cook-Lynn refers to an address made by an African writer, Wole Soyinka, in 1960. Soyinka said that an author who did not function as his society's conscience must deny himself or become merely a "chronicler and post-mortem surgeon." The radical conscience in her short fiction illustrates Elizabeth Cook-Lynn's similar commitment to her people.

Norma C. Wilson

SELECTED BIBLIOGRAPHY

Works by Elizabeth Cook-Lynn

Then Badger Said This. New York: Vantage, 1977.

Seek the House of Relatives. Marvin, S.D.: Blue Cloud Abbey, 1983.

The Power of Horses and Other Stories. New York: Arcade Publishing, 1990.

"The Radical Conscience in Native American Studies." *Wicazo Sa Review* 7/2 (1991): 9–13.

"The American Indian Fiction Writer: Cosmopolitanism, Nationalism, the Third World, and First Nation Sovereignty." *Wicazo Sa Review* 9/2 (1993): 26–36.

"A Journey Into Sacred Myth." *IKCE WICASTA: The Common People Journal* 1/1 (1998): 5–8.

Critical Studies

Allen, Paula Gunn. *The Sacred Hoop: Recovering the Feminine in American Indian Traditions.* Boston: Beacon, 1986.

Bruchac, Joseph, ed. *Survival This Way: Interviews with American Indian Poets.* Tucson: University of Arizona Press, 1987.

Ruppert, James. "The Uses of Oral Tradition in Six Contemporary Native American Poets." *American Indian Culture and Research Journal* 4/4 (1980): 87–110.

ROBERT COOVER
(1932–)

Born in Charles City, Iowa, in 1932, Robert Coover spent his childhood in Iowa and his adolescence, during the war years, in Indiana and Illinois (his father was managing editor of the Herrin, Illi-

nois *Daily Journal*). On graduation from
Indiana University in 1953, Coover was
drafted into the navy and served in Europe, where he met his wife-to-be, a University of Barcelona student, Maria del
Pilar Sans-Mallafré. In 1957 Coover began
what became his first collection of stories,
Pricksongs & Descants (1969). Meanwhile,
between 1958 and 1961 he worked toward a general humanities master's degree at the University of Chicago. Studying philosophy and religion, he meditated
on how "to struggle against myth on
myth's own ground." Coover's first novel,
The Origin of the Brunists, about an American religious cult, was published in 1966
and has been succeeded by seven more
novels. He also has produced two more
books of collected short stories, three
long short stories (each published as a
separate volume), a book of plays (*A Theological Position*), and numerous stories, as
yet uncollected. He has won many prizes,
including the Dugannon Foundation Rea
award for his lifetime contribution to the
short story. Between 1960 and 1980
Coover resided and wrote mostly abroad,
in England and Spain. He has since been
a professor of creative writing at Brown
University and has lived in Providence,
Rhode Island. At Brown he has champi-
oned hypertext fiction—open-ended fiction written for computers and utilizing
hypertext linking technology. The ultimate structure of such fiction is determined by the reader, not the writer.
"Unlike print text," Coover explains,
"hypertext provides multiple paths between text segments" and favors "a plurality of discourses over definitive utter-
ance."

Coover's interest in hypertext is the

outgrowth of his entire work, which must
be seen in contrast to an older tradition
of fiction. The older tradition paradoxi-
cally divides fiction into two neat kinds:
it designates some made-up stories, such
as myths, fables, and fairy tales, as purely
fictive; it designates other made-up stories, the ones called "realistic" or "realist,"
as true to life, less fictive than veracious.
The realist side invites us to see ourselves
in factitious stories and characters, and to
appropriate imaginary experiences as if
they were ours. Realist fiction intends to
edify us with knowledge of ourselves. But
a younger countertradition of storytelling, one that owes itself in part to Hawthorne's "Twice-Told Tales" and Melville's wilder fancies and that includes the
work of Gertrude Stein, James Joyce, Virginia Woolf, Samuel Beckett, Jorge Luis
Borges, Julio Cortázar, John Barth, Donald Barthelme, William Gass, and Coover,
opposes separating fictions into what is
true and not true, what we can and cannot
identify with, what edifies self-knowledge
and what does not. The countertradition
produces exhilarating, unnerving inter-
minglings of reality and fiction, inventions
that evade the fixed distinctions we live
by as well as read by.

To shake up the distinction between
fictions that are fables and fictions that are
true, Coover's *Pricksongs & Descants* begins
with "The Door," in which Little Red Riding Hood is the daughter of Jack the Giant-
killer. To these fairy-tale materials Coover
attaches a device commonly called "stream
of consciousness," which realist writers
developed to secure art's lifelikeness. At
the portal of his collection, Coover thus
seems a realist himself, who will retell and
humanize fables in terms of ordinary psy-

chology and experience. But the collection's second story, "The Magic Poker," undoes the first impression. The opening sentence of "The Magic Poker," "I wander the island, inventing it," equates the given reality of the tale—its island setting—with fabrication. The realist is an imposter. He makes everything that can happen in a story, and his authorial fiat makes reality. He is an illusionist, a magician. Yet the inventor-imposter also announces that "anything can happen," because in truth he is not fully in command. The imposer is imposed upon by the movement of fictional narrative, which word by word, event by event, produces uncontrollable possibilities of form and significance. "The Magic Poker" becomes, simultaneously (and by the separation of every paragraph from every other by a fence of asterisks), a story of two women exploring a deserted island, on which they find a rusty poker; a story of two women exploring a deserted island, on which they find a rusty poker, while unbeknownst to them they are stalked by a potential rapist; a story of two women exploring a desert island, on which they find a rusty poker that turns into a prince when one of the women kisses it; and so on—for there are even more storylines than these. So, by the fiat of the inventor and by the autonomy of words and narrative structures, a realistic story becomes a fairy tale, just as in "The Door" a fairy tale becomes realism.

By making reality fablelike, Coover does not suggest that fable or myth alone is truth. He maintains a contrast between myth and truth, but he shows that truth slides between the contrasts, and that myth and reality are equally states of enchantment. And "'there *are* no disen-

chantments,'" as a character in "The Magic Poker" says, "merely progression and styles of possession. To exist is to be spell-bound." Essential to the spell is narrative. Although by fissioning his storylines Coover uproots the logic whereby we follow the unity of a story's complications, his aim is not an antinarrative one. He pulverizes single-minded storytelling in order to give us all the more story to be interested in. Moreover, narrative's spellbinding power is suspense, which Coover intensifies by multiplying the unresolved intrigues whereby narrative entrances us.

Another spellbinding aspect of existence is Eros. Coover's stories interweave erotic glamour into the magic of his pluralized storylines. Our culture's narratives of male-female desire maintain fables wherein men characteristically master women, by force, by stealth, or by merely eyeing them; and wherein women characteristically are passive objects of male desire, are without desires, or even personal agencies, of their own. Are these stories true or false? Coover makes us wonder at how they are true-false. In *Spanking the Maid* (1982), a maid orders the world according to her master's ruthless directives. But she can't get it right, a deficiency for which he repeatedly punishes her. He insists that the pains he wants her to take, the pains he inflicts, express a "divine government of pain," whose agent he is. This is an old tale of male behavior; and we recognize it again in the prince who quests for Sleeping Beauty in *Briar Rose* (1996). She is a "mystery" the male will solve; when he declares to the sleeper that "You are Beauty" and "I am he who will awaken Beauty," he is performing his stereotyped narrative function. Yet Coover overturns these more-than-twice-told male myths. The narratives unfold the demise of male initiative, and the ascendancy of the maid and Briar Rose. The unfolding goes farther: it interidentifies male and female, hero and antihero, heroine and antiheroine; and, in *Briar Rose*, good fairies and bad. One good-bad fairy is the fiction writer, who makes the reader feel awake and dreaming, active and passive, female and male; whose knowledge of enchantment's persistence shows when Briar Rose says, "Now that I am awake . . . the truth is more hidden than before." Coover's initial repetition of the gender stereotypes searches for a possibility of remaining enchanted by Eros without remaining enchained by its clichés.

The tie between Coover's new forms of narrative and his work's erotic tension and intensity shows the wide appeal of Coover's material: for Eros is the stuff of popular culture. In America, however, movies are even more popular than sex. In *A Night at the Movies* (1987) Coover allies his artistry with film traditions. In "The Phantom of the Movie Palace," Coover claims that his fiction is no different, no more avant-garde than Hollywood's "great stream of image-activity," which seeks an "impossible mating, the crazy embrace of polarities as though the distance between the terror and the comedy of the void were somehow erotic." Replicating stock movie scenarios and characters, *A Night at the Movies* most of all apotheosizes the magics of cartoon animation and special effects. "Lap Dissolves" (one of *A Night*'s "Selected Short Subjects") contains a dream narrative that is Coover's typical magic act—a typical Coover story,

in other words—and that also is pure Loony Tunes and Dreamworks: "There were these midget baseball players who turned out to be prehistoric monsters, and all of a sudden they attacked the city, only even as they went on eating up the people, the whole thing turned into a song-and-dance act in which the leading monster did a kind of ballet with the Virgin Mary who just a minute before had been a lawn chair." Of course, when we are at the movies with Coover we go back to the primary production site: the great stream of language activity, whose spellbinding stunts and illusions are the original special effects.

Coover's stories are as much saturated by American politics as by pop culture. *A Political Fable* (1980) was written in 1968, a year of assassinations, riots, and U.S. disaster in Vietnam. For his hero Coover borrows Dr. Seuss's Cat in the Hat, and he shows the Cat running for president. The Cat's essential ambiguity, whereby he changes shapes at will and works magical special effects on the media and the nation, is a double for the ambiguities of Coover's fictions. "The Cat breaks the rules of the house, even the laws of probability, but what is destroyed except nay-saying itself, authority, social habit, . . . violence in the name of love?" The electorate responds with wild enthusiasm to the Cat's "Tricks and Voom and Things like that," which are "unencumbered by pseudo-systems" and by "the madness of normalcy." That madness possesses the Cat's opponent, who spouts "all the old clichés about 'free enterprise' and . . . 'the American Way of Life' . . . and 'government is a business and should be run like one.'" The opponent is an unconscious pile of incoherent American clichés; the Cat too exemplifies the same incoherence, but he also consciously unmasks and exhibits it, in order to carry us "out to something new where these old ways of identifying ourselves will seem sad and empty." Unfortunately for America, reaction sets in: it settles for the old fixed distinctions and condemns the Cat's lack of realism. In the end the Cat is torn apart. But the fable suggests that Robert Coover's stories—his version of Voom—will survive their own fission and can contribute to their reader's liberty.

Robert L. Caserio

SELECTED BIBLIOGRAPHY

Works by Robert Coover

Pricksongs & Descants. New York: E. P. Dutton, 1969.
A Political Fable. New York: Viking, 1980.
Spanking the Maid. New York: Grove Press, 1982.
In Bed One Night & Other Brief Encounters. Providence, R.I.: Burning Deck Press, 1983.
A Night at the Movies or, You Must Remember This. New York: Simon & Schuster, 1987.
Briar Rose. New York: Grove Press, 1996.

Critical Studies

Coover, Robert. "The End of Books." *New York Times Book Review,* June 21, 1992.
Gordon, Lois. *Robert Coover: The Universal Fictionmaking Process.* Carbondale: Southern Illinois University Press, 1983.
Kennedy, Thomas E. *Robert Coover: A Study of the Short Fiction.* New York: Twayne, 1992.

LYDIA DAVIS
(1947–)

Lydia Davis was born in 1947 in Northampton, Massachusetts, the daughter of two writers, Robert Gorham Davis and Hope Gale Davis. She grew up in Massachusetts, where her parents taught at Smith College, moving to New York at the age of ten, when her father began teaching at Columbia University. At fifteen she went to study music in Vermont, and at eighteen she began a bachelor of arts in English at Barnard College. Shortly afterward she met Paul Auster, then a student at Columbia. Auster introduced her to a variety of French writers, including Maurice Blanchot, large portions of whose work she has subsequently translated. During the early seventies Davis and Auster lived, traveled, and wrote in Europe. They were married in 1974. Davis's first collection of stories, *The Thirteenth Woman,* was published in 1976, followed by *Sketches for a Life of Wassilly* in 1981, when Davis and Auster split up. *Story and Other Stories* appeared in 1983. *Break It Down*, containing a selection from the previous volumes as well as some new stories, was published to acclaim in 1987, when Davis married the painter Alan Cote. Her novel *The End of the Story* brought her to the attention of a new readership in 1995, and *Almost No Memory,* published in 1997, once again collected recent and older stories. Davis, who has two sons—Daniel (from her first marriage) and Theo (from her second)— has taught at Bard College since 1986. At this writing she is translating Marcel Proust's *À Côte du Swann* for Penguin and working on a new novel in the form of a French grammar.

Lydia Davis's distinctive voice has never been easy to fit into conventional categories. Admired by poets (particularly the Language poets), and indeed often shelved in the poetry section of bookstores, her stories have bemused as many readers as they have enchanted. When *Break It Down* was first published, *New York Times* critic Michiko Kakutani wondered in an article attacking "minimalism's dead end" why Davis was publishing "the sort of fragments that writers like F. Scott Fitzgerald used to relegate to their notebooks." Defending the "short short" in an anthology entitled *Sudden Fiction* (1986), Davis noted that we are "more aware of the great precariousness and the possible brevity of our lives than we were in the past. . . . Perhaps we express not only more despair but also more urgency in some of our literature now, this urgency also being expressed as brevity itself."

While *The End of the Story* is a full-length novel that incorporates and retells several of Davis's shorter stories, here too her concerns are very different from those of most novelists. Challenging the boundaries between fiction and the meditative essay, Davis is concerned with narrative and the ways (and whys) that narratives are constructed. Many of her stories are, in fact, parables about storytelling, concerned, like Kafka's, with the difficulties involved in messages reaching and being correctly interpreted by their intended recipients.

While not writing fiction, Davis is a translator (notably of Michel Leiris and Blanchot), and much of her fiction aspires to reflect what she sees as the provisional and "curiously unlocated" status of the translated text. In early stories she uses the translation metaphor directly as her protagonists are frequently placed in foreign settings. In later works she takes linguistic estrangement to be the province of everyone who depends on language to communicate. Her characters speak as if they have suddenly found themselves in a foreign country. "I feel cut off from the other people in this country—to mention only this country," says the narrator of "The Professor." There is a pervasive sense that they are impersonating others, that their voices are ventriloquized, emanating from somewhere outside and detached from their own consciousnesses. It is as if the typical Davis narrator is, to quote John Ashbery's poem "No Way of Knowing," "waking up / In the middle of a dream with one's mouth full / of unknown words."

Davis's parables are most successful when they examine the problems of communication between men and women, and the strategies each uses to interpret the other's words and actions. In stories such as "The Letter," "Break It Down," "Story," and more recently, "Agreement" and "Disagreement," the lover tries to "figure out" the behavior of the loved one. In "Go Away," she concludes that when he says "Go away and don't come back," she is still hurt, "even though he does not mean what the words say, even though only the words mean themselves mean what they say." In "Story," "she" phones "him," receives no answer, goes to his house, finds his car but not him, writes him a note, goes home, receives his call, argues with him about his "story" of the evening's events, goes to his house, confronts him and returns home. The piece is littered with the markers of analytical reasoning: connectives such as "for example," "either . . . or," and "because" proliferate; precise time keeping is emphasized; and every emotion is quantified: "how angry is he," "how much" does he love her. These logical processes are intended to lead her, and us, to the truth. Indeed, the word "truth" appears six times in the final paragraph. But each repetition only weakens the chances of its attainability. That there might be rational choices to make does not mean that it is possible to make them.

This episode forms part of *The End of the Story,* and its progress is characteristic of the progress of the novel itself. The move from short story to novel does not mean, however, that readers learn more about the history or context of the affair and its protagonists. Indeed, the increased scope provided by the novel simply allows the obsession to be more fully expressed. The very length of the protagonist's narration reveals her inability to end her story. If Davis's novel questioned the nature of ending, her stories explore other constraints of narrative, genre, and interpretation. A random sampling of Davis's titles suggests some of these concerns: how does one find "The Center of the Story," one piece asks, while another posits, "What Was Interesting" about it? Indeed, is the notion of "Story" itself simply one of many "Other Stories" with which we torture and comfort ourselves?

"The Letter" (from *Break It Down*) exemplifies many of Davis's methods and compulsions. The story examines translation on many levels, between men and women, between languages, and finally, between genres. The story's narrator is herself a translator and while engaged in translating "a difficult prose poem," she receives a letter from an ex-lover. "Though of course," she soon has to acknowledge, "it is hard to call it a letter, since it is nothing but a poem, the poem is in French, and the poem was composed by somebody else."

The narrator attempts analysis at several levels. First she examines the letter as a physical object, noting such details as the smell of the paper and "a small ink blot in the curve of one letter" of her name. When this proves not to yield the meaning she requires, she moves on to consider the poem itself, and its significance as her lover's choice. Three things bother her, however: first, that he has sent a poem instead of a letter; second, that it is "the kind of poem it is"; and third, and most important, that he is using words "composed by somebody else" in a language that belongs to neither of them, instead of his own, to communicate with her. Indeed the narrator sees her lover's choice of a French prose poem as signaling a reluctance to be responsible for his "letter" at all.

Her initial scruples are suspended, however, when, on a second reading, she notices "the date, her name, comma, then the poem, then his name, period." Armed with these new data, she willingly accepts that the text should be read as a "letter" after all. Next she begins to analyze the poem itself, to perform, in other words, an exercise of practical criticism. The poem is not reproduced in the story, and all the reader has access to are the few words she singles out for attention: *pures, obscures, la lune, compagnon de silence, nous nous retrouvions*. But these are enough to situate the poem within an established Romantic paradigm of lost love and regeneration. Having transformed the poem into a letter, however, the narrator attempts to read it solely in relation to her own situation. Her first interpretation is positive: that they will one day be reunited; her second negative: "perhaps he does not really expect to see her again," and finally she has to admit to herself that perhaps the poem does not signify anything at all about their affair. It cannot be translated into the letter she requires.

But this is not where the story ends. Instead, all these hermeneutical contortions are simply dismissed in favor of an erotic response. "Half-dreaming," the narrator inhales the paper believing she can smell the scent of her lover, although as Davis reminds us (not allowing our disbelief full suspension) "she is probably smelling only the ink."

The structure of relationships as well as texts fascinates Davis. Many stories examine designated roles and how they contain us: what it is to be "the mother" or "the daughter," "the husband" or "the wife," or even "Wife one" or "Wife two." One narrator struggles to understand how "the angry man" whom she regards as her "enemy" can be the same person as "the playful man," "the serious man," and "the patient man" whom she loves. A recurring concern is the difference between how one appears to oneself and to others. One narrator realizes that the gap between how

"A Friend of Mine" sees herself and how others see her also applies to herself; another, with "Almost No Memory," reads old notebooks and wonders "how much they were of her and how much they were outside her." The protagonist of "Five Signs of Disturbance" distinguishes herself from "her voice," which she fears "will communicate something no one will want to listen to." What "if I were not me and overheard me from below, as a neighbor," thinks one narrator, while another worries that someone learning that she has "A Position at the University" will think she is "the sort of person who has a position at the university," whereas "a complete description of me would include truths that seem quite incompatible with the fact that I have a position at the university." Identities are the slipperiest of things.

Supremely self-conscious and intellectually playful, Davis's work is nevertheless often very moving, perhaps never more so than when it reveals the cost of that very self-consciousness. What a relief it would be, thinks one character, if, after all, "what I feel is not very important." "The Professor," meanwhile, "a woman in glasses," dreams of marrying a cowboy because she is "tired of so much thinking." "I thought that when my mind, always so busy, always going around in circles, always having an idea and then an idea about an idea, reached out to his mind, it would meet something quieter." She says this on the third page of her story; by page nine, after many "ideas about ideas," the "daydream" collapses. The story must either "end, or begin" (and that very ambiguity opens up a whole other series of questions about questions) with her husband and herself "standing awkwardly there in front of the ranch house, waiting while the cow-boy prepared our room." Escape from the life of the mind is inevitably futile for Lydia Davis's ever so slightly manic intellectu-als, and while readers may also occasion-ally long to escape, they will be sorry when they do.

Kasia Boddy

SELECTED BIBLIOGRAPHY

Works by Lydia Davis

The Thirteenth Woman and Other Stories. New York: Living Hand, 1976.
Sketches for a Life of Wassilly. Barrytown, N.Y.: Station Hill, 1981.
Story and Other Stories. Great Barrington, Mass.: Figures, 1983.
Break It Down. New York: Farrar, Straus & Giroux, 1986.
Almost No Memory. New York: Farrar, Straus & Giroux, 1996.

Critical Studies

McCaffery, Larry. *Some Other Frequency: Interviews with Innovative American Authors.* Philadelphia: University of Pennsylvania Press, 1996.
Perloff, Marjorie. "Fiction as Language Game: The Hermeneutic Parables of Lydia Davis and Maxine Chernoff." In Ellen G. Friedman and Miriam Fuchs, eds., *Breaking the Sequence,* pp. 199–214. Princeton, N.J.: Princeton University Press, 1989.
Ziolkowski, Thad. "Lydia Davis." *Dictionary of Literary Biography,* vol. 130, pp. 104–108. Detroit: Gale Research, 1993.

CHITRA BANERJEE DIVAKARUNI
(1953–)

Chitra Banerjee Divakaruni, a short story writer, poet, novelist, and essayist, was born in 1953 in Calcutta, grew up bilingual in Bengali and English, and earned her doctorate in English literature from the University of California, Berkeley (1984). She divides her time between the Bay Area and Houston. She published a collection of short stories, *Arranged Marriage,* in 1995, and her first novel, *The Mistress of Spices,* in 1997. Divakaruni has published four collections of poetry, *Dark Like the River* (1987), *The Reason for Nasturtiums* (1990), *Black Candle* (1991), and *Leaving Yuba City: Poems* (1997) and edited two volumes of readings: *Multitude: Cross-Cultural Readings for Writers* (1993) and *We, Too, Sing America: Readings for Writers* (1997). Her second novel, *Sister of My Heart* (1998), carries echoes of the short story "The Ultrasound," from *Arranged Marriage.*

Divakaruni's works, written and set within the context of the United States, should be read and discussed within the larger area of world literature written in English in the second half of the twentieth century. The parallels between her work and that of other twentieth-century South Asian and South Asian American writers need to be acknowledged. For example, her narratives about women's lives often read like echoes from one of India's greatest short story writers, Ismat Chugtai. But while Chugtai seizes the reader's attention with the strength and near savagery of her short stories, Divakaruni uses lyricism and understatement to present her point of view. In her literary portraits of South Asian families in the United States, Divakaruni can be counted among South Asian American women writers such as Tahira Naqvi, Susham Bedi, and Usha Nilsson, whose stories are often based against the background of South Asian American communities. In her best-crafted works, Divakaruni's techniques of storytelling remind the reader of writers from India such as Rabindranath Tagore, R. K. Narayan, and Santha Rama Rau.

In the introductory statement to her poetic narrative "Yuba City Wedding," Chitra Divakaruni says that writing in America is a challenge for her "to bring alive, for readers from other ethnic backgrounds, the Indian—and the Indian American—experiences, not as something exotic and alien, but as something human and shared." She also sees her work as an attempt to make her own South Asian community aware of the main subject of her work: "the plight of women of Indian origin struggling within a male-dominated culture, even here in America."

The women in *Arranged Marriage* are portrayed as strong and willing to change their situation in life. In the story "Meeting Mrinal," Asha, a newly divorced wife, decides that she and her son will not remain caught in silent, shocked grief in the face of their abandonment. In "Affair," a quiet, stereotypically traditional wife decides to leave her flamboyant, subtly cruel husband and make a life of her own. "The Disappearance" portrays a woman from the point of view of her husband, who is un-

able to understand why she has left him. After all, he had treated her very well. He had gone along with her color scheme for the kitchen and her plans for a vacation. When she had wanted to go back to school and to get a job, he had forbidden her to do either because it was his duty to take care of her. He was equally firm about his role as the husband who knew what was best for both of them as far as sex was concerned. And then, "the quiet, pretty girl" he had chosen to be his wife and to live with him in the States left him and abandoned her beloved son without a word of explanation.

With the exception of two stories, "The Maid Servant's Story" and "The Bats," the main narratives and episodes in *Arranged Marriage* are set in the United States. But India, even if it is in the form of memories, is present throughout the book. The pervasive imagery in *Arranged Marriage* is of physical landscapes—of homes, gardens, fields, rivers, cities, and villages—where the women live out their lives, and of clothes—the colors, the textures, the saris, *shalwar kameez,* dresses, skirts, and blouses—worn by the women. And despite its title, the relationships between the women in the stories are more striking than the portraits of marriages, failed or otherwise.

"The Maid Servant's Story" is the longest and the most intricately crafted narrative in *Arranged Marriage*. Using the device of a story within a story, of different stories told by different voices, Divakaruni presents the web of relationships between two generations of women and between women from different socioeconomic classes. The framing story is narrated by Manisha, a young professor at a

California university, who is visiting her home in Bengal. It begins with a conversation between Manisha and her beloved maternal aunt (*mashi*), Deepa Mashi, about the possibility of Manisha marrying a Bengali colleague in California. As the story unfolds, we become aware of the life-long tension between Manisha and her mother. It is a tension hidden behind the soft sounds of birds in the garden, the lighthearted banter between Manisha and her aunt, and the descriptions of the calm, familiar landscape of home. As far as Manisha is concerned, her aunt's life is uncomplicated, carefully codified, "constructed of simpler lines, its shapes filled with primary colors that do not bleed together."

This imagery of colors and patterns is extended when Manisha laughingly announces that she might agree to wear a traditional Banarasi silk sari if she ever gets married, but she will not wear "any of those traditional gaudy colors. . . . Maybe saffron would be nice—a pale saffron." She is surprised when her aunt tells her it would be best not to wear a saffron-colored sari. At this point, the story takes a different direction and is no longer about Manisha. As if she has pulled a thread out of Manisha's imagined saffron silk sari, Deepa Mashi unravels a story about the close relationship between a mistress and her maidservant. The symbolic colors— the white and red sari Deepa Mashi is wearing, the saffron silk of Manisha's imagination, the saffron sari given to the maid by her mistress in Deepa Mashi's story—collide when the maid spits "a bloodred wad of betel leaf" against her former mistress's palm.

The story concludes with Manisha's re-alization that her mother is the mistress of Deepa Mashi's story and the object of the maid's contempt. Images of color and of light and dark return as Manisha and her aunt sit together, "watching where the last light, silky and fragile, has spilled itself just above the horizon like the *palloo* of a saffron sari."

"Clothes," one of the most lyrical of the stories in *Arranged Marriage,* begins with a description of a young woman bathing in a lake: "The water of the women's lake laps against my breasts. . . . The little waves . . . make my sari float up around me, wet and yellow, like a sunflower after rain." "Clothes" is also one of the best examples of Divakaruni's subtle use of classical Indian mythology in a contemporary South Asian American story. Sumita, the protagonist of "Clothes," is a reminder, as well as a re-creation, of the heroine Savitri. Living in America with her husband and his parents, Sumita has been as traditionally a virtuous wife and daughter-in-law as the legendary Savitri. But when death comes for Sumita's husband, it is not in the form of the God of Death who in Savitri's story is willing to engage in a contest of riddles and even give back a husband's life. For Sumita's husband, death comes in the shape of a bullet fired by a robber in the store where her husband works. Savitri fights to regain her husband's life. Divakaruni's Sumita decides to fight for herself and the life she and her husband had planned for themselves in the United States. Instead of dutifully returning to India with her parents-in-law, Sumita decides to stay in the States, go to a college, and become a teacher. She is determined not to wear the traditional white sari of orthodox Hindu widows she

describes as "doves with cut-off wings."
As she looks at herself in a mirror, she
wonders how she will manage her life
without her husband in this dangerous
new land. She takes a deep breath and says,
"Air fills me—the same air that traveled
through [my husband's] lungs a little while
ago. . . . In the mirror a woman holds my
gaze, her eyes apprehensive yet steady. She
wears a blouse and skirt the color of al-
monds."

Many of the stories in *Arranged Marriage,* such as "The Maid Servant's Story,"
"Clothes," "The Ultrasound," "The Word
Love," and "Meeting Mrinal," can be read
as a stereotyping of the polarized concept
of freedom for a woman in America versus
loss of freedom for a woman in India. But
Divakaruni is too perceptive and skillful
a writer and her narratives are much too
complicated for such generalizations. In
writing about South Asian women's
struggles, defeats, and successes both in
India and in the United States, Divakaruni
proves her courage as a writer who is willing to address difficult issues through her
stories and her poetry. Divakaruni's narratives, which defy the traditionally held
distinctions between the genres of prose
and poetry, reveal her ability to manipulate the traditions and the craft of writing
from both India and the United States of
America.

Roshni Rustomji-Kerns

SELECTED BIBLIOGRAPHY

Divakaruni, Chitra Banerjee. *Arranged Mar-
riage.* New York: Doubleday, 1995.
Rustomji-Kerns, Roshni. "Chitra Banerjee
Divakaruni, *Arranged Marriage." Journal of
South Asian Literature* 30/1 & 2 (1995):
281–287.
Ghosh, Bishnupriya. "*Arranged Marriage* by
Chitra Banerjee Divakaruni." *Weber Stud-
ies* 13/2 (spring/summer 1996):157–
158.
Sen-Bagchee, Sumana. " 'Mericans, Eh?"
The Toronto Review of Writing Abroad 14/
3 (1996): 72–73.

ANDRE DUBUS
(1936–1999)

Andre Dubus experienced himself as
a man living in a violent America. He
wrote as a Catholic who believed in God.
The majority of his stories concern lower
middle-class families living in the old industrial towns of northeast Massachusetts. These men and women are often
lapsed "cradle-Catholics" who live with
uneasy decisions about lust, birth control,
and abortion. Although many of his characters are unbelievers, in their stories the
concepts of love, redemption, and sin have
meaning. The thrice-divorced Dubus,
however, was hardly an orthodox Catholic: he did not accept the authority of the
pope, and his most devout characters have
their quarrels with the church. The young
hero of "If They Knew Yvonne" tells one
priest that he no longer believes that masturbation is a sin, but confides in another
that he believes making love with his girlfriend was a sin, not because of the act
but because he did not love her. Re-

demption, for Dubus, comes less from accepting the authority of the church than from accepting the weightiness of a fully committed love for another human being. Abortion is problematic in such stories as "Miranda Over the Valley," "Falling in Love," or "Finding a Girl in America" not because it violates church teachings but because it is used to maintain a coldly calculated, emotionally detached freedom. Similarly, marriage itself matters less than the nature of a sexual relationship; in "Adultery," marriage becomes wrong when it becomes only a friendly and convenient means for servicing one's sexual and emotional needs. Parenthood and the relationship between husband and wife are central concerns for Dubus. He sees anything used to avoid these primary bonds—including the professionalism of the artist ("Adultery," "Falling in Love"), the soldier ("The Misogamist," "The Shooting"), or the athlete ("The Pitcher")—as perverse. He is critical of any view of masculinity that compels men to deny the emotional and spiritual centrality of their lives as husbands and fathers.

Born in Lake Charles, Louisiana, in 1936, Dubus moved eight years later with his family to Lafayette, where he attended the Christian Brothers School. He returned to Lake Charles to enter McNeese State College. After graduation, he joined the U.S. Marine Corps. During his five years in the military, four children were born to Dubus and his wife, Patricia Lowe. In 1963 Dubus took the risky step of resigning his commission and moving his young family to Iowa City, where he entered the University of Iowa graduate writing program. In 1966 Dubus accepted a teaching post at Bradford College in Massachusetts. His novel The Lieutenant was published the following year.

During the next twenty years Dubus published seven volumes of short stories and novellas. His stories were regularly selected for the major prize anthologies, and he received a National Endowment for the Arts grant and a Guggenheim Fellowship. Dubus was committed to the novella and short story forms. He resisted pressure from publishers to write novels; even though such longer works as Voices from the Moon were issued as short novels, Dubus himself regarded them as long short stories. Dubus nevertheless found ways to build larger, more architectural structures within the body of his work. Three of his most important novellas ("We Don't Live Here Anymore," "Adultery," and "Finding a Girl in America") revisit the same characters at different moments and from different points of view, thus tracing the course of their marriages over time. The early Paul Clement stories provide snapshots of a boy raised in a divided marriage; his competing loyalties to his mother and to his father prepare him for betrayal of those he loves and for the limited view of masculinity he adopts as a marine recruit in "Cadence," a story in which he celebrates a physical endurance that his friend Munson questions. In "Goodbye," the young Lieutenant Clement visits his family with his new wife, only to endure once again the bitterness between his parents. Dubus also found more oblique ways to establish connections among his short works so that they began to constitute a larger fictional world. The protagonist of one short story may appear as a minor figure in another (Roy Hodges in "The Misogamist" and "Waiting"). The same bar, Timmy's, is a major or minor setting in half a dozen works. A comment by the narrator of "Rose" suggests why so many stories revolve around this establishment; he notes that Timmy's is a place for workingmen, despite the college students who have taken it up. The same might be said of Dubus's fiction.

In 1986 Dubus lost one leg above the knee and was in a wheelchair until his death of a heart attack in February 1999. He had stopped to help two people who had driven over an abandoned motorcycle, and a car hit him while he was pushing a young woman away from its path, probably saving her life. This difficult time also brought the breakup of his marriage to his third wife, Peggy Rambach, with whom he had fathered two more children. A grant from the MacArthur Foundation helped provide financial support as Dubus published a volume of short stories and a collection of personal essays. It is tempting to read Dubus's later work in light of such dramatic events, particularly such stories as "The Colonel's Wife," in which Robert Townsend must accept that both his legs, badly broken in a riding accident, will never be the same again and that his wife has had affairs as well as he. But in fact stories like "The Colonel's Wife" only make more graphic themes that occupied Dubus long before his own accident: separation between body and spirit, and love predicated upon the acceptance of failure and pain. Violence, however, continues to be the most obvious subject in his fiction.

In a 1987 interview, Dubus described life in the United States as violent and said that he doubted he would write so much about violence if he lived "in Canada or Denmark." He was most interested in violence as a response to an attack on one's self or loved ones. From his first published story, "The Intruder," to the recent "Out of the Snow," Dubus tried out a variety of responses to attacks on one's self, on other innocent people, and on loved ones. This common issue links the three groups of stories that might otherwise seem very different: those that draw on his childhood in Louisiana and its atmosphere of racial tension, those that draw on his years as a professional soldier, and those that reflect his later life in the Merrimack Valley of Massachusetts. This continuing preoccupation suggests Dubus's intense personal investment in the matter; he does not view violence as only a detached cultural observer. In the essay "Giving Up the Gun," Dubus describes how he began to carry a gun in 1977 after "someone I love was raped in Boston by a man who held a knife to her throat." Echoing the concerns and even the language of his own stories, Dubus declared "that no woman would ever be raped if I was with her." In 1985 he found himself about to shoot a white man who was threatening a black man with a knife. No one was injured, but Dubus was shaken by what he might have done. Appalled that "a young man could be dead by my hand because of one moment on a Friday night," he still felt he had no choice but to protect the black man: "I understand turning the other cheek. But what about me turning that guy's cheek?" After his accident, Dubus wrote, he felt even more need for a gun, until one day on a train when a vision of himself killing someone was so strong that "I gave up answers that are made of steel that fires lead, and I decided to sit in a wheelchair on the frighteningly invisible palm of God." For Dubus, giving up the gun also signified giving up "the protection I believed they gave people I loved, and strangers whose peril I might witness, and me."

"The Intruder," first published in 1963 but collected in the 1996 *Dancing After Hours,* describes young Kenneth Girard's killing of a man prowling outside his sister's bedroom window. After the shooting Connie runs outside, calling, "Douglas, Douglas, Douglas!" Kenneth "knows" that he has killed not a prowler, but his sister's boyfriend. Though Kenneth's father assures his distraught son that he has shot a threatening prowler, Kenneth and the reader both believe Mr. Girard is lying to protect his son from knowing what he has done. For Connie's behavior both before and after the accident clearly implies a plan for Douglas to return in secret to her bedroom. Kenneth seems to have acted out of a desire to protect those he loves, his parents and his sister. Mr. Girard assures his son that the man he killed represented a threat: "It was a prowler. You did right. There's no telling what he might have done."

Even though the desire to protect others seems a valid motive, Kenneth's fantasies about doing so are disturbing. At the beginning of the story, when he heads for the woods where he indulges in these thoughts, Kenneth himself feels "as if he had left the house to commit a sin." Moreover, his daydreams connect heroic protection with sex and violence. He imagines "that he had saved a beautiful girl from a river" and that, after leading soldiers through the woods, he "slapped

a hand over the guard's mouth and stabbed him in the back." Specific references to movies and television programs merge the fantasies of the thirteen-year-old with cultural fantasies of westerns and heroic warfare.

Kenneth's desire to protect is entwined with his young sexuality and with his anger and aggression. He considers his sister "the most beautiful girl he knew," and Douglas is an "intruder" in more than one sense. Kenneth resents the intrusion of the boyfriend into his own plans to spend the evening alone with Connie: "He liked being alone, but, even more, he liked being alone with his sister." When the thought of Douglas's arrival makes him "nervous," Kenneth gazes at a magazine photograph of a girl in a bikini while cleaning his rifle with a sexually suggestive motion. Though Kenneth does not like Douglas and is never consciously aware that the man he later hears outside the house might be him, his instant comprehension when Connie calls "Douglas!" may suggest that he had a latent sense of the lovers' plan. Moreover, a faint ambiguity about the dead man's identity that Dubus creates may reflect Kenneth's view that Douglas, like the anonymous "prowler," is a threat to his sister and an intruder.

The story leads the reader to believe with Kenneth that Mr. Girard is lying when he tells Kenneth that the dead man was not Douglas. Dubus implies that Kenneth's strength resides in his refusal to accept the comfort of his father's lie. He knows and continues to insist that the dead man is Douglas. He knows his guilt, rejects his action, and, anticipating Dubus's own later gesture, he gives up the gun. Moreover, the last line of the story shows Kenneth's understanding that his guilt goes far beyond a tragic mistake in identity: "He saw himself standing on the hill and throwing his rifle into the creek; then the creek became an ocean, and he stood on a high cliff and for a moment he was a mighty angel, throwing all guns and cruelty and sex and tears into the sea." This fantasy begins on the same hill where Kenneth earlier indulged in thoughts of heroic manhood. He senses that he is rejecting the structures of his earlier dreams as much as the gun itself; he senses that "cruelty and sex" as well as guns are part of heroic dreams of protection. The "sex" he rejects is not just his sister's, but also his own. His final vision suggests both a moral judgment more mature than his father's *and* a childish and naive wish to escape his own adulthood.

"Killings," written approximately fifteen years after "The Intruder," also concerns a shooting and its consequences. Matt Fowler and his friend Willis Trottier execute Richard Strout, the young man who has killed Fowler's son, Frank. This seems to be an act of private vengeance rather than of protection, but Matt's act has been partially motivated by his wish to protect his wife, who suffers every time she encounters the seemingly unrepentant Strout on the streets of their small town. "She can't even go out for cigarettes," he tells Willis. "It's killing her." While it is obviously too late to "protect" Frank, Matt experiences his son's murder as an assault on his own fatherhood and on his wish to protect his children. But Dubus himself, in a 1987 interview, rejected Fowler's "sympathetic" violence: "Once he [Matt] kills a human being, he has violated nature and is forever removed from it." Indeed,

the title of the story itself—"Killings"— seems to link both the original slaying of Fowler's son and Matt's retaliation, suggesting that there may be finally no important moral distinction between the two acts, and it may further imply the effect on Matt himself. Matt seems isolated by his act at the end of the story. He cannot tell his other children the truth, and he cannot make love with Ruth.

Like Kenneth in "The Intruder," Matt is saddened by his act. In this story, Strout, the man who is shot, is clearly guilty, but he is still a human being, and that is the knowledge Matt has to suppress in order to kill him. Moreover, Strout is part of human connection. As Willis puts it, "Ever notice even the worst bastard always has friends?" At the end of the story, Matt thinks of Strout's current girlfriend, imagining her sleeping, as yet unaware that her boyfriend has been killed. In this story, if not in "The Intruder," the villain and the boyfriend are one and the same. To comfort Kenneth, Mr. Girard relies on distinctions between innocent men and guilty, anonymous prowlers who presumably deserve to die, but Matt cannot draw such clear moral lines. At the end of "Killings," Matt seems to blur distinctions between the innocent and the guilty, the loved and the unknown; he thinks instead of all the dead, who were once living.

However clear Dubus and Matt may be about the consequences of Matt's violence, the story is unsettling precisely because most readers will enter to some degree into Fowler's desire to snuff out the careless, self-indulgent Richard Strout. But in carrying out the deed, Matt becomes isolated even from those who sympathize with his violence. He is finally most human in his divided reactions; readers can sympathize with the part of him that desires nothing more than to kill Strout and the part of him that is horrified by his own desire. Dubus feels, and can make his readers feel, both what is compelling and what is wrong about Matt's act.

"Out of the Snow," a story in Dubus's recent collection *Dancing After Hours,* is far more explicit in its probing of "protection" as a reason for violence. LuAnn Arceneaux is a housewife who confronts "doom walking out of the snow": two men who have followed her from the market and entered her house. Seeing "hatred and anger" in the eyes of the man in the red sweatshirt, she is afraid to run: "Her body would not turn its back on them; it knew that if it did, it would die." Instead she fights both men, first kicking one in the testicles, then swinging a heavy skillet with both hands at the heads of both men, breaking bones in their faces and hands.

What violence could be more defensible? When LuAnn later remarks to her husband, "I know what I couldn't do. I couldn't turn the other cheek," Ted's reply is essentially that of Kenneth's father in "The Intruder": "You did what you had to do. It's a jungle out there. . . . You *had* to. For yourself. For the children. For me." He emphasizes her violent response to violence as an act of protection not only for herself but also for others. LuAnn, like Kenneth, is not comforted, and "Out of the Snow" also ends with the protagonist's consideration of the self as a killer: "I don't know how close I came to killing them." This knowledge, even more than the two men, is the "doom" that comes "out of the snow" to disrupt her harmony, a snow that

echoes the winter Matt Fowler imagines as his fate in the last sentence of "Killings": "he saw red and yellow leaves falling to the earth, then snow: falling and freezing and falling."

All three stories end with a sympathetic family member comforting an actual or potential killer. While the images that conclude their stories imply that Kenneth and Matt reject the solace that their violence was justified or necessary to protect others, LuAnn is the only protagonist to do so with an explicit speech: "I didn't hit those men so I could be alive for the children or for you. . . . And if it's that easy, how are we supposed to live? If evil can walk through the door, and there's a place deep in our hearts that knows how to look at its face, and beat it till it's broken and bleeding, till it crawls away. And we do this with rapture."

We do this with rapture. Here LuAnn uncovers a vision of human nature that Dubus only implies in the other works: however necessary violence may be to protect themselves and others, however sincere the part of them that does shrink from violence, another part of human beings resonates with the original physical aggression because it corresponds to inner aggressive desires. For Dubus, redemption lies in the fear of their own violence that is as authentic as enjoyment of it. What his characters fear *is* their enjoyment.

In all three stories, the protagonists deploy their weapons against a threat to love and family harmony, but "Out of the Snow" differs from the other two stories in important ways. LuAnn's violence is in response to a direct attack on the self. Her attack on the men is the most extended and physical, if least lethal, response to threat. She is a woman deploying a skillet rather than a gun. Thus the story implies that performing violence "with rapture" is a human rather than an exclusively male or exclusively American problem, and it suggests an aspect of Dubus unusual in a writer so preoccupied with masculinity: he often adopted a female point of view, and he was interested in the inner lives of women, not just in the ways women influence and define the values of his male characters.

Most important, LuAnn responds to violence as a committed Catholic. (Kenneth is a Catholic, but his guilty Hail Mary's when he looks at photographs of women seem perfunctory, as does his family's discussion of Mass.) Like Dubus in his personal essay, she uses the biblical metaphor of "turning the other cheek" to weigh her response to attack. The importance Dubus attaches to LuAnn's beliefs explains what otherwise seems a strangely slow start to a dramatic story. The men enter the story only in the last eight pages; the first thirteen detail the minutiae of LuAnn's everyday activities. LuAnn views the morning toast and oatmeal as "a sacrament" she offers to her family and to God; she returns the supermarket cart instead of leaving it in the parking lot because with even such a small action "you join the world. With your body. And for those few moments, you join it with your soul." LuAnn does not separate what she *does* from who she *is*. Because she lives "by trying to be what I'm doing" and does not separate her spirit from her body, LuAnn cannot write off her aggression as an aberration: "All afternoon I was amazed by my body. But

that was me hitting them." LuAnn views even giving up cigarettes as a spiritual struggle, so what would it mean for her to kill another human being?

Dubus's treatment of LuAnn demonstrates both his tendency to characterize his protagonists through their daily rituals and his belief that such rituals can separate the secular and divine or merge the two. Like military drill and protocol, personal routines of exercise, reading, coffee, newspapers, and cigarettes are both a discipline and a way to manage pain. Such regular activities may allow protagonists to keep pain at a distance without ever confronting its spiritual sources. On the other hand, as "Out of the Snow" suggests, actions regularly performed can also rise to the level of sacramental devotion, creating as well as dulling feelings. For Luke Ripley, ritual seems an attempt to mediate spiritual imperfection. In "A Father's Story," in *The Times Are Never So Bad,* Luke rises every morning for an hour of silence before Mass, but though he receives the Eucharist, thoughts of his daily life often distract him from the words of the Mass: "I cannot achieve contemplation, as some can; and so . . . I have learned . . . [that] ritual allows those who cannot will themselves out of the secular to perform the spiritual." Ritual, however, cannot prevent spiritual failure. At the end of the story, Luke has "to face and forgive" his failure to report an accident in which his daughter has run down a young man who was possibly still alive. Though he also fails to confess this action, Luke continues to receive the Eucharist, believing in God's love for him even in his weakness. Like LuAnn, he gives up "a peace I neither earned nor deserved" to understand his human limitations and consequent need for grace.

The final sentence of "Out of the Snow" also balances love and human failure. It describes LuAnn sitting with her husband: "Their legs touched, their hips, their arms; and they sat looking at the fire." The sentence weighs their connection, centered on the fire, against the violence that came "out of the snow." One may choose to emphasize either their connection or its limitations. They have just disagreed, and only their bodies touch, bodies separated into parts: legs, hips, arms. Despite her domestic "sacraments," LuAnn recognizes her own imperfection. Her rituals provide no answer to violence. Horrified by her fight with the men, and the dilemma they represent, she uses the same words Luke uses to insist on a human action that neither can justify to God: "I would do it again."

Other Dubus stories suggest that inaction in the face of violence can be as problematic as responding to it with force. A sense of failure pervades "The Curse," in which a middle-aged bartender looks on helplessly as a group of young men gang-rape a young girl in his presence. Despite the assurances of those around Mitchell that any resistance on his part would have been useless, the bartender insists that "I could have stopped them," and he feels he deserves the victim's curse. The dual possibilities of paralysis in the face of violence and of meeting it with an equally violent private vengeance preoccupied Dubus since his first stories. In fact the two seemingly opposed responses are often oddly conjoined. In "The Bully," the young Paul Clement's passivity when a bully attacks him and a friend is clearly

linked to Paul's later compulsion to hang a kitten. Rose's spiritual paralysis as her husband beats their young children precedes not only her heroism in saving her daughters from a burning apartment but also her deliberate choice to back over her fallen husband with the family car ("Rose"). Polly Comeau in "The Pretty Girl" shoots the husband who has previously raped her but also ensures his death by her passivity, a fact not lost on Ray's brother, who wonders, "how you can be like that with a guy, then shoot him and leave him to bleed to death while you sit outside."

Only occasionally preachy, Dubus at his best is morally serious without subordinating aesthetic concerns to any moral purpose. His stories employ more long passages of perceptive, reflective narration than do those of most contemporary American writers, but he also has an ear for dialogue, particularly for the exchanges between regulars in bars, between military men, between parents and children, and between those long married. Perhaps nothing better illustrates the way Dubus's spiritual vision subtly permeates his realistic portrayal of a secular world than does his frequent use of language that operates simultaneously in both contexts. "Get something sinful," LuAnn's friend tells her, when LuAnn reports she is going out for groceries. Similarly, Dubus's close observation of the strong emotions of fatherhood never disappears into allegory, even when "A Father's Story" reminds the reader of a heavenly as well as an earthly father. A simple "Jesus" uttered in a bar is first a realistic curse. The division between its profane and its spiritual meanings suggests the potential Andre Dubus often discovered in even his most unlikely characters, a potential that may be manifested only in their dissatisfaction with their lives.

Suzanne Hunter Brown

SELECTED BIBLIOGRAPHY

Works by Andre Dubus

Separate Flights. Boston: David R. Godine, 1975.
Adultery and Other Choices. Boston: David R. Godine, 1977.
Finding a Girl in America: A Novella and Seven Short Stories. Boston: David R. Godine, 1980.
The Times Are Never So Bad: A Novella and Eight Short Stories. Boston: David R. Godine, 1983.
We Don't Live Here Anymore: The Novellas of Andre Dubus. New York: Crown Publishers, 1984.
The Last Worthless Evening: Four Novellas and Two Stories. Boston: David R. Godine, 1986.
Selected Stories. Boston: David R. Godine, 1988.
Broken Vessels. Boston: David R. Godine, 1991.
Dancing After Hours. New York: Alfred A. Knopf, 1996.
"Giving Up the Gun." *The New Yorker,* February 24 and March 3, 1997.

Critical Studies

Kennedy, Thomas E. *Andre Dubus: A Study of the Short Fiction.* Boston: Twayne, 1988.
Kennedy, Thomas E. "Raw Oysters, Fried

Brain, the Leap of the Heart: An Interview with Andre Dubus." *Delta* (February 1987 [special issue devoted to Dubus's work]): 21–77.

DEBORAH EISENBERG
(1946–)

"I like the bristling, sparky, kinetic effect you can get from condensing something down to the point where it almost squeaks." Deborah Eisenberg's description, to a reporter, of the short story's attractions suggests the energy with which her own fiction is charged, though its cool, ironic surface masks the intensities below. The details of each story's world are recorded with witty precision, in sharp contrast to the tentative perceptions and emotions of the characters. The narrative's characteristic understatement leaves a disquieting doubt about whether the characters have seen what the reader sees—though sometimes the endings deftly, surprisingly reveal just how far the protagonist has silently traveled.

The title of Eisenberg's first collection, *Transactions in a Foreign Currency,* suggests the basic situation in which her central characters, mostly young women, find themselves. They must negotiate an unfamiliar environment, but the currency in question involves less the exchange of money than of styles, idioms, implicit understandings—ultimately, of selves that seem constituted as much by the need to accommodate such mores, "to adhere to the slippery requirements of distant authorities," as by any internally shaping impulse. Nevertheless, having mastered the local patois, these characters often achieve a moment of self-assertion or at least resistance that the code itself cannot predict or circumscribe.

In "Flotsam," Charlotte, the first-person narrator of the opening story in this collection, is rejected as "sentient protoplasm" by her boyfriend Robert: "'Have you ever had an intention?' he said. 'Have you ever had a desire? Have you ever even had what could accurately be described as a reaction?'" Drifting to New York, Charlotte finds a roommate named Cinder (that is, Lucinda, but transitory flares of metropolitan fashion—and passion—have left Cinder a burned-out residue). In the East Village orbit of Cinder and her friends, Charlotte acquires, frequently through humiliation, tidbits of information about dress (Cinder's shop sells both used clothing and her own creations), drugs, urban males and their sexual requirements, and various hip bigotries— "meaningless fragments," Charlotte says, "until enough flotsam accretes to manifest, when one notices it, a construction." Although Charlotte herself initially appears to be flotsam, her accumulation of small insights enables her not only to tear up her vainly cherished photograph of Robert but to walk out on Cinder— her "heart racing with a dark exultation, as if [she'd] just, in the grace of an instant, been thrown wide of some mortal danger."

The alien terrains that subsequent protagonists navigate include postadolescent sexuality ("What It Was Like, Seeing Chris," narrated by a schoolgirl whose literal vision is endangered by eye disease), gym culture ("Days"), and the geography and rhythms of Canadian or Latin American cities ("Transactions in a Foreign Currency," "Broken Glass") and, above all, the personal entanglements of other lives that impinge on ours without revealing the history or competing allegiances that will eventually preclude sustained connection. The initially perplexing world of a soap opera proves alluring to the narrator of "Rafe's Coat," because with repeated viewing its mysteries *can* be resolved and its relationships decoded. The motives and desires of those around her—not to mention her own—remain more opaque.

The narrator of "Rafe's Coat" is treated with more irony than most of Eisenberg's protagonists, even though their characteristic receptivity, verging on passivity, might seem an invitation to satire; for them, ordinary activities—going shopping, quitting smoking, even sleeping through the night—become arduous achievements, especially in "Days." Almost heroically, they must improvise selves adequate to a world that is still revealing itself.

Although Eisenberg describes "Days" as her only autobiographical story—it was also the first—*Transactions in a Foreign Currency* frequently mirrors the New York she must have found when she moved there at the age of twenty-six. She was born in Winnetka, Illinois; after two years at Marlboro College in Vermont and an interval of travel, she yielded to New York's seemingly inevitable pull and pursued further studies at the New School for Social Research. There she also met the playwright and actor Wallace Shawn, whom she credits with first prompting her to write. Remarkably, Eisenberg's unforeseen career as a writer did not begin until the age of thirty. She says it took her three years to write "Days," and for the next five or six years she seldom wrote more than one story a year. Nevertheless, generous payments by the *The New Yorker* helped to free her from work as a secretary and waitress. In addition to her three collections of short stories, *Transactions in a Foreign Currency, Under the 82nd Airborne,* and *All Around Atlantis,* she has produced a noteworthy commentary on the paintings of Jennifer Bartlett, *Air: 24 Hours.* In the verbal vignettes that complement Bartlett's images, Eisenberg is stunningly alert to their "enigmatic and highly charged atmospheres." Her discussion of Bartlett's "struggle against resolution" is no less suggestive in relation to her own fiction.

Frank Conroy's invitation to read at the Iowa Writers' Workshop and encouragement from the novelist and short-story writer Francine Prose helped to initiate Eisenberg's teaching career; she has led writing workshops at various universities, and while still living in New York with Shawn, she has since 1992 taught one semester at the University of Virginia. Among other honors, she has received the American Academy of Arts and Letters Award in Literature, a Whiting Writer's Award, and a Guggenheim Fellowship.

Eisenberg's protagonists' resistance to premature certainties admirably evinces a kind of "negative capability," especially in contrast to the intellectual operations of characters who are complacently equipped with categories and explanations for all human phenomena—explanations most readily applied to those on the other side of a social, ethnic, or national divide. The political implications of these contrasting approaches to experience, tacit in the stories of *Transactions,* are foregrounded in Eisenberg's second collection, *Under the 82nd Airborne,* which is clearly influenced by the time that she and Shawn spent in Mexico and Central America during the 1980s. This political turn is already anticipated by the portrait of American émigrés—a failed leisure class who inexpensively maintain their status abroad—in "Broken Glass," the last of the stories in *Transactions.* For once the transaction is economic as well as cultural: the disparity in wealth between even "failed" Americans and the Latin Americans who tend their needs makes the pleasures of the elite an extortion; willed incomprehension and indifference disguise the nature of the bargain—at least from its beneficiaries.

Initially this casual imperialism seems merely opportunistic, apolitical, but the title story of *Under the 82nd Airborne,* as well as "Holy Week" and "Across the Lake" (in *All Around Atlantis*) makes its complicity with political repression inescapable; the gunrunners, the missionaries, the diplomatic attachés of "Under the 82nd Airborne" are only more aggressive exponents of the narrow and self-serving vision of the émigrés or the countercultural traffickers in native handiwork ("Across the Lake"). In "Someone to Talk To" or "Tlaloc's Paradise" (both in *All Around Atlantis*), the ways in which exiles imaginatively appropriate these exotic locales also become suspect. Even in the most politically charged stories, what is truly frightening is not so much the visible apparatus of state terror as the sense of the unknown—intimations of violence which the outsider will never be able to read. Nor, on the other hand, will she be able to read the ways in which the life of the indigenous population accommodates itself to the exigencies of poverty and force, flowing in hidden channels and maintaining its own forms of beauty, gravity, and grief.

The widening frame of Eisenberg's fiction makes more visible the forms of violence implicit in domestic settings (in both the familial and national sense). In the Cheeveresque milieu of "The Robbery," the violation of a neighbor's house makes wealthy suburban life seem suddenly vulnerable, but dinner guests restore a sense of security by locating the "obvious" culprit in the ne'er-do-well brother of the maid; the rectification of middle-class order seems tacitly, if only discursively, as violent as its rupture. The dreams of the protagonist hint that she is dissatisfied with this resolution by elaborating childhood memories of Vernon and Evaline ("each had a grandparent, or grandparents, who had been slaves") and transporting her to an imagined scene of communal life, more impoverished but more vital than the one she knows.

Accompanying Eisenberg's attention to the politics of the family is an increased focus on teenaged characters, precociously perceptive but ill equipped to fend off illegitimate encroachments of grownup authority. Jim Shepard's review of All Around Atlantis shrewdly compares Eisenberg to the Henry James of What

Maisie Knew, and comments that "the tension between vocabulary and perception creates in Eisenberg's young people a kind of uncanny eloquence of the nearly articulate."

Both fictional and actual violence haunts the adolescents who appear in All Around Atlantis. In "Mermaids," a fat unhappy girl colors a plane trip to New York by telling her unwilling companion about bodies in lagoons that are visible from the sky: "Their hair floats, and their legs are green and slimy," and of course they are imagined as "beautiful little girls" who are the victims of sex crimes. This imagined glimpse of horror condenses and displaces the adult cruelty, masquerading as beneficence and parental discipline, to which both girls are exposed in the course of the story. Francie, the title character of "The Girl Who Left Her Sock on the Floor," discovers only upon her mother's death that her father's vividly narrated death in a traffic accident is untrue. She flees the casual condescensions of her boarding school, where "dazzling, razor-edged splinters" tinkle in the voices of well-meaning teachers.

Francie arrives at the apartment her father shares with his gay lover. There the story leaves her, at a literal and metaphorical threshold. For Eisenberg's adolescent characters, the vista of adult experience is daunting but heady (Francie's final thought is that her father is "going to have to deal with her soon enough," and not vice versa). On the other hand, the compelling title story of All Around Atlantis is shadowed by the past, rather than the future, and by violence on a much larger scale. The historical violence of the Holocaust, which compromises the narrator's American innocence, goes unspoken. After her mother's funeral she looks back at her incredulous adolescent discovery of an unnamed past whose presence, felt rather than known, has shaped the household in which she grows up. The household consists of her mother Lili, subject to recurrent black depressions, and her "uncle" Sándor, actually a cousin, who had brought her mother from Europe as a one-and-a-half-year-old child, a small remaining fragment of his shattered family; in Hungary Sándor had been a poet, and both mother and uncle have their circle of admirers, drawn by some residual luster of European style and high culture.

Atlantis, a book of Sándor's poetry whose title evokes a mythical lost world, is resurrected and translated by Peter, who represents a later (and more politically acceptable) wave of Hungarian refugees in the 1950s. Peter's "rediscovery" of Sándor is also a betrayal: "Absolutely every poor shnook seemed to be out there scrounging up some piece of art with which to beat up some ideological adversary or intellectual competitor. . . . Now, of course, no one wants art for any purpose whatsoever—let alone for its own. . . . But *Sándor*? A *bastion* against *Communism*? Oh, please, Peter. For shame." The narrator worries that her own curiosity about Lili's and Sándor's histories, sharpened by the inquiries of her wealthy friend Paige (to whom the whole household seems exotic), is also pruriently invasive. The two sides of the historical divide permit only spectral habitation: "We were the ghosts in the ghost of Lili's city, just as she and Sándor were ghosts in mine." Both art (Sándor's book *Atlantis*)

and historical experience (the Atlantis of prewar Europe and the events that destroyed it) are opaque but potent, exerting a force field whose contours cannot be reliably mapped. This pressure of the unknown is felt with particular power by Americans; as Eisenberg has commented, "We are all the things that happened to our grandparents, and yet we don't know what those things are." Yet at the same time the story cautions against the mystification of such differences. The narrator, grown older, visits her son in Los Angeles; when she observes the most recent immigrants, "Ma, Eric says, not every manicurist or waiter here used to be the most promising poet or physicist in Nigeria or Guatemala or Korea, you know."

"All Around Atlantis" is the most recent of Deborah Eisenberg's stories, and perhaps her most brilliant and emotionally capacious. Its complex orchestration of differences—between past and present, Europe and America, biographer and subject, art and its social uses, as well as among economic classes, ethnicities, and historical generations—might stand as a virtual summation of her work to date. Positioned like "Broken Glass" at the end of a collection, it may also mark new directions for her subsequent fiction.

Barry Weller

SELECTED BIBLIOGRAPHY

Works by Deborah Eisenberg

Transactions in a Foreign Currency. New York: Alfred A. Knopf, 1984.
Under the 82nd Airborne. New York: Farrar, Straus & Giroux, 1992.

Air: 24 Hours. Jennifer Bartlett. New York:
  Harry N. Abrams, 1994.
All Around Atlantis. New York: Farrar, Straus
  & Giroux, 1997.
The Stories (So Far) of Deborah Eisenberg. New
  York: Farrar, Straus & Giroux, 1997.

Critical Studies

Sharkey, Nancy. "Courting Disorientation."
  New York Times Book Review, February 9,
  1992.
Shepard, Jim. "In the Absence of Language."
  New York Times Book Review, September
  21, 1997.

STANLEY ELKIN
(1930–1995)

Although Stanley Elkin's reputation as
a virtuoso prose stylist and creator
of mordantly funny, oddly affecting fictions rests on ten novels and two collections of novellas, he published one volume
of short stories early in his career that is
likely to have enduring appeal. After the
appearance of Criers and Kibitzers, Kibitzers
and Criers in 1966, however, Elkin pretty
much abandoned the short story for
longer forms that better allowed him to
explore his themes of obsession and excess
and to conduct his highly original experiments with a pop-culture-inspired, Yid-
dish-inflected, Joycean-rich language.
Among his most admired novels are The
Dick Gibson Show (1971), The Franchiser
(1976), The Living End (1979), George Mills

(1982), The Magic Kingdom (1985), and
Mrs. Ted Bliss (1995). The two collections
of novellas, Searches and Seizures (1973) and
Van Gogh's Room at Arles (1993), are brilliantly written, beautifully crafted books.
Pieces of Soap, thirty entertaining essays,
appeared in 1992.

Stanley Lawrence Elkin was born on
May 11, 1930, in New York City, the
eldest son of Zelda Feldman Elkin and
Philip Elkin, a traveling salesman of costume jewelry. The family moved to Chicago when the boy was three and he was
educated in the city school system and
then at the University of Illinois, Urbana.
In 1953 Elkin married Joan Marion Ja-
cobson, an artist, with whom he had three
children. After serving in the army
(1955–1957), he received a doctorate in
English from his undergraduate alma mater in 1961. From that year until his death
on May 31, 1995, he taught writing at
Washington University in St. Louis,
where he was Merle Kling Professor of
Modern Letters. Over the course of his
career Elkin received many awards: from
the Paris Review (1963), the Guggenheim
Foundation (1966), the Rockefeller Foundation (1968), the National Endowment
for the Arts and Humanities (1972), the
Raymond and Hilda Rosenthal Foundation (1979), and the Southern Review
(1981). George Mills and Mrs. Ted Bliss were
judged the best novels of their years by
the National Book Critics Circle, and in
1982 Elkin was elected to the American
Academy and Institute of Arts and Letters.

Elkin began writing short stories as a
child. His first published works—"The
Sound of Thunder" and "The Party"—
appeared in the small literary magazines
Epoch and Views in 1957 and 1958, and

have since been gathered with other fugitive pieces to demonstrate, as he amusingly said in *Early Elkin,* "some up-from-nothing quality about life which says a good word for human possibility." In his preface to a 1990 reprint of *Criers and Kibitzers, Kibitzers and Criers,* Elkin explains why he has given up writing short fiction: "I'm trying to tell what turned me. Well, delight in language as language certainly. . . . But something less delightful, too. It was that nothing very bad had happened to me yet. . . . Then my father died in 1958 and my mother couldn't take three steps without pain. Then a heart attack . . . when I was thirty-seven years old. Then this, then that [the onset in 1972 of the multiple sclerosis that crippled him] . . . and maybe that's what led me toward revenge—a writer's revenge anyway; the revenge, I mean, of style."

Criers and Kibitzers, Kibitzers and Criers is an extraordinary display of style, or to be more precise, of many styles. Comprising nine very different pieces, it remains the most valuable single showcase of his many gifts as a writer of fiction. The title story is a graphic study of Jake Greenspahn, a grocery store owner sodden with grief and rage at the death of his son, as well as at his shrinking business and his perception that employees and customers are cheating him. One afternoon he catches his produce manager shaking down a shoplifter for a ten-dollar bribe, but when he tries to fire him, Frank blurts out that he saw Jake's dead son slip money from the cash register. That night the grocer has a startling dream of being in a synagogue surrounded by the ten men necessary for worship. Comforted by the thought that there is at least one place where prayers

are always being said, he is confounded by his inability to conjure up the face of his dead son. Urged on by the rabbi, the grocer in the dream finally sees his suffering son's face in the coffin, "before the undertakers had time to tamper with it." When the smiling rabbi turns away, Greenspahn shouts for the congregants to look at his son's "smug smile of guilt" at the moment he turned, his hand in the till, to see Frank watching him. At first, this startling ending seems bruisingly bleak, but in the dense context of the story, it mixes hope with despair, for Greenspahn is having a revelation that links him to the all-too-human employees and customers he had so bitterly reviled.

"I Look Out for Ed Wolfe" is a bizarre, insinuating piece about a fired bill collector who sells everything he owns in an effort to come to a bottom-line dollars-and-cents accounting of his own worth. At the end, confused and alienated, he purchases freedom at the price of spiritual death, and his story becomes an unnerving little parable about the equation of money and value in late twentieth-century American consumer society. "Among the Witnesses" is an acerbic comedy about pleasure-seeking Jewish vacationers who are forced to face hard questions about blame and responsibility in the wake of a small girl's accidental drowning in the resort swimming pool. "The Guest" is more extravagant: a wild, discomfiting farce about Bertie, a screwball, down-on-his-luck trumpeter who wheedles a chance to housesit alone for vacationing friends. Puttering about, getting high on drugs, talking to himself in other people's voices, he gleefully trashes the apartment and, when burglars steal appliances and clothes, pretends to have performed the theft himself. Readers are likely to be intrigued (and perhaps even envious) of Bertie's anarchic energy, but appalled too by his transgressive cruelty in the name of paying back respectable people for having patronized him as a zany failure.

Something of this same provocative doubleness occurs in "In the Alley." Waking one morning to realize his doctor's prediction that he will be dead of cancer by this date has not come true, the schlemiel Feldman decides to take a more active role in choosing how he will live and die. Checking into a hospital to join a "fraternity of the sick," he finds the suffering patients unresponsive to his noble purpose. Afterward, in a working-class bar, he tries to establish connection with a woman by confessing his illness, but she mistakes him for an inept seducer and, with the help of companions, beats him unconscious, leaving him to die in a stinking alley with a note pinned to his jacket: *STAY AWAY FROM WHITE WOMEN.* Yet despite his wretched fate, Feldman achieves a certain dignity by having actively tried to die in a purposeful way.

Three of the last four stories in *Criers and Kibitzers* are comic/serious experiments with narrative voices that Elkin would later develop more successfully in his novels. "On a Field, Rampant" is a deft ironic parody of the familiar seventeenth- and eighteenth-century plot device in which a lowborn figure, believing he is of royal birth, goes in search of his high destiny. "Cousin Poor Leslie and the Lousy People" is a brassy anecdote of rivalries among Jewish children in the 1940s. In "Perlmutter at the East Pole" an endearingly eccentric anthropologist goes on a worldwide search for the key to all mythologies, a journey that ends with him addressing other zealots at an open-air forum in Manhattan's Union Square.

"A Poetics for Bullies," however, is *echt* Elkin. In an outlandish, self-delighting monologue, Push the bully reveals the secrets of his art. "I'm best," he tells us, "at torment," a "chink-seeker" who exploits the vulnerable: fat kids, cripples, dummies, nerds, slobs. Never violent, and quick to confess his own covetousness and envy, he works by "sleight-of-mouth," deploying all the trickster's tools to harass and manipulate. Forced to confront the charismatic John Williams—a boy superb at sports, academics, romance, and defending the weak—Push devises a catch-22 scheme. He challenges Williams to a fight to trap him. If the paragon accepts, his image as peacemaker is tarnished; if he loses to Push, he forfeits his reputation for mastery; if he wins, he himself becomes a bully. Although Williams whips Push and claims virtue by having punished a tyrant, the bully has the last word: "I will not be reconciled, or halve my hate. *It's* what I have, all I can keep. My bully's sour solace. . . . I can't stand them near me. . . . I shove them away. I force them off. I press them, thrust them aside. *I push through.*"

Here, early on, is the signature of the mature Stanley Elkin: comic ingenuity, linguistic brilliance, and a surprising twist on conventional morality. At first, readers are likely to recoil at the narrator's blatant self-advertisement of his own nastiness, but they soon come to realize that this bully's quick-witted art reveals his solicitude as well as his vulnerability. He is closer to his impaired victims, more connected to and fonder of them than the faultless Williams can ever be. Stanley Elkin, like Wallace Stevens, believes that "the imperfect is our paradise . . . in this bitterness, delight. / Since the imperfect is so hot in us, / Lies in flawed words and stubborn sounds."

Lawrence Graver

SELECTED BIBLIOGRAPHY

Works by Stanley Elkin

Criers and Kibitzers, Kibitzers and Criers. New York: Random House, 1966.
Early Elkin. Flint, Mich.: Bamberger Books, 1985.

Critical Studies

Bailey, Peter J. *Reading Stanley Elkin.* Urbana: University of Illinois Press, 1985.
Bargen, Doris G. *The Fiction of Stanley Elkin.* Frankfurt am Main: Peter Lang Verlag, 1980.
Dougherty, David C. *Stanley Elkin.* Boston: Twayne, 1991.

GEORGE P. ELLIOTT
(1918 – 1980)

George P. Elliott was born near Knightstown, Indiana, the son of a Quaker farmer and a Methodist mother. The rural environment and the religious moralism that saturated his childhood experience strongly color Elliott's literary work, particularly in his characteristic emphasis on moral ideas. When he was ten, financial difficulties forced Elliott's family to resettle in southern California, which would provide the setting for many of his narratives. After attending a junior college, Elliott went on to study English at the University of California at Berkeley (A.B. 1939, M.A. 1941). In 1941, he married Mary Emma Jeffress, with whom he had one daughter (Nora, born 1943). Elliott acknowledged that his wife, for many years an editor of the *Hudson Review,* provided "severe, particular, and acute criticisms [that] diverted me from egregious error innumerable times." An appointment, in 1947, at the all-male St. Mary's College (near Berkeley) marked the beginning of a thirty-three-year teaching career. In 1955 Elliott taught for a year at Cornell, moving on to Barnard (1957–60), the University of Iowa at Ames (1960–61), UC Berkeley (1962), and then back again to St. Mary's (1962–63). In 1963 he accepted a post in the Creative Writing Program at Syracuse University, where he remained until his death in 1980.

A versatile author, Elliott produced two collections of short stories, four novels, two books of essays, and six volumes of poetry. He left one unpublished novel (set in ancient Byzantium) and a number of uncollected reviews, essays, and short stories scattered in periodicals such as *Harper's, New Republic, American Scholar, Nation, Writer,* and *Esquire.*

Critics have found Elliott's poetry "serious . . . demanding and rewarding" (Victor Howes) and "by turns sensual, meditative, witty" (John T. Irwin). He himself termed the composing of verse "a way of connecting things which can be known better than they can be talked about." *Fever and Chills* (1961), Elliott's most notable poem, is a compelling 734-line verse narrative that traces, in the third person, an adulterous affair from the perspective of a married man who has taken up with a friend's wife.

Hailed as a leading American essayist, Elliott was widely praised for both stylistic innovations and the "calm suavity" and "easy authority" of his prose (Joseph Epstein). "A Piece of Lettuce," "A Brown Fountain Pen" (both collected in *A Piece of Lettuce*), "Snarls of Beauty" (in *A George P. Elliott Reader*), and "Never *Nothing*" (in *Conversions*) are among the most original and impressive of all his literary productions. Reflecting the influence of Montaigne and Bacon, these and a half-dozen other pieces compare favorably with the work of leading contemporary essayists such as Joan Didion and Annie Dillard. Elliot explained that he experimented with essays "constructed poetically and narratively rather than logically and expositorily."

Like his essays and short stories, Elliott's four published novels—*Parktildon Village* (1958), *David Knudson* (1962), *In the World* (1965), and *Muriel* (1972)—evoke a vivid sense that we are "sharing the company of a lucid and highly cultivated author" (Epstein). They tend to emphasize moral ideas (often tied to social criticism) over characterization and plot development—an emphasis that also typifies Elliott's short fiction.

Elliott's short stories—twenty-three of which appeared in two collections, *Among the Dangs: Ten Stories* (AD) and *An Hour of Last Things and Other Stories* (HLT)—exemplify a variety of subgenres: from brief parables such as "The Well and the Bulldozers" (HLT) and Kafkaesque fantasy such as "In a Hole" (HLT) to both conventional science fiction and "semi-scientific" narratives—the former exemplified by "Invasion of the Planet of Love" (HLT) and the latter by "Into the Cone of Cold" (HLT) and "Femina Sapiens" (*Esquire,* March 1970). Among Elliott's most thought-provoking short stories are his sociocultural fables, especially "Faq'" (AD), "Sandra" (HLT), and "Among the Dangs" (AD). Perhaps Elliott's best-known tale, "Among the Dangs" is a "long-short story" (a form Elliott favored) about a black American graduate student, and later professor, who out of economic and vocational necessity twice volunteers to live incognito with a remote Ecuadorian tribe to gather anthropological data. When, some years later, he independently makes a third trip, he abandons his university position to become a high prophet among the Dangs. Facing ritual death, however, he escapes back to a conventional marriage and a secure if self-alienating career as an academic. He confesses, in the end, that more than the physical danger, he fled the prospect of having "reverted until I had become one of them . . . [had] taken in all ways the risk of prophecy . . . until I had lost myself utterly," to a state in which "my consciousness had become what I was doing." In the end, ironically, he faces losing himself utterly in his marriage and tenured professorship. Elliott described his black protagonist as "torn between two cultures . . . in but not of either of them" ("Discovering the Dangs," in *Conversions*).

"Better to Burn" and "Miracle Play," two neglected masterworks, showcase Elliott at his virtuoso best as writer of realistic short fiction. "Better to Burn," another long-short story, takes the form of a series of journal entries. The diarist is Julia—thirty-six years old, clinically depressed, and holed up in a California motel, "a stucco tomb," after breaking up with her lover. Mature, compulsively reflective, Julia spends most of her time in bed, "either to die or to gather strength for going back to life." Her confessions and self-scrutiny powerfully dramatize the revelatory efficacy of the process of autobiographical writing. At the same time, they disclose, through the medium of Julia's tortured and ultimately warped consciousness, the devastating consequences of a consuming, five-year affair that has failed. The lovers, who had moved in together after four years, soon discovered to their horror that they loved merely "the demon" in each other and that they were incapable of experiencing together "the trust of giving yourself up finally to another." As a moralist, Elliott foregrounds in stories such as this the limits of a decency that contains an "injunction against using others as things for one's private ends and against wasting one's self in overindulgence and existential despair" (Blanche Gelfant).

By any measure one of Elliott's finest productions, the eight-page "Miracle Play" is comparable in tone and reflective depth to such fictionalized autobiography as Joyce's "Araby" or, in the American idiom, the episodes in Paul Horgan's *Things as They Are*. The story, told by the protagonist as an adult, concerns three pivotal events that occurred when he was a child of five and that culminated in an epiphany whereby "I learned to my wonder that there was an invisible world perfect with the one I saw." The first episode centers on the child's perceptions of his father and his aunt while he is kept separated from his mother, who is giving birth to his brother. The second event is his experience of the death of his grandmother, who had proved a nervous, inadvertently harsh caretaker during his mother's confinement. The climactic episode is a Christmas nativity play in which his father is Herod and his aunt an angel. He tells how he sat with his mother awestruck, marveling at his father who "wasn't only my dad, he was Herod too. . . . Dad was trusting and warm, but Herod was full of hate." His epiphany occurs "at the end as I listened to the invisible angel, visible Aunt Rebecca, warn Mary and Joseph . . . I realized that it was far more important that these people had done what they had done, and that God wished it so, than that actually they were church members and my family." This scene, largely autobiographical, discloses the formative impact that religious drama has on the consciousness of a child with the sensibility of the artist and intellectual. Overall, Elliott's short stories reflect an admitted penchant for "making moral-psychological discriminations" and an unswerving commitment to the principle that "a good story . . . incarnates an idea of moral reality."

Phillip Stambovsky

SELECTED BIBLIOGRAPHY

Works by George Elliott

Among the Dangs: Ten Stories. New York: Holt, 1961.

An Hour of Last Things and Other Stories. New York: Harper, 1968.

A George P. Elliott Reader: Selected Poetry and Prose. Edited by Robert Pack and Jay Parini. Hanover, N.H.: University Press of New England, 1992.

Critical Studies

Gold, Herbert. "A Short-Story Bonanza." *New Republic,* January 16, 1961.

Janeway, Elizabeth. "Love and Lack of Love." *New York Times Book Review,* June 30, 1968.

Poss, Stanley. "Private Responsibility." *Nation,* August 26, 1968.

JOHN FANTE
(1909–1983)

If the Italian immigrant experience has a presence in anthologies of multicultural American literature, it is usually through a short story by John Fante. He published fully half of his lifetime production of short stories before 1940, in national magazines such as *American Mercury, Atlantic Monthly, Harper's Bazaar,* and *Scribner's.* He had also published two novels and *Dago Red,* a collection of his stories, which was described in a review in the *Nation* as "plotless sketches of the type written by William Saroyan."

John Fante was born in Denver, Colorado, on April 8, 1909, to a father who had immigrated from Abruzzi, Italy and a mother born in Chicago to immigrant parents from Potenza, Italy. He was one of four children raised in Boulder, where his father, a stonemason and bricklayer, found work in the building trades. Fante had always dreamed of becoming a great writer; at an early age, he says, he was encouraged by Catholic nuns to write. He attended Regis College and the University of Colorado at Denver and left before completing a formal degree to hitchhike out to California. There he took jobs in fish canneries and on shipping docks to help support his mother and siblings after his father had run away, for a period of time, from the family. From these experiences came his earliest short stories, which he sent to H. L. Mencken, then editor of the *American Mercury.* Fante's debut as a storywriter, in 1932, was aided by Mencken's desire to combat the WASP hegemony of the New England literary establishment. As it turned out, some of these stories came from the letters Fante had attached to the manuscripts he had submitted.

One of the earliest American writers of Italian descent, Fante adapted the oral tradition of southern Italian peasants to a literary culture. His sentence structure is simple and characteristic of the language used in oral storytelling, which depends on memory for the maintenance of important information. In crisp, clean, accessible language, he mingles realistic images of working-class characters with the youthful romanticism of a protagonist longing for love or the accolades of success.

Fante's stories are usually set in Denver or Los Angeles, and are populated by family members, neighbors, and local authority figures. Most of his stories show the effects of assimilation upon the children of Italian immigrants, children lured away from their identities as Italian in hopes of gaining full membership in American culture. In stories such as "A Wife for Dino Rossi," "A Bricklayer in the Snow," and "A Kidnapping in the Family," Fante depicts Italian immigrants as heroic figures whose struggles to stay alive, to raise families, and to deal with the stress of immigrant life tell a new American story. His representation of *italianità*, or "Italianness," is usually found in three figures: the father, the mother, and the grandmother. Against these foreign characters he sets up the Americans through the likes of bankers, landlords, and business owners. Caught somewhere between these two extremes of identity are the children, who must achieve a synthesis of Italian and American identity.

Fante's stories represent unparalleled insights into American Catholicism, which is often portrayed through cultural conflicts between an Irish clergy and Italian American parishioners. "Altar Boy," his first publication, presents a young Italian boy's crisis of faith, which erupts into childhood pranks played in church and into acts of petty thievery in the community. He returned to Catholicism in later stories such as "My Father's God," in which an old Italian succumbs to his wife's pleas and decides, after many years, to reunite with the church. When told that he must confess his sins, he asks if he can do it in writing, a request the young Italian American priest allows. When presented with a long confession written in Italian, the young priest, who cannot read the language of his ancestry, can only laugh when he realizes he has been tricked and shamed at the same time.

In 1933 his signature story, "Odyssey of a Wop," appeared in the *American Mercury*. The story traces the evolution of the identity of a protagonist of Italian origins from youth, when he learns that calling an Italian a dago is an insult that can only be redressed by fisticuffs, to young adulthood, when he realizes that the ethnic slurs can be useful in referring to lazy parasites who live off the hard work of others. In his simple, trademark style, he writes: "From the beginning, I hear my mother use the words Wop and Dago with such vigor as to denote violent distaste. She spits them out. They leap from her lips. To her they contain the essence of poverty, squalor, and filth. . . . Thus, as I begin to acquire her values, Wop and Dago to me become synonymous with things evil." The odyssey that the immigrant must complete, in the move away from the old country to the new, is to transcend the stereotype created by others and to fashion an identity that allows one to laugh at one's shortcomings and gain the inner strength to disarm insults.

Fante's writing is very much concerned with the relationship between the individual and his family and community and the subsequent development of a single protagonist's American identity that requires both an understanding and a rejection of the immigrant past represented by parental figures. An interesting development occurs in Fante's later stories. In

"Helen, Thy Beauty," and "Mary Osaka, I Love You," he begins to use Filipino Americans as his main characters. These new immigrants allowed him to address again the social concerns of his generation: how best to become American. At the same time, he could dramatize the survival concerns of the immigrant generation.

While Fante's earlier years were spent writing stories and novels, in later years he turned to screenwriting, earning a living that would bring him a beautiful home on Malibu beach for his wife Joyce Smart and their four children. As a contract writer for Hollywood, Fante achieved his greatest success with an adaptation of his 1952 novel *Full of Life*, a film starring Judy Holiday and Richard Conte that was nominated for an Academy Award. Among his many screen credits as a writer are *East of the River, Youth Runs Wild, Jeanne Eagels, The Reluctant Saint,* and *A Walk on the Wild Side*. Stories such as "The Wrath of God," which recounts the 1933 Long Beach earthquake, served as rehearsals for scenes in his novels. His Colorado childhood is reflected in his first novel, *Wait Until Spring, Bandini* (1938); his young adulthood in the Bunker Hill area of Los Angeles is the basis for the novels *Ask the Dust* (1939), *Dreams from Bunker Hill* (1982), and *The Road to Los Angeles* (1985). His Hollywood experiences are portrayed in his novella *My Dog Stupid,* published posthumously in *West of Rome* (1986).

In 1955 Fante was stricken with diabetes, which eventually blinded him. However, he continued producing stories and novels by dictating to his wife. In the late 1970s, Black Sparrow Press rediscovered Fante through the poet and novelist Charles Bukowski. Since then the press has brought back into print all his earlier writings and has published some previously unpublished works. This revival led to his work's being translated into French, Italian, Spanish, and German. By the time of his death, in 1983, Fante had been referred to as "national treasure" and had established a worldwide reputation as a novelist and storywriter. He left a rich literary legacy of humorous, often self-ironic, explorations of American immigration, ethnicity, Catholicism, and assimilation.

Fred L. Gardaphe

SELECTED BIBLIOGRAPHY

Works by John Fante

"Mary Osaka, I Love You." *Good Housekeeping,* October 1942.
The Wine of Youth: Selected Stories. Santa Barbara, Calif.: Black Sparrow, 1985.

Critical Studies

Collins, Richard. *John Fante: A Literary Portrait.* Toronto: Guernica Editions, 1999.
Cooper, Stephen. *Full of Life: A Biography of John Fante.* New York: Farrar, Straus & Giroux, 2000.
Cooper, Stephen. "John Fante's Eternal City." In David Fine, ed., *Los Angeles in Fiction: A Collection of Essays,* pp. 83–99. Albuquerque: University of New Mexico Press, 1995.
Cooper, Stephen, and David Fine, eds. *John Fante: A Critical Gathering.* Madison, N.J.: Farleigh Dickinson University Press, 1999.
Gardaphe, Fred L. *Italian Signs, American*

Streets: The Evolution of Italian American Narrative. Durham, N.C.: Duke University Press, 1996.

Green, Rose Basile. *The Italian-American Novel: A Document of the Interaction of Two Cultures*. Madison, N.J.: Farleigh Dickinson University Press, 1974.

Wills, Ross B. "John Fante." In Seamus Cooney, ed., *John Fante: Selected Letters 1932 to 1981*, pp. 329–338. Santa Rosa, Calif.: Black Sparrow, 1991.

JAMES T. FARRELL
(1904 – 1979)

In the second half of the twentieth century, James T. Farrell was regarded as one of the strongest realist writers of the 1930s. Known primarily for novels grouped together as trilogies, tetralogies, and pentalogies, he began his career as a writer of short stories. Two hundred and fifty stories were published in fifteen volumes during his lifetime, many of which can be appreciated today for their strong characterizations and contemporary themes. Among his collections are *Chicago Stories* (1998), *Childhood Is Not Forever and Other Stories* (1969), and *An Omnibus of Short Stories* (1957), which reprints pieces from several of the earliest volumes.

Born in 1904 to a lower middle-class Irish Catholic family, Farrell started to attend the University of Chicago in 1925, while working at a gas station. He became a voracious reader, influenced by the economics of Thorstein Veblen and the prag-

matism of John Dewey, among others. Farrell and his first wife, Dorothy, left Chicago for a year in Paris and returned to New York in time for the publication of his first novel, *Young Lonigan,* in 1932. Though he traveled widely in the United States and abroad, he resided for the rest of his life in New York, which became the setting of his later novels.

Farrell's best fiction uses as source material the life of the South Side streets he knew growing up. At the age of seven he was sent to live with his grandparents, to make way for new siblings, whom his parents could ill afford. He felt estranged from his family as siblings suffered at home, one of them dying, while he experienced a materially more comfortable life. Despite a close relationship with his grandmother (fictionalized in the Danny O'Neill novels), the distance from his parents made his boyhood painfully memorable.

Adolescence is a frequent focus in Farrell's fiction. "Helen, I Love You" (1930) portrays a twelve-year-old boy's confusion about love and the formation of personal identity. Dan wants to win back the affection of Helen Scanlan, which he lost because of his shyness. Returning home after a day with Helen, Dan is chastised for spending his hard-earned money on her. After an argument, he "sat in the parlor crying and cursing . . . the family just hadn't understood at all." To make matters worse, Helen comes around to his front steps, and when he is told of her presence, he says he "doesn't care if she was there or not. After that, Helen hadn't paid any attention to him." In looking back at his own adolescence, Farrell writes in the introduction to *Short Stories* (1946), "So of-

ten I seemed lost in an inner state of bewildered loneliness."

Farrell's sensitivity enabled him to develop a growing awareness of the spiritual
poverty of his neighborhood, in turmoil
after World War I. The influx of blacks to
the South Side threatened the insularity
of the Irish Catholics, who had little tolerance for different groups. Farrell described their racism and anti-Semitism in
stories such as "For White Men Only"
(1934), "The Fastest Runner on Sixty-first
Street" (1948), and "Tommy Gallagher's
Crusade" (1939).

"The Fastest Runner on Sixty-first
Street" is a resonant and poignant story of
racism and the American Dream. Morty
Aiken, at the age of fourteen, shows the
promise of becoming a track star, a possible Olympic champion. He is an only
child whose father saves for his son's college education. However, one day Morty
joins a gang of bored friends to chase two
black youths out of Washington Park.
They lose the blacks behind a funeral procession but find another one to chase.
Morty breaks far ahead of his gang and is
led deep into the black neighborhood,
where he is jumped in an alley and his
throat is slashed. Ironically, Morty is victimized by racism beyond his awareness,
personified by his best friend, Tony Ra-
buski, whose protector he had become.
Tony, often picked on as a "Polack," initiates the chase that climaxes with Morty's
death. The reader grieves not only for
Morty but also for his parents, who have
lost their only chance to see a child succeed
economically and socially. However, the
reader must confront racism and the spiritual void that drives it.

A prolific writer of short stories and
novels, Farrell also published several
works of nonfiction, among them *A Note
on Literary Criticism* (1936) and *Reflections
at Fifty and Other Essays* (1954). His work
fulfills an aim he stated in a lecture at
Miami University (Oxford, Ohio) in
1957: "I have tried to write in such a way
that there is no author intervening—that
there [are] only . . . the characters, whom
you see, and believe are real, and in whose
fate you are interested." Influenced by
Joyce, Chekhov, Proust, Conrad, and
Hemingway, Farrell's stories illustrate a
confident sense of aesthetics and his rebellion against Victorian convention and
the slick magazine formulas of the time.
In particular, he resented the idealized
portraits of children, like Booth Tarking-
ton's entertaining Penrod stories. He considered these stories daydream fiction designed to sell advertising, their heroes
obtaining goals without personal cost,
with no troubling emotions.

"Helen, I Love You" embodies Farrell's
rebellion and provides an introspective
look at adolescence far different from Tar-
kington's. The story opens with Dan trad-
ing insults with Dick Buckford on the
street. Farrell juxtaposes the verbal contest with Dan's inner struggle. Dan's confusion stems, in part, from his pop culture
ideas of heroism: if he beat up Dick in
Helen's sight, "everything would be all so
swell, just like it was at the end of the
stories he sometimes read in the *Saturday
Evening Post*." However, the boys do not
fight. Dan remembers the family argument and how he lost Helen. Nothing else
happens. The story illustrates Farrell's
lack of concern with traditional plot. "Action," he said in a 1965 speech, "can be of
the mind. It can be a psychological pro-

cess. It can be some hurt or sudden joy." "Helen, I Love You" offers none of the satisfactions of a love story or well-turned tale. Its conclusion leaves Dan alone with his "strange feelings" in the growing darkness, afraid of the wind. He is poised on the precipice between childhood and adulthood, needing love and understanding, needing to prove himself, and struggling to create an identity with confusing mass-media models.

A number of Farrell's stories connect the inner turmoil of youth to the problems of urban culture. "The Scarecrow" (1930) achieves an objectivity Farrell strove for in contrast to the autobiographical introspection of "Helen, I Love You." He considered the story "a leap into originality." Scarecrow is the only name, other than Nickel Nose, of an abused fourteen-year-old girl who gives herself willingly to any boy who will have her. She lives with her mother, who beats her regularly with a rubber hose. The Scarecrow's life contrasts to her daydreams—in a long passage the adjective *beautiful* precedes every item on her list of material desires, indicating her limited imagination. She has sex with a boy who takes her to a Halloween party, where he abandons her among his friends as they get drunk. The Scarecrow is ridiculed, and before the party breaks up, she strips to reveal her welts and bruises. One girl shows compassion and wants to take her home with her but is told, "I tried that once. You'll never get her out." The story ends with the Scarecrow, having forgotten her dress, wearing only her underclothes and a coat, alone and shivering.

The story's depiction of squalor was shocking at the time, but understated and tame compared to its progeny. It is a significant link in the development of American fiction, connecting the 1890s to the 1930s, claiming as an ancestor Stephen Crane's *Maggie, A Girl of the Streets*. "The Scarecrow" is also a progenitor of stories by Hubert Selby, Jr., in *Last Exit to Brooklyn* (1964) and Buddy Giovinazzo in *Life Is Hot in Cracktown* (1993). Selby's Tralala, like the Scarecrow, does not have an ordinary name, suggesting that she too is less than human. Tralala is fifteen when the story opens, living among friends with whom she "puts out" and rolls drunk sailors. Her downward slide is inevitable. The story crescendos with a gang rape, where Tralala is left naked and bleeding, as good as dead in an empty lot. *Life Is Hot in Crackdown* opens with fourteen-year-old Londa, a direct descendent of Tralala and the Scarecrow. Londa has survived for seven years by performing oral sex to obtain crack; by "firing the bazooka" (smoking crack) she is able to withstand her father's physical and sexual abuse. Her inevitable death is mentioned in a later, related story.

The criticism that such fiction is not art but documentary journalism or sociology has impugned Farrell's reputation since his first novel, *Young Lonigan*, was published in 1932. Farrell's fiction, and that of the dire realists who followed him, overturn self-satisfied notions about the quality of life in America. Their work causes the reader to empathize with society's outcasts such as Farrell's Scarecrow, Selby's Tralala, and Giovinazzo's Londa—all sexually abused young women. Farrell, his predecessor Stephen Crane, and his successors presaged a social problem widely discussed today. As Blanche Gelfant has noted, much of Farrell's work criticizes society for its "reprehensible indifference to the waste of human life."

Farrell's stark, often shocking approach to the street life of Chicago's South Side had an immediate influence on Depression-era novelists and successive generations, including fellow Chicagoans Richard Wright and Nelson Algren. Farrell's stories express the empathy he believed necessary to the writing of fiction, giving voice to the voiceless, primarily the working-class Catholic Irish. Farrell's stories do not allow complacency, they provoke troubling questions. Though the early pieces take place in the 1920s, they are relevant today, reflecting as they do an urban way of life dominated by consumerism and dehumanizing images from a mass-market entertainment industry. James T. Farrell empathized with ordinary people who could not live up to the glamorous images of beautiful people surrounded by "beautiful things." His stories include a wide range of protagonists: working men, abused and abusing women, priests, nuns, the patriarch of a prosperous middle-class family, a homeless man. Such diverse voices enable the reader to connect with all of humanity.

Robert Fox

SELECTED BIBLIOGRAPHY

Works by James T. Farrell

A Note on Literary Criticism. New York: Vanguard Press, 1936.
The League of Frightened Philistines and Other Papers. New York: Vanguard Press, 1945.
Literature and Morality. New York: Vanguard Press, 1945.

Reflections at Fifty and Other Essays. New York: Vanguard Press, 1954.
An Omnibus of Short Stories. New York: Vanguard Press, 1957.
Childhood Is Not Forever and Other Stories. New York: Doubleday, 1969.
Eight Short Stories & Sketches. Edited by Marshall Brooks. Newton, Mass.: Arts End Books, 1981.
Hearing Out James T. Farrell: Selected Lectures. Edited by Donald Phelps. New York: The Smith, 1985.
Chicago Stories. Edited by Charles Fanning. Urbana: University of Illinois Press, 1998.

Critical Studies

Branch, Edgar M. *James T. Farrell.* New York: Twayne, 1971.
Branch, Edgar M. *A Paris Year: Dorothy and James T. Farrell, 1931–1932.* Athens: Ohio University Press, 1998.
Gelfant, Blanche H. *The American City Novel.* Norman: University of Oklahoma Press, 1954.
Gelfant, Blanche H. "Studs Lonigan and Pop Art." *Raritan* 4 (spring 1989): 111–120.
Salzman, Jack, and Dennis Flynn, eds. *James T. Farrell.* Special issue of *Twentieth Century Literature* 22/1 (February 1976).

WILLIAM FAULKNER
(1897–1962)

No other writer in this century has been at once so provincial in his subject matter and so sophisticated in his narrative technique as William Faulkner. Nor has anyone been so influential or so widely imitated. Born in Mississippi in 1897, Faulkner came of age understanding that his family's reduced circumstances corresponded to the South's decline; his own father was the mediocre successor to a legendary grandfather of Civil War heroics. Faulkner himself was undistinguished as a student at Ole Miss, though fortunate in having a friend who inspired him to read Melville, Henry Adams, Lawrence, Cather, Huxley, and Fitzgerald. By the 1920s, a series of odd jobs as house painter, carpenter, and postmaster freed him to write—first poetry, then fiction. Three conventional novels appeared before the breakthrough innovations of *The Sound and the Fury* (1929), which was followed by a decade of extraordinary literary experiments that would transform the twentieth-century novel: *As I Lay Dying* (1930), *Light in August* (1932), *Absalom, Absalom!* (1936), and *Go Down, Moses* (1942).

Royalties from novels, however, were slim during the Great Depression, which was, ironically, an era when mass-market magazines could offer top dollar for short stories. In 1930, newly married, Faulkner began publishing short fiction as a means of paying bills while working on novels (he would also write screenplays in Hollywood for similar mercenary motives). A decade later, most of his books were no longer in print, and his reputation revived only with Malcolm Cowley's *The Portable Faulkner* (1946), which reprinted a handful of major stories as well as excerpts from novels. Renewed recognition led to the award of the Nobel Prize in 1949, and

Faulkner spent the 1950s in relative retirement, giving long interviews as writer-in-residence in Virginia, Japan, and West Point.

Faulkner always had a conflicted response to the idea of short fiction, partly because his expansive imagination made it hard for him to keep his stories story-length. Yet he could not ignore the market, having earned less from his first four novels than from the sale of four stories to the *Saturday Evening Post*. He may have carped that such writing interfered with his more serious longer work, but he felt that way even as he created his greatest short stories. These stories demarcate familiar Faulknerian terrain, a terrain so characteristic that his name is one of the few to have become a writerly adjective. Part of the reason for this is his thematic obsession with the tragedy of southern racial relations, a product of the "peculiar institution" of slavery, which forced blacks and whites to live together yet apart. All his later novels and most of the stories occur in an imagined Yoknapatawpha County, the "little postage stamp of native soil" that allowed Faulkner to reconsider the tormented history of his region. The saga he created, which stretches from early Native American possession to World War II, mires ghostly heroes together with embittered survivors, privileged planters with stalwart sharecroppers, ambitious renegades with overly principled ascetics in a community always required to define itself as essentially black and white.

Another more obvious "Faulknerian" quality—the tropical lushness of his style, the wrenched syntax, the stark repetitions—tends to be less characteristic of the stories, perhaps because they were intended for a more clearly commercial market. But Faulkner's concern with meanings delayed and constructed by the reader is as apparent in "A Rose for Emily" and "The Bear" as in *The Sound and the Fury*; his concern with the violent legacy of racism as obvious in "Dry September" and "That Evening Sun" as in *Light in August*. And his realization that narratives are never complete or finished but always open to further revision is apparent in the recasting of stories in new guises, retold in such later novels as *The Unvanquished* and *Absalom, Absalom!* (though an economic incentive was always at work in this process of recycling). Indeed, so committed was Faulkner to the expansive possibilities of the short story form that in *Go Down, Moses* he created what he always insisted was a novel composed entirely of interrelated stories previously published separately.

"Barn Burning" (1939) is among Faulkner's finest stories and the best introduction to issues that recur in his fiction, including most importantly the conflict between family ties and community abstractions. More poignantly than almost any other figure Faulkner created, ten-year-old Sarty Snopes is tormented by "the old fierce pull of blood," caught in the tension between preadolescent loyalty to his father Abner and a growing awareness of Abner's moral savagery in defying community standards. Present and preterite tenses shift abruptly in the story, with Sarty's immediate anxieties conveyed by exclamatory italics that interrupt a straightforward chronicle of his developing moral integrity. The theme of a child's anxiously coming to terms with

the need for social mores has fascinated the best of American authors (James, Crane, and Hemingway, among others), and was masterfully explored in *The Adventures of Huckleberry Finn,* which succeeds through Mark Twain's ironic trick of *not* allowing Huck to understand his own moral heroism, keeping his narrative always in the first person.

By contrast, Faulkner dramatizes the problem of having a hero too young to grasp a larger moral order by deliberately shifting the narrative perspective outside Sarty's consciousness at a number of important junctures. Once, when Abner realizes Sarty would have told the truth if given a chance, an authorial voice intrudes with an insight well beyond the boy's capabilities: "Later, twenty years later, he was to tell himself, 'If I had said they wanted only truth, justice, he would have hit me again.'" This foreshadowing of a calmly retrospective view registers Sarty's own gradual recognition of his developing independence, his growing need to stand up for something larger than sheer family solidarity. The difficulty of this evolution is conveyed in the fabric of the narrative, in an ambiguous dependence on the pronoun "he" that occasionally confuses Sarty with his father, mirroring the process by which people are entangled in the history of their families and dramatizing the inherent difficulties in any attempt to escape paternal authority.

The story begins with a fiercely loyal boy immersed in his father's perspective but already conflicted at the prospect of testifying on Abner's behalf in court. Sarty both endorses his father's irrational perspective against the judge ("*Enemy! Enemy!* he thought") and reveals deep reservations

(*"He aims for me to lie,* he thought, again with that frantic grief and despair, *And I will have to do hit.*"). Later, when the family is forced to move, the image of Major de Spain's mansion triggers in Sarty a silent acknowledgement of the value of self-respect, honesty, honor, human integrity—in short, the "peace and dignity" he has never associated with his father. Still, filial loyalty prompts him to fierce defense of a man whose sly viciousness he cannot fathom until the moment kerosene is poured in preparation for torching de Spain's barn. At that point, Sarty races unself-consciously to warn of the danger, troubled by only the most fleeting pang of regret (*"Father. My father."*).

The fact that even now the meaning of his father's actions escapes Sarty is clarified wonderfully in the ironic distance between Sarty's final testament—"He was brave"—and the deflating account provided by an authorial voice detailing Abner's mercenary Civil War ventures. That distance in perspectives enhances our appreciation of Sarty's development, dramatizing through narrative voice itself the story's thematic conflicts in levels of knowledge. That Sarty, unaware of these facts or their meaning, departs at the story's conclusion reinforces the weight of the dramatic transformation that has ensued since the story began only weeks before. Its final words, "He did not look back," register a sense of closure for both the story and the boy.

Though "Barn Burning" is most importantly about a boy's coming of age, it raises other related issues, one of them economic: uneducated sharecroppers are kept impoverished by a system that allows rich landowners to indulge their taste in carpets imported from France. Abner's acts of retaliation, motivated by resentment of that system, are craven, even sociopathic (scarring rugs, burning barns), and hardly gestures of heroic defiance. But an implicit part of postbellum life in the rural South is the exploitative economics that offers less and less to such as the Snopes, and Abner's brutal behavior is in some measure the result of his brutalized condition. As the narrator says, "fire spoke to some deep mainspring of his father's being . . . as the one weapon for the preservation of integrity, else breath were not worth the breathing." However misshapen Abner's sense of "integrity," Sarty achieves his own principled independence by an ability to emulate his father, transforming a destructive urge into something more socially responsible and sustaining.

Along with class, gender is highlighted in the story, in the distinct set of relations between Abner, Sarty, and his brothers on the one hand, and the women of the family on the other. The unnamed mother's "hopeless despair" is matched by the ineffectiveness of his aunt and "big, bovine" sisters, whose collective helplessness against Abner's destructiveness becomes a source of mild contempt. Yet Sarty's final awareness that his father is deeply wrong derives in part from his mother's moralizing example. And if his departure at the end is wholly commendable, the redemptive possibilities of his transformation are partially undercut by the cyclical reminders in the story's concluding paragraph ("The slow constellations wheeled on"), which imply a repetition of the patriarchal conditions represented in the story.

"Barn Burning" relies on a fairly

straightforward narrative voice that actively assists the reader in understanding the consciousness of a ten-year-old boy as he comes to grips with his father's inadequacies. A decade earlier, Faulkner had created a more elusive and tantalizing narrative voice in "A Rose for Emily" (1930). The story works retrospectively, circling back from its opening sentence—"When Miss Emily Grierson died, our whole town went to her funeral"—through a biography of Emily Grierson, to the moment immediately following the funeral when the town and narrator discover the corpse of her poisoned lover in her bed. The final revelation of murderous necrophilia comes as a shock, especially given the unidentified narrator's dispassionate tone. At no point does he or she reveal emotional involvement in the events recounted, as if to forestall the excess emotional engagements that structure the circular narrative—engagements between Emily and her father, between Emily and her lover Homer Barron, between Emily and the taxpaying town. Faulkner's story evokes Henry James's novella, *Washington Square,* in which a young woman is caught between a domineeringly suspicious father and a fortune-hunting suitor. But the closer literary legacy may be Charles Dickens's Miss Havisham, whose disappointed bridal hopes in *Great Expectations* lead to her self-immuring in an imminent pre-wedding moment, with clocks symbolically stopped at twenty to nine, wedding cake left on the table, and a bridal gown worn unchanged until her fiery death years later.

Emily Grierson's desire to arrest time is reflected in the narrative itself, which circles back from its opening sentence as the last event in a chronology yet to be determined. The entire story seems intended to bring the reader more thoroughly to an understanding of the opening line, and thus to participating fully in the initiating moment of death. Frequent adverbial clauses beginning with "when" contribute to a repeated breaking of narrative motion that, even as it moves time along, marks it as past. Emily's strongest motive, to refuse any acknowledgment of time and its consequences, is established in scenes of her resistance to burying her father's corpse, paying taxes, and accepting free postal delivery. That motive, however, is made more immediate through the hesitations and backward shiftings of the narrative itself. And the attempt on the part of the unidentified townspeople (invoked sometimes as "we," sometimes "they") to make sense of her life matches our readerly efforts.

While the reader partakes in Emily's obsession through a circuitous chronology that accentuates time by forestalling it, the narrative also enhances her mysteriousness by delaying knowledge of the facts. We may have become jaded by poststructuralist claims that fictional texts are always about their own interpretative quandaries, but there is no avoiding that classic critique in this case: "A Rose for Emily" engages the problem of reading itself in the distinction between Emily's actual biography and the accounts of the townspeople. The tension between these two possibilities is defined as a conflict in the narrative modes of gothic tale and detective story, which structure the story even as they introduce narrative unreliability. Only as readers carefully detect the relevant clues can they anticipate the gothic revelation of the closing sentence.

If the conflict between Emily's secret and the town's complacency produces a certain ironic tone, it also disguises the remarkable similarity between the deranged spinster who imposes her murderous marriage plot and the town that likewise imposes an indulgently misplaced homage on its proud senior citizen. The town's satisfied self-assurance about the eccentric spinster, moreover, is paralleled in the reader's confidence over the self-contained narrative voice. This helps explain the frequent effort among critics to devise a chronology of Emily's life based on a series of temporal markers and only one stated date (1894, the year her taxes are remitted), as a means of gaining control over a narrative that seems incapable of controlling itself (interestingly, no two of these critical accounts quite agree on dates). Clearly, Faulkner intended this response, since early draft versions are much more explicit about the story's events.

Again, however, Faulkner is interested in more than mere narrative-making, and the story can be read in a number of thematic ways, perhaps especially as a perverse monument to the southern heritage. Emily is admired by the town, considered "a tradition, a duty, and a care," and only her death fosters a reconsideration of her life. The townspeople have applauded not a madwoman and a murderess but a heroic figure to whom they have a "hereditary obligation," deserving its noblesse oblige. Like the South itself, she has earned respect for the dignity with which she has faced adversity. To them, her fostering of traditional cultural talents (teaching painting to young girls) as well as her antagonism to industrial modernization (refusing free postal delivery) have transformed her into a model of Confederate persistence. As the narrator intones, "Thus she passed from generation to generation—dear, inescapable, impervious, tranquil, and perverse." That her intrepid eccentricity covers for necrophilia and murder—albeit of a Yankee suitor lacking in honor—complicates any interpretation of Faulkner's meaning in the story. But the description of her "iron-gray" fortitude suggests a certain wry admiration for Emily, who achieves through death the status of an honorable icon; the color may even quietly refer to her association with Confederate values. She wins from fellow townspeople, at least before the story's conclusion, the respect they hold for the best of southern tradition. And ironically, her death achieves for both town and reader precisely the suspension of time that she had striven to achieve through Homer Barron's murder.

Various readers have pointed to the formal symmetry of "A Rose for Emily." The opening invasion by the Board of Aldermen is matched by the final breaking into Emily's bedroom that discloses the corpse; only in the third, middle section is her isolation left fully intact. This thematic alteration between isolation and intrusion plays out the contest between Emily and the town to reveal, or conceal, the facts of her life. The more vivid tension, however, occurs in the story's suppression of action, as details of the past fall into place to form a portrait monstrously different from any we had assumed. The narrative creates an overall rhythm of slow-motion revelation, with each aspect of personality laid bare before the surprising jolt of the story's final sentence.

A startling aspect of Faulkner's achievement in the short story form is that his most brilliant successes succeed with quite different materials in narratively various ways. "Red Leaves" (1930), for example, is often acknowledged as his most extraordinary story, not least because of the nuanced use of a selectively omniscient point of view in describing the bizarre Indian ritual of burying his slave with a leader. Other authors might have played up the exotic features of these materials, but Faulkner quickly moves beyond such concern by manipulating the narrative perspective (sometimes in the slave's consciousness, at others with the pursuers, at still others quietly omniscient) to enforce the reader's conflicting sympathies both with and against tradition. The narrative develops just the opposite of "A Rose for Emily" and achieves a different effect, at once gut-wrenchingly suspenseful and hilarious, culturally alien and yet movingly familiar on the subjects of death and tradition.

The purely comic strain in Faulkner is revealed nowhere better than in "Spotted Horses" (1931), which introduces the Snopeses, the clan whose ratlike persistence and witless endeavors animate Faulkner's late novelistic trilogy, *The Hamlet* (1940), *The Town* (1957), and *The Mansion* (1960). The story is told by Ratliff, a sewing-machine agent, who recounts in humorous dialect the wily, inscrutable Flem Snopes's rise in life: "That Flem Snopes. I be dog if he ain't a case, now." A month after wedding the local merchant's daugh-ter, Flem takes his wife to Texas to conceal a premature pregnancy, returning a year later with twenty wild horses to sell. In fact, Flem never admits to owning the horses, much less profiting from their sale, and in the equine havoc wreaked on the town, he avoids any blame. Once sold, the horses cannot be caught, racing through houses, roaming the countryside, leaving broken wagons and legs behind. The rare mix of satiric comedy and pathos that Faulkner achieves in the story is represented best in the character of Mrs. Armstid, who had resisted her foolish husband's purchase of a horse, had even won the Texas salesman's promise of a refund, and yet can only passively accept Flem Snopes's patent lie that he had nothing to do with the trade. After all, the Texas salesman has left town and therefore Flem cannot help her, save for a nickel candy for her young "chaps." The story ends with Ratliff's admiring view of Flem Snopes's brazen sales triumph: "If I had brung a herd of wild cattymounts into town and sold them to my neighbors and kinfolks, they would have lynched me. Yes, sir."

Among short story practitioners, William Faulkner is nearly unique in his fascination with action-laced narratives, coupled with a commitment to literary experimentation. Perhaps the author he most resembles is Stephen Crane, whose preoccupation with bizarre experiences seemed only to reinforce his skepticism about the potential of any supposedly straightforward account. Just as narrative for Faulkner nearly always begins with peculiar events—of barn-burning fathers, necrophilic old maids, and hysterical Indian slaves, among others—his fiction also makes us acutely aware of the form in which those events are represented, the narrative voice and temporal succession that makes them "peculiar" to begin with. Few other authors invite such self-consciousness in the process of reading, or display in the course of a story how firmly readerly judgments emerge from the reader's own predilections. This open-ended, revisable quality of Faulkner's aesthetic may help us understand why so many of his novels began as stories and why so many of his stories appear again in novels. But it does not explain the peculiar and continuing power the best of William Faulkner's stories have in transforming sharply observed episodes of human behavior, however fantastic, into triumphant fictional explorations of universal experiences.

Lee Mitchell

SELECTED BIBLIOGRAPHY

Works by William Faulkner

Collected Stories of William Faulkner. New York: Vintage Books, 1950.
Uncollected Stories of William Faulkner. Edited by Joseph Blotner. New York: Vintage Books, 1979.

Critical Studies

Ferguson, James. *Faulkner's Short Fiction.* Knoxville: University of Tennessee Press, 1991.
Skei, Hans H. *William Faulkner: The Novelist as Short Story Writer.* Oslo: Universitetsforlaget, 1985.

F. SCOTT FITZGERALD
(1896 – 1940)

Although F. Scott Fitzgerald's fame rests primarily on his two major novels, *The Great Gatsby* (1925) and *Tender Is the Night* (1934), he wrote more than 160 short stories during his lifetime. At least six of his stories are considered classics, among the best American short stories published in the twentieth century, and are widely anthologized. Although Fitzgerald thought of himself primarily as a novelist, the stories represent a literary legacy that equals his novels. The connection between the two forms was clear to Fitzgerald, for whom short stories not only provided the income that supported his family over the years—and allowed him to write his novels—but also served as a kind of fictional laboratory. In his stories Fitzgerald developed his style and the themes that he would develop in the novels; in many cases, after a story had been published in a mass-circulation magazine, he would copy passages that seemed to him particularly felicitous into a notebook for possible use later in a novel. From the time he was a young boy in school until his death in Hollywood in 1940, Fitzgerald never ceased writing the short stories that gave him financial and literary sustenance.

F. Scott Fitzgerald was born September 24, 1896, in St. Paul, Minnesota, to Edward and Mollie McQuillan Fitzgerald. He was always proud that he was named for his second cousin, three times removed, Francis Scott Key, composer of "The Star-Spangled Banner." When he was two, the family moved to Buffalo, New

York; two years later to Syracuse; then back to Buffalo in 1901. In 1908, after his father lost his job, the family returned to St. Paul, where he attended St. Paul Academy and began to write short stories. The family moved several times in St. Paul, always living in rented houses; indeed, throughout his lifetime, Fitzgerald never owned a place of residence. The years of his childhood and early youth were indelibly etched in his memory. He would always feel like the outsider, the poor relation, dependent on his mother's family, admitted to but never really a member of St. Paul's social world. This sense of estrangement is characteristic of his fiction, from the short stories of his school years to those he wrote shortly before his death in Hollywood.

In September 1911 he enrolled in the Newman School in New Jersey, where he wrote and published his stories in the *Newman News*. In 1913, he entered Princeton University, where he established friendships with writers Edmund Wilson and John Peale Bishop. At Princeton he joined the major literary and dramatic clubs, and his work appeared in the *Nassau Literary Magazine* and *Princeton Tiger*. In 1914, while home for a school break, he met and fell in love with Ginevra King, who became the model for the unattainable girl who appears frequently in his early short stories. Fitzgerald left Princeton and joined the army in 1917. While stationed in Montgomery, Alabama, he fell in love with Zelda Sayre, whom he married in 1920, the same year that his first novel, *This Side of Paradise,* was published. The success of that novel and the personal celebrity Fitzgerald and his beautiful wife achieved made them icons of the "Jazz

Age," the term Fitzgerald popularized to describe the 1920s. In the same year, his first short story collection, *Flappers and Philosophers,* was published. The Fitzgeralds' daughter, Frances Scott (Scottie) was born in 1921. During the next four years the Fitzgeralds moved to Great Neck, New York, and twice to the French Riviera. His second novel, *The Beautiful and Damned,* was published in 1922, as well as a second collection of short stories, *Tales of the Jazz Age.* In 1926 his third collection of stories, *All the Sad Young Men,* appeared. Fitzgerald completed his next novel, *The Great Gatsby,* in France, where the couple settled until 1927, when he made his first trip to Hollywood to try his hand at screenwriting. Later that year, the family moved to Ellerslie, a rented home in Delaware, and Zelda Fitzgerald started to take ballet lessons. Returning to France, with an interval at Ellerslie and a trip to North Africa in 1930, they took an apartment in Paris, where Zelda suffered her first nervous breakdown and entered a nearby clinic. Later, she was moved to clinics in Switzerland until she was deemed able to return to the United States, to Montgomery. In the next few years, Zelda would experience several breakdowns, and Fitzgerald made a second trip to Hollywood (1931), all the while publishing the short stories that made it possible for him to meet the enormous cost of his wife's illness. In 1934 his novel *Tender Is the Night* was published, and the following year saw publication of his fourth collection of short stories, *Taps at Reveille*. During the years 1935–1937, living in North Carolina close to Zelda's hospital, he was deeply in debt, drinking heavily, and despondent about his wife's condition and his own health. In July 1937 he was given a contract as screenwriter for Metro-Goldwyn-Mayer for $1,000 per week, and he left for Hollywood, where he would remain for the rest of his life. His romance with gossip columnist Sheilah Graham began shortly after his arrival in Hollywood and lasted until his death. He continued to write short stories, notably the Pat Hobby stories, and completed a screenplay for *Three Comrades* (1937), released by MGM. His drinking while in Dartmouth, New Hampshire, with Budd Schulberg, his cowriter on *Winter Carnival,* led producer Walter Wanger to fire him from that film project. In 1939 he began work on a novel about Hollywood, *The Last Tycoon,* but it remained incomplete, for he died of a heart attack at Sheilah Graham's apartment on December 21, 1940.

Although Fitzgerald's writing style and language were not notably idiosyncratic, as were those of his contemporaries Ernest Hemingway and William Faulkner, his fiction is recognizable by its romantic rhetoric, settings, characters, and social issues. His early stories are notably different from those of his late period in both style and subject. The stories reveal a pattern of development and may be divided into three groups: the early tales about golden flappers and idealistic philosophers, his "sad young men," who confront the problems of young people living in the hedonistic 1920s (e.g., "May Day," "Winter Dreams"); the middle stories of the early to mid-1930s, a time of trial and error, of struggle for a new style and new fictional forms that could accommodate the emotions and needs of a mature man and tragic life. The middle period may be de-scribed as Fitzgerald's artistic crisis, when his subjects were as serious as those the nation confronted during the Depression, but his plots were outworn, stale, and mechanical ("A New Leaf," "The Intimate Strangers"). Nevertheless, during this period he produced two of his greatest short-story masterpieces, "Babylon Revisited" (1931) and "Crazy Sunday" (1932), both incorporating the matter rather than the manner of his more commercial contemporary work. The third period, his late works, from the late 1930s until his death, are highly allusive and deeply moving, marked by new techniques—ellipsis, compression, and suggestion. These works are often brief, autobiographical sketches, semifictional attempts to reinterpret his life and art. The tone is almost flat, essayistic; the narrative is unemotional and economical, yet strangely haunting in its dry precision. Among the late stories are "The Lost Decade" (1939), "Afternoon of an Author" (1936), and "News of Paris . . ." (1940). Similar to these, but distinctly separate, stand the Pat Hobby stories, where the old vitality has become corrosive bitterness in a literature of humiliation.

Most of Fitzgerald's stories employ standard fictional techniques used in the novels: central complication, descriptive passages, dramatic climaxes and confrontations, reversals of fortune. Like the novels, the stories rarely turn on the action; more often, even in the shortest, slightest story, there are several actions of equal weight. Fitzgerald's major difficulty is with plot; he will often begin with a good idea, create dramatic scenes, and then let the story limply peter out, or resolve the complications mechanically, as in "A

Change of Class" (1931). But his lyrical prose and his ability to create a protagonist who is at once a participant and observer of the action (like Nick Carraway in *The Great Gatsby*) make even the slightest story memorable. Fitzgerald's gifts as a short story writer were primarily lyric and poetic; lapses in plot and characterization did not concern him nearly as much as using the wrong word. His descriptive gifts are strikingly apparent; with a few selected details usually in atmosphere or decor, he creates a mood against which the dramatic situation stands out in relief. The line describing Miles Calman's house in "Crazy Sunday" is illustrative: "Miles Calman's house was built for great emotional moments—there was an air of listening as if the far silences of its vistas hid an audience, but this afternoon it was thronged, as though people had been bidden rather than asked." Through his language, Fitzgerald created another world in his stories, a kind of dreamland replete with its own conventions and milieus. He often projected his imagination though the rhetoric of nostalgia into the past, creating a world of beauty, stupefying luxury, and fulfillment, a world that is a refuge from fear and anxiety, satiety and void, his answer to death and deterioration. Through imagery, through sensory appeals, through the evocative recreation of an idealized past and fabulous future, Fitzgerald's stories as a whole have the effect of lifting and transporting readers past the restrictions of their own world.

The world of Fitzgerald's stories is most frequently the world of the very rich. Milieus and manners constitute the backdrop against which a rags-to-riches story may unfold, as a struggling young man is rescued by a benevolent tycoon, or a beautiful Cinderella meets her handsome, wealthy prince. Even in the more somber stories, manners and milieu are as important as the plot or the characters. Whatever the form of the story, Fitzgerald's range of subjects is wide and varied. Within the larger themes of life, love, death, and the American myth of success there are incalculable shades and variations. Most of these themes were adumbrated in his apprentice fiction (1909–1917).

The major subjects of his short stories are the sadness of the unfulfilled life and the unrecapturable moment of bliss; the romantic imagination and its power to transform reality; love, courtship, marriage, and problems in marriage. He writes too of the plight of the poor outsider seeking to enter the world of the very rich, and of the cruelty of beautiful and rich young women, as in "The Rubber Check" (1932). He treats other serious subjects like the generation gap; the moral life, manners, and mores of class society; heroism in ordinary life; emotional bankruptcy and the drift to death; the South and its legendary past; and the meaning of America in the lives of individuals and in modern history. To these subjects, which intrigued him from adolescence, he added Hollywood, where the American dream seemed to so many of his generation to have reached its apotheosis. Mass-circulation magazines such as *Saturday Evening Post, Redbook,* and *Women's Home Companion* were strong outlets for his work from the 1920s through the early 1930s, and at his peak (1929–32), his stories commanded fees of $4,000 apiece. By the mid-1930s his stories no longer appealed to readers, and his chief outlet was *Esquire* magazine, where he received only $250 per story.

One of Fitzgerald's most moving stories from his early period is "Winter Dreams" (1922). Like *The Great Gatsby,* published three years later, and "The Rich Boy" (1926), it concerns the conflict between the very rich and a protagonist from the middle class, a contrast explored through careful scrutiny of social gestures, moods, conventions, and customs. In "Winter Dreams," Dexter Green is a golf caddy at the luxurious club serving the wealthy inhabitants of Sherry Island. He meets Judy Jones, daughter of a member of the club, and she and her summer world become the focus of his dreams. In the beautiful, cold, imperious, and unattainable Judy Jones, Fitzgerald embodies both the allure and the cruelty of the very rich. Dexter pursues her, but she eludes him; the effort to attain her is for him the struggle to realize his dreams of entering the glittering world of those enchanting summers. But her world—which ultimately symbolizes both the beauty and the meretriciousness of Dexter's dreams—is cruel and destructive. Dexter, listening to music floating over the lake at Sherry Island, felt "magnificently attuned to life." His memories of the summer sustained him throughout the winter, and his winter dream was simply to recapture the ecstasy of that golden moment at the lake when he felt that "everything about him was radiating a brightness and a glamour he might never know again." That ecstasy, which is linked with the vision of Judy Jones, is Dexter's vision of immortality, just as Daisy Buchanan is Gatsby's. Had

he succeeded in capturing Judy, he believed he could have preserved his youth and the beauty of a world that seemed to "withstand all time." When her beauty fades with the years, his hopes fade with it, along with that sense of wonder he had cherished over the years. They are both lost "in the country of illusion . . . where his winter dreams had flourished."

Perhaps Fitzgerald's greatest short story, certainly one of his best known, is "Babylon Revisited," which was filmed by MGM in 1954. Written in 1930, it reflects the writer's meditative sadness as he looks back from the gloom of the Depression on the waste and dissipation of the 1920s. The story is about Charlie Wales, who, caught up in the frivolity of American expatriate life in Paris of the boom years, once made a mistake that resulted in his wife's death. He has become sober, has a well-paying job, and has come back to the scene of his earlier indiscretions to reclaim his daughter, Honoria, who has been living with his in-laws, Marion and Lincoln Peters. Charlie must prove to the Peterses that he is now stable and, indeed, that he adheres to their values. His difficulty is that Marion actively dislikes him and wishes to continue to punish him for his past behavior. Fitzgerald constructs the story around a series of contrasts: between Charlie and his in-laws, past and present, illusion and reality, dissipation and steadiness, gaiety and grimness, Paris and America, adults and children—and most of all, between the world gained and the world lost. The author's tone, detached, critical, and ironic, merges with Charlie's self-critical but not self-pitying awareness. Every brief observation resonates throughout the story: "I spoiled this city for myself. I didn't realize it, but the days came along one after another, and then two years were gone, and everything was gone, and I was gone."

The mature Charlie Wales is not the same young man who locked his wife out of their hotel during a drunken brawl on that fateful night years ago. The story is about his exploration of the problems of character and responsibility, particularly about the power of one's past to shape and ultimately determine his future. Against a background of change and dislocation caused by the Crash and the Depression, the story of Charlie Wales becomes a search for enduring values within the individual, the values that enable someone to find the courage and stamina to remake a life that has been squandered in dissipation. Charlie admits that he "lost everything I wanted in the boom," and his one hope for future redemption is continuity of character, as if by passing on to his daughter some of his own lessons from the past he will preserve at least part of himself in her.

"Babylon Revisited" is a complex, compressed story, with one of the most mature and important messages in Fitzgerald's work: character may not bring Charlie happiness along with his newly discovered values, and it may even intensify his despair and corrode his hopes. The ending of the story has been the subject of much discussion—and the fate of Charlie Wales is ambiguous, yet curiously, all the more satisfying to the reader in its ambiguity. It reveals F. Scott Fitzgerald as a mature artist and a consummate short story writer.

Ruth Prigozy

SELECTED BIBLIOGRAPHY

Works by F. Scott Fitzgerald

Flappers and Philosophers. New York: Charles Scribner's Sons, 1920.

Tales of the Jazz Age. New York: Charles Scribner's Sons, 1922.

All the Sad Young Men. New York: Charles Scribner's Sons, 1935.

The Stories of F. Scott Fitzgerald. New York: Charles Scribner's Sons, 1951.

Afternoon of an Author: A Selection of Uncollected Stories and Essays. New York: Charles Scribner's Sons, 1957.

The Pat Hobby Stories. New York: Charles Scribner's Sons, 1962.

The Apprentice Fiction of F. Scott Fitzgerald. Edited by John Kuehl. New Brunswick, N.J.: Rutgers University Press, 1965.

The Basil and Josephine Stories. Edited by Jackson R. Bryer and John Kuehl. New Brunswick, N.J.: Rutgers University Press, 1965.

Bits of Paradise: 21 Uncollected Stories by F. Scott and Zelda Fitzgerald. Edited by Scottie Fitzgerald Smith and Matthew J. Bruccoli. New York: Charles Scribner's Sons, 1973.

The Price Was High: The Last Uncollected Stories of F. Scott Fitzgerald. Edited by Matthew J. Bruccoli. New York: Harcourt Brace Jovanovich, 1978.

The Stories of F. Scott Fitzgerald. Edited by Matthew J. Bruccoli. New York: Charles Scribner's Sons, 1989.

Critical Studies

Bryer, Jackson R., ed. *New Essays on F. Scott Fitzgerald's Neglected Stories.* Columbia: University of Missouri Press, 1996.

Bryer, Jackson R., ed. *The Short Stories of F. Scott Fitzgerald: New Approaches in Criticism.* Madison: University of Wisconsin Press, 1982.

Kuehl, John. *F. Scott Fitzgerald: A Study of the Short Fiction.* Boston: Twayne, 1991.

Mangum, Bryant. *A Fortune Yet: Money in the Art of F. Scott Fitzgerald's Short Stories.* New York: Garland, 1991.

Petry, Alice Hall. *Fitzgerald's Craft of Short Fiction: The Collected Stories, 1920–1935.* Ann Arbor: UMI Research Press, 1989.

Prigozy, Ruth. "F. Scott Fitzgerald." *Dictionary of Literary Biography,* vol. 86, pp. 99–123. Detroit: Gale Research, 1993.

RICHARD FORD

(1944 –   )

Richard Ford's moving and eloquent stories emerged in the wave of blue-collar realism that swept American fiction in the 1970s and 1980s. Ford was influenced by his friend Raymond Carver, a gifted and original craftsman, who wrote about self-destructive deadbeats and losers who eke out marginal lives in the Pacific Northwest. Misunderstood as a minimalist, Carver evoked failure and unhappiness in a flat, understated tone that reflected the featureless surroundings and numb emotional lives of his characters. Building on Carver's spare technique and bleak portraiture, Ford's stories seek a wider emotional range; they focus on the buried feelings, mysterious losses, and aching transitions that mark the destinies of ordinary individuals.

Richard Ford was born in Jackson, Mississippi, in 1944 and lived for a time opposite the home of Eudora Welty, one of the South's most respected writers. (He would later become her literary executor and coedit the Library of America edition of her work.) Ford's father had a heart attack when his son was eight and died when he was sixteen, which meant that Ford spent a great deal time on the road or with his grandparents, who ran a hotel in Little Rock. He graduated from Michigan State University in 1966 and tried several careers—school teaching, police work, law school, and the Marine Corps among them—before deciding to become a writer. Ford married his college girlfriend, Kristina Hensley, in 1968. Because of her work in urban planning and his teaching jobs—at the University of Michigan, Williams College, and Princeton, among others—they moved frequently, setting down roots in different parts of the country. Peripatetic by choice, they had no children.

After finding little success with short fiction, Ford published *A Piece of My Heart* (1976), a lushly written Faulknerian novel that takes place in his native Mississippi and Arkansas. His second book, *The Ultimate Good Luck* (1981), was a violent existential thriller set in Mexico that reminded some reviewers of the hard-boiled male fiction of Hemingway and Robert Stone. Though *A Piece of My Heart* was well received, Ford did not gain significant readership or critical attention until *The Sportswriter* (1986), a first-person novel set in suburban New Jersey about a man coming to terms with loss and regret as he mourns the death of his son and the dissolution of his marriage. Not much happens in this dreamy book, written with a musing inwardness that echoes the reflective voice of Walker Percy's *The Moviegoer* (1961). Ford's narrator, Frank Bascombe, like Percy's, takes remarkable satisfaction in the small rituals of daily life. Thus Ford came into his own by turning from the melodramatic to the quietly suggestive; he learned from Carver and Percy how to find meaning, even deep feeling, in banal situations and seemingly uneventful lives.

Rock Springs (1987), a collection of ten stories, marked another striking shift in Ford's fiction, for it combined the grim, occasionally violent world of his early work with the bare manner and quotidian atmosphere of *The Sportswriter*. Each phase of Ford's work plays off a different region; these tales are set in Montana, not far from Carver country, where the Fords have had a home since 1983. Much of *Rock Springs*—along with the short novel *Wildlife* (1990) and the long story "Jealous" in *Women with Men* (1997)—reads like variations on a single submerged story, almost a fragmentary novel, unfolding in the vicinity of Great Falls, Montana: A man in his early forties looks back to the turning point of his life, a moment when he was fifteen or sixteen, the time his parents' marriage went awry, when death or violence, sexual waywardness or simple misunderstanding came between them, and he himself, though young and confused, was initiated into the mysteries of the adult world.

The mood of *Rock Springs* is best expressed by the opening of "Great Falls": "This is not a happy story. I warn you." Most of the stories are told in the first person, in a tone of portentous simplicity—mournful, resigned—at times touching, even heartbreaking, but also occasionally mannered and unconvincing. Ford learned from Carver how to pull the reader right into the story, to pare it down to elemental details and put an unexpected spin on every sentence. But Ford's stories are long and more complex than Carver's; their narration reaches, not always successfully, for an emotional pitch that Carver implies but rarely underlines. "Great Falls" ends with just such a large gesture, an appeal to "some coldness in us all, some helplessness that causes us to misunderstand life when it is pure and plain, makes our existence seem like a border between two nothings, and makes us no more or less than animals who meet on the road, desperate and without patience and without hope."

The story as a whole is little more than an anecdote, though it involves the end of a marriage. The boy's father comes home to find his wife with a gentleman caller; he holds a gun to the man's neck as he threatens and rags him but then simply sends him away. The son's recollections, many years later, are strung together with short, declarative sentences: "The house itself is gone now—I have been to the spot." "It is a true thing that my father did not know limits." They are so uninflected that they sound like pieces of folk wisdom: the narrator reaches for insight he did not have when these events took place. His memories reflect not only what happened then, which marked him forever, but also other nameless blows life had in store for him. This brooding sense of the unspoken prepares us for the story's final lines and gives them surprising resonance.

Like Hemingway in his Nick Adams stories, Ford uses such silences to lend weight to the young man's initiation into unhappy manhood. This rite of passage, which sometimes involves hunting and fishing, or drinking and women, but also a tremulous fear and sensitivity, takes place in the heart of Hemingway territory, in a Montana that seems more like a great emptiness than a natural paradise. Nature offers moments of almost sublime beauty, like the flight of the wild geese in the last story, "Communist," but the towns and cities, with their transient inhabitants, become in memory "a place that seemed not even to exist, an empty place you could stay in for long time and never find a thing you admired or loved or hoped to keep." Here, aimless people make the wrong choices, or no choices, on the way to their own special form of unhappiness.

Though Ford's stories focus on ordinary lives in commonplace settings, what happens in them, however trivial or arbitrary it may seem, becomes a turning point, the moment when hope began to fail, when a marriage fell apart, when a boy was suddenly thrust out on his own, first glimpsing life in all its darker shadings. At such times, always matter-of-factly described, the fault lines of character, the stresses of a relationship, suddenly come to the surface, and the narrator discovers that "the most important things of your life can change so suddenly, so unrecoverably." As he later wrote in "Good Raymond," a brief memoir, Ford shared with Carver a sense "that life goes this way or life goes that way; that chance is always involved, and that living is usually just dealing with consequences."

In another story, "Optimists," the fa-ther comes home to find his wife not with a lover but simply playing canasta with friends. But he himself is terribly upset: the labor situation on the railroad is bad, hard times are coming, and he has just seen a man die under the wheels of a boxcar. When one of the guests goads him provocatively, he kills the man with a single punch, setting in motion a train of consequences that transform all their lives. Though the father had not meant to do what he does, it lands him in prison, destroys his marriage, and changes his son's outlook: "I saw him as man who made mistakes, as a man who could hurt people, ruin lives, risk their happiness. A man who did not understand enough." The same could be said about all the men in Ford's stories. They educate the young protagonist to a world of violent impulses, thoughtless behavior, and irretrievable effects. And people simply drift apart, as if something in the western air kept them from staying together. By the end of the story, when the narrator runs into his mother at a convenience store, he has seen neither of his parents for many years.

The one undoubted masterpiece in *Rock Springs* is "Communist," an initiation story that strikes a fine balance between unspoiled natural beauty and the wayward human presence. Here the father is already dead and the main character is the mother's boyfriend, Glen Baxter, who takes the young man hunting for wild geese—creatures that, unlike people, are said to mate forever. The mother is not happy: "Hunt, kill, maim. Your father did that too." But the boy is enthralled. His father has already taught him to box; Glen will teach him to kill. He is enraptured by the sight and sound of the geese, "a sound that made your chest rise and your shoulders tighten with expectancy." Ford gives the young man's voice an accent all its own: "It was a thing to see, I will tell you now. Five thousand white geese all in the air around you, making a noise like you have never heard before. And I thought to myself then: this is something I will never see again. I will never forget this. And I was right."

"I don't know why I shoot 'em," says Glen. "They're so beautiful." But in a decisive moment, Glen refuses to finish off a goose he has wounded, then kills it in a burst of fury, and this undoes him in the eyes of both mother and son. "You don't have a heart, Glen," she says. "There's nothing to love in you. "And the boy, now grown older, sees Glen not as "a bad man, only a man scared of something he'd never seen before—something soft in himself—his life going a way he didn't like. A woman with a son. Who could blame him there?" Like many of Ford's stories, "Communist" turns on almost nothing but makes it everything, a defining moment that shifts the course of people's lives. The boy's eagerness to become a man leads him to the manly perception that life is more complicated than he knew; an initiation into the hunt becomes an initiation into the mysteries of life, as the boy discovers how "a light can go out in the heart."

Ford's portentous endings test the limits of introspection for characters that are not obviously insightful. The narrator of "Rock Springs," a petty car thief with a daughter and girlfriend in tow, inspects his life from every angle, but when he appeals for the reader's empathy in the final line ("Would you think he was anybody like you?"), he speaks for the author more than for himself. Despite its unity of tone and setting, its strong characters and memorable atmosphere, *Rock Springs* is an uneven collection. There is something factitious and literary, an aura of unearned wisdom, about the poker-faced simplicity of weaker stories such as "Winterkill."

Ford once told an interviewer that "I'm probably never going to write out of one voice and don't wish that I could," but the ruminative tone of *Rock Springs* can be less persuasive than the casual, quotidian voice of *The Sportswriter* and its acclaimed sequel, *Independence Day* (1995). The reverse can be seen in *Women with Men,* where the first and the third stories, written more in *The Sportswriter* voice, seem slack, while the middle story, "Jealous, " belongs with the most effective writing in *Rock Springs*. "Jealous" adds an impressive chapter to Richard Ford's episodic sequence about a boy's coming of age in a world where love and pain, tenderness and violence, intimacy and estrangement, are opposite sides of the same coin.

Morris Dickstein

SELECTED BIBLIOGRAPHY

Works by Richard Ford

"My Mother, in Memory." *Harper's,* August 1987.

Rock Springs. New York: Atlantic Monthly Press, 1987.

The Granta Book of the American Short Story. (Editor.) London: Granta Books; New York: Viking, 1992.

Women with Men. New York: Alfred A. Knopf, 1997.

"Good Raymond." *The New Yorker,* October 5, 1998.

The Granta Book of the American Long Story. (Editor.) London: Granta Books, 1998.

Critical and Biographical Studies

Dickstein, Morris. "The Pursuit of the Ordinary." *Partisan Review* 58 (summer 1991): 506–513.

Lyons, Bonnie. "The Art of Fiction CXLVII: Richard Ford." *Paris Review* 38 (fall 1996): 42–77.

Weber, Bruce. "Richard Ford's Uncommon Characters." *New York Times Magazine,* April 10, 1988.

MARY GAITSKILL

(1954–)

Mary Gaitskill is the author of two story collections, *Bad Behavior* (1988) and *Because They Wanted To* (1997); a novel, *Two Girls, Fat and Thin* (1991); and essays and reviews in such mainstream magazines as *Mirabella, Vogue,* and *Harper's* and such avant-garde Internet journals as *Word.* Her work is cerebral, representing thinking as central to living; visceral, located in affect-laden scenes of intimacy and aversion; passionate, about pain and survival. It is feminist work, where the wounds of romance feel familiar and confirming to the female characters, in contrast to male confusion, surprise, or resentment. It has also been identified as "queer" work, meaning that Gaitskill rep-resents desire as a state of feeling alive rather than a choice of one side or the other of the heterosexual/gay and lesbian divide. Finally, for all of Gaitskill's icon-oclasm, her work is conventional too, in both its minimalist style and its saturation by romantic fantasy.

The centrality to intimacy of fantasy and misrecognition distinguishes Gaitskill's fiction, as well as her essays and reviews. Her characters form habits of obsession or cruelty that alternate with warmth, empathy, and erotic optimism, but mainly they experience the uncertainties of intimacy in states of numbness or confusion. Encountering failure engenders pain, which they both receive and inflict. Gaitskill's critical detractors sometimes respond to her depiction of pain by suggesting that her characters are simply incompetent for living, for they seem not to learn from their mistakes. But Gaitskill disclaims the usual indices of ethical intimacy and healthy self-regard, focusing on in-between or inarticulate states of feeling: "She didn't understand what moved beneath her own words. It seemed too big to be chipped off in word form, but it didn't matter. . . ." When someone's optimism is confronted by the unlovable within love, her hopefulness can feel pathetic or even perverse. At the same time, there is something courageous and affirming about it: a person's openness to attachment makes a space for change, the outcome of which cannot be predicted.

This image of desire's optimism requires an energetic intelligence, a monitoring mind that pays attention to detail, although knowing something never conquers the instability of attachment: "it seemed that I had been very stupid to see such complexity in what had happened between us," the narrator of "Stuff" says. "It seemed equally possible, though, that he was even more stupid not to see it." These paradoxes of knowledge and mis-understanding can make Gaitskill's stories tragic and dark—but also very funny: sometimes in a sly way; sometimes through the shock of a hilarious image; always as a measure of the absurd drama of the moment when one is overwhelmed by a scene that one wants to be in, is halfway in, and yet that one is fleeing too.

One might call this tangle of longing and posturing "the private," in that the world of the stories is personal, organized and energized by the will to love. How-ever, these works are also about how in-timacy builds worlds: not just psycholog-ical but material worlds, involving networks of friends, lovers, families, col-leagues, acquaintances, and strangers who live in places made memorable by detail, food and smells and conversation.

Little of the how, why, and where of this larger cluster of concerns has been engaged by Gaitskill's critics. Distracted by the sex and love plots, they have not found interest, for example, in the class relations she is always tracking: the din-giness and contingency of life on the eco-nomic bottom; the social and economic marginality of temporary workers and clerks; the murky liminality of students' lives; the too-shiny, stable and unsatisfying worlds of college professors and lawyers; the blurry chaos of drunken and drug-addicted survival. Yet for Gaitskill eco-nomics and occupation powerfully shape the way one grasps the world, even sex-ually. As Gaitskill writes in "Other Fac-tors," one's relation to "sex" and to "the

job" expresses not only one's relation to survival but also a notion of "success" that, while rarely enumerated, shapes and mo-tivates a person's core wants and needs.

Instead, Gaitskill has been particularly linked by critics with the prose of sado-masochism. In this she tends to associate herself with Nabokov, whose seeming cruelty, she says, masks his rich compre-hension of and engagement with human suffering. In terms of contemporary lit-erary culture she is linked with Valerie Martin, Amy Bloom, Angela Carter, Kathy Acker, and Catherine Texier. *Bad Behavior* and *Two Girls, Fat and Thin* explic-itly represent characters whose sexual practices are organized by rituals or fan-tasies involving pain; even her more "con-ventional" women tend to experience desire as a rush of subordination to some-thing (an ideal, a fear) or someone (a lover). How does she distinguish between a healthy and a pathological relation to being open to the pain of intimacy? For Gaitskill this is a feminist question, but also one that marks sexuality in general, for men and for women. Two exemplary stories in this mode are "A Romantic Weekend" and "Stuff."

The New York-based scene of "A Ro-mantic Weekend" is an adulterous tryst between a nameless sadistic man whose desire to "torture" women is enumerated in all its conventionality, and a woman, Beth, whose masochistic fantasies are taken straight from the "seductive puff-ball" of romance narrative. He imagines her "bound and naked in an S&M bar," while she imagines herself "helpless and swooning, in his arms." While she dis-appoints him because she has "too much ego" to be a successful "slave," he disappoints her because he's a "pathologically insecure . . . hostile moron." He reconsiders his sexual history throughout, experiencing "in a queasy scramble" his movement between a placid marriage and sadistic affairs. Meanwhile, Beth reveals that she "can't have sex normally" because a lover hurt her physically during sex in college, but she also embraces the way it "opened [me] up" and seeks to reexperience her loss of control on her own terms.

The displeasure that radiates from their sexuality notwithstanding, the lovers fight desperately to keep their fantasies alive. Beth is "smitten" with the attention the man fixes on her. When he realizes that she needs to hear that his cruelty is motivated by a fear of love, he thinks, "This could work out fine," and the story ends on an optimistic note. The affair becomes a contract for deception, Beth consenting to her negation in order to feel loved, the man consenting to don the veil of love's promise in order to make it seem that it is *her* need that engenders his violence.

Gaitskill's sympathy for and aversion to these contortions is evident. But how can one understand the lovers' desire for an unsatisfying arrangement that will always disappoint their particular fantasies of subordination? As they sit in a bar, they see that "most of [the patrons] were men in suits who sat there seemingly enmeshed in a web of habit and accumulated rancor that they called their personalities." The fear of becoming one of the living dead, numbed by the incorporation of normalcy's forms, haunts all of Gaitskill's main characters: and pain is much closer to the feeling of really living than is fantasy or its partner, loneliness.

In Gaitskill's later story, "Stuff," other facets of the relation between pain and attachment emerge. "Stuff" is the last in a series of four stories clustered within *Because They Wanted To,* collectively titled, "The Wrong Thing." These are mainly San Francisco stories in which the narrator moves between heterosexuality and lesbianism. But this shift denotes not a movement from pain to pleasure, or subordination to freedom. The biggest shift is in the norms of the sexual culture in which the attachments take place. What is markedly "heterosexual" in "Stuff" is the privateness of heterosexuality. Kenneth sees Susan, the narrator, at a colleague's party; he pursues her on dates and on the phone, telling her lightly ironic stories of his sexual vulnerability; he takes her to his private hoard of thrift shop and garage sale treasures, lavishing on her things irrelevant to how she lives. Even their intensely personal conversations make restaurants seem private: it is as though each table is a separate room in which a couple sits, an invisible wall making the others around them barely exist.

Meanwhile, as in "A Romantic Weekend" and many other Gaitskill stories, we encounter in "Stuff" scenes of endless talking that perform paradoxical functions. Foremost, they are boring and predict erotic disappointment. Yet, the white noise of verbosity holds open a space for intimacy to be generated: it enables the hope that the two might talk their way into a true feeling. Yet because intimacy destabilizes, this exposed feeling propels some characters, especially Gaitskill's men, back into abstraction or an exaggerated stance of self-possession and assertion of control. This reaction formation is especially evident in the stories that feature male physical brutality, "Secretary," "Trying to Be," "The Girl on the Plane," and "Kiss and Tell."

In contrast, the lesbian world of "Stuff" takes place in bars and among groups of friends, as well as in private apartments. Rather than seek out a bubble of privacy, lesbian attachment here emerges from a less-defended physicality that short-circuits the defenses of language and enables a more open sexual pedagogy, including a more ritualized and self-conscious relation to S/M sexual practice. Susan is involved, off and on, with Erin, who "just want[s] somebody to hurt me and humiliate me." When Susan tells Erin that she deserves better than intimate pain, Erin laughs: "'Susan,' she said, 'you're so sweet I just want to tie you up and torture you. But that stuff is what gets me off. It's not about self-hate or anything icky. It just gets me off."

The self-accepting simplicity of Erin's perceptions here distinguishes her from almost everyone in these two short story collections. As the epigraph to *Because They Wanted To* (from Carson McCullers) suggests, "the state of being beloved is intolerable to many." Elsewhere, Susan wishes "she could grab . . . happiness and mash it into a ball and hoard it and gloat over it, but she couldn't. It just ran around all over the place, disrupting everything" ("The Blanket").

As a stylist Gaitskill has been associated with the "expressionless eighties' deadpan" and minimalism of American literary culture. She writes from the relatively privileged class of white Americans whose familial and sexual struggles have been massively documented starting in the post–World War II generation. Born in Lexington, Kentucky, Gaitskill grew up in the suburbs of Detroit and graduated from the University of Michigan in 1981. Although she has not married, is not especially rooted in any city, and has lived in the risky worlds of stripper and sex worker, her work is nonetheless saturated by conventional baby-boomer concerns about the isolating traumas of ordinary experience. Stylistically, the strange proximity of antithetical affects is marked in the way the rhythms, sounds, and silences of her prose denote what language cannot do. The careful, fine pacing of the sentences provides a sense of scale for unworked-through intensities. The prose itself does not get heated when it describes heat, but assures without saying it that *this* feeling, whatever it is, will be succeeded by another, and that only tracking it over time will enable a more reliable understanding of it. The fear of psychological numbness can also be linked to the performative effects of this style: the proliferation of detail in Gaitskill's work marks the fear and desire to be overwhelmed by events and sensation, since true living is located in the resistance to repetitions that petrify personality. It is as though in Gaitskill's world a person identifies with his/her own emotional impossibility more than any other aspect of identity: even in the case, as with "Walt and Beth: A Love Story," when there is a happy ending.

"Walt and Beth," cowritten by Gaitskill and Peter Trachtenberg, is a crayon-illustrated adult/children's book, published in cyberspace. It is about two lovers with a history of violent sexuality and failed therapies for it and for the damage they do to themselves and each other. Yet the crayon drawings and the primary colors that illuminate the story, along with the many happy cats who populate the rooms of the lonely lovers, suggest in advance the happy ending.

Each lover blames the other for his or her own frustration: both are endlessly fascinated with the other's refusal to give them what they want. Beth wants beauty, Walt spiritual peace. Their trouble is not that they are simply depressed, masochistic, or destructive, but that their ambivalence has disabled their capacity to feel a simple feeling: this leads them to the childlike feeling of being overwhelmed, only with the adult capacity to obsess and destroy. Gaitskill's celebrated essay, "On Not Being a Victim: Sex, Rape, and the Trouble with Following Rules," addresses the complexities of women's capacity to accept the relation of pleasure and pain in their own sexuality, arguing against a certain conservative and feminist tendency to project sexual discomfort onto an external predator (a man, usually). In "Walt and Beth," both lovers' intense and conflicted desire to feel leads them through dark sexual degradations and to various therapies for their anger and violence; in the end, they resolve to see their love in the simultaneity of their therapeutic project.

Trauma for Gaitskill means an incapacity to learn, and thus to sustain love. Happiness, in contrast, requires the live mind to work through the details of emotional inconsistency, patiently making possible moments of decision that feel, simply, right. As a character notes in Gaitskill's story "Veronica," "You've got to decide whether you want to live, or not. . . . Because if you do, you're going to have to start fighting for it."

Lauren Berlant

SELECTED BIBLIOGRAPHY

Works by Mary Gaitskill

Bad Behavior. New York: Vintage Books, 1988.
"Modern Romance: A Lesson in Appetite Control." *Ms.,* May 1989.
Two Girls, Fat and Thin. New York: Vintage Books, 1991.
"On Not Being a Victim: Sex, Rape, and the Trouble With Following Rules." *Harper's,* March 1994.
Because They Wanted To. New York: Scribner, 1997.
"Veronica." *POZ* (http://www.thebody.com/poz), August 1998.
"Walt and Beth: A Love Story." (With Peter Trachtenberg.) *Word* (http://www.word.com), July 7, 1999.
"Suntan." *Word* (http://www.word.com), July 12, 1999.
"Sorcerer of Cruelty (My Inspiration: Vladimir Nabokov)." *Salon* (http://www.salon1999.com), July 12, 1999.

WILLIAM H. GASS
(1924–)

A much admired and highly esteemed writer, William Howard Gass was born in Fargo, North Dakota, on July 30, 1924, and grew up in Warren, Ohio. He majored in philosophy at Kenyon College (B.A., 1947) and received his Ph.D. in philosophy from Cornell University in 1954. In 1952, he married Mary Patricia

O'Kelly and had three children. In 1969, he married Mary Alice Henderson and had two more children. He taught at the College of Wooster (1950–54) and Purdue University (1954–69). Since 1969 he has taught in the philosophy department at Washington University, where he is David May Distinguished University Professor in the Humanities and Director of the International Writers Center in Arts and Sciences. His works include a collection of short stories, *In the Heart of the Heart of the Country*, as well as more than fifteen uncollected short fictions; a series of four novellas, *Cartesian Sonata*; two novels, *Omensetter's Luck* and *The Tunnel*; and influential critical writings: *Willie Masters' Lonesome Wife* (a blend of fiction and theory), *On Being Blue, Fiction and the Figures of Life, The World Within the Word, Habitations of the Word,* and *Finding a Form*. Two of Gass's keen interests, reflected in his writing, are photography and architecture.

Gass has been awarded a Rockefeller Foundation grant for fiction (1965–66), a Guggenheim Fellowship (1969), and the Academy and Institute of Arts and Letters Award for Fiction in 1975 and its Medal of Merit for Fiction in 1979. *The Tunnel* was nominated for the 1996 PEN/Faulkner Award. In 1985 and 1996 he won the National Book Critics Circle Award for *Habitations of the Word* and *Finding a Form*; and he received the 1997 Lannan Foundation Lifetime Achievement Award, a $100,000 prize.

William Gass's metafictional short stories are best understood in terms of their own processes, the "world within the word," as Gass says, rather than as a mirror of the external world. Metafiction is concerned more with its own processes than

with objective reality and life in the world. In Gass's collection *In The Heart of the Heart of the Country,* what appear to be character, setting, and plot are not mimetic representations of the natural world; they are actually devices for capturing the readers' attention and directing it to linguistic structures of the text's creative process—language, repeated rhythms, and sounds. As Gass points out, "the novelist now better understands his medium . . . language," and literature calls attention to "the world within the word."

Gass begins the title story of *In the Heart of the Heart of the Country* with a reference to Yeats's "Sailing to Byzantium":

And therefore I have sailed the seas
    and come
To the holy city of Byzantium.

Gass writes:

So I have sailed the seas and
    come . . .
to B . . .
a small town fastened to a field in
    Indiana.

The reader wonders if the small town actually is Byzantium, the eternal city that makes "soul clap its hands and sing, and louder sing." The narrator's "B" is "fastened to a field," to land, to earth, to the dying world trapped in time. The narrator's soul, sick with desire, seems to want life. In his house, the narrator continues, "Leaves move in the windows. I cannot tell you yet how beautiful it is, what it means. But they do move. They move in the glass." Gradually we appreciate that in Gass's story we are not moving in a real world. Gass creates a universe of sounds and rhythms, a verbal world: "this house in B in Indiana with its blue and gray bewitching windows, holy magical insides. Great thick evergreens protect its entry . . . . My house, this place and body, I've come in mourning to be born in." The narrator continues, "I dreamed my lips would drift down your back like a skiff on a river. I'd follow a vein with the point of my finger, hold your bare feet in my naked hands." The narrator, pursuing assonantal and alliterative constructions, asserts: "I must organize myself. I must, as they say, pull myself together." "I'm empty or I'm full," the narrator states, "depending; and I cannot choose. I sink my claws [trying to be catlike] in Tick's fur and scratch the bones of his back until his rear rises amorously. . . . And Mr. Tick rolls over on his belly, all ooze."

In the narrator's house the window looks within to the creative act. This window opens to patterns of the story—unusual referential patterns. Explains Gass: "[It is] as though each word were itself a window through which I could see other words, other windows." For example, in the section of the title story called "House, My Breath and Window," at the same time that the outer reality is deteriorating, the vision seen through the inner window is described as growing: the writer, looking through the window, indicates that winter seems to be deadening the landscape: "No snow is falling. There's no haze." The external world is dead, but gradually the poetic rhythms grow and soar with energy. An expanding set of alliterations and assonances and inner rhythms glides into awareness. The narrator explains: I have seen the sea slack, life bubble through a body

without trace, its spheres impervious as soda's. Downwound, the whore at wagtag clicks and clacks." In the same sentence there is the alliteration of words and new words ("downwound," "wagtag"); the narrator creates an echo in the text as the lines overflow with inner rhymes—"I find I write that only those who live down grow; and what I write, I hold, whatever I really know."

In addition, on the literal level, there is a series of perplexing contradictions. On one hand, we are told: "My window is a grave, and all that lies within it's dead." On the other hand, this is followed by, "It is not still." The statement, "there is no haze" is followed by images of "befog" and "mist." Earlier, the narrator uses contrarieties to describe his beloved (poetry). She is both on a raft with him and the river on which he floats: "we are adrift on a raft; your back is our river." These paradoxes help to point toward the mystery of the world within the word, the world developed by the alliterations and assonances and rhythms that are the texture of the new poem/story. The "inscape" gradually replaces the traditional referential world of reality.

In the collection's first story, "The Pedersen Kid," the structure of the detective story is introduced. The adolescent narrator, Jorge Segren, goes with Big Hans, the hired man, to the barn and sees the Pedersen Kid, their neighbor's son, who is unconscious. Later, the young boy tells them a story about his escape from a criminal who may have murdered his family. After hearing the report, Jorge, Big Hans, and Jorge's father leave for the Pedersen house. As the action progresses, Jorge fantasizes about doing "something special and big—like a knight setting out." The trappings of a mystery and a quest are set up as Jorge, his father, and Big Hans—each in competition with the other—journey in the snow to the Pedersen house. They find the killer's dead horse in the snow; the killer shoots Jorge's father; Hans runs away; Jorge hides in the Pedersen cellar; and when he hears the killer leave, he goes upstairs in the house. The next morning, the sun is out and Jorge feels happy, "warm inside and out, burning up, inside and out, with joy."

The "structure" or "manifest content" of the story stresses Jorge's successful completion of his mysterious quest. He is his own person, "free" from the control of his sadistic, whiskey-drinking father. He even is able to look outside of his own concerns and shows interest in another: "I really did hope that the kid was as warm as I was now." The experience also seems to take on religious significance, as though the Pedersen Kid has been resurrected. Jorge feels that the Pedersen kid had done him "a glorious turn," causing Jorge to muse, "Well it made me think how I was told to feel in church." These signs connect to imagery patterns that, as Bruce Bassoff argues, describe the resurrection of the Pedersen Kid: after finding the near-dead Pedersen Kid, Big Hans places him "on the kitchen table in all that dough. . . . Getting him ready to bake." This evokes the Christian image of symbolically breaking bread to share in the body of Christ. This image is repeated toward the end of Jorge's quest, as he waits for the killer in the snow. He fantasizes, "the Pedersen Kid was there too, naked in the flour." This image of resurrection connects to Jorge's rebirth.

Simultaneously, however, details work to parody these traditional aspects of the story. The mystery is never solved, for no information is given at the end as to whether the Pedersens really have been murdered or whether the killer is present at the end or has escaped. Jorge ponders: "He'd gone off this way yet there was nothing now to show he'd gone; . . . he might be lying huddled with the horse . . . nothing even in the shadows shrinking while I watched to take for something hard and not of snow and once alive." And it is not clear whether the killer shoots Jorge's father or whether Jorge does: "And pa—I didn't touch you, remember—there's no point in haunting me. He did. He's even come round maybe." As readers, we may not feel troubled by these ambiguities. We are compelled by the use of language to feel the warmth of Jorge's newfound energy: "warm inside and out, burning up, inside and out, with joy."

The repeated rhythms and sounds have successfully developed a satisfying subtext to which we respond without concern for mimetic references to the natural world. This tuning in to the subtext is evident early in the story when the lonely Jorge, living with his alcoholic, brutal father, his passive mother, and Big Hans, expresses the frustration, hatred, and rage in an interior monologue.

For the reader, however, the anapestic rhythms and echoing sounds of the words overshadow the anger in Jorge's monologue. The harmonious melody of the subtext can cause us to soar in excitement at the world within the word, pulling us back from what seems to be the world of external reality, frequently a grotesque world, filled with pain and suffering. Gass has indicated that it often is a challenge to "write beautifully about the grotesque." The rhythmic language becomes an appeal to the auditory imagination and invites readers to perceive emotionally. We appreciate the aesthetic value of the world of words, which may possibly be a refuge for us.

At the close, Jorge says: "There was *no need* for me to grieve. . . . The snow would keep me. . . . The winter time had finally got them all, and I really did hope that the kid *was* as *warm* as I *was* now, *warm inside* and out, burning up *inside* and out with joy." That the beautiful alliteration and assonance come from Jorge, an uneducated boy, adds to the opposition of texture and structure.

In "Representation and the War for Reality," Gass offers a theoretical explanation of the "word" and the "world" of fiction: "A word begins as a small sound *fastened to a thing*—a thought—like a balloon tied to the worried finger of a child; it is a nearly nothing noise." Gass's theoretical explanation gives us insight into the way the musical rhythms of the short story develop a world of their own, much as a balloon can sail into its own magical world.

Elaine B. Safer

SELECTED BIBLIOGRAPHY

Works by William Gass

Omensetter's Luck. New York: New American Library, 1966.

In the Heart of the Heart of the Country. New York: Harper & Row, 1968.

Fiction and the Figures of Life. New York: Alfred A. Knopf, 1970.

Willie Masters' Lonesome Wife. New York: Alfred A. Knopf, 1971.

On Being Blue. Boston: David R. Godine, 1975.

The World Within the Word. New York: Alfred A. Knopf, 1978.

Habitations of the Word. New York: Simon & Schuster, 1985.

The Tunnel. New York: Alfred A. Knopf, 1995.

Finding a Form. New York: Alfred A. Knopf, 1996.

Cartesian Sonata. New York: Alfred A. Knopf, 1998.

Reading Rilke. New York: Alfred A. Knopf, 1999.

Critical Studies

Bassoff, Bruce. "The Sacrificial World of William Gass: *In the Heart of the Heart of the Country*." *Critique* 18 (summer 1976): 36–58.

Holloway, Watson L. *William Gass*. Boston: Twayne, 1990.

McCaffery, Larry. *The Metafictional Muse: The Works of Robert Coover, Donald Barthelme, and William H. Gass*. Pittsburgh: University of Pittsburgh Press, 1982.

Saltzman, Arthur. *The Fiction of William Gass*. Carbondale: Southern Illinois University Press, 1986.

ELLEN GILCHRIST
(1935–)

Born in Vicksburg, Mississippi, in 1935, Ellen Gilchrist spent her childhood in the midst of an extended southern family. Her father had to take his family out of the South to pursue his career during World War II, but Gilchrist kept her southern roots alive by returning each summer to the family's estate in Mississippi, where the facts and fictions of Gilchrist's career were spawned. Gilchrist's college education and writing career were interrupted by marriage, and she moved to New Orleans, a city that inspired many stories the world would later come to know. In 1976 Gilchrist took the crucial step to establish herself as a writer when she entered the University of Arkansas MFA program in creative writing. Although she did not finish a degree, work begun there resulted in her first book of poems and her first collection of short stories, *In the Land of Dreamy Dreams*. She went on to write six more collections of short stories, including *Victory Over Japan,* which won the National Book Award for short fiction. Gilchrist has also written four novels, another book of poetry, a play, and a collection of commentaries, drawn from her broadcasts on National Public Radio. Continuing her life-long love of literature, Gilchrist currently lives in Fayetteville, Arkansas, where she is writing a series of novellas for adolescents.

Like many of her women protagonists who are often accused of talking too much by the men in their lives, Ellen Gilchrist is not about to compromise her convictions as she goes about the business of telling the truth as she sees it. Even as a child she displayed supreme confidence in her opinion. She was outraged that anyone, even God, might dare to limit her passion for life. Gilchrist states, "I was

obsessed with death—a good beginning for a writer. . . . I was mad at God. . . . I hated him. I sat up in a magnolia tree . . . and dared him to make me fall." Her protagonists, displaying a kindred outrage at limitation, are often furious at husbands, lovers, brothers, any personification of a patriarchal power. But Gilchrist shuns the feminist label, stating, "I like men because they protect me. All my life they have protected me and I believe they will go on doing it as long as I love them in return." The central conflicts of Gilchrist's protagonists dramatize this contradictory impulse toward men. Gilchrist's women resent the male authority they steadily crave.

Hunger is at the heart of many Gilchrist characters. They are forever eating, or wanting to eat with craving limited by self-imposed diets. Gilchrist's women are hungry for experience and passion; when those desires are frustrated, they console themselves with sweets, drinks, and recreational sex. The women are rarely satisfied, and if so, not for long.

Throughout Gilchrist's body of work, she continuously returns to the lives of characters conceived in early stories; a reader can watch these young women mature with each new book Gilchrist writes, revealing shifts in the writer's concerns. Critics have often noted the similarities between the life of Gilchrist and her characters. Mary McCay observes, "Ultimately many of Gilchrist's themes can be summarized in terms of a quest. Gilchrist's own life has been a quest for identity, wholeness, artistic freedom and love, and her quests are mirrored in those of her characters." The women are tenacious and ambitious; like their creator, they plot and scheme, but above all, they dream.

Gilchrist's first collection, *In the Land of Dreamy Dreams,* is a collection that primarily maps the frustrations and passions of adolescent girls. Rhoda Manning in particular dramatizes Gilchrist's own preoccupation with self-definition in a southern society that expects its girls to grow up thin, discreet, and indulgent toward men. Rhoda resists. Set in the heart of the Mississippi Delta, "Revenge" begins with Rhoda on a quest to resolve an injustice. In first-person point of view, a grown Rhoda recalls the summer she learned she would live her life battling to prove herself to the opposite sex, and on occasion she would win.

"It was the summer of the Broad Jump Pit," she begins, instantly reminding us of how we recall our lives through a telescopic memory, focusing in on a key moment, and bringing to that moment months, sometimes years of emotional history. Rhoda recalls observing the boys at play, and re-creates the scene in such vivid detail that we are there gazing though Rhoda's eyes with the precise attention envy provides: "Next comes my thirteen-year-old brother, Dudley, coming at a brisk jog down the track, the pole-vaulting pole held lightly in his delicate hands, then vaulting, high into the sky. His skinny tanned legs make a last desperate surge, and is clear and over." The narrator's personality and intense desire filter through her observation. She wants to achieve that desperate surge, vault high into the sky. The ten-year-old narrator sits in lonely exile on top of a chicken coop at her family's estate, wanting to compete with the boys, to join in their naive and optimistic training for the Olympics.

The war is almost over, a letter from Rhoda's father has explained. The Allies will prevail, and soon the global competition will shift away from the deadly battlefield to an arena of sports. War serves as a backdrop to many stories in Gilchrist's first two collections, contributing to her theme of the struggle for power; the presence of war also provides a narrative space to illustrate the innocence of characters caught in private battles while ignorant of the ultimately deadliness of war. Gilchrist renders her characters deliberately naïve, a naiveté that often saves them from despair. Their rebellions and small victories have deep significance but limited consequence. Creating a distance between how the characters and readers perceive the personal struggles of the story, Gilchrist establishes a place of dramatic irony where we observe the humor and pathos of passionate characters locked in naive notions of victory.

"Revenge" also illustrates Gilchrist's southern comic style, exaggerated emotion ironically fixing on a mundane thing, while pain and rage whir steadily, unseen. The story begins with Rhoda arguing to participate in digging the broad jump pit. With the boys in control, she throws threats and racist slurs as well as fistfuls of dirt. Defeated, she seeks comfort in the feminine world of her grandmother's arms, plates of pound cake and happy distraction in taking dancing lessons from the black cook. Restricted from the world of action, Rhoda dreams of revenge. She prays that "the Japs [will] win the war . . . and take [the boys] prisoners, starving them and torturing them, sticking bamboo splinters under their fingernails." She imagines herself allied with the conquering "Japs." Like many Gilchrist protagonists, she imagines a script of conquest.

She briefly feels satisfied through a more feminine strategy when she is invited to be maid of honor in her aunt's wedding. But only temporarily pleased, she sneaks a drink from the bar, slips into the night, strips the fancy dress off and practices pole vaulting alone in the dark. This gesture of sneaking and honing strategy is typical of Gilchrist's women. Rhoda discovers she is a natural at handling that male pole. She successfully launches a vault just as the wedding party discovers she has broken free of polite social restraints. Her strength is bared in the moonlight. But recalling that moment of victory, a mature Rhoda reflects, "Sometimes I think whatever has happened since has been of no real interest to me," suggesting that a woman's personal war for independence has momentary victories, but that her life is to be filled with battles quietly lost.

Whereas Rhoda is driven by a need for revenge, another regularly appearing character dramatizes an additional concern of the author: the quest for romantic love in a distinctly fallen world. Nora Jane Whittington, a resourceful daughter of an alcoholic mom, has raised herself and continues on her personal quest. It is love, not revenge, that motivates her to commit a robbery in "The Famous Poll at Jody's Bar." After locking the men in the ladies room, she steals cash to pay for her road trip to San Francisco to be with her irresponsible but one true love. She is an enterprising and resolute romantic.

In *Victory Over Japan,* a collection that again depicts women caught in emotional battles while operating in a larger world at war, we learn that the boyfriend abandons Nora Jane. But she manages to survive with the support of a man she meets by chance. He adores Nora Jane, but still hopelessly in love with the wrong guy, she soon finds herself pregnant with twins and uncertain of the father. Such a predicament could be the source of tragedy for other writers, but for Gilchrist it is another occasion for creative adjustment to a capricious world.

In this collection, we meet another recurring protagonist, Crystal Weiss. She is a southern debutante fallen from grace and the family fortune, but she clings to an upper-class life style through a loveless marriage. Crystal's fury borders on self-destruction. Cynical, hard-drinking, indifferent to her daughter, only her razor-sharp sense of humor and the love of her black maid, Traceleen, save her from ruin. We learn of Crystal through the eyes of Traceleen, who, like the author, knows Crystal's every virtue and vice, loves her dearly, and assists in Crystal's escapades without judgment.

Crystal, like most of Gilchrist's women, is privileged in terms of class and wealth and yet is still restless, hungry, and miserable. Crystal is lonely in the midst of her well-heeled social set and frustrated by limits in a world still run by men. But in "Traceleen, She's Still Talking" Crystal has her day. Furious at her brother's irresponsibility with the family wealth, resentful that he inherited money while she was expected to marry it, she steals her brother's Mercedes to crash a fence and liberate the antelope he has purchased for private hunting expeditions. She temporarily saves the antelope from a predatory game rigged against them, and for a moment she liberates herself.

In this collection, Rhoda, like many Gilchrist women, learns to use her sex as a tool instead of letting it be a liability. Romantic perhaps in their quests for individual expression of self, they are hardly romantic about sex. Usually referred to as "fucking," the act of sex is rarely one of making love. Rather it is a sport, a pastime where one can distract oneself, feel a little surge of power by laying a claim on someone. In "The Lower Garden District Free Gravity Mule Blight or Rhoda, a Fable" Rhoda calculates and uses the technique of sexual strategy as skillfully as she once took a pole and vaulted on male terrain. The story opens with "Rhoda woke up dreaming," a line that evokes a theme in many Gilchrist stories. Women often awake to themselves, first envision their power through dreaming, and then act. But here the dreams are of crushing skulls, particularly the skull of her ex-husband. Again Rhoda wants revenge, and she gets it by making a false claim on her engagement ring. The insurance agent is fully aware of her deception and agrees to it, knowing he is very likely to be rewarded with sex. Screwing in her kitchen, they both admit their lies—he's married; she's a thief. With the truth out, lies flutter like torn flags on a battlefield as they indulge in an act of sex that seals their deception, each taking dull pleasure in having manipulated the other.

In a later collection, *The Age of Miracles,* the protagonists are middle-aged. They may not be as attractive as they once were, but they are still keenly aware of their appetites. The quest for romance and power is less desperate. Their cynicism has been worn away by sense of humor about the whole process of getting and pleasing men. In "A Statue of Aphrodite" Rhoda appears again with her usual hunger for sex and food. Although facing the restraints of age, as well a deep fear of AIDS, Rhoda is stronger than ever. She has become the successful writer she has hoped to be; but still she finds herself paying a price as she slips back into a role of pleasing men. And when a rich doctor invites her to visit his home and play as hostess for his daughter's wedding, she reluctantly tries to squeeze her personality and her healthy body into a petite Laura Ashley dress as well as a persona he has ordered for her. She pays the price of the plane ticket to visit him, but she gets her orgasm though the skill of his hands, not the penis she would rather enjoy. But she only briefly plays the role of good wedding guest and demands to be driven to the airport before the festivities are over. As always, Rhoda values herself far too much to be made to behave for long. She escapes, finds another lover, and in a tumble of sheets and condoms and protective gels and creams, she exacts the pleasure and power she craves. But, well raised, she does not neglect to send a wedding gift: a tasteless statue of Aphrodite. With deliberate kitsch, she obtains her need for poetic justice as well as revenge.

Gilchrist, like her characters, greatly values defining her self and her world through action, but more importantly, through words. Her first-person narratives continually depict women using the form of storytelling to give shape to their worlds. Gilchrist's characters often face the task of adjusting to disruption by trying to hang on to a social fabric that too often rips. Strategies for survival usually entail scripting oneself. Gilchrist's women routinely imagine the way their lives should be, but they do not stop with visualization. They act. Victims of forces beyond their control, they turn predator, adapting to the male environment and using tools of rhetoric, sex, lies, and sometimes plain physical strength like the men who only sometimes rule.

In her most recent collection, *Flights of Angels,* Gilchrist gives us some new characters and some familiar from previous stories, but the attitude toward the old power struggle has changed. The inevitability of death renders the old domestic battles for power and money somewhat diminished in light of the need for peace of mind and happiness. Fear of AIDS hovers like an angel of death in many stories. People are dying everywhere from cancer, strokes, and murder, and as a result the daily battle with life has changed. In "Phyladda, or the Mind/Body Problem," an ex-actor now playing diagnostician in a New Age clinic offers an insight that recurs throughout the collection: "We're all going to die when this is over . . . we need to be nice while we wait." He may as well be speaking for Gilchrist, who takes a turn away from the need for revenge and has moved to a place of transcending battles. The gifted diagnostician observes, "There are only two things you can have wrong with you. One is illness. The other is fear. Fear is the real killer. It evades all known drugs, all kindness, all care." His treatment for fear is based on a magical belief

that random acts of kindness—if kept secret—bring us luck, health, happiness. While the same old frustrations with life abound, Gilchrist's characters are now capable of walking away from a fight. No angels intervene to save suffering souls in *Flights of Angels.* The characters find ways to redeem themselves by embracing instead of battling life. The idea that a moment's grace can arrive to calm a worried soul becomes a possibility in this latest world of Gilchrist. The grace is not from God—or angels—but rather from people. Ellen Gilchrist's characters seem to have learned that peace cannot be gained by conquest, but by a letting go of fear and turning compassion toward a world inevitably slipping away.

Jane Bradley

SELECTED BIBLIOGRAPHY

Works by Ellen Gilchrist

The Land Surveyor's Daughter. Fayetteville, Ark.: Lost Roads Press, 1979.

In the Land of Dreamy Dreams. Fayetteville: University of Arkansas Press, 1981.

The Annunciation. New York: Little, Brown, 1983.

Falling Through Space. New York: Little, Brown, 1984.

Victory Over Japan. New York: Little, Brown, 1984.

Drunk with Love. New York: Little, Brown, 1986.

Riding Out the Tropical Depression. New Orleans: Faust Publishing, 1986.

Light Can Be Both Wave and Particle. New York: Little, Brown, 1989.

I Cannot Get You Close Enough. New York: Little, Brown, 1990.

Net of Jewels. New York: Little, Brown, 1992.

Anabasis. Jackson: University of Mississippi Press, 1994.

Starcarbon. New York: Little, Brown, 1994.

The Age of Miracles. New York: Little, Brown, 1995.

Rhoda: A Life in Stories. New York: Little, Brown, 1995.

The Courts of Love. New York: Little, Brown, 1996.

The Anna Papers. New York: Little, Brown, 1998.

Critical Studies

Mandelbaum, Paul, ed. *First Words: Earliest Writing from Favorite Contemporary Authors.* Chapel Hill, N.C.: Algonquin Books, 1993.

McCay, Mary A. *Ellen Gilchrist.* New York: Twayne, 1997.

Schramm, Margaret. "Ellen Gilchrist." *Dictionary of Literary Biography,* pp. 178– 187. Detroit: Gale Research, 1993.

HERBERT GOLD
(1924–   )

B orn in Cleveland, Ohio, Herbert Gold received his B.A. from Columbia University in 1946 and his M.A. from the Sorbonne in 1948. Like Philip Roth and John Updike, he belongs to a group of writers who came into prominence during the 1950s. During that period,

Gold made his mark as a literary chronicler of the places and people that, taken together, represented a significant pattern of contemporary American experience. At his best, Gold could blend the social realism that had been the identifying mark of naturalists such as Theodore Dreiser and John Steinbeck with the literary modernism associated with James Joyce. The result was a fictional voice at once edgy and ambivalent, as nuanced as it was evocative.

Many of Gold's early novels and stories were set in his native Midwest and clustered around such standard themes as initiation, family quarrels, and male-female relationships. In each case, however, Gold created characters that readers could believe in and care about; and in a rendering of the smaller shocks of discomfort and recognition, he created in his fiction a subtle vehicle for crafty wordplay, finely tuned observations, and deeply rooted sympathy.

In the late 1960s Gold moved to California, a state of mind as well as of place. California served as the setting and cultural ambiance for much of his fiction from the 1970s onward. The author of nineteen novels, four collections of short fiction, and five books of nonfiction, Gold has established his reputation most from his short fiction, in particular, from several signature stories.

Perhaps no single story is more indicative of Gold's keen attention to human detail and ability to render complex emotion than "The Heart of the Artichoke." Included in his first collection, *Love & Like* (1960), it was the story that, Gold said, "was personally crucial because it gave me a sense that I was now my own man."

Gold's remark is intriguing on a number of levels, but perhaps none more revealing than the ways that "becoming a man" is reflected in the story itself. Daniel Berman, the story's twelve-year-old protagonist, relates a tale that, on its surface, has much in common with Jerome Weidman's haunting tale of estrangement, "My Father Sits in the Dark" (1932), and Delmore Schwartz's justly famous "In Dreams Begin Responsibilities" (1939). At bottom, all of them concentrate on the tensions, spoken and unspoken, that separate the experiences and attitudes of immigrant Jewish fathers from the cultural rebelliousness of their Americanized sons.

In Gold's story, however, the subtle shifts from Daniel's youthful pride to his final heart-cracking guilt take the initiation tale to a new level. Berman's father, a shopkeeper, has known about hard work since the day he first arrived in America: "his first job . . . selling water to the men building the skyscrapers, teetering across the girders for fifteen cents a pail." He also knows how to peel an artichoke until he arrives at its very heart: "he peeled an artichoke with both hands simultaneously, the leaves flying toward his mouth, crossing at the napkin politely tucked at the master juggler's collar, until with a groan that was the trumpet of all satisfaction he attained the heart."

Like his father peeling an artichoke, Daniel peels away the leaves of his embarrassment over his parents' highly inflected patois of Yiddish and English until he arrives at the "heart" of his conflict—namely, that their love is as fierce as it is unconditional, and that to arrive at manhood requires a delicate balancing of independence and accommodation.

Thus, Gold's story is an unpeeling of the layers that hide or otherwise disguise the human heart. Central to the dramatic tension is what constitutes a proper education for an immigrant Jewish son. Not surprisingly, a part of Daniel craves irresponsibility, while another part pursues Patti Donahue, the object of his youthful ardor. Gold's account spares neither parents nor child: as Daniel's father puts it, with the certainty of a Biblical prophet: "*Some kits* [read: kids] *help out in the store. . . .* Moreover, they "*remember their father and mother.*" By contrast, Daniel tries (unsuccessfully) to find a suitable rhyme for Patti Donahue's last name and to memorize Edgar Allan Poe's "Ulalume," a poem he secretly reads over and over at work, but remains unsure about how to pronounce the title character's name.

What Daniel *is* sure about, however, is how badly his parents want him to "be a man" as they define the term. To them, a man is someone who "learn[s] of a dollar," who "know[s] what's what in life." Appropriately enough, Daniel is nearly thirteen years old when the conflicts in the Berman household boil over into a physical confrontation between an immigrant Jewish father and his acculturated son. On the very edge of becoming a bar-mitzvah, literally a "son of the commandments"— and therefore one whose new religious obligations make him ipso facto a man— Daniel explodes with the rage of the unfairly treated: "I won't, I *won't* work in your store. I don't want it. It's not my life. I hate it!" Though the passage contains echoes of James Joyce's *A Portrait of the Artist as a Young Man,* especially in those sections where Stephen Dedalus announces his Irish Catholic *non serviam,*

Gold does not call undue attention to the allusion, leaving it subtly for suggestion.

The final paragraphs of "The Heart of the Artichoke" create a species of catharsis as Daniel's heartbroken father weeps behind the bathroom door and his anguished son sums up the lessons learned. Here, Daniel skims away the postures and childish certainties that had blinded him to larger human truths, and listens, possibly for the first time, to his father's poignant cry, "What's happening to us all?"

After a series of rejection slips, "The Heart of the Artichoke" was accepted by the editors of *Hudson Review,* then a new, untested publication. Subsequently, Gold became a regular contributor to its pages, even as his stories began appearing in such mass-circulation magazines as *Harper's, Playboy,* and *The New Yorker.* More important, the alternating currents between fathers and sons—sometimes very close to love, sometimes perilously close to hatred—continued to engage Gold's attention and his imagination. With *Fathers: A Novel in the Form of a Memoir* (1968), a book that brought Gold to the best-seller list for the first (and only) time, he managed to blend the best aspects of fiction with nonfiction, and thus tell the story he hinted at provocatively in "The Heart of the Artichoke." Granted, other Jewish American writers continue to explore this rich territory, but in ways that grow ever paler as the reservoir of ethnic material (what the Berman family eats, how they speak, what has formed their respective values) fades from memory. In this sense, "The Heart of the Artichoke" will continue to be highly regarded, first as a consummately rendered piece of short fiction and then as a chronicle of those times, those places, when sons of immigrant Jews struck out against parochial limitation only to discover that its protective folds had more merit than they once imagined.

"Love & Like," the title story of Gold's first collection, brings much the same ambivalent spirit to a tale chronicling the aftermath of a marital breakup. Twice divorced, Gold resists the easy equations sometimes drawn between his protagonist, the thirty-two-year-old Dan Shaper, and himself. Rather, Shaper's account of returning to his former home in Cleveland to see his children should best be thought of, in Gold's words, "as a cautionary tale," one in which the character's last name— Shaper—is no doubt important. After all, what artists do is "shape" the material of their lives, relying on actual experience as a launching point for the imagination. In "Love & Like," Dan learns the distinctions between *love* and *like* as he tries to explain the subtle distinctions to his young daughters. "Mommy says you don't love her any more," the six-year-old Paula announces in the middle of Dan's visit from New York City, where he lives now. Dan explains that he likes her mommy (and that she likes him), but that he no longer loves her as she no longer loves him. Nonetheless, they both like and love their two wonderful daughters. Dan's explanation is yet another installment in a long series of miscommunications, all the more ironic because his job is to put technical manuals on long-range walkie-talkies into clear English. By contrast, his wife puts her faith in psychiatric terminology (*"relate, transfer, orient"*) and an expensive private school oriented toward "difficulties, special problems, broken homes."

If the Shapers' divorce is now a legal fact complete with settlement obligations and new lovers on both sides of the equation, what to do about the children remains a "puzzler," the last word in Gold's anguished, highly nuanced tale of how modern marriages often fall into ruin. Nothing expresses these thoughts more poignantly than the moment when Shaper links the language of technical manuals with his futile hope that love and like can be the building blocks of a newly constituted relationship between his ex-wife and his daughters: "he had labored with a Signal Corps semantics expert on further explanations of how to keep contact open under conditions of vital stress. . . . Condition of stress not total chaos if received flashes emergency transistor filters out static toward coded meaning (see Fig. 3), Put into heart's English. Also see resources of regret, hope, and desire for possible decoding toward good conscience."

Gold's short stories specialize in the "heart's English." The capacity to strip away the cant and public certainties of contemporary life enables his fiction to reach those vulnerable spots in the human psyche that psychiatry alone often misses. Best of all, Gold relies on such unexpected metaphors as an artichoke's heart and the language of technical manuals to dramatize his nuanced account of people at odds with one another.

"San Francisco Petal," a story that takes the complicated measure of the counterculture as it once thrived in the early 1970s, reflects not only Gold's newly acquired West Coast sensibility but also the various attractions and repulsions that came with the territory. Included in *Lovers*

and Cohorts, the story revolves around the curious relationship between Frank, who narrates the tale, and Linda, a leftover '60s flower child, who contributes the pastiche of cultural detail. She is a waitress at the Natural Sun, a with-it restaurant that Frank describes as "soya and no-meat dining for philosophic dope dealers and their clientele." He then goes on to say that "the teller of this history must stop to admit that he is not merely a historian. He is connected. He has a certain responsibility. He is attracted to the girl in the Mexican Marine shirt who told cute stories of perversion, dope, and troubles with her blue VW bus." In the process Frank strips away Linda's various petals and comes to the rueful conclusion that "Linda was finished as a pretty little thing. Whatever came next, it wouldn't be pretty. Frank could go back to saying I about himself."

Gold's short stories were often written when work on a novel sagged ("Aristotle and the Hired Thugs") or when he was trying out themes ("A Celebration for Joe") that ultimately found full expression in a novel. But regardless of their genesis, Gold's stories continue to haunt long after their specific cultural moment has passed. As Gold puts it in the introduction to *Lovers and Cohorts,* after four decades of writing short fiction, "my passions as a teller of tales have remained: love, family, Jews, Bohemia, wanderlust, and the meaning of life." The last item is clearly the most important of all, pointing to a quest the writer must find unending. With tongue firmly in cheek, Gold writes that if he finds "the meaning of life, I'll be sure to let you know." Meanwhile, his stories are surely one of the best records we have of a short story writer wrestling with the complicated, exasperating world in which he lives.

Sanford Pinsker

SELECTED BIBLIOGRAPHY

Works by Herbert Gold

15 x 3. New York: New Directions, 1957.
Love & Like. New York: Dial, 1960.
The Magic Will: Stories and Essays of a Decade. New York: Random House, 1971.
Lovers & Cohorts: Twenty-seven Stories. New York: Donald I. Fine, 1986.

Critical Studies

Moore, Harry T. *The Fiction of Herbert Gold.* Carbondale: Southern Illinois University Press, 1964.
Smith, Larry. "Herbert Gold: Belief and Craft." *Ohioana Quarterly* 21 (1978): 148–156.
Walden, Daniel, ed. *Herbert Gold and Company: American Jewish Writer as Universal Writer.* Special issue of *Studies in American Jewish Literature* (1991).

ERNEST HEMINGWAY
(1899 – 1961)

One of the great innovators of the twentieth-century form, Ernest Hemingway continues to be among the most widely read, frequently taught, and carefully studied of American short story writers. Much of the material for his fiction came from his life. Born and raised in Oak Park, Illinois, the second child and first son of Grace Hall, a music teacher, and Clarence Hemingway, a doctor, Hemingway eventually had four sisters and one younger brother. The family summered in northern Michigan, where the boy learned from his father to hunt and fish. A restless student, he graduated from high school as an aspiring writer/adventurer, wanting to join the army and fight in World War I, but an eye problem disqualified him. However, Hemingway soon got to the war by enlisting with the Red Cross in Italy as an ambulance driver. The job brought him to the front lines, where within weeks he was badly wounded. Though not a soldier, his courage under fire made him a recognized war hero.

After the war and recuperation, he returned home and to newspaper work, and married his first wife, Hadley Richardson. Rather than settle down, the fledgling writer wanted to be a reporter/poet in the tradition of Mark Twain and Stephen Crane, and he thought that the best place to learn his craft was Europe. Living primarily in Paris, with a letter of introduction from Sherwood Anderson, the newlyweds got to know Gertrude Stein, Ezra Pound, F. Scott Fitzgerald, and other American expatriates. At this point, Hemingway went rapidly from a brief apprenticeship to early literary fame as the voice of the postwar "lost generation." His first full collection of stories, *In Our Time* (1925), and his first serious novel, *The Sun Also Rises* (1926), were quickly followed by a second story collection, *Men Without Women* (1927), and a World War I novel, *A Farewell to Arms* (1929).

In the 1930s, on his second of four marriages, Hemingway began to embrace celebrity and the active lifestyle of bull-fighting, deep-sea fishing, and big-game hunting. He also engaged in the period's politics, working as a pro-Loyalist foreign correspondent during the Spanish Civil War. His efforts at fiction disappointed some critics. Nevertheless, he published a new collection of significant short stories, *Winner Take Nothing* (1933), and in 1938 added four more accomplished selections to the otherwise retrospective edition, *The Fifth Column and the First Forty-Nine Stories*. This book would be Hemingway's last collection of short fiction published in his lifetime; it marked the end of an exceptionally productive sixteen years. He wrote more stories afterward, but none matched the technical brilliance and thematic audacity of those he had composed from 1922 to 1938. His reputation as a master of the form rests securely on this period's distinguished body of work.

In 1940 he published his ambitious novel about the war in Spain, *For Whom the Bell Tolls*. During the 1940s and 1950s, Hemingway, the father of three sons, adopted the public persona of "Papa," the macho authority figure. This role seemed to define him more and more, as he wrote and published less. But he staged a proud comeback with the enormous success of *The Old Man and the Sea* (1952), which won the Pulitzer Prize, and he was awarded the Nobel Prize for Literature in 1954. In his final years, physical ailments and severe depression made it impossible for Hemingway to write. He committed suicide, with one of his favorite shotguns, in 1961. His death barely slowed his career. A large collection of unpublished manuscripts, along with uncollected stories and journalism, have resulted in several posthumously published books, including *The Fifth Column and Four Stories of the Spanish Civil War* (1969) and *The Nick Adams Stories* (1972), the latter of which combines previously unpublished pieces and reprinted stories about the recurring character, Nick, along with stories that *might* be about him. Finally, *The Complete Short Stories of Ernest Hemingway: The Finca Vigía Edition* (1987) joins previously published work with assorted manuscript materials.

"I always try to write on the principle of the iceberg," Hemingway said. "There is seven-eighths of it underwater for every part that shows." This axiom provides an approach to the strategies behind both the exacting manner and the hard-edged matter of his short fiction. A Hemingway story's depths of meaning and feeling are often submerged in words composed in a detached, clipped, journalistic method of description, with little narrative commentary, little context for the dialogue, and little explanation for changes of scene. It often seems at first that not very much has happened during the events of such a story, that something is missing. In order to begin to "get it," the reader must join in composing the narrative, paying careful attention to each word and phrase, noting important repetitions and oppositions, filling in the text's strategic gaps. This "minimalist" style, with its deceptively simple surface, invites and challenges readers to draw on their knowledge and experience in order to discover what deeper meanings and emotions there might be below.

And the stories do not disappoint.

Their various worlds confront one with limited but forceful truths that get, in vividly convincing ways, to the essence of certain kinds of human desires, anxieties, and behaviors. Keeping in mind Hemingway's "iceberg principle," the attentive reader recognizes that these stories' characters often try to keep most of their thoughts and emotions hidden below the surface, displaying only a deliberately reserved exterior. They may induce others and even themselves to believe that this cool and controlled persona is the real thing; however, the "little" they seem to exhibit is actually a great deal, and will reveal the complexity, anguish, and pain of these characters' inner lives, the humanity that emerges from between the lines of the precise prose.

Some of the most powerful stories share certain contours of character, setting, and theme. Among these distinct (if overlapping) configurations, critics have discerned the following groups of stories: *In Our Time,* the "odd and original" group of unified pieces and the author's first sustained book; the Nick Adams stories, variously tracing their character's "life lessons" from boyhood to fatherhood; the "marriage tales" of women and men at odds with each other and themselves; the assorted "grace under pressure" narratives, in which embattled, aging male protagonists are put to the test; and the two daringly ambitious and vividly realized "African Stories."

Living up to its title's promise, *In Our Time* is an intricately structured book whose parts—fifteen stories and sixteen brief "interchapters"—are threaded together in ways that make for a strikingly unified whole, presenting a vision of the 1920s and, perhaps, of contemporary times with a selective but incisive cumulative record of the state of things. The stories, usually featuring young male protagonists, tend to be concerned with the personal and domestic, particularly the enduring tensions of American white middle-class family life and the disappointments of relations between the sexes, which are somewhat compensated for the sustenance of "uncomplicated" same-sex friendships and revivifying journeys into nature. The interchapter sketches, on the other hand, are political and public, with a wide-ranging pattern of culturally sanctioned violence: brutal war episodes, official and unofficial executions, and the bullring's bloody rituals.

"Indian Camp," the second story in the book and the first of seven to feature Nick Adams, brings together several of the images and themes that make up *In Our Time.* Like many of Hemingway's early stories, it is set in the upper peninsula of Michigan, beginning with the brief nighttime journey that young Nick and his father, a physician, make by rowboat to the title destination. Dr. Adams has brought his son along to help with a caesarean section that he must perform on an Indian woman who has been in labor for two days. The rough operation and delivery are done with a jack-knife and without anesthetic, while the woman's husband, his foot injured, remains in the bunk above his wife. Before beginning, the doctor explains to Nick that the woman's "screams are not important. I don't hear them because they are not important." The child is successfully born and the mother's life is saved, but the screams turn out to be significant nonetheless: the Indian husband/father has not been able to endure them, and has slit his throat with a razor. Dr. Adams tries to keep his son from seeing this self-inflicted butchery, but "Nick, standing in the door of the kitchen, had a good view of the upper bunk when his father, the lamp in one hand, tipped the Indian's head back." Witnessing the simultaneous violence of birth and death, the boy has learned something about the severe nature of existence. He asks his father why this particular father killed himself. "He couldn't stand things, I guess," is the reply. The story closes with Nick and Dr. Adams heading homeward, "In the early morning on the lake sitting in the stern of the boat with his father rowing, he felt quite sure that he would never die."

The precise and haunting quality of "Indian Camp," with its detached, subtle prose and enigmatic resistance to "easy" interpretation, demonstrates one of Hemingway's greatest gifts and one of In Our Time's greatest pleasures: the expert ability to pull readers into a story's world and force them to make meaning out of it, while concurrently forcing them to face certain harsh and treacherous truths. The carnage that Nick witnesses—with its evocative connections to deep uncertainties about how we come to live, to give birth, and to die—may shock and disturb us nearly as much as we think it should the boy. By directing the reader's focus to Nick's naive, unformed response, the story compels one to consider the impact of the events on him, and on oneself. The reader joins the character in a process of initiation and in the loss of a certain innocence. On the other hand, the reader may also be wondering about the perspective that is largely left out: the Amer-

ican Indian father, mother, and child, who have suffered a much more immediate and vicious loss.

With its emphasis on witnessing violent suffering, "Indian Camp" sets the tone for the brutality depicted in many of the interchapter sketches of In Our Time. And with its emphasis on the response of a boy (or young man) to an encounter with difficult truths, the piece also shares much in common with many of the book's other stories: "My Old Man" concerns a boy who learns about his father's corruption, "A Very Short Story" and "Soldier's Home" are sharply etched portraits of disturbed young men back from the war, and "Out of Season" depicts a "young gentleman" whose relationship with his wife has soured. This pattern of "male education" is also in the other stories that trace the growth of Nick Adams, as he witnesses the strains in his parents' marriage in "The Doctor and the Doctor's Wife," experiences the complications of early romance and the solace of male friendship in "The End of Something" and "The Three Day Blow," encounters strange dangers on the road in "The Battler," faces the burden of impending fatherhood in "Cross Country Snow," and retreats into nature, where "nothing could touch him," in "Big Two-Hearted River." Some critics have seen the physical and psychological "escape" in this latter two-part story, which ends In Our Time, as an unstated response to wounds from the war; others have seen it as a retreat from unnamed family tensions. Whatever one's interpretation of the cause of Nick's damaged psychological condition and his need for the "separate peace" of a solitary fishing trip, it pays to keep in mind something that Hemingway once said: "The position of the survivor of a great calamity is seldom admirable." "Big Two-Hearted River" is about a character in such a position, a protagonist in painful crisis, who is experiencing the frightening feeling of "losing it," while trying to reassert some semblance of control. If stories are equipment for living, this one provides the reader with a fitting conclusion to a book that cumulatively describes modes of coping with how things are "in our time."

Hemingway continued writing the life lessons of Nick Adams, an invented "alter ego" who bears some obvious resemblances to the author. Together, this varied group of stories illustrates a character's development over a near-lifetime. Nick is a sensitive adolescent whose "heart's broken" in "Ten Indians," a curious and complicated young man witnessing violence and despair in "The Killers," a badly shaken soldier trying his best to hold on in "Now I Lay Me" and "A Way You'll Never Be," and a concerned parent who is still working out his relationship with his own father in "Fathers and Sons." In this latter story and in the posthumously published "The Last Good Country," there is a distinctly painful sense of emotional and ecological loss, an elegy for a better time and place that no longer exist, save for in prose memories. As their author put it, "All stories, if continued far enough, end in death, and he is no true story-teller who would keep that from you."

The various "marriage tales" also deal with loss, although of a markedly different kind. However offensive some critics may find Hemingway's "hyper-masculine" reputation, his writing often presents a nuanced exploration of his version of the truth about relations between men and women: "If two people love each other, there can be no happy end to it." These stories collectively engage that valid, albeit gloomy, premise; the most interesting of them often do so from the point of view of a female character. Challenging the reader with their determined emphasis on the contrasts between female and male desires and perspectives, and with their questioning of what such constructed identities mean, these dispatches from the front lines of the "gender wars" usually refuse to take sides, and, in the most illuminating of them, Hemingway is decidedly *not* a defender of male opinion or conduct.

"Hills Like White Elephants" is a representative Hemingway marriage tale, and its deceptively detached style and subtle yet powerful substance make for an unforgettable example of the essence of the author's "iceberg" method. A casual reader might think that he or she were going over the transcript of an overheard, banal conversation, but an active reader will fill in the gaps that the story has strategically left amidst its spare descriptions and "reported" lines of dialogue. An American couple in Spain sits at a table in a hot and dusty railroad station, waiting for their connecting train to arrive. The woman, Jig, suggests that the hills across the valley "look like white elephants," but the man is unresponsive. They order a drink, and she says that, "It tastes like licorice. . . . Everything tastes of licorice. Especially all the things you've waited so long for, like absinthe." This remark, with its tone of resigned disappointment and edge of resentment, signals the direction in which the tale is headed. Jig's male companion offers further clues when he tries to assure her that, "It's really an awful simple operation. . . . They just let the air in and then it's all perfectly natural. . . . I've known lots of people that have done it." At this stage (about halfway through the four-page story), a careful reader has perhaps pieced together that Jig is pregnant and her companion wants her to have an abortion.

Once again, Hemingway's indirect style gets the reader to participate in the story's creation by contemplating the vital things that the couple are leaving unsaid. Jig seems to want to have the child and worries about what will happen to their relationship in either case, while the man clearly does not want the child, though insisting that, "I'm perfectly willing to go through with it if it means anything to you." Perhaps his greatest fault is this callous desire to have it both ways: convince Jig to make the decision he wants, but have it appear that she has made her own choice. "I know it's perfectly simple," he insists. Jig seems to know better, to know that it is anything but "simple." Although the story ends with her saying, "There's nothing wrong with me. I feel fine," one realizes that this couple, regardless of what they do about their unplanned pregnancy, has lost whatever it was that first made them fall in love. Their inability to communicate, conspicuous throughout the story, is the ultimate evidence of their relationship's failure and of the inherent difficulties of all female-male partnerships. In just a few pages of dialogue and description, Hemingway provides a remarkable amount of knowledge and emotion. A couple's inability to communicate and a relationship's downward spiral are

the stuff of which the marriage tales are made. Similar examples include: the brutal relationship of "Up in Michigan," the troubled couple on a train to Paris in "A Canary for One," the grotesque peasant episode of "An Alpine Idyll," the woman leaving a man for another woman in "The Sea Change," and the desperate wife of "One Reader Writes."

Notwithstanding the essential importance of the marriage tales to an understanding of the scope of Hemingway's short fiction, there is also a distinctive group of stories that concern "men without women," male protagonists for whom the Hemingway expression "grace under pressure" fits. These characters tend to live and work in the lower depths, among the "second rate" or worse of their professions, and they are usually well past their prime, suffering from the painful, accumulated damages that life can inflict. Nevertheless, in worlds of moral corruption and decay, they maintain a sense of dignity and a shabby honor through their responses to adversity. The primary function of their code of conduct is to impose a sense of order on what would otherwise be chaos. These characters possess a certain sense of "style," the qualities of which often vary, but constant in most of these stories are protagonists who display a willingness to endure pain without complaint and a devotion to doing one's job as well as one can under the circumstances. Among these figures, who rarely achieve physical victories but are sometimes allowed moral ones, are the unyielding bullfighter of "The Undefeated," the graceful major of "In Another Country," the defiant boxer of "Fifty Grand," the sarcastic ambulance surgeon of "God Rest You Merry,

Gentlemen," and the suffering-but-silent gambler of "The Gambler, the Nun, and the Radio."

If some of the stories in this group come dangerously close to empty celebrations of heroism for heroism's sake, "A Clean, Well-Lighted Place" portrays a main character with a genuinely courageous and profoundly moving sensibility. The story begins with three characters in a cafe: a lonely old man who has recently tried to commit suicide because "He was in despair"; a sympathetic older waiter who is aware of how valuable a clean and pleasant cafe with good light can be; and a younger, self-centered waiter who thinks that the old man had "nothing" to despair about. Later, after the others have gone, the older waiter closes the cafe and considers why he and certain others need such a place of refuge: "What did he fear? It was not fear or dread. It was a nothing that he knew too well. It was all a nothing and a man was nothing too. It was only that and light was all it needed and a certain cleanness and order." He then launches into a parody of the Lord's Prayer—"Our *nada* who art in *nada*," etc.—while searching the nocturnal streets for an appropriately bright and polished establishment in which to face "*nada*." Clearly, this experienced man's "nothing," unlike the younger waiter's earlier use of the word, actually means *something*: a refusal to flinch at the arbitrary, chaotic, and unpredictable state of existence. The character's authentically existential heroism is found in his recognition of this "nothing," and in his efforts to develop a response to it, while appreciating the need for a proper place to exhibit such grace under pressure.

Toward the end of his successful sixteen-year period with the short story, Hemingway wrote two works, each set in Africa, that are generally considered his most ambitious attempts in the genre. "The Short Happy Life of Francis Macomber" combines and transforms several of the most significant elements of Hemingway's short fiction. Its title character bears a striking resemblance to Nick Adams, as the story appears to provide him with a valuable and much-needed life lesson, but the ironic nature of this particular lesson's end marks a major difference. The portrait of unrest that is Francis and Margot Macomber's marriage is more complex and deeply ambivalent than any of the relationships depicted in the marriage tales. And Robert Wilson, the big-game hunter, is a figure in the grace under pressure mode, but the validity of his code of conduct is directly challenged at key moments in the story. A reader familiar with Hemingway's earlier work will likely feel that the writer, deciding to combine many of his major characters and themes in "Macomber," also decided to reevaluate them. It stands as an amazing prose performance, as does "The Snows of Kilimanjaro." Many (including its author) have noted that "Snows" encompasses the scope of a novel, and that the account of a dying writer's reminiscences includes several intriguing sketches of stories that might have been. However, unlike the invented case of Harry, the failed writer of "Snows," Ernest Hemingway should not invite thoughts of what might have been. His brilliance as a short story writer is clear and his art fully realized.

Peter Mascuch

SELECTED BIBLIOGRAPHY

Works by Ernest Hemingway

Three Stories and Ten Poems. Paris: Contact, 1923.
in our time. Paris: Three Mountains Press, 1924.
In Our Time. New York: Boni and Liveright, 1925. Revised edition, New York: Charles Scribner's Sons, 1930.
Men Without Women. New York: Charles Scribner's Sons, 1927.
Winner Take Nothing. New York: Charles Scribner's Sons, 1933.
The Fifth Column and the First Forty-Nine Stories. New York: Charles Scribner's Sons, 1938. Reprinted as *The Short Stories of Ernest Hemingway.* New York: Charles Scribner's Sons, 1954.
The Fifth Column and Four Stories of the Spanish Civil War. New York: Charles Scribner's Sons, 1969.
The Nick Adams Stories. Edited by Philip Young. New York: Charles Scribner's Sons, 1972.
The Complete Short Stories of Ernest Hemingway: The Finca Vigia Edition. New York: Charles Scribner's Sons, 1987.

Critical Studies

Benson, Jackson J., ed. *The Short Stories of Ernest Hemingway: Critical Essays.* Durham, N.C: Duke University Press, 1975.
Benson, Jackson J., ed. *New Critical Approaches to the Short Stories of Ernest Hemingway.* Durham, N.C: Duke University Press, 1990.
Smith, Paul. *A Reader's Guide to the Short Stories of Ernest Hemingway.* Boston: G. K. Hall, 1989.
Smith, Paul, ed. *New Essays on Hemingway's Short Fiction.* New York: Cambridge University Press, 1998.

AMY HEMPEL
(1951–)

Amy Hempel is among a small group of contemporary American writers who have achieved an international reputation for short fiction alone. Her stories have appeared in *Best American Short Stories, The Pushcart Prize,* and prestigious anthologies; they have also been translated into more than a dozen languages. Hempel's first collection, *Reasons to Live* (1985), established her reputation as a poetic and meticulous observer of small but resonant moments in the lives of seemingly unremarkable people. Two subsequent volumes, *At the Gates of the Animal Kingdom* (1990), and *Tumble Home* (1997), extended and refined her reputation.

Born in Chicago in 1951, Hempel spent most of the 1960s in Denver, and the 1970s in San Francisco; in California she received what she has termed "a nonlinear college education" at five institutions, including Whittier College. The consistent feature of those years was her journal-keeping. In the early 1980s Hempel moved to New York, where she took the most important step in her formal education by enrolling in a seminar at Columbia University run by writer and editor Gordon Lish. She remained Lish's student for a number of years, "cannibalizing the journals of [her] twenties" and producing stories that became her first book.

Although she speaks of a happy childhood, Hempel insists that her creativity derives from a darker side of life, and that loss, pain, and anxiety are the main subjects of her fiction. She features anxious and fearful characters, usually young women, whose reasons for suffering the stories do not take pains to explain. Instead, her narratives attempt to record human consciousness as fluctuation and uncertainty. A representative Hempel short story might be described as an extreme example of V. S. Pritchett's description of the genre: "the glancing form of fiction that seems to be right for the nervousness and restlessness of contemporary life." Hempel has spoken of how her fiction creates situation through a fragment or an image: "I don't . . . think up a whole new world. I capitalize on the little perfect details." This technique puts causes and contexts in the story's background, where their ambiguity helps to create the tensions readers conventionally derive from plot. Some reviewers were unreceptive. An unsympathetic Sven Birkerts chastised her for lacking "comprehensiveness and scope . . . [and] a prose that can face chaos and master it with vision." Robert Phillips in the *Southern Review* criticized *At the Gates of the Animal Kingdom* for neglecting "the three elements traditionally associated with a successful story: exposition, development, and drama." Yet Hempel admits to having no interest in "the sort of dramatic writing that would be necessary to give you the

wreck, the murder, the whatever," and offers through her fiction no advice on mastering circumstance. She has suggested that her intentions and methods have "more to do with poetry than with conventional short stories." Her stories do not present meanings by plot resolution, epiphany, or other dramatic character change. Rather, they pose questions they do not answer.

Hempel's first published story, "In the Cemetery Where Al Jolson Is Buried," illustrates her interest in extreme emotional situations, her poetic indirection for rendering them, and her ironic rejection of the self-help clichés applied to grief and guilt. Narrated by a young California woman, the twenty narrative fragments recount her hospital visit to a terminally ill friend, their comic and evasive conversations, her callous flight and failure to return, and her later thoughts on memory and self-assessment. Hempel structures the story as if to mimic a conventional progression from problem to resolution: it begins with the dying friend's asking, "Tell me things I won't mind forgetting," and it ends with a vignette on grief. In between, however, a jumble of narrative sections presents shocking, contradictory emotions associated with friendship and dying, neither narrating the death nor suggesting an acceptable attitude toward it. The dying friend tells a nurse that the narrator is a "Best Friend," but the visit is an insincere, self-conscious performance, and it is two months late. The narrator's self-absorption is so extreme that she considers even looking at the sick friend a kind of heroism, "hoping that I will live through it." During a beach break from her acting, she thinks of the sea as filled with sharks and the land as potential earthquake; her Richter scale seems to measure only internal vibrations. Returning to find a bed prepared for her in the hospital room, she regards her dying friend as a predator: "She wants every minute, I thought. She wants my life." At the end of the story, the narrator feels no catharsis, and moves further into ambiguity: "[Departing,] I felt weak and small and failed. / Also exhilarated." This reaction is a startling but also ironic contrast to the concluding but only marginally relevant vignette of a chimpanzee's fully rendered maternal grief. Despite claiming to feel an internal earthquake and an inability to assemble these fragments of experience, the narrator candidly reveals a callous and calculating self by suggesting other options: "It is just possible I will say I stayed the night. / And who is there that can say that I did not?"

In interviews, Hempel invites biographical readings of her stories. "Most of [Reasons to Live]," she has said, "is first-hand." She speaks in vague terms about her own losses and pains, of writing as "a kind of revenge on people [parents, men, teachers, just about anybody] who did not take me seriously." At the same time, she cautions that every successful work "stops being [an autobiographical] story and becomes the story's story." Hempel illustrates this process of transformation in "The Harvest," a two-part story from At the Gates of the Animal Kingdom. A fictional narrative paired with an equally long factual exposition of its autobiographical sources, the story concerns a young California woman who, like Hempel, had her leg broken in a traffic accident. The fictional portion is compressed, fragmented,

and in the end deceptive—its first-person narrator does not actually describe the accident; she tells not of feeling pain, only of fearing it. She will not exaggerate her injuries for financial gain, but will lie to create a narrative climax of self-display: at the beach-site of her accident, she melodramatically shows her scars and pretends to be a shark-attack victim. The narrator's wisecracking, deceptions, and claim that she was with a married man when the accident occurred seem designed to stifle a reader's sympathy. By contrast, the factual exposition of Hempel's accident presents her sympathetically and disarms with its candor: "I leave a lot out when I tell the truth. The same when I write a story." Like her fictional narrator, Hempel exaggerates her injuries but presents herself as dominated by a context of circumstance and ironic coincidence that, if included, would have thematically dominated the fictional version as well. For example, the reporter whose car hit her on Mount Tamalpais wrote an exposé causing Jim Jones's flight to Guyana, and later covered the Jonestown mass suicide; Hempel's traumatic accident raised his insurance premium by twelve dollars. Her hospital stay also coincided with that of victims of a murderous San Quentin riot; and in a drugged trance in her room with a view of Mount Tamalpais, she watched televised reports and thought her own death was being announced. By excluding such related, if peripheral, circumstances, the fictional version supports Hempel's poetics, which claim for the writer a freedom to prevail for that moment over the circumstances in her life.

Hempel has been frequently mentioned in the cultural and critical debates about minimalism in American fiction because, with the exception of a single epistolary narrative, "Tumble Home," her stories are brief and, in their understatement, deceptively easy to read. Although Hempel has spoken against the term *minimalism* as a "lazy" imprecision, it reminds readers that, in Cynthia J. Hallett's phrase, "an esthetic of exclusion" governs all short fiction, and that the short story has resisted prescriptive genre theories and the mandates that literature represent the social world and contextualize social meanings.

The novella "Tumble Home" is as close as Hempel has come to representing a social world. Its first-person narrator, in a long letter addressed to a man she loves, writes not only of her internal struggles, but also of Chatty, Warren, and Karen, other voluntary patients in a mental institution. She measures with emotional pain her distance from the social and material status of the man who haunts her, a painter whose work she sees in galleries and the Tate Museum, whose house is featured in a glossy magazine, and whose last words to her were untrue: "We'll see each other again." Yet whereas the narrator's feelings are clearly strong, the story does not endorse them or verify them by any reference outside the narrative consciousness: an objective reader must consider that she has spent only "an hour" with the man, and that there is something ominous in her remark, "The certainty I feel—it is something to hit back with." The narrator, moreover, even has her title wrong: "tumble home" is not, as she reports, in the flare of a ship's bow, but rather in the opposite, inward curve of the hull amidships. Such details signal a distance that is typical between Hempel and even her most sympathetically drawn characters. Hempel has suggested that her art is the answer to feelings of powerlessness. Her characters have no such answer, but her interest in them comes from their membership in a "submerged population" whose neglect by conventional fiction Frank O'Connor wrote of in *The Lonely Voice*. "I'm not very comfortable out in the world," Amy Hempel once said. "Being a kind of peripheral figure all my life has been a way to get material."

Kerry Ahearn

SELECTED BIBLIOGRAPHY

Works by Amy Hempel

Reasons to Live. New York: Alfred A. Knopf, 1985.
At the Gates of the Animal Kingdom. New York: Alfred A. Knopf, 1990.
Tumble Home. New York: Scribner, 1997.

Critical Studies

Birkerts, Sven. "The School of Lish." *The New Republic,* October 13, 1986.
Hallett, Cynthia J. "Minimalism and the Short Story." *Studies in Short Fiction* 33 (1996): 487–495.
Phillips, Robert. "Difficulties and Impossibilities: New American Short Fiction." *The Southern Review* 28 (1992): 420–429.
Sapp, Jo. "An Interview with Amy Hempel." *The Missouri Review* 16 (1993): 76–95.
Schumacher, Michael. "Amy Hempel." In *Reasons to Believe,* pp. 28–45. New York: St. Martin's Press, 1988.

MARY HOOD

(1946–)

How Far She Went, Mary Hood's first collection of stories (1984), won the Flannery O'Connor Award for Short Fiction and the *Southern Review* Louisiana State University Short Fiction Award. From that volume, "Inexorable Progress" was selected for inclusion in *Best American Short Stories 1984,* and two years later *And Venus Is Blue,* Hood's second collection, won the Townsend Award for Fiction and the Dixie Council of Authors and Journalists Author-of-the Year Award. "Something Good for Ginnie" won a Pushcart Prize in 1986, and Mary Hood was given a Whiting Writers Award in 1994. Her stories have appeared in prestigious magazines, and her first novel, *Familiar Heat* (1995), was translated into several foreign languages to move beyond the geographical setting of her fiction, the South of the past three decades.

Mary Hood has lived in Georgia all her life. She was born in Brunswick, in the Golden Isles of the southern coastal region, but since 1976 has lived in Woodstock, a small town in Cherokee County at the foothills of the Appalachians. Once rural and undisturbed by progress, this north Georgia county has in the past decade been transformed into a Sunbelt exurb of Atlanta, boasting a huge golf community and a manmade lake, obliterating cotton fields and old mills, and introducing lawn chemicals and car exhaust. Hood is not married and lives with her mother, her cats, and her Labrador retriever in a house filled with books and music and surrounded by flowers and tall hedges to mute the sounds of traffic. She earned her bachelor's degree in Spanish at Georgia State University in 1967; she has taught high school, worked as a library assistant, and painted pet portraits on handsaws. She has been writer in residence at Berry College and earns her living today by writing and teaching.

In a 1986 article in *Harper's,* Mary Hood cites her parentage as the single most important influence on her writing. Her father, a native New Yorker and aircraft worker, and her mother, a native Georgian and Latin teacher, give her the northern conscience that demands brevity, asking with every plot turn, "So?" while the southern storyteller relishes the irrelevant detail and family history. Fifteen of the sixteen stories in her two short story collections are set in the past three decades in Georgia, reflecting the natural and the asphalt landscape. The characters in these stories speak the colloquialism of the southern talker of all social classes. In a theme common to Faulkner and Welty, the bonds of family strengthen and nourish, but they also bind and even damn Hood's characters, whose sins persist through generations in such stories as "How Far She Went," "And Venus Is Blue," "A Man Among Men," and "Manly Conclusions."

In *How Far She Went,* seven of the eight stories are set in rural north Georgia. The concrete details make real the landscape and frame the conflicts of characters whose lives are simple only on the exterior. In the first story, "Lonesome Road Blues," a lonely widow goes to the county fair to see the lost country arts, hear the Grape Arbor Pickers, and to take home and nurture a travel-worn bluegrass picker who accepts her hospitality and abandons her. She is left alone, where she began, resting her eyes on the "blue-green mountains beyond and beyond." In "Solomon's Seal," the red clay of the Georgia foothills is the barren ground for a country woman's marriage. A bitter wife, she nurtures her pepper plants, tomato seedlings, and potato slips, coaxing them from the hard ground with water and love, while cursing her husband's big boots and hunting dogs that crush her tender plants. Divorce ends this forty-year marriage, with the woman breaking every plate from her hope chest ("That's one he won't get") and lamenting that she has never learned how to root the six-leafed plant of magical powers, Solomon's Seal. It takes patience to survive in these hills, the girl in "A Country Girl" tells the city reporter who comes to the shrine of the famous lady writer of north Georgia, Corra Harris: "You mustn't resist the brambles," she tells him as they struggle through the blackberry bushes; "just back out of them"; "it's no country for a man with a temper."

In *How Far She Went,* two of Hood's most powerful stories remind readers that unhappy families are, in many ways, alike. The title story is about a mother who fails to love her daughter; "A Man Among Men" is about a father who fails his son. The sins in both are generational, ending only when an act arrests the cycle, breaking down the barrier of old hurts. In "How Far She Went," the granny and her fifteen-year-old granddaughter are forced together by the girl's mother's death and her father's abandonment. The old woman did not love her own daughter, the girl's mother: "she knew and the baby knew: there was no love in the begetting. That was the secret, unforgivable, that not another good thing could ever make up for, where all the bad had come from . . . a child who would be just like her, would carry the hurting on into another generation." When drunks whom the girl has teased pursue the grandmother and granddaughter on motorcycles, the old woman makes the choice to sacrifice her little dog to keep them safely hidden. They both hurt, but now it is different: the girl sees that the old woman cares about her, wants her. They walk home, the old woman bearing her lifeless dog: "The girl walked close behind her, exactly where she walked, matching her pace, matching her stride, close enough to put her hand forth (if the need arose) and touch her granny's back where the faded voile was clinging damp, the merest gauze between their wounds." Though the connection is thin and tenuous, the sacrifice establishes the bond of family that protects and heals.

It takes a literal and figurative reaching across generations for father and son to connect in "A Man Among Men." Thomas, rejected by his father in favor of his profligate brother Little Earl, refuses to love his own rebellious son, Dean. His recognition comes when he thinks for just a moment that the boy he finds dead of a drug overdose is his son. As a law officer, he goes to report the death to the boys' mother and is moved by her keening: "You don't love them for it, but you love them. There's good in between the bad times. . . . The Lloyd Jesus knows I love all my boys!" Each of the story's three sections has opened with a different angle of Thomas's father lying in the casket, the inevitable burial ahead. At the story's end, Thomas and Dean stand at the gravesite, and it is here that they reach across the emotional divide: Dean "stepped across Little Earl's grave and brushed the chalk dust off Thomas' shoulders, brushed and brushed. That was when Thomas began to cry."

Countryside gives way to trailer parks, subdivisions, new shopping centers, and beltways in Hood's second collection, *And Venus Is Blue,* but her characters retain their uniqueness of place and of speech. The language of these characters rings true because Hood has imitated what she hears in her daily life, the talk of her own family and of her neighbors. Realistic setting and diction work together with narrative perspective to create believable characters in Hood's "post-minimalist fiction." The trend labeled minimalism, which dominated the 1980s with the stories of Ann Beattie, Raymond Carver, and Bobbie Ann Mason, was characterized by the ironic, detached narrator who told a story from the first-person point of view in the present tense and ended it with no resolution. In contrast, Mary Hood's third-person narrator "appears gracious and unselfish, though ever present," her point of view remarkable in a literary period, in David Baker's words, "marked by minimal expression and first-person confessionalism." Her characters, Dan Pope observes, have a history of people and place and their situations are resolved at the end of the story. For example, in "The Desire Call of the Wild Hen," the reader greets

Candy at birth, sees her through a failed marriage, and leaves her screaming like the bird of the story's title. In "Nobody's Fool," Hood reveals in a childhood vignette the daughter's shame about her father's millworker background, and in "Finding the Chain," a visit to the mother's old home place links birth family and blend family.

The endings, though, are bleaker in *And Venus Is Blue.* While families do mend, the damage can be permanent, as it is in "The Goodwife Hawkins," a story of wife abuse, and in the novella "And Venus is Blue," a story of a father's suicide. Vinnie is the good wife to Hawk Hawkins, but her only redemption from their sick marriage lies in her husband's death. Hawk's behavior might be explained by brain damage sustained in the car accident, but his insistent cruelty remains: "Hawk taped her mouth shut with two-inch-wide adhesive and stood her against the refrigerator door, at attention, while he sat at the dinette table, pouring whiskey into his coffee and aiming the pistol at her good heart." Debilitated by strokes, Hawk has stained walls, carpet, and furniture in his various struggles over mealtime; his incontinence keeps Vinnie going up and down the stairs to wash the clothes. When Vinnie leans over to pick up his TV remote, he kicks her; when she throws him a surprise birthday party, after the guests leave he slits her arm with the serving knife. The story opens with Hawk's death and Vinnie's release, the verbs setting up the juxtaposition with his violent acts against her: "She hauled the drapes back, raised the blackout shades, cranked open the jalousies, shoved the patio door wide open on its reluctant track, and ran his musty old pointer, She-lah, out into the fresh air. These were her first free acts." Her last act in the story is to sling Shelah's gift of a dead bunny over the hedge, the audience of neighbors watching: "'Bury that thing,' she said, disgusted."

In the complex and lyrical novella "And Venus Is Blue," Delia looks at the past through the present to comprehend her loss. The story's epigraph prefigures Delia's torment: "Imagine a photograph album, with a bullet fired pointblank through it, every page with its scar. Murder attacks the future; suicide aims at the past." Delia must confront the fact of her father's suicide, which calls up the old pain of separation and abandonment she has felt since her mother left them, came back, and left them again. The narrative moves from daybreak to midnight, the span of a day and of a lifetime; every intense moment as remembered in Delia's life is shot through with her father's death. To Delia, Venus is blue, love is pain, and she "could always control her behavior more easily than her feelings. . . . She even kept her dead kitten an extra day, holding out against hope, against all odds."

Mary Hood's careful execution and attention to small detail give life to her landscape and her characters. Alice Mc-Dermott writes that if Hood "offers her characters few comforts in their struggle to live, neither does she provide her stories with false epiphanies or literary redemptions. She is consummately honest. She does not fear the bleak conclusions of some lives or the quiet, fleeting triumphs of others."

Dede Yow

SELECTED BIBLIOGRAPHY

Works by Mary Hood

How Far She Went. Athens: University of Georgia Press, 1984.
And Venus Is Blue. New York: Ticknor & Fields, 1986.

Critical Studies

Aiken, David. "Mary Hood: The Dark Side of the Moon." In Jeffrey J. Folks and James Perkins, eds., *Southern Writers at Century's End,* pp. 21–31. Lexington: University Press of Kentucky, 1997.
Baker, David. "Time and Time Again." *The Kenyon Review* (Winter 1987): 137–142.
McDermott, Alice. "Love Was All They Knew to Call It." *New York Times Book Review,* August 17, 1986.
Pope, Dan. "The Post-Minimalist American Story or What Comes After Carver?" *Gettysburg Review* 1/2 (1988): 331–342.

LANGSTON HUGHES
(1902 – 1967)

Born February 1, 1902, in Joplin, Missouri, James Mercer Langston Hughes grew up in the Midwest in a college-educated African American household. As an adolescent, however, when thousands of blacks were migrating out of the agricultural South, Hughes went to Mexico to visit and work with his father James, who had divorced his mother Carrie when Langston was a toddler. Hughes's fluent Spanish and racially ambiguous looks allowed him to live comfortably among Mexicans, but in 1920 he decided to move to New York City to attend Columbia University. After a year, disappointed academically and socially, he left to travel, sleeping, as he once wrote, in "ten thousand beds." For several years he worked as a merchant sailor along the coast of West Africa, and for a few months in a restaurant in Paris.

Hughes launched his writing career in the mid-1920s, at the height of the Harlem Renaissance. His unsolicited pieces were quickly accepted for publication, even though sent by an unknown young man from abroad. He first gained recognition as a poet, winning literary competitions sponsored by the NAACP and the National Urban League, and publishing eleven poems in Alain Locke's groundbreaking anthology *The New Negro* (1925). His distinctive use of black idiom and jazz rhythms in the volumes *The Weary Blues* (1926) and *Fine Clothes to the Jew* (1927) brought him literary fame and such appellations as "the bard of Harlem" and "the Negro Poet Laureate."

Sponsored by white patrons, Hughes graduated from Lincoln University in Pennsylvania in 1929. He quickly seized opportunities to visit Cuba, Haiti, the Soviet Union, China, and Japan. In 1937 he covered the Spanish Civil War for the Baltimore *Afro-American* and was active in radical politics throughout the decade and afterward. Hughes's nomadic travels, his race, his profound sense of social justice, and his extraordinary literary versatility flavored all his writing. Even though he staked his claim on representations of Af-

rican Americans, Hughes's work captures human nature in many races and nationalities.

Hughes stood apart from other noted African American writers of the time because he remained in Harlem, buying a brownstone and establishing a home among the black masses rather than in the affluent suburbs. He also distinguished himself from some other writers of the Harlem Renaissance because he did not stop writing even after white patrons' fascination and financial support waned. Early on Hughes had determined to earn a living as a writer, and he quickly accomplished that goal. Besides uncollected dramas, comedies, musicals, opera librettos, newspaper columns, essays, and random contributions to magazines, he published more than sixty books in nearly every genre: poetry, novels, autobiography, short fiction, histories, biographies, essays, and translations. Editing many anthologies of short stories, poems, folklore, and humor, he also assisted visual artists in publishing their work. Since his death on May 22, 1967, collections of his works have been edited and published, and future projects are planned. A literary society and related journal in his name were founded in 1981. He is now widely regarded as one of the most important and influential American writers of the twentieth century.

Hughes began writing and publishing short stories in his teens. As a high school student in Cleveland, he empathized intensely with the people in the tales of Guy de Maupassant, which he read in French. Spurred by this reading, Hughes published a few short stories in his high school literary magazine. Despite the early appearance of these pieces, however, he did not focus on the genre until the 1930s.

His first collection of short fiction, *The Ways of White Folks,* appeared in 1934, after the Harlem Renaissance was no longer in vogue and the Depression had subdued the artistic and hedonistic excitement of the "roaring" twenties. The volume represented his own astonishment and anger regarding the behavior of white folks, including his own literary patron. In 1952 Hughes published a second volume of short stories, *Laughing to Keep from Crying,* followed by *Something in Common* (1963). In 1996, *Langston Hughes: Short Stories* brought together all the previously collected fiction other than *The Ways of White Folks* (which remains in print), plus many pieces that originally appeared only in periodicals. Altogether, including the Simple stories, ten books of Hughes's short fiction have been published.

The protagonists in Hughes's short stories include males and females of all ages, many of whom experience loneliness, isolation, or financial distress. These characters form relationships—often only temporary. Although these relations may not salvage the character's sanity or stabilize his or her success, they inevitably help the reader to imagine new and varied ways of finding common ground with others. A character may suffer bruises or a knife may be brandished, but violence is minimized in these stories. Instead, Hughes's characters reveal injuries to their hearts and egos. Sometimes, as in "One Friday Morning," a secondary character emerges to order the protagonist's chaos. At other times, as in "Little Dog," the troubled protagonist disappears and is soon forgotten.

Hughes's settings range from big cities such as New York and Chicago to isolated, nondescript farm regions. Most often set in the United States, the stories also take place in such diverse locations as Mexico City ("Tragedy at the Baths"), Havana ("Little Old Spy"), Hong Kong ("Something in Common"), and on the shore of the Niger River ("African Morning"). Often focusing on sound, Hughes captures linguistic nuances of these places, including phrases in French and Spanish and dialogue using various dialects of English.

"Slave on the Block," Hughes's first mature, professional short story, exemplifies his work in the genre. The introductory paragraph sets the scene in the home of Michael and Anne Carraway, a wealthy couple in New York's Greenwich Village. The narrator reveals that Michael, who composes for piano, and Anne, who paints, both enjoy an artistic fascination with Negroes. Because the names of actual writers, artists, and songs are listed, the story manifests an authentic Harlem Renaissance context. Because of their realism, Hughes's stories often illustrate and humanize historical and sociological data.

The Carraways developed patronizing relationships with Mattie, their "new colored maid," and Luther, the nephew of their deceased maid and cook. When Luther arrives to collect the dead cook's belongings, Michael and Anne adore him, "the most marvelous ebony boy . . . a boy as black as all the Negroes they'd ever known put together." Anne paints Luther seminude, and Michael "went to the piano and began to play something that sounded like 'Deep River' in the jaws of a dog, but Michael said it was a modern slave plaint, 1850 in terms of 1933. Vieux Carré remembered on 135th Street. Slavery in the Cotton Club." Hughes captures the distorted aesthetic venture succinctly, representing with similes and titles many layers of meaning.

In typical Hughes fashion, even when intimate physical relationships are implied—as between Mattie and Luther—graphic details never appear. Glaring, however, are the vulgarities of human nature, as when Michael's hostile and haughty mother arrives. Mother Carraway's presence disrupts the household. The boundaries between employer and servant are suddenly sharply defined, and a major conflict forces a choice regarding Luther: "Either he goes or I go," demands Michael's mother. Both Luther and Mattie leave, their departure more a triumph than a dismissal. Such underdog victories often figure in Hughes's works.

During the 1940s Hughes shifted into a unique literary form, often considered a short story but also discussed as a hybrid between serialized novel, short story, satirical sketch, and muted autobiography. This form developed from a newspaper feature and grew into five volumes known as the Simple stories. The episodic fiction first appeared in Hughes's weekly column for the *Chicago Defender* in February 1943. The first book-length collection, *Simple Speaks His Mind,* was published in 1950. Four more collections appeared by 1965. In 1994 an edited collection, *The Return of Simple,* retrieved from obscurity some out-of-print or unpublished Simple stories.

Unlike any of Hughes's other short fiction, the Simple stories all center on one character, Jesse B. Semple, better known as "Simple." This streetwise, deceptively untutored Harlem Everyman dominates dialogues, most often conversing with a college-educated writer, Ananias Boyd. Boyd functions as a foil while Simple recalls his childhood or philosophizes about women, labor, politics, landladies, dogs, or anything else that catches his fancy. Frequently humorous, the stories nevertheless present poignant analyses of issues seen from the average Harlem resident's point of view in the 1940s, 1950s, and 1960s. Platitudes about American pride and democracy seem shallow and fallacious after Simple has blasted them with the harsh realities of his own daily struggles.

A typical Simple story, "Possum, Race, and Face," begins smack in the middle of a conversation, in this case over beer in a bar. As usual, the foil is never named, merely called "I." When Boyd enters the bar at 2 A.M., Simple asks him to stay a while and hear how he and girlfriend Joyce have revived their romance. Unlike Hughes's other short stories, his Simple pieces generally have very little third-person narration. In "Possum, Race, and Face," Simple explains in delicious detail the virtues of soul food, dating back to his youth as a "passed around" child. In his own fashion, he connects food to church and startlingly announces: "If I was to pray what is in my mind, I would pray for the Lord to wipe white folks off the face of the earth. Let 'em go! Let 'em go! *And let me rule awhile!*" Simple's prayer may seem foolish or hostile, but his world without white folks reveals economic and educational equality, along with an end to colonial rule in Africa and Asia. He goes on to wish, "colored folks should have the same right to get drunk as white folks," not being judged "a disgrace to our group." In typical Simple fashion, he has moved back and forth from important global issues to seemingly mundane details. However, careful consideration reveals a germ of truth in Simple's assertion: "I see plenty of white men get on the buses drunk, and nobody says that a white man is a disgrace to his race." Boyd chides Simple for his "ordinary desire," insisting that instead of wanting the right to get drunk, "You ought to want to have the right to be President, or something like that."

"Very few men can become President," said Simple. "And only one at a time. But almost anybody can get drunk. Even I can get drunk."

"Then you ought to take a taxi home, and not get on the bus smelling like a distillery," I said, "staggering and disgracing the race."

"I keep trying to tell you, if I was white, wouldn't nobody say I was disgracing no race!"

"You definitely are not white," I said.

"You got something there," said Simple. "Lend me taxi fare and I will ride home."

Typical of a Simple story, this ending shows the protagonist cleverly surrendering his point but gaining something important: in this case, taxi fare—a loan that he typically never gets around to repaying. The exchange also illustrates the discernible vernacular distinctions between the diction of Simple and Boyd. While Simple uses black vernacular English and Boyd uses standard English, both men show intelligence and both deserve respect.

Hughes's representations in short sto-

ries range from the multiple volumes of the Simple stories, which describe one man's life, to abbreviated fictional scenes—prose poems—in which whole lives are captured in unspoken words, as in "Saratoga Rain." The short fiction of Langston Hughes delves into human nature, usually leaving the reader better able to bridge the gaps between self and other.

Donna Akiba Sullivan Harper

SELECTED BIBLIOGRAPHY

Works by Langston Hughes

The Ways of White Folks. New York: Alfred A. Knopf, 1934.

Simple Speaks His Mind. New York: Simon & Schuster, 1950.

Laughing to Keep from Crying. New York: Henry Holt, 1952.

Simple Takes a Wife. New York: Simon & Schuster, 1953.

Simple Stakes a Claim. New York: Rinehart, 1957.

The Best of Simple. New York: Hill & Wang, 1961.

Something in Common and Other Stories. New York: Hill & Wang, 1963.

Simple's Uncle Sam. New York: Hill & Wang, 1965.

The Return of Simple. New York: Hill & Wang, 1994.

Langston Hughes: Short Stories. New York: Hill & Wang, 1996.

Critical Studies

Berry, Faith. *Langston Hughes: Before and Beyond Harlem.* New York: Citadel, 1992.

Harper, Donna Akiba Sullivan. *Not So Sim-*

ple: *The Simple Stories by Langston Hughes.* Columbia: University of Missouri Press, 1996.

Ostrom, Hans. *Langston Hughes: A Study of the Short Fiction.* New York: Twayne, 1993.

Rampersad, Arnold. *The Life of Langston Hughes.* 2 vols. New York: Oxford University Press, 1986–1988.

ZORA NEALE HURSTON
(1891 – 1960)

Zora Neale Hurston was born in Notasulga, Alabama, in 1891, a birth date that she sometimes erased by as much as a dozen years and a birthplace she always supplanted with Eatonville, the all-black Florida town that her father helped to found and that, according to Hurston's autobiography, was "the first attempt at organized self-government on the part of Negroes in America." Hurston returned to Eatonville often as an adult and she drew inspiration from it throughout her career, using it not only for her well-known images of healthy, autonomous, racial self-definition and nurturing community life but also for her less noted images of the petty, suffocating judgments of self-satisfied small-town morality. At the height of the Harlem Renaissance in the 1920s, Hurston joined many other black intellectuals and artists in moving to New York. There, while associating with the leading intellectual lights of New York's "New Negro" movement, she began to publish witty, comedic, highly styled stories and plays that both mocked and celebrated African American life. At the same time, Hurston studied anthropology at Columbia University with Franz Boas, launching many years of folklore collecting in the South, Jamaica, and Haiti, and she also embarked on a complex relationship with a white literary patron, Charlotte Osgood Mason. The constraints of this patronage relationship—which sometimes left Hurston begging for stomach medicine, shoes, and the right to perform her own materials—delayed publication of her earliest writing.

But in the 1930s she burst forth with two groundbreaking collections of folklore, *Mules and Men* (1935) and *Tell My Horse* (1938), challenging conventions of anthropological objectivity. She also published her first three novels. *Jonah's Gourd Vine* (1934) drew heavily—and often quite critically—on the lives of her hard-working, strong-willed mother and her charismatic, too-worldly, self-destructive, preacher father. *Their Eyes Were Watching God* (1937), a stunningly lyrical love story that violates norms of sexual restraint by offering a bold quest for female fulfillment, is largely responsible for the current Hurston revival. *Moses, Man of the Mountain* (1939) is a humanizing retelling of the Moses legend in the tradition of paralleling the plight of biblical Jews and contemporary African Americans. Hurston continued to publish a range of ethnographic, fictional, dramatic, and surprisingly conservative political writings throughout the 1940s, when she brought out her celebrated but cagey autobiography *Dust Tracks on a Road* (1942) and *Seraph on the Suwannee* (1948), an odd, sympathetic romance about southern whites and gender miscommunication. When she died in 1960, in poverty, neglect, and obscurity, she left behind a wealth of unpublished writing: work for the Federal Writers' Project, nearly a dozen full-length plays, numerous stories and essays, and a number of unpublished novels, full copies of which remain to be found.

Although Hurston's reputation has rested largely on her innovative and unconventional work as a novelist and anthropologist, the short story was her original medium. She began to publish linguistically rich yet conventionally plotted short fiction almost fifteen years before she published *Jonah's Gourd Vine,* and she continued to publish short fiction—ranging from traditional stories to vernacular dialect pieces, from retold folktales to modernist experiments in language, narrative, and point of view—long after her final book-length publication, *Seraph on the Suwannee* (1948). Taken together, her short fiction explains a great deal about why Hurston's aesthetic and political preoccupations set her askew of fellow writers associated with the literary traditions (realist, modernist, folklore, or Harlem Renaissance) on which she drew. Hurston worked, for example, in a black intellectual context that emphasized celebrating, defending, and explicating collective black life in ways that would mount a united front against white portrayals of rural innocence, urban depravity, and extreme cultural difference. Yet, her short fiction is often marked by a fierce defense of individualism, a determined focus on cultural difference, representations of

sexuality, and a general avoidance of the disputatious strategies used by her peers.

In "John Redding Goes to Sea," for example, Hurston's first published story, the main character is immediately set off against the townsfolk's narrow-minded view that "John Redding was a queer child." This story focuses compassionately on John's wanderlust and the women in his life who thwart adventure. "Hometied," John makes a last effort to "be a man" by accepting dangerous work on a bridge that "the white folks" are stupid enough to build at flood time. John is killed and found with a gaping side wound and his arms outstretched, floating Christ-like on a piece of lumber. His wife and mother wail and wring their hands. But John's father knowingly floats John off "on the bosom of the river," where he can finally pilot "his little craft" toward "the sea, the wide world—at last." Many features mark this story as early work. But this naive and sentimental portrayal of the frustrated, misunderstood individual establishes a trope in Hurston's writing, from *Their Eyes Were Watching God*'s Janie, who finds "a jewel down inside herself" but cannot "gleam it around," to *Dust Tracks on a Road*'s description of "a feeling of terrible aloneness." "Drenched in Light," Hurston's second published story, picks up this theme by introducing Isie Watts, a "joyful," black female child whose natural playfulness and joi de vivre are squelched by both her grandmother and Eatonville. In *Dust Tracks on a Road,* Hurston recycles this character to depict her childhood self.

Whether for self-description or the pursuit of a theme, Hurston is prone both to recycle her own material and to rely on stock or stereotyped characters. Isie Watts, for example, in all of her various incarnations, leaps right off the minstrel stage as a "shining little morsel," who loves nothing better than to dance and preen for whites. And playing on modernist tropes of primitivism, Hurston ends "Drenched in Light" with a white woman's desire to have "a little of [Isie's] sunshine to soak into my soul." "I need it," she declares. It is often unclear whether in deploying such images—happy pickaninnies, shrewish women, manly men, life-deadened whites—Hurston is taking refuge in convention and prejudice or thumbing her nose at it, pandering to her audience or exposing its predilections.

The best of Hurston's stories seem to be less conscious of audience and to offer more substantial characters. Hurston's third story, "Under the Bridge," for example, is a simple, effective tale of romantic triangulation among three nicely rendered characters: Luke, his young wife Vangie, and his son Artie. Although the plot of conflicting loyalties and the father's choice of suicide to enable his son and wife's happiness can certainly be read as hackneyed, all three characters emerge as believable figures caught in a genuine dilemma. "Spunk" and "Sweat," two of Hurston's best and best-known stories, pick up this theme of romantic triangulation and give it a much more tragic turn. In "Spunk," Lena Kanty is seduced away from a husband the townsfolk judge meek and passive by a "giant of a brown skinned man" who seems as large and untouchable as God. But after her husband is killed trying to get Lena back, the townsfolk are forced

to acknowledge that "Joe wuz a braver man than Spunk." Joe's bravery shows posthumously in an inexplicable, grisly sawmill accident that cuts Spunk in half. The townswomen are last seen gathered at Spunk's funeral, discussing Joe's ghostly revenge, and wondering "who would be Lena's next." "Spunk" seems to inaugurate a kind of moral realism, a fable narrated with the focus and detail of carefully observed ethnography.

"Sweat," another of Hurston's best stories, also tells a tale of terrible cruelty and terrible revenge. Not content merely to flaunt his mistresses and disparage the labor that feeds, clothes, and houses him, Sykes Jones tortures his battered, unhappy, hard-working wife by bringing home a pet snake, what Delia fears most in the world. "You done starved me an' Ah put up widcher, you done beat me an Ah took dat, but you done kilt all mah insides bringin' dat varmint heah," she warns him. Pushed beyond her breaking point when she realizes that Sykes plans to kill her with the snake and install his mistress in her place, Delia ambushes Sykes with his own trap and "with a surge of pity too strong to support" listens to his death moans from far outside their bedroom window. Male marital infidelity is punished exactly in Hurston's fictional world. But neither is her world a place which promises women "sweet things wid . . . marriage," as Janie puts it in *Their Eyes Were Watching God*.

Not all of Hurston's stories of romantic triangulation are quite so grim. Plots of romantic betrayal often work as comedic backdrops for anthropological reportage of the social and linguistic rites of courtship, as in "Muttsy," "The Eatonville Anthology," or "Story in Harlem Slang," a sketch of the verbal hijinks of two pimps, which gives us the dozens—"If you trying to jump salty, Jelly, that's your mammy"—and courting dialogue—"'But baby!' Jelly gasped. 'Dat shape you got on you! I bet the Coca Cola Company is paying you good money for the patent!'" In "The Gilded Six-Bits," another of Hurston's most frequently reprinted stories, the power of the true love between Eatonville's Missie May and Joe triumphs over the sordid materiality of Otis D. Slemmons and his seductive false gold. Although more sentimental than "Spunk" or "Sweat," this story suggests that when romance *does* succeed, any happiness it offers will be paid for in corresponding difficulty.

If outcomes are not necessarily happy, it is important in Hurston's stories that innocence triumph over corruption. In "The Conscience of the Court," Hurston's last published story, the beleaguered innocent is Laura Kimble, the black servant of white Mrs. Celestine Clairborne, to whom Laura is unreservedly devoted. With Mrs. Clairborne out of town, Laura is faced with a strange white man laying claim to her mistress's property. In the role of faithful retainer, Laura "jumped as salty as the 'gator when the pond went dry. I stretched out my arm and he hit the floor on a prone. . . . All I did next was to grab him by his heels and frail the pillar of the porch with him a few times." Laura is arrested and brought to trial. It comes out in court that "the purpose of the loan was to finance the burial of Thomas Kimble," Laura's husband, and that its due date

is still more than three months away. To make up for a momentary loss of faith in her mistress, Laura, who is of course dismissed from court, makes "a ritual of atonement" by polishing and repolishing Mrs. Clairborne's silver. And this is how the story ends. Again, the story draws on conventions that may make the reader queasy. Is Hurston assuring whites of black loyalty? Blacks of white protection? Elsewhere, as in stories like "Black Death," Hurston warns that "white folks are very stupid about some things. They can think mightily but cannot *feel*," and they are outwitted over and over again in stories like "High John De Conquer," one example of the sort of folklore Hurston loved to collect.

Naive sentimentalism and hard-nosed moral realism. Apparent racial pandering and blanket indictment of whites. Women as shrews, women as victims. That all are characteristic of Hurston's fiction is, perhaps, not surprising, given her constant propensity to lean into contradiction. As the late Toni Cade Bambara put it, "the woman, quite simply, did not play." Hurston's stories are playful and provocative but somehow they never quite conform, never seem to play by any rules. Which is hardly to say that these stories are not valuable, both for students of Hurston and for students of the short story. In her short fiction, especially, Hurston could put herself forward as a writer, test out material and themes to expand later, and rework anthropological materials, even re-create characters taken directly from her fieldwork. The least of her short stories provide testing grounds for her struggles with divergent constituencies, and the best of them can stand on their own alongside any of the short fiction of her contemporaries and should be included in anthologies of classic American short stories as fine examples of the genre. Zora Neale Hurston was deeply interested in the form of the short story, particularly its adaptability to oral traditions, folklore, and the vernacular, and she returned to it again and again throughout her life, experimenting with its possibilities and bringing to bear on it all of her varied and complex interests.

Carla Kaplan

SELECTED BIBLIOGRAPHY

Published Stories

"John Redding Goes to Sea." *Stylus* 1 (May 1921): 11–22. Reprinted in *Opportunity* 4 (January 1926): 16–21; Cheryl A. Wall, ed., *Zora Neale Hurston: Novels and Stories* (New York: Library of America, 1995), pp. 925–939; Henry Louis Gates, Jr. and Sieglinde Lemke, eds., *Zora Neale Hurston: The Complete Stories* (New York: Harper Perennial, 1996), pp. 1–16.

"Drenched in Light." *Opportunity* 2 (December 1924): 371–374. Reprinted in *Spunk: The Selected Short Stories of Zora Neale Hurston* (Berkeley: Turtle Island Foundation, 1985), pp. 9–18, under the title "Isis"; Wall, ed., pp. 940–948; Gates and Lemke, eds., pp. 17–25.

"Under the Bridge." *The X-Ray: The Official Publication of Zeta Phi Beta Sorority* (December 1925). Reprinted in *American Visions* 11 (December/January 1997): 14–19.

"Spunk." *Opportunity* 2 (June 1925): 171–173. Reprinted in Alain Locke, ed., *The New Negro* (New York: Albert and Charles Boni, 1925), *Spunk*, pp. 1–8; Wall, ed., pp. 949–954; Gates and Lemke, eds., pp. 26–32.

"Possum or Pig?" *Forum* 76 (September 1925). Reprinted in Gates and Lemke, eds., pp. 57–58.

"Magnolia Flower." *Spokesman* (July 1926): 26–29. Reprinted in Gates and Lemke, eds., pp. 33–40.

"Muttsy." *Opportunity* 4 (August 1926). Reprinted in *Spunk*, pp. 19–37; Gates and Lemke, eds., pp. 41–56.

"The Eatonville Anthology." *Messenger* 8 (September–November 1926). Reprinted in Alice Walker, ed., *I Love Myself When I Am Laughing and Then Again When I Am Looking Mean and Impressive: A Zora Neale Hurston Reader* (New York: The Feminist Press, 1979), pp. 177–178; Gates and Lemke, eds., pp. 59–72.

"Sweat." *Fire* 1 (November 1926): 40–45. Reprinted in Walker, ed., pp. 197–207; *Spunk*, pp. 38–53; Wall, ed., pp. 955–957; Gates and Lemke, eds., pp. 73–85.

"The Gilded Six-Bits." *Story* 3 (August 1933): 60–70. Reprinted in Walker, ed., pp. 208–218; *Spunk*, pp. 54–68; Wall, ed., pp. 985–996; Gates and Lemke, eds., pp. 86–97.

"The Fire and the Cloud." *Challenge* 1 (September 1934): 10–14. Reprinted in Wall, ed., pp. 997–1000; and Gates and Lemke, eds., pp. 117–121.

"Cock Robin, Beale Street." *Southern Literary Messenger* 3 (July 1941): 321–323. Reprinted in *Spunk*, pp. 69–74; Gates and Lemke, eds., pp. 122–126.

"Story in Harlem Slang." *American Mercury* 55 (July 1942): 84–96. Reprinted in *Spunk,* pp. 82–96; Wall, ed., pp. 1001–1007; Wall and Lemke, eds., pp. 127–138.

"High John De Conquer." *American Mercury* 55 (October 1943): 450–458. Reprinted in Wall and Lemke, pp. 139–148.

"The Conscience of the Court." *Saturday Evening Post* (March 18, 1950): 22–23, 112–122. Reprinted in Wall and Lemke, pp. 162–177.

Unpublished Stories

"Black Death." Reprinted in Gates and Lemke, eds., pp. 202–208.

"The Bone of Contention." Reprinted in Gates and Lemke, eds., pp. 209–220.

"Book of Harlem." Reprinted in *Spunk,* pp. 75–81; Gates and Lemke, eds., pp. 221–226.

"Harlem Slanguage." Reprinted in Gates and Lemke, eds., pp. 227–232.

"Now You Cookin' with Gas." Hurston's unedited version of "Story in Harlem Slang." Reprinted in Gates and Lemke, eds., pp. 233–241.

"The Seventh Veil." Reprinted in Gates and Lemke, eds., pp. 242–260.

"The Woman in Gaul." Reprinted in Gates and Lemke, eds., pp. 261–283.

Critical Studies

Bone, Robert. *Down Home: Origins of the Afro-American Short Story.* New York: Columbia, 1988.

Chinn, Nancy, and Elizabeth E. Dunn. "'The Ring of Metal on Wood': Zora Neale Hurston's Artistry in 'The Gilded Six Bits.'" *Mississippi Quarterly* 49/4 (fall 1996): 775–790.

Gates, Henry Louis, Jr., and Sieglinde Lemke. "Introduction: Zora Neale Hurston: Establishing the Canon." In Henry Louis Gates, Jr., and Sieglinde Lemke, eds., *Zora Neale Hurston: The Complete Stories,* pp. ix–xxiii. New York: HarperCollins, 1996.

Jones, Evora W. "The Pastoral and the Picaresque in Zora Neale Hurston's 'The Gilded Six-Bits.'" *College Language Association Journal* 35 (1992): 316–332.

SHIRLEY JACKSON
(1916–1965)

*T*he *New Yorker* published Shirley Jackson's "The Lottery" on June 26, 1948, and hundreds of readers recorded their stunned reaction to the tale of a woman's ritualistic death by stoning in a twentieth-century American town square. "By the next week," Jackson wrote in her "Biography of a Story," "I had to change my mailbox to the largest one in the post office, and casual conversation with the postmaster was out of the question, because he wasn't speaking to me." Although she joked about the more upset correspondents, who included her own mother, Jackson was unnerved by the sudden notoriety.

Discussed as fable and folklore, praised for its chilling ironies and subtle symbolism, "The Lottery" has become one of the most widely reprinted works of American literature. Maya Angelou stressed its skillful plotting for an Insight Media program in 1978; Richard Ford selected it for *The Granta Book of the American Short Story* in 1992. Establishing Jackson's artistry in a genre that S. T. Joshi has called "domestic horror," "The Lottery" inevitably shaped readers' expectations for the five novels and the many stories that followed. When she died after a heart attack on August 8, 1965, the *New York Times* headlined her long obituary "Shirley Jackson, Author of Horror Classic."

Although Jackson lived in Vermont for much of her adult life and is often identified as a New England writer, she was born on December 14, 1916, in San Francisco. Her father, Leslie Jackson, had emigrated from England; her mother, Geraldine Bugbee Jackson, was related to noted California architects—a probable factor in Shirley Jackson's fascination with buildings in her novels and in stories like "The Little House," "A Visit" (formerly "The Lovely House"), and "The House." "Home" (1965), the last work Jackson published before her death, describes an outsider's dangerous encounter with the ghost of a small boy who is trying to return to the country house she and her husband have innocently purchased. Jackson's childhood in suburban Burlingame is reflected in her first novel, *The Road Through the Wall* (1948), and in the semiautobiographical story "Dorothy and My Grandmother and the Sailors," an account of two twelve-year-old girls who experience a few moments of panic on an eventful trip into San Francisco. In 1933, Jackson's executive father was promoted, and she strongly resented the cross-country move

to Rochester, New York. Mentally depressed (a condition that would recur later in her life), she withdrew from the University of Rochester after two years.

Several of Jackson's early stories appeared in Syracuse University publications, including the *Spectre*, a magazine she founded with her fellow student Stanley Edgar Hyman. Their outspoken editorials on civil rights anticipated "After You, My Dear Alphonse" (1942), a critique of a middle-class housewife who foolishly assumes that her young son's African American friend comes from a large, poor, and lazy family. It was Jackson's first story for *The New Yorker*. Jackson and Hyman were married on August 13, 1940, in New York City, and her jobs at a radio station, an advertising agency, and Macy's department store supplemented his modest income from the *New Republic* and *The New Yorker*. When Hyman joined the faculty of Bennington College in 1945 and they moved to Vermont, Jackson's sense of dislocation paralleled that of many of her lonely characters. She wrote several hours a day, typing manuscripts between P.T.A. meetings, baseball games, and pajama parties for her four children. Family activities inspired more than thirty semiautobiographical comic stories, which Jackson sold to *Ladies' Home Journal, Good Housekeeping, Harper's,* and other magazines. The most frequently anthologized of these is "Charles," which ends with an O. Henry twist when the startled mother of a new kindergartener realizes that the terror of the classroom is her own son. Another popular story is "The Night We All Had Grippe," which Jackson called "the most direct translation of experience into fiction that I have ever done." Written in a fever, while the author coped with the demands of her flu-stricken husband and children, the farce of switched beds and a missing blanket is strongly reminiscent of James Thurber's "The Night the Bed Fell." Jackson was an innovator in the field of family comedy, and she skillfully pieced most of these stories into the fictionalized memoirs *Life Among the Savages* (1953) and *Raising Demons* (1957), yet she discounted the literary merit of such work. As recent scholars have demonstrated, however, the popular domestic narratives of writers like Jackson, Betty MacDonald, and Jean Kerr are a major branch of American women's humor and a mirror of post–World War II culture.

Jackson's family stories also bear the hallmarks of her more serious short and long fiction. Ordinary situations turn strange, even nightmarish. A young mother and her two small children meet a sinister man on a train in "The Witch"; in "The Daemon Lover," a young woman with dreams of marital bliss is apparently abandoned by her fiancé on their wedding day; the unhappy housewife of "The Beautiful Stranger" falls in love with her husband's mysterious and hallucinatory double and then gets lost, perhaps permanently, while trying to find her way home to him. Jackson's work "has a pervasive atmosphere of the odd about it," says S. T. Joshi, who ranks Jackson with Ramsey Campbell as H. P. Lovecraft's successors in the field of "weird fiction." The haunted tower of a country mansion in "A Visit" and the demonic stranger who mesmerizes a young woman in "The Rock" are among Jackson's occasional gothic touches, but the oddness of her fiction

more often inheres in the everyday. In "The Summer People," for example, an elderly husband and wife stay at their lake cottage after Labor Day, only to find themselves cut off from the outside world, awaiting probable death at the hands of resentful villagers—a violent defense of tradition that parallels the action of "The Lottery."

The Lottery; or, The Adventures of James Harris (1949), the only collection that Jackson made of her short fiction, capitalized on the impact of the title story in *The New Yorker*. Jackson grouped her twenty-five tales into four sections, inserted transitional passages from a witchcraft treatise, revised stories to emphasize a mysterious stranger named James Harris, and appended the "demon lover" ballad to clarify the subtitle of the book. Jackson's most famous story opens on a beautiful June 27 as villagers gather for an annual lottery that is held concurrently in other towns. According to the biographer Judy Oppenheimer, Jackson's own town of North Bennington was the model for both its modern setting and its characters. Playful children arrive on the square before their busy parents, and the boys make a large pile of the "smoothest and roundest" stones, whose grim purpose is revealed only at the story's conclusion. Other foreshadowings are equally unobtrusive. The townspeople keep their distance from the lottery equipment and hesitate when Mr. Summers asks them to steady the black box so he can mix up the slips of paper inside. The degree of ceremony is puzzling: families line up together, lists of kinship networks have been prepared, and every able-bodied person must attend. People seem reluctant to get the winning ticket, and there are rumors that other villages are going to stop holding the lottery; but Old Man Warner counters with a proverb: "Lottery in June, corn be heavy soon." When Bill Hutchinson draws the slip with a black spot, his wife shatters the morning calm, shouting that Mr. Summers rushed Bill's selection. Tessie herself receives the marked paper after the five Hutchinsons draw to determine which family member will win the final round. As the desperate woman screams, "It isn't fair," the town advances against her, armed with stones from the boys' stockpile.

"The Lottery" has provoked a variety of critical responses, including mythic, feminist, and Marxist approaches. Jackson told her *New Yorker* editor that "The Lottery" was "just a story" with no special theme, but Oppenheimer says she told a friend it was about "the Jews," recent victims of Nazi terror in World War II. A student of folklore, Jackson employed archetypes of scapegoating and seasonal sacrifice, timing the lottery near the summer solstice, when farming communities labor to ensure a rich harvest. The three-legged stool that supports the ominously black box could be a modern version of the Greek tripod of prophecy, and the container itself recalls Pandora's box of woes. A neighbor reminds the distraught Tessie that each villager "took the same chance"; however, in Jackson's fiction, women have a knack for drawing disaster.

The disaster is not so macabre in the symbolically titled "Flower Garden," but once again, the weight of tradition brutally crushes a woman's poignant challenge.

Mrs. MacLane seems to bring the spring with her when, in late March, she moves to a New England town with five-year-old Davey. A young urban widow, she freshens the rooms of her little cottage with pretty colors, attracting the villagers' friendly attention. Helen Winning, who lives in the "old Vermont manor house" up the hill, is especially helpful. Long ago, she yearned to plant a garden and to make the cottage into a home for her own family, but over the past eleven years she has so thoroughly adjusted to life in her husband's big ancestral house that she is beginning to look like her mother-in-law. The older Mrs. Winning clearly holds the authority in the three-generation household, and the arrival of the free-spirited Mrs. MacLane sparks a crisis in young Mrs. Winning's well-ordered existence.

Like the repressed women in many of Jackson's other stories ("The Daemon Lover," "The Tooth," and "Elizabeth"), Helen Winning finally breaks out. Her resistance is mild but significant as she pays a lengthy call at the cottage and extends warm invitations to the MacLanes, "all without the permission of her mother-in-law." The young women's friendship blossoms, and the days become "miraculously long and warm," with the first colors in the MacLanes' new garden "promising rich brilliance for the end of the summer, and the next summer, and summers ten years from now."

Abruptly, the villagers' kindness turns to cruelty, and the promise tokened by the garden is never fulfilled. Shocked when Davey joins in the taunts that little Howard Winning directs against a mulatto boy from the edge of town, Mrs. MacLane makes her son apologize to Billy Jones. The defensive Helen Winning is "incredulous," "indignant," and "embarrassed" when Mrs. MacLane then employs Billy's father to do the heavy garden work. With "the weight of the old Winning house" in her voice, Helen publicly dissociates herself from the newcomers in the cottage. Her insinuation that Mrs. MacLane is having an affair with Mr. Jones seals the community's rejection of Davey and his mother, but the lie also shows Helen's desperate conformity with the prejudiced neighbors she has known all her life. After a storm throws a huge branch across the MacLanes' ruined garden, the "tired" Mrs. MacLane decides to leave, and Helen Winning turns her back on the destruction without a word of comfort. Like Tessie Hutchinson in "The Lottery," the estranged women are both terribly defeated by village ways.

Stanley Hyman has observed that Jackson's "fierce visions" are "a sensitive and faithful anatomy of our times, fitting symbols for our distressing world of the concentration camp and the Bomb." Safe haven is an ideal in Jackson's fiction, but, in the spirit of the 1940s and the Cold War decades, her characters are more likely to discover heart-wrenching betrayals. Whether the genre is domestic comedy, gothic horror, or realistic narrative, Jackson pulls the rug from under her precariously balanced housewives and career women. Drawing on myth, ritual, and literary antecedents, these modern tales of loss and bewilderment create an atmosphere of quiet threat that was promptly recognized as the signature of a Shirley Jackson story.

Joan Wylie Hall

SELECTED BIBLIOGRAPHY

Works by Shirley Jackson

The Lottery; or, The Adventures of James Harris. New York: Farrar, Straus, 1949.

The Magic of Shirley Jackson. Edited by Stanley Edgar Hyman. New York: Farrar, Straus & Giroux, 1966.

Come Along with Me: Part of a Novel, Sixteen Stories, and Three Lectures. Edited by Stanley Edgar Hyman. New York: Viking Press, 1968.

Just an Ordinary Day. Edited by Laurence Jackson Hyman and Sarah Hyman Stewart. New York: Bantam Books, 1996.

Critical Studies

Hall, Joan Wylie. *Shirley Jackson: A Study of the Short Fiction.* New York: Twayne, 1993.

Joshi, S. T. "Shirley Jackson: Domestic Horror." *Studies in Weird Fiction* 14 (winter 1994): 9–28.

Oppenheimer, Judy. *Private Demons: The Life of Shirley Jackson.* New York: G. P. Putnam's Sons, 1988.

JAMAICA KINCAID
(1949–)

Poverty and the lack of educational opportunity for girls in the late 1960s compelled Antigua-born Jamaica Kincaid to immigrate to the United States to work as an au pair. Yet with her agile mind and iconoclast's personality, the soon-to-be writer did not long remain in this position. Kincaid held several jobs, earned her high school degree, and studied photography in and around New York City between 1966 and 1973. A chance elevator ride with George W. S. Trow, then a "Talk of the Town" columnist for *The New Yorker,* proved to be the watershed event in Kincaid's writing career. With Trow's encouragement and contacts, she began as a featured columnist for *Ingenue* and *The New Yorker* and subsequently wrote four works of fiction—*At the Bottom of the River* (1983), *Annie John* (1985), *Lucy* (1990), and *Autobiography of My Mother* (1995)—and two works of nonfiction—*A Small Place* (1988) and *My Brother* (1997). The experimental nature of her magazine writing—Kincaid has described some of her columns as "weird"—is duplicated in her only collection of short fiction, *At the Bottom of the River.* In a bio-bibliographic article on Kincaid, Susan Andrade states that *At the Bottom of the River*'s allusive narrative structure and "mythopoetic" language may alienate some readers. To mitigate this effect, readers have been encouraged to see the book as a companion to Kincaid's novel *Annie John*; both texts share themes and characters, but the latter renders them in a more accessible manner. Nevertheless, the honor Kincaid won for her short story collection (the Morton Dauwen Zabel Award, granted by the American Academy and Institute of Arts and Letters in 1983) attests to its artistry and literary value.

If one wanted to define the pieces in *At the Bottom of the River,* the familiar terms "short story" or "prose poem" would be the most precise. Yet by whatever name, Kincaid makes form accommodate her concerns, whether she proffers a critique of systems of power (parental authority, colonialism, or even narrative form) or articulates the reality of her Antiguan home and childhood. The work's refusal to be explicitly categorized signals two of the author's concerns: a defiance of limiting categories and an interest in self-fashioning. Similarly, this collection resists interpretation from any one critical position. Although it has often been described as a multifaceted vision of an Antiguan girlhood, one must not neglect *At the Bottom of the River*'s anticolonial critique or its modernist and postmodernist sensibilities.

Born in St. John's, Antigua, on May 25, 1949, Elaine Potter Richardson changed her name to Jamaica Kincaid when she published her first article. She offers various reasons for the change: in a 1993 interview with Alan Vorda, Kincaid claims that the pseudonym enabled her to write the "truth" as she saw it. In a 1990 interview with Selwyn Cudjoe she says that she changed her name because she hated the name "Elaine." In both interviews, the writer states that she desired anonymity as protection from bad reviews and familial censure. In the 1993 interview, Kincaid admits that the change allowed her to play around with her identity and to foreground her connection to the Caribbean ("'Kincaid,'" she says, "just seemed to go together with 'Jamaica'"). These diverse "reasons" and her claim to randomness notwithstanding, Jamaica Kincaid's name change signals her rejection of externally imposed conventions; the nom de plume also identifies the author's investment in empowerment through self-construction. In *At the Bottom of the River,* "Girl" and "In the Night" effectively represent both concerns. The process of uncovering the reasons for her name change, while offering insight into the writer and this collection, also prepares readers for the interpretive work needed to find meaning in these stories.

At the Bottom of the River's poetic, almost encoded, language requires interpretation; therefore, readers must work to understand the author's language and imagery. In addition, Kincaid relies heavily on an Antiguan cultural context, which may alienate non-Antiguan readers; however, this alienation is part of the author's intention. Her stylistic choice, rather than merely an off-putting technique, encourages readers to engage this text critically and to join Kincaid in her desire to make meaning through active interrogation of established norms.

Kincaid's use of Antiguan cultural practices has led some critics to describe *At the Bottom of the River* as a work of "magical realism." The author claims, however, that the collection is "magic" and "real," but not necessarily a work of "magical realism." *Magical realism* is a term that describes fiction that uses imaginary, improbable, and fantastic material in a realistic manner and/or setting. But what if a writer's reality embraces magical elements? Kincaid tells Alan Vorda that her Antigua is unreal and "goes off into fantasy all the time." She also claims that she is not an imaginative writer, merely one whose background is "fantastic." In saying this, Kincaid does not seek to replace the "real" with the "unreal"; she intends to dismantle the boundaries between the

two and foreground the notion that "reality" is plural.

Other literary critics classify Kincaid's culturally specific and experimental style as "modernist." Selwyn Cudjoe argues that writing like Kincaid's attempts to express an alternative reality over which modern and scientific societies have little control. It is certainly true that *At the Bottom of the River* is modernist in its experimental, enigmatic, and sometimes ambiguous features. It can also be defined as a postmodernist work in that Kincaid writes against limiting notions of history and identity; but merely to define this collection by either term would discount the inherent ambiguity and "unreality" of Jamaica Kincaid's cultural experiences. What is "real" for her—an African-descended, female writer from a formerly colonized country—is not necessarily "real" for others. Kincaid's form reflects and elaborates on her context; in other words, a modernist/postmodernist style and magical-realist perspective are tools that articulate her concerns most efficiently.

It is through her use of culturally specific features that Jamaica Kincaid shares her childhood experiences and offers her critique of hegemonic power. Although one will find both issues in "Girl" and "In the Night," the former represents a vexed power relationship between a mother and daughter (between the powerful and the powerless), and the latter exemplifies Kincaid's interest in formations of identity.

The first story in *At the Bottom of the River,* and Kincaid's most anthologized work, "Girl," is a series of dependent clauses separated by semicolons; in effect, it is a three-page sentence. This piece tests the boundaries of the short story form and can be read as an examination of the shape and limits of power. Written in roman and italic fonts, "Girl" is a series of declarative statements (punctuated by two questions) through which a mother instructs a girl on how to be a proper lady. Through the girl's two brief responses, readers learn that the mother's views on womanhood are not as benign as they first appear. The mother tells the girl: "soak salt fish overnight before you cook it; is it true that you sing benna [a type of calypso] in Sunday school?; always eat your food in such a way that it won't turn someone else's stomach; on Sundays try to walk like a lady and not like the slut you are so bent on becoming; don't sing benna in Sunday school." These "rules" are very restrictive and brook little argument. The large number of the mother's roman-text instructions diminish the girl's short responses: the girl says, *"I don't sing benna on Sundays at all and never in Sunday school,"* and later in the story, after the mother advises her to "always squeeze bread to make sure it's fresh," the girl asks, *"but what if the baker won't let me feel the bread?"* The mother seemingly ignores the fact and import of the girl's tentative responses. The first response appears after the mother expresses her own concerns about the girl's Sunday school behavior, and the last is followed by, "you mean to say that after all you are really going to be the kind of woman who the baker won't let near the bread?"

As tentative as they appear, the girl's responses are a movement away from her mother's stifling definition of womanhood. Readers learn that the command not to sing benna on Sunday is unwarranted; the second response reveals that the girl's interest is in her relationship with the baker and his goods, and not with the freshness of bread. These responses, therefore, lead readers to reevaluate the mother's rules: they seem to convey an English domestic reality, something peculiar to the mother's experience and by no means universal. Mother continues: "this is how you set a table for tea; this is how you set a table for dinner; this is how you set a table for dinner with an important guest." One must also consider that Mother and Girl straddle two different times, the former a product of an Antigua ruled by English mores, and the latter from an Antigua moving into the "formerly colonized" period.

But even within this apparently obvious power relationship, Kincaid reveals her inclination toward modernism's ambiguity: while imposing English and gendered norms on the child, the mother concurrently transmits Antiguan foodways, belief systems, and the like. The mother instructs: "when you are growing dasheen, make sure it gets plenty of water or else it makes your throat itch when your are eating it; . . . don't throw stones at blackbirds, because it might not be a blackbird at all; this is how to make a bread pudding; this is how to make doukona; . . . this is how to make a good medicine to throw away a child before it even becomes a child." Singing benna, growing dasheen, knowing when blackbirds might not be blackbirds, and herbal remedies mark "Girl" as an Antiguan story and as one that subverts accepted rules of behavior.

"In the Night" is a seven-page sketch that combines Kincaid's description of the sublime character of an Antiguan night with her discussion of the activities of supremely ordinary individuals. But unlike "Girl," "In the Night" does not advance a distinct plot; rather, it may be interpreted as a vehicle through which Kincaid enacts her belief in the "real" aspect of the magical and the "magical" aspect of the real. This story also demonstrates the author's concern with convention and issues of identity. Without a plot as a guide, readers must focus on the author's ideological motivations and reconsider their own beliefs about reality, tradition, and identity.

Toward the end of this story, the narrator says, "I am a girl, but one day I will marry a woman—a red-skin woman with black bramblebush hair and brown eyes, who wears skirts that are so big I can easily bury my head in them." By allowing that females can marry females, Kincaid posits that one's sexual identity is a matter of self-creation rather than of biology. Readers may find the narrator's assertion provocative, yet it builds upon the idea of self-fashioning that Kincaid addresses in "Girl." Contrary to the order that defines the girl's reality in the previous story, the narrator of "In the Night" covets the disorder that the red-skin woman's hair represents. The narrator does not find this disorder threatening, however, as she also finds safety in the woman's skirts. Kincaid continues in this vein by demonstrating that cultural "truths" are similarly malleable.

Kincaid draws on a folkloric figure, the jablesse, that is most often negatively represented. Traditionally speaking, the jab-

lesse is a beautiful woman with one goat's hoof who lures the unsuspecting to their death. But in "In the Night" (as well as in "Letter from Home" and "My Mother"), this woman is a transformative figure: she is "a person who can turn into anything." In light of the restrictions placed on the girl in "Girl," one can clearly see the value of such a model. "In the Night" also features the night-soil man, someone who collects and disposes of the contents of chamber pots and latrines. Here, Kincaid elevates the figure from the lowly position assigned him because of his job. Night-soil men "come and go, walking on the damp ground in straw shoes. Their feet in the straw shoes make a scratchy sound. They say nothing." The author presents these as perfectly "normal" tasks, and yet these men also "can see a bird walking in trees. It isn't a bird. It is a woman who has removed her skin and is on her way to drink the blood of her secret enemies." In both cases, Kincaid reclaims these denigrated figures and, additionally, questions the belief in the immutability of culture and tradition. When read as a colonial critique, "In the Night" demonstrates that those who have been designated as lowly or inferior (the colonized) need not claim or remain in that position.

Finally, Kincaid's depiction of night-soil men supports the idea that At the Bottom of the River is not necessarily a work of magical realism. Through this character, the writer reveals the everyday nature of the fantastic and the fantastic nature of the everyday. Kincaid embeds references to spiritual beliefs and practices in paragraphs that detail perfectly ordinary events. The woman who removes "her skin and is on her way to drink the blood of her secret enemies" is also "a woman who is reasonable and admires honeybees in the hibiscus. It is a woman who, as a joke, brays like a donkey when he is thirsty." Later in the story, while a man makes "his wife a beautiful mahogany chest, someone is sprinkling a colorless powder outside a closed door so that someone else's child will be stillborn." Anne Tyler, who reviewed *At the Bottom of the River* for the *New Republic,* addresses this feature of the collection when she says that Jamaica Kincaid's scrutiny of apparent minutiae affords them mystical importance.

Jamaica Kincaid has said that her creative process involves using and then reinventing reality. This allows her to lay bare the artificial nature of categories and the structures that thrive on categorization. In her oeuvre, she worries the boundaries of various "truths"; ultimately, her process teaches readers to do the same. *At the Bottom of the River* illustrates this idea most lyrically.

Rhonda Denise Frederick

SELECTED BIBLIOGRAPHY

Bloom, Harold, ed. *Jamaica Kincaid: Modern Critical Views.* New York: Chelsea House, 1998.

Cudjoe, Selwyn R. "Jamaica Kincaid and the Modernist Project: An Interview." In Selwyn R. Cudjoe, ed., *Caribbean Women Writers: Essays from the First International Conference.* Wellesley, Mass.: Calaloux Publications, 1990.

Ferguson, Moira. *Jamaica Kincaid: Where the Land Meets the Body.* Charlottesville: University Press of Virginia, 1994.

Simmons, Diane. *Jamaica Kincaid.* New York: Twayne, 1994.

Vorda, Allan. "'I Come from a Place That's Very Unreal': An Interview with Jamaica Kincaid." In Allan Vorda, ed., *Face to Face: Interviews with Contemporary Novelists,* pp. 77–105. Houston: Rice University Press, 1993.

RING LARDNER
(1885–1933)

In the 1920s, Ring Lardner was one of America's most acclaimed writers of short fiction. Virginia Woolf hailed his baseball stories as "the best prose that has come our way." H. L. Mencken declared, "There is more of sheer reality in such a story as 'The Golden Honeymoon' than in the whole canon of Henry James, and there is also, I believe, more expert craftsmanship." And Dorothy Parker, reviewing a retrospective collection of his fiction, wrote, "It is difficult to review these spare and beautiful stories; it would be difficult to review the Gettysburg address."

With the exception of "Haircut," still included in anthologies of short fiction, Lardner's "spare and beautiful stories" are now mostly forgotten. But as the admiration of readers as sharp-eyed as Woolf, Mencken, and Parker should suggest, his work deserves another look. Lardner did not always produce fiction that rose above the ephemeral level of the columns, reports, and comic strips that he turned out during his long career as a newspaperman.

But in stories like "A Busher's Letters Home," "My Roomy," "Champion," "Haircut," "The Love Nest," and "Some Like Them Cold," Lardner combined an unusual gift for vernacular literature with an alternately hilarious and agonizing examination of who gets to appear in the American limelight, who does not, and why.

He was born Ringgold Wilmer Lardner on March 6, 1885, the ninth of nine children. He enjoyed a secluded and privileged boyhood on an estate in Niles, Michigan, where he was cared for by his own private maid and educated, largely by his mother, until the ninth grade. But by the time he graduated from high school, his family's fortune had collapsed. At his father's insistence, he entered engineering school, an experiment that lasted less than a semester. After a year spent starring as a blackface performer in Niles (he would retain a lifelong love of musical theater and a lifelong belief in the inferiority of black people), he moved on to a career in journalism, working first in South Bend, Indiana, and then in Chicago. On the basis of his witty, unconventional coverage of the local baseball teams, the *Chicago Tribune* hired him as a regular columnist in 1913. The next year, he published six stories in the *Saturday Evening Post* about a brash, semiliterate pitcher named Jack Keefe, and achieved instant national fame.

The first of these stories, "A Busher's Letters Home," is the best and can be read without reference to any of its many sequels. (After chronicling Jack Keefe's first two seasons in *You Know Me Al* [1916], Lardner would send him into the army in

Treat 'Em Rough [1918] and *The Real Dope* [1919], and bring him back to the playing field in a daily comic strip called *You Know Me Al,* syndicated in 1923 and 1924.) In a series of seventeen brief letters from Jack to a hometown friend, Lardner records the quick rise and equally quick fall of a "busher," a minor leaguer attempting to break into the major leagues. Jack has what he calls "stuff"—a smoking fastball—but he refuses instruction in the craft of pitching. Just before the start of the season, his manager takes him aside and says, "Boy why don't you get to work? I says What do you mean? Ain't I working? He says You ain't improving none . . . you don't go after bunts and you don't cover first base and you don't watch the baserunners. He made me kind of sore talking that way and I says Oh I guess I can get along all right."

Like many other Americans in an era typified by the rapid growth of complex, impersonal networks of production and publicity, Jack wants to believe that he can acquire a professional identity without accepting a position within an existing system. His incessant bragging—"I have a world of speed and they can't foul me when I am right"—is one manifestation of this belief. Another is his inability to play cards. In one letter, he describes to Al a game of draw poker in which he is dealt three sevens and picks up the fourth on the draw. Rather than increase the pot with raises, he simply calls Kelly's fifty-cent bet, takes his modest winnings, and quits. When Kelly mocks his incompetence, Jack says, "I got a notion to take a punch at you." Kelly says, "Oh you have have you? And I come back at him. I says

Yes I have have I? I would of busted his jaw if they hadn't stopped me. You know me Al."

That tag phrase—"You know me Al"—neatly encapsulates the guiding principle of Jack's character: the desire to be, and be recognized as being, always already identical to himself. Though Lardner clearly sympathizes with this desire, he also wants us to recognize its limitations. Because Jack's ideal of autonomous selfhood prevents him from entering, or even acknowledging, the organizational structure of games, he is, despite his tremendous natural abilities, a terrible baseball player. "A Busher's Letters Home" ends with Jack's being sent back to the minors, complaining to the end about the "luck" of those who get to stay in the majors.

In satirizing Jack's shortcomings as a player of games, Lardner implicitly aligns himself with the philosophy of identity that was promoted in the early decades of the twentieth century by a group of writers and reformers that the critic William Gleason has dubbed the "play theorists." According to one of these theorists, Joseph Lee, you are only fully an "individual" when you are "holding down the part assigned to you in the economy of the social whole to which you may belong, as the boy in the school team holds down third base." In the 1910s and 1920s, when the highest form of individuality was generally conceded to be, in Gleason's words, "a by-product of corporate membership," Jack Keefe's version of selfhood could hardly help but seem, at the very least, archaic.

At the very most, it could seem a form of insanity. In "My Roomy" (1914), the focal character is again a "busher" with extraordinary raw talent who refuses to field (when asked why he doesn't try to catch the balls that are hit to him in the outfield, he replies, "Because I don't want 'em"). But this time this first-person narration is handled by the busher's roommate, and the busher, Elliot, turns out to be more than just eccentric. When he is exposed as an incompetent poker player, he sings at the top of his lungs until the rest of the players leave. "You're some buster!" the narrator says to him. "You bust up ball games in the afternoon and poker games at night." "Yes," Elliot says, "that's my business—bustin' things." As if to prove it, he "picked up the pitcher of ice-water that was on the floor and throwed it out the window—through the glass and all." It is an act of violence against figuration itself, a defensive literalization of a metaphor that had threatened to displace and condense his identity. Because his identity is resolutely individual, rather than corporate, Elliot distrusts representations that do not remain attached to the things they represent (including his own first name, Buster, which he keeps a secret from the team). In most twentieth-century American literature and film, that distrust is the admirable expression of a vestigial but nostalgically preserved Americanness; in "My Roomy," it is a prelude to self-annihilation. When the manager loses patience with him and has him sold to another team, Elliot "goes up to the lookin'-glass and stares at himself for five minutes. Then, all of a sudden, he hauls off and takes a wallop at his reflection in the glass." After smearing a handful of blood on the narrator's face, he runs out of the hotel; the next—and last—we hear of him is a letter from an asylum. The narrator's pronouncement on him at the beginning of the story ultimately serves as a kind of epitaph: "he'd be the greatest ballplayer in the world if he could just play ball."

The distance that Lardner establishes between his narrator's normality and El-liot's abnormality should not be mistaken for an unequivocal repudiation of what Elliot stands for. It is worth noticing, in this context, that the narrator's judgment on Elliot is virtually identical to the judg-ment that Lardner's critics had begun to pass on him by the mid-1920s. Initially drawn to Lardner by his virtuoso powers as a vernacularist, they began to wish aloud that he would expand his stylistic range. But he would not "play ball"; he would not do what it took to enter the literary version of the major leagues. After a long night of drinking with his Long Island neighbor F. Scott Fitzgerald and the lit-erary critic Edmund Wilson in the early 1920s, Lardner told Wilson that "the trou-ble was he couldn't write straight En-glish." When Wilson asked him to clarify, Lardner said, "I can't write a sentence like 'We were sitting in the Fitzgeralds' house and the fire was burning brightly.'" In the words of Abe North, the character mod-eled on Lardner in Fitzgeralds' *Tender Is the Night,* there was something in him whose business was "to tear things up." But if this interior something, this "roomy," kept him out of the major leagues, it also made him an extraordi-narily vital, unpredictable writer. Take, for instance, his list of the ten most beau-tiful words in the English language, writ-ten down as part of a parlor game in the 1920s: "Gangrene, flit, scram, mange, wretch, smoot, guzzle, McNaboe, blute and crene." In its violent swerving away from the canons of beauty, and in its in-dulgence in a purely syllabic pleasure, it captures, prismatically, the light, restless, destructive spirit of Lardner's finest work.

The ambivalence generated by the op-position of "busting" to "playing ball" did not extend to the other important op-positions that structured Lardner's sto-ries: the opposition of "straight" to "fixed" matches and the opposition of critical to uncritical spectatorship. Especially after the Black Sox scandal, in which a group of Chicago White Sox players were paid to throw the 1919 World Series, Lardner made it his mission to rail against every-thing that conspired to make the American playing field something other than level. And as the mass media he worked in be-came more sophisticated and pervasive, Lardner became increasingly contemp-tuous of the passive, insatiable spectators it cultivated and fed, a crowd of nonpar-ticipants lost in what he called, in a 1922 essay, "an excess of anile idolatry."

Accordingly, the stories that focus on fixed matches and uncritical spectators might seem to have little to recommend them. In "Champion" (1916), for in-stance, Lardner clearly wants the reader to loathe the various fixes that make it possible for the brutal Midge Kelly to be-come an admired boxing champion, and to disdain the fans who believe that the fights and the reports of the fights are "straight." Rather than suggest, compli-cate, and work through its central the-matic conflicts, in the manner of realist or modernist fiction, "Champion" lays out conflicts that are decided in advance, in the manner of sentimental reform fiction. What this means, of course, is that the story itself is fixed, no less than the matches it wants to deplore.

Lardner's genius is to have recognized this, and to have brought the fix inherent in the genre of sentimental reform fiction to the surface of his narrative. The story opens with a scene in which Midge spies a half dollar belonging to his brother Connie, "three years his junior and a cripple." Connie tries to cover the coin with his hand, "but the movement lacked the speed requisite to escape his brother's quick eye." "Watcha got there?" asks Midge. "Nothin'," says Connie. "You're a one legged liar!" says Midge, and knocks his brother cold. With that final, ridiculously broad stroke, we enter the bitterly comic fictional universe that Nathanael West would soon make his own. Midge goes on to knock down his mother; to deliver "a crushing blow on [his] bride's pale cheek"; to run out on his wife and baby; to knock down his brother-in-law when he asks for child support; to jilt his manager for a new one; to jilt his girlfriend for the wife of his new manager; and to become the welterweight champion of the world. Incapable of being ambivalent about his subject and incapable of trusting unambivalent representation, Lardner chooses, perversely, to rev his worn-out narrative vehicle until it smoots, blutes, and crenes.

In the world of the story, Lardner's closest likeness is Midge's last manager, Wallie Adams. When asked by a reporter for the story of Midge's life, Wallie "step[s] on the accelerator of his imagination": "Just a kid; that's all he is; a regular boy. Get what I mean? Don't know the meanin'

o' bad habits. Never tasted liquor in his life and would prob'bly get sick if he smelled it. Clean livin' put him up where he's at. Get what I mean?" Over the course of the interview, Wallie interrupts himself eight times, after a perfectly evident and ordinary statement, to say, "Get what I mean?" The phrase becomes an instrument of humiliation, because what it really asks, with an insinuating nudge, is, "Don't you know the shape of this narrative in advance?" Of course we do; it is one of those culturally privileged tunes whose incessant airings and equally incessant requests have lodged it in each of our brains. That, for Lardner, is the problem with the encomiums to champions that get printed in the sports pages *and* with the debunkings of champions, like "Champion," that get printed in literary magazines.

That is not to say that "Champion" represents the only conceivable way of making interesting art out of an obsession with fixers and idolaters. In "Haircut" (1925), Lardner complicates his theme by suggesting that certain kinds of fixing and idolizing may be ethically acceptable. The town "half-wit," Paul Dickson, idolizes a woman named Julie Gregg, who feels nothing but pity for him. She, in turn, idolizes the town's new physician, Doc Stair, who thinks of her as "just a young lady that wanted to see the doctor." When her crush is exposed and ridiculed by Jim Kendall, a "jokesmith" who has it in for her because she has repeatedly refused his advances, she retreats in embarrassment to her home. After finding out who is responsible for the disappearance of his idol, Paul Dickson gets Jim to take him duck shooting, borrows his gun, and shoots him dead. Doc Stair, who has previously told Paul that anyone who would play a joke like that on a girl like Julie "ought not to be let live," declares, in his capacity as coroner, that there is no need for a jury, "as it was a plain case of accidental shootin'."

Because Jim is an unusually detestable character, the reader's sympathy can hardly help but be drawn in the direction of the fiercely uncritical idolater, Paul, and the behind-the-scenes fixer, Doc. Lardner seems to want his readers to consider the possibility of exceptions to rules: Might the uncritical idolatry of a woman be a good thing, even if it leads to the murder of her oppressor? Might the fixing of the evidence of a shooting be a good thing, even if it allows a murderer to evade trial?

But even as he raises these questions, Lardner interferes with the inclination to grant such exceptions. The primary source of the story's humor, after all, is the incongruity between Jim's derivative, mean-spirited self-aggrandizement and the first-person narrator's insistence that Jim is exceptional—a "card," a "character," and a "caution." The narrator, Whitey, remembers at one point that Jim used to call Paul "cuckoo; that's a name Jim had for anybody that was off their head, only he called people's head their bean. That was another of his gags, callin' head bean and callin' crazy people cuckoo. Only poor Paul ain't crazy, but just silly." Whitey takes each of Jim's commonplace slang words to be "an expression of Jim's himself," a sign of his irreducible sense of self. Though Whitey does not believe that Paul is crazy, he willingly brackets the question of Paul's sanity when Jim calls him cuckoo, because, as he says of another of Jim's gags, "Nobody could of thought it up but Jim Kendall." A Jim Kendall gag may sometimes be a "raw thing," but Whitey believes that Jim's character is constructed in such a way that he "couldn't resist no kind of a joke, no matter how raw. . . . He was all right at heart, but just bubblin' over with mischief."

If readers decide that Doc and Paul are properly exempt from criminal law because Jim is exceptionally wicked, they merely invert Whitey's "excess of anile idolatry," attributing to Jim a "bubblin' over" diabolism that legitimates any assault on his person or his rights. If they decide that Doc and Paul are exempt because their immediate motive is exceptionally pure, they again put themselves in the position of the uncritical idolater; by making an exception for Doc and Paul because they are championing affronted womanhood, readers set aside a "bubblin' over" chivalry—a mode of idolatry in its own right—as an always excusable object of worship. In either case, moreover, readers fail to remember that everything they know about the interiors of these characters comes by way of Whitey, and that Whitey, by profession and by temperament, is a handler of the surfaces of people's heads. The last words of the story— "Comb it wet or dry?"—serve as reminders that in the real time of the narrative, Whitey has been clipping and arranging the hair of a stranger who has done nothing but sit silently in his chair. It is a signature Lardner move; he gives us a story whose moral dimension seems to depend on some knowledge of what is going on in the minds of its central characters, but accompanies the story with the running image of a head whose interior is beyond the reader's grasp.

In the last years of his life, Ring Lardner produced very little memorable work. He was diagnosed with tuberculosis in 1926, but he did not begin a serious course of treatment for another four years. As the tuberculosis progressed, so did his alcoholism. By the time of the stock market crash, his extended drinking bouts were ending in hospital stays. To protect his wife and four sons, he checked into a hotel whenever he felt a bender coming on and invested heavily in life insurance. In *Tender Is the Night,* Fitzgerald would write, "All of them were conscious of the solemn dignity that flowed from [Abe North], of his achievement, fragmentary, suggestive, and surpassed. But they were frightened at his survivant will, once a will to live, now become a will to die." To all appearances, that something in him that was driven to bust things had curled around and burrowed into his vitals. He died of a heart attack on September 25, 1933.

Geoffrey Sanborn

SELECTED BIBLIOGRAPHY

Works by Ring Lardner

The Portable Ring Lardner. Edited by Gilbert Seldes. New York: Viking, 1946.
Selected Stories. Edited by Jonathan Yardley. Harmondsworth: Penguin, 1997.

Critical Studies

Lardner, Ring, Jr. The Lardners: My Family Remembered. New York: Harper & Row, 1976.
Robinson, Douglas. Ring Lardner and the Other. New York: Oxford University Press, 1992.
Yardley, Jonathan. Ring: A Biography of Ring Lardner. New York: Random House, 1977.

DAVID LEAVITT
(1961–)

David Leavitt "came out in *The New Yorker* in more ways than one," he has said, when he was only a college junior: his short story "Territory" was the first that magazine had ever published on gay experience. That debut in 1983, quickly followed by the publication of his short story collection *Family Dancing* in 1984, earned him a literary reputation both impressive and burdensome. Prodigy, gay pioneer, spokesperson for a generation, Leavitt has experienced both the glamour and the detraction that come with early media attention. He returned to the short story after writing two novels, *The Lost Language of Cranes* (1986) and *Equal Actions* (1989), and in 1990 published a second collection entitled *A Place I've Never Been* (1990). His reputation suffered a jolt with the publication of his next novel, *While England Sleeps,* a venture into historical fiction modeled in part on Stephen Spender's autobiography that drew charges of plagiarism from the elder writer. Since then Leavitt has written a collection of novellas entitled *Arkansas* (1997), in one of which ("The Term Paper Artist") he responds to the Spender incident. His most recent novel, *The Page Turner* (1999), revisits the subject of his early fame, though with the figure of a musician rather than a writer. Leavitt has also coedited two anthologies of gay writers, *The Penguin Book of Gay Short Stories* (1994) and *Pages Passed from Hand to Hand: The Hidden Tradition of Homosexual Literature in English from 1748 to 1914* (1997).

David Leavitt was born in Pittsburgh on June 23, 1961, the son of Harold Jack Leavitt and Gloria Rosenthal Leavitt. The family, which also included older siblings John and Emily, soon moved to Palo Alto, California, where his father was a professor of organizational behavior at Stanford University and his mother was active in political causes. In 1979 Leavitt went to Yale University, where he met his creative writing mentors, Gordon Lish and John Hersey. After graduation, Leavitt moved to New York and worked briefly in publishing. More recently, he has been living in Italy, writing and coediting anthologies of gay writers with his partner Mark Mitchell.

On *Family Dancing*'s cover is a collage of photographs of suburban houses. This is Leavitt's "territory," as the first story in the collection is titled, a landscape of upper middle-class suburbs and families, but also an exploded or fragmented version of that world. In "Territory," a young gay man returning to his suburban California home invites his New York lover for a visit, only to recognize that this relationship does not fit in his mother's "territory." In the setting of mothers and dogs and middle-aged women playing Mozart trios, Leavitt's protagonist and his lover are sexual marauders. What the nuclear family can house, what needs it fails to meet,

how its exiles survive in the aftermath of its various devastations: these are the topics and themes of Leavitt's collection of stories.

The incommensurable "territories" of a solitary mother and her gay son are followed by other solitudes and separations. In "Counting Months" and "Radiation," women with cancer, deserted by their husbands and weighted with fears for their children's own vulnerable lives, learn to live on with things that would once have been unendurable to them, past their death sentences, past their memories of youthful bravado. Survivors of cancer, divorce, abandonment, the mothers of Leavitt's stories seem to take all the punishment, bear all the burdens. The fathers, if they appear at all, are distant and emotionally absent. In "The Lost Cottage," a family gathers, at the mother's insistence, for a Cape Cod reunion even though her husband has divorced her and remarried six months earlier. When one of the sons endorses her commitment to family tradition, his clear-eyed sister responds, a bit sententiously, "Tradition can become repetition . . . when you end up holding onto something just because you're afraid to let it go. I am ready to let it go."

But few can "let it go" entirely. In "Family Dancing," the title story of the volume, a graduation party culminates in a grotesque dance of the shattered nuclear family. Like planets that have not lost their gravitational attractions (and repulsions), they are drawn to one another, careen around, stumble. The abandoned ex-wife clings to her ex-husband; their closeted gay son, newly graduated, is drawn in as a buffer between them, and their angry, obese daughter is pushed against her will "into the center of the circle, into the reeling inner circle of her family."

The last story, "Dedication," introduces a group of characters, friends from college, who will become benchmark figures for Leavitt, appearing again in *A Place I've Never Been* and in one of the novellas in *Arkansas*. In this their first appearance, Celia and her two gay friends Nathan and Andrew form a triad: Celia, in love with Nathan, fond of Andrew, becomes first the conduit and then the excluded middle of their relation. The prohibition that exiles her is like the voice of the bouncer at the gay bar: "Sorry . . . no women allowed." As Celia wonders about her "dedication" to these men, she registers the lure and inadequacy of Nathan's jesting tribute: "You know . . . you're wonderful. When I write my book, I'm dedicating it to you."

Family Dancing is, in fact, dedicated to women—Leavitt's mother and Deborah Reade, presumably his friend. Yet its depiction of women is troubling. Their bodies are, with a few exceptions, fat or cancer-ridden. Their husbands desert them, or they are the defeated rivals of gay men and younger women for the attentions of men they desire. Is it sympathy or animus that motivates these portraits? Their abjection seems at times gratuitous, even ornamental. The gay sons suffer a guilt toward women that might seem more compassionate than the indifference of their heterosexual fathers, but the guilt itself often seems a cover for their own independent cruelties.

In *A Place I've Never Been* Leavitt shifts his focus from the family to the lives of young single men and women in New York, California, and Europe. Place is still a crucial metaphor, but now it signifies something about the nature of experience for this generation: both its "been there, done that" reductive worldliness and its new geography as remapped by the spread of AIDS. For the first time, Leavitt acknowledges the inescapable presence of AIDS in his "territory" as a gay male writer. In the title story, Nathan and Celia, now on the verge of thirty, are reassessing the terms of the game of life. Nathan, whose ex-lover has tested positive for HIV, and who avoids finding out about his own status just as he avoids sexual encounters, lives in a place of fear that Celia "has never been." Celia, meanwhile, is moving new places in her own life; during the long months of Nathan's absence in Europe—his attempt to escape the virus—she has shed weight as well the shelter of Nathan's frustrating companionship, and now she is on the verge of a love affair herself. The crossed purposes of this homosexual-heterosexual pair, the mismatch of their desires and longings, comes out with a poignancy and anger here, as if in response to the reticences of that earlier story about their "dedication" to each other.

In other stories in the volume, the unvisited places takes a variety of other forms. In "AYOR," an acronym used in the *Spartacus Guide for Gay Men* for "at your own risk," the narrator avoids places of risk and desire, experiencing them instead second hand through the forays of his friend Craig. Like a classic tale of the double, "AYOR" makes Craig a kind of picture for the narrator's Dorian Gray; Craig's body suffers the damage of living out desire in this era, while the narrator "always end[s] up at home—alone, but unscathed. Safe."

Several stories, following the lead of the title story, balance the claims of homosexual and heterosexual lives. In "Married to Vengeance," a woman attends the wedding of her former lover and registers the tremendous social power of heterosexual life choices. Seated at a table with the social misfits, she watches the bride, gleaming and beautiful, draw the eyes of the assembled guests. Later, in the women's room, the ex-lover sheds tears and reveals doubts, but the narrator knows that there is much in that conventional choice to make for her former lover's happiness. In "Houses," by contrast, the male narrator is coming out of just such a marriage; closeted and married to a childhood friend, he is torn with ambivalence about the domestic life that sustains him and the man of his dreams who would take him out of it.

Two stories at the end of the volume move away from the American settings—New York, East Hampton, northern California—to Italy. The first of these "international theme" tales (shades of Henry James), "I See London, I See France," brings Celia in contact with lives and worlds painfully different from her own. When her fiancé rather presumptuously offers one such exquisite world to her, she insists on its inaccessibility: "It's not that I want to live here *now,* it's that I want to *have* lived here . . . to be the sort of person who grew up in this sort of place." But when she finds that the inhabitants of this beautiful Italian villa also long for something they have missed, she feels a link between her mundane past and this present, a "mysterious thread" that connects the Queens of her childhood to this enchanted Tuscany.

The volume's concluding story, "All Roads Lead to Rome," picks up the "mysterious thread" that binds America to Europe. An American ingenue—in Leavitt's version a gay man—visits his lover's complex Italian family when the matriarch is dying, prompting reflections on the courses their lives have taken, the losses they have suffered, the way things might have gone. Guilt over a son who committed suicide mingles with nostalgic memories of liberating American soldiers at the end of World War II. Now, bathing again in the healing waters of the spring where the soldiers once came, the old woman sees liberation again in this young American, sees both the lost son and the distant rescuers. But what salvation can this young man possibly bring? If "all roads do lead to Rome," the volume ends with a great forgiving cosmopolitanism, an insistence not on "the road not taken" or the "place I've never been" (the experience that one has missed), but on the generous convergences of lives whatever the paths that have led them to that place.

Leavitt has been both criticized and praised for making gay writing mainstream. By detailing gay life in the context of the upper middle-class family or the privileged postgraduate worlds of Ivy League-educated urban sophisticates, by moving with ease between the lives of male and female, gay and straight characters, he has clearly fallen short of the political expectations of certain readers. David Leavitt's "territory" is not, as he is quick to acknowledge, that of the gay writers of the 1970s whose work documents the sexual frontiers of a gay urban scene. But if that "mainstreaming" of gay writing is his defect, it is also his virtue; and in his short stories, in particular, one senses an imagination of all kinds of "other places" and of the roads that lead there, even if they are places he has never been.

Julie Rivkin

SELECTED BIBLIOGRAPHY

Works by David Leavitt

Family Dancing. New York: Alfred A. Knopf, 1984.
A Place I've Never Been. New York: Viking, 1990.

Critical Studies

Harned, Joe. "Psychoanalysis, Queer Theory, and David Leavitt's *Lost Language of Cranes.*" *South Central Bulletin* 11/4 (winter 1994): 40–53.
Lawson, D. S. "David Leavitt (1961–). In Emmanuel S. Nelson, ed., *Contemporary Gay American Novelists: A Bio-Bibliographical Critical Sourcebook,* pp. 248–253. Westport, Conn.: Greenwood, 1993.
Lo, Mun-hou. "David Leavitt and the Etiological Maternal Body." *Modern Fiction Studies* 41/3–4: 429–465.

URSULA K. LE GUIN
(1929–)

U rsula K. Le Guin achieved national recognition for her short stories and novels in the 1970s. She is revered for her world building, lyrical style, character-centered stories, experimental structures, and moral concerns. Her primary themes are political rebellion and freedom, self and other, loyalty and betrayal, liminality and alienation, and communication.

Le Guin was born in 1929 into a family that not only encouraged her independence and development, evidenced by her submitting her first science fiction story at the age of twelve to *Amazing Stories,* but also provided a milieu of cultural study and relativism. Her father, Alfred Kroeber (1876–1960), was one of the founders of modern anthropology; her mother, Theodora Kracaw Kroeber (1897–1979), was a psychologist and writer, the author of the best-selling *Ishi in Two Worlds.* Studying new worlds, writing, reading *Tao Te Ching,* living in California on the edge of the continent, were all formative influences.

After completing a bachelors of arts degree at Radcliffe College and a master of arts and doctoral work at Columbia University in French and Italian renaissance poetry, Le Guin received a Fulbright scholarship to France, where she met and married the historian Charles A. Le Guin in 1953. She and her husband have three children and several grandchildren and live in Portland and Cannon Beach, Oregon.

Her career as a professional writer began in 1962 when she sold her first science fiction story. After three apprenticeship novels, she published *A Wizard of Earthsea* in 1968 and *The Left Hand of Darkness* in 1969, each launching a series of related works—the Earthsea quartet and the

Hainish future history stories. To date she has published eight short story collections, sixteen novels, two nonfiction collections, five books of poetry, and ten books for children, and she has won numerous awards, including the National Book Award, the Newbery Silver Medal, five Hugos, five Nebulas, the Kafka Prize, and the Pushcart Prize.

She published her first collection of short stories, *The Wind's Twelve Quarters*, in 1975, followed the next year by a collection of linked stories, *Orsinian Tales*. These two collections set the patterns for all but one of her short story collections; the books contain either groupings of short stories previously uncollected (*Compass Rose*, 1982; *Fisherman of the Inland Sea*, 1994; *Unlocking the Air*, 1996) or linked stories (*Searoad*, 1991; *Four Ways to Forgiveness*, 1995). The one exception is *Buffalo Gals and Other Animal Presences* (1987), a thematic collection of poems and stories, some previously collected. Her increased interest in short fiction, ranging in length from the parable to the novella, is evident: since 1991 she has published four of her eight collections as well as more than a dozen stories, as yet uncollected.

Le Guin has published more than one hundred short stories along a literary spectrum that includes fantasy, science fiction, and realism. The spectrum is a particularly useful metaphor because Le Guin has experimented with an increasing variety of story forms. Although she does not mix science fiction and fantasy, she does hybridize fantasy and realism when she writes magical realism ("Ether, OR"), mixes realism and essay ("Limberlost"), revisions old myths and tales ("The Poacher"), and writes narrative jokes in the form of nonfactual reports ("Ascent of the North Face").

Besides genre, Le Guin's stories are known by their fictional worlds: the Hainish universe, Earthsea, Orsinia, and the future and present American West. Le Guin's work has become a touchstone for cohesive, resonant world building through the details of invented languages, architecture, topography, food, clothing, political structures, literature, cultural rituals, climate, history, major cities, and technology and tools.

The Hainish universe consists of more than one hundred planets on which the people of Hain established some form of humanoid life over a million years ago and with which the Hainish, Le Guin imagines, are now trying to reestablish contact. Here Le Guin has created thought experiments for social and political models. "Semley's Necklace" (1964) and "Winter's King" (1969) were her earliest Hainish short stories; many of her major science fiction novels (1969–1974) are set in this world, and several new stories have appeared in the 1990s.

Earthsea is an archipelago, the setting for Le Guin's four fantasy novels (1968–1990); except for two early short stories, "The Word of Unbinding" and "The Rule of Names," she has not used Earthsea for her short fiction. Orsinia, on the other hand, is predominantly a setting for her short fiction; it is a landlocked, central European country that she invented very early in her apprenticeship. Le Guin treats the place and the people realistically, including their sharing of central European history from the twelfth century to the mid-twentieth century, during which small countries like Czechoslovakia were frequently conquered by powerful neighbors. *Orsinian Tales* was followed by the novel *Malafrena* (1979); "Unlocking The Air," the title story of Le Guin's latest short story collection (1996), is her most recent excursion to Orsinia.

The future and the contemporary American West have been settings for science fiction short stories and semirealistic stories, respectively. Le Guin used both settings in the 1970s, most notably in the science fiction novella "The New Atlantis" (1975) and in the realistic story "Malheur County" (1979). *Searoad* (1991) is a collection of linked stories set in the fictional town of Klatsand on the Oregon coast. Ordinary people facing the death of a parent or partner, sexual preference, troubled marriage, thwarted dreams and ambitions look for ways to deal with their losses and each other.

Le Guin's stories raise questions about the relationships between individuals and various political structures, between humans and the rest of existence, about the nature of gender differences, of reality, and of human nature itself. But her stories do not definitively answer the questions that she raises. Le Guin's metaphor for her work is the drafty house. As she said in a 1998 interview, "Opening doors in walls is the image I always get back to. If I have any particular job as a writer, it's to open as many doors and windows as possible and to leave them open. So the house gets drafty."

Her characters are often on the threshold of society or knowledge or personal change: a scientist working on a new theory in "Another Story or the Fisherman or the Inland Sea"; a diplomat entering forced or chosen exile, an artist trying to represent new perceptions in paint or words, a woman bearing a new stage of development in "Quoits." Her stories resist the traditional male hero who is tested by adventures and violence. Risk, in a Le Guin story, is apt to be the act of reaching out to the other, the stranger, in love or trust or cooperation. The images of touching and of the outstretched or the wounded hand recur, and in her 1988 collection Le Guin has referred to the "space between us (in which both cruelty and love occur)" as "the sacred place."

Le Guin's lyrical style puts the weight of the meaning of the stories on images and metaphors, cadence and rhythm, tone and repetition. The image of hearth or house, the structure that holds the smallest unit of any social or political system, is prominent. Walls call attention to the rewards and costs of political freedom and security, while trees and rocks portray the solidity of the material world, wild grasses portray the fragility of the environment, and the ocean's edge portrays the fragility of human existence. Woven goods, art objects that use the network or web, and maps of roads or stars suggest the interrelatedness and flux of something as encompassing as all existence or as focused as the experiences of a person's life. Language itself is frequently a subject of her stories—the importance of naming, words as acts, gendered language, and the irony in the figurative made literal (in "Ether, OR," the town of Ether is "a real American town, a place that isn't where you left it" because it literally shifts its location while the residents sleep).

In a statement made in a 1994 interview, Le Guin said that art opens up the world; "We're drawn in—or out—and the windows of our perception are cleansed, as William Blake said." In her experimentation with point of view, Le Guin challenges her readers' comfortable perspectives and assumptions about reality. The story may be told from the perspective of a tree ("Direction of the Road"), a female wolf whose husband is transformed into human shape ("The Wife's Story"), or an intelligent alien who is forced to run mazes by the scientist studying it ("The Mazes"). More frequently, she has been using multiple perspectives for a single story, such as "Hernes"; writing paired stories such as "A Man of the People" and "A Women's Liberation"; and using magical realism as in "Buffalo Girls Won't You Come Out Tonight?" Sometimes, as in "The Shobies' Story," her stories are about storytelling itself.

Readers of one or several Le Guin stories can appreciate the richness of her work by considering it in the context of her own fiction, her times, and literary history as can be seen in an early, a middle, and a late story. Study of "A Week in the Country" (1976), one of Le Guin's first Orsinian stories, will reward the reader with a sense of how Le Guin weaves in image, character, and politics to make a story and how that single unit connects outward to her other stories. Stefan Fabbre's coming-of-age experiences are traumatic: while on vacation with his best friend, he falls in love with his friend's sister, experiences the murder of his best friend by the police who supposedly mistake him for a political rebel, and endures a brief imprisonment and torture. In an atmosphere of political oppression, Fabbre must choose what to do in the face of such pain and loss. Images of house and

road capture the tensions between security and journey, duration and change. Connections to Le Guin's other stories are numerous. Members of the Fabbre family also appear in "Brothers and Sisters" and "Unlocking the Air," while the themes of political freedom and rebellion figure in nearly every Hainish story. The community and house that signify home calls to mind the long Klatsand story "Hernes," while vowing fidelity in the face of tragedy is also found in her earliest Hainish short story, "Winter's King." In fact, Le Guin has commented that "underneath everything I write there is this sense of the tragic."

"Sur" (1982) illustrates Le Guin's lyrical style, genre experimentation, and feminism. In this story of a women's secret exploration of the South Pole a few months before the expeditions of Amundsen and Scott, Le Guin explores women's ways of doing and perceiving in work, art, friendships, and writing. Because Le Guin is challenging a variety of assumptions, readers can research the history of polar explorations; discussions of gendered languages, narrative structure, and perceptions of reality; women's use of private journals; arguments about genre definitions; and the author's other published works of the same period. Consideration of Le Guin's lyrical style, evident in the poetic descriptions of Antarctica and the journey, also leads to an analysis of tone and the differences between the sadness and joy felt by the fictional writer and by the actual reader.

"The Shobies' Story" (1994) focuses on the crew members of the spaceship *Shoby*, who will be the first humans from the Hainish world to travel through space instantaneously, due to the development of the churten drive. The story is bileveled, comprising both space adventure and metafiction. The crewmembers and their social structure, mission, and response to crisis can be fruitfully contrasted to the more traditional space adventure story. With the churten drive, like the ansible (Le Guin's previous Hainish invention— a device for near-instantaneous communication across space), Ursula Le Guin explores the relationship between a technological tool and the cultures that use it. Furthermore, the churten drive can be considered as a metaphor, and the entire story can be read as a story about the nature of fiction; the leap across space is also the leap from the everyday world to the fictive world.

Elizabeth Cummins

SELECTED BIBLIOGRAPHY

Works by Ursula K. Le Guin

The Wind's Twelve Quarters. New York: Harper & Row, 1975.

Orsinian Tales. New York: Harper & Row, 1976.

The Compass Rose: Short Stories. New York: Harper & Row, 1982.

Buffalo Gals and Other Animal Presences. Santa Barbara: Capra Press, 1987. Reprint, New York: New American Library, Plume, 1988.

Searoad: The Chronicles of Klatsand. HarperCollins, 1991.

A Fisherman of the Inland Sea: Science Fiction Stories. New York: HarperCollins, 1994.

Four Ways to Forgiveness. New York: HarperCollins, 1995.

Unlocking the Air and Other Stories. New York: HarperCollins, 1996.

Critical Studies

Abrash, Merritt. "'The Field of Vision': A Minority View on Ultimate Truth." *Extrapolation* 26 (spring 1985): 5–15.

Attebery, Brian. "Gender, Fantasy, and the Authority of Tradition." *Journal of the Fantastic in the Arts* 7/1 (1996): 51–60.

Bittner, James W. "Persuading Us to Rejoice and Teaching Us How to Praise: Le Guin's *Orsinian Tales*." *Science-Fiction Studies* 5 (November 1978): 215–242.

Rass, Rebecca. *Ursula K. Le Guin's* The Left Hand of Darkness: *A Critical Commentary.* New York: Simon & Schuster, 1990.

Slaughter, Jane. "Ursula K. Le Guin." *The Progressive* 62 (March 1998): 36–39.

Spivack, Charlotte. *Ursula K. Le Guin.* Boston: Twayne, 1984.

White, Jonathan. "Coming Back from the Silence." *Talking on the Water: Conversations About Nature and Creativity.* San Francisco: Sierra Club Books, 1994.

MERIDEL LE SUEUR
(1900–1996)

Meridel Le Sueur was born in Iowa in 1900 and lived through nearly all of the twentieth century to become a voice of conscience for her time. Her mother, socialist educator Marion Wharton, and her Puritan grandmother Antoinette McGovern Lucy, a leader of the Women's

Christian Temperance Union, raised her in the turbulent era of radical populism on the plains until the family relocated to St. Paul, Minnesota, in 1917. By the time Meridel was seventeen, she had met many of the famous "Reds" of her day, including Eugene Debs, Big Bill Haywood, and Emma Goldman, and she was inflamed with stories of the labor wars across the land. In succession she joined the Industrial Workers of the World, the Non-Partisan League, the Populist Party, and the Communist Party, and began writing for *The Masses* (later *New Masses*) and *The Worker*.

Though devastated by the execution of anarchists Nicola Sacco and Bartolomeo Vanzetti in 1927, Le Sueur married and had two daughters against the advice of friends who claimed that a woman should be free to agitate against the coming disaster. Living alone through the Depression, she wrote for the radical press as well as for commercial magazines, such as *The Dial, Scribner's,* and *American Mercury*. Her first story collection, *Salute to Spring,* appeared in 1940. More stories appeared in *Yale Review* and *Kenyon Review,* along with a popular history of the upper Midwest, *North Star Country,* in 1945. Then she was blacklisted by major publishers because of her Communist Party affiliation. Between 1947 and 1958 she published articles in left-wing magazines; her family's history, *Crusaders;* and a privately printed story collection, *Corn Village*.

After 1970 Le Sueur was "rehabilitated," in large part by the feminist movement. A women's collective produced a film about her life and work, *My People Are My Home,* in 1973, and Patricia Hampl interviewed her for *Ms.* A collection of

poems, *Rites of Ancient Ripening,* appeared in 1975. West End Press published two story collections, *Harvest* and *Song for My Time,* in 1977, as well as two novels, *The Girl* in 1978 and *I Hear Men Talking* in 1984. Feminist Press produced *Ripening,* collected writings with a critical introduction by Elaine Hedges, in 1982. Her short story "Annunciation" was anthologized in both the *Norton Anthology of Literature by Women* and the *Heath Anthology of American Literature*. She and Toni Morrison delivered the keynote speeches at the American Writer's Congress in 1981 in New York, and she lectured tirelessly on college campuses until 1990. She published an experimental novel, *The Dread Road,* with West End Press in 1991, and left portions of three other novels in manuscript at her death in 1996.

Le Sueur's short stories fall into several thematic types. Her early work was passionately psychological. Believing she had suffered abandonment by her mother and victimization at the hands of the male world around her, she retold the story of Demeter and Persephone in "Persephone" (1927). The predatory male archetype in this story is more fully developed in her later fiction, reemerging as Butch in the novel *The Girl* and as Bac in *I Hear Men Talking*. Another early influence was D. H. Lawrence—especially in what Le Sueur called his "passional" writings. Lawrence's voice and subject matter can be most strongly felt in Le Sueur's novella *The Horse* (1939).

Even Le Sueur's most political writings were highly subjective, written from the point of view of a first-person narrator who was frequently an actor in her own story. Although the personal journalism called "reportage" was commonly employed by other radical writers of the 1920s and 1930s, Le Sueur made her narrative voice more emotional, even disruptive in its overtones. Her reportage included works of realism, such as "Women on the Breadlines" (1932); strike reporting, such as "I Was Marching" (1934); dramatized interviews with working-class heroes and heroines, such as "Eroded Woman" (1948); and reflections on the McCarthy period, such as "The Dark of the Time" (1956). Sometimes this mode of writing was transmuted into nightmarish, hallucinatory fiction reminiscent of Poe, as in "Summer Idyll, 1949."

An early story, "Corn Village" (1930), depicts a theme common to midwestern women writers, the harshness of the land and the raw prairie towns. Le Sueur's story reflects her struggle for spiritual existence in a place that terrified her soul. It begins, "Like many Americans, I will never recover from my sparse childhood in Kansas. The blackness, weight and terror of childhood in mid-America strike deep into the stem of life. Like desert flowers we learned to crouch near the earth, fearful that we would die before the rains, cunning, waiting the season of good growth."

The story continues with many scenes illustrating this bleakness, one scene leading to another. Incapable of acting meaningfully against the tyranny of weather and land, the farmers admire the violence of tornadoes, as one of which takes all the buttons off a man's coat. A rejected suitor goes mad and shoots his lover and then himself on the main street of town; an outpouring of grief at the funeral is followed by lethargy, as the families disperse and the men return in silence to their trades. Later, at a revival meeting, even the narrator's Puritan grandmother is stirred, though she believes that sensation of any kind is wicked. But when the evangelist leaves town, the sinners forget they have been saved. At the end, the narrator again evokes Kansas, "your country with its sense of ruin and desolation like a strong raped virgin." She concludes, "I have come from you mysteriously wounded. I have waked from my adolescence to find a wound inflicted on the deep heart. And have seen it in others too, in disabled men and sour women made ugly by ambition, mortified in the flesh and wounded in love." Her Puritan origins have nothing to offer but a warning. Stingy, life-denying forces, bare like the land at winter solstice, assault the innocent heart, pervert the impulse toward growth, and defeat the isolate individual. This is the very negation of life.

In "Annunciation" (1935), Le Sueur moves beyond the figure of the endangered soul to the new image of an expectant mother peering into a dim and dangerous future. In this story, the young girl's radicalism consists of her holding her thoughts in private as she waits in a rented room for her child to be born. While her husband searches for work, she contemplates the pear tree in the garden, the symbol of recurrent beauty in the world, reminding her of the fruit of her womb. Did we all once hang, she wonders, from such a pear tree, awaiting birth into an unknown world? She remembers her argument with her husband, a radical, over having the child. He opposed bringing a child into the world when the world itself needs a revolution. "Why don't you take something?" he says. "Get rid of it. This isn't the time to have a child. Everything is rotten. We must change it."

Seeking somehow to harmonize her vision of the creation of life and her sense that the world must be saved, the young woman writes a letter to her unborn child. "Tonight, the world into which you are coming . . . is very strange and beautiful. . . . The dark glisten of vegetation and the blowing of the fertile land wind and the delicate strong step of the sea wind, these things . . . will be familiar to you. I hope you will be like these things. I hope you will glisten with the glisten of ancient life, the same beauty that is in a leaf or a wild rabbit, wild sweet beauty of limb and eye. . . . I hope you will be a warrior and fierce for change, so all can live." Near the end of the story, her vision complete, the future mother sees herself as a fruit hanging from a tree. Thus she joins the common destiny of women all over the world, fighting for life and the continuity of life.

Le Sueur's later short fiction has not received as much attention as her early stories. But her writing, particularly in the McCarthy period, develops in important ways, taking on a new darkness and shattering distinctions of genre so that reportage becomes nearly incoherent, the stream of consciousness of the lost soul in a world now governed by the atomic bomb and the anticipation of total destruction. In "The Dark of the Time" (1956), Le Sueur takes a bus from St. Paul and joins the people of America on their migrations: the city's wounded returning to the ruined farms, the young mothers fleeing poverty and destitution, the Korean War

soldiers on furlough with nowhere to go. Again, the piece works by a montage of interspersed scenes and short passages of recorded speech. Le Sueur's mastery of description is brought to bear on the ruination of the landscape, the parallel ruination of poverty, and the spiritual ruin of those trying to recover a world now buried under the debris of the Cold War.

"The Dark of the Time" describes Le Sueur journeying south and east to Elizabethtown, Kentucky, where Nancy Hanks gave birth to Abraham Lincoln; then west to Kansas City, where she boards a crack train north again to St. Paul. The train is very slow, because coffins bearing the war dead are being dropped off at prairie towns. The soldiers on board, seeing their comrades going to their final rest, drift from memory to despair. One soldier cries, "Bring me back, that's all I ask. Receive me, furrow. Plow deep for me, Indian Valley, bring me home around the world. O! he cries, this country! O my country. . . . O let me come back to you, roll me back earth, around the world, roll me backward earth and roll me home!" Le Sueur ends this powerful story with a meditation on the role of the artist, who must return a true vision of America to the people.

As a woman writer, Le Sueur insisted on her own version of the radical experience. She emphasized birth and survival over destruction and death, the negative pole of revolution. She advocated the sensual, lived experience over the coldness of the intellect. She fought for the liberation of all people from illusion, whether induced by Puritan values or the new puritanism of Marxism-Leninism. She believed in the word, the use of language as a means of education and agitation. Finally, Meridel Le Sueur affirmed the radicalism of the heart—the idea that passion saves us, passion for life, for change, for seeing our efforts reflected in a better world to come.

John Crawford

SELECTED BIBLIOGRAPHY

Works by Meridel Le Sueur

Corn Village: A Selection. Sauk City: Stanton and Lee, 1970.

Salute to Spring. New York: International Publishers, 1977.

*Ripening: Selected Work, 1927–*1980. Edited by Elaine Hedges. Old Westbury: Feminist Press, 1982.

I Hear Men Talking: Stories of the Early Decades. Minneapolis: West End Press, 1984.

Harvest Song: Collected Essays and Stories. Albuquerque: West End Press, 1990.

The Girl. Revised edition. Albuquerque: West End Press, 1991.

Critical Studies

Coiner, Constance. *Better Red: The Writing and Resistance of Tillie Olsen and Meridel Le Sueur.* New York: Oxford University Press, 1995.

Gelfant, Blanche H. "'Everybody Steals': Language as Theft in Meridel Le Sueur's "The Girl." In Florence Howe, ed., *Tradition and the Talents of Women,* pp. 145–166. Urbana: University of Illinois Press, 1996.

Rabinowitz, Paula. *Labor and Desire: Women's Revolutionary Fiction in Depression America.* Chapel Hill: University of North Carolina Press, 1991.

SHIRLEY GEOK-LIN LIM
(1944–)

Shirley Geok-lin Lim, professor of English and women's studies at the University of California, Santa Barbara, has published three collections of short stories, *Another Country and Other Stories* (1982), *Life's Mysteries: The Best of Shirley Lim* (1995), and *Two Dreams: New and Selected Stories* (1997). Lim also writes poetry, memoir, and literary criticism. Her first collection of poetry, *Crossing the Peninsula and Other Poems* (1980), received the Commonwealth Poetry Prize for a best first book of poetry, and her memoir *Among the White Moon Faces: An Asian-American Memoir of Homelands* (1996) won the 1997 American Book Award. One of her coedited books, *The Forbidden Stitch: An Asian American Women's Anthology* (1989), received the 1990 American Book Award. She is also the author of *Nationalism and Literature: English-Language Writing from the Philippines and Singapore* (1993) and *Writing S.E./Asia in English: Against the Grain, Focus on Asian English-language Literature* (1994).

Lim was born in the town of Malacca, on the west coast of the Malay peninsula, a multiethnic, multicultural society where Malays live alongside Chinese and Indian minorities. Though Lim's parents were both South Seas Chinese, each belonged to a different linguistic community. Her father spoke Hokkien, a dialect from the Fujien province of China, while her mother's language was *baba* Malay, spoken by assimilated Chinese. Lim was never comfortable with Hokkien and was called a "Malay devil" by Chinese-speaking Malayans because she spoke Malay, the language her mother used to speak to her. Malay for Lim, however, was only a childhood tongue, her mother's language, not hers. English was, and still is, the language of Lim's passion and imagination, the language in which she finds comfort and power, and the language she has mastered and claims as hers.

Lim's relation to the English language is shaped by her British colonial education. At the time of her birth in 1944, Malacca was under Japanese occupation. When World War II was over, Great Britain reestablished its long-standing colonial rule over the region until 1957, when Malaysia became an independent state within the British Commonwealth. Lim's childhood was marked by instability, hunger, and loneliness. Her father's failed business plunged the family into poverty; her mother abandoned the family soon after. Despite being the only girl among five brothers, Lim received little attention from her father. But she found comfort and pride at the Catholic convent school, where she began to develop her literary talent and earned distinction by her excellent academic performance. Later Lim received a B.A. with First Class Honours in English from the University of Malaya in Kuala Lumpur. She taught English for two years at the university while working on her M.A. before coming to the United States to complete her master's degree.

She eventually earned her Ph.D. at Brandeis University in Waltham, Massachusetts.

Lim's immigrant experience in the United States has become part of the rich sources of her writings. In her short stories such as "Transportation in Westchester," "A Pot of Rice," and "Two Dreams," Lim writes about the experience of exile, dislocation, and struggle for a better life. The unique aspects of these stories are her portrayals of academic immigrants' struggles, including the challenge they face in dealing with interracial relationships and intercultural conflicts both socially and at home. Her professional protagonists and their experiences reflect a new phase in the changing demographics of Asian American communities and of North America as well. In this respect, Lim's immigrant stories have a closer connection to the works of a younger generation of Asian American writers such as Gish Jen Wang Ping and Chang-Rae Lee, rather than to the stories of Hisaye Yamamoto, Wakako Yamauchi, or Maxine Hong Kingston. Yet Lim's stories share much with the older generation of Asian American women writers, especially in their thematic concerns of the female experiences and their social conditions, including patriarchy and racial hierarchy.

Most of Lim's stories are set in Malaysia, each story opening a window to a particular segment of that richly diverse, fascinating world and its peoples. Yet their subject matters and themes are not restricted to the local. One recurrent theme is the impact of Western ideas—"more dangerous than seducers or midnight lovers"—on the old social structure and moral values of Asian communities, and the subsequent effects on the lives of individuals, as illustrated in stories such as "Mr. Tang's Girls," "Sisters," "The Good Old Days," "All My Uncles," and "Thirst."

Other important subject matters and themes in Lim's stories include gender relations and the impact of colonialism. Lim explores the process of gender identity formation and the effect of institutionalized sexism on women's lives in stories such as "Native Daughter" and "Life's Mysteries." Rather than being merely helpless victims of patriarchy, women in these stories are complex individuals, masterful at manipulating power relations. Issues of gender are intersected by class and ethnic divisions in their everyday lives. Just as Lim's portrayal of gender relations is not reduced to a binary paradigm, her representation of the intervention of British colonialism in Malaysian lives is complicated and multifaceted, as stories such as "The Touring Company," "The Farmer's Wife," and "The Bridge" indicate.

Lim's stories are notable for their wide range of styles and voices. Though never radically experimental, Lim constantly searches for new possibilities in unfolding narratives, portraying characters, and capturing complex experience through different points of view. This effort is particularly evident in the changes she makes in "Sisters," which rewrites "Mr. Tang's Girls." The latter ends with the climactic action of the killing of Mr. Tang by his daughter Kim Li, but the narrative point of view never allows us to see anything of Kim Li from within—except her carefully guarded exterior—so that we have no way to sympathize with her action, which remains an unconvincing shock.

"Sisters" revises the circumstances and cause of Mr. Tang's death, and more importantly, the narrative point of view. As a result, we can experience with more intimacy the daughters' lives and feelings as we witness the battle between old customs and new attitudes.

Lim is particularly skillful in propelling her readers immediately and sensually into the world her characters inhabit, through commonplace images endowed with startling power. To a large extent, the power of these ordinary things derives from Lim's wonderfully controlled point of view. In "Hunger," everything we see and experience is filtered through the eyes of a hungry but proud child, Chai. Her hunger is accompanied by loneliness; both are related to the absence of her mother, the devastating effect of which the child is living through without being consciously aware of it. Lim weaves Chai's hunger and longing for her mother seamlessly through a combination of "stream of consciousness" and descriptive narrative from the third-person point of view. This combination creates a free passage between the inner world of the child and the outer world she encounters, thus enabling Lim to show us a chunk of life through the child's experience and at the same time tell us more than the child is aware of:

Only two days since Mother left. The freedom seemed forever. More room for running. More time for staying awake, games, play. Was she glad? Was she sad? There was never time for thinking although the day was long, longer as the afternoon drew on and on toward meal time, longest in darkness when the odours of soy, pork, ginger, garlic and sweet cooked rice lingered on and on in the empty rooms downstairs, like a vague ache in her crotch, a burn in her chest, sensations that follow her to the bedroom. . . .

Mother would be gone three days next morning.

Lim achieves an intensity and depth of the child's vaguely felt pain of loneliness by arranging words and images in such a way that they take on an implied undercurrent of meaning—the child goes to bed hungry, missing her mother more than she realizes.

On the other hand, Lim is able to maintain the intensity and depth of Chai's feelings by extending her sense of loneliness together with her hunger through various locations and incidents, which unfold the narrative while expanding Chai's world. While allowing us to observe the world through the eyes of a hungry, lonely child, Lim knits the narratives together with a brisk tempo that matches the rhythm of the child's activity and thought. These details also serve to enhance Chai's vulnerability and to intensify our anxiety when Chai is seduced and molested by an old man who lures her with a guava. Hence, we feel particularly relieved and surprised when Chai refuses the old man's seduction with money, despite her unbearable hunger. Still, Lim keeps us on edge by rendering Chai's refusal unsettling. The narrator asserts that the old man's ten-cent coin could not "make up for the [child's] terrible pleasure of ignoring his pleading eyes and waving hand." Something has changed in the child, who enjoys the pleasure of power over someone else's desire.

This realization is refreshingly unlike the epiphany in James Joyce's stories. What is happening to Chai is illuminated by something she cannot fathom.

Shirley Geok-lin Lim's art enables us to see the extraordinary in the ordinary and to be at once surprised and moved. It is largely this capacity that makes her stories so compelling. Her stories offer more than moments of insight and delight; they open up a space bordering on different cultures, as an alternative cognitive site for us to understand our world and ourselves.

Zhou Xiaojing

SELECTED BIBLIOGRAPHY

Works by Shirley Geok-lin Lim

Another Country and Other Stories. Singapore: Times, 1982.

Life's Mysteries: The Best of Shirley Lim. Singapore: Times, 1995.

Two Dreams: New and Selected Stories. New York: Feminist Press, 1997.

Critical Studies

Edelson, Phyllis. Review of *Crossing the Peninsula and Other Poems* (1980), *No Man's Grove* (1985), and *Another Country and Other Stories* (1982). In Shirley G. Lim and Mayumi Tsutakawa, eds., *The Forbidden Stitch: An Asian American Women's Anthology,* pp. 255–258. Corvallis: Calyx, 1989.

Knowlton, Edgar C., Jr. Review of *Another Country and Other Stories. World Literature Today* 58 (winter 1984): 167.

Manaf, Nor Faridah Abdul. "More Than Just A Woman." *Tenggara* 34 (1995): 75–86.

Wang, Jennie. "Interview with Shirley Lim." In Farhat Iftekhamddin et al., eds., *Speaking of the Short Story*, pp. 153–166. Jackson: University Press of Mississippi, 1997.

JACK LONDON
(1876–1916)

Interest in the writings of Jack London is often inseparable from a fascination with his biography. Born in San Francisco on January 12, 1876, the illegitimate son of an itinerant astrologer, Jack London was raised by his hard-working but poor mother and stepfather, from whom he took the name London. From these beginnings, London fought his way to success by means of a strong body, a quick intelligence, and above all a tenacious will. After leaving school at the age of fifteen, he worked as a San Francisco Bay oyster pirate. During the next seven years he served as a seaman on a Pacific sealer, labored in a series of factories and mills, participated in the march of Coxey's Army of the unemployed on Washington, spent a semester at the University of California, and searched for gold in the Klondike. Although he was later to draw upon all of these early experiences in his fiction and autobiographies, the most significant of them was his year in the Klondike— from mid-1897 to mid-1898—during which he did little mining but much observing and listening. On his return to the Bay Area he sought, like many others, to

exploit the "matter of the Klondike" by transforming it into saleable fiction, and in late 1898 he sold his first Klondike story, "To the Man on Trail," to the *Overland Monthly*. Similar stories followed: two collections of Klondike short fiction (in 1900 and 1901), and in 1903 the short novel *The Call of the Wild*, which made him world-famous.

In 1902 London spent six weeks in the East End of London acquiring firsthand experience for his *People of the Abyss*. Later (to cite only the most noteworthy of his travels) he journeyed to Japan and Korea to report the Russo-Japanese War; undertook a voyage around the world in his schooner, the *Snark*, which foundered in the South Pacific after two horrendous years; and toward the end of his life made frequent and lengthy trips to Hawaii. London's brief first marriage collapsed in 1903, and in 1905 he married Charmian Kittredge, who shared his enthusiasm for the outdoors and travel and who accompanied him on all his later journeys.

The hardships of London's early life and his later reading had made him a committed socialist. He ran twice for mayor of Oakland on the Socialist Party ticket and lectured widely in support of the socialist movement. From 1909 until his death in 1916, he devoted much time and energy to his large ranch at Glen Ellen, California, in the Sonoma Valley. Despite his peripatetic existence and extraordinary range of interests, London produced prolifically throughout his career. On November 22, 1916, Jack London died of uremic poisoning.

Of the fifty-odd books by London published during his lifetime and posthumously, nineteen are collections of short stories. The recently published *Complete Short Stories of Jack London,* in three volumes, adds a sizeable number of previously uncollected stories for a total of 197. This large body of work is mixed in several senses. It is extremely uneven in quality, ranging from formulaic potboilers to stories considered among the best in the genre. It also varies in subject matter, theme, and technique.

Throughout his career, London was aggressively open in stating his belief that a professional writer's first commitment was to produce saleable material. When he was at the top of his form, his stories created their own market. However, when he was tired, or busy with other projects, or strapped for cash—all of which happened often—his knowledge of the market, coupled with the salability of his name, helped him produce fiction that was sure to be accepted whatever its quality. As a result, it is generally acknowledged that London "at his best" can be reduced to roughly thirty stories.

London began his career almost exclusively as a writer of Klondike stories with a powerful Darwinian theme of man's limitations in the face of natural forces. His initial six collections, from *The Son of the Wolf* to *Lost Face,* are made up of Klondike stories written from 1898 to 1906, and constitute, in conjunction with his Klondike novels of the same period, what has come to be called London's Northland Saga. With the depletion of this vein, London turned for material to his recent South Sea adventures and to his formative years in the San Francisco Bay area, the latter stories often infused with openly displayed socialist themes. By late 1911, however, he felt himself written out in the short story form. His most recent stories, as collected in *A Son of the Sun* and *Smoke Bellew,* were derivative of earlier work to the edge of self-parody, and he had reached the point of having to employ other writers, including a youthful Sinclair Lewis, for plot ideas. Dissatisfied with this state of affairs, London gave up the short story form from late 1911 to 1916. But in early 1916 he experienced a remarkable reengagement with the possibilities of the form at its best, a rebirth of interest generated largely, it would seem, by his recognition of the relationship of the ideas of Carl Jung, which he had recently encountered, to Polynesian and Hawaiian settings. Two posthumous collections, *The Red One* and *On the Malakoa Mat,* reflect this last phase of London's career as a writer of short fiction.

London's early Northland stories and short novels were so immediately successful that his arrival on the literary scene at the turn of the century has often been called an "explosion." His impact on contemporary readers, however, was no accident, as London himself often noted in later years. On his return from the Klondike in 1898, London carefully surveyed the current market for short fiction. Two staples of magazine fiction—sentimental and local color stories—were, he decided, both tired and unreflective of the contemporary code of manly vigor as was soon to be epitomized by Theodore Roosevelt. On the other hand, Rudyard Kipling, in his extremely popular *Plain Tales from the Hills* (1888), had demonstrated the market strength of the story of action and adventure set in an exotic locale. A good many of London's early Klondike stories are therefore Kiplingesque, often, however, in a negative sense. As well as resiting the Kipling formula in the far North, they overindulge in authorial commentary, establish too blatant a center of value in a codified hero whose western-based beliefs clash with the moral system inherent in a harsh environment, and introduce a discordant mix of raw comedy and purple-passage lyricism. Other stories, however, such as "The Law of Life" and "Love of Life," while still occasionally labored, explore freshly and powerfully, within the archetypes of experience implicit in the Klondike setting, the eternal question of man's place in nature.

Almost from the very first, even as he was successfully exploiting Kipling's loose short story form, London was drawn to a more dramatic technique. As he wrote to a friend in an often-cited letter of mid-1900, the function of the writer is not to "tell the reader. Don't. Don't. Don't. But **HAVE YOUR CHARACTERS TELL IT BY THEIR DEEDS, ACTIONS, TALK, ETC.** . . . The reader doesn't want . . . your observations, your knowledge . . . your ideas—**BUT PUT ALL THOSE THINGS WHICH ARE YOURS INTO THE STORIES, INTO THE TALES, ELIMINATING YOURSELF**."

By 1902 London had achieved this goal in his best Klondike stories by both subduing his authorial voice and omitting his code hero authorial spokesman, the Malemute Kid. He did not always maintain this ideal of fictional form, especially after 1906, when pressures to produce resulted in much careless work. But in the stories for which he is best known, his technique of a dramatically rendered, action-centered, yet thematically dense narrative

provided a significant anticipation—most obviously fulfilled in the short fiction of Ernest Hemingway—of one of the major strains in the twentieth-century American short story.

"The White Silence," which appeared originally in the *Overland Monthly* in February 1899 and was collected in *The Son of the Wolf,* is typical of the kind of Klondike story that catapulted London into fame. Three people—Mason, a hardened miner; his Indian wife, Ruth; and the Malemute Kid—are on trail in the frozen Northland. Their food is running low, the dogs are becoming vicious, and all around them the natural world is not only physically threatening in its frozen emptiness but also psychically fearful in its unresponsiveness to man's desire for meaning—the natural world as White Silence. The story plays itself out in a mix of sentiment and brutality characteristic of this early phase of London's work. Mason is severely injured in an accident, and though, as he requests, the Kid must eventually kill him to save himself and Ruth, all three figures are softened and humanized by a realization of his impending death. There is only the White Silence in the natural world, but men can nevertheless communicate in human terms.

"To Build a Fire," probably London's most famous and widely reprinted Klondike story, appeared initially in *Youth's Companion* in 1902, was radically revised for the *Century* magazine in 1908, and was collected in *Lost Face*. Despite an extraordinary cold snap of 75 degrees below zero, an unnamed newcomer to the Klondike undertakes what he believes to be a routine journey across the wastes, accompanied only by a dog. A series of mishaps, however, climaxed by an inability to build a fire, results in his death. In the face of the danger inherent in the natural world, the man had lacked both the experience of the Old Sourdough who had sought to advise him and the instinctive wisdom of the dog. Man can and does survive in an often hazardous world, but he does so only with knowledge and humility. The story owes much of its power to London's capacity to blend the journey motif and its ominous setting into an expression of impending disaster heightened by the controlled tragic irony of the narrative voice. In addition, London's unconscious adoption of the parable form, in which plot, character, and setting join to express, with allegorical clarity, a paraphraseable moral, provides the story with its effect of seamless perfection.

"The Red One," one of London's last and most problematical stories, appeared posthumously in *Cosmopolitan* in 1918 and was collected in *The Red One*. It was neglected until the early 1970s, but has recently received more attention than any other short story by London. Bassett, an English scientist, is severely wounded in an encounter with a native tribe of the Solomon Islands. He is rescued and returned to partial health by another tribe, but in the end, when close to death, he accepts a ritual beheading by the tribe's "devil doctor." The focus of the story, however, is less on these events than on a huge orb of iridescent red metal that emits a powerfully evocative sound when struck and that serves the tribe as a sacred object. Bassett is drawn to the mystery of the red one—its origin, its color and sound, and its function in the tribe. Eventually, he acknowledges that it somehow constitutes

a source of meaning and even affirmation, despite the horror of its role in the tribe's sacrificial rituals. The undefined nature of the "somehow" in Bassett's conversion to belief, the complex and rich Freudian and Jungian implications of the symbolism of the story, and its relationship to London's late fascination with the subconscious— all have contributed to the recent interest in "The Red One."

Donald Pizer

SELECTED BIBLIOGRAPHY

Works by Jack London

The Son of the Wolf. Boston: Houghton Mifflin, 1900.

The God of His Fathers and Other Stories. New York: McClure, Phillips, 1901.

Children of the Frost. New York: Macmillan, 1902.

The Faith of Men and Other Stories. New York: Macmillan, 1904.

Moon Face and Other Stories. New York: Macmillan, 1906.

Love of Life and Other Stories. New York: Macmillan, 1907.

Tales of the Fish Patrol. New York: Macmillan, 1910.

Lost Face. New York: Macmillan, 1910.

When God Laughs and Other Stories. New York: Macmillan, 1911.

South Sea Tales. New York: Macmillan, 1911.

The House of Pride & Other Tales of Hawaii. New York: Macmillan, 1912.

A Son of the Sun. New York: Doubleday, Page, 1912.

Smoke Bellew. New York: Century, 1912.

The Night-Born and Other Stories. New York: Century, 1913.

The Strength of the Strong. New York: Macmillan, 1914.

The Turtles of Tasman. New York: Macmillan, 1916.

The Red One. New York: Macmillan, 1918.

On the Makaloa Mat. New York: Macmillan, 1919.

Dutch Courage and Other Stories. New York: Macmillan, 1922.

The Complete Short Stories of Jack London. Edited by Earle Labor, Robert C. Leitz, and I. Milo Shepard. Stanford: Stanford University Press, 1993.

Critical Studies

Labor, Earle, and Jeanne Campbell Reesman. *Jack London.* New York: Twayne, 1994.

McClintock, James T. *White Logic: Jack London's Short Stories.* Cedar Springs, Mich.: Wolf House Books, 1976.

Sherman, Joan R. *Jack London: A Reference Guide.* Boston: G. K. Hall, 1977.

DAVID WONG LOUIE
(1954–)

David Wong Louie was born in Rockville Center, New York, in 1954. He attended Vassar College and the University of Iowa and began publishing in midwestern and western literary magazines such as the *Iowa Review, Kansas Quarterly,* and *Quarry West.* He is the recipient of a National Endowment for the Arts fellowship and has been a fellow at the McDowell Colony and Yaddo. His stories have been anthologized in *The Best American Short Stories 1989* and *The Big Aiiieeeee!: An Anthology of Chinese American and Japanese American Literature* (Penguin, 1992). Louie's collection of short stories *Pangs of Love* received the *Ploughshares* John C. Zacharis First Book Award and the *Los Angeles Times* Art Seidenbaum Award for First Fiction in 1991. In his acceptance speech for the Seidenbaum Award, Louie noted that he began sending the book out himself after several years of having it rejected by agents. Knopf picked it up quickly and the collection of short stories was published to much acclaim and notice. Louie has taught at Vassar College and at the University of California, Los Angles.

Louie's parents owned a Chinese laundry in a Long Island suburb, and Louie's short stories reflect that marginalized labor force, as well as the conflicts and tensions between Chinese immigrants and a U.S. mainstream, chiefly white, population that neither understands nor appreciates them. Sometime in the mid-1970s, Louie, responding to rejection slips, decided to make his fiction non-ethnic-Chinese-specific. "What I'd do is write in the first person about somebody like myself, but I wouldn't identify him as Chinese American. . . . I was trying to satisfy my paranoia about what people wanted to read or what editors thought people wanted to read. And I didn't see anything out there to tell me differently."

Addressing the apparent success of Asian American writers in the late twentieth century, Louie complains in his introduction to his anthology *Dissident Song* that "while [publishing] houses are undeniably more receptive to our work, their tastes remain circumscribed: their appetite for the exotic, the 'oriental' is bottomless." His short stories demonstrate his resistance to the contemporary cultural movement both to fix Chinese Americans in an orientalist fantasy and to assimilate them into U.S. culture as model minorities. His stories destabilize these two stereotypes of the Chinese American, whether first-generation immigrant or American-born, and offer instead a richly imagined gallery of characters, odd, nonconformist, insistently individualized, and even bizarre.

The stories that treat recognizably Chinese American themes are among Louie's most original. In "Displacement," Mr. and Mrs. Chow, an immigrant Chinese couple, pay for their lodging by working as housekeeper and nurse to their landlady, a frail, elderly widow. Mrs. Chow pretends not to understand English and maintains her self-esteem even as she hears herself slandered by the widow, who accuses her of theft. Unlike her husband, whose presence in the United States is "built from a vocabulary of deference and accommodation," Mrs. Chow prefers unassimilated silence. Yet, ironically, she is "the one better equipped to escape," the partner who chooses every Friday night to ride the roller coaster, which is figured as an image of her risk-taking approach to her new country: "Oh, this speed, this thrust at the sky, this UP! Oh, this raging, clattering, pushy country!"

The theme of male ethnic identities at disjuncture is sounded throughout the book. In "Birthday," Wallace Wong's thwarted aim, to take his ex-girlfriend's son for a birthday baseball game, symbolizes the Chinese American male's desire to become, as it were, the father of an American (white) family. Wallace's refusal to accept his outsider position, his desperation for a relationship with a (white) son and (white) girlfriend, operates as a hyperbolic trope for the place of Chinese American men in white America, absent as father and husband. Frustrated paternity is a repeated motif in stories as divergent as "The Movers" and "One Man's Hysteria Real and Imagined in the Twentieth Century."

In the title story, "Pangs of Love," which plays on the Chinese family name Pang, a Chinese mother has to maneuver the uncertain territory of her sons' sexuality. The first-person narrator has a Caucasian girlfriend who wants him to move out of the apartment he shares with his mother. The story picks up the comic tremors of a visit to the youngest son's country home in Bridgehampton. Billy, a successful commercial artist, has surrounded himself with his au courant homosexual companions for the weekend, and Mrs. Pang, the perennial outsider of metropolitan American culture, wants to know if "all the men in this house have good jobs, they have money, why don't they have women?" Mrs. Pang worries over the cost of everything and, anxious for grandchildren, has "offered to take all the boys on bride safaris in Hong Kong." Mother and son can communicate only through Chinese; as the son says, "once I went to school, my Chinese vocabulary stopped growing; in conversation with my mother I'm a linguistic dwarf."

"Love on the Rocks" is structured on multiple shifting points of view, illustrating the novelistic stylistics that M. M. Bakhtin had theorized in *The Dialogic Imagination*. Undermining the notion that ethnic identity can be expressed or reflected as a single, fixed subject or an orientalist other, Louie's writing gestures toward a multiplicity of identities at play in the ethnic subject. Composed of ten short sections, the story focuses on the mystery of Buddy Lam, a model, if stereotypical, Chinese American presented in the first section through the first-person point of view of a male acquaintance, Bruce Chin. The name of this minor narrator-character is not immediately revealed, and this withholding of information contributes to the "puzzle" of ethnic character central to the story. Chin's betrayal of his friend Buddy Lam, when he callously blips Buddy off the employment roster, serves as an overarching signifier for the response of the community surrounding Buddy, from his contemptuous mother-in-law to his adulterous wife, to the narcissistic tease Miriam and her fanatical husband.

The narrative unfolds using multiple points of view, in first and third person. The opening motif of relationships characterized by competition, of subjects whose loss of employment figures the absence of a sociable context, sets the theme developed through the other nine sections. In the third section, for example, the first-person voice is that of Etsy, a white American female, whose representation of Buddy and Miriam's "affair" echoes the orientalist fantasy of a majority white culture. Hearing that Buddy is prone to buying six bags of party ice each time he visits Miriam, Etsy "wondered if the stuff had anything to do with his Ori-

ental love technique." Similarly, in the fourth section, Buddy's mother-in-law's prejudice against her daughter's Chinese American husband is seen both in her approval of Cookie's affair with a "Yale grad, tall, bearded, feet planted firmly in the financial world" and in her overt racism. Whether imagined as an exotic sexual partner or an ineffective provider, the Chinese American male is never permitted legitimate entry into the social material world that white American women control. This devaluing of the Chinese American male as male is underlined again in the sixth section, where the first-person voice of Miriam elaborates on the difference between Buddy and her white husband Al. Like Buddy, Al is not successful as a provider, but Miriam understands his failure to be a triumph of the spiritual, satirized in Al's chosen profession, as a salesman who sells Christianity: he is considering putting video games that are "truly Christian amusements" into his store. Al characterizes the intermixing of commerce and faith, capitalism and love, that Louie repeatedly satirizes as emblematic of U.S. cultural discourses.

Through its use of elements of the bizarre, the supernatural, and the irrational, its depiction of unnatural sexuality and necrophilia, the story refers to a tradition of American gothic epitomized in Flannery O'Connor's stories and William Faulkner's classic "A Rose for Emily." Like Buddy, Al, as a type of white American male, appears a grotesque; just as Buddy's obsessive passion for Miriam is a displaced revenge passion against his unfaithful wife Cookie, whose corpse he keeps on ice in the bathtub in a hallucinatory dimension of the living dead, so Al's Christian fervor borders on the realm of irrationality and religious madness. "Love on the Rocks" is a late twentieth-century rewriting of Faulkner's theme of passion in conjunction with social anomie, indistinguishable from psychotic excess and rigid communalism, only at this moment to imagine the ethnic male as Miss Emily, in the gendered position of the dominated other. The multiple point of view, climaxing in the ninth section in the first person plural, when the plot approaches discovery of the horror of necrophilia, like the communal point of view in Faulkner's story, serves to satirize and ironize a community's moral narrowness and immoral complacency.

The final story, "Inheritance," offers an explanation for the persistence of Chinese culture in second-generation characters who resist their parents' resistance to assimilation, and yet cannot free themselves entirely of their parents' immigrant culture. Edna, the sole surviving child, is living in Buffalo, where her immigrant Chinese husband is doing graduate work. A defiant political activist, she rejects both her father, Edsel, and her husband's desire for a child. Told in the first-person voice of Edna, the story revolves around the theme of regeneration. Having lived through a series of deaths in the family, Edna and her father Edsel take different positions on the prospect of motherhood for Edna. Even as these deaths haunt the father and daughter, so also both struggle with their notions of an affirmative life, viewed by Edsel in traditional terms as the birthing of babies. Composed of flashbacks to an early self, the story pieces

together the multiple meanings of its title. "Inheritance" suggests heirlooms, valuable objects, values transmitted through the family, but it also signifies the death of parents, death resulting in the concept of "an inheritance." The story instates the added dimension of the problem of cultural inheritance, in the absurdity of Edsel's Americanization (he names himself after a car that was a dismal market product) and the differences between the American-born daughter and her partially assimilated father. Although the plot revolves around Edna's relationship with her father, its central problematic is that of the reproduction of mothering. Edna did not cry at her mother's funeral, but when she comes across Mrs. Woo, who has been abandoned by her children, Edna's grief at Mrs. Woo's fate signals the possibility of reconciliation to her abusive mother. Remembering her mother in Mrs. Woo's house, Edna also remembers her mother's violence, miserliness, and absence of love. In recognizing this unloving mother, she now understands why she has not wanted to be a mother herself and thus rejected or repressed her femininity. The story suggests a resolution to Edna's struggles over her identity when she turns away from her suicidal impulse and, smelling gas in Mrs. Woo's kitchen, opens a window and "breathed what seemed like my first breath."

The stories of *Pangs of Love* are situated between the crosshairs of postmodern narrative, characterized by collage, parody, bricolage, decentered narrators, nonlinearity, multiple voices and registers, and traditional themes of parent-child conflict, cross-cultural miscommunications, immigrant sorrows, and romantic and sexual mishaps. The themes are not new to Asian American and immigrant American literature; but the imagined characters and the prose style are original, fresh with satirical energy, and full of elegantly ironic layerings that disavow conventional sentiment and stale disclosures of ethnic identity. In their lapidary reconfigurations of Euro- and Chinese American themes, Louie's stories compel reading by their very attention to the shifting and ambiguous nature of cross-cultural lives and situations.

Shirley Geok-lin Lim

SELECTED BIBLIOGRAPHY

Works by David Wong Louie

Introduction to Dissident Song: A Contemporary Asian American Anthology. Special issue of Quarry West, 1991.
Pangs of Love. New York: Alfred A. Knopf, 1991.
The Barbarians Are Coming. New York: G. P. Putnam's Sons, 2000.

Critical Studies

Feldman, Gayle. "Spring's Five Fictional Encounters of the Chinese American Kind." Publishers Weekly, February 8, 1991: 25–27.
Manini, Samarth. "Affirmations: Speaking the Self Into Being." Parnassus: Poetry in Review vol. 17, no. 1 (spring 1991): 88–101.
Simpson, Janice C. "Fresh Voices Above the Noisy Din." Time, June 3, 1991.

NORMAN MAILER
(1923–)

As one of the most prolific and notorious writers of the late twentieth century, Norman Mailer is both highly distinctive in his style and in many ways representative of his time. Indeed, Mailer's writing reflects the literary history of the last hundred years, from early naturalism to later experimental works that blend fact and fiction, history and the novel. Short stories such as "A Calculus at Heaven," "The Language of Men," "The Time of Her Time," and "The Man Who Studied Yoga" suggest the arc of this development. They give a sense of Mailer's voice as it developed in his early novels, and also provide an interesting transition between the modernism of Hemingway and Fitzgerald and the postmodernism of Coover and Barth.

In The Armies of the Night, Mailer says that he was raised "a nice Jewish boy from Brooklyn." Born in 1923 to first- and second-generation immigrants, he was the beloved elder child of his middle-class parents. He read at a young age, loved building model airplanes, and in 1939 entered Harvard as an engineering student. After graduating in 1943 he was drafted into the army, and served in the Philippines and occupied Japan. His first novel, The Naked and the Dead (1948), was a critical and popular success, propelling him into a celebrity status that he groomed assiduously for half a century. His next several novels received mixed reviews, but Mailer kept himself in the public eye

by political and social commentary, including a stint as columnist for the *Village
Voice* (which he helped found). In the
1960s he came into his own with several
book-length works of New Journalism,
notably *The Armies of the Night* (1968),
which won a Pulitzer Prize and a National
Book Award. For decades he has been one
of America's best-known writers, dab-
bling in filmmaking, getting in public debates (and sometimes public brawls), and
being arrested for stabbing his wife. After
making the hero of the novel *An American
Dream* (1965) a man who kills his wife and
sodomizes his maid, Mailer was labeled
by Kate Millet and other early feminists
as one of America's arch-sexists. His
books became steadily bigger—sometimes, as in the Pulitzer Prize-winning *The
Executioner's Song* (1979), running over a
thousand pages. By the late 1990s, settled
with his sixth wife, and having lived down
his disastrous parole sponsorship of the
prison writer Jack Abbott, Mailer seems
to have mellowed at last. But he remains
deeply at odds with what he sees as the
relentless tendency of American life toward faith in technological progress and
the pursuit of a sanitary world. His most
recent novel, *The Gospel According to the
Son* (1997), a first-person account of Jesus' life, demonstrates that he has lost
none of his confidence or ambition. In *The
Time of Our Time* (1998), a retrospective
anthology on the fiftieth anniversary of the
publication of *The Naked and the Dead*,
Mailer organizes the selections as a kind
of late twentieth-century American history, and perhaps some of the excerpts
from his novels can be considered addi-
tions to the canon of his short fiction.

The best place to begin talking about
Mailer's short stories may be with his own
disingenuous claim that he agrees with
critics who find his short fiction "neither
splendid, unforgettable, nor distinguished." He admits that "he does not have the
interest, the respect, or the proper awe
[for the form]. The short story bores him
a little" (introduction to *The Short Fiction
of Norman Mailer*). In a typical move,
Mailer thus preempts his harshest critics
and demonstrates his modesty by denying
his skill, while at the same time arrogantly
calling into question the value of the short
story as a literary form. Even granting
some truth to Mailer's self-evaluation, his
stories, while few and uneven, are more
important than he suggests, both for their
intrinsic merit and for their literary-
historical importance.

The chief virtue of Mailer's best writing is honesty, and its chief method is the
exploration of intense experience. He says
that his short stories "are all excursions
and experiments," and claims in *The Armies
of the Night* that he learned his most important lesson from Hemingway and
Aquinas: "If it made you feel good, it was
good," and "Trust the evidence of your
senses." As an existentialist, Mailer believes that every individual is radically
alone and forced to struggle for survival
against a host of physical and spiritual
threats. But as a mystic, Mailer also believes that every individual is part of a
larger whole, of which we are given
glimpses in transcendent moments of
dream, sexual union, guilt, fear, artistic
insight, and religious perception. Anyone
who claims to be sanitizing or rectifying
life, freeing it from guilt or sickness, is

actually attacking humanity and individ-uality under the aegis of a falsely utopian vision of "Technology Land." Mailer sees twentieth-century society as bent on con-verting people into machines, whether through the crude force of communism or the subtler suasion of consumerism. His handful of published short stories, all written between the early 1940s and the early 1960s, reveal the progress of his ideas about the courage, resolve, and imagi-nation needed to keep one's spirit alive in a world bent on quashing it. "The Greatest Thing in the World," a prize-winning stu-dent story, depicts a naturalistic universe of constant struggle in a social jungle, in which a moment of sensual satisfaction is the most that can be asked of life. "The Last Night: A Story," a movie "treatment" published twenty-two years later, de-scribes a series of difficult moral and in-tellectual choices, with the fate of the en-tire human race at stake. Between these two stories, Mailer expanded his view of the human condition from the narrowly materialistic to something much more spiritually complex. Mailer seems to have decided that moral decisions have tangible effects on the universe, and that the senses provide a key to, but not a limit on, the spiritual world.

In America, the theme of doomed courage is, of course, associated with Hemingway, and many of Mailer's short stories clearly show Hemingway's influ-ence. An example of this influence and of Mailer at his best is "The Time of Her Time." Narrated by a bullfighting instruc-tor who has taken on the task of sexually liberating the women of Greenwich Vil-lage one at a time (but three or four a

week), the story is about what happens when this "kindly cocksman" encounters a worthy opponent. By the time he figures out that he might be able to learn from her, and thus love her, she is gone. She has gotten from him the training she came for, has become "a real killer," and true to his teaching she has moved on. Contempo-rary readers may find Mailer's protagonist unsympathetic: "A phallic narcissist she had called me. Well, I was phallic enough, a Village stickman who could muster enough of the divine It on the head of his will to call forth more than one becoming out of the womb of feminine Time, yes a good deal more than one from my fifty new girls a year, and when I failed before various prisons of frigidity, it mattered little."

From the perspective of the 1990s, it may not be obvious how radically Mailer was attempting to advance the American cultural conversation about sex and re-lationships, as Hemingway had tried to do a generation earlier. Taboos that seemed inviolable forty years ago have all but dis-appeared. Mailer's writing played no small role in that process. But whether this story has enduring value beyond its place in the history of American literary sex may be an open question.

The most frequently anthologized of Mailer's stories is also his favorite: "The Man Who Studied Yoga." Originally con-ceived as the preface to an ambitious series of eight novels, of which only The Deer Park (1955) was ever written, "The Man Who Studied Yoga" is an image of life as a long, pointless joke with a predictable punch line. Perhaps closest to the themes and imagery of such important contemporaries as Bellow and Updike, though still unmistakably his own, Mailer's story tells of a single Sunday afternoon and evening in the life of a would-be novelist, Sam Slovoda. Distinguished only by his honest acceptance of his own fate, surrendering to his bourgeois impulses even while despising them, Sam may be Mailer's own worst nightmare. The story's omniscient narrator, who might be God or Sam's therapist thinking of himself as God, speaks in a voice Mailer will use again in several novels. Sam, his wife, and four of their friends watch a pornographic movie, behavior that seems rather quaint from the jaded perspective of the late nineties, but that for Sam calls into question the "womb of middle-class life" in which he has embedded himself. The story's title refers to a shaggy dog story told by one of Sam's friends, which in turn echoes a scene in *Moby-Dick* in which Pip refers in passing to the old joke about what happens when you unscrew your navel. Mailer demonstrates his scorn for self-absorbed navel-gazing through dialogue between Sam and his wife, in which they speak in a kind of psychobabble as a substitute for real communication. As Sam struggles at the end of the story to put himself to sleep, Mailer suggests that Sam's refusal to take risks drains his life of significance. Despite a mystical hint of optimism whispered by the narrator into Sam's ear, the story ends on a note of lament: "So Sam enters the universe of sleep, a man who seeks to live in such a way as to avoid pain, and succeeds merely in avoiding pleasure. What a dreary compromise is our life!" This ending again echoes Melville, especially the last words of "Bartleby, the Scrivener":

"Ah Bartleby! Ah humanity!" Like Melville, Norman Mailer is a writer who has always taken chances in his work and been unwilling to settle for doing the same thing he has done before. Though he ultimately found the short story insufficient for the scope of his ambition, he used it early in his career to test the limits of realistic fiction and of what could be said about sex and personal identity in American literary discourse.

Eric Heyne

BIBLIOGRAPHY

Works by Norman Mailer

Advertisements for Myself. New York: G. P. Putnam's Sons, 1959.
The Short Fiction of Norman Mailer. New York: Pinnacle Books, 1967.
The Time of Our Time. New York: Random House, 1998.

Critical Studies

Busch, Frederick. 1973. "The Whale as Shaggy Dog: Melville and 'The Man Who Studied Yoga.'" *Modern Fiction Studies* 19: 193–206.
Miller, Gabriel. "A Small Trumpet of Defiance: Politics and the Buried Life in Norman Mailer's Early Fiction." In Adam J. Sorkin, ed., *Politics and the Muse: Studies in the Politics of Recent American Literature*, pp. 79–92. Bowling Green: Bowling Green University Press, 1989.
Solotaroff, Robert. *Down Mailer's Way*. Urbana: University of Illinois Press, 1974.

BERNARD MALAMUD
(1914 – 1986)

Bernard Malamud was the finest short story writer produced by Jewish culture in America, and was, indeed, one of the classic American writers of short fiction. The five collections of short stories he published in his lifetime— *The Magic Barrel* (1958), *Idiots First* (1963), *Pictures of Fidelman: An Exhibition* (1969), *Rembrandt's Hat* (1973), and *The Stories of Bernard Malamud* (1983)—make a persuasive case for our ranking him with Hawthorne or Poe or Flannery O'Connor, who, upon reading *The Magic Barrel* in 1958, wrote to a friend: "I have discovered a short-story writer who is better than any of them, including myself." The publication in 1997 of *The Complete Stories,* a roundup of all his known short fiction, fifty-five stories written between 1940 and 1984, offers the essence of Malamud, a lifetime of eloquent and poignant vignettes. Though Malamud published seven novels before his death in 1986, each one touched with his distinctive melancholy grace, the short story remains the purest distillation of his abiding leitmotif: the still, sad music of humanity. Typically, the Malamud story is an epiphany of disappointment, a document of the half-life—the shabby region of mediocre existence just shy of disaster. By and large, his characters and their predictable sorrows were too frail to bear the weight of longer constructions, but in the short story, where Malamud achieved an almost psalmlike compression, the life-defying stringency of his characters' existences seems at home. He has been called the Jewish Hawthorne, but he might also be thought a Jewish Chopin, a composer of preludes and nocturnes in prose.

Because he was a retiring man who resented the intrusions of literary celebrity, Malamud did not open up his life for inspection. As a result, we know only the broad strokes of his life and career. Born in Brooklyn on April 26, 1914, to Russian-Jewish immigrant parents, Max and Bertha (Fidelman) Malamud, he was raised in the kind of circumstances described by the grocery store scenes of his novel *The Assistant* and an early short story, "The Grocery Store." Hard work, late hours, a cold flat, and empty shelves were the daily fare, and Malamud's imagination was marked by a sense of life as deprivation. Looking back on his childhood, Malamud would recall that there were no books in his home, no cultural nourishment at all, except that on Sundays he would listen to someone else's piano through the living-room window. His mother's suicide when he was fifteen was a blow that he never completely recovered from, and one senses in much of his writing, in his creation of haunted and tragic women, an homage to her. He attended City College of New York and received his B.A. in 1936; he took his M.A. from Columbia in 1942, writing a thesis on Thomas Hardy. During this period he worked at odd jobs—hotel waiter and entertainer in the Catskills, worker in a yarn factory, high school teacher, clerk for the Census Bureau—and wrote steadily. His first stories appeared in print in 1943, and in 1950 he found his way into *Harper's Bazaar, Partisan Review,* and *Commentary*. Though Malamud was not a man of ideas, his character as a writer was shaped in the orbit of the New York intellectuals, who took him up in the 1950s and promoted him as the voice of their own particular weltsch-merz.

What we know of Malamud's domestic and professional lives is simple and straightforward. He married Ann de Chiara in 1945 and had two children, Paul, born in 1947, and Janna, born in 1952. After nine years of teaching high school English, he found a job at Oregon State University in Corvallis, Oregon, where he taught composition—four sections a semester—from 1949 until 1961. When Oregon State refused to give him regular literature courses, even though while working there he had written more than a dozen stories and three novels, *The Natural* (1952), *The Assistant* (1957), and *A New Life* (1961), he decamped for Bennington College, where a lightened teaching schedule afforded him an opportunity to devote himself to writing. With breaks for travel and a two-year visiting lectureship at Harvard during 1966–68, Malamud would remain on the Bennington faculty until just before his death in 1986. What such a profile suggests is a life of hard work and steady habits, whose major dramas were internal ones, dramas of the soul and of the imagination, played out on the pages of his books rather than in the experiences of his life. This is largely true; Malamud defined his life by what he did, which was to write. Malamud was a man of obstinate will and iron self-discipline, and from start to finish he worked tirelessly at his writing, producing in the end seven novels and fifty-five short stories.

Much of this writing was rooted deeply in depression, and during Malamud's lifetime this was taken to be the very ensign of his Jewishness. Especially in the first two decades after the Holocaust, when, with the publication of *The Natural, The Magic Barrel, The Assistant,* and *Idiots First,* his reputation was at its peak, the note of lamentation in his stories tended to be equated with their Jewish element, indeed their "Jewish-universal" element. In those days one could say, "All men are Jews," and be thought to have spoken the last word on the human condition. From a vantage point beyond universalism, one can see clearly how such a sentiment befitted a moment in American history when Jews and other Americans—at least literary-intellectual Jews and Americans—sought rapprochement on terms beyond the inconveniences of cultural particularity, passed off as the inheritance of less enlightened times. Malamud was a "non-Jewish Jew," though not precisely as historian Isaac Deutscher described that figure: prophetic, cosmopolitan, transnational, revolutionary. He was rather Jewish by mood, by a kind of internal chord structure, and one thinks of him now as a typical product of Reform Judaism, even though Malamud kept as aloof from that denomination as he did from all formal religion. Malamud knew nothing of Torah and Talmud, of ritual and ancient lore. Of the folklore of Ashkenazi Jewry, he knew his generation's share but no more. In his stories, Israel does not exist, while Italy and its art loom large. Malamud may have been a profoundly ceremonial writer, but his rituals came more out of Western art than Jewish culture.

Bernard Malamud was a major writer with an abiding devotion to the small voice, typical enough of short story writers. Though he wrote in the manner of a folklorist, especially in stories like "Angel Levine," "The Jewbird," and "The Magic Barrel," he remained open to the possibility and freedom of literary modernism and experimented with form to create an oeuvre that ran from conventional fables to self-parodying constructions. Indeed, from an early story titled "Spring Rain," written in 1942 (but first published in *The Complete Stories* in 1997), with its palpable echoes of James Joyce's "The Dead," to the very late "In Kew Gardens," about the last days of Virginia Woolf, modernism entered his work both as style and theme; Malamud aspired to the oblique, the atonal, and the nonrational. Sometimes the tension between the little people who populate his stories and the modernist imperatives behind the storytelling lends his stories a strange angularity, as in that oddest of his productions, the story-cycle *Pictures of Fidelman,* in which a Jewish American painter, decamping to Italy, undergoes adventures that remind us of Kafka in their hallucinatory absurdity.

The Malamud character is one readers have long since come to recognize: the hunger artist transposed into a small merchant, retiree, or pensioner. He is commonly alone or beset by family, creditors, or customers. He wants us to admire his fasting, though he has never found a food that he liked. Of warm human companionship he knows only rumors. He runs a grocery, a deli, or a candy store where the cash register is empty and the accounts-receivable book full. His sons avoid him; his daughters are wayward and ungrateful. He may have a heart condition, like Mendel in "Idiot's First," Marcus the tailor in "The Death of Me," or Mr. Panessa in "The Loan," or he may take his own life, like Rosen the ex-coffee salesman in "Take Pity," Oskar Gassner in "The Jewish Refugee," or Virginia Woolf in "In Kew Gardens." (Malamud was no Camusian existentialist; suicide was always an option.) From marriage he derives no joy, and of sex he knows only the ache of longing. At his most wretched he is a Jewbird, black as a caftan, fishy as a herring, and cursed/blessed with the powers of flight, his face pressed hungrily to the window at the comforts of home life within. In one story, indeed, "Take Pity," death releases one such man into a chamber of heaven that looks like a furnished room. Even the grave brings no ease.

So deeply ingrained is this woe that it seems virtually biological, bound in helixes within every cell. But in the first postwar decade, it had the full sanction of the times and was well nigh universal among Jewish writers and intellectuals. The sorrow that penetrates to the bone in Malamud was the mood of a generation of Jewish writers who had been raised on immigrant poverty and worldwide depression and brought abruptly to adulthood by the Holocaust. Low spirits came as naturally to them as hunger or ambition or breath.

What could be the enduring appeal of a writer so obstinately depressive, who peoples his stories with characters out of our worst nightmares? That is not a simple question to answer, but we might begin with Malamud's own words. In the story

"Man in the Drawer," an American journalist, Howard Harvitz, while touring Russia, is enticed by Levitansky, a Russian-Jewish writer whose work cannot be published in the Soviet Union, to read some of his stories. Harvitz, after much shilly-shallying, reads them and renders an approving judgment: "I like the primary, close-to-the-bone quality of the writing. The stories impress me as strong if simply wrought; I appreciate your feeling for the people and at the same time the objectivity with which you render them. It's sort of Chekhovian in quality, but more compressed, sinewy, direct, if you know what I mean."

Sinewy, direct, simply wrought, close to the bone—Malamud's own writing is all that—but an appreciation of his simplicity takes one only so far toward understanding his appeal, which has, I think, other sources: his terror, his music, and his mystery. The music of Malamud's writing, its taut, concise adagios of woe, is solemn, troubled, and not always reliably melodic. He was no Bellow or Roth or Updike, primed with repartee and capable of a mot more juste on every page. His idiom was limited: a basic English that calls to mind Isaac Babel in its regard for simple truths and studied lack of ornamentation. Within that limited budget of words, however, Malamud achieved a small night music, a simple tonal weariness as thick as oil and dark as blood. The Malamud story has a soundtrack before it has a plot.

In a very late story, "Zora's Noise," a woman newly married to a widower begins to hear unhappy noises: "a vibrato hum touched with a complaining, drawn-out wail that frightened her because it made her think of the past, perhaps her childhood oozing out of the dark." Her husband, a cellist named Dworkin, tries listening in the night: "[Dworkin] leaned on his arm and strained to listen, wanting to hear what she heard. The Milky Way crackling? A great wash of cosmic static. . . . As he listened the hum renewed itself, seeming to become an earthly buzz—a bouquet of mosquitoes and grasshoppers on the lawn, rasping away. . . . Then the insects vanished, and he heard nothing: no more than the sound of both ears listening. . . . Dworkin sometimes heard music when he woke at night—the music woke him."

What the two are hearing might be the unconscious, the return of the repressed, the dread of aging and approaching death, childhood oozing out of the dark. With or without a name it is dread and mystery made audible: the blues in the night. Here as elsewhere, Malamud seems to have learned his method from a handbook of Freudian principles: his characters present symptoms, dreams, or sudden terrors that they cannot decipher. Malamud was shrewd enough a writer to refrain from giving that dread a label.

The initial impression Malamud gave in the 1950s, with his early stories in *The Magic Barrel* and the novels *The Natural* and *The Assistant,* was of being a purveyor of Jewish admonitions. The novels in particular cast long, didactic shadows and ask the reader to judge their characters as deserving of their trials. Moreover, *The Natural* and *The Assistant,* as well as stories like "The Lady of the Lake," "Girl of My Dreams," and "The Magic Barrel," broadcast suggestions of a sexual moralism as well, though its exact nature is never spelled out. Indeed, the element of sexual admonition in Malamud's writing is usually a reluctant prescription for abstinence based not upon conscience but upon impossibility. One should not, the lesson goes, because one must not, and one must not because one cannot. Characters fail, not because they transgress, but because it is in their blood to fail.

And yet, Malamud was a moralist and an insistent one, though the law to which he bound his characters had little in it of specifically Jewish content. It is the law of simple charity and compassion. Most of his characters either earn their misery through hard-heartedness or are the victims of others. Kessler, the former egg candler of "The Mourners," is quarrelsome and a troublemaker and is self-isolated in his tenement apartment. Rosen, the ex-coffee salesman in "Take Pity," has been driven to the grave by a widow who, out of misplaced pride, rejects his charity. Glasser, the retired shamus in "God's Wrath," has had poor luck with his children, and we may guess that they all had no better luck with him. In story after story rejection is returned for devotion, a warm heart is battered by a cold one. The word *no* is the most powerful and bitter in Malamud's lexicon.

For all that, Malamud could be funny. When in a mood to break out of this sorrowfulness, he could tap a theatrical strain of humor, as in the six stories that make up the volume published as *Pictures of Fidelman*: "The Last Mohican," "Still Life," "Naked Nude," "A Pimp's Revenge," "Pictures of the Artist," and "Glass Blower of Venice." There, Malamud simply kicked out the jambs and threw together a raucous comedy of art, art criticism, sex, and desire gone berserk in, of all places, Venice, Italy. These stories stand apart from the main line of Malamud's fiction and show what he could do when he eased back on the controls. There is one hilarious scene in "Pictures of the Artist" in which the impecunious street artist Artur Fidelman tries to explain the aesthetics of a hole in the ground in a parody of art crit jargon as fine as anything I know.

Finally, beyond the alternating cycle of comedy and despair in Malamud's stories is a mystique: a secret heart to which they all beat, a remote fire around which they dance a private ritual whose meaning is never precisely disclosed. We know only that it has to do with love and the hardness of finding it. If Malamud knew what was behind the veil, he refused to lift it, as if he were in mourning and the mourning had its own sanctity. This secret heartache led Malamud to an identification with the tears of the Jewish past and an affection for a world that his father's generation tried to flee: the tenement, the candy store, the hand-to-mouth hardships of the confined life. All Jewish writers of Malamud's generation were washed in this backflow of ghetto misery, but only Malamud made a monument to it. His stories symbolize hidden wounds in search of metaphors, and it is a validation of Malamud's art that he found metaphors that retain their power to galvanize the reader. That so many of his stories remain fresh decades after their first publication is a reminder that Bernard Malamud was, after all, a lifelong apprentice to his craft who was always striving to renew himself and did so, happily for us, time after time.

Mark Shechner

SELECTED BIBLIOGRAPHY

Works by Bernard Malamud

The Magic Barrel. New York: Farrar, Straus & Cudahy, 1958.

Idiots First. New York: Farrar, Straus, 1963.

Pictures of Fidelman: An Exhibition. New York: Farrar, Straus & Giroux, 1969.

Rembrandt's Hat. New York: Farrar, Straus & Giroux, 1973.

The Stories of Bernard Malamud. New York: Farrar, Straus & Giroux, 1983.

The Complete Stories of Bernard Malamud. Edited by Robert Giroux. New York: Farrar, Straus & Giroux, 1997.

BOBBIE ANN MASON

(1940–   )

Bobbie Ann Mason's first collection of short stories, *Shiloh and Other Stories* (1982), won her the prestigious PEN/ Hemingway Award for First Fiction in 1983. Her stories had appeared in such widely circulated magazines as *The New Yorker, Atlantic Monthly,* and *Mother Jones.* By the time *Love Life* appeared in 1989, Mason had contributed her stories to awards anthologies (*Best American Short Stories* 1981 and 1983) and won the Pushcart Prize (1983 and, later, 1996) and O. Henry Award (1986 and 1988). Her 1985 novel *In Country* was made into a Warner Brothers film by director Norman Jewison in 1989, while her third novel, *Feather*

Crowns, won the Southern Book Award in 1993. Yet critics and readers agree that the compact form of the short story conveys most successfully her "slice of life" realism.

The inner life of the characters in Mason's stories is defined by their outer circumstances. Mason, like short story writer Raymond Carver, illuminates the interior with meticulous surface detail. Using third-person point of view, specific and concrete language, and present-tense narration, Mason creates a world as immediate as the air we breathe. Set in her native rural Kentucky, an area fast giving way to suburbs and shopping malls, the stories in her two collections depict the emotional landscape of characters whose expanding world not only poses change but also threatens extinction of a social and moral order that had prevailed for generations. The best known of all her books, *In Country,* deftly evokes the Civil War through Vietnam as it powerfully conveys the moral and physical dislocation of an entire generation.

The literal, physical changes—farms become subdivisions, parking lots, malls—mirror the emotional and psychological changes in the social order and in marriage and the family. Stranded between the two worlds, the older, more mature characters grapple with changing roles and the younger generation with redefining duties and responsibilities. In the title stories "Shiloh" and "Love Life," Mason creates perfectly furnished worlds where her characters deal, some successfully, some not, with the changes that have come into their lives.

"Shiloh" is the most anthologized of all Mason's stories. The opening sentence,

"Leroy Moffit's wife, Norma Jean, is working on her pectorals," sets the stage for the internal and external conflicts the story chronicles. For the fifteen years that they have been married, Leroy has been on the road driving a truck and Norma Jean has sold cosmetics at the Rexall drugstore. Grounded by an accident, Leroy sits home all day smoking dope and making things from craft kits. His most recent creation, a log cabin from notched Popsicle sticks, has inspired him to build a real log cabin for his wife, an interest Norma Jean does not share. In fact, the couple shares little save the distant memory of their child's death. Born a few months after they married at eighteen, the baby died of sudden infant death syndrome in the back seat of the car at the drive-in as they watched a double feature, *Dr. Strangelove* and *Lover Come Back*. Leroy muses at one point that "they have known each other so long that they have forgotten a lot about each other."

Leroy's stasis after his years of "flying past scenery" are in direct contrast to Norma Jean's movement: "Something is happening. Norma Jean is going to night school. She has graduated from her six-week body-building course and now she is taking an adult-education course in composition at Paducah Community College." Norma Jean's mother tells Leroy, "Y'all need to get out together, stir a little. Her brain's all balled up over them books." But the trip they decide to take together is their last one. They pack a picnic lunch and go that Sunday to Shiloh, a Civil War battleground bearing witness to the death of 3,500 soldiers, and now, with Norma Jean's announcement, to the death of their marriage. "I want to leave you," Norma

Jean tells Leroy, and walks to the bluff that overlooks the Tennessee River. The story closes with Norma Jean waving her arms at Leroy: "She seems to be doing an exercise for her chest muscles."

The parallel opening and closing images of the story illustrate Mason's structural and thematic artistry. While Norma Jean has strengthened her body and mind to move on, Leroy's body and his will have atrophied. Immobile with his bad leg, Leroy cannot get up and follow Norma Jean to the edge. Norma Jean's position, though, is more equivocal, leaving the story, as Mason often does, open-ended and for that reason subject to criticism. Readers who want an affirmation, or at best a resolution on the part of the characters at the end of the story, can see how well that technique works in Lee Smith's stories in *Cakewalk* (1981) or Mary Hood's stories in *How Far She Went* (1984). Yet, Mason's analysis of her endings bears consideration: "I think my stories tend to end at a moment of illumination. . . . Leroy recognizes that his life has got to change. His situation is difficult, but he now knows he can't just deny it or ignore it, and I think that knowledge is hopeful. I see the excitement of possibility for a lot of my characters at the end of their stories" (Lyons and Oliver 469–470).

The women tend to fare better than the men, finding a source of strength in the possibilities of their expanding circle. Sandra in "Offerings" finds living with her cats and ducks in a natural wilderness preferable to spending her weekends with her husband in Louisville, watching go-go dancers in smoky bars. Linda in "Old Things" takes her children and moves in with her mother because "she don't feel like hanging around the same house with somebody that can go for three hours without saying a word." When her mother, Cleo, tells her, "people just can't have everything they want all the time," Linda's response is that "people don't have to do what they don't want to as much now as they used to." Cleo says that she should know that, "it's all over television." Mason herself says, "people are getting free of a lot of baggage."

But freedom has its price in Mason's world—the disappearing familiar landscape leaves rootless wanderers in the second collection, *Love Life*. In the title story, Jenny, a sophisticated traveler, seeks the security symbolized by the old family quilt her favorite Aunt Opal has stuffed in the closet. Jenny has no place to call her own, so she buys a one-acre lake lot at an auction because she "wants a place to land," and marriage is not the place for her. Opal, on the other hand, has been grounded for years, her retirement from teaching high school finally freeing her to sip her peppermint-liqueur spiked Coke and explore the wide world of MTV, blaring songs with "balloons and bombs." "Rock and roll," Opal quotes from a song she has heard, "is never too loud." Opal's speech is typical of Mason's characters, whose vocabulary is fed by TV lingo but is true to their situation—"country speech," Mason calls it, "blunt Anglo Saxon" with no pretensions.

Like many writers, Mason draws on her own experience. She lived on the family dairy farm until she left for college and graduate school (she holds a Ph.D. from the University of Vermont). "I grew up," she told Dorothy Combs Hill in 1986, "absolutely immersed in pop culture.

Mainly the radio, but movies too. We went to movies all the time." But a greater influence than the twelve movies a week she saw in the summer was the early rhythm and blues music she heard from WLAC in Nashville from 1950 to 1954: "it really sank deep in my soul." The rock and roll that resonates in her stories, the songs of Bruce Springsteen and her veneration of the Beatles (her first novel, written at age eleven, was about the band) come from this early influence. Mason's early attunement to the larger world beyond her far smaller world provides her the vision to create the vignettes her stories offer of the inevitable conflict that occurs between the two. "The family's my source; my anchor, my way of finding out what's going on with people and connecting with the region" (Lyons and Oliver 454).

Mason's region, the rural South, is the particular place from which she draws the universal. Like southern writers before her—Flannery O'Connor, Carson McCullers, Zora Neale Hurston, William Faulkner, Richard Wright—and those who are her contemporaries—Lee Smith, Mary Hood, Alice Walker, Clyde Edgerton—she sees herself as "reclaiming materials that otherwise would be lost or ignored." For Bobbie Ann Mason, writing about her own postage stamp of soil allows her to "reclaim a measure of pride and identity for my people." While her fiction is southern in setting and language, it is American in subject and theme. The gradual deterioration of a simple world order gives birth to a more complex and chaotic world, with only shadow lines to mark the new and uncharted territory.

Dede Yow

SELECTED BIBLIOGRAPHY

Works by Bobbie Ann Mason

Shiloh and Other Stories. New York: Harper & Row, 1982.
Love Life: Stories. New York: Harper & Row, 1989.
Midnight Magic: Selected Stories of Bobbie Ann Mason. Hopewell, N.J.: Ecco, 1998.

Critical Studies

Hill, Dorothy Combs. "An Interview with Bobbie Ann Mason." *Southern Quarterly* 31/1 (fall 1992): 85–118.
Lyons, Bonnie, and Bill Oliver. "An Interview with Bobbie Ann Mason." *Contemporary Literature* 32/4 (winter 1991): 449–470.
Ryan, Maureen. "Stopping Places: Bobbie Ann Mason's Short Stories." In Peggy Whitman Prenshaw, ed., *Women Writers of the Contemporary South,* pp. 283–294. Jackson: University of Mississippi Press, 1984.

MARY McCARTHY
(1912 – 1989)

In form and theme, Mary McCarthy's writings have extraordinary range. Her enduring work includes scores of novels, short stories, autobiographies, and books of cultural criticism, as well as hundreds of essays and reviews. Throughout her writing, McCarthy has exhibited a deep concern for civil rights and social responsibility; she wrote penetrating and astute essays on the Vietnam War and the Watergate trials; more privately, she discussed her philosophical and intellectual concerns in letters to her close friend, political philosopher Hannah Arendt. Deeply engaged with cultural events and intellectual trends, Mary McCarthy's novels and short stories reflect dramatic shifts in American culture during a century characterized by rapid urbanization, bureaucratization, and the radicalization of the political consciousness of artists and intellectuals. With intellectual rigor, rich detail, and keen wit, Mary McCarthy's work boldly examines traditional assumptions about gender, class, and race.

McCarthy provides stories of her own life in her many autobiographical writings, among them *Memories of a Catholic Girlhood* (1957), *How I Grew* (1987), and the posthumously published, unfinished *Intellectual Memoirs* (1992). She was born in Seattle in 1912 and orphaned at the age of six when both parents died of influenza on a train bound for Minnesota. After her parents' death, McCarthy lived with relatives in both Minnesota and Seattle and was an accomplished writer at a very young age, writing short stories and winning school prizes for her expository essays. She went on to college at Vassar, where she began writing reviews for the *Nation* and married Harold Johnsrud, an aspiring playwright.

When McCarthy and Johnsrud decided to divorce in 1936, three years after they married, McCarthy moved to New York and began work as an editorial assistant for the publishing company Covici-

Friede. While in New York, she wrote book reviews for the *Nation* and the *New Republic,* as well as the theater chronicle for the *Partisan Review.* In the mid-1930s McCarthy joined with Marxist intellectual Philip Rahv to revive the *Partisan Review.* Living in a small apartment in Greenwich Village, McCarthy was surrounded by other artists and intellectuals; writers such as Sherwood Anderson, Erskine Caldwell, John Dos Passos, and Upton Sinclair debated the politics of communism, taking positions for and against Stalinism. These political debates and McCarthy's allegiance to the anti-Stalin Trotskyists became the subject matter of two short stories, "The General Host!" and "Portrait of an Intellectual as a Yale Man," both later collected in *The Company She Keeps.* In the latter story, protagonist Margaret Sargent's outspoken Trotskyist views unsettle Jim Barnett's seeming liberalism. While Sargent speaks forthrightly about her political convictions, Jim ends up working for a mainstream magazine called *Destiny*; he continues to think about Margaret and tries to justify his abandonment of political principles by blaming his wife and children or by claiming that his new life retains some of its old liberalism: "It was true that the publisher of *Destiny* was a reactionary in many ways—potentially he might even be fascist—but in certain points he was progressive."

Like her character Margaret Sargent, McCarthy wrote many works of political and cultural analysis in which she spoke openly about her sometimes unpopular political views. Throughout her career, McCarthy expressed her social criticism,

without reservation, in reviews and essays; in the 1960s and 1970s she began writing larger works on political issues, including *Vietnam* (1967), *Hanoi* (1968), *Medina* (1972), *The Seventeenth Degree* (1974), and *The Mask of State: Watergate Portraits* (1974). McCarthy's ability to speak with unflinching candor is also crucial in her fiction and autobiographical writings, in which her examination of taboo subjects often created considerable controversy. She spoke unreservedly about sexual experiences, admitted to having abortions, and provided details about obtaining and using a diaphragm in her best-selling novel *The Group,* in which free love, adultery, misogyny, divorce, and insanity are confronted openly. Similarly, in the interlocking short stories of *The Company She Keeps,* Margaret Sargent drinks, gets divorced, has affairs, and goes through psychoanalysis, thereby challenging the norms of traditional femininity.

Mary McCarthy's own relationships often became part of her fictional writing. In the first year of her rocky marriage to literary critic Edmund Wilson in 1938, he insisted that she stay in the study until she had written a short story. The result was "Cruel and Barbarous Treatment," about John Porter, for whom McCarthy left her first husband. Another brief fling with a man she met on a train en route to Reno provided the plot to her short story "The Man in the Brooks Brothers Shirt." Although Wilson productively pushed McCarthy to write fiction, her self-esteem suffered greatly during their marriage. She finally left Wilson and married Bowden Broadwater in 1946. Wilson entered the world of Mary McCarthy's fiction in

A Charmed Life in 1955, where she writes in a thinly veiled portrait of him: "He casts a long shadow. I don't want to live in it. I feel depreciated by him, like a worm, like a white grub in the ground." In 1961, McCarthy married James West, with whom she remained until her death from cancer in 1989.

When McCarthy published *The Group* in 1963, critic Elizabeth Hardwick praised the author for writing the novel "from a women's point of view, the comedy of Sex." From its beginnings, McCarthy's work has been concerned with the politics of gender. In particular, McCarthy exposes the destructive paradigms on which traditional gender roles are based by revealing the harmful distortions of characters tied to traditional notions of masculinity and femininity. In this context, only women who stand outside these conventions survive with integrity.

McCarthy's earliest autobiography, *Memories of a Catholic Girlhood,* is a series of interrelated stories that problematizes the difference between fiction and autobiography. An autobiographical essay that explores issues of memory, creative reconstruction of past events, and the role of imagination prefaces each "story." The characters in *Memories* share many characteristics and themes with the characters of her fictional story collection, *The Company She Keeps*. In particular, the character of Uncle Myers becomes a prototype of dominating brutality and excessive masculinity that appears throughout McCarthy's work. Abusive, bestial, and unintelligent, Myers is cruel to the McCarthy children and embodies the distorted aggression inherent in the traditional mas-

culine role. In "A Tin Butterfly," included in *Memories of a Catholic Girlhood,* Myers sits "in a brown leather armchair in the den, wearing a blue work shirt stained with sweat. . . . Below this were work man's trousers of a brownish-gray material, straining at the buttons and always gaping slightly . . . to show another glimpse of underwear. . . . On his fat head, frequently . . . were the earphones of a crystal radio set, which he sometimes, briefly, in a generous mood, fitted over the grateful ears of one of my little brothers." Throughout *The Company She Keeps,* characters that embody the exaggerated aspects of Uncle Myers's masculinity appear foolish and ridiculous. Characters such as Mr. Sheer in "Rogue's Gallery" and Pflauman in "The Genial Host" seem infantile and self-indulgent. Pflauman's name means "prunes" in German, underscoring the absurdity of his position as a social middleman. In "Portrait of an Intellectual as a Yale Man," Jim Barnett's status as a glamorous, liberal intellectual rests on the unstable ground of his inflated self-importance. He comes to despise Margaret Sargent, the female protagonist, for making him aware of his limitations: "He had never been free, but until he had tried to love the girl, he had not known that he was bound. . . . Through her he had lost his primeval ignorance, and he would hate her forever."

Margaret Sargent appears in all of the stories in McCarthy's collection, drawing them together into an interlocking whole. She is the embodiment of the modern woman, trying hard to find ways of combining work and love, family and career, and finding it tough going. She encounters a double standard everywhere, in both work and love. Although Sargent has had an elite education at one of the nation's best colleges, her choices are limited to being a secretary or an assistant. The irony is not lost on her. *The Company She Keeps* chronicles the isolating and frustrating experiences of a young woman whose culture does not provide her with opportunities to develop and advance.

Although McCarthy's female characters are often sexually liberated and independently mobile, many have not completely escaped nineteenth-century Victorian norms of passivity and dependence. Not only are the women often constrained by fears of exploitation or loss of reputation, but they also lack economic opportunities to achieve self-sufficiency. Bound by these socioeconomic limitations, many of McCarthy's female characters still await the gallant knight who will rescue them from life's concerns. "Ghostly Father, I Confess," included in *The Company She Keeps,* depicts the liberated woman, Margaret Sargent, turning in desperation to this mythology: "The mind was powerless to save her. Only a man. . . . She was under a terrible enchantment, like the beleaguered princess in the fairy tales."

Margaret Sargent's achievement of such modern freedoms as the ability to divorce, to live and travel alone, to work and freely express political convictions, and to remarry are not enough to temper her need for male approval. Not only does she wait for a man to save her in "Ghostly Father, I Confess," but also she assumes the role of nurturer for many men, even those who are morally defective, psychologically unbalanced, and sexually inept.

In "Rogue's Gallery," she works for a charlatan who sells miniature portraits of dogs and Italian paintings with fake signatures, a man who does not pay her salary and avoids his debts. Nevertheless, Sargent is intent on redeeming him: "All my efforts were bent on keeping Mr. Sheer in a state of grace, and I stood guard over him as fiercely, as protectively and nervously, as if he had been a reformed drunkard. And, like the drunkard's wife, I exuded optimism and respectability." While exposing Mr. Sheer's weakness, McCarthy reveals Margaret Sargent's frustrated need to fulfill the role of redemptive womanhood, satirizing her attempt to attain moral superiority through the salvation of unregenerate men.

In "The Man in the Brooks Brothers Shirt," Mr. Breen refuses to let Margaret Sargent play the romantic heroine who will redeem him with a nurturing woman's love. Despite her valiant efforts, he remains unchanged. Throughout the story, she feels disgust and revulsion for her seducer: "The attraction was not sexual, for, as the whiskey went down in the bottle, his face took on a more and more porcine look that became so distasteful to her that she could hardly meet his gaze." Nevertheless, Sargent is carried away by traditional notions of romantic love and assumes the role of redemptive womanhood. Her own feelings become inconsequential as seduction turns into a performance in which the romantic heroine must adjust every gesture, every facial and vocal nuance, to support her leading man: "She found that she was extending herself to please him. All her gestures grew overfeminine and demonstrative." The charade forces her into a role of powerlessness and self-abnegation as "she helped him take off the black dress, and stretched herself out on a berth like a slab of white lamb on an altar."

The consequences of feminine passivity are confining and destructive, but McCarthy also creates characters that open up new possibilities for women, embodying options completely outside of established visions of womanhood. For example, in *Memories of a Catholic Girlhood,* McCarthy depicts Rosie Morgenstern Gottstein, her great-aunt, as an alternative to her grandmother's domesticated ornamentality. She "was a short, bright, very talkative, opinionated woman, something of a civic activist and something of a Bohemian." McCarthy feels a connection with this "excitable" aunt and perceives the woman as evidence of multiple possibilities for women's lives in the twentieth century. Not only does Rosie suggest that women can express their opinions and act them out, but also she is "something of a Bohemian," indicating that she disregards convention and lives outside of mainstream society. The power that Rosie evokes is that of alternatives, a woman's ability to live in a way different from her mother, grandmother, neighbor, or peer. This is particularly important for the young McCarthy in *Memories of a Catholic Girlhood* because her social environment is one dominated by silenced and often ineffectual women.

By turning her life stories into fictional episodes, McCarthy admits such alternatives and possibilities. She emphasizes the possibilities Rosie offers and demonstrates the limits of more conventional routes. Throughout her autobiographical works, memory plays only a part in the creation of narrative. Whether she begins with a story from her own life or an entirely fictional episode, McCarthy's primary interest becomes the ability to shape a story and to make it into a coherent, aesthetically unified whole. In this way, she becomes the author of her own life, forming and shaping it as she writes. In an interview for the *Paris Review* in 1962, McCarthy acknowledged the possibilities inherent in the act of writing: "I think I'm really not interested in the quest for the self anymore. . . . What you feel when you're older, I think is that . . . you really must make the self. . . . I don't mean in the sense of making a mask, a Yeatsian mask. But you finally begin in some sense to make and choose the self you want." Be defying genre categories, her writing becomes a series of exercises in self-formation, or performances, through which female and male readers can glimpse alternatives to conventional gender paradigms. Mary McCarthy began writing autobiography in an effort to find the truth, in an objective sense, but she finally realized that one must make the self through the imaginative rendering of stories.

Wendy Martin

SELECTED BIBLIOGRAPHY

Works by Mary McCarthy

The Company She Keeps. New York: Simon & Schuster, 1942.

Memories of a Catholic Girlhood. New York: Harcourt Brace, 1957.

The Hounds of Summer and Other Stories. New York: Avon Books, 1981.

Arendt, Hannah. *Between Friends: The Correspondence of Hannah Arendt and Mary McCarthy, 1945–1975.* New York: Harcourt Brace, 1995.

Brightman, Carol. *Writing Dangerously: Mary McCarthy and Her World.* New York: Clarkson Potter, 1992.

Epstein, Joseph. "Mary McCarthy in Retrospect." *Commentary* 95(5) (May 1993): 41–47.

Gelderman, Carol W. *Conversations with Mary McCarthy.* Jackson: University Press of Mississippi, 1991.

Gelderman, Carol W. *Mary McCarthy: A Life.* New York: St. Martin's Press, 1988.

Hardwick, Elizabeth. "Mary McCarthy in New York." *New York Review of Books,* June 11, 1987.

Niebuhr, Elizabeth. "The Art of Fiction: Mary McCarthy." *Paris Review* 27 (winter–spring 1962): 58–94.

ELIZABETH McCRACKEN

(1966–)

Elizabeth McCracken is the author, to date, of two books: a collection of short stories, *Here's Your Hat What's Your Hurry* (1993), and a novel, *The Giant's House* (1996). *Here's Your Hat What's Your Hurry* was an American Library Association Notable Book of 1994. *The Giant's House* was a finalist for the 1996 National Book Award in fiction and is the work that earned her a place on *Granta* magazine's much-touted Best Young American Novelists list, a lineup of twenty of America's up-and-coming young writers, seven of whom were women. Daphne Merkin claimed in *The New Yorker* that "although McCracken is as original a writer as they come, her novel can be placed in a vaguely Southern tradition, which combines Christian sentiment with an air of rueful secularism." Merkin is reminded of writers like Harper Lee, Marjorie Kellogg, Carson McCullers, and Walker Percy, authors who share "a confiding and idiosyncratic tone that comes to seem as natural as the way one talks to oneself. What they also share is an embrace of the anomalous . . . as a means of recasting our notions of what human redemption might look like."

Elizabeth McCracken was born in Brighton, Massachusetts, on September 16, 1966. Both her parents are academics. McCracken, who has called herself "a lapsed librarian," has worked in libraries since the age of fifteen and has a degree in library science from Drexel University. She also has degrees in English literature from Boston University and in fiction writing from the University of Iowa. She now lives in Somerville, Massachusetts, and avows she "has not lived a life of particular note and frequently vacations in Des Moines, Iowa." She has received grants from the Michener Foundation, the Fine Arts Work Center in Provincetown, and the National Endowment for the Arts.

In "Here's Your Hat What's Your Hurry," the title story of McCracken's collection, the character Aunt Helen Beck migrates from family to family, staying with whomever will have her for as long as they will have her, claiming distant kinship and bestowing upon arrival in any new home an artifact stolen from the last. She explains that the picture or the candlestick holder is of historical and familial importance; she is, in actuality, related to no one she claims to be and has lived this subterfuge for nigh on forty years. The implications of Aunt Helen Beck's long success at sustaining such a life is that family—and a sense of family—is an amalgam brought together by desire and need, not by relationship or blood. One of the fine ambiguities of the story arises at the end when Aunt Helen Beck is looking into a little boy's eyes and she sees "an old, familiar expression: I could go now, it wouldn't make any difference, my family album might as well be the phone book, so long." It is a moment of connection between the little boy Mercury and Aunt Helen Beck, a ready construction of family; it is the suggestion that they are now kin regardless of convention. But the old, familiar expression is perhaps also a look Aunt Helen Beck has seen in other people's eyes as they tell her good-bye, as they send her on her way, "so long," relegating her to the vast though "illegitimate" possibilities of the phone book as family album. Aunt Helen Beck is at once everyone's aunt and that aunt we all have whose relation to us is oblique, probably a second cousin once or twice removed. Aunt Helen Beck is also an infiltrator, not of the tribe, the ostracized. She gives rise to feelings that terrify, perhaps primally so, connectionless solitude, banishment, the erosion of familial identity.

In the story "It's Bad Luck to Die," the character Lois is six feet tall, a Jewish girl from Des Moines, and though she is not as outsized as the acromegalic James

Sweatt is in *The Giant's House,* she too must learn how to live in her body, how to take up occupancy in so much space. Lois is eighteen when she meets Tiny, a forty-year-old tattoo artist who falls in love with Lois's wide open spaces. She becomes his canvas, and the artistry of his tattoos allows her to at last move into her physique instead of feeling "like a ghost haunting too much space." "It's Bad Luck to Die" is yet another story in which identity or belonging is found unashamedly where convention does not reside.

The narrator's mother in "What We Know About the Lost Aztec Children" comes in one day, kicks the door shut with her foot, and announces, "Steven, this is your Uncle Plazo." Uncle Plazo's chin is barely higher than a doorknob, and until recently he has been a circus act with his now deceased brother, Zleeno. Steven and his two sisters discuss at which point in their lineage they might have acquired their Uncle Plazo: "He could be a great-uncle," or "He could be from Tennessee. Ma was originally from Nashville." Uncle Plazo is in fact from the mother's past, a member of the Ten-in-One sideshow, along with Seal Boy, the Tattooed Beauty, The Skeleton Dude, and a pair of "angry Siamese twins." Later in the story Uncle Plazo informs Steven that his mother was the "most beautiful armless girl in the world." The identity that Steven has constructed of his mother, one aided greatly by her gift of letting him forget that she is abnormal, broadens to include a family and stories he did not know she had, and for which he must learn compassion.

"What We Know About the Lost Aztec Children" is a dramatized discussion of the stories people tell about themselves and the identities they construct. Many of those constructions are forced upon them, many are in retaliation—all are as significant as genetic identity, perhaps even more so. "The man from Mars," Uncle Plazo said, "was from Kentucky. I always liked him." Being both from Mars and from Kentucky is not a paradox for Uncle Plazo, nor for many of McCracken's characters for whom a point of origin necessitates another geography, one hospitable to the anomalous.

Issues of imposed or negotiated identity are also vividly at the center of the story "Mercedes Kane." Ellen, the divorced mother of Ruthie, the story's narrator, one day brings home a woman who might be indigent, homeless, though we learn she's "got a room, but she won't say where." Ellen is convinced the woman is Mercedes Kane, a child prodigy whose magnificent intellectual accomplishments dominated the news when Ellen was growing up. Ruthie, no stranger to identity wars, watches from the sidelines as her mother's intractable desire for the woman butts up against the caffeine quaffing, chain-smoking, talk-show obsessed cipher who just happens to call herself Mercedes and who is more like a louche sphinx than a person capable of speaking "six real languages plus Esperanto." One of the story's most interesting aspects is Ruthie's emergence as both a character and a self during the respite Mercedes's arrival provides from her mother's intense focus.

"Some Have Entertained Angels, Unaware" is the story of Annie and Jackie, two children brought up, for the most part lovingly, by an odd assortment of boarders to whom their father has relinquished their large and dilapidated Victorian house. Several years pass before the father's return, which, when it happens, the reader comes to learn, is not for sentimental or familial reasons but rather to sell the house because he needs the money. Both the motley group of people who have come to constitute a family for Annie and Jackie and the context within which this has happened are almost instantly dissolved. "Some Have Entertained Angels, Unaware" is arguably the story within McCracken's collection that most overtly questions origins, pedigree, genetic history, particularly those conventionally given legal and societal credence. "The family tree . . . begins with me," Annie and Jackie's father insists when entreated to tell a story about his own family, their ancestry. Perhaps in the father's reluctance to divulge their "actual" history, he has given them the gift of self-creation, a gift that both Annie and Jackie must learn to embrace.

Common to many of the stories in Elizabeth McCracken's collection is the tension surrounding acts of self-creation, either as insisted upon by outside forces or as an internal dictum arising out of feelings of alienation or displacement.

Michelle Latiolais

SELECTED BIBLIOGRAPHY

Works by Elizabeth McCracken

Here's Your Hat What's Your Hurry. New York: Random House, 1993.

McCracken, Elizabeth. *The Giant's House.* New York: Dial Press, 1996.

Critical Studies

Jack, Ian. "The Best of Young American Novelists." *Granta* 54 (summer 1996): 171.

Lodge, David. "O Ye Laurels." *New York Review of Books,* August 8, 1996.

Merkin, Daphne. "Big: A decade of unlikely happiness." *The New Yorker,* July 29, 1996.

O'Rear, Joseph Allen. "The Giant's House." *The Review of Contemporary Fiction* XVII (1997): 208.

CARSON McCULLERS
(1917 – 1967)

Carson McCullers was born Lula Carson Smith to Lamar and Marguerite (Waters) Smith on February 19, 1917, in Columbus, Georgia. The precocious child began writing plays at an early age but held music to be her calling. By 1934, however, she abandoned her dreams of becoming a concert pianist, and she instead traveled to New York City to study creative writing at Columbia and New York University. On a return trip to the South, Carson met Reeves McCullers, also an aspiring writer, who soon relocated to New York. The couple married in 1937 and moved to North Carolina. There, before resettling permanently in New York in 1940, McCullers wrote most of her acclaimed first novel, *The Heart Is a Lonely Hunter* (1940), a tale of two male deaf mutes and the devotion that one of them, ironically named Singer, elicits from four unlikely characters. McCullers's second novel, *Reflections in a Golden Eye* (1941), received scant praise, as critics damned the story of murder, voyeurism, and homosexuality as too bizarre for even the southern gothic school. No less perverse is the novella "The Ballad of the Sad Café," a dark fairy tale of triangulated desire between the Amazonian Amelia Evans, her demonic ex-husband, and a hunchback, but its 1943 publication in *Harper's Bazaar* and prominence in McCullers's subsequent collections met with general acclaim. So too did *The Member of the Wedding* (1946), a novel about the lonely Frankie Addams's search for a "we of me" in her southern family and community. The less successful *Clock Without Hands* (1961), McCullers's final novel, presents dual plots focusing on an autobiographical figure dying of leukemia and an interracial pair of would-be young male lovers.

McCullers's plays similarly drew mixed responses. The 1949 dramatization of *The Member of the Wedding,* starring Julie Harris and Ethel Waters, was nothing short of a triumph and, like *The Heart Is a Lonely Hunter, Reflections in a Golden Eye,* and "The Ballad of the Sad Café," was eventually filmed. In contrast, *The Square Root of Wonderful* (1958), largely based on McCullers's destructive marriage, was a dismal failure, closing on Broadway after only forty-five performances. In addition to these works and twenty short stories, McCullers also produced a handful of obscure poems and a series of essays collected by her sister, *Mademoiselle* editor Margarita Smith, in *The Mortgaged Heart* (1971).

The inescapable theme of McCullers's

fiction is unrequited love. She held the bleak opinion that love is rarely, if ever, reciprocal, as she famously explains in "The Ballad of the Sad Café": "First of all, love is a joint experience between two persons . . . the lover and the beloved, but these two come from different countries." "The most outlandish people can be the stimulus for love," McCullers clarifies: "The beloved may be treacherous, greasy-headed, and given to evil habits. Yes, and the lover may see this as clearly as anyone else—but that does not affect the evolution of his love one whit. A most mediocre person can be the object of a love which is wild, extravagant, and beautiful as the poison lilies of the swamp." Therefore, McCullers concludes, "the value and quality of any love is determined solely by the lover himself. It is for this reason that most of us would rather love than be loved. In a deep secret way, the state of being beloved is intolerable to many. The beloved fears and hates the lover, and with the best of reasons. For the lover is forever trying to strip bare his beloved."

McCullers's own life suggests why she maintains this dismal perspective in so much of her writing. Her tumultuous marriage to Reeves, complicated by alcoholism and homoerotic attachments on both their parts, ended in divorce in 1941. When they reconciled and remarried four years later, they were no more well suited for each other, but the relationship ended only when Reeves committed suicide in France in 1953. Throughout these years, Carson nursed a number of crushes, typically on unresponsive women such as Annemarie Clarac-Schwarzenbach and Katherine Anne Porter. McCullers's an-

guish in her personal relationships was accompanied by an attempted suicide and a lifetime of illness: rheumatic fever, pleurisy, pneumonia, paralytic strokes, and breast cancer. A virtual invalid in her last years, she died on September 29, 1967, and was buried at Nyack, New York, where she had lived with her mother and sister since 1945.

Like many other writers known primarily as novelists, including fellow southerners Truman Capote and Eudora Welty, McCullers began her career by writing short stories that were later eclipsed by her longer fiction. Some stories are, in fact, prototypes of novels— "The Aliens" and "Untitled Piece," for instance, both prefigure *The Heart Is a Lonely Hunter*—but most differ significantly from the longer works of fiction in several ways. The latter are set in the South and often address interracial social relationships; the stories, on the other hand, most frequently take place in the North or in an unspecified geography and focus almost exclusively on white characters. With the exception of "The Orphanage" and "Madame Zilensky and the King of Finland," the stories are also far less gothic than the longer fiction and typically depict the mundane rather than the eerie, bizarre, or grotesque. Nevertheless, even the earliest short pieces reveal a fairly narrow focus that does not vary from the longer fiction's themes of loneliness, abandonment, and rejected affection. McCullers includes all of these, for instance, in "Sucker," an apprentice story written at seventeen but not published until 1963. Here the narrator Pete recounts how he simultaneously but unsuccessfully negotiates his attraction to an older girl and the adoration of his orphaned male cousin. When abandoned by both Maybelle and Sucker, Pete, anticipating the sentiments of "The Ballad of the Sad Café," concludes, "If a person admires you a lot you despise him and don't care—and it is the person who doesn't notice you that you are apt to admire. This is not easy to realize."

Besides introducing this preoccupation with unsatisfying relationships, "Sucker" also establishes two recurring subjects in McCullers's fiction: men or boys who must cope with vaguely articulated same-sex desire, and children awkwardly poised between adolescence and adulthood. Gay or quasi-gay relations like the homoerotic bond between Pete and Sucker are particularly prominent in the longer pieces, structuring all of them except *The Member of the Wedding,* but they figure into shorter ones as well. "The Jockey," for example, is a bitter indictment of the callous rich that centers on Bitsy Barlow's devotion to his injured "particular pal." It was with her adolescent characters, however, that readers and critics most closely associated McCullers. Teenagers—and especially young tomboys—agonizing over their uncertain social roles appear in *The Heart Is a Lonely Hunter, The Member of the Wedding,* and *Clock Without Hands* as well as in many stories: "Poldi" and "Wunderkind," tales of young musicians; "Breath from the Sky," an autobiographical piece about a girl suffering an unnamed illness; "Correspondence," McCullers's only epistolary story; "Like That," a treatment of menstruation so frank that editors considered it unpublishable until the 1970s; and "The Haunted Boy," a story of failed suicide.

Both "Poldi" and "Wunderkind," McCullers's first published story, not only

use teenage protagonists but draw upon her early musical training and relationship with her childhood piano teacher, Mary Tucker. "Wunderkind" details a young girl's dismay upon realizing that her musical talents are limited and that she is not the prodigy she originally seems. Crucial here is the complex mutual investment between Frances and her idealized instructor, Mr. Bilderbach, just as Hans's unacknowledged infatuation with the older female cellist is central in "Poldi." In both stories the author uses fiction to process what she believed was her abandonment by Mary Tucker; moreover, McCullers begins to explore in them how multiple and variable the forms of love may be.

While the young McCullers's stories tend to highlight adolescents, the older writer's works perhaps not surprisingly feature a large number of dysfunctional marriages. Of these stories, the brief "Art and Mr. Mahoney" is the lightest, with its focus on a socially unrefined husband who embarrasses his wife by clapping at an inopportune moment. In contrast, however, are "Instant of the Hour After," "A Domestic Dilemma," "The Sojourner," and "Who Has Seen the Wind?" The first, a devastating depiction of an alcoholic, eerily foreshadows Reeves McCullers's ultimate fate, even hinting at an attraction to other men, while consistently maintaining sympathy for the put-upon wife. The second story reverses these roles, casting the wife and mother Emily Meadows as the alcoholic who threatens an otherwise charming family. And yet even this character's atrocious drunken behavior (she feeds her children toast peppered with cayenne rather than cinnamon) does not wholly eradicate her husband's love for her. The story ends with him slipping into bed with his sleeping wife and tenderly touching her, a moment in which "sorrow paralleled desire in the immense complexity of love." This complexity similarly characterizes John Ferris's feelings in "The Sojourner" as he struggles with his ex-wife's ideal family and his own brittle relationship with his new girlfriend's son. Love seems to be missing altogether, however, in "Who Has Seen the Wind?" In that story, a fictional parallel to *The Square Root of Wonderful,* McCullers forthrightly attacks Reeves through the character of the failed writer Ken Harris.

The Square Root of Wonderful has a second parallel in "The Haunted Boy," a chilling story featuring yet another adolescent protagonist. As the title suggests, the anxious young Hugh Brown is haunted by memories of his mother's failed suicide— "the other time" is the only way he can allow himself to phrase it—and the threat of a second attempt. The majority of the narrative therefore details his desperate efforts to find companionship with a friend when his mother is unexpectedly absent one afternoon. The story ends on an atypical note of reassurance: Mrs. Brown has only gone shopping, and Hugh ultimately masters his fears with the assistance of his father's kind words. But McCullers hints that this resolution is both temporary and equally crippling for Hugh, since he must repress not only fear but all emotion— "the anger that had bounced with love, the dread and guilt"—to cope with his mother's presence.

The position in which Hugh finds himself is not unlike that of the unnamed drunken protagonist of "A Tree. A Rock. A Cloud," whose devotion is rejected by his wife rather than a suicidal parent. After a futile pursuit of her, the man arrives at what he terms the "science" of love. People, he maintains, "start at the wrong end of love. They begin at the climax." They should instead slowly work up to the love of another human being, investing first in inanimate objects such as those listed in the story's title or in other minor things. McCullers's plot suggests, however, that this understanding is as potentially flawed as Hugh's negation of emotion. Because the drunken man convinces himself that these loves are as gratifying as that for his wife, he refuses any greater expression where there is the risk of rejection. "I go cautious," he explains when asked if he has since fallen in love with another woman. "I am not quite ready yet."

Carson McCullers remained secure of her creative powers throughout her career, once asserting, "Surely I have more to say than Hemingway, and God knows, I say it better than Faulkner." Mid-century critics agreed that she had exceptional talent, and her numerous grants and awards included two Guggenheim fellowships, three O. Henry prizes, an American Academy of Arts and Letters grant, a New York Drama Critics Circle award, and membership in the National Institute of Arts and Letters.

Gary Richards

SELECTED BIBLIOGRAPHY

Works by Carson McCullers

"*The Ballad of the Sad Café*": *The Novels and Stories of Carson McCullers.* Boston: Houghton Mifflin, 1951.

"The Ballad of the Sad Café" and Collected Short Stories. Boston: Houghton Mifflin, 1955.

The Mortgaged Heart. Boston: Houghton Mifflin, 1971.

Critical Studies

Carr, Virginia Spencer. *Understanding Carson McCullers.* Columbia: University of South Carolina Press, 1990.

Clark, Beverly Lyon, and Melvin J. Friedman, eds. *Critical Essays on Carson McCullers.* New York: G. K. Hall, 1996.

McDowell, Margaret B. *Carson McCullers.* Boston: Twayne, 1980.

Westling, Louise. *Sacred Groves and Ravaged Gardens: The Fiction of Eudora Welty, Carson McCullers, and Flannery O'Connor.* Athens: University of Georgia Press, 1983.

THOMAS McGUANE
(1939–)

Thomas McGuane was born in Michigan in 1939. He earned a bachelor of arts degree in English from Michigan State University and a master of fine arts degree from the Yale School of Drama, and he held a Wallace Stegner Fellowship at Stanford University. McGuane's fiction is set in Michigan, the Florida Keys, and Montana, places where he has lived. Since the late 1960s, McGuane has owned and operated a working ranch in southwestern Montana. Currently he ranches near McLeod, Montana, where he lives with his third wife, Laurie, and their children. An avid sportsman, McGuane has written extensively about ranch life, hunting, and fishing.

Recognized primarily as a novelist, with eight published novels to date, McGuane has also written screenplays, essays, and numerous short stories, many of which are collected in *To Skin a Cat,* published in 1986. With the publication of his first novel, *The Sporting Club,* in 1969, McGuane was off to an auspicious start. His second novel, *The Bushwhacked Piano* (1971), won him a laudatory review in the *New York Times Book Review* and the Rosenthal Award from the National Institute of Arts and Letters. While his first four novels were largely satiric, his subsequent Montana novels have been less so, and their language has become less pyrotechnic and more attentive to the nuanced details of working and sporting men. In the past few years, McGuane has published mostly in essay form, with a limited-edition collection of essays on fishing and several magazine pieces.

McGuane's collection of short stories, *To Skin a Cat,* received generally positive reviews. McGuane had prepared extensively before attempting a short story collection, a project that took three years to complete. The collection represents an experiment unlikely to be repeated, for McGuane believes that "short stories are basically read only by other short story writers." Nevertheless, a few stories have appeared since his collection in magazines as disparate as *The New Yorker* and *Boy's Life.*

The stories in *To Skin a Cat* cover ground familiar to readers of McGuane's novels: many of the protagonists are financially comfortable but socially and spiritually dislocated, their families are fractured, they cling to or are tied to virtues and values associated with another time, and they often struggle against corruption by a materialist society. Sometimes their attempts to accommodate their desires within a rigidly structured contemporary world manifest in manic or outlaw behavior, as in "Like a Leaf" and "The Rescue." Mid-life crises, fatal attractions, and "grace under pressure" form the thematic core of the stories collected in *To Skin a Cat*. If these characters, such as Jack in "Two Hours to Kill," find any sort of refuge, it is most often through the rituals of physical labor or sport, and it is nearly always outside, in nature.

Although McGuane has never embraced regionalism, his work consistently links his characters, especially in moments of self-discovery, to place. Since the 1970s that place has most often been Montana, a landscape that suits his characters' emotional and spiritual dislocation. For McGuane, Montana seems to be a place where the old mythic West and the new commercial West still struggle for cultural power. Although the old West myths cannot sustain McGuane's protagonists, they cling to many of the values associated with it anyway. In the story "Partners," the values associated with masculine outlawry allow both the escape from conventionality for Dean Robinson and his recapture by conventional society. Robinson, recently made partner in a Montana law firm, has been mentored by Edward Hooper, a senior member. Hooper includes Dean in a dinner at an important client's home. When Dean discovers that the client's wife is an old girlfriend, he rejects his role as upwardly mobile lawyer for the role of rival to Terry Bidwell and suitor to his wife Georgeanne. He offends Hooper in the process and courts ruin at the firm by pursuing Georgeanne with abandon. The two go for a drive into "a vast, mainly unpeopled area with scattered small impoverished ranches," where Dean and Georgeanne grow comfortable with each other for the first time after years apart. Out of town, where "plovers hunted along the plowed ground, and the sky was extremely blue," Dean suddenly understands that he and Georgeanne are not lovers, but good friends. Here it is the West of nature and not of commerce, the prairie and not the city, that allows for Dean's revelation. But Dean has played the outlaw's part too well, for when he returns Georgeanne to her home, he and her husband Terry exchange blows. At first the injured Dean thinks of a legal response, "attempted homicide," but he still clings to the old codes and enters the house to defend his and Georgeanne's honor. In dialogue worthy of a classic Western, Terry says to the bleeding and battered Dean, "I hope this has been worth it to you, pardner." While the spelling is old West dialect, the meaning is multiple, and forecasts Dean's complicity in the system he strives to reject. Dean refuses to quit his job, and his outlaw attitude extends to his workplace, where he describes legal work as "shitwork" and stands up to Hooper. The outlaw becomes an office hero, finding that his bad behavior "seems merely to have advanced [his] career." Dean's attempts to escape the monotony and conventionality of his job have only made him more successful and more deeply entrenched. The old codes, though deeply imbedded, can be made to serve the new commercial West.

The story "Road Atlas" presents another rivalry, this time between brothers. Bill Berryhill is in business with his two brothers, but remains unsatisfied with the new West and its RV distributors, gasohol plants, and grain elevators. Both brothers speak a clichéd language of "level playing fields, a smoking gun . . . who was on board and what was on line." Both want Bill to be a team player, finding that his "search for meaning is a bore." But as the descriptions of the brothers, with their MBAs, cigars, bow ties, and their language make clear, McGuane wants his readers to find them, and not Bill, the bores. Though the brothers, and by implication the culture, render Bill and his old-fashioned sense of values superfluous, Bill is at his best—direct, focused, productive—when he engages the old-fashioned rituals of the West. Bill, and the story, come alive as McGuane describes Bill in his role as small-time rancher. When out on the ranch Bill loses the indecision and passivity that mar his relationship with Elizabeth, the woman in his life, and he loses the cynicism that marks his relationship with his brothers. He knows how a haystack ought to be constructed and most important, how to work as one with a fine cutting horse. In a detailed rendering of cutting a steer from a small herd, McGuane shows what the old West still has to offer: "This time, Red [the horse] lowered himself and waited; and when the cow moved he sat right hard on his hocks, broke off, stopped hard, and came back inside the cow. Now he was working, his

ears forward, his eyes bright. . . . Bill was pleased to be reminded that this was a horse you could call on and use. After a minute more, Red was blowing and Bill put his hand down on his neck to release him. The colt's head came up as though he were emerging from a dream, and he looked around." McGuane has said that "the close study of all animals teaches us that we're not the solitary owners of this planet," and the old ways of the West, through raising livestock or hunting, allow for that closeness between human and animal. Bill's resistance to his brothers' world is worth making, for Bill's attention to ranching resists self-indulgence and self-delusion, the twin vices of the commercial new West.

Bobby Decatur, the protagonist of the collection's title story, "To Skin a Cat," offers no such resistance. "To Skin a Cat," written and published earlier than the other stories in the collection, looks backward to McGuane's earlier satirical work, with its dark humor and violence. Nominally a Montanan, Bobby's only connection to the family ranch in Deadrock, Montana, is the income he derives from it. While both Bobby and his mother in New York display themselves as Westerners—Emily Decatur answers the door of her suite at the Carlyle Hotel in a "Dale Evans cowgirl suit," and Bobby "exudes privilege in his tweed jacket, Levi's, and cowboy boots"—neither retains any connection to the land or the work done at the ranch. McGuane introduces readers to Bobby, in London to sell a falcon, where he meets another American, Marianne, there to visit her fiancé. Bobby admires birds of prey, Marianne, and pimps. He sells his falcon, seduces Marianne, and sets out to become her pimp. They return to the United States, head west, and rent a place in San Francisco. Both Bobby and Marianne, with too much money and too little to do, seem attracted to a contemporary version of outlaw life which takes the form of prostitution. For Bobby the outlaw is the pimp; for Marianne, it is the whore. In McGuane's stories the outlaw position is nearly always defined through sex.

McGuane lambastes modern urban culture throughout the story, while alluding to the debased urbanized alternatives. In San Francisco, the most western place Bobby can go, Marianne suggests a trip to Golden Gate Park. The park too shows only nature debased, ritualized, and commodified. At the park they find the casting pools of the Golden Gate Angling and Casting Club. While elsewhere McGuane has written elegiacally of the club, here the "well-dressed anglers," who cast where there are no fish, only inspire terror in Bobby. The buffalo paddock offers no solace either, for the sight of "the great mementos" only makes Bobby feel weak. Given that the redemptive West, of outdoor sports and work, remains elusive for both Bobby and Marianne, their fate is sealed. Bobby and Marianne manage to become involved in prostitution, though not in the way they planned. Marianne is kidnapped by a rival pimp, becoming his prize—an unwilling sex partner for his clients. Throughout the story Bobby remains dissatisfied with his life, unable to live authentically, but both Bobby and Marianne pay for their outlaw impulses. When Bobby finally finds Marianne, she kills him.

Many readers find "To Skin a Cat" extremely distasteful and indicative of McGuane's insensitivity to women characters in his work. In the only major review of the collection, and generally a positive one, in the New York Times Book Review, Elizabeth Tallent criticized both "Like a Leaf" and "To Skin a Cat" as too bleak, even repelling. In both stories sexually active women pay a hard price for their sexual outlawry. But in both stories, the men too pay a price for their misguided allegiance to a bankrupt western mythology. When freedom is construed as license, McGuane seems to say, the results will be disastrous. McGuane follows a deeply worn path when he links sexual license with the exploitation of the land, but while the characterization by gender is conventional, the language, and often the imagery, are not. Neither Bobby Decatur nor Marianne (who is given no last name) becomes sympathetic in the way many of McGuane's characters do, because they have been given nothing to do. While Bobby might be a good falconer, McGuane never shows him at work with a hawk. Readers see Marianne only as prey: we learn that she has been a lobbyist for meat byproducts, but never see Marianne do anything but perform sexually. While McGuane seems to suggest that both characters deserve readers' scorn, it seems Marianne pays more dearly, because she pays so conventionally.

Ironically, by its absence in "To Skin a Cat," readers may come to recognize that McGuane's stories offer some of the best depictions of men at work in contemporary literature. Few, if any, contemporary writers are as attentive to language as

Thomas McGuane. For McGuane, self-discovery is linked to place, and place is evoked through the precise language of its customs, its work, and its inhabitants. It is such attention to the minutiae of his characters' lives, what they own, how they work and speak, that makes his work distinctive. At his best, McGuane reveals the dignity in the details of our working lives, no matter what the stature of that work within the culture at large.

Nancy Cook

SELECTED BIBLIOGRAPHY

Cook, Nancy. "Investment in Place: Thomas McGuane in Montana." In Barbara Meldrum, ed., *Old West-New West: Centennial Essays,* pp. 213–229. Moscow: University of Idaho Press, 1993.

Gregory, Sinda, and Larry McCaffery. "The Art of Fiction 89." Interview with Thomas McGuane. *Paris Review* (fall 1985): 34–71.

McGuane, Thomas. *To Skin a Cat.* New York: Dutton, 1986.

Morris, Gregory L. "How Ambivalence Won the West: Thomas McGuane and the Fiction of the New West." *Critique* 32/3 (spring 1991): 180–189.

Westrum, Dexter. *Thomas McGuane.* Boston: Twayne, 1991.

JAMES ALAN McPHERSON
(1943–)

Born in Savannah, Georgia, in 1943, James Alan McPherson grew up in a working-class African American community and attended racially segregated public schools. After graduating from high school, he enrolled at Morris Brown College in Atlanta. In the summer of 1962 he was hired as a waiter for the Great Northern Railway, a job that allowed him to observe at close range the habits, speech, and values of a diverse range of Americans, and that provided him with material for some of his best early stories. Although McPherson had begun writing fiction while still an undergraduate, his real promise as a writer emerged soon after he entered Harvard Law School. The *Atlantic Monthly* accepted "Gold Coast," quickly printed it as one of the "Atlantic Firsts," and collaborated with McPherson in publishing *Hue and Cry* (1969), his first collection of short stories.

Although McPherson graduated from Harvard Law School in 1968, he decided not to pursue a career as a lawyer. Instead, he enrolled in the Iowa Writers' Program and received a master of fine arts degree in 1969. In the meantime, he maintained his association with the *Atlantic Monthly* and was invited to join the editorial board as a contributing editor. In the 1970s, McPherson continued writing fiction and essays and taught at the University of California, Santa Cruz, Morgan State University, and the University of Virginia. He was awarded a Guggenheim Fellowship in 1972, and in 1977 his second collection of short stories, *Elbow Room,* won the Pulitzer Prize for fiction. In 1981, he received a MacArthur Prize Fellowship.

Among the many critics and writers to praise *Hue and Cry* was Ralph Ellison, who observed that McPherson "is a writer of insight, sympathy and humor and one of the most gifted young Americans I've had the privilege to read." Like Ellison, McPherson is primarily concerned with the ironies and contradictions of American life, particularly when racial issues are involved; and he is also fascinated by the diversity of American culture, especially the challenge for a writer to do justice to the extraordinary range of American types. Consequently, in *Hue and Cry* and *Elbow Room,* McPherson's cast of characters, settings, and aesthetic techniques are impressively varied. He makes use of his own training and wide experience in several tales. "An Act of Prostitution," in *Hue and Cry,* and "A Sense of Story," in *Elbow Room,* deal with characters involved in courtroom scenes. Some stories are set in the South, while others take place in New York, Boston, San Francisco, and London. Many works involve a first-person narrator (usually an African American male) who is more an observer than a participant. The narrator records the appearance, speech, habits, and predicaments of individual characters no less than the defining characteristics of specific places. The meaning of the stories is usually revealed through a series of revelatory details rather than dramatic action or sensational turns of plot. McPherson's technique often invites the reader to play a collaborative role as onlooker and even as eavesdropper.

Like many of McPherson's best stories, "Gold Coast" is a quiet but powerful exploration of the complex forms of American prejudices and their insidious consequences. Robert, a young African American writer, tells how—to gather material for fiction—he once took a job as an apprentice janitor in a building near Harvard Square. "Conrad Aiken had once lived there," he notes, and "before Harvard built its great houses, it had been a very fine haven for the rich." Now, however, the building is inhabited by nondescript tenants: "old maids, dowagers, asexual middle-aged men, homosexual young men, a few married couples and a teacher." Robert studies the tenants with the detachment of an anthropologist and the irony of a satirist, "noting their perversions, their visitors, and their eating habits." Given his relentless search for stories, he even jokes about having to restrain himself from going through their garbage scrap by scrap.

Absorbing most of Robert's attention is James Sullivan, the old Irish superintendent, who has lived in the basement and collected garbage for thirty years. Sullivan's fixation is Jews: "the biggest eaters in the world. . . . Don't ever talk about them in public. You don't know who they are and that Anti-Defamation League will take everything you got." Similarly, another tenant, Miss O'Hara, a spinster with airs, stereotypes lower-class Irish, detesting Sullivan and his wife for their coarse ways and heavy drinking. Robert too is a victim of prejudice. Blacks and whites on Boston's subways and sidewalks snub and scowl at him and his white girlfriend.

As the story develops, the persistence of the bigotry, the oppression of the impoverished lives of the tenants, and the singularity of Robert's own steely absorption with material for fiction harden and age him in understandable yet unnerving ways. Although he had become something of a confidante and pal for Sullivan, he mechanically moves from the building and coldly rejects the old man when he passes him, encumbered by bundles, on a Cambridge street. By the end of the story, the irony earlier directed at the hapless tenants is turned on the narrator, whose detachment is seen to be an edgy defensiveness and a source of his own isolation, as well as a necessary tool for survival.

Several other stories in *Hue and Cry,* notably "On Trains" and "Solo Song for Doc," have an Ellisonian component. Each piece explores a world in which African Americans, presumed to be placed outside or beneath the threshold of American social life, are actually in the middle of the important action. "On Trains" cuts through the curtain of racial fictions to the core of the strengths, shortcomings, and basic desires of individuals—whether white passengers or black Pullman porters. One woman passenger objects to a black porter's customary station at the back of the sleeping compartment. The porter explains that he is simply doing his job: "I'm a Pullman Porter. . . . I been a Pullman Porter for forty-three years." The woman angrily summons the conductor and says, "We have a right to sleep here without these people coming in doing things." When the conductor asks what the porter has done, the woman screams, "He's black! He's black!" and insists on sitting in the coach section for the night. In contrast, another woman has chatted up John Perry, the club car's black bartender, throughout the evening. As she leaves the club car, she says seductively, "See you later on." When Perry steals into the dark sleeping car, he passes the old porter, who has fallen asleep. "Then he knocked very softly on the door to Com-

partment G. And after a while it was opened and closed very quickly behind him."

Doc Craft, the hero of "Solo Song for Doc," has, like the old porter, his own high professional standards. Considerably more than an affable menial, he is a walking personification of a way of life, expressing a quintessential African American point of view in which personal dignity is rarely confused with the necessary compromises and inconveniences endured because of white prejudice. As Doc schools a young recruit in the art of being a waiter, McPherson captures this special sense of dignity and personal value by allowing Doc Craft to brag about the standards he and his fellow porters and waiters had created and maintained. Without their imagination, patience, and profound understanding of some of the social absurdities of race in American life, the American experience of being "On Trains" would not have existed. They were that experience.

"Why I Like Country Music," as well as other stories in *Elbow Room,* makes similar points about the inextricability of American and African American cultures. Here, one of McPherson's nameless narrators tells the story of his childhood sweetheart, Gweneth Lawson of Brooklyn. The reader is forced to appreciate how the South comprehensively influences the North, and vice versa. The black narrator grew up in South Carolina and is married to a third-generation New Yorker. He tries to explain to his urbane black wife why he likes country music. "I like banjo," he says, "because sometimes I hear ancestors in the strumming. I like the fiddlelike refrain in 'Dixie' for the very same reason. But most of all I like square dancing—

the interplay between the fiddle and the caller, the stomping, the swishing of dresses, the strutting, the proud turnings, the laughter." A flashback takes the reader to the narrator's elementary school days in South Carolina, where he square dances with the beautiful Gweneth Lawson. One might draw the conclusion, among others, that the South is in his blood and asserts itself culturally in the music he enjoys and he women he admires. But more profoundly, McPherson has depicted the complex fate of African Americans whose genesis is in the American South.

After the publication of *Elbow Room* in 1977, McPherson returned to the University of Iowa, where he is a professor of English. He has not published another collection of short stories, but he has written many essays, several of which have been included in annual anthologies of distinguished nonfiction. McPherson is also the coeditor of *Fathering Daughters* (1998). His book *Crabcakes* (1998) is a memoir of his life in Iowa and his experiences in Japan. McPherson's *A Region Not Home: Reflections from Exile* (2000) is a collection of cultural and personal essays. McPherson's profound interest in Japanese culture partly appears to be an attempt to reach even beyond the horizon of his predecessor Ellison and think comparatively about people who exist beyond the confines of the American imagination. In the end, however, he seems, in all his stories and essays, to project a vision summed up in the title story of *Elbow Room,* which depicts the marriage of Virginia Valentine, an idealistic young black woman from Tennessee, to Paul Frost, a young white from Kansas, and their families' complicated responses to their relationship. Some of the complications eventually appear to be settled after the birth of their son. McPherson's narrator describes Virginia's quest as "an epic of idealism." Before she marries Paul and after she returns home from a stint with the Peace Corps, the narrator observes: "She entered the areas behind the smiles of Arabs, Asians, Africans, Israelis, Indians. In the stories they told she found implanted different ways of looking at the world."

Horace Porter

SELECTED BIBLIOGRAPHY

Works by James Alan McPherson

Hue and Cry. Boston: Little, Brown, 1969.
Elbow Room. Boston: Little, Brown, 1977.

Critical Studies

Beavers, Herman. *Wrestling Angels Into Song: The Fictions of Ernest J. Gaines and James Alan McPherson.* Philadelphia: University of Pennsylvania Press, 1995.

NICHOLASA MOHR
(1938–)

In many ways, the life of New York Puerto Rican (Nuyorican) author Nicholasa Mohr, born in 1938 in Spanish Harlem, mirrors the experiences of her fictional characters. While not strictly autobiographical, Mohr's work is intimately tied to her own working-class Puerto Rican childhood at the height of the Puerto Rican migration to New York City during the 1940s and 1950s. Originally trained as a graphic artist at New York's Art Students League, the Brooklyn Museum of Art School, and the Pratt Center for Contemporary Printmaking, Mohr began writing in the early 1970s at the suggestion of an art collector, and soon earned a contract with Harper & Row. Shortly after the publication of her critically acclaimed first novel *Nilda* (1973), Mohr set aside her prosperous career as a visual artist in order to pursue writing exclusively, publishing four volumes of short stories, *El Bronx Remembered* (1975), *In Nueva York* (1977), *Rituals of Survival: A Woman's Portfolio* (1985), and *A Matter of Pride* (1997); three novels, *Felita* (1979), *Going Home* (1987), and *The Magic Shell* (1995); a memoir, *In My Own Words: Growing Up Inside the Sanctuary of My Imagination* (1994); a biography of Evelyn López Antonetty, *All for the Better: A Story of El Barrio* (1995), and two illustrated children's books, *The Song of El Coquí* (1995) and *Old Letivia and the Mountain of Sorrows* (1996). Since the onset of her writing career, Mohr has been the recipient of numerous awards, and her writing, popular with both children and adults, is widely anthologized.

As part of the "second generation" of Nuyorican authors, Nicholasa Mohr's work was often initially compared with that of her Nuyorican contemporaries, most notably Piri Thomas, author of the classic *Down These Mean Streets* (1967). In contrast to the themes of violence and drug abuse among Nuyoricans that predominate in Thomas's novel, Mohr's work is often noted for its thematic emphasis on the everyday struggles and achievements of working-class Puerto Ricans, particularly women. As Mohr states in her essay "The Journey Toward a Common Ground: Struggle and Identity of Hispanics in the U.S.A.," her efforts to portray Puerto Rican women in a believable fashion are rooted in her long-time dissatisfaction with their existing characterizations (or lack thereof): "There were no positive role models for me out there in the great society at large when I was growing up. When I looked and searched with the need to emulate a living person, preferably a woman with whom I could identify, my efforts were futile. As a Puerto Rican female in the U.S., my legacy was either one of a negative image or invisibility."

Aside from its strength of characterization, Mohr's work is also noteworthy in terms of its language. Inspired by the Puerto Rican culture's respect for the art of storytelling, Mohr seeks to document daily life among mainland Puerto Ricans in a realistic manner previously unknown to mainstream audiences. In this documentary style, Mohr reproduces Nuyoricans' daily speech, be it in Spanish, English, or Spanglish, though her relatively infrequent use of Spanish has aroused discussion among some literary critics. However, Mohr defends her decision to write English-dominant texts about Puerto Rican characters, citing greater reader accessibility and the need to reflect the linguistic realities of Puerto Ricans who permanently reside on the mainland. Indeed, in Mohr's work language is not the sole nod to the complex relationship between island and mainland Puerto Ricans: conflicting cultural norms (particularly with regard to gender roles), mainland constructions of the island as a mythical paradise, and Puerto Rico's unique status as a U.S. commonwealth are central themes as well.

One of Nicholasa Mohr's most widely discussed short stories, "The English Lesson," part of the collection *In Nueva York* (1977), takes place on New York's Lower East Side during the 1970s. The story focuses on the relationship between William ("Chiquitín") and Lali, both recent Puerto Rican immigrants and employees at a luncheonette owned and operated by Lali's older husband Rudy. When the two express their desire to take a basic English course, Rudy reluctantly agrees to allow his wife to participate; the subsequent attraction that develops between William and Lali serves as the story's centerpiece, and complements its themes of gender roles, immigration, and language politics.

For young Lali, the opportunity to learn English independently of Rudy offers her the chance to forgo her usual passivity and take advantage of the new possibilities afforded her in New York. Like many of Mohr's female protagonists, for Lali intellectual independence precipitates emotional fulfillment, in contrast to Rudy's notion that the key to a happy marriage is financial stability. Unlike Rudy, William encourages Lali's pursuit of intellectual independence and by extension her abandonment of the private sphere (her place in front of the stove at her hus-

band's restaurant) for the public sphere (as an individual exploring horizons beyond the luncheonette).

In "The English Lesson" Mohr anticipates the rapidly shifting demographics of New York's Latino immigrant population, as well as their frequent rejection of previous assimiliationist models. With language functioning as the principal marker of national origin, the classroom of Mrs. Hamma, the patronizing though well-intentioned English teacher, becomes a site for examining the prejudices toward and differences between the various immigrant populations. Far from ignorant of their unique position as U.S. citizens who nevertheless retain a Latin American identity, Lali and William combat daily obstacles by relying on each other for humor and companionship.

As attested to in many of Nicholasa Mohr's published interviews, her story "The Artist," part of the volume *Rituals of Survival* (1985), is decidedly semiautobiographical in nature and has consequently been the subject of much critical attention. The women featured in the stories of *Rituals* live their lives as the title indicates: they do whatever is necessary to adapt and survive, regardless of the circumstances. "The Artist" chronicles Nuyorican Inez Otero's early marriage to the abusive Joe Batista in order to escape the tyranny of the stingy Aunt Ofelia, Inez's legal guardian since she was orphaned at the age of eleven. In spite of Joe's violent nature, Inez struggles to realize her dream of attending art school and eventually achieve the intellectual, emotional, and financial independence she craves. Told in a chronological order interrupted by occasional flashback sequences, the story is divided into five parts, climaxing in Joe's discovery of Inez's secret life as an art student and concluding with the end of their marriage. "The Artist" well exemplifies the feminist thrust of *Rituals of Survival,* inasmuch as it concentrates on Inez's experiences with such issues as sexuality, domestic violence, and the process of self-realization.

In "The Artist," as in much of Mohr's short fiction, men are afforded a sexual freedom not permitted to women, as evidenced by Aunt Ofelia's tolerance for her pubescent son Papo's constant public masturbation. Joe's insistence on sex with "his" Inez whenever and however he pleases also plays a role in Inez's gradual progress towards ownership of her own sexuality. Throughout "The Artist," Inez's art enables her to cope with her own difficulties regarding her sexuality and violent marriage. As the story progresses, artistic creativity and self-expression displace marriage as Inez's bridge to self-realization. Ultimately, Inez rejects her abusive spouse's verbal and physical abuse and manages to break from Joe by lying to him about her sexual past. Although the lie does momentarily liberate Inez, it also erases any possibility of a completely happy ending, as once again Inez's desirability as a woman is dictated by her sexual purity.

The character of Inez Otero is revisted at a later stage of her life in "My Newest Triumph," a story in Mohr's latest volume, *A Matter of Pride and Other Stories* (1997). While treating many of the same issues touched upon in "The Artist," this time Mohr abandons her traditional third-person narrative in favor of a first-person perspective. The action in "My Newest Triumph" takes place twenty-five years af-

ter the end of Inez's marriage to Joe Batista. Inez, now a successful artist, is in Puerto Rico preparing to present a one-woman show when her ex-husband Joe resurfaces. For readers not familiar with "The Artist," Mohr recounts the tale of Inez's life with Joe, as well as her subsequent remarriage, motherhood, and divorce via a series of flashbacks. Much like "The Artist," the aptly titled "My Newest Triumph" culminates in a scene in which Inez once again employs her own cleverness to thwart Joe's manipulative intentions.

In general, "My Newest Triumph" echoes many of its predecessor's primary themes: art as a means to self-realization and men's sexual "ownership" of women. In this latest story, Inez truly uncovers the path to her own fulfillment and eliminates her own sense of being no one, or "nobody's child." Whatever power Joe still wields over Inez vanishes at the end of "My Newest Triumph," as Inez, no longer the introverted virgin of more than twenty-five years ago, forces her ex-husband to confront his own naiveté and inflated sense of self-importance. The title of the story in fact refers to two triumphs: that of Inez's prosperous artistic career, and more important, her victory over a painful episode in her personal life.

Mohr's work mirrors the tensions inherent in the existences of her hybrid subjects, particularly with regard to gender roles. As part of one of the first waves of widely published Nuyorican authors, her willingness to address "taboo" issues while faithfully portraying the daily lives of her characters has made Mohr a key predecessor of current U.S. Latina/o literature.

María Elena Cepeda

SELECTED BIBLIOGRAPHY

Works by Nicholasa Mohr

El Bronx Remembered. New York: Harper &
Row, 1975.
In Nueva York. New York: Dial Press, 1977.
Rituals of Survival: A Woman's Portfolio. Hous-
ton: Arte Público Press, 1985.
"Puerto Rican Writers in the United States,
Puerto Rican Writers in Puerto Rico: A
Separation Beyond Language." *The Amer-
icas Review* 15/2 (summer 1987): 87–
92.
"The Journey Toward a Common Ground:
Struggle and Identity of Hispanics in the
U.S.A." *The Americas Review* 18/1 (spring
1990): 81–85.
A Matter of Pride and Other Stories. Houston:
Arte Público Press, 1997.

Critical Studies

Hernández, Carmen Dolores. "Nicholasa
Mohr." In Carmen Dolores Hernández,
ed., *Puerto Rican Voices in English: Interviews with Writers,* pp. 85–94. Westport,
Conn.: Praeger, 1997.

LORRIE MOORE
(1957–)

In 1998, Lorrie Moore's third collection
of short stories, the most moving of
which focus on motherhood and mortality, was chosen as one of the best books
of the year by the *New York Times Book
Review.* The citation for *Birds of America*
succinctly summarized Moore's comic yet
dark style, which reviewers over the years
have characterized as "ruefully" and "painfully" funny, "gallows humor," "sardonic,"
"mordant," and full of "deadpan wit."
"Moore, like Samuel Beckett," the editorial board noted, "sees that nothing is
funnier than unhappiness." In reviewing
the collection, critics lauded a new assurance and "full maturity" in her writing,
especially welcome praise for a writer
who was called "young" and "precocious."
With this volume, Moore, known for her
portrayal of young urban professionals
("yuppies"), became an acclaimed observer of the human condition.

Success in both her writing and academic careers came early for Moore. Born
Marie Lorena Moore in 1957, she was
raised in the small Adirondacks town of
Glens Falls, New York. Her father was an
insurance executive, her mother a nurse
turned housewife, and she has described
their comfortable household as "politically minded" and "culturally alert." At
nineteen, while a student at St. Lawrence
University, she won *Seventeen* magazine's
short story contest with the first story she
submitted. Her first collection, *Self-Help*
(1985), largely comprising stories from
her master's thesis at Cornell University,
was published when she was twenty-eight.
At the time she was a creative writing
instructor at the University of Wisconsin.
Today she is a professor of English there
and lives in Madison with her husband and
five-year-old son. The midwestern college campus is one of most Moore's most
frequently used and effectively satirized
settings, and the longing of intellectuals
in the Midwest for the "sophisticated" East
is a common theme in her fiction.

Self-Help received glowing reviews, and Moore was hailed as a new "voice of her generation." She was promptly compared to a wide variety of writers and humorists; her "brisk ironic tone" was considered reminiscent of Grace Paley; her wisecracking, continual insertion of one-liners and mock philosophy suggested Woody Allen to some; and her examinations of unhappy romantic relationships drew comparisons to Ann Beattie. When asked about her influences at the collection's publication, Moore chose a writer whose descriptions of female adolescence she would evoke with her second novel, *Who Will Save the Frog Hospital?* "When I was 18 or 19 my favorite writer was Margaret Atwood," she said in an interview with journalist Caryn James. "For the first time I read fiction about women who were not goddesses or winners. In some ways they were victims, but they weren't wimps. They were stylish about their victimization."

Moore's typical protagonist in her first two story collections is a thoughtful and intelligent woman, often a student, academic, or writer, who thrives on wordplay and wit and is keenly aware of the cinematic and literary traditions that inform her life. She is frequently neurotic, self-deprecating, self-destructive, or glaringly self-absorbed. For all of her intellectual gifts and general financial well-being, she is almost always a victim. The plagues she suffers from range from cold and unfaithful fathers, lovers, and husbands to chauvinistic employers and pink-collar ghettos to cancer. In reading Moore's three collections of stories chronologically, however, a victorious journey emerges for this character as she enjoys a passage out of victimization. This trajectory makes *Birds of America* particularly satisfying for Moore's readers and critics as she refines her dark humor, and offers stories that are vastly more hopeful and life-affirming.

In *Self-Help*, Moore's focus is on young girls and young single women, an unhappy lot trying to deal with their parents' painful legacies or the puzzle of maternal love, or trying to negotiate their own unsuccessful romantic relationships. The collection's two older characters, both married women with children, are in even worse shape than their younger counterparts. In "Go Like This," the fortyish writer heroine is dying of breast cancer and planning a preemptive suicide, and in "To Fill" the thirty-five-year-old narrator ends up in a mental institution after stabbing her philandering husband. *Self-Help* offers little possibility for enduring or redemptive love between men and women, and its portraits of men as adulterers and unfeeling mates may seem like angry male-bashing. Moore's subsequent collection, *Like Life* (1990), features women— and one male protagonist—in romantic and career dilemmas, and focuses on a thirtyish or older group. Material prosperity is an important issue in these stories, as couples battle over it and others desperately seek it. These stories strongly suggest the television program *Thirtysomething,* especially in "Vissi d'Arte," where an idealistic young playwright is tempted to write for a slick program featuring "babies and blenders." The TV series was alternately embraced and reviled by viewers and critics for its yuppie and "whiny" characters, and their desires to meld newfound prosperity and the perfect family life, criticisms that might be applied to some of Moore's characters. The characters in *Like Life* share disbelief in what their lives have become and a terror of how they have lost control of their fate. A cheese store manager whose only companion is her cat says, "You could look at your life and no longer recognize it." A young woman torn between two boyfriends has a "subtle" nervous collapse and cannot comprehend how she ended up in this place in her life. "How did one's eye-patched rot-toothed life," she asks, "lead one along so cruelly, like a trick, to the middle of the sea?" In *Birds of America,* Moore's protagonists are mainly middle-aged, and they have become stronger, wiser, and more self-aware. In the collection's best three stories, ordinary women become warriors as they battle cancer, fight off intruders, and struggle to rebuild their lives after tragedy. While the differences between the genders are still important, more sympathetic male characters emerge and relationships are healthier. Men can be saints and saviors as they support both their spouses and families through difficult times, and parents seem less obsessed with themselves and more nurturing of others.

In *Self-Help*'s "What Is Seized," Moore examines what daughters inherit from their mothers, and how daughters become, and fear becoming, their mothers. The narrator, Lynn, has seen her beautiful mother destroyed by marriage to an emotionally frigid and unfaithful man, and she vows to avenge this wrong in her own relationships. "I will leave every cold man, every man from whom music is some private physics and love some unsteppable

dance," she thinks; "I will try to make them regret." As her mother goes mad and eventually dies from cancer, the daughter examines her distressing legacy. "And when your mother starts to lose her mind, so do you," she laments, and she realizes that in addition to the inheritable objects like "pearls, the blue quilt, and some original wedding gifts," she has also collected "the touches and the words and the moaning the night she dies." These are the pains that the daughter seizes and "carries around in little invisible envelopes" that will "not stayed glued." In the story, Moore aims to capture the lyricism and tragedy of a Greek myth and uses the images of Ceres and her kidnapped-to-hell daughter as a guiding metaphor for a mother and child in peril. Lynn's meditation is rich with memorable metaphors. Rooms in a house are like "songs," a soul is a "drafty, cavernous, empty ballroom," false "I love you's" are like "tiny daggers," and the future is "some hoop-skirted belle that must gather up its petticoats." If the story's language is beautiful, its meanings offer a chillingly grim contrast. Lynn's psyche is depicted as having been irreparably damaged by the memory of her mother's descent into mental illness and cancer, a pattern she feels helpless to break.

"How to Be an Other Woman" portrays another young woman, a recent college graduate frustrated in her career and burdened with her parents' ambition for her. She is also distressed at seeing herself turn into a cliché of a mistress. When she discovers that she is not her lover's only mistress, she realizes that a man will not be her salvation, and she begins to try to save herself. "How to Be an Other Woman" is one of several stories in *Self-Help* written in the second person, in the form of a how-to manual. These are as much how-not-to advice as they are ironic commentaries on the 1980s trend of books on self-improvement, sexual guidance, and popular psychology.

Although Moore considers "the essence of her work to be sad," her writing sparkles with the love of wordplay and the Dorothy Parker-like verbal cleverness of her women. Beginning in *Self-Help,* and throughout her stories and novels, she features characters who mishear, misspeak, play word games, or simply cannot resist a good pun. When the overeducated assistant in "How to Be an Other Woman" is asked if she is a "secretary," she quips, "More like a sedentary." The collegiate aspiring writer in "How to Become a Writer" updates Melville by creating the "fish-eat-fish" world of a depressed suburban husband. Her "Mopey Dick" begins with the line, "Call me Fishmeal." Moore's jokesters are frequently questioned on their persistent and defensive wisecracking. The unfaithful husband of "To Fill" complains that to his wife "Everything's a joke. You're always flip-flopping words, only listening to the edge of things." "Life is a pun," she counters. "It's something that sounds like one thing but also means something else." The young mistress touches on the smile-that-hides-the-tears humor that abounds in the collection when she tells her paramour, "I suffer indignities at your hands. And agonies of duh feet. I don't know why I joke. I hurt."

The many humorous exchanges based on mishearing or mangling words also signify a disconnection between the genders in Moore's stories, and suggest that they speak an essentially different language. When Trudy and Moss in "Amahl and the Night Visitors" argue, for example, they seem incapable of hearing each other correctly. "Moss. I usually don't like discussing sex," she says, and he replies, "I don't like disgusting sex either."

In *Like Life,* Moore's humor advances beyond puns and wisecracks, which some readers found tiring in their preponderance. Three motifs emerge in their stead: the academic world with its hilariously vapid students, bureaucratic administrators, and pretentious or poorly qualified scholars; the distrust and regional differences between easterners and midwesterners; and the modern single woman's conflicting desires for independence and professional success and for the perfect relationship with a man. These themes are all deployed in *Like Life's* "You're Ugly Too." The story takes its title from a doctor joke told by its protagonist, but finds its true humor in a smart feminist's bewilderment about what men in the 1990s may want from a woman, and what a woman needs to be fulfilled. Zoë Hendricks is an American history professor at an Illinois college where her laughably stupid students are "good Midwesterners, spacey with estrogen from large quantities of meat and cheese," and "armed with a healthy vagueness about anything historical or geographic." They are only slightly better than her previous pupils in New Geneva, Minnesota, where "everyone was so blond" that "brunettes were often presumed to be from foreign countries," and she is viewed suspiciously for her lack of complacency and assumed to be from Spain. Hilldale-Versailles College has hired Zoë primarily to provide defense against a sexual discrimination suit. What they really want her to be, she thinks, is a polite, unthreatening "Heidi." After a series of depressing dates with local men, which Moore sketches quickly and savagely like sitcom vignettes, she begins to suspect that "all men, deep down, wanted Heidi. Heidi with cleavage. Heidi with outfits." Moore creates in Zoë a woman who is both pitiable and sympathetic. She is more neurotic than most, and yet she experiences longings with which her female readers can identify. She desires a man who can appreciate wit and intelligence and not crave a "Heidi" or "Barbie," and she needs to be taken seriously in a male-dominated workplace. She also hears the ticking of the "biological clock" that marks her childless years.

In *Birds of America*, Moore's first publication since becoming a mother herself, the stories move away from the depiction of adolescents and young career women and couples, and explore the emotions of parents and those seeking parenthood. Moore's yuppies, the notoriously self-absorbed college graduates who enjoyed the 1980s environment of "material prosperity, sexual liberation, and unparalleled personal choice," are choosing in the 1990s to care about somebody other than themselves. Many of these stories feature children in peril from disease or broken homes, and parents who believe that their lives are not worth living without their children. Mac in "What You Want to Do Fine" fears his life would be "wrecked completely" if divorce separates him from

his young son; and parents in "People Like That Are the Only People Here" confess to having a second child to prevent themselves from suicide if they lost the first. The cancer that has killed many of her earlier characters has returned. This time, however, the characters engage in a gripping battle with the disease that has both violent and joyous consequences. Her heroine in "Real Estate" buys a gun and begins taking shooting lessons because she does not want to resign herself to being a victim of animal intruders or other forces that could invade her life as her disease has.

"People Like That Are the Only People Here," a clinically detailed drama, has become one of Moore's most celebrated works. It was selected for the compendium *Best American Short Stories of 1998* and won first prize for the year in the O. Henry short story competition. Through a mixture of first- and third-person narration, it explores the rapidly escalating horror of a writer and her husband who learn that their infant son has a tumor in his kidney. From its opening sentence—"A beginning, an end: there seems to be neither"— the reader is immediately thrown into the family's sense of the surrealism of the situation, the alternating numbness and panic, and the guilt of the parents at the "inconceivable fate." While the illness of a child brings out courage and camaraderie in the community of parents, Moore is unflinching in displaying the darker and less noble side of their emotions as they value their own child's survival above all the others', and as they begin to long to be away from each other.

The "Mother," referred to only as such, at first cannot believe her son's condition, and hopes that somehow the malignancy was actually found in an X ray of her own body. If she cannot absorb the disease from him, she believes she must absorb the blame for its existence. Her husband suggests that she take notes on the experience for a journalistic piece whose sale they might need to finance the rounds of medical treatments, but the idea of accurately describing their ordeal makes her doubt her skills as a writer. Moore satirizes her own skills as the mother protests, "I'm not that good. I can't do this. I can do—what can I do? I can do quasi-amusing phone dialogue. I can do succinct descriptions of weather. I can do screwball outings with the family pet." Despite this modesty, we see that the mother, like Moore, is a literary success. A surgeon at the hospital asks her to autograph a copy of her latest novel, a story of teenage girls that suggests *Who Will Save the Frog Hospital?* The pursuit of Moore's women of career achievement and professional respect has come full circle. The mother has achieved fame as a writer, and yet it seems inconsequential compared to her role as parent.

"People Like That Are the Only People Here" ends with the mother's triumphant departure from the hospital with a recovering baby whose heart "drums with life." The story is followed significantly by "Terrific Mother," the ironically titled tale of a woman who accidentally causes the death of a friend's baby. Retreating into a cocoon of guilt and seven months of isolation in her apartment after a fall from a picnic bench kills the child she is holding, Adrienne experiences a spiritual rebirth on an academic retreat in Italy. Her professor husband Martin, one of the most sympathetic men Moore has created, convinces Adrienne that a normal marriage and life are possible for her, and in his patient and supportive eyes she finds both forgiveness and absolution. While *Birds of America* features a rogue's gallery of bad men like the philanderers and criminals in "Willing," "Community Life," and "Real Estate," it offers an even wider array of men who care about their children passionately and are willing to support their mates through any crisis. Cal in "Dance in America" is an equal partner with his wife in weathering their son's cystic fibrosis, and Jack in "Four Calling Birds, Three French Hens" may not fully understand his wife's grief at her cat's demise, but he helps her through therapy and a healing memorial. It is in these visions of sensitive men who are as deeply realized and human as their female counterparts that Moore finally allows for the possibility of meaningful and lasting relationships for her women. This hope of romance and true companionship makes Lorrie Moore's often bleak observations on the hazards of the modern world more embraceable, and gives her long-time readers the satisfaction of finding a light at the end of her long, dark tunnel.

Janet R. Raiffa

SELECTED BIBLIOGRAPHY

Works by Lorrie Moore

Self-Help. New York: Alfred A. Knopf, 1985.

Anagrams. New York: Alfred A. Knopf, 1986.

Like Life. New York: Alfred A. Knopf, 1988.

Who Will Run the Frog Hospital? New York: Alfred A. Knopf, 1994.

Birds of America. New York: Alfred A. Knopf, 1998.

Critical Studies

James, Caryn. "New and Improved Lives," *New York Times,* March 24, 1985.

Kakutani, Michiko. "And What Have They Done with Their Lives?" *New York Times,* September 11, 1998.

Kakutani, Michiko. "Books of The Times: Observations on Failures in Passion and Intimacy." *New York Times,* June 8, 1990.

Kakutani, Michiko. "Self-Help." *New York Times,* March 6, 1985.

Lee, Don. "About Lorrie Moore." *Ploughshares,* Fall 1998.

McCauley, Stephen. "Love Is Like a Truck on the Interstate." *New York Times,* May 20, 1990.

McInerney, Jay. "New and Improved Lives." *New York Times,* March 24, 1985.

McManus, James. "The Unbearable Lightness of Being." *New York Times,* September 20, 1998.

TOSHIO MORI
(1910 – 1980)

In Toshio Mori's 1941 story "The Sweet Potato" is this brief but meaningful exchange:

On the last day of the Fair we walked much and said little. . . . Hiro was almost crying. "Here's this wonderful thing called the Fair ending tonight. . . . Tomorrow the Island will be empty and dark . . .

"What do you think?" he asked me suddenly. "Do you think our people will ever be noticed favorably? What can we Japanese do? Must we accomplish big things here in America?

"Little things can accomplish big things too. I think," I said.

"That's right," he agreed. "But it's so slow. It takes time."

No single excerpt can encapsulate the entire corpus of a writer whose work is as subtle and varied as that of Toshio Mori. And yet this passage is striking for what it says about the ambitions Mori had for his fiction and the obstacles he faced as an American of Japanese descent. Taken within the context of Mori's career as a whole, his narrator's conviction that "little things can accomplish big things" is not so much a naive expression of optimism as it is a realistic assessment of the circumstances of his community—an assessment that has served as the foundation for his art. His short stories are consistently marked by the ability to uncover something worthy of a reader's attention in even the most ordinary lives or most mundane acts. They seldom deal with earth-shattering events or major personal crises in the lives of his characters, but instead linger over the quotidian details of lived lives and the nuances of relationships that reveal so much about human nature precisely because they seem so near to hand. As Mori put it near the end of "Tomorrow and Today": "When one has been around the neighborhood a while, the routine is familiar and . . . appears dull and colorless. But in this routine there is the breathtaking suspense that is alive and enormous, although the outcome and prospect of it is a pretty obvious thing."

Toshio Mori was born in Oakland, California. His parents were Japanese emigrants from Otake in Hiroshima prefecture. They had two sons before Mori's father moved first to Hawaii, where he worked on a sugar plantation, and then to Oakland, where he bought and operated a bathhouse. After the family was reunited they eventually sold the bathhouse and went into the garden nursery business. In 1915 they moved to San Leandro, where Mori lived, except for the war years, for the rest of his life.

Mori attended school in Oakland, but like many Nisei (second-generation Japanese Americans) he also attended Japanese language school. Thus, although he never expressed a desire to visit Japan, his understanding of Japanese culture was deep and had a formative influence on his development as an artist. He demonstrated a gift for writing at an early age and was encouraged by his mother and teachers to pursue the dream of becoming a writer. He was also a gifted athlete who was offered a tryout with the Chicago Cubs almost two decades before Jackie Robinson broke the color line. At the request of his mother, Mori did not take up the challenge to try to make the Cubs. Perhaps he knew too well the difficulties he would have faced had he tried to become a professional athlete. To wonder what might have been is wistful speculation of the kind that Mori himself did not often indulge, but it is worth noting this incident for the light it sheds on him as an individual and on his social environment, where institutionalized racism was a significant part of the cultural landscape.

Mori spent his young adult life working in the family nursery and writing in his spare time in the evenings. The 1930s was a period in which many writers strove for the creation of an essential American narrative; and in spite of Mori's penchant for focusing on the small details of everyday life in his own community, he nevertheless saw himself as sharing the literary ambitions of his generation. The clearest evidence of his desire to move into the mainstream lies in his admiration for Sherwood Anderson's *Winesburg, Ohio,* which at the time was one of the most influential works of American fiction. These two writers are temperamentally very different, and Mori never brings to his work quite the same drive to expose the hypocrisies of average American life. For all their differences, however, Mori explicitly cites Anderson in a number of his early stories, and he models his general approach on *Winesburg, Ohio,* using the accumulation of details from story to story to create a larger sense of community and thus provide a context out of which the reader can begin to sense the significance of lives that otherwise might seem of little interest.

Unlike many prewar Japanese American writers, who published mainly in local papers or journals targeted at a narrow readership, Mori's desire to be read as a mainstream writer led him to submit his work to publications with wide circulation. At the age of twenty-eight, he received his first acceptance from *The Coast* magazine, and over the next four years he published in a variety of journals, including *Common Ground, Current Life, New Di-*

rections, and *The Clipper*. As a result, his work began to attract the attention of established figures in the literary world, most notably William Saroyan, who wrote the introduction to Mori's first collection of short stories, *Yokohama, California*. This collection was scheduled to be published in the spring of 1942.

The war wrecked these plans. Caught up in one of the most shameful episodes in American history, the forced relocation of Japanese Americans to concentration camps, Mori was moved, along with his family and neighbors, to the Central Utah Relocation Camp in Topaz. He stayed there for most of the war, working in the documentation section of the camp and trying to keep his career as a writer afloat. The pressures on him were tremendous, since he felt responsible for his family, especially his mother, during this long ordeal. The family was finally permitted to return to San Leandro so that they could be near and care for his younger brother, Kazuo, who was seriously wounded in the fighting in Italy.

Because of the anti-Japanese sentiments aroused by the war, *Yokohama, California* did not appear until 1949. When it finally came out, it was a different collection, changed by the addition of two stories: "Tomorrow Is Coming, Children" and "Slant-Eyed Americans." The first story is an old woman's reminiscence of her life in America. Although she is telling her story to her grandchildren in a relocation camp, she puts a positive spin on the hardships she has faced and affirms her belief that she belongs in America. The other story, which is autobiographical, is set at Sunday lunch in a Japanese American household on December 7, 1941. On hearing the news about the attack at Pearl Harbor, the members of the family discuss the uncertain future, though again the tone is positive and asserts the Americanism of the family. One of the characters, a young friend of the family named Tom, tells of his feelings: "Sometimes I feel all right. You are an American, I tell myself. Devote your energy and life to the American way of life. Long before this my mind was made up to become a true American. This morning my Caucasian American friends sympathized with me. I felt good and was grateful. . . . Then I got sick again because I got to thinking that Japan was the country that attacked the United States. I wanted to bury myself for shame."

These stories were added at the publisher's request in an effort to give the collection a patriotic, sentimental appeal, but because they were written after the start of the war they seem out of place in the collection in terms of both tone and conception. Moreover, these stories cannot conceal the anguished emotions of people who, though no longer Japanese, were not permitted to be "true" Americans. In the end the attempt to make *Yokohama, California* more acceptable to a wider readership in the immediate postwar period was not successful, and the delay of its publication marked a serious break in Mori's career. The outbreak of war and the forced relocation shattered the Japanese American community that had been the site and inspiration of Mori's collection; and the inclusion of these two later stories is emblematic of this shattering. After the war, Mori continued to write, publishing dozens of short stories and one short novel, *Woman from Hiroshima*. However, it was not until near the end of his life, in the 1970s and 1980s, that collections of his work became widely available and he finally gained a wider audience.

Given the sheer variety of his stories, it is difficult to classify their characteristics. Although his style is generally matter-of-fact in tone and realistic in technique, some works, such as "The Chauvinist" or "It Begins with the Seed and Ends with a Flower Somewhere," are strikingly experimental in their use of terse, imagistic language and tightly controlled perspective that verges at points upon a stream-of-consciousness narrative. Many stories reflect the tendency toward autobiographical, or "I-novel," fiction that dominates twentieth-century Japanese literature. The presence of Mori's Japanese heritage, in the form of Zen religion and aesthetics, is also apparent in stories such as "The Trees" and "Abalone, Abalone, Abalone." But perhaps the most consistent element of Mori's work is the tone of gentle understanding his narratives assume as they reveal to us both the comedy of human foibles and the sad, muted desperation hidden beneath the banality of ordinary life. Far from presenting a sentimental view of life, many of Mori's stories—"The Finance Over at Doi's," "The Chessmen," "Operator, Operator!" or "Tomorrow and Today"—are deeply unsettling because the sense of loneliness and desperation they create is grounded in situations that are immediate and familiar. Mori himself perhaps best sums up the source of his aesthetic appeal in the story "He Who Has the Laughing Face" when his narrator observes: "Every little observation, every little banal talk or laughing matter springs from the sadness of the earth that is reality; every meeting between individuals, every meeting of society, every meeting of a gathering, of gaiety or sorrow, springs from sadness that is the bed of earth and truth."

Mori endeavored to enter the mainstream of American fiction through the critical and sympathetic depiction of his own parochial community. His success was acknowledged early on by Saroyan, who called him "the first real Japanese-American writer." The muscle-bound language of this assessment sounds almost laughably dated now, but it indicates the seriousness with which Saroyan took the aspiration of minority writers to be accepted in the world of American letters. The fact that Mori needed the patronage of an established figure, who was himself seen as an "ethnic" writer, is a measure of the predicament he faced in trying to be at once true to his experience and not marginalized by it. When we consider how Toshio Mori dealt with this predicament in his life, the question he raised in 1941, "What can we Japanese do?" is a poignant reminder of the difficulties of being a minority writer in America. His short stories are also a beautiful response to that question.

Dennis Washburn

SELECTED BIBLIOGRAPHY

Works by Toshio Mori

Yokohama, California. Introductions by Lawson Fusao Inada and William Saroyan. Caldwell, Idaho: Caxton Printers, 1949.

Reprint, Seattle: University of Washington Press, 1985.

Woman from Hiroshima. San Francisco: Isthmus Press, 1978.

The Chauvinist and Other Stories. Introduction by Hisaye Yamamoto. Los Angeles: Asian American Studies Center, University of California at Los Angeles, 1979.

Critical Studies

Bedrosian, Margaret. "Toshio Mori's California Koans." *MELUS* 15/2 (summer 1988): 47–55.

Mayer, David R. "Toshio Mori and Loneliness." *Nanzan Review of American Studies* 15 (1993): 20–32.

Palumbo-Liu, David. "The Minority Self as Other: Problematics of Representation in Asian-American Literature." *Cultural Critique* 28 (fall 1994): 75–102.

BHARATI MUKHERJEE

(1940–)

Bharati Mukherjee is the best-known and most-anthologized contemporary North American fiction writer of South Asian origin, with two important volumes of stories and five novels to her credit. Her second collection, *The Middleman and Other Stories,* won the National Book Critics Circle Award in 1988, bringing her to prominence as an energetic, aggressively optimistic voice of the late twentieth-century waves of immigration to the United States. However, Mukherjee sees herself as an American rather than an Indian or Asian American, and most of her work reflects her conviction that immigrants remake themselves when they come to America, breaking with their pasts, infusing their various cultures and worldviews into the American cultural mix, and transforming both themselves and America itself in the process. The protagonists of her earlier stories are often South Asian women, and her stories most commonly speak of the immigrant experience, although her reach and narrative voice have extended to encompass Americans of all kinds, men and women, young and old, natives and newcomers, from successful professionals to illegal aliens working in restaurants, from white racists to immigrants who refuse to assimilate. But her most potent and characteristic narrative is the romance of the female immigrant who, having cut loose from her past, falls in love with the dangerous, free-floating gamble of America, and plays the game wholeheartedly, risking all—and winning.

Born in 1940 in Calcutta, Mukherjee was educated at Loreto Convent School. She took her bachelor of arts in English from the University of Calcutta and her master of arts in English and ancient Indian culture from the University of Baroda. In 1962 she came to the United States to attend the University of Iowa Writer's Workshop, receiving her master of fine arts a year later. Soon afterward she married Clark Blaise, a Canadian fellow student. The couple moved to Montreal, where Mukherjee taught at McGill University while completing her doctorate in English and comparative literature from Iowa. She also wrote two novels, *The*

Tiger's Daughter (1972) and *Wife* (1975), and, with Blaise, a nonfiction book, *Days and Nights in Calcutta* (1977). Writing this last book was a turning point for Mukherjee, as she came to see herself as an immigrant rather than an expatriate. The following year she won a Guggenheim Foundation award and left McGill in 1980, moving to the United States. She taught creative writing at various colleges and universities in the New York area, where her stories began to win awards. Her first collection, *Darkness*, was published in 1985, and was followed by *The Middleman and Other Stories* (1988). She collaborated with Blaise on another nonfiction work, *The Sorrow and the Terror: The Haunting Legacy of the Air India Tragedy* (1987). Her novel *Jasmine* was published in 1989, followed by *The Holder of the World* (1993) and *Leave It to Me* (1997). Since 1990 Mukherjee has been professor of English at the University of California, Berkeley.

In a 1991 essay, "Love Me or Leave Me," the title of a favorite Doris Day movie of her youth, Mukherjee discusses the vision of America that the film presented to her as an aspiring young writer. It is the success story of a naive but ruthlessly ambitious chorus girl who "had what it takes" to get to the top and was determined to get there. Mukherjee points out the protagonist's moral ambiguities, saying that she learned from her "that it was not at all unethical for the Woman as Artist to lie and cheat and use men on the way to stardom." Mukherjee's own typical female protagonist is a woman who does just that, employing manipulative survival tactics that powerless women have long been forced to use. Their seeming compliance,

their ability to mold themselves into what is expected of them, becomes a powerful weapon in the hands of her heroines. Many of her female immigrant characters are thus able to adjust to life in America more easily than their male counterparts. As one says, "I've been trained to adapt."

"Love Me or Leave Me" also invokes another of Mukherjee's central themes: the romance with America. In a 1997 article in *Mother Jones*, she makes the allegory literal by draping herself in an American-flag sari. Many of her female characters free themselves from the traditional constraints on women by releasing their powerful female desire, and abandoning the security of fixed traditional roles and identities for a more fluid sense of self. Mukherjee has spoken of her own need to dispense with "the stagnant steadiness of the Calcutta upper classes." In so doing, she uses disturbing images of violence and sexuality to convey the urgency of her characters' desire. "Even more than other writers," she says, "I must learn to astonish, even to shock." And, indeed, shocking images abound in her work, evoking the violence that attends her characters' self-transformations, from "leeches gorging" on women's breasts to rape and bloody murder.

With some important late twentieth-century differences, Mukherjee advocates the melting-pot model of assimilation that accompanied earlier waves of European immigration. Critical of the Canadian policy of "multiculturalism," which she sees as reinforcing ethnic differences, she subscribes instead to the U.S. model. She does not, however, see assimilation as conformity to a unitary, Eurocentric image of

America, but promotes a multicultural America that at once assimilates its new immigrants and is transformed by them. She also firmly rejects nostalgia for the old country. In order to be able to embrace the New World, her successful characters often sever ties decisively with the Old, dismissing "back home" as "a nothing place" or "a hellhole." The past serves merely as an oppressive backdrop against which the immigrant triumphs by redefining him/herself.

Reshaping of self involves reshaping of language as well. Mukherjee uses neither contemporary Indian English nor colonial British English in her stories, but instead employs a hard-nosed, "tough-cookie" American English, full of computer-age neologisms, short, clipped sentences, and pithy phrases describing sex, violence, and money. In her earlier work, she takes V. S. Naipaul as a model, a writer whose narrative stance is postcolonial homelessness. Later, with her immigration to the United States, it is Bernard Malamud whom she invokes. "I see myself as an American writer in the tradition of other American writers whose parents or grandparents had passed through Ellis Island," she writes in the introduction to her first collection of stories, Darkness, which is dedicated to Malamud.

The dozen stories that make up Darkness include six previously published pieces, several of which are set in Canada. "The World According to Hsu" is Naipaulian in both tone and setting. A couple from Canada, Ratna and Graeme Clayton, are on holiday on an unnamed postcolonial island somewhere "off the coast of Africa" where a coup of some kind appears to be in progress. For all the chaos and regression (as in Naipaul, the island seems to have seen its best days during the colonial period), Ratna, who does not want to return to Canada, feels "safer than she had in the subway stations of Toronto." "Isolated Incidents" and "Tamurlane" also address Canadian government treatment of Asian immigrants and reflect Mukherjee's feelings of alienation after her long sojourn in Canada. At this stage in her career, Mukherjee feels that a certain dynamism in the United States has stimulated her creative work as a writer. She takes a jaundiced view of Canada and romanticizes the United States, for all its own racist violence.

In her introduction to Darkness, Mukherjee invokes Whitman as she declares, "It's possible . . . to hear America singing even in the seams of the dominant culture." With the publication of this collection, her first in the United States, she celebrates "a movement away from the aloofness of expatriation to the exuberance of immigration." Nevertheless, by no means all of the mostly South Asian characters in Darkness are immigrant success stories. "A Father," one of the most disturbing stories in the collection, is a portrait of a man who feels he has lost control over his life and at last loses control of himself as well in an act of violence. It depicts the differing responses of the members of an Indian immigrant family to suburban life in the United States. In contrast with his wife and daughter, who are quick to Americanize themselves, Mr. Bhowmick, a passive, cautious man, withdraws into prayer and paranoia, worshipping the goddess of death, Kali, at a large shrine he has erected for her in his bedroom. He feels emasculated as he sees his daughter Babli becoming an unfeminine, ultrarationalistic engineer and his agnostic and ambitious wife continually shopping, nagging him, and analyzing him with self-taught American pop psychology. He neither loves nor understands them and fails to interact with them as a father or a husband. The shocking climax comes in a confrontation over Babli's out-of-wedlock pregnancy. From the perspective of his daughter and the second generation, Mr. Bhowmick could be seen as the stereotypical Old World patriarch, upholding tradition even more rigidly than he might have back home. But in Mukherjee's story, we see from his own perspective that he is at sea, dangerously adrift.

Two stories in *Darkness,* "Nostalgia" and "Saints," make an interesting pairing. "Nostalgia" anatomizes an Indian immigrant who has paid a price for his success. Manny Patel is a conservative psychiatry resident in New York with an American wife from Camden, New Jersey, and a teenage son at Andover "who has recently taken to wearing a safety pin through his left earlobe." Wealthy and patriotic Dr. Patel has always been resolutely against romanticizing the old country, but today he succumbs to the lures of nostalgia in a form of a doe-eyed Indian goddess, "the girl of his dreams." He meets this vision working at the India Sari Palace and worshipfully invites her to dinner at the adjoining New Taj Mahal restaurant. After dinner, she takes him to a hotel room above the restaurant and seduces him. Just as his nostalgia for India, his mood of "regret filtered through longing," is at its height, the maitre d' interrupts, announcing that the woman is under age and he is her uncle; it has all been a setup, and Dr. Patel must comply with the "uncle's" demands and make his escape back home.

"Saints," the companion story to "Nostalgia," is set "back home" in the New Jersey suburbs after the Patels' divorce, and is told from the second-generation perspective of their unhappy teenage son Shawn, who is living with his mother. Shawn feels the pain of her loneliness and his father's distance, and watches helplessly as his middle-aged mom is two-timed by an abusive younger man. He plays chess by day and places prank sex-calls by night with an equally disaffected Vietnamese friend who is haunted by nightmares of his traumatic past. His father sends him a book about an Indian saint who, upon attaining enlightenment in a mystic trance, felt no difference between love and pain. At night, making himself up ritually with his mother's cosmetics, Shawn floats in trance through the suburban streets, peering in at the windows of Indian immigrant families, reaching for that state of grace where he is both in touch with and insulated from love and pain.

In the eleven stories of her second collection, *The Middleman and Other Stories,* which sealed her reputation as a major American writer, Mukherjee confidently takes on a wide range of voices that includes her characteristic South Asian heroine but also reaches beyond her gender, class, and particular immigrant group, from a Jew in South America in the Naipaulian title story to a Vietnam vet in Miami in "Loose Ends." In "A Wife's Story," the first-person narrator is a "well-bred" Indian woman, the wife of a wealthy businessman. She is ostensibly in the United States to pursue higher education, but in fact has no intention of returning to her old life. Sharing an apartment with a Chinese American model, dating a Hungarian émigré whose wife is back in the old country, she is fast becoming part of the multiethnic milieu of New York and growing irrevocably apart from her husband. On a brief visit to her, he plays the tourist, she the guide. He does not know her any longer, and she hardly knows herself; changing faster than she can keep up with, she is becoming an outsider to herself. The well-crafted story ends on the night before his return to India, with the narrator waiting naked for him while he bathes. She looks at herself in the mirror as a voyeur might look at a total stranger: "The body's beauty amazes. I stand here shameless, in ways he has never seen me. I am free, afloat, watching somebody else." While displacement made Mr. Bhowmick feel fearful and adrift, uprooting from a settled social milieu has unleashed this Indian wife's desires. Thrust into the swirling cultural mix of New York, both her personality and her sexuality have become free-floating. No longer is there any essential self; set in motion, she is going places, she knows not where.

"Loose Ends" also employs first-person narration, this time from the "other side," in the voice of a tough-talking white mercenary and Vietnam veteran who feels that America is being overrun by Asian and Latin American immigrants. Haunted by an image of a gigantic caged python sleeping on a bed of its own turds, he shudders at the thought of "all that coiled power," equating it with images of America's self-defeating foray into Vietnam. On the run, he stops at an Indian-owned motel in Florida and bursts into a private room where an intimate group of extended family members are eating together. Suddenly, he is the alien: "I feel left out, left behind. While we were nailing up that big front door, these guys were sneaking around the back. They got their money, their family networks, their secret language." When "jailbait," as he calls one of the teenage daughters, shows him to his room, he strikes, raping her, and blasts away in a stolen car, wanting to "squeeze this state dry and swallow it whole." Like the python wallowing in its own waste, he has become what he most dreads.

The voice in "Orbiting" is that of Rindi, a young Italian American woman from New Jersey, the occasion Thanksgiving, when her family meets her new lover Ro, an Afghani war refugee. Mukherjee captures the charged, intimate atmosphere of the Thanksgiving dinner and the nuances of the different voices, tensions, and body language as they meet with mutual incomprehension. Rindi's lower middle-class suburban family is simple, even crass, while Ro comes from the Afghani elite. Ro has skied in St. Moritz, yet here he is the one whose clothes and mannerisms seem all wrong. "He's sophisticated," thinks Rindi, squirming with embarrassment on behalf of her family; "he could make monkeys out of us all, but they think he's a retard."

Two of Mukherjee's stories contain the germ of later novels, and a third is based on information gathered for a longer nonfiction work. "Courtly Vision," the closing story in *Darkness*, is *The Holder of the World* in miniature. "Jasmine," in *The Middleman*, is the story of an ambitious young Trinidadian woman who immigrates illegally to America to make good. It later developed into the novel of the same name, although the latter Jasmine was an Indian woman. "The Management of Grief," also in *The Middleman,* is derived from Blaise and Mukherjee's research for *The Sorrow and the Terror.*

Each of the female protagonists of Mukherjee's three most recent novels is a woman who continually "remakes herself." In a 1997 interview in *Jouvert,* Mukherjee notes that her displaced, "unhoused" characters respond in a variety of ways to their changing environments. She expresses the hope that "these characters help to piece together an unsentimental portrait of the United States. I certainly know what I love about the spirit of America, but I've also written at great length about the underside of the American Dream . . . the guts, imagination and assertiveness of that American spirit, and its underside—the will to imperialize." Moving away from racial, ethnic, or narrowly South Asian constructions of identity, which she looks upon as forms of self-imposed ghettoization, Bharati Mukherjee claims America, warts and all. Like her vision of America, her characters are at once creative and destructive; they both confront and perpetrate violence and exploitation; they defy their fates and survive.

Josna Rege

SELECTED BIBLIOGRAPHY

Works by Bharati Mukherjee

Darkness. New York: Penguin, 1985.
The Middleman and Other Stories. New York: Grove Press, 1988.

"Love Me or Leave Me." In Wesley Brown and Amy Ling, eds., *Visions of America: Personal Narratives from the Promised Land,* pp. 187–194. New York: Persea Books, 1993.

Critical Studies

Alam, Fakrul. *Bharati Mukherjee.* New York: Twayne, 1996.
Chen, Tina, and S. X. Goudie. "Holders of the Word: An Interview with Bharati Mukherjee," *Jouvert* 1(1), 1997 (http://social.chass.ncsu.edu/jouvert/vlil/bharat.htm).
Nelson, Emmanuel, ed. *Bharati Mukherjee: Critical Perspectives.* New York: Garland, 1993.

VLADIMIR NABOKOV
(1899–1977)

By the time he died in 1977, Vladimir Nabokov had secured his place among the twentieth century's greatest writers. He had lived in six countries but ultimately considered himself "an American writer." "In America," he declared in *Strong Opinions,* "I found my best readers, minds that are closest to mine. . . . It is a second home."

Nabokov's first home was Russia, where he was born into a wealthy St. Petersburg family in 1899. His father, a prominent politician opposed to the Bolshevik revolution, led the family to exile—eventually in Berlin—in 1919. That year, Nabokov entered Trinity College, Cambridge, earning his degree in Russian and French literature in 1922. He returned to Berlin, and in 1925 married Véra Slonim, who would become an important literary advisor and assistant. Their only child, Dmitri, was born in 1934. Nearly destitute, and alarmed by Hitler's rising power, the Nabokovs moved to France in 1937, but fled the Nazi advance again in 1940.

They came to America, settling in the Boston area and becoming citizens in 1945. From 1941 to 1948, Nabokov was a research fellow at Harvard's Museum of Comparative Zoology (an expert and passionate collector, he published numerous scientific papers about butterflies), and lectured on Russian language and literature at Wellesley College. In 1948 he moved to Ithaca, New York, where he taught literature at Cornell. He wrote there his most controversial novel, *Lolita*; the fame and fortune it brought allowed Nabokov to resign his Cornell post in 1959 and devote his time exclusively to writing. From 1961 until his death in 1977, he lived at the Hotel Montreux Palace in Switzerland.

Bilingual from an early age, and remarkably prolific, Nabokov wrote mostly in Russian until 1940, and thereafter in English. His works include seventeen novels (the most celebrated in English are *Lolita, Pnin, Pale Fire,* and *Ada*); several volumes of poems and plays; collections of letters, lectures, and interviews; the screenplay for Stanley Kubrick's film of *Lolita*; four English translations of works by Russian writers (most prominently, of Pushkin's *Eugene Onegin*); and *Speak, Memory,* his autobiography to 1940.

Nabokov wrote some sixty-five short stories—only nine (all written in America) initially composed in English. Most Russian stories, under the pseudonym "Vladimir Sirin," appeared during the 1920s and 1930s in Europe's émigré newspapers and magazines. His English stories appeared primarily in the *Atlantic Monthly* and *The New Yorker*. He wrote his last in 1951, abandoning the form to concentrate on novels. But after *Lolita* stimulated interest in his stories, Nabokov, in collaboration with his son, Dmitri, translated most of his Russian stories into English and published them in four collected volumes. In 1995, Dmitri published an authoritative edition, *The Stories of Vladimir Nabokov*. Along with the fifty-two stories collected in his father's lifetime, this edition includes Dmitri's translations of thirteen additional Russian stories, only two of which had appeared before in English; Nabokov's notes from the earlier volumes; and bibliographical information. (The quotations from the stories that follow are from this edition.)

Most of Nabokov's stories are set in Russia, Germany, or elsewhere in Europe; only a few are set in America. Nabokov lavished special care on his settings, cataloguing the objects that fill them, and attending carefully to the quality of light, as in "The Seaport": "Here and there, like the colored flames of some petrified fireworks display, cafés blazed in the purple twilight. Round tables right out on the sidewalk, shadows of black plane trees on the striped awning, illuminated from within." His style unites fact and feeling, science and art (Nabokov's twin passions): precise, concrete, and elegantly economical, it is also densely evocative, adjecti-

vally expansive, and sensorially suggestive.

Nabokov uses, in roughly equal measure, first- and third-person narrators; occasionally, as in "Torpid Smoke," he surprisingly combines the two forms. Some
writers efface or minimize a narrator's
presence; Nabokov typically features it.
His narrators sometimes intrude to highlight the story's status as a fictional construct ("The Leonardo," "Recruiting,"
"The Assistant Producer," "Lance"). They
can be opinionated, mentally or emotionally overwrought, crisply judgmental, fer-
vently sympathetic—strong presences, in
any case, mediating the reader's experience of the story. Conversations among
characters are more often described than
represented in the form of direct dialogue,
thus enhancing the power and primacy of
the narrative voice (and distinguishing
Nabokov from such writers as Raymond
Carver).

Some readers find Nabokov's works
too tricky or self-conscious, and his attitude toward his characters emotionally
detached. But as Dmitri Nabokov points
out in his preface to the 1995 collection,
the most persistent theme of these stories
is "Nabokov's contempt for cruelty—the
cruelty of humans, the cruelty of fate."
Although rarely sentimental, Nabokov's
stories affectingly explore the pathos of
characters—often lonely and frightened
exiles—who struggle to maintain their
fragile dignity and emotional composure.
He catches them in moments of crisis: a
boy consumed by fear that his father is
about to fight a duel ("Orache"); parents
grieving over the actual or potential loss
of their children ("Christmas," "Breaking
the News," "Lance"); men on the verge of

death desperately trying to interpret the
sudden forms of clarification too briefly
dangled before them ("Terra Incognita,"
"Perfection"). Nabokov's characters are
typically brought to the edge of possessing
what they desire most—a lover, a secure
home, a reinvigorated life, a recovered
memory—only to have what they want
denied by violence or death, human indifference, or cosmic treachery.

"Signs and Symbols" and "Spring in
Fialta" are among Nabokov's finest stories; in an interview with Stephen Jan
Parker, Nabokov listed them—along
with "Cloud, Castle, Lake" and "The Vane
Sisters"—among his own favorites. One
of his shortest, most widely anthologized
works, "Signs and Symbols" (1948) is a
complex masterpiece of economy and
emotional power. Set in America and told
by a third-person narrator, the story seems
initially simple enough: elderly immigrant
parents try to bring a birthday present to
their "incurably deranged" son in a sana-
torium, but are sent away because he has
tried yet again to kill himself. After a silent, dejected journey home, they resolve
to rescue their son the next morning and
care for him themselves. Quietly celebrating around midnight, they are startled
by three phone calls. The first two—from
a girl asking for "Charlie"—are, the
mother insists, wrong numbers. As the
father reexamines the undelivered present, the phone rings again—and there the
story ends.

Readers know—and suspect the parents know—what that third call por-
tends: the son has tried again, probably
successfully, to kill himself. Conventional
notions of irony, and the ominous atmosphere of a story that flamboyantly strews

in the parents'—and readers'—paths a variety of foreboding "signs" and "symbols" (for example, a "half-dead unfledged bird"), strongly point toward that conclusion. By interpreting the story's suggestive signs, the reader participates in the deeper loss these already sad parents will experience in the unwritten moment beyond the story's end.

"Signs and Symbols" involves the reader in other, more unusual ways. The son's disease is a form of paranoia called "referential mania." Seeing the natural world in "conspiracy" against him, he believes that even "pebbles or stains or sun flecks form patterns representing in some awful way messages which he must intercept," and that he must "devote every minute" to "decoding" their meaning. An aggressive interpreter, he invests random, perhaps trivial, details with signifying power, building them systematically into a story of which "he is the theme."

Readers may be engaging in essentially the same sort of activity that defines the son's illness when they confidently interpret the story's last call as something more than another wrong number, or identify patterns in the story's other signs and symbols. Characteristically for a Nabokov story, "Signs and Symbols" operates on multiple levels, each intensifying the other: it evokes, with remarkable tenderness, the pain and freight of its characters' lives, while sharply challenging readers to examine the methods of storytelling and interpretation that provide access to those lives.

"Spring in Fialta" (1938) is perhaps Nabokov's most luminous, textured, and brilliantly realized story. It is narrated by Victor, a businessman who encounters again, on an Adriatic town's hazy streets, a woman he first met fifteen years earlier on a snowy Russian night. His and Nina's paths have briefly crossed several times since; once, in Paris, they made love. Nina is a warm but elusive figure: her tenderness "did not commit her to anything," and she "had always either just arrived or was about to leave." Yet she has long inhabited Victor's imagination, emblematizing a set of possibilities more "lovely" and "delicate" than his happy but conventional marriage allows.

Like the streets they wander in Fialta, where "past and present are interlaced," the story weaves between Victor's remembered history with Nina and this present morning. After lunch together with Nina's husband (described by Victor with brutal humor), and alone again on a terrace as the sun illuminates Fialta, Victor suddenly asks Nina: "Look here—what if I love you?" Nina gives a puzzled glance, and Victor retreats: "I was only joking." It is their last conversation; minutes later, outside town, Nina dies in a fiery car crash.

Their life together, such as it was, had been lived in transitional locales: on railway platforms, on steps and terraces surrounded by "half-built" or "half-ruined" houses, amidst the shifting weather of Fialta. All this, for Victor, created a "life-quickening atmosphere" in which "everything is something trembling on the brink of something else, thus to be clutched and cherished."

But Nina's death, and Victor's last question, have put an end to imminence; their relationship can never become something more than what it was—except, perhaps, through the vehicles of memory and art. Like so many Nabokovian characters bereft of what they cherish, Victor turns to what he calls "the music box of memory" in order to reconstruct, understand, celebrate, mourn, and—above all—preserve his past. The music counts more than the memory: his actual memories can be of nothing more than brief, random encounters with Nina. But he can try to endow them with a kind of permanence and consequence through this story's dense lyricism, and to locate in art a woman who could never be precisely located in life. Victor attains what Nabokov's autobiography—invoking musical imagery—defined as "the supreme achievement of memory": "the masterly use it makes of innate harmonies when gathering to its fold the suspended and wandering tonalities of the past."

Taken together, "Spring in Fialta" and "Signs and Symbols" embrace the thematic concerns and narrative strategies that shape many of Vladimir Nabokov's stories. They powerfully evoke a persistent sense of possibility and loss, and explore the complex ways in which language is used—by characters, storytellers, and readers—to illuminate the past, preserve memory, confront death, and sustain at least provisional hope in lives where "everything is something trembling on the brink of something else."

Stephen Fix

SELECTED BIBLIOGRAPHY

Works by Vladimir Nabokov

Nabokov's Dozen. Garden City, N.Y.: Doubleday, 1958.

Speak, Memory: An Autobiography Revisited. New York: Putnam's, 1966.
A Russian Beauty and Other Stories. New York: McGraw-Hill, 1973.
Strong Opinions. New York: McGraw-Hill, 1973.
Tyrants Destroyed and Other Stories. New York: McGraw-Hill, 1975.
Details of a Sunset and Other Stories. New York: McGraw-Hill, 1976.
The Stories of Vladimir Nabokov. New York: Knopf, 1995.

Critical Studies

Alexandrov, Vladimir E., ed. *The Garland Companion to Vladimir Nabokov.* New York: Garland, 1995.
Boyd, Brian. *Vladimir Nabokov: The American Years.* Princeton, N.J.: Princeton University Press, 1991.
Boyd, Brian. *Vladimir Nabokov: The Russian Years.* Princeton, N.J.: Princeton University Press, 1990.
Nicol, Charles, and Gennady Barabtarlo, eds. *A Small Alpine Form: Studies in Nabokov's Short Fiction.* New York: Garland, 1993.
Parker, Stephen Jan. "Vladimir Nabokov and the Short Story." *Russian Literature Triquarterly* 24 (1991): 63–72.

JOYCE CAROL OATES
(1938–)

Joyce Carol Oates was born in Lockport, Erie County, New York, on June

16, 1938 (Joyce's Bloomsday), the daughter of Frederic and Caroline (Bush) Oates. In 1959 she won the *Mademoiselle* college fiction contest with "In the Old World." The following year she graduated with a bachelor of arts in English from Syracuse University; she took a master of arts at the University of Wisconsin in 1961. At Wisconsin, she met and married Raymond Smith, who now runs the Ontario Review Press. In 1963 her story "The Fine White Mist of Winter" was included in Martha Foley's *Best American Short Stories.* Coming across the volume while browsing in a library, Oates decided to abandon her doctoral thesis and concentrate on fiction. She is now the author of more than seventy books—novels, plays, poetry, essays— and nearly five hundred short stories. She has edited many anthologies, including, in 1992, *The Oxford Book of the American Short Story.* She is the recipient of many awards, including the PEN / Faulkner Bernard Malamud Lifetime Achievement Award for the Short Story and the Rea Award for "a significant contribution to the story as an art form." Teaching since 1966, she is now Roger S. Berlin Distinguished Professor in the Humanities at Princeton University.

In a 1971 essay, Oates notes that "any remarks about the short story made by a writer of short stories are bound to be autobiographical, if they are at all honest. For me the short story is an absolutely indecipherable fact." Echoing Flannery O'Connor, an important early influence, she has emphasized the essential mystery of the form: "The short story is a dream verbalized, arranged in space and presented to the world, imagined as a sympathetic audience. . . . The dream is said

to be some kind of manifestation of desire, so the short story must also represent a desire, perhaps only partly expressed, but the most interesting thing about it is its mystery."

The feeling of a "dream verbalized" informs many stories, perhaps most famously "Where Are You Going, Where Have You Been?" which in characteristic Oates style marries the details of realism with the atmosphere of the fairy tale. First published in 1966, it remains one of Oates's most frequently anthologized stories. Connie, a fifteen-year-old girl, is left home alone one sunny Sunday afternoon. She is disturbed by a man who calls himself Arnold Friend and offers to take her for a ride in his gold convertible. The story ends on a threshold marked by the house's screen door, as Connie hovers between innocence and experience, and perhaps life and death.

Short stories are classically concerned with the individual, with what Frank O'Connor described as "the lonely voice," on such thresholds of contact with other, often disturbing, lonely voices. Sometimes these are strangers, as in the case of Arnold Friend or the man who appears on the doorstep of a house in which he had once lived (only to change everything) in "Where Is Here?" Often, however, they are people who should not seem strange to the reader. "In the Region of Ice," for example, a dedicated teacher, Sister Allen, is distressed to find her student "trying to force her into a human relationship." "What Is the Connection Between Men and Women?" asks a 1970 story, and the problem of that particular connection is an enduring concern. "But what could she understand of his experience, having had no part of it?" thinks the narrator of "Upon the Sweeping Flood" about his wife.

Often the gap between men and women is one of bodily experience. In "Raven's Wing," a man who is unafraid when a dangerous horse lunges at his hand is amazed that his wife can bear to put earrings into her ear lobes. "He knew it was a trick he could never do if he was a woman." He also cannot understand why she is depressed, why in her pregnancy she is "ruining her looks to spite him." Pregnancy is presented as widening the gap between men and women in many stories, memorably in "Golden Gloves," where an ex-boxer broods on his career and then looks at his sleeping pregnant wife and thinks, "You'll be going to a place I can't reach."

Writing itself, however, Oates has observed, is about illuminating "*what it feels like* from a position alien to my own." Men and women in particular are each other's doppelgangers, the "shadow selves" who often represent "crystallization[s] of . . . [our] own loneliness."

Oates's fiction is concerned also with "memorializing people," in particular the people of her childhood "back there" and "back then" in Erie (often renamed as Eden) County. The stories she tells are often those that, as the narrator of "The Swimmers" puts it, "go unaccountably wrong and become impermeable to the imagination. They lodge in the imagination like an old wound never entirely healed." Many of the best of these stories share the quality of fable. "Upon the Sweeping Flood," for instance, begins "One day in Eden County . . . a man named Walter Stuart was stopped in the rain." What follows is an exploration, worthy

of Flannery O'Connor, of what it is to save and be saved. Driving home after his father's funeral, Stuart is warned by the sheriff's deputy of the threat of flood. He decides to help and eventually finds two teenagers abandoned by their father. In the chaos of the storm, he comes to recognize "the incompleteness of his former life" and is tipped into madness and murder.

Oates often seems reluctant to speculate about the distinctive nature and value of the short story as a form. In most of her statements she refuses to be pinned down to a definition ("There is no nature to it, but only natures"), and maintains that "any short story can become a novel, and any novel can be converted back into a short story or into a poem." "As for telling or writing stories, short stories in place of novels," as she has said, "I seem to have been unaware of the form until many years had passed and I had written several thousand pages of prose." At other times, however, she has stressed the specific qualities of the genre. In the introduction to *The Oxford Book of the American Short Story* she notes categorically that the short story "is no more than 10,000 words" and is "an intensification of meaning by way of events." Most important, "it achieves closure—meaning that, when it ends, the attentive reader understands why." Epiphany, or at least "a tangible change of some sort," is crucial.

Although rightly lauded for her short fiction and obviously drawn to its variety, Oates has described the novel as "the most human of all art forms." "It may well be," she has said, "that all the short fiction in existence cannot match a single great novel: Hardy's *Tess,* for instance." "Technique holds a reader from sentence to sentence, but only content will stay in his mind," she goes on, and perhaps in reading short fiction, we inevitably become too aware of technique. In the short story, as the critic Tzvetan Todorov says, "there is no time . . . to forget it is only 'literature' and not 'life.'" With a novel, Oates maintains, one can "get so deep into character," its "an emotionally involving experience," while "with short fiction, and of course poetry, you don't have any character."

The two forms are, however, not always so distinct for Oates. She remembers, as a sophomore in high school, discovering Hemingway's *In Our Time* and seeing "how chapters in an ongoing narrative might be self-contained units, both in the service of a larger structure and detachable, in a manner of speaking, from it." Apart from her earliest books, Oates's short story collections have all been carefully constructed around distinct themes or ideas: "wholes, with unifying strategies of organization." The "fifteen tales" of *Crossing the Border* (1976) are all set on the American-Canadian border and explore the ways that individuals cross many kinds of boundaries that they themselves hardly recognize. Seven stories focus on a single couple, providing a narrative thread whose episodes parallel and gather resonance from the other stories. The twenty-five stories of *Heat* (1991) are grouped into three sections, exploring, in quite different contexts, the inevitability of violence, mostly male, largely sexual, and the ways in which it is tolerated. If the organization becomes chronological as well as thematic, a group of stories can even grow into a novel. After writing "Ghost Girls," Oates's self-confessed "fas-

cination with [her] parents' lives" led her to write another four pieces, then to see that "the stories constitute a single story, a novel built out of images and episodes titled *Man Crazy*" (a process that recalls Virginia Woolf's experience of several stories "taking hands and dancing in unity" to become *Jacob's Room*). On the difference between the two forms, Oates suggests that it is simply a question of "the degree of complexity: how long a story will take and how many characters are involved. Anything that takes place over a period of time obviously involves a novel because the short story usually can't accommodate time."

While de-emphasizing character and chronological development, the short story instead allows greater freedom for thematic and stylistic experimentation, qualities that Oates fully exploits. "How I Contemplated the World from the Detroit House of Correction and Began My Life Over Again" is written in the form of notes for an essay, while "Unmailed, Unwritten Letters" is just what the title suggests. Oates meanwhile describes "the floating paragraphs" of "Heat," the story she chose to represent herself in the Oxford anthology, as resulting from experiments with " 'tone clusters' in prose." "The tone of 'Heat,' she wrote, "is that of a piano used as a nonvibrating instrument, without the use of the pedal, in which chords struck and lifted, do not resonate or echo but exhibit an eerie disconnection with each other."

"Heat" is a story of doubles, eleven-year-old twin girls, "Rhea-and-Rhonda," cheeky, sassy, "the same girl," murdered by a local simpleton, Roger Whipple, in the heat of the day. Recalling Camus's *The*

Stranger, Oates presents a crime in which the summer heat is itself somehow complicit. The sense of disconnection in the telling of the story belongs to the consciousness of the narrator, who had been a child of the same age as the twins. It is she who needs to tell the tale but cannot bear to construct a narrative, cannot bear to have its events happen all over again. She therefore moves back and forth in time, suggesting at once the moment when it is all over and the moment when it could still have been otherwise. (Oates would also use this technique to powerful effect in her 1992 novella, "Black Water.") Inevitably, however, the narrator recognizes that "a story . . . has to go its own way." Toward the end, the reader learns why. Many years later, she had an adulterous affair near the ice house where the girls died, and looking back on that, she feels unable "to recognize that woman, as if she was someone not even not-me but a crazy woman I would despise, making so much of such a thing, risking her marriage and her kids finding out and her life being ruined for such a thing, my God." Recognizing her own crazy heat, also in the proximity of ice, she is unable to refrain from re-creating the girls' final moments. In her lover's car, after making love, she is able to empathize not only with the girls' fear but also with the crazy compulsion that overtook Whipple, and with her parent's subsequent desire to keep her safe. "I wasn't there, but some things you know."

Introducing the story of her uncle's love affair in 1959, the narrator of "The Swimmers" similarly confesses that while "some of it I was part of, aged thirteen . . . much of it I have to imagine." In these cases, the "prism of technique" is no gimmick, but rather the means by which Oates can interrogate not only character and consciousness but the very nature of storytelling.

In her contributor's notes to various anthologies, as well as in interviews and essays, Oates distinguishes different ways in which her short stories came into being. For example, she describes "Is Laughter Contagious?"—included in *The Best American Short Stories 1992*—as a "concept story," "a fiction whose genesis is an idea, not images or people." "Ghost Girls," in *The Best American Short Stories 1996,* on the other hand, originated "purely out of an image." The afterword of *The Poisoned Kiss* speaks of stories that "came from nowhere," while the origin of each of the miniature narratives of *The Assassination,* on the other hand, "lay in desire."

Some stories begin with existing works of literature. Allusion is, after all, another way of making connections between two lonely voices. Although most of Oates's work is in some way informed by a gothic perspective—which she defines simply as involving "extremes of emotion" being "unleashed"—some collections draw directly on a gothic tradition. In collections from *Night-Side* (1977) to *The Collector of Hearts* (1998), the reader encounters "tales" in the Poe and Hawthorne tradition. A group of stories in *Marriages and Infidelities* (1972) most directly refer to their "inspirations"—Joyce's "The Dead," Kafka's "The Metamorphosis," Chekhov's "The Lady with the Pet Dog" and Henry James's "The Turn of the Screw"—yet allusion is a constant in Oates's work. "The Seasons," for example , is a wonderfully unexpected rewriting and expansion of

Hemingway's story of kittens and abortion, "Cat in the Rain." The marriage between texts as well as people allows one to "transcend the limitations of the ego," but it also opens the way to infidelity. As the title of *The Poisoned Kiss* suggests, the most intimate connection can also be the most deadly.

Refusing to pin herself down, Oates has stretched and shrunk the short story in all directions. She has written several novellas, including "Black Water" (1992) and "I Lock My Door Upon Myself" (1990), which Richard Ford, who also dislikes the constraints of genre definitions, recently included in *The Granta Book of the American Long Story* (1998). Oates is also attracted to the short-short story as the "miniature narrative . . . more akin to poetry than to conventional prose, which generally opens out to dramatize experience and to evoke emotion; in the smallest, tightest places, experience can only be suggested." *The Assignation* (1989) and *Where Is Here?* (1992) are collections of "miniature narratives" that Oates wrote over a number of years. She describes them as "radical distillations of story," and compares their constraints to those of the sonnet. "In such adventures of the imagination 'form' precedes 'content': one might feel 'form' as an emptiness, an ache, a void-to-be-filled, and the 'content' as narrative generated by this phenomenon." The stories emphasize the immediacy of process: "he was laughing, maybe he was crying and his nose was running, I just lay there thinking, All right, kid, all right you bastards, this is it."

Characters in these, the shortest of stories, are often presented on a threshold, moving toward decisions, as one puts it, "like sleepwalkers, propelled by a rough shove." "This is it," ends "The Boy," the story of an afternoon's fooling around between a teacher and a seventeen-year-old pupil. In "Slow," a woman hears her husband come home at "the wrong time" and sees him sobbing into the steering-wheel, "and in that instant she knows that their life will be split in two though she doesn't, as she makes her slow way to him, know how, or why." In "Tick," another woman refuses to answer her husband's phone calls. He has moved out after she refuses to accept certain unnamed "conditions" for their life. One day, though when she finds a tick in her hair and is "close to hysteria," she finally answers the phone, knowing the full implications of her action: "She foresees a reconciliation, love-making both anguished and tender. She foresees starting a child. It's time."

In nearly forty years of story writing, Joyce Carol Oates has moved through the complete gamut of genres and styles available to the writer and created a few new ones along the way. In other respects, she has continued to explore, from all possible perspectives, the deep obsessions that informed her earliest work. Indeed, in the introduction to a 1993 collection of early stories, she described her career as one of "rings that emerge out of rings, with *By the North Gate,* my first book, at its core." For every story that concludes, *this is it,* another comes forth to ask, *is it really?* And so every story, every collection, yields to another, itself in turn poised on the threshold between memory and desire, knowledge and skepticism.

Kasia Boddy

SELECTED BIBLIOGRAPHY

Works by Joyce Carol Oates

By the North Gate. New York: Vanguard Press, 1963.

Upon the Sweeping Flood and Other Stories. New York: Vanguard Press, 1966.

The Wheel of Love and Other Stories. New York: Vanguard Press, 1970.

Marriages and Infidelities. New York: Vanguard Press, 1972.

The Goddess and Other Women. New York: Vanguard Press, 1974.

The Hungry Ghosts: Seven Allusive Comedies. Los Angeles: Black Sparrow Press, 1974.

Where Are You Going? Where Have You Been? Stories of Young America. Greenwich, Conn.: Fawcett, 1974.

The Poisoned Kiss and Other Stories From the Portuguese. New York: Vanguard Press, 1975.

The Seduction and Other Stories. Los Angeles: Black Sparrow Press, 1975.

Crossing the Border: Fifteen Tales. New York: Vanguard Press, 1976.

Night-Side: Eighteen Tales. New York: Vanguard Press, 1976.

All the Good People I've Left Behind. Santa Barbara: Black Sparrow Press, 1979.

A Sentimental Education: Stories. New York: E. P. Dutton, 1980.

Last Days: Stories. New York: E. P. Dutton, 1984.

Wild Nights. Athens, Ohio: Croissant, 1985.

Raven's Wing. New York: Dutton, 1986.

The Assignation. New York: Ecco, 1988.

Oates in Exile. Toronto: Exile Editions, 1990.

Heat and Other Stories. New York: Dutton, 1991.

Where Is Here? Hopewell, N.J.: Ecco, 1992.

Where Are You Going? Where Have You Been? Selected Early Stories. Princeton, N.J.: Ontario Review Press, 1993.

Haunted: Tales of the Grotesque. New York: Dutton, 1994.

Will You Always Love Me? and Other Stories. New York: Dutton, 1996.

The Collector of Hearts: New Tales of the Grotesque. New York: Dutton, 1998.

Critical Studies

Bastian, Katherine. *Joyce Carol Oates's Short Stories Between Tradition and Innovation.* Frankfurt: Bern, Lang, 1983.

Johnson, Greg. *Invisible Writer: A Biography of Joyce Carol Oates.* New York: E. P. Dutton, 1998.

Johnson, Greg. *Joyce Carol Oates: A Study of the Short Fiction.* Boston: Twayne, 1994.

TIM O'BRIEN

(1946–)

Tim O'Brien's literary reputation emerges from seven books and several award-winning short stories. Praised for his sensitive and imaginative treatments of American soldiers' experiences in the Vietnam War, O'Brien is often placed in the company of other prominent Vietnam soldier-authors such as Philip Caputo, Larry Heinemann, Robert Olen Butler, and John M. Delvecchio. O'Brien, a self-described "strict realist" who dismisses critics' labels of "surrealist" or "magical realist," argues, and rightfully so, that he is much more than a "war writer." He explores the broader themes of the daily war of the living. He also examines in a postmodernist fashion the problematic nature of truth and reality as he forces readers to separate actuality from possibility, truth from lies, facts from fiction, one perspective from another, and the author from his fictional characters.

O'Brien's many literary prizes include the 1978 National Book Award for his novel *Going After Cacciato*, the French Prix du Meilleur Livre Etranger for *The Things They Carried* (1990), and the James Fenimore Cooper prize for his 1994 novel *In the Lake of the Woods*. In addition, several of his short stories (usually a chapter from one of his published books or a new story later revised and incorporated into a book) have received critical acclaim and appeared in editions of *The Best American Short Stories* and *Prize Stories: The O. Henry Awards*. Three of O'Brien's books in particular have provided frequently anthologized short stories—the nonfictional war autobiography *If I Die in a Combat Zone* (1973) and his two novels *Going After Cacciato* and *The Things They Carried*. The latter, because of its twenty-two linked sections of story, memoir, confession, character sketches, and lyric prose poems, has received the most attention and praise from readers interested in the short story.

Tim O'Brien, born in Austin, Minnesota, in October 1946, moved at the age of ten with his family to Worthington, Minnesota, a town of approximately ten thousand people located on Lake Okabena in the southwest part of the state and the setting for some of his stories. In 1968, O'Brien graduated Phi Beta Kappa and summa cum laude as a political science major from Macalester College, where he served as student body president during his senior year. He was drafted into the army in August 1968 and served thirteen months as an infantryman in Quang Ngai province, South Vietnam. During this tour of duty, he was awarded a Purple Heart and a Bronze Star for valor. After his discharge from the army in 1970, O'Brien entered the Ph.D. program in government at Harvard University, taking a leave on three occasions to work as a journalism intern and national affairs reporter for *The Washington Post*. While publishing his war autobiography and a novel, *Northern Lights* (1975), O'Brien remained in the graduate program until 1977, when he left with an unfinished dissertation called "Case Studies in American Military Interventions" to become a full-time writer.

Readers familiar with details from O'Brien's personal life will find intriguing thematic links between his art and life. As a child he played war games on the local golf course and Little League baseball. His mother, an elementary school teacher, taught him at an early age the importance of clarity and precision in writing, and his father, an insurance salesman, encouraged wide reading. But to escape the pain of his alcoholic father's dinnertime taunts, the adolescent O'Brien sought solace in performing magic. The defining moment in O'Brien's life, however, occurred in the summer of 1968 after his college graduation and receipt of a draft notice. Having actively supported antiwar candidate Eugene McCarthy in the 1968 presidential primaries and believing that American involvement in Vietnam was wrong ("certain blood was being shed for uncertain reasons"), O'Brien agonized about whether to ignore or accept his draft notice. After a decision described in his war autobiography as a "sleep-walking default," O'Brien entered the army. Ever since, he has struggled with his guilt over submitting to obligations to others rather than to an obligation to himself. Consequently, this life-altering decision and its aftermath have become prominent subjects and influences in much of O'Brien's writing, including *The Things They Carried*.

Readers and critics have disagreed about appropriate descriptions for the creative and unconventional form and content of *The Things They Carried*, O'Brien's fifth book. Is it a collection of short stories, a short-story cycle, a series of loosely connected vignettes (similar to his nonfictional *If I Die in a Combat Zone*), or a unified novel emerging from twenty-two stories carefully linked through style, structure, content, themes, narrative iteration, and a first-person narrator? Is it, as the author claims, an anti-Vietnam war book? Is it a thinly veiled nonfiction war autobiography of soldier-author Tim O'Brien as told through the words of a forty-three-year-old soldier-author who also happens to be named "Tim O'Brien"? The real O'Brien, in responding to this last question about autobiographical connections, notes that the use of his own name in the book emerged from a serendipitous moment of emotional intensity rather than from a conscious decision on his part to create a narrator who was the author's alter ego. More important, according to O'Brien, in using these interrelated sections of facts, story, confession, commentary, and narration of other peo-

ple's experiences, he forced himself to invent a new form that blurs the boundaries between fact and fiction, short story and novel, memory and imagination.

Despite ongoing questions about the book's form, critics agree on the skill with which O'Brien has woven together the diverse content through point of view, structure, and recurring situations viewed from different literary and human perspectives. In addition, critics praise the emotional power of the stories as O'Brien strives for what he labels in the book "story-truth" (making the reader's stomach believe) as opposed to "happening-truth" (the facts of events). Also distinguishing this collection of stories is their metafictional content as O'Brien uses several of these pieces to examine the process and purposes of storytelling, as well as the elusive nature of a story's truth. Three representative sections from the book illustrate these qualities.

The title story, "The Things They Carried," which like many of the others is self-contained, is one of the most anthologized of the twenty-two sections and received the 1989 National Magazine Award in Fiction. As the book's first story, it is also intricately linked with the remaining pieces—a prologue for the rest of the book. Within the framing story of Lieutenant Jimmy Cross's unrequited love for a college girl named Martha, author O'Brien mixes storytelling with narrative enumeration to introduce characters and events frequently reappearing in the other stories. He also lists weighted physical objects (personal and military items ranging from Martha's letters to a 6.7-pound flak jacket) that these American soldiers carry with them as they slog through the Vietnam jungles. Most significant, he catalogues the "unweighed" spiritual burdens, fears, and memories that these men also "hump" during and after their tours of duty—"the burden of being alive." This love story with its digressions, "heavy" accumulation of details, realistic portrayal of a soldier's existence, and probing of a soldier's heart and mind presents subjects, style, form, and basic tensions recurring throughout the book: facts versus feelings, memory versus imagination, certainty versus ambiguity, independence versus obligation, and courage versus cowardice.

This last tension becomes the subject of another frequently anthologized story—"On the Rainy River"—that has autobiographical links. In this narrative-confessional piece, author O'Brien imaginatively reworks an event from his own life, his post-graduation draft notice, to explore the moral confusion surrounding fictional narrator Tim O'Brien's dilemma of whether to flee from or fight in the Vietnam War. Escaping to a northern Minnesota fishing resort on the Rainy River, which forms the border with Canada, the fictional Tim spends six days pondering issues of heroism, courage, and responsibility. Like the central character in Stephen Crane's Civil War novel *The Red Badge of Courage,* he also analyzes his fears—of the war, exile, ridicule, and censure. At a time in America when young men were burning their draft cards to protest the Vietnam War, this O'Brien, aided by the sympathetic efforts of the camp's elderly and fatherlike owner, eventually decides to fight. Years later, he recounts living with the guilt that results from having submitted to his fear of shame rather

than to the dictates of his conscience: "I was a coward. I went to the war."

This judgment, presented earlier in *If I Die in a Combat Zone,* focuses readers' attention on one of the recurring subjects examined throughout this collection—the essence of physical and moral courage. As in his other books, O'Brien explores this topic within various contexts and from different angles to create an intentional ambiguity about notions of cowardice and courage. Is a soldier's mere endurance of war also courageous? In "On the Rainy River" and other stories in *The Things They Carried,* significant parallels between O'Brien's life and the fictional narrator's also lead to questions regarding the personal authenticity of the stories. For O'Brien, however, uncertainty surrounding a story's literal truth is inconsequential when compared to the verity of the emotions the work conveys to its readers.

O'Brien's indirect consideration of the nature of good storytelling and the meaning of the word "true" becomes more overt in another of the book's twenty-two stories as the author, through his fictional narrator, examines the relationship between literary lies and story truths. In "How to Tell a True War Story," the fictional soldier-author, reflecting on his war experiences twenty years earlier, examines the essential qualities of war stories. To accomplish this, he mixes commentary and personal confession, along with a self-described war "love story," one relating the accidental death of soldier Curt Lemon, killed during a bit of battlefield horseplay with a friend. Also included is a retelling of another war story told to the narrator by one of his fellow soldiers. Interspersed with these tales are the narrator's commentaries about the process of creating a war story ("making up a few things to get at the real truth"), the amorality of war stories ("a true war story is never moral"), and the ways for readers and listeners to gauge the truth in war stories ("A true war story, if truly told, makes the stomach believe"). This fictional soldier turned author also plays with narrative perspective as he retells the central story about Curt Lemon and changes its effect by adding or subtracting information. Consequently, each of the multiple versions of the story has a different emotional impact for the reader—love, hate, beauty, ugliness, wonder, disgust, understanding, or confusion. The purpose for this narrative iteration with changes is to show that truths in war stories are contradictory and that ultimately war stories are not about war but about universal feelings and conflicts. Furthermore, the goal of a war story, and for that matter any story, remains constant: "to get at the real truth," which is situated in the emotions conveyed and not in the accuracy of the details.

Such principles of storytelling become the standards by which Tim O'Brien believes readers should judge all the stories in *The Things They Carried*. In doing so, readers will also find that the author is able to combine realistic details, narrative playfulness, a seriousness of subject matter, and shifting viewpoints in a form and content that challenge readers and lead to insights about the elusiveness of truth and the power of feelings. Along the way, these stories also become glimpses into the souls of the narrator and the author.

Tobey C. Herzog

SELECTED BIBLIOGRAPHY

Works by Tim O'Brien

The Things They Carried. Boston: Houghton Mifflin, 1990.

Critical Studies

Calloway, Catherine. "Pluralities of Vision: *Going After Cacciato* and Tim O'Brien's Short Fiction." In Owen Gilman Jr. and Lorrie Smith, eds., *America Rediscovered: Critical Essays on the Literature and Film of the Vietnam War,* pp. 213–224. New York: Garland, 1990.

Herzog, Tobey C. *Tim O'Brien.* New York: Twayne, 1997.

Smith, Lorrie. "'The Things Men Do': Gendered Subtext in Tim O'Brien's *Esquire* Stories." *Critique* 36 (fall 1994): 16–39.

FLANNERY O'CONNOR
(1925–1964)

Few storytellers are as initially appealing and ultimately inaccessible as Flannery O'Connor. Her clear, energetic style, humorously delineated cartoonlike characters, and wild mixture of narrative ingredients make an irresistible combination. Take, for example, Mrs. Freeman's introduction at the opening of "Good Country People," the story of the lady Ph.D. who has her artificial leg stolen by a Bible salesman. The impervious Freeman has two public expressions, forward and reverse: her forward was "like the advance of a heavy truck. Her eyes never swerved" but "turned as if they followed a yellow line down the center." When she occasionally used reverse, "her face came to a complete stop," and her black eyes seemed to recede; "though she might stand there as real as several grain sacks on top of each other, [she] was no longer there in spirit." As inviting as beginnings like this are, however, their corresponding endings are marked by murders, suicides, strokes, devastating self-revelations, abandonment, and rejection. Between her beginnings and endings O'Connor introduces mysteries of Christian grace frequently more fathomable to her characters than to her readers. "You should be on the lookout for such things as the action of grace," she advised the latter, "and not for the dead bodies." O'Connor was an allegorist in the tradition of Hawthorne, but with meanings defined by orthodox theology rather than by moral speculation. Interpreting an O'Connor story requires an understanding of the Christian concept of grace, just as understanding *Oedipus the King* requires an idea of the Greek concept of fate.

Mary Flannery O'Connor was born on March 25, 1925, in Savannah, Georgia, to Edward and Regina (Cline) O'Connor, genteel members of Georgia's minority Roman Catholic community. After attending Catholic schools in Savannah and, briefly, in Atlanta, Flannery (who dropped her first name in college) entered Peabody High in Milledgeville, Georgia, the mainly Protestant hometown of her mother, where the family took up residence in 1938. In high school, Flannery drew car-

toons, wrote for the school newspaper, and developed a taste for Edgar Allan Poe's stories. Her father died in 1941 after a long battle with lupus (the disease that would claim his daughter's life), and the following year Flannery joined the freshman class at Georgia State College for women, a block from her Milledgeville home. While at college, she contributed to the literary magazine, became art editor of the yearbook, and received a scholarship to the University of Iowa, where she enrolled in the Writers' Workshop.

During her years in Iowa City (1945–48), O'Connor encountered the fiction of Joyce, Kafka, and Faulkner; had stories published in *Accent*, *New Signatures*, *Mademoiselle*, and *Sewanee Review*; struggled with her vocation in a religious sense; and started to attend daily Mass. She began her first novel (published in 1952 as *Wise Blood*) at Iowa under the influence of Eliot's *The Waste Land* (and, later, Paul's conversion in Acts 9 and the final scenes of *Oedipus the King*), receiving the Rinehart-Iowa Fiction Award in 1947 for sample chapters. O'Connor worked on her novel at Yaddo, the artists' colony near Saratoga Springs, New York, in 1948–49; then, after a brief sojourn in Manhattan, took up residence in Connecticut with classicist Robert Fitzgerald and his wife, Sally (who would become O'Connor's editor and biographer). While returning by train to Milledgeville for Christmas in 1950, O'Connor was stricken with what was subsequently diagnosed as lupus and, surviving a brush with death, moved with her mother to Andalusia, a 1,500-acre dairy farm outside Milledgeville they had recently inherited. With help from Caroline Gordon, who began serving as O'Connor's literary mentor, *Wise Blood* was published and almost universally misunderstood and condemned by reviewers as immoral, violent, and gothic. However, John Crowe Ransom appreciated it enough to get O'Connor a *Kenyon Review* fellowship, which brought her $2,000 to pay for blood transfusions.

Resigned to her illness and responding to cortisone treatments (which eventually caused bone deterioration), O'Connor bought a pair of peacocks to raise for aesthetic pleasure (the male with full tail spread she compared to the transfiguration of Christ) and enjoyed a burst of creative energy. Inspired now by the country folk that came to the farm rather than by literary prototypes, she completed the nine stories collected as *A Good Man Is Hard to Find* in 1955 and won O. Henry Awards for two of them. Besides "Good Country People" and the title story of the frivolous grandmother who accepts kinship with her killer at the moment of death, other noteworthy stories include "The Artificial Nigger," about an alienated grandfather and grandson who recognize their connection through a miserable lawn statue, and "The Displaced Person," the tale of a farmer's widow implicated in the death of a Polish immigrant who, like Christ, has upset the status quo. Reviewers responded with enthusiasm, recognizing a first-rate talent even as they mistakenly read the stories, and the collection sold four thousand copies in three printings between June and September. In October the first chapter of her second novel, *The Violent Bear It Away* (1960), previewed in *New World Writing*, and O'Connor continued to work on subsequent chapters while she completed some of the stories that would be included in her posthumous collection, *Everything That Rises Must Converge* (1965).

As her physical condition deteriorated, O'Connor took to the crutches she called her flying buttresses. Determined to be active when able, she accepted speaking engagements at a variety of colleges and universities, among them Notre Dame, Georgetown, and Chicago. In 1958 she made a pilgrimage to Lourdes, France, visited the Fitzgeralds in Italy, and had an audience with Pope Pius XII. When *The Violent Bear It Away* appeared, O'Connor was discouraged that her intentions had been misunderstood by both favorable and unfavorable reviewers. By 1961, her periods of relative wellness decreased as she suffered hip and jaw problems, anemia, a fibroid tumor, and kidney infections, but she continued to work on her stories. A poignant interaction between art and pain is revealed in her last letters. In her final one to friend Maryat Lee, written a few days before her death on August 3, 1964, O'Connor writes in an illegible scrawl, "Dont know when I'll send those stories. I've felt too bad to type them. Cheers, Tarfunk."

Her final nine stories were published a year later, in 1965, as *Everything That Rises Must Converge,* a title she had selected from the Jesuit theologian Teilhard de Chardin. Outstanding among them are "Greenleaf," in which Christ as predator-bull pierces an agnostic widow's heart; "A View of the Woods," the story of a grandfather damning himself by killing his look-alike granddaughter, his vehicle of grace; "Revelation," the discovery by a self-satisfied lady hog farmer that she is at the tail of the line to Paradise; and "Parker's

Back" (Connor's last story), in which a prophet in flight is reborn when rejected by his wife for having a Byzantine Christ tattooed on his back. Other posthumous publications include *Mystery and Manners* (1969), Sally and Robert Fitzgerald's gathering of O'Connor's occasional prose; *The Complete Stories of Flannery O'Connor*, winner of the National Book Award for 1971; and *The Habit of Being* (1979), a thick volume of letters edited by Sally Fitzgerald that assures O'Connor a niche next to Emily Dickinson in the pantheon of American letter writers.

Flannery O'Connor's apologia as a storyteller can be gleaned from the lectures and articles in *Mystery and Manners,* a collection that reveals O'Connor's theological subject matter and the New Critical principles she applied to it. O'Connor profiles herself in explaining that the Catholic writer overcomes disconnections between faith and vision when "the Church becomes so much a part of his personality that he can forget about her—in the same sense that when he writes, he forgets about himself." Recognizing that piecemeal approaches to her work, which made it essentially absurd, nihilistic, violent, or regional, were unpreventable, she issued a qualifying disclaimer for her readers in a lecture at Hollins College in 1962, insisting that the basic assumptions underlying her stories are "the central Christian mysteries," sin, redemption, grace, salvation, and adding "that there are perhaps other ways than my own in which [the stories] could be read, but none other by which [they] could have been written."

To establish the storyteller's initial duty to his art, O'Connor combines New Critical principles and statements from Thomas Aquinas defining art as reflective of God and as "reason in making." She favors the aesthetic complexities in modern fiction that deemphasize the author and plunge the reader into dramatically rendered experiences, but she cautions against absorption in processes of consciousness neglectful of the sacramental world outside. The particular challenge in short fiction is a completeness within brevity requiring a beginning, middle, and end (in some order), adequate motivation and meaning, as well as revelation of the mystery of life, an O'Connor essential. What makes a short story long, or significant, is its unstated meaning, its illumination of small history in universal light, its fusion of the regional and the ultimate, of manners and mystery. Such meaning reaches beyond the human intellect and its theories, including those of Freud, to transfigure a particular personality through an unexpected but appropriate action "on the anagogical level . . . which has to do with the Divine life and our participation in it."

As the crisp visual details of her fiction would suggest, O'Connor emphasizes the eye as the evaluating organ that involves the writer's whole personality and world, agreeing with Romano Guardini "that the roots of the eye are in the heart." Because seeing includes moral vision and judgment, it makes a difference in a story, she insists, if the writer believes in creation by an intelligence or by cosmic accident, in humanity being made in God's image or God in its, in human wills being free or bound like those of other animals. Rather than narrowing the writer's field of vision, as secularists contend, religious belief expands vision through mystery, reveals a supernatural world in the natural one, and thus adds to rather than diminishes the field of observation. The storyteller of faith is invited, like the blind man touched by Christ (Mark 8:24), to deep and strange visions. As a citizen of the defeated South, a storyteller might be culturally conditioned to the loss of innocence and need for restoration, but as a Christian he can mystify this through the biblical Fall of Man and "Redemption . . . brought about by Christ's death and by our slow participation in it."

Because contemporary readers have domesticated despair, and consequently demanded from fiction a reflection of life devoid of mystery, O'Connor believes the serious writer must search within to develop a realism deeper than the typical, one similar to Hawthorne's efforts in the direction of "romance." Such realism requires the writer to manipulate vision through shock and distort surfaces to reveal truth and the discrepancies of life— "to the hard of hearing you shout, and for the almost-blind you draw large and startling figures." This strategy attracts O'Connor toward the grotesque in southern fiction (and the influence of Faulkner), the grotesque becoming for her the literal tracing of spiritual lines of motion or the action of grace; it also clarifies her use of the freak and of violent encounters. The freak is intended to reflect the fallen human condition and disturb those "afflicted with the doctrine of the perfectibility of human nature by its own efforts," to show us "what we are, but what we have been and what we could become." The divine offer of grace to elevate and heal the human freak is inextricably linked to Christ's sacrificial death and emphatically reflects what theologian Karl Rahner terms God's "universal salvific will." O'Connor depicts the urgency of this salvific will in "Greenleaf," when agnostic Mrs. May is pursued and pierced through the heart at her moment of vision by a runaway bull, a story probably indebted to Victorian poet Francis Thompson's "The Hound of Heaven," which psychologizes the theology of human flight from the divine predator. "With the serious writer," O'Connor explains, "violence is never an end in itself. . . . [The] extreme situation [rather than "the tenor of our daily lives"] best reveals what we are essentially."

All these essential components of the Christian mystery are dramatized repeatedly in O'Connor's stories. The call to transcend the sinful human condition is given with increasing urgency to self-satisfied Ruby Turpin in "Revelation," to vindictive Mr. Fortune in "A View of the Woods," and to the vain and flighty grandmother in "A Good Man Is Hard to Find." O'Connor delineates the fallen state of each subject, depicts the urgency of God's salvific will, and analyzes the process of grace according to her reading of Thomas Aquinas's theory in the *Summa Theologica* of the "double act" of operating and co-operating grace, of how we are at once opened to grace and assisted by grace to respond (Question 111, Article 2).

Ruby Turpin unmindfully boasts of her fallen state to her audience in the doctor's waiting room: "When I think who all I could have been besides myself and what I got, a little of everything, and good disposition, besides, I just feel like shouting, 'Thank you, Jesus, for making everything the way it is!'" That "the way it is" is the way of sin startles Ruby when she is hit in the eye with a book titled *Human Development* and attacked by a psychotic college student named Grace. Subsequently, in her conflicting encounter with grace, Ruby recognizes herself as seriously flawed, as someone placed at the very end of the purgatorial procession to Paradise, well behind "whole companies of white-trash . . . and bands of black niggers in white robes, and battalions of freaks and lunatics shouting and clapping and leaping like frogs." O'Connor distances the readers from the interaction of operating and cooperating grace in this story, perhaps because that process is a mystery; we are confined to the surface as the route to the supernatural. Although resentful at being called an "old wart hog" and directed "back to hell where you came from" by the psychotic girl, Ruby later seems aware of her opportunity for grace and vision: "she bent her head slowly and gazed, as if through the very heart of mystery . . . she were absorbing some abysmal life-giving knowledge." Her subsequent actions indicate affirmative response to the divine offer, a moment of human transcendence, and the resolve to begin the painful process of reform: "At last she lifted her head. . . . She raised her hands . . . in a gesture hieratic and profound. . . . She lowered her hands and gripped the rail by the hog pen, her eyes small but fixed unblinkingly on what lay ahead."

In "A View of the Woods," which reverses the positive outcome of Ruby Turpin's story, O'Connor gets inside Mr. Fortune as he is given the opportunity to fathom the eternal consequences of selling property to spite his son-in-law Pitts, whom the old man considers trash, and

block out his family's view of the woods. Puzzled that his nine-year-old, lookalike granddaughter, Mary Fortune, opposes the sale, old Fortune repeatedly gets up from an afternoon nap to contemplate the woods; however, each time he stifles God's self-communication. Fortune's final contemplation is the most emphatic: "The third time he got up to look at the woods . . . the gaunt trunks appeared to be raised in a pool of red light that gushed from the almost hidden sun setting behind them." That the divine appeal is being made through Christ becomes obvious in the sunset description of the woods O'Connor specified in a letter to "A" as "the Christ symbol." "The old man stared for some time, as if . . . he were . . . held there in the midst of an uncomfortable mystery. . . . He saw it, in his hallucination, as if someone were wounded behind the woods and the trees were bathed in blood." In closing his eyes against this "unpleasant vision," Fortune is rejecting the grace of atonement in favor of the damnation adumbrated in the transposing of crucifixion and inferno imagery: "against the closed lids hellish red trunks rose up in a black wood." However, the "universal salvific will" is not so easily dismissed and violently turns itself on Fortune through granddaughter Mary, who attacks him and tries to force him to accept through her his human bond to Pitts. The only way grace can be stifled is by dashing Mary's head against a rock until "his conquered image . . . [is] absolutely silent. . . . The eyes had rolled back down and were set in a fixed glare that did not take him in." Mr. Fortune is one of the damned, according to O'Connor, damning himself by emphatically rejecting divine communication.

In "A Good Man Is Hard to Find," O'Connor has explained the meaning she intended in her depiction of the grandmother's response to grace, when she reaches out to a murderer and identifies him as "one of my babies . . . one of my own children." That response, O'Connor said, is an "unexpected" and yet "totally right" gesture that is "in character and beyond character," that is "on the anagogical level . . . which has to do with the Divine life and our participation in it." This gesture signifies her realization that "she is responsible [accountable in her sinfulness] for the man before her who has murdered . . . the members of her family" and joined to him by ties of kinship. Though she is shot to death, her soul is saved. As O'Connor explains, "The old lady's gesture, like the mustard-seed [Matt. 17:20], will grow to be a great crow-filled tree in the Misfit's heart, and will be enough of a pain to him there to turn him into the prophet he was meant to become."

No American storyteller made clearer than Flannery O'Connor individual human absurdity and collective need, or dramatized so shockingly the psychological operation of grace and so comically the miserable condition of the human territory where grace operates. The strength of her stories lies in her sacramental theology as well as narrative skill, her ability to discover ultimate reality in the natural world and present it through observable details, to "reveal" in manners the "mystery of our position on earth." Properly understood, her economy of grace becomes universal rather than sectarian or even confined to Christians. O'Connor largely sought subjects among the unchurched, among those "in the invisible Church" whose "discoveries . . . have meaning for us who are better protected . . . and . . . often too lazy and satisfied to make discoveries at all."

John J. Murphy

SELECTED BIBLIOGRAPHY

Works by Flannery O'Connor

A Good Man Is Hard to Find and Other Stories. New York: Harcourt, 1955.
Everything That Rises Must Converge. New York: Farrar, Straus & Giroux, 1965.
Mystery and Manners: Occasional Prose. Edited by Sally and Robert Fitzgerald. New York: Farrar, Straus & Giroux, 1969.
The Complete Stories of Flannery O'Connor. New York: Farrar, Straus & Giroux, 1971.
Flannery O'Connor: Collected Works. Edited by Sally Fitzgerald. New York: Library of America, 1988.

Critical Studies

Friedman, Melvin J. and Beverly Lyon Clark, eds. *Critical Essays on Flannery O'Connor.* Boston: Hall, 1985.
Giannone, Richard. *Flannery O'Connor and the Mystery of Love.* Urbana: University of Illinois Press, 1989.
Whitt, Margaret E. *Understanding Flannery O'Connor.* Columbia: University of South Carolina Press, 1995.

JOHN O'HARA
(1905 – 1970)

A prolific writer of novels, novellas, plays, and journalism, John O'Hara was also the author of fifteen substantial collections of short stories. O'Hara's fiction commanded a vast popular readership for four decades, despite the reservations of reviewers who criticized his work as superficial, too detailed, and limited in range. Such objections notwithstanding, however, O'Hara nonetheless produced a considerable body of short stories that are masterworks of social realism and narrative irony.

The son of Dr. Patrick H. and Katherine Delaney O'Hara, John O'Hara was born and raised in Pottsville, the small industrial town in the eastern Pennsylvania mining region that he made famous as the fictional Gibbsville in numerous stories and in novels. O'Hara was a rebellious, heavy-drinking adolescent whose behavior got him expelled from three prep schools between 1920 and 1924. This deeply disappointed his father, who wanted him to pursue a career in medicine. Instead, the young O'Hara took to journalism, a line of work that would have a formative influence on his literary style (as it did that of established authors of the time such as Hemingway and Anderson, with whose fiction O'Hara's has stylistic affinities). While in the employ of his hometown paper, O'Hara nurtured a passionate ambition to attend a prestigious university. When he managed to get accepted at Yale in 1925, however, his father died and left the family unable to afford

the costs. (Yale and other Ivy League institutions would figure prominently as symbols of prestige, personal achievement, and privileged social standing in the many O'Hara stories that focus on social stratification and class rivalry.)

O'Hara's career as a journalist began with the Pottsville *Journal* in 1924. Setting out on his own in 1928, he worked for the most part in New York, where alcoholism, a volatile temper, and irregular work habits kept him moving from job to job until 1934. In that year O'Hara's first novel, *Appointment in Samarra,* appeared and quickly became a popular best seller, catapulting the young author to literary fame. O'Hara's most significant early success as a short story writer had come in 1928 with "The Alumnae Bulletin," the first of 225 O'Hara stories that were to appear in the pages of *The New Yorker*.

In 1931, O'Hara married Helen Petit, an actress and graduate of Wellesley; but his drinking and unpredictable temper caused Petit to divorce him within two years. The popular success of *Appointment at Samarra* led to scriptwriting opportunities on the West Coast; and from 1934 through the mid-1940s, and for a time in the mid-1950s, O'Hara divided his year between New York and Hollywood. These locales provided the settings of the generally undistinguished show-business narratives collected mostly in *Files on Parade* (1939), *Pal Joey* (1940), and *Pipe Night* (1945). In 1937, O'Hara married his second wife, Belle Wylie, with whom he had one child, Wylie Delaney O'Hara (b. 1945). After Belle's premature death in 1954, O'Hara moved permanently to Princeton, New Jersey, where in 1955 he married Katherine Bryan.

A source of perennial bitterness for O'Hara (who was twice passed over for a Nobel Prize) was the conviction that his work never received the full measure of critical acclaim that it merited. Still, O'Hara did garner a number of awards, including the New York Drama Critics' Circle Award and the Donaldson Prize for the 1952 Broadway revival of *Pal Joey*, the National Book Award for the Gibbsville novel *Ten North Frederick* (1955), and the American Academy of Arts and Letters Gold Medal Award of Merit (1964).

O'Hara's literary style is notable for its reportorial economy, narrative irony, and hard-edged social realism. The latter comes to life most dramatically in his expert rendering of dialogue and in the abundance of material and symbolic details (club and school insignias, for example, and particular makes of automobile) that indicate social status. A "social historian," O'Hara produced Thackerayan depictions of pretentiousness, hypocrisy, arrogance, cruelty, and stupidity—individual, collective, and normative. His habitual focus on the breakdown of human relationships often illuminates, from various angles, the social realities—typically conflictive—of what he saw as America's "spurious democracy." A perennial theme of O'Hara's is inveterate ethnic and class antagonism and the resulting instability in which "any social situation is likely to blow up in one's face." Among the most salient features of O'Hara's narrative style is his heavy reliance on dialogue to delineate character. He once declared, as "O'Hara's Law," that an author who lacks either the skill or concern to create convincing, realistic dialogue—which he felt should stand on its own, with a minimum of mod-

ifiers—fails sufficiently to grasp "character and his creation of character." And character, for O'Hara, is central: the writer of fiction is "most effective," he argued, "perhaps even *only* effective, when his concern is for his character rather than for his conditions."

O'Hara's novels had a huge popular appeal thanks to their hard-boiled realism, their documentary presentation of class tension, and their treatments of ungoverned passions and social scandal. His fictional exposés of manners and caste get played out in three different and yet uniquely American sociocultural settings: the sharply stratified, multiethnic mining region of his "Lantenengo County" in Pennsylvania (which O'Hara conceived as his equivalent of Faulkner's Yoknapatawpha County); the world of the wealthy and upper-middle class in and around Philadelphia, New York, and Boston; and the social milieu of actors and writers in Hollywood.

O'Hara's short fiction shares the settings of his longer work and is widely recognized as his most significant literary achievement. Three of the finest and most characteristic stories from O'Hara's early period are "The Doctor's Son" (1934), "Over the River and Through the Wood" (1935), and "Lunch Tuesday" (1937). "The Doctor's Son" is the quintessential introduction to the world of Gibbsville and to the narrator, Jimmy Malloy, O'Hara's semiautobiographical persona. Jimmy Malloy was to be a presence in novels and stories over the next thirty years, as a child, an adolescent, a young journalist in the fictional Lantenengo County and New York City, and as a Hollywood scriptwriter. (His final appearance is as narrator in the consummately observed "A Man to Be Trusted," a posthumously published long-short story about his extended relationship with a couple who lost a son his age, and how at thirteen Jimmy became sexually involved with the wife.) "The Doctor's Son" concerns a series of events, narrated by Malloy, that occur in the coal-mining district during the 1918 influenza epidemic. Jimmy, at fifteen, has been enlisted to drive a medical student called in from Philadelphia to spell Doctor Malloy, who has dropped from exhaustion. Accompanying the substitute doctor on his father's rounds, young Malloy witnesses firsthand in the saloons (where many of the working poor collect for treatment) and in ramshackle Collieryville houses the panic, rage, horror, and death that the epidemic precipitates. The perception of unpredictable disaster sharply intensifies, along with that of betrayed trust, when Jimmy discovers that the young practitioner has taken up with a mining official's wife, to whose home he drives the man. The adultery stands in counterpoint to the "pure" love that the boy nurtures for the woman's daughter. Ironically, the girl's father dies of the flu and she subsequently refuses to speak with Jimmy, eventually leaving town and eloping later with someone else. The tensions and betrayal that blight both professional and personal relationships in the story, including that of Jimmy and his father, not to mention the random suffering and death of the innocent and the good, are hallmarks of O'Hara's bleak vision of the human lot.

"Over the River and Through the Wood" (1935), with its startling ending, is the best-known early story in which O'Hara demonstrates his ability richly to develop the inner life of a character. The portrait of the loneliness and infirmities that accrue with aging looks forward, along with the theme of facing one's mortality, to many of the stories collected in the volumes beginning with Assembly (1961).

"Lunch Tuesday" (1937) exemplifies the sort of New Yorker fiction that O'Hara is often credited with having perfected. Set in "one of those good, characterless restaurants in the East Fifties," it is about two friends, married women, having drinks together and discovering by chance that one is having an affair with the other's husband. The piece is vintage O'Hara in its unforgiving narrative irony, the effective use of delayed revelation, and in the theme of sexual betrayal.

O'Hara's skill as a short story writer developed considerably over the decades, and from 1960 on (following an eleven-year hiatus during which he wrote copiously in other genres) he began producing short fiction that is more discursively amplified, psychologically nuanced, and superbly paced than most of the early work. Although still traditionally realistic and focused on O'Hara's staple themes, the short stories of the 1960s reveal a greater concern with the capacity to love and with the experience of aging. Two stories that exemplify the degree to which O'Hara's art matured in his late phase are "The House on the Corner" and "School," both from 1964. The former showcases O'Hara's skill as a master of dramatic irony as it unsentimentally portrays a son's filial love and loyalty to the values of middle-class parents who live close to the bone so that their son could rise above their financial and social stratum. "School," a study of the betrayal and emotional cruelty that adultery incites between father and son, illustrates the impressive dramatic power that O'Hara was capable of achieving in his late stories through remarkably deft narrative pacing.

O'Hara's readership declined sharply in the decades after his death. One reason is that he consistently refused permission to anthologize his short stories. Another is the consensus among literary scholars and critics that his work lacks distinction for the reasons enumerated above and, on more general grounds, because it is unregenerately "conservative" and stylistically reactionary. Such judgments prove far from the mark, however, in the many John O'Hara stories—especially in the eight collections that begin with *Assembly*—that display a combination of bold social realism, masterly narrative pacing, trenchant irony, and dialogue that brings character and incident compellingly to life.

Phillip Stambovsky

SELECTED BIBLIOGRAPHY

Story Collections

The Cape Cod Lighter. New York: Random, 1962.
The Hat on the Bed. New York: Random, 1963.
The Horse Knows the Way. New York: Random, 1964.
Waiting for Winter. New York: Random, 1966.
And Other Stories. New York: Random, 1968.
The Time Element and Other Stories. Edited by Albert Erskine. New York: Random, 1972.
Good Samaritan and Other Stories. Edited by Albert Erskine. New York: Random, 1974.
Gibbsville, Pa. Edited by Matthew J. Bruccoli. New York: Carroll & Graf, 1992.

Critical Studies

Grebstein, Sheldon N. *John O'Hara*. New York: Twayne, 1966.
Long, Robert Emmet. *John O'Hara*. New York: Ungar, 1983.
MacShane, Frank. "Introduction: The Power of the Ear." *Collected Stories of John O'Hara*. New York: Random, 1984.

TILLIE OLSEN
(1913?–)

The author of a small but powerful body of work, Tillie Olsen is best known today for *Tell Me a Riddle* (1962), a volume of short stories; *Yonnondio*, a novel written in the 1930s but not published until 1974; and *Silences* (1978), a collection of critical essays and reflections that have the density of poetry. Her short fiction is highly regarded for its consummate craft and transformative vision.

Tillie Olsen's parents, Samuel Lerner and Ida Beber Lerner, were born and raised in Russia. Drawn to the Bund, a Jewish socialist organization with a humanist and internationalist perspective, they participated in the 1905 Revolution, a mass uprising protesting the tyranny of the regime. When it failed, they emigrated separately to the United States, eventually marrying and settling in the Midwest. Born in 1912 or 1913, the second of six children, Tillie Lerner grew up in Omaha, Nebraska, understanding the experiences of her working-class immigrant family in the context of global human struggles for survival and dignity.

Omaha was a surprisingly diverse world of native-born and newly immigrant workers, visiting socialist activists and intellectuals, and black families in the Lerners' integrated neighborhood. Olsen's ability to recall and inscribe the different rhythms of language—the cadences of black sermons, the multiethnic exchanges of factory workers, the inflections of Yiddish-influenced English—make her prose a rich evocation of multicultural America. Passionately literate even as a young girl, she read widely in fiction, poetry, criticism, and social theory. Her work fuses modernist experimentation in style with the commitment to social change expressed in what she calls the "larger tradition of social concern": writers ranging from Tolstoy, Chekhov, and Victor Hugo to Rebecca Harding Davis, Elizabeth Maddox Roberts, and Walt Whitman. In the notes for her essay on Davis's *Life in the Iron Mills,* Olsen tells how an encounter with the story when she was fifteen taught her that "literature can be made out of the lives of despised people," and "You, too, must write."

Olsen's commitment to writing and her social engagement unfolded simultaneously. She became a political activist in her teens, joining the Young People's Socialist League and, in 1931, the Young Communist League. In the 1930s, when America was in the midst of a devastating depression, communism seemed to many to offer a more humane, and more socially successful, vision than the laissez-faire capitalism of the pre-New Deal United States. Jailed for helping to organize a strike in a packinghouse, she contracted tuberculosis. Recovering in Minnesota, she began work on the novel that would become *Yonnondio.* In 1933, now a single mother, she moved to California, meeting and eventually marrying Jack Olsen, a YCL activist and labor organizer. Her 1930s writing voices the angers, the longings, and the hopes of working men, women, and children.

As the decade wore on, and Olsen bore her second daughter, she became increasingly absorbed in mothering her family and working for pay. She stopped work on *Yonnondio,* not rediscovering the completed chapters and preparing them for publication until the 1970s. She did not begin to write fiction again until the 1950s. A time of material prosperity, the 1950s were also an era haunted by the memory of Nazism and war and by the threat of nuclear annihilation. The Cold War against the Soviet Union provided the context for a fierce anticommunism in the United States and the systematic repression of the left activist politics and culture of the previous decades. Like many activists, the Olsens lost their jobs and suffered harassment from FBI surveillance.

Ironically, for Olsen, this was also a time of passage from her busiest years as a mother and an activist to the moment when, her fourth and youngest child in school, she was able to find a little writing time. She enrolled in a writing class at San

Francisco State University, finishing one story, "I Stand Here Ironing," and completing the first draft of a second, "Hey Sailor, What Ship?" On the basis of this work, she received a fellowship in creative writing to Stanford, and, there "as the exiled homesick come home," she found "the comradeship of books and writing human beings." In her eight months at Stanford, she completed "Hey Sailor, What Ship?", wrote "O Yes," and finished the first third of "Tell Me a Riddle." These four stories constitute Olsen's only collection of fiction, published as *Tell Me a Riddle* in 1962. Conceived as sections of a novel, the stories portray the lives of members of an extended family over three generations. Set within the home, constructed from the rhythms and language of daily familial life, they constantly expand in scope to illustrate the location of the family within a larger set of social relations and historical contexts. The dilemmas of mothering, particularly for poor women, are central in both *Yonnondio* and the stories of *Tell Me a Riddle*. Few other writers have rendered so fully the profound contradictions of maternity: its calling forth of all one's love, patience, humor, and sometimes, when the resources for furthering growth are nonexistent, despair; its absorption of one's attention, time, thought; its transformation of one's creative capacities from the boldly visionary to the carefully nurturing.

"I Stand Here Ironing" introduces a voice rarely heard in fiction until this time, the voice of a poor single mother. The monologue that constitutes the story is her response to the concern of a teacher or school counselor, who tells her that her daughter Emily "needs help." It depicts all the anguish and guilt of a mother who, in order to work to support her children, has been forced to leave them in inadequate care. Vulnerable and serious, Emily unexpectedly has developed gifts as a mime. "You ought to do something about her with a gift like that": the suggestion echoes in the mother's thoughts as a rebuke, for "without money or knowing how, what does one do?" Images of fluidity and lightness—Emily's early animation, physical quickness, movement on the stage—are juxtaposed with a heavier language of clogging and clotting, as her gift eddies within, imperfectly fulfilled. But this mother's pain is both relieved and deepened by her understanding that Emily is far from alone in being one for whom "all that is in her will not bloom." Emily is a "child of her age, of depression, of war, of fear." Refusing to accede to the counselor's well-intentioned but inadequate intervention, the mother's response is "Let her be." Yet her stance is ultimately not resignation or hopelessness. She prays fiercely at the end that her daughter's will to live fully will transcend the hard soil of her youth: "Only help her to know—help make it so there is cause for her to know— that she is more than this dress on the ironing board, helpless before the iron." Like much of Olsen's work, this story explores the "hidden injuries of class," acknowledging the harm done by poverty and powerlessness but also insisting on the presence of creativity among those in whom it is least nurtured socially.

Like "I Stand Here Ironing," "O Yes" revolves around mother-daughter relationships, in this case two mother-daughter dyads, Helen and her daughter Carol, and their African American friends

Alva and her daughter Parialee. The story is structured in two parts. The first section narrates a single episode in which Carol attends Parry's baptism at a black church. The words, music, and motion of the church service are performed textually as the congregation responds to the preacher's sermon, swelling into "an awful thrumming sound . . . like feet and hands thrashing around, like a giant jumping of a rope." The passion of the parishioners, enacting a ritual of liberation from bondage that Carol cannot understand, disturbs and frightens her. She longs to be able to compress the sound and motion "into a record small and round to listen to far and far." The final vision of horror for her is the spectacle of a schoolmate, writhing against the ushers "with the look of grave and loving support" on her face. Overcome by the unfamiliar emotionality of the service, Carol faints, subsequently retreating from Alva's attempts at comfort and explanation.

In the second section, Helen unwillingly witnesses her daughter grow increasingly estranged from Parry, as they are impelled in different directions by the formal and informal tracking system of the American public school. But "O Yes" concludes with an episode that marks Carol's maturation into, identity with, and compassion for a larger human community. Feverish with the mumps, she races downstairs shrieking for her mother to turn off the radio, which is playing the same "storm of singing" that led to her fainting in the church. Finally wanting to know "why . . . they sing and scream like that," she confesses her shame at the betrayals of her friendship with Parry, and for the first time names and recognizes

her relatedness to and social estrangement from Vicky, the "bad girl" of her school, whose ecstasy at the church has triggered her fainting spell. "Oh why is it like it is," she cries," and why do I have to care?" Holding her silently, her mother thinks, "*Caring asks doing. It is a long baptism into the seas of humankind, my daughter. Better immersion than to live untouched. . . . Yet how will you sustain?*" This passage transforms Carol's estrangement at Parry's baptism, an instance of the alienation of different cultural communities from one another, into the possibility for her participation in another form of baptism, a continuous process of immersion in the "seas of humankind," implying the mutual responsibility of one human being for another across class and racial lines.

As in "I Stand Here Ironing," a discourse of bodily constriction and expression permeates the text, most obvious in the church scene but working throughout to render the girls' different trajectories into separate adulthoods. In the most joyous moments, Carol and Parry play physically together, "leaping, bouncing, hallooing . . . in the old synchronized understanding." This joyousness is reversed in a scene when Parry brings the homebound Carol her homework. Here, Parry's fast jive talk and frantic motion conceal her pain; their teacher has assumed Parry to be the daughter of Carol's maid, and has given her instructions with a patronizing racism. Carol is tracked on the upwardly mobile course that severs most children like her from the less racially differentiated world of their childhood and indoctrinates them with a sense of propriety and decorum appropriate to their rising status in the white middle classes. Parry's energy and physicality are molded increasingly by her maturation into a black working-class culture whose linguistic and bodily forms signal and produce her increasing distance from social approval and social power. Hence Olsen's name for her, Parialee.

This complex story rewrites maternality as a process far different from rearing one's own children for success in the existing social order. Each section of the story ends with the internal monologues of, respectively, Alva and Helen. Alva's monologue recalls a vision she had at fifteen, pregnant and alone. Framed in the language of African American spiritual discourse but infused as well with images of nurturance merging the identities of mother and child, the vision encompasses a spiritual journey from death to rebirth and culminates with a revelation of freedom. During her journey, a voice calls to Alva, "Mama Mama you must help carry the world." Maternality becomes, then, a process both spiritual and social, entailing responsibility for the well-being of a larger human community. The black church, a location where an oppressed people can share their suffering and celebrate their bonds with one another in safety, suggests the possibility for community and resistance. At the conclusion of the story, the reader learns that Helen, while silently comforting her weeping daughter, yearns herself for "the place of strength that was not—where one could scream or sorrow while all knew and accepted, and gloved and loving hands waited to support and understand." The conclusion mourns the absence of community in Helen's life, an absence more fully articulated in "Hey Sailor, What Ship?" Neither Alva nor Helen in their silences can give Carol the

answers she demands, nor protect their children against the rigid stratifications of 1950s American society. Yet the story affirms what they can give: the example of their own friendship and of a will to transcend more traditional and limited notions of maternal desire.

In the more overtly elegiac "Hey Sailor, What Ship?" Whitey, an old sailor friend of Lennie's and Helen's, comes to shore on leave and collapses of alcoholism and illness in their home before disappearing once again. The very intrusiveness of his visit measures the degree of loss the story records, the loss of an earlier time when men and women—including Lennie and Whitey, the sailor—united to struggle as progressive union activists for better working conditions and for a better world. Through Whitey's fragmented internal monologues, through his exchanges with family members, through their references to his past visits and shared history, and through his declamation of "The Valedictory," by the condemned Philippine revolutionary Jose Rizal, the text enables the reader gradually to reconstruct the able seaman and social activist Whitey once was. Olsen contrasts his lost heritage, a time of brotherhood, to the diminished present, when even his union has no place for him and a dominant anticommunism relegates sentiments like those in "The Valedictory" to nostalgic renditions in private living rooms. "Hey Sailor" is linked to "Tell Me a Riddle" both thematically and formally. Both stories comment on the alienation and disengagement from public life that characterized the 1950s and explicitly mourn the loss of a radical political culture and vision. In both, a narrative unfolds in the present

but is continuously disrupted by intimations of the past, revealed in fragments of conversation and memory, as
though the experience of the past is too
different for the present to contain but too
important for it utterly to repress. The
very form of the stories, then, simultaneously reproduces and protests the social and historical silencings characteristic
of the 1950s.

"Tell Me a Riddle" won the O. Henry
Award for best American short story in
1961. The most sustained and complex
of the pieces in the *Riddle* volume, it addresses the nature of human bonding; the
quest for, in Olsen's words, "coherence,
transport, meaning"; the aspiration toward justice; the confrontation with
death. Like Olsen's other work, the story
celebrates the endurance of human love
and of the passion for justice, in spite of
the pain inflicted and the limitations imposed by poverty, racism, and a patriarchal
social order. Its power derives from its
distillation of themes of such large compass in evocative and precise language, at
once poetic and performative of the specific rhythms and idioms of Yiddish-born
English, and from its structure, which
only gradually reveals the relevance to the
lives of one poor aging immigrant Jewish
couple of a past embracing the struggles
and horrors of modern history.

"Tell Me a Riddle" begins with a deadly
battle of wills between an old man and
woman, married forty-seven years, over
whether to sell their home and move to
a cooperative. The conflict is shaped by
the different ways their poverty has affected each of them. David longs to be
free of responsibility and surrounded by
friends; Eva longs only to be left alone.

The years of struggle to keep her family
fed and clothed have transformed her capacity for engagement in the lives of others
into its obverse: the terrible need for solitude, for "reconciled peace."

When Eva falls ill with terminal cancer,
David finds himself compelled to become
a caretaker. Concealing her condition
from Eva, but fearing to stay home alone
with her in her dying, he takes her to visit
a daughter in Ohio, and then to Venice,
California, which in those years was home
to a community of older, working-class
Jews. As her condition deteriorates, she
becomes delirious, pouring out fragments
of poetry and song from her youth. Tended
in her illness not only by David but also
by her granddaughter, Jeannie, a nurse,
Eva passes on to Jeannie the legacy of her
earlier years. It is crucial to the way "Riddle" works as art that Olsen reveals the
dimensions of that legacy only gradually.
Slowly, the reader realizes that this silent,
bitter grandmother was an orator in the
1905 revolution, that she and her husband
met in Siberian prison camps, that she had
once publicly articulated a passionate vision of human possibility and human liberty. Through this narrative strategy, Olsen suggests the tragic dimensions of social
silencings, imposed on working-class people by physical and intellectual deprivation, isolation, and routinized work, and
imposed on women by role-related demands and gender ideologies. Read this
way, Eva's coming to speech again at last
becomes an act of resistance and creation,
both cathartic and political. Rachel Du-
plessis sees Eva as a silenced artist whose
last work is the "cantata" she composes in
dying. In this reading, the granddaughter's
practice of her art, similar in its ethical

motivation to Eva's activism, will realize the creative potential left unfulfilled in the grandmother's life.

Eva's deathbed oration forces David to acknowledge not only what has been lost and destroyed in her, but also what is lost in American society of the 1950s, with its grasping materialism, atomic nightmares, and repression of radical culture. This narrative counterpoint reveals that Eva's withdrawal, though grounded in personal circumstances, has deeper causes still: a disillusionment with the ravages of modern history and an overpowering sense of the disparity between her youthful revolutionary idealism and the complacency of contemporary life. One of the resonant words of "Riddle" is "betrayal," and David's changed consciousness at the novella's conclusion must encompass "the bereavement and betrayal he had sheltered—compounded through the years—hidden even from himself." In dying, Eva awakens David (and the reader) out of an accommodationist stance into a potentially oppositional one.

Olsen continued to struggle with the circumstances imposing silence in her own writing life: the need to work for pay; the interruptions occasioned by family life; the loss of the habit of writing. "Requa," published in 1970, was her first story in almost ten years. A stylistically complex work set in the Depression, "Requa" narrates a thirteen-year-old boy's slow recovery from the devastating loss of his mother. Though "Requa" is literally the American Indian place name of the North Pacific town where the boy, Stevie, comes to live with his clumsily nurturing uncle, a junkyard worker, the word also connotes a requiem for and commemoration of the

dispossessed and forgotten. "Requa" implies, in its simultaneous difficulty and beauty of form, an order won from disorder. As Blanche Gelfant suggests, its ultimate coherence, wrought from a chaos of fragments, blank spaces, catalogues of junkyard sounds and implements, connects "a child's renewed will to live" and "an artist's recovered power to write."

The reclamation of lives and words from silencing becomes Olsen's greatest theme. The essays that she wrote in the 1970s simultaneously theorize the effects of silencings in writers' lives and pay a special respect to writers who have rescued from oblivion the otherwise invisible and silent lives of others. *Silences* (1978) weaves together her previous essays with excerpts from the work of other writers and an extended gloss. The book catalogues all the various forms of silencing that befall writers—especially women and those who must struggle for sheer survival. For Tillie Olsen, creativity is a human gift accorded to most of us; it is the "circumstances" of gender, of race, and of class that too often deform and impede its expression. Her work, in mourning the loss of all that does not bloom in an inequitable world, inspires a consciousness of human possibility and a commitment to social justice.

Deborah Silverton Rosenfelt

SELECTED BIBLIOGRAPHY

Works by Tillie Olsen

Tell Me a Riddle. Philadelphia: Lippincott, 1961.

Critical Studies

Coiner, Constance. *Better Red: The Writing and Resistance of Tillie Olsen and Meridel Le Sueur.* New York: Oxford University Press, 1995.

Hedges, Elaine, and Shelley Fisher Fishkin, eds. *Listening to Silences: New Essays in Feminist Criticism.* New York: Oxford University Press, 1994.

Nelson, Kay Hoyle, and Nancy Huse, eds. *The Critical Response to Tillie Olsen.* New York: Greenwood Press, 1994.

Orr, Elaine Neil. *Tillie Olsen and a Feminist Spiritual Vision.* Jackson: University Press of Mississippi, 1987.

Rosenfelt, Deborah Silverton, ed. *"Tell Me a Riddle," by Tillie Olsen.* New Brunswick, N.J.: Rutgers University Press, 1995.

SIMON ORTIZ
(1941 –   )

Simon Ortiz's life and writing center on Acoma, New Mexico. The stark southwestern landscape and the open skies form the backdrop for the culture and perspective of the Pueblo people whose agricultural acumen and stable sociopolitical structure have endured for centuries. Simon Ortiz was born into these people and this landscape on May 27, 1941, in Albuquerque. His parents were both from Acoma Pueblo and raised a large family in nearby McCartys. He was schooled locally, learning English as a sec-

ond language. In the sixth grade he enrolled in a Bureau of Indian Affairs (BIA) school in Santa Fe. Later he graduated from the Albuquerque Indian School. In 1961, he attended Ft. Lewis College in Durango, Colorado. After a tour in the army from 1963 to 1966 and some time in a veteran's hospital in Colorado, he attended the University of New Mexico. In 1969 he received a master of fine arts degree from the University of Iowa.

Over the years, Ortiz has taught at a variety of institutions, including San Diego State University, Institute of American Indian Arts, Navajo Community College, College of Marin, University of New Mexico, Sinte Gleska College, and Lewis & Clark College. He has been a newspaper editor for the National Indian Youth Council, a consulting editor for Pueblo of Acoma Press, and an editor of an anthology of contemporary Native American fiction, *Earth Power Coming.* Ortiz has even served as lieutenant governor of his beloved Acoma Pueblo.

Ortiz's writing first reached a wide audience with the publication of *The Man to Send Rain Clouds,* edited by Kenneth Rosen, in 1974. Ortiz's fiction and that of Leslie Marmon Silko stood out in the volume and influenced many Native writers of the day. They created a richly textured fiction that brought to life surprising Native characters, motivated by a value system different from the dominant society, but intact and in the process of negotiating the boundaries with the white world. Ortiz published four short stories in *The Man to Send Rain Clouds,* including "Kaiser and the War" and "The Killing of a State Cop," that introduced conflicting worldviews.

Four other stories appeared in the small volume *Howbah Indians* (1978), which includes "Men on the Moon." His volume *Fightin': New and Collected Stories* (1983) contained nineteen stories, three of which were published in earlier volumes, including "To Change in a Good Way."

Ortiz received much national attention in 1976 with the publication of his volume of poetry *Going for the Rain*. He has become associated with what has been called the "Native American Renaissance," the flowering of Native writers after N. Scott Momaday's 1969 Pulitzer Prize for *House Made of Dawn* that continued through the 1970s. Other volumes of poetry followed, among them *A Good Journey* (1977), *Fight Back* (1980), *From Sand Creek* (1981), *Woven Stone* (1991), and *After and Before the Lightning* (1994).

Well known as a poet, Ortiz has been acclaimed and influential as a fiction writer, his stories widely anthologized and critically celebrated. *Howbah Indians* includes stories depicting the everyday life of Indian people struggling with common problems, such as a woman leaving her home to find work in "Home Country" and a crippled war veteran's suffering in "Something's Going On." In "Men on the Moon," young Pueblo relatives try to explain television and the 1969 landing on the moon to their aged grandfather. The result is a humorous, poignant juxtaposition of Indian worldview and modern technological assumptions.

The stories in *Fightin'* are more sophisticated, more conscious of cultural politics than those in *Howbah Indians*. As always, Ortiz explores the makeup and consequences of cross-cultural interactions, but not merely to essentialize the gap between Native and Western perspectives. Rather, he seeks to show the universal human circumstances that undercut such divisions, and he is respectful of the potential of individuals to appreciate their connections to the human community and to perceive the spiritual nature of our existence.

Much of the interest in Ortiz's short stories lies in his skillful use of the storyteller persona. Many of the stories are told in the first person, so that the reader becomes accustomed to an insider's look at the Pueblo world. Ortiz often resists psychological analysis in favor of developing the observable details of the event, in much the same ways traditional oral narratives do, as in "Men on the Moon" or "Kaiser and the War." Regularly, he foregrounds the role of traditional mythic material, tells a story inside a story, or juxtaposes various voices as in "The Killing of a State Cop" or "Pennstuwehniyaahtsi: Quuti's Story." His narrators divulge much with revealing details and a well-tuned ear for dialogue. It is vital that his readers see the events through Pueblo eyes, for storytelling is an essential source of cultural continuance, one of the main fibers that weave Pueblo life. To tell stories is to further that tradition of Pueblo life and strengthen it in a world that ignores and devalues Pueblo understandings. In the preface to *A Good Journey,* he deliberately writes, "The only way to continue is to tell a story and there is no other way."

One of his best-known stories is "Kaiser and the War." The story revolves around a Pueblo Indian who refuses to be inducted into the army. The narrator, a member of the pueblo, recalls much of the action from his childhood. When the draft board men come, Kaiser runs away to the remote Black Mesa to hide. The community is divided about his behavior, partly because some people think he is crazy. However, the narrator remembers Kaiser as someone who acts more childlike than crazy and notes his almost childlike appreciation of the old oral narratives. The government agents and the sheriff try to get the pueblo elders to bring Kaiser in, but they will not comply with such coercion. The authorities deputize a number of the men observing the confrontation, and they spend a couple of days wandering around in the sun over inhospitable ground, while the Indians laugh at them and collect some easy money. Eventually the deputies get discouraged and quit. Soon afterward Kaiser decides to join the army, but when he tries to, he is put in the state penitentiary. The pueblo awaits his return, but an alleged attempted murder keeps Kaiser in jail for many years. When he is released, he is changed, and quite subdued. Every day, he continues to wear the dress suit given to him on release until he becomes the talk of the pueblo. Just before he dies of natural causes up at sheep camp, he wraps the suit up and tells his sister to send it to the government. She does not do so because she cannot figure out exactly to whom Kaiser wanted her to send the suit.

Ortiz's frequent use of the third-person, limited perspective forces the reader to interpret the motivation behind Kaiser's action. However, the Indian and the authorities are also forced into that position. Some of the community allow his actions to speak for themselves, reflecting a traditional respect for an individual's pursuit of his own path in life, but others reject any interpretation, label him crazy, and wish to ostracize him. Interpretation is built on knowledge and compassion. The actions of the government show neither, but rather a complete misunderstanding of the Pueblo perspective, a perspective the reader is led to adopt. Readers are allowed to make up their own minds.

No one, not even his relatives, knows why Kaiser continues to wear the suit, though many have their own interpretations. The Pueblo perspective may not always generate complete knowledge, but it allows room for individuals to create some understandings of their own and to live with them. The Western manipulative and coercive perspective closes off those possibilities of cross-cultural understanding. In the end, the suit comes to represent the self-limiting desire to ignore that which is not understood and to mold it into an existing perspective. As such, Kaiser believes that the suit belongs to the government.

Another popular story, "To Change in a Good Way," tells of two Okies, Bill and Ida, who have moved to a small New Mexico town to work in a mine. They become friends with Pete and Mary, Indians from a nearby pueblo, because Pete and Bill work together. Not long after he had come to visit, Bill's younger brother Slick dies in Vietnam after stepping on an American landmine. Pete and Mary bring the grieving couple an ear of corn and a cornhusk bundle prepared in keeping with Pueblo religious traditions for the dead. Pete says, "You and Ida are not Indian, but it doesn't make any difference. It's for all of us, this kind of way, with corn and this, Bill." Pete tells them the corn is to help their lives go on, and the cornhusk bundle is for Slick and his travels in the other world. He informs Bill that he should put the bundle "some place important" where Slick can be helping us "to change life in a good way." After the funeral, Bill and Ida return to New Mexico. Ida plants the corn in her garden, and Bill, who has become disillusioned with the hollow, patriotic justifications surrounding Slick's death, decides to place the bundle in the mine. There, he asks Slick to help them all, but especially to help hold the mine rafters up because the company will not supply adequate materials to guarantee the miners' safety.

As Ida and Bill begin to appreciate the Pueblo spiritual perspective, the reader moves past simple stereotypes of superstitious savages or New Age healers. Compassion and friendship move people beyond superficial differences, and the Native worldview is revealed. Ortiz places the departed Slick in a role similar to that of the katchina spirits, some of which are departed Pueblo ancestors. Their job, after death, is to work for the living, to make things better. Bill, disillusioned with the empty spiritless world he encounters at Slick's funeral, concludes that the Indians were "righter than we've ever been led to believe. And now I'm trying too." Ortiz's short stories do not minimize the distance between cultures, but they do not give in to despair. The universal concerns with spirit and compassion can bridge the widest cultural rift. For Simon Ortiz this is the work of stories.

James Ruppert

SELECTED BIBLIOGRAPHY

Works by Simon Ortiz

"The Killing of a State Cop," "The San Francisco Indians," "Kaiser and the War," and "A Story of Rios and Juan Jesus." In Kenneth Rosen, ed., *The Man to Send Rain Clouds: Contemporary Stories by American Indians.* New York: Viking, 1974.

Howbah Indians. Tucson: Blue Moon Press, 1978.

Fightin': New and Collected Stories. Chicago: Thunder's Mouth Press, 1983.

Critical Studies

Scarberry-Garcia, Susan. "Simon J. Ortiz." In Kenneth Roemer, ed., *Native American Writers of the United States.* Detroit: Bruccoli Clark Layman, 1997.

Wiget, Andrew. *Simon Ortiz.* Boise: Boise State University, 1986.

CYNTHIA OZICK
(1928–)

From a distance, Cynthia Ozick's biography looks as if it was cut from that pattern unique to an earlier generation of so-called New York intellectuals. Born in New York in 1928, on the eve of the Depression, Ozick was a child of Russian-Jewish immigrants who owned a drugstore. Doing odd jobs about the store, she first became aware of the long hours and grinding work of small business people.

But there too she discovered wonders, the human and chemical smells, the window displays of balanced goldfish bowls, and the books that came around with The Traveling Library, a big green truck that passed periodically through the neighborhood, bringing literacy to wherever people lived and worked. A working-class environment, hers was also a literate one, a world in which ideas had a special and cherished place.

Out of loneliness and a fierce curiosity about the world, Ozick became bookish, reading, she has said, *Little Women* a thousand times, while also writing poetry in imitation of an uncle, Hebrew poet Abraham Regelson. Later, with a B.A. from New York University and an M.A. from Ohio State University (and an M.A. thesis on Henry James), she copyedited advertising for a newspaper while writing a massive modernist novel, *Trust,* which would eventually be published in 1966. A precociously difficult book and a rap on the door of the palace of art, it was written in a language of "sinewy, grand undulations" (a phrase she has applied to James) and was in general too challenging, too intense and abstract to gain more than a token readership. Ozick's career as a writer of importance would not begin until the publication of her first collection, *The Pagan Rabbi and Other Stories* (1971), which brought her the acclaim that the novel had failed to do and established the voice that would be her trademark ever after: the voice of wisdom in distress, bookish and also worldly, encyclopedic in reference, jagged in rhythm, swift in velocity. It is recognizable as the voice of the New York intellectual brought to bear on the composing of fiction.

For all that, Ozick has not been the standard-issue New York intellectual at all, at least not in the mold of those writers who a generation earlier gathered around *Partisan Review* and the *Commentary* magazine of the immediate postwar years. The niece of a Hebrew poet and daughter of a Talmudic rationalist who also knew Latin and German, she refused, even under the pressure of the Great Books, to be a "non-Jewish Jew," preferring to write a fiction that would keep her in some working relation to normative Judaism. It is that relation that has made her fiction both distinctive and, for the general reader, difficult of access.

The reader of Cynthia Ozick's stories is likely to wish for a volume or two of her essays close by for reference. As often as not, Ozick's stories read like ethical treatises in narrative form, for which basic understanding might be supplied by the essays. Sometimes, to be sure, the homiletic content is stated in the stories themselves, like the much-quoted "All that is not Law is levity" in the story "Usurpation (Other People's Stories)." Without such evident prompting, readers may feel that they are missing a clue. Thus early stories like "The Pagan Rabbi" and "The Dock Witch" (in *The Pagan Rabbi and Other Stories*), which force a comparison between Jewish/monotheistic and pagan/polytheistic ethics, seem to call for Ozick's own commentary for interpretation. When written in this modality, Ozick's stories resemble the Aggadah of Jewish lore, those imaginative elaborations of Talmudic strictures or biblical tales through which the Jews have historically told themselves what was enduring and morally relevant in their holy texts. This makes

Ozick unique among contemporary American fiction writers. Her stories are glosses not usually upon experience but upon precept and text. "I believe that stories ought to judge and interpret the world," she writes in her preface to the collection *Bloodshed*. Nor are they, for the most part, stand-alone structures, autobiographical romans à clef, Chekhovian microdramas, or astringent Joycean dissections of the dear and the dirty. They seem rather to be outcroppings of some durable vein of values that "mean" in relation to each other and in relation to the great magma of lore, precept, and liturgy, to which they stand as commentary.

A bird's-eye view of Ozick's career reveals essays, novels, and stories as evenly distributed and interdependent. From the start, Ozick has been a writer for intellectuals, after the fashion of earlier writer-intellectuals like Henry James, Virginia Woolf, and George Eliot, for whom she expresses admiration. That may help to explain the industry of critical exegesis that has grown up around her work; it feels sturdy enough to support the weight of continual interpretation.

The writing itself calls to mind William Butler Yeats's saying that of our quarrels with others we make rhetoric, while of our quarrels with ourselves we make poetry. It is the quarrel with the self that fuels the Ozick story, objectified though it is as characters in collision. Her stories are noisy: the narrative is roiled and clamorous, as characters nervously work out their disputes in terms that stir the emotions to a boil. The nervous system itself may even move to stage center, being not only a seismograph for ideas in struggle but itself an issue, as characters in her stories tend to break down under extreme tension.

Thus, in Ozick's best-known story, "Envy; or, Yiddish in America" (in *The Pagan Rabbi*), the issue is the fate of a disappearing language and its literature, though what the reader experiences is the despair and rage of one Edelshtein, a Yiddish poet who feels that he has died along with Yiddish, because, in America, he cannot find a translator. The story is a penetrating X ray of the fate of Yiddish, a language crushed in Europe, suppressed in Israel, and abandoned by the Jews in America. Edelshtein is one of those writers who set out to join world modernist culture between the two great wars only to find themselves unknown to the world, indeed to the Jews themselves. "To speak Yiddish," he says, "is to preside over a funeral." The exception is fellow writer Yankel Ostrover, who has found translators and become a best-selling author while Edelshtein reads his poems in retirement homes. (It is speculated that Edelshtein and Ostrover are modeled on the actual Yiddish writers Jacob Glatstein and Isaac Bashevis Singer. Possibly so, but the story still must be read as a fiction in which Ozick freely improvised around contrasting historical symbols.) There had been bad blood between Edelshtein and Ostrover, and privately Edelshtein and friends refer to Ostrover as *der chazer,* the pig. His secret to finding translators has nothing to do with qualities intrinsic to his writing; he woos them and keeps them in envy of each other.

The story gains its particular traction from the figure of Edelshtein, who is a believable symbol for a vast tragedy. His injury resonates against the murder of the

Jews and their language, and if Edelshtein cannot distinguish his own agony from the calamities of the past, he need not; he is a product of them. (Like many Jewish writers, Ozick is obsessed by the literature that was lost when the Jews of Europe were killed. Her novel *The Messiah of Stockholm* concerns the loss of a book that Polish-Jewish writer Bruno Schulz was known to be writing at the time of his death in 1942.) As Edelshtein dissolves in rant and accusation at the end of the story, the reader absolves him of his misdemeanors, including harassing telephone calls to Ostrover. He is the underground man as emblem of tragic history, and the last thing we ask of him is to be a good sport.

Not every Ozick story engages the tensions of history so concretely. However, many of the elements of "Envy" run through all the fiction: the Holocaust, the fate of literature, the burden placed by the dead upon the living, the seductions of the secular life, the raw nerves and ready exasperations of marginal living, the search for a liturgical literature in modern America. "The Pagan Rabbi," the title story from the same collection, features Isaac Korngold, a rabbi who has hanged himself in a public park, leaving behind notebooks that reveal him to have been a closet nature lover, a passionate reader of landscape poetry, and a follower of "the Great God Pan." The story is often cited, along with "The Dock Witch," as a *midrash* (commentary) on the second commandment, God's prohibition against graven images, which Ozick has generalized in essays into a warning against the enchantments of literature itself. Indeed, no small part of the story is its caution against the imagination

as Moloch, capable of misleading even the most pious, if unopposed by a stout resistance to mere pleasure. Korngold, by responding at first to lyric poetry and the green world it celebrates, is led down the slippery slope to sporting with "dryads" and other figures of vegetable passion, eventually abandoning his wife, his senses, and his life.

It is a curious performance: an artist's tract against art, underscoring Ozick's difference from every other fiction writer in America. What does a writer stand for but the salutary effect of art upon the human spirit and the body politic? Of course, Ozick is working from within a tradition of suspicion that is not only Jewish but a constant of Western culture from Plato to Puritanism. If Adorno declares poetry barbaric after Auschwitz, Ozick asks, "Why just after Auschwitz?" As for the story itself, a parable of self-delusion ending in death, it does not entirely bear the weight of its prescriptions, being too much the abstract contratext and lacking anchors of the commonplace to render it credible to readers.

A later story, "Usurpation (Other People's Stories)," is Ozick's contratext par excellence. As she says in her preface to the book in which it appears, *Bloodshed and Three Novellas,* "It is against magic and mystification, against sham and 'miracle,' and, going deeper into the dark, against idolatry. It is an invention directed against inventing—the point being that the story-making faculty itself can be a corridor to the corruptions and abominations of idol-worship, of the adoration of the magical event." The story itself, involving living writers (Bernard Malamud), ghosts of dead ones, magic crowns, prophetic powers, and talking goats, would not seem at first blush to be a cautionary fable at all so much as a mid-1970s postmodern fabulation or post-Marquezian minuet of the real and the magical. However, despite its helping itself to the compulsory playfulness and licensed incoherence of those modes, it is less a case of "art for art's sake" than of "contra-art for contra-art's sake," about which—and here arises the reader's need for double consciousness—one needs to be told.

All of this makes Ozick sound formidable, and indeed she makes stiff demands on her readers: emotional, intellectual, and spiritual. That she has a devoted academic following is some indication that in demanding of readers both concentration and patience she has found fertile ground in a sector of that population. It should not be thought, however, that Ozick cannot entertain when she chooses. The most recent collection of stories, *The Puttermesser Papers,* is writing of a very different order from many earlier stories, being more relaxed, more genial, more reader-friendly, and in places authentically funny.

A loose-knit assembly of stories featuring Ruth Puttermesser (Yiddish for butter knife), *The Puttermesser Papers* is a comedy of city dreams and city sorrows. At first glimpse, Puttermesser is a single lawyer in her mid-forties with a nondescript job with the New York City Office of Receipts and Disbursements, a place as nondescript as nondescript can get. She herself is an unprepossessing figure who describes herself as "not bad looking," though the Breck girl she is not. She carries an umbrella, has periodontal disease, reads thick nineteenth-century novels,

dreams up imaginary daughters, and has been left by her lover, a married man. In the longest and arguably the most vigorous story, "Puttermesser and Xantippe," Ruth Puttermesser is demoted from her patronage job and returns home to find a naked girl, her skin resembling clay, on her bed. It is a golem such as the one created by Rabbi Loew in the sixteenth century to save the Jews of Prague; it calls itself Xantippe, calls Puttermesser "mother," and seems capable of any service from housekeeping to city planning.

Rapidly and predictably, Puttermesser is restored to her post and more; she becomes mayor, brings an end to crime and corruption, and establishes New York as the gleaming city on the hill. However, because golems will be golems, that is, out of control, the dream is shattered almost as quickly as it is dreamed. The story is fresh but also a return to a formula Ozick had used with success years earlier, in "Envy." "Puttermesser and Xantippe" may or may not be a *midrash* upon social values or extravagant dreaming, but it is also a fiction of striking particularity, following the adventures of a plausible character in a sadly recognizable world. Here is the dreamy, harried Puttermesser, with her bad gums, her struggling houseplants, her marginal existence in an empire of patronage, her collection of Balzac, Dostoevsky, and Dickens, reminding us of the steaming, devastated Edelshtein with his unheard poems and unlived triumphs. The story reworks Jewish legend, but it is also a vivid slice of contemporary life, just as Xantippe is a reworking of Jewish lore but also a well-loved daughter run amok, and New York is the city on the hill but also a tangle of mean streets and an empire of sleaze. In all these late stories, including "Puttermesser: Her Work History, Her Ancestry, Her Afterlife," "Puttermesser Paired," "Puttermesser and the Muscovite Cousin," and "Puttermesser in Paradise," Ozick's claim to be taken as a writer in the main line of moral realism finds its justification, for here is a free-standing fiction at last, self-interpreting and parallel to the essays rather than dependent upon them. One sees the imperative of "all that is not law is levity" relaxed, so that law and levity coexist and complement each other rather than compete. Ozick's fiction, it appears, has evolved in her quarter century plus of story writing, from being nervously homiletic to being confident enough of its moral grounds to open itself up to other of Cynthia Ozick's strengths: her comic, narrative, and intellectual abilities. As a result, her most recent fiction is her best.

Mark Shechner

SELECTED BIBLIOGRAPHY

Works by Cynthia Ozick

Trust. New York: New American Library, 1966.

The Pagan Rabbi and Other Stories. New York: Alfred A. Knopf, 1971.

Bloodshed and Three Novellas. New York: Alfred A. Knopf, 1976.

Levitation: Five Fictions. New York: Alfred A. Knopf, 1982.

The Cannibal Galaxy. New York: Alfred A. Knopf, 1983.

Art and Ardor. New York: Alfred A. Knopf, 1983.

The Messiah of Stockholm. New York: Alfred A. Knopf, 1987.

The Shawl. New York: Alfred A. Knopf, 1989.

Metaphor and Memory. New York: Alfred A. Knopf, 1989.

What Henry James Knew and Other Essays on Writers. London: Jonathan Cape, 1994.

Fame and Folly. New York: Alfred A. Knopf, 1996.

Portrait of the Artist as a Bad Character, and Other Essays on Writing. London: Pimlico, 1996.

The Puttermesser Papers. New York: Alfred A. Knopf, 1997.

Critical Studies

Bloom, Harold, ed. Cynthia Ozick: Modern Critical Views. New York: Chelsea House, 1986.

Cohen, Sarah Blacher. Cynthia Ozick's Comic Art: From Levity to Liturgy. Bloomington: Indiana University Press, 1994.

Finkelstein, Norman. The Ritual of New Creation: Jewish Tradition and Contemporary Literature. Albany: State University of New York Press, 1992.

Friedman, Lawrence S. Understanding Cynthia Ozick. Columbia: University of South Carolina Press, 1991.

Kauvar, Elaine M. Cynthia Ozick's Fiction: Tradition and Invention. Bloomington: Indiana University Press, 1993.

Lowin, Joseph. Cynthia Ozick. Boston: Twayne, 1988.

Pinsker, Sanford. The Uncompromising Fictions of Cynthia Ozick. Columbia: University of Missouri Press, 1987.

Shapiro, Michael, editor. Divisions Between

Traditionalism and Liberalism in the American Jewish Community: Cleft or Chasm. Lewiston, N.Y.: Edwin Mellen Press, 1991.

Strandberg, Victor H. *Greek Mind / Jewish Soul: The Conflicted Art of Cynthia Ozick.* Madison: University of Wisconsin Press, 1994.

Walden, Daniel, ed. *The World of Cynthia Ozick: Studies in American Jewish Literature.* Kent, Ohio: Kent State University Press, 1987.

GRACE PALEY

(1922–)

Born in the Bronx on December 11, 1922, Grace Paley has a quintessential New York voice. Its vitality, its sheer imaginative energy, an amalgam of the rhythms of urban English, Yiddish, and Russian (with an occasional dip into African American, Irish, and Puerto Rican street talk) is the triumph and defining characteristic of her art. The stories seem to generate from the narrative voice. It is as if the language invents them, each story seemingly making itself up as it finds its ideal form. An improvisatory casualness is one of the disguises of her fiction. A high degree of technical sophistication is its true condition. Paley's stories, though not without virtuoso turns, rarely insist on their own achievement, deny their own audacity, her craft covering its own traces.

Paley's career is an anomaly among twentieth-century American writers. She started late, publishing her first story when she was thirty-four (an age when Hemingway's and Fitzgerald's best work was behind them), and she has not been prolific, much of her potential writing time sacrificed to frontline antiwar and feminist/humanist activism. She is also probably the only major American writer of her time never to have published a novel. In a culture in which fiction is often admired for its size—the "great" American novel being famous for its grandiose bloat—Paley offers us the alternative of encapsulated (sometimes seemingly fragmentary) tales. She is at her best often—her fiction at its most consequential—in the shortest space.

Paley is indeed a major writer working in what passes in our culture as a minor form. The encapsulated aspect of her fiction (the world in a phrase, the breadth of a novel in five pages) has at times deceived the media, that system of mirrors that tends to discover the very things it advertises to itself, into taking it for less than it is. This is not to say that she has not had her share of honors and recognition, but that they are just beginning to catch up with her accomplishments. The short story at its best is more closely aligned to the precision of the poem than to the novel, which is a more forgiving genre. Paley's fiction might be seen as an exemplification that confirms this rule. She started out as a poet; many of her stories in fact include poems written by her characters. The short story was the poetic form that best accommodated her talent, which is to say she is a poet who tells stories, which is also to say she writes stories that are driven by language (and secondarily, character) as opposed to plot. The stories are surprising, work out their destinies in ways that defy conventional expectations. In her own quirky way, Paley has probably redefined the possibilities of the short story as much as, say, Donald Barthelme, a more obviously radical writer, who was, incidentally, a good friend and near neighbor in Greenwich Village.

Paley has to date produced three volumes of tales, which have been assembled as *The Collected Stories,* published by Farrar, Straus & Giroux in 1994. With each succeeding volume the stories have seemed more improvisatory and casual in their structure, more risky and unexpected. The later stories also tend to be more overtly political (while avoiding the tendentious) and also more implicitly personal. Many are told in the first person by her mock alter-ego, Faith. Characters recur and redefine themselves from story to story so that the stories seem after a while pieces of a larger design. An argument can be made that taken all together, Paley's stories evoke a microcosm not so different from that of a nineteenth-century novel.

Her first collection, *The Little Disturbances of Man,* was brought out by Doubleday in 1959. The sassy voice establishes itself in the opening lines of the first story, "Goodbye and Good Luck," the only one in the volume to be previously published. "I was popular in certain circles, says Aunt Rose. I wasn't no thinner then, only more stationary in the flesh." And Rose goes on to tell the story of her feckless life to her niece, Lillie. After she becomes a ticket-taker for the Russian Art Theater of Second Avenue, she is taken up by the company's leading actor, Vlashkin. In op-

position to her mother's unhappy life, Rose elects "to live for love." She becomes Vlashkin's mistress, but breaks up with him after she meets his wife. Many years later, after his wife has divorced Vlashkin (for adultery), Rose, still unmarried, renews her romance with the aging actor. The story's ironic happy ending has Rose marrying Vlashkin so she'll "have a husband, which, as everybody knows, a woman should have at least one before the end of the story." The listener, Lillie, is the filter of the story, the author's alter-ego. Rose's quixotic devotion is finally rewarded, but she has to sacrifice most of her life to achieve her triumph. Lillie's aunt is no artist, but her integrity—her uncompromising commitment to the heart's desire—offers a kind of paradigm for the artist's life.

In "A Woman Young and Old," the almost fourteen-year-old narrator, Josephine, has a crush on her aunt's boyfriend Brownie (Corporal Brownstar), and ultimately persuades him to marry her. When told of Josephine's plans to marry, her mother accuses her of treachery. "That's not nice to take him away from her. That's a rotten sneaky trick. . . . Women should stick together." At the end it is not Josephine who gets a husband but the mother, who violates her own stricture by usurping the next soldier her sister brings around. It is a love-starved, desperate world we see through the perspective of Josephine's precocious innocence. "Living as I do on a turnpike of discouragement, I am glad to hear the incessant happy noises in the next room," she tells us. While her mother and her new husband make love, Josephine gets to cuddle with her kid sister who, in the new sleeping accommodations, has moved in with her. As in many of Paley's works, the engaging comic voice temporarily distances the reader from the disturbing events that lie just beneath the story's surface.

"An Interest in Life," from which the book's title derives, is in conventional terms the most fully realized story of the first collection. A story initially about a husband's desertion of a wife and four children, it opens, "My husband gave me a broom one Christmas. That wasn't right. No one can tell me it was meant kindly." The matter-of-fact, ironic voice of the protagonist, Ginny, distances the reader from the conventions of her pathos, makes light of easy sentiment. Ginny, in a particularly desperate moment, makes a list of her troubles in order to get on the radio show "Strike it Rich." When she shows the list to John Raftery, a former suitor unhappily married to someone else, he points out to her that her troubles are insufficient, merely "the little disturbances of man." Paley's comic stories deal in exaggerated understatement, disguise their considerable ambition in the modesty of wit. Ginny's nosy, officious neighbor, Mrs. Raftery, who once stabbed herself to keep her son John from marrying Ginny, becomes Ginny's unlikely ally. To get back at John's wife for taking her son to the suburbs, she sends John to Ginny's apartment to comfort her. Inevitably, John and Ginny become lovers, the devout John placing "his immortal soul in peril" with no apparent pang of conscience. "It's still hard to believe that a man who sends out the Ten Commandments every year for a Christmas card can be so easy buttoning and unbuttoning." Ginny survives by be-

coming a kept woman, though at the end she imagines her feckless husband's return, the pair making love on the kitchen floor, "so happy . . . we forgot the precautions."

The closing story, "The Floating Truth," the most surreal in the collection, makes us aware that all of the stories are more or less dreamlike. The narrator just out of school, equipped to do nothing, visits her agent ("vocational counselor"), who works out of a hearse. A man named Stubblefield (called Edsel by the agent) hires the narrator subject to getting her résumé, which the anonymous vocational counselor—identified by several different names—fabricates for her. The résumé is a paradigm of capitalism at its most manipulative, showing the narrator as having through contrivance and ingenuity created a demand for nonexistent products and services. The job she gets requires sharpening pencils, studying the morning and afternoon newspaper, and perseverance. When a second assistant is hired by her boss, our heroine complains that "there isn't enough work to go around. . . . There's nothing to do." "It's my company, isn't it?" Edsel tells her in high dudgeon. "If I want to, I can hire forty people to do nothing." This odd anticapitalist fable, somewhat uncharacteristic for the first volume, anticipates some of the narrative tropes of the second.

"Distance," in the second collection, *Enormous Changes at the Last Minute,* published in 1974, is a retelling of some of the materials of "An Interest in Life" through the self-justifying (also self-denying) point of view of Ginny's neighbor, Mrs. Raftery. It also makes us aware that Paley has been in the process of creating an ongoing imagined world richer and more compelling than its ostensibly real counterpart. Each time Paley denies us the comforting illusion of conventional fiction by making us aware that she is telling a story, the illusion reestablishes itself with even greater persuasiveness.

Themes and characters move into one another from story to story. Life is too short, moving too quickly (all of us going in private directions) to do all the things one means to do. "Living" is about a missed connection, about the distraction of being caught up in one's own life. At the start, a friend, Ellen, calls Faith, the narrator of many of the later stories, to announce that she's dying. Faith reports, not altogether metaphorically, that she is dying too. Ellen dies; Faith recovers, her own dying (and living) precluding involvement in Ellen's. At the end, when Ellen's loss has etched itself into her feelings, she tells us, "I often long to talk to Ellen, with whom, after all, I have done a million things in these scary private years. Two weeks before last Christmas, we were dying." The economy of the story—it runs barely two and a half pages—makes it all the more powerful, avoiding, as Paley almost always does, easy emotional appeals or inflated sentiment.

"The Burdened Man" also deals with survival and renewal. A man, anxious about money, which is to say loss of self, becomes friends, outgrowth of a financial squabble, with a neighbor's wife. "Now," he decides, "it was time to consider different ways to begin to make love to her." He goes to the woman's house one Sunday and is confronted by her husband, a policeman, who shoots up the kitchen and wounds the burdened man. Passion and survival unburden the title character of his displaced obsessions. "Until old age startled him, he was hardly unhappy again."

Although all of Paley's stories have metafictional elements, "A Conversation with My Father" definitely treats the process of making fiction (Paley's fiction in particular). The narrator's father asks her why she doesn't write simple stories like de Maupassant or Chekhov. "Just [describe] recognizable people and write down what happened to them next." To please her father, to prove the task hopeless, she offers him (and us) in abbreviated form a plain story, a self-fulfilling failure since the narrator holds that "Everyone, real or imagined, deserves the open destiny of life." The father complains that she leaves everything out, and Paley's narrator invents another, more elaborate version of the same story. The longer version is not much closer to the kind of story the father wants, and he berates her for making jokes out of "tragedy." The story ends on a dark note. "How long will it be?" the father asks. "Tragedy! You too. When will you look it in the face?"

Three of the best fictions in *Later the Same Day* (1985) are about storytelling— the sharing of personal stories— and as such are also about their own imagining. Paley insists on making us aware that we are reading stories here, and stories within stories within stories. "The Story Hearer" is perhaps the most complex example of this predilection. The story starts with Faith telling us, "I am trying to curb my cultivated individualism, which seemed for years so sweet. . . . So when

Jack said at dinner, 'What did you do today with your year off?' I decided to make an immediate public accounting of the day, not to water my brains with time spent in order to grow smart private thoughts." The story Faith tells Jack of her day is full of digressions, including stories some of the people she encounters tell her, memories jogged loose by these stories including Jack's contentious responses to her news, the piece ending with Jack and Faith in bed together, arguing and consoling, celebrating their long-term (through many other stories) companionship. "Listening" is another story about storytelling (and listening to stories), another work in which politics and esthetics struggle toward the synthesis of common ground. The tale, which has a kind of intuitive structure (characteristic of the more recent pieces), ends with Faith's friend, Cassie, wanting to know why she has been excluded from Faith's stories. Cassie's challenge recalls an earlier story, "Debts," which is about the obligation Faith feels to keep the people close to her alive by giving voice to their stories and the stories of their families. "How can you forgive me?" Faith asks Cassie. And Cassie, seemingly forgiving her with a laugh, says, "I won't forgive you. . . . From now on, I'll watch you like a hawk. I do not forgive you." Paley through Faith offers us here (and elsewhere), seriously and in partial jest, a sense of her role as writer to chronicle her microcosmic world through the reimagined life and times of herself and her friends.

In Paley's longest story, "Zagrowsky Tells," roles are reversed and Faith is the listener, a distrustful former customer of the story's druggist-narrator, a man with a history of being a bigot. Faith, who once picketed his store because he mistreated black customers, questions him suspiciously about the black boy at his side. The boy is his grandson, Emanuel, and Zagrowsky, in his role of storyteller, feels obliged to satisfy Faith's officious curiosity. His daughter Cissy, confined to a mental hospital, became pregnant as the result of a liaison with the institution's black gardener. As Cissy's sanity was at issue, Zagrowsky and his wife agreed to keep the baby, innate decency overriding innate prejudices. And so Zagrowsky is rewarded, Emanuel becoming "his little best friend." The story, which rides dangerously close to sentimentality, is saved by Paley's language and the tartness of the closure—Zagrowsky's impatience with Faith's moralistic presumptions. Humanity and love in these stories take precedence in the long haul over honorable political gestures. Though she may be committed politically to one side of an issue, Paley as an artist is also aware that the other side is not without its own justice.

Grace Paley writes about families, about political commitment, about lost and found love, about divorce, marriage, death, ongoing life—the most risky and important themes—in a style in which words count for much, sometimes for almost all. The stories—in some cases, the same stories—deal on the one hand with their own invention and, on the other, profoundly (and comically) with felt experience. In this sense, and in a wholly unschematic way, Paley combines what has been called the "tradition of new fiction" in America with the abiding concerns of the old.

Jonathan Baumbach

SELECTED BIBLIOGRAPHY

Works by Grace Paley

The Collected Stories. New York: Farrar, Straus & Giroux, 1994.

Critical Studies

Isaacs, Neil D. *Grace Paley, A Study of the Short Fiction.* Boston: Twayne Publishers, 1990.
Klinkowitz, Jerome. "Grace Paley: The Sociology of Metafiction." *Delta* 14 (May 1982): 81–85.
Malin, Irving. "The Verve of Grace Paley." *Genesis West* 2 (fall 1963): 73–78.

AMÉRICO PAREDES
(1915–1999)

Américo Paredes, ethnographer, poet, and fiction writer, is best known for his study of the Mexico/United States border culture, especially that of the region known as the Lower Rio Grande. To the study of the popular literature of that part of Texas he has dedicated several publications. His book *With His Pistol in His Hand* (1958), which marked a new direction in Chicano scholarship, is a study of the *corrido* (ballad) of the legendary border figure Gregorio Cortez. Before that Paredes had written a novel and some short stories, unfortunately not published until much later, for they represent the transition of Mexican American fiction from early writers such as Fray Angélico Chávez to the fiction of post–Chicano movement writers such as Tomás Rivera, Miguel Méndez-M, and Rolando Hinojosa.

Born on September 3, 1915, in Brownsville, on the Texas-Mexican border, the son of Justo Paredes and Clotilde Manzano, Paredes attended school in his hometown. He worked as a newspaperman for the *Brownsville Herald* from 1936 to 1943. The following year he joined the armed forces and was sent to Japan in 1945 with the occupation army. There he wrote some of his short stories while serving as one of the editors of the army's newspaper *Stars and Stripes*. Back home, he attended the University of Texas at Austin, receiving his B.A. in 1951, his M.A. in 1953, and a Ph.D. in 1956, all in anthropology. The following year he became director of the University of Texas Center for the Study of Folklore, and in 1970 he was appointed professor of English and anthropology, as well as director of the Mexican-American Studies Program. He retired from that institution in 1985 as professor emeritus of anthropology and English. Paredes died in 1999.

Most of Paredes's research in ethnography has been published in learned periodicals and books, among them *A Texas-Mexican Cancionero* (1976) and *Folklore and Culture on the Texas-Mexican Border* (1993).

Very few of his literary compositions were published before his retirement. *The Shadow,* his first novel, which won a prize in a fiction contest, was not published until 1998. His first short story, "The Hammon and the Beans," written in 1939, was finally published in 1953. His second novel, *George Washington Gómez,* written between 1936 and 1940, did not appear until 1990. Some of his poems, however, began to appear in southwestern newspapers (*Brownsville Herald, La Prensa* of San Antonio) as early as 1934 but were not collected in a volume until 1990, under the title *Between Two Worlds.*

Like his novels and poems, Paredes's short stories were not published in book form until after his retirement in 1994, when seventeen of them appeared under the title *The Hammon and the Beans.* In 1952, however, six of them had won first prize in a contest on the short story held by the *Dallas Times Herald.* Some of the seventeen stories collected in 1994 were written in Brownsville during the 1940s and 1950s. "Revenge" was written between 1940 and 1944; "Little Joe," "Rebeca," "Brothers," "The Gift," "When It Snowed in Kitabamba," and "Ichiro Kikuchi" were written in Japan between 1945 and 1950; others, although they are also set in Japan, like "Sugamo," "The Terribly High Cost," and "Getting an Oboe for Joe," were completed in Austin.

Paredes's short stories can be classified into two groups, one consisting of those set in the Lower Rio Grande borderland, the other dealing with Japanese life and culture. One of the stories of the second group, "Ichiro Kikuchi," takes place in Japan, but its protagonist is a Mexican of Japanese descent.

The Border stories take place in a fictitious town, Johnsville-on-the-Grande, which represents the author's hometown, and the characters are Texans of Mexican descent who had been living in the valley since the eighteenth century. By trying to preserve their culture, they come into conflict with the Anglo-American members of the community. This cultural/racial conflict prevails in most of Paredes's early stories. The tragic story of "The Gringo" takes place in the nineteenth century at the time of the U.S.-Mexican War. The protagonist, a young Mexican called El Gringo by his people because of his blond hair and blue eyes, is taken for an American until his speech gives him away and he is killed.

Similar conflicts structure some of the other stories of this first group. In "The Hammon and the Beans," the conflict reflects historical events that occurred during the second decade of the twentieth century, when the United States invaded Mexico for a second time, landing troops in Tampico and Veracruz on the Gulf of Mexico. The antagonism against the United States was reflected along the border, where a group led by Aniceto Pizaña (a historical character mentioned in the story) declared war in his Plan de San Diego against the Texas Rangers. However, the story deals mainly with the struggle of the people to survive during this period of national conflict. The two motifs in the title of the story, the "hammon" (ham, for the Spanish *jamón*) and the "beans," become symbols for affluence and poverty. The soldiers eat ham while the

Mexican people eat beans. The protagonist, Chonita, begs the soldiers to give her "the hammon and the beans." The narrator says, "I thought it was a pretty poor joke. Every evening almost, they would make her get up on the fence and yell, 'Give me the hammon and the beans!' And everybody would cheer and make her think she was talking English." The irony is that Chonita becomes the spokesperson of the Texas Mexican community.

In these early stories, Paredes goes beyond the racial/cultural conflicts between the two ethnic groups and focuses on the conflicts among the native Texas Mexicans. In "Over the Waves Is Out," the main conflict between father and son is resolved by the Anglo sheriff; in "Macaria's Daughter" and "Rebeca" it is between husbands and wives. In "Revenge," Paredes introduces a conflict with another ethnic group. A young Chicano is prevented from taking revenge on an Italian who suddenly dies. The irony is that the Italian's father meets the Chicano at the funeral of his son, and, much to the Chicano's embarrassment, believes that the avenger was his son's best friend.

In the stories written in Japan, Paredes writes about the nation's struggle to recover from the shame of defeat. The subservience of the Japanese characters in "When It Snowed in Kitabamba" contrasts with the arrogance of the American officer who loses face when he trips and falls in the snow. In "The Terribly High Cost," Paredes describes the predicament of dying after the war, a time when the Japanese people could not afford to die, for it was so expensive. Contrasting with these tragic stories, the last two, "Getting an

Oboe for Joe" and "The American Dish," are humorous, revealing another facet of Paredes as a short story writer. His humor is based on the picaresque adventures of Johnny Picadero, a character that appears in both stories.

"Ichiro Kikuchi" integrates the Mexican American, the Mexican national, and the Japanese into a powerful story about cultural identity. A first-person narrator tells the life of the protagonist, born in Cuernavaca, Mexico, of a Japanese father and a Mexican mother, who is named José Guadalupe (Lupe) according to his mother's wishes, a name that would later save his life because of a medallion of the Virgin of Guadalupe that he wears around his neck. His father, who calls him Ichiro, sends him to Japan, where he is drafted and sent to the Philippines. There he is made a prisoner of war by the Americans and is about to be executed when the Mexican American sergeant notices that he has a pendant of the Virgin of Guadalupe around his neck and saves his life. Ichiro had been sent to Japan because his father wanted him to maintain his Japanese identity. Ironically, it is his Mexican identity that saves him.

In all of Paredes's stories, wherever the setting, and whatever the nationality of the characters, the world is always observed from the perspective of a Mexican American. Paredes accomplishes this by drawing on the history, the customs, the traditions, and the ideology of the Mexican Americans. His conflicts are mostly cultural, but he does not limit himself to those between Mexican Americans and Anglo-Americans. He is perhaps the only fiction writer of Mexican American origin who introduces into his stories the cultures of other ethnic groups. He is sensitive not only to the weaknesses of others but also to those of his own people. They can be good and they can be bad, because they are universally human. Enriched by a variety of characters, settings, and plots, Américo Paredes's stories are steeped in tragedy, humor, pathos, and irony.

Luís Leal

SELECTED BIBLIOGRAPHY

Limón, José E. "Américo Paredes: A Man from the Border." *Revista Chicano-Riqueña* 8/3 (summer 1980): 1–5.

Paredes, Américo. *The Hammon and the Beans and Other Stories.* Houston: Arte Público Press, 1994.

Saldívar, Ramón. *Chicano Narrative: The Dialectics of Difference.* Madison: University of Wisconsin Press, 1990.

DOROTHY PARKER
(1893 – 1967)

Although Dorothy Parker is known best for her sassy repartee around the Algonquin Round Table, she was an accomplished writer of poetry, stories, plays, and film scripts, as well as of drama and book reviews. Although her sardonic poetry was extremely popular when it was published and remains readable today, her short stories are her greatest accomplishment. Through them, Parker depicts the complexities of cultural transformation in the early twentieth century.

Born in West End, New Jersey, Dorothy Parker grew up in New York with parents from two very different worlds. Her father was a descendent of German Jews who emigrated after the unsuccessful revolution of 1848, and her mother came from British ancestry. From the age of twelve, Parker cultivated a literary persona; she wrote poetry and imagined herself as the eccentric English aristocratic poet, Edith Sitwell. After her father died, she supported herself by playing piano at a dance school and submitted her poetry to such magazines as the *Saturday Evening Post* and *Vanity Fair*. She soon began writing captions for photographs and illustrations at *Vogue* magazine and married stockbroker Edwin Pond Parker II. Their marriage fell apart, however, when he returned from World War I a morphine addict and alcoholic.

Meanwhile, Dorothy Parker had been contributing frequently to *Vanity Fair* and joined the staff of the magazine as a drama critic. When the humorist Robert Benchley was hired as managing editor, Parker formed a friendship with him that would last their lifetimes. The playwright and editor Robert Sherwood joined the staff and, before long, the three had lunch together every day at the Algonquin Hotel in midtown Manhattan. They formed the nucleus of what was to become the Round Table, a celebrated gathering of journalists, writers, and celebrities known for their witty conversation. An astute observer of contemporary social and sexual mores, Parker delivered acerbic witticisms that are still quoted today. When asked, for example, to use "horticulture" in a sentence, she replied, "You can lead a horticulture, but you can't make her think."

Parker continued to write essays and book reviews for the *Saturday Evening Post, Smart Set,* and *The New Yorker.* Her reviews were often merciless and clever: she described one book as "second only to a rubber duck as the ideal bathtub companion . . . it may be neatly balanced back of faucets, and it may be read before the water has cooled. And if it slips down the drain pipe, all right, it slips down the drain pipe." Her 1927 collection of poems, *Enough Rope,* had widespread appeal and sold well. At this time, Parker also made an enormous effort to write a novel, convinced that this was the mark of a serious writer. In a state of utter panic, she drank a bottle of shoe polish and was hospitalized as a result. In an effort to recoup its losses on the contract for Parker's novel, in June 1930 Viking published *Laments for the Living,* a collection of thirteen of Parker's short stories.

In 1934, Dorothy Parker married actor Alan Campbell. They worked collaboratively as screenwriters and were nominated for an Academy Award. The 1930s was also a decade of political awakening for Parker. She protested the execution of Italian immigrants Nicolà Sacco and Bartolomeo Vanzetti and participated in a wide range of Communist Party events. As a result, she was blacklisted as a screenwriter, along with Campbell, Donald Ogden Stewart, Lillian Hellman, and Dashiell Hammett. Marriage to Campbell seemed to agree with Parker, and she was delighted to discover that she was pregnant at the age of forty-three and deeply unhappy when she miscarried in the first trimester. The relationship began to deteriorate when Campbell joined the army during World War II. After he returned to New York in November 1946, they decided to divorce. They remarried in 1950, but their relationship remained conflict-ridden.

Parker rebelled against the role of feminine passivity, and her provocative humor was a bold attempt to dissociate herself from traditional values. Nevertheless, her poems and stories express the discomfort and dismay of women dependent on men. Continuing to write short stories, Parker published "I Live on Your Visits" in *The New Yorker* in January 1955. The story explores an alcoholic divorcee's preoccupation with visits from her son, who lives with his father and stepmother. Mercurial and manipulative, she desperately clings to her son for her sense of reality, yet becomes defensively angry when he rejects her. The protagonist lacks the ability to shape her own life and instead lives vicariously through a man—this time the adolescent son eager to escape her. "Lolita," another story published in *The New Yorker* in the same year, tells of a young woman who escapes her domineering mother by marrying a handsome and successful man. In a fit of jealousy, the mother perversely hopes that her daughter's marriage will fail. Parker's final two stories, "The Banquet of Crow," and "The Bolt Behind the Blue," focus on primitive rage and envy that are scarcely concealed by the facade of gentility. The first story is a merciless portrait of a husband and wife who loathe each other while pretending to have a happy marriage; the second probes the patronizing relationship of a wealthy woman and her secretary.

In 1958, Parker received an award from the prestigious National Institute of Arts and Letters, and the following year she was elected a member. Her final years were filled with invitations to lecture and to teach at colleges, but when she accepted a visiting position at California State College in Los Angeles, she felt overworked and underappreciated. She continued to drink heavily and alienated her few remaining friends. Parker died in 1967 and bequeathed her literary estate and what little money she had to Martin Luther King Jr.

When Parker emerged on the literary scene in New York City in the 1920s, women were becoming more active in public and more culturally visible than in previous decades. Her writing often satirized the vanities as well as the uncertainties of a decade characterized by rapid transformations in gender relationships resulting, in part, from a growing concern among women to have careers as well as families. In her irreverence and her ability to speak quickly and freely, Parker embodied the possibilities of independent women in early twentieth-century America. Her fiction and poetry, however, capture the many complexities of this cultural transformation, portraying female protagonists who are poised precariously between shifting value systems or who lose their balance entirely.

The 1920s, after all, was the decade that began with the passage of the Twenty-first Amendment, which gave women the right to vote. It is not surprising that extraordinary changes in women's participation in the public sphere would follow in the wake of this landmark event. On a more sensational level, the flapper represented new versions of female style: with bobbed hair, bound breasts, and streamlined clothes designed by Chanel and Erté, the flapper projected an image of mobility and modern efficiency. In addition, the flapper broke the rules of traditional female decorum by wearing makeup—"paint," previously worn only by prostitutes—and by drinking, smoking, and dancing with abandon in public. In the arts, flapper poets like Edna St. Vincent Millay and H.D., along with Parker, charted these experiences from a female, often feminist, perspective and, in doing so, explored a largely unknown emotional terrain. Parker challenged rules of feminine decorum and codes of passivity and submission. As her poem "Unfortunate Coincidence," published in *Enough Rope,* indicates, her emphasis was openly and consistently satiric:

> By the time you swear you're his,
> Shivering and sighing,
> And he vows his passion is
> Infinite, undying—
> Lady, make a note of this:
> One of you is lying.

Many of Dorothy Parker's short stories capture the tensions of the modern woman caught between the claims of the private and public spheres. This dislocation can be seen most clearly in "Big Blonde," a narrative of a woman who is brought up in the tradition of nineteenth-century femininity but who must live in the public arena without any of the protections or guarantees traditionally given in return for feminine self-sacrifice and adornment. The protagonist, Hazel Morse, "prided herself upon her small feet and suffered for her vanity boxing them in snub-toed, high heeled slippers of the shortest bearable size." Her entire personality has been shaped by the need to please men: she laughs at their jokes and flatters them, desiring more than anything to be popular, the only form of success she perceives for herself. When she finally marries Herbie Morse, she is relieved to be exempt from the need to entertain men, and she embraces the role of maternal tenderness instead. This shift in emphasis comes as an unpleasant surprise to her husband, and they soon divorce. As a displaced homemaker, Hazel frequents bars looking for a man to "pay all of her bills" in return for her total devotion. Even though the traditional obligation of men to shield women no longer holds, women are nevertheless expected to defer to men in the public sphere as in the private. In this story, Parker makes it clear that the loss of male protection is the price extracted for the entrance of women into public life. The sharp irony of "Big Blonde" is that Hazel Morse is caught in a profound shift in cultural values without the resources necessary to leap from old to new paradigms.

Other stories, such as "The Waltz," "You Were Perfectly Fine," and "A Telephone Call," depict the ways in which modern women are still involved in nineteenth-century courtship rituals, calling attention to the disparity between women's personal responses and social behavior. "The Waltz" is a savagely funny narrative of a woman's response to her extremely clumsy dancing partner. While remaining outwardly composed and charming, the narrator endures a bone-crushing embrace with a man who has no sense of rhythm, bruises her shins, and shouts into her ear. Even though she describes the experience as a *danse macabre,* she is unable to say no when he asks her for an encore.

Many of Parker's other short stories expose the excesses of the feminine nurturing ethos. In "You Were Perfectly Fine," a wife comforts her husband, who cannot remember his drunken behavior of the previous evening. Even though he was boorish, hostile, and rude, she reassures him that he was "perfectly fine." "A Telephone Call" captures the extraordinary anxiety of a woman waiting for her lover to call; it is a subtle narrative of the distribution of power in the couple's relationship. Although she very much wants to talk to him, she is terrified to call because she fears it will anger him. Like her nineteenth-century counterpart, this protagonist must wait passively for the man to make the first move. This story takes a particularly ironic twist when she begins to pray for help to resist the impulse to call him. So embedded are the gender roles and their power relationships that the possibility of reversal is terrifying.

In other stories, the disappointments and compromises of marital relationships are exploded with unblinking realism. Through the skirmishes of newlyweds en route to their honeymoon, "Here We Are" depicts the emotional uncertainty and sexual jealousy that often persists in marriage. The bride wants reassurances of her attractiveness, while the groom ogles other women in an effort to demonstrate his virility. Similarly, in "The Lovely Leave," a husband and wife spend their few days together quarreling instead of enjoying a brief reunion. The satiric intensity of the narrative makes it clear that the husband and wife have divergent expectations; she wants to be reassured of his affection for her because love is the focus of her life, while he feels compelled to return to military duty as soon as possible because courage and duty are the center of his. "Mr. Durant" presents a portrait of a forty-nine-year-old family man who has an affair with his twenty-year-old secretary. While smugly enjoying the domestic comforts provided by a wife who bores him, Mr. Durant enjoys Rose's sexual favors until she becomes pregnant, whereupon he dismisses her as a nuisance.

Much of Parker's work demonstrates a preoccupation with the complexity of gender relationships during a time when the paradigms shaping the politics of sexuality were shifting. Although Parker was fiercely committed to professional achievement, she also wanted a satisfying emotional and sexual life. Unfortunately, it was not easy to balance love and work during the years that Dorothy Parker lived. In general, it was a matter of choosing one or the other; the woman who functioned effectively in the professional sphere was expected to relinquish private fulfillment, while the woman who stayed home to care for a husband and family was barred from the public arena. In effect, the first two-thirds of the twentieth century did not offer a dramatic improvement in women's choices; instead, the modern woman glimpsed possibilities, improvised her life, and tried to make sense of what often seemed an episodic existence. Nevertheless, it is important to acknowledge the achievements of women like Dorothy Parker whose experimental lives created possibilities for subsequent generations.

In effect, Dorothy Parker's short stories and poems explore new emotional geography, demarcating areas that are no longer psychologically viable for thinking women while staking a claim in the borderlands for future women to inhabit and cultivate. In her public life, Parker transformed the nineteenth-century role of the nurturing woman who guides the family in the private sphere into the role of the intellectual colleague who makes her convictions known to the world at large, thereby shaping twentieth-century public opinion.

Wendy Martin

SELECTED BIBLIOGRAPHY

Works by Dorothy Parker

Laments for the Living. New York: Viking, 1930.

After Such Pleasures. New York: Viking, 1933.

Here Lies. New York: Viking, 1939.

Collected Stories of Dorothy Parker. New York: Modern Library, 1942.

The Portable Dorothy Parker. New York: Viking, 1973.

The Penguin Dorothy Parker. Harmondsworth: Penguin, 1977.

Critical Studies

Keats, John. *You Might as Well Live: The Life and Times of Dorothy Parker.* New York: Simon & Schuster, 1970.

Kinney, Arthur. *Dorothy Parker.* Boston: Twayne, 1978; revised edition, 1998.

Meade, Marion. *Dorothy Parker: What Fresh Hell Is This?* New York: Penguin, 1987.

Melzer, Sondra. *The Rhetoric of Rage: Women in Dorothy Parker.* New York: Peter Lang, 1997.

JAYNE ANNE PHILLIPS
(1952–)

Jayne Anne Phillips was born in Buckhannon, West Virginia, on July 19, 1952. She graduated in 1974 with a bachelor of arts degree from the University of West Virginia and in 1978 with a master of fine arts degree from the University of Iowa, where she has also taught. She is the recipient of many awards, including, in 1977 and 1979, the Pushcart Prize; in 1978, a National Endowment for the Arts Fellowship; and in 1980 the Sue Kauffman Award for First Fiction for *Black Tickets.* She has also received a Bunting Institute Fellowship from Radcliffe College. Her first novel, *Machine Dreams* (1984), was nominated for many prizes, including the National Book Critics Circle Award. A second novel, *Shelter,* was published in 1994. In recent years, she has taught in the Creative Writing Program at Boston University. Jayne Anne Phillips married Mark Stockman in 1985; they have three sons.

Jayne Anne Phillips's career has in some ways followed a typical modern trajectory—starting with poetry, moving on to very short prose pieces, then longer stories, and finally novels. In a 1995 interview given shortly after the publication of *Shelter,* Phillips said that she no longer really wrote short stories: "I seem to be more interested now in a form that I can really live with—for years! When I get involved in a book I don't want to break the spell in any way, and everything that I do has to do with that book."

To separate Phillips's work into collections of short fiction and novels is, however, to miss much of what is distinctive about her style. The story collections for which she is best known, *Black Tickets* and *Fast Lanes* (she has also published four volumes with small presses), are highly integrated. Her novels *Machine Dreams* and *Shelter,* meanwhile, rely on multiple narrators and "nests of stories," the phrase Katherine Mansfield used of Dorothy Richardson's *Pilgrimage.* "There's a real similarity," Phillips has said, "between the way that a book of stories and a novel are put together." Furthermore, she readily acknowledges "a thread of obsession that runs through all the work; it's a way of seeing the world. When you look at all of a writer's work there should be a sense of that world enlarging, in a different way each time."

Black Tickets, which brought new stories together with previously published pieces to create a new whole, is a kind of woman's

In Our Time of the post-Vietnam generation. The pieces move from first to third person, from long monologues or narratives to short sketches often rooted in photographs or other images. Although some critics dismissed the later pieces as "writing school exercises," they work in much the same way as Hemingway's "interchapters," which he described as "like looking with your eyes at something, say a passing coast line, and then looking at it with 15x binoculars." According to Phillips, "*Black Tickets* works like a novel because of the way that it was organized. It wasn't just put together in any order. The short pieces introduced the long ones, and they tipped the reader off and taught the reader how to read the work." For example, the short piece "Wedding Picture," almost a prose poem, introduces the more traditional narrative "Home," and, Phillips notes, "it clearly could be the character in 'Home' speaking this piece. They're connected in those kinds of ways, and in terms of echoes. I think I had a kind of intuitive or thematic organization, which happened when I put them together."

One connection is that of the different kind of "Souvenir" (the title of one of the strongest stories in the collection) that prompts memory. Souvenirs can be photographs or objects, but dreams are most often the trigger for a character's memories and secrets. Indeed, the collection's preface announces that "these stories began in what is real, but became, in fact, dreams." Many memories are of family relationships—of daughters and fathers, daughters and mothers, of illness and uneasy sexuality, of things unspoken yet un-

derstood. (*Machine Dreams* too is structured as a series of the dreams and memories of different members of a single family.) The child, of course, is the ultimate souvenir of the parent—whether as just "one reminder" of a casual affair ("Bluegill") or, more often, as "a secret in her blood making ready to work against her" ("Souvenir"). "Maybe I was in training to become my mother," thinks the narrator of a later story, "Blue Moon."

"Place comes to me very strongly," Phillips has said, and *Machine Dreams* and *Shelter* explore in detail the constraints and security of a small town and a summer camp in West Virginia, respectively. The short stories, on the other hand, often present their characters between places, in various liminal zones. They are "about rootlessness or what identity is when there is no place, which is another way of saying how important place is." In "The Heavenly Animal," for example, Janey visits her home town "five years after the divorce" of her parents and is torn between them, lunch with one, dinner with the other. Her father's attentions are fixed on her car. "I won't stay in one place all my life out of fear I'll get crippled if I move," she tells him. But asked about what she'll do next, she answers, "I don't know. . . . How can I know?"

The seven linked stories of *Fast Lanes* continue to explore themes of family, restlessness, wandering, and anxiety about the future. "How Mickey Made It," which won the Pushcart Prize in 1983, ends with Mickey telling his girlfriend to put away her fortune cards: "I believe in that shit, don't scare me"; but then the next story, "Rayme," opens, "In our student days we were all in need of fortune tellers." In the final story, "Bess," the narrator sees a look in her brother's face that "foretold everything" between them: "Whatever we did from then on was attempted escape from the fact of the future."

"Rayme" fully exploits the self-conscious and seemingly arbitrary nature of the short story form. Describing her student housemates, the narrator says, "This story could be about any one of those people, but it is about Rayme and comes to no conclusion." After hearing about Rayme's background, one learns that "the facts she referred to at different times seemed arbitrary, they were scrambled, they may have been false or transformed." The notion of a coherent "us"—of a communal rather than individual experience—is undermined at the end of the story. The reader learns that "most of us would leave town in a few weeks," "some of us were going to Brazil," "some of us were going to California," "a few were staying in West Virginia." But in this list is inserted, "and I had been recently pregnant." She quickly moves on, but the story concludes with the friends, "as close to family as most of us would ever get," swimming in the lake, where Rayme asks the narrator, who is finally named as Kate, "when you had your abortion, did you think about killing yourself?" The question is dismissed, and yet it hangs there and colors a reading of the stories that follow.

Kate's feeling that "our destinations appeared to be interchangeable pauses in some long, lyric transit" is the central concern of the title story, which explores one such pause. Another first-person woman narrator travels home, accompanied by

her friend Thurman. "Only one story . . . we've been in that truck three weeks," he says at the end of their journey. "I lose track of where I am," she says. The "floating" images of "Rayme" intensify: "when I met Thurman he was floating and I was floating home"; he'd been in "all the western floater's towns" and shares with her "the floater's only fix," an ability never to look back. Yet this is no simple masculine "on the road" experience. She seeks Thurman because "it was time to sleep with someone" and she's "twenty-three and American and . . . can't drive." Moreover, her journey to discover America does not take her away but toward home. Her parents and grandparents "stayed in one place and sank with whatever they had." Her generation, on the other hand, has "roads. Sensation, floating, maps into more of the same." Anxiety about what the future may hold, what direction to take, persists. All that Thurman can advise is to "check your mirrors. Always know what's coming up on you." "Don't close your eyes. Keep watching every minute. . . . If you're careful you can make it: . . . the one right move. Sooner or later you'll see your chance." What "the right move" or her "chance" may be remains a mystery.

The notion of the writer as a historical or familial witness is crucial for Phillips. "I think the person who ends up being a writer," she says, "is often the child who's chosen to hear the secrets or stories, who is handed the task of redeeming the family or redeeming the parent. It is a burden, but it's also a blessing." Indeed often the past seems as close, and as uncertain, as the future for Phillips's protagonists. This is particularly true of "Blue Moon" and

"Bess," stories featuring characters from *Machine Dreams,* but published later. Both are first-person stories of the love between brother and sister, and an epiphanic moment that "foretold everything." Eighty years later, Bess recalls the year 1900, "the summer I was twelve, the summer Warwick got sick and everything changed." It is a summer of watching and of the loss of innocence, for as Bess recognizes, "no love is innocent once it has recognized its own existence." In "Blue Moon," through telling the story of her brother Billy's love affair with Kato, the summer before he goes to Vietnam, Danner finds herself more than simply a straightforward witness: "the boundary I'd imagined between myself and anything I saw, or touched, was gone." In its place comes the storyteller's gift of empathy.

As a kind of disclaimer to *Black Tickets,* Phillips wrote that her characters "bear no relation to living persons, except that love and loss lends a reality to what is imagined." This is far from the supposed credo of "dirty realism," the style her work reputedly exemplifies. Phillips never leaves her reader with a view of surfaces. Instead her narrators compulsively interpret, imagine, and invent. In "Wedding Picture," the daughter quickly goes beyond her description of what is captured by the camera (clothes, smiles, skin) to see what she knows to be there beneath the surface: that the woman is pregnant, that her true love is dead five years, her mother is sick, and "it's time." Phillips's aesthetic seems closer to that proposed by Mickey in the opening story of *Fast Lanes* ("all you can do is turn the bad stuff into something else and not flake out on what it costs you")

than to any version of unvarnished realism. "The bad stuff" is never simply presented but is transformed by an insistent lyricism into something that offers the possibility of change and sometimes even hints of salvation. For it is salvation that is demanded not only by her floating individuals and their broken-down families, but also, ultimately, Jayne Anne Phillips suggests, by America itself.

Kasia Boddy

SELECTED BIBLIOGRAPHY

Works by Jayne Anne Phillips

Sweethearts. Short Beach, Conn.: Truck Press, 1976

Counting. New York: Vehicle Editions, 1978.

Black Tickets. New York: Delacorte, 1979.

How Mickey Made It. St Paul, Minn.: Bookslinger, 1981.

The Secret Country. Winston-Salem, N.C.: Palaemon, 1982.

Fast Lanes. New York: E. P. Dutton, 1987.

Critical Studies

Adams, Michael. "Jayne Anne Phillips." In Karen Rood, ed., *Dictionary of Literary Biography Yearbook: 1980,* pp. 297—300. Detroit: Gale Research, 1981.

Lassner, Phyllis. "Jayne Anne Phillips: Women's Narrative and the Recreation of History." In Mickey Pearlman, ed., *American Women Writing Fiction,* pp. 192—210. Lexington: University Press of Kentucky, 1989.

Schumacher, Michael. *Reasons to Believe: New*

Voices in American Fiction. New York: St. Martin's Press, 1988.

KATHERINE ANNE
PORTER
(1890 – 1980)

Katherine Anne Porter ranks with William Faulkner, Flannery O'Connor, Ernest Hemingway, and Eudora Welty as a twentieth-century master of modern American short fiction. A consummate artist, she wrote stories marked by unflinching treatment of painful material, deft control of narrative perspective, exquisitely precise details, firmly realized characters, and a finely crafted style. Born Callie Russell Porter on May 15, 1890, in the frontier community of Indian Creek, Texas, she was the fourth of five children of Mary Alice Jones and Harrison Boone Porter. When Porter's mother died in 1892, the family moved to Kyle, in south-central Texas, to live with Porter's paternal grandmother Catherine Anne Skaggs Porter. "Aunt Cat," as the family called her, had been born into a Kentucky family of some means; but her fortunes declined after her marriage to an economically imprudent husband who had died young. Through her strict management of children, grandchildren, and money, Aunt Cat recouped some of the family's financial losses while providing its chief source of discipline, stability, and strength. By her example, Aunt Cat helped teach her granddaughter that a woman could be self-sufficient and independent. A great storyteller, Aunt Cat also nurtured the development of Katherine Anne's narrative ability.

After her grandmother's death in 1901, Porter spent a year in a private school and held several short-lived part-time jobs. She then began a restless moving from place to place and an equally restless involvement with people, whether husbands, relatives, or friends, that would characterize much of her life and repeatedly interrupt her concentration on her writing. In 1906, at the age of sixteen, she married a railway clerk, John Henry Koontz, whom she divorced in 1915, at that time legally assuming the name Katherine Anne. Despite tuberculosis during 1915–1917 and influenza in 1918, she worked as a movie extra in Chicago, read poetry and sang on the Lyceum Circuit, and worked for newspapers in Dallas and Denver. In 1919 she moved to Greenwich Village, where she wrote children's stories and met various writers, artists, and prominent Mexicans. Offered a job with a magazine, she moved in 1920 to Mexico, where she began to accumulate the material that would go into some of her most admired tales, including "María Concepción," "Flowering Judas," and "Hacienda." Later in the 1920s and in the early 1930s she lived in New York, Connecticut, Massachusetts, Bermuda, and Mexico again; was married briefly to an Englishman, Ernest Stock; and published a collection of highly acclaimed short stories, *Flowering Judas* (1930).

A Guggenheim fellowship enabled Porter to go to Europe, where she lived and traveled during 1931–1936. Divorced from Stock, in 1933 she married Eugene Dove Pressly, whom she divorced five years later. In 1934 she published a limited edition of *Hacienda*, and in 1935 an expanded one of *Flowering Judas*. Meanwhile, in Europe, she had started to reflect upon her youth in Texas and Colorado, a past she would eventually describe in a series of semiautobiographical works: "The Old Order" stories, "Old Mortality," and "Pale Horse, Pale Rider." In 1939 the last two of these tales were issued with "Noon Wine" as *Pale Horse, Pale Rider: Three Short Novels,* a volume that solidly established Porter's reputation as a major author. Reviewers for influential newspapers and journals praised the excellence of her work, compared her to Nathaniel Hawthorne and Henry James, and ranked her among the greatest writers America had produced.

In the meantime, back in the United States, Porter married for the fourth and final time. Her new husband, more than twenty years her junior, was Albert Erskine, the business manager of the *Southern Review,* who would later become a renowned editor at Random House. Erskine learned the actual discrepancy in their ages at the marriage ceremony and grew furious at what he saw as Porter's deception. As a result, Porter was to claim that their marriage ended on the day it began. Later, she said that marriage had starved her heart and that she had found it incompatible with the pressures and demands of authorship.

After separating from Erskine in 1940, Porter lived for nearly two years at the Yaddo artists' colony near Saratoga Springs, New York, where she became friendly with Eudora Welty, whose literary career she helped to launch by writing the introduction to Welty's first volume of short fiction, *A Curtain of Green* (1941). She bought a house in the Saratoga Springs area while working on a volume of short fiction, *The Leaning Tower*; an early version of her novel *Ship of Fools*; and a book, never completed, about the colonial New England divine Cotton Mather. Increasingly, her need for money to support herself while writing dictated where she lived and worked and to some extent what she would publish. Hence in the middle 1940s she resided briefly with authors Allen Tate and Caroline Gordon, completed the ill poet John Peale Bishop's stint as consultant at the Library of Congress, published *The Leaning Tower and Other Stories* (1944), and moved to Hollywood, where, like William Faulkner and F. Scott Fitzgerald somewhat earlier, she helped write film scripts. Late in the decade she turned to guest lecturing and university teaching as sources of income, assuming her first position at Stanford University in 1948–1949. Throughout the 1950s she continued to supplement her income in this manner, holding posts at several universities and colleges.

Meanwhile, Porter continued to work on *Ship of Fools,* a laborious task that diverted her from the short fiction in which she excelled. Realizing that she must protect her reputation by continuing to publish books, she collected many of her previously published stories in her important volume of the 1950s: *The Old Order: Stories of the South.* The book contained such well-known narratives as "The Jilting of Granny Weatherall," "Old Mortality," and six of the seven pieces based on her Texas girlhood that she would later assemble in *The*

Collected Stories of Katherine Anne Porter (1964, 1965).

During the 1950s, Porter continued to lecture and teach in order to secure sufficient income for her writing. She spent 1952–1953 at the University of Michigan and the University of Liège and rounded out the decade with posts at the University of Texas, the University of Virginia, and Washington and Lee College. After receiving a Ford Foundation grant in 1959, she moved to Washington, D.C., to finish *Ship of Fools.* In 1961 she secluded herself in Cape Ann, Massachusetts, to complete the book, which she delivered to her publisher for publication on April Fool's Day, 1962. She had worked on the lengthy, long-awaited novel for over twenty years. Although it received mixed reviews, it became an immediate best-seller and was made into a commercially successful film with an international cast that included Vivien Leigh, Simone Signoret, and Jose Ferrer. In 1966, Porter won both the Pulitzer Prize and the National Book Award for *The Collected Stories of Katherine Anne Porter.* In that year she also received an honorary doctorate from the University of Maryland, an event with important repercussions for her future life and the disposition of her literary estate.

With its triple accolades, the year 1966 was perhaps the high point of the public recognition accorded Porter. Her period of greatest literary productivity, however—the 1920s and the 1930s—had long since passed, her creative energies gradually siphoned off by repeated involvements with relatives, husbands, cultural activities, lecturing, teaching, and travel. She had once wryly remarked that there were only three ages—young, ma-

ture, and remarkable—and at age seventy-six, with *Ship of Fools* and *The Collected Stories* behind her, she had accomplished a great deal of what she had long been striving to attain. (Important books she would go on to publish— *The Collected Essays and Occasional Writings of Katherine Anne Porter* [1970] and *The Never-Ending Wrong* [1977], about the 1920s Sacco-Vanzetti case—had their origins in earlier times.) For the rest of her life she lived mainly in the South, graciously accepting public honors and bravely attempting to combat the repeated illnesses that beset her as she grew older. Settling in Maryland, in 1968 she deposited her papers in the McKeldin Library at the University of Maryland, where a handsome room was named for her. In her late eighties, she suffered a series of incapacitating strokes. She died on September 18, 1980. After her cremation, her ashes were buried at her Texas birthplace.

Like many writers, Porter drew upon the circumstances of her life—her upbringing, discouragements, and triumphs—for some of her most memorable fiction. She treats these matters with exquisite artistry in stories based on her youth in Texas and Colorado: "The Old Order" pieces, "Old Mortality," and "Pale Horse, Pale Rider," which may be studied together as a single work portraying the evolution of the semiautobiographical character Miranda Gay; and in her Mexican tales, most notably "María Concepción." "The Old Order" series and the two long tales related to it trace the development of the imaginative, sensitive, inquisitive, and independent Miranda from childhood and adolescence to early maturity. In the seven pieces of "The Old

Order" series, Porter shows the motherless Miranda being cared for by her grandmother, her father, and family servants, who discipline the girl strictly, deride her fears, and unwittingly fail to give her the affectionate support she requires for stability and maturation.

In "The Fig Tree," for instance, Miranda's grandmother and father rush the grieving child off to the family farm before she can determine whether a chick she has buried is actually dead, while in "The Circus" several family members unsympathetically reproach her for leaving the circus, terrified by a sneering tightrope walker and a cruel dwarf. As Miranda approaches adolescence, she and her older brother Paul increasingly distance themselves from their adult relatives. Hence in "The Grave," the last and one of the most frequently reprinted of the "Old Order" pieces, she and Paul are hunting alone in the woods when they unexpectedly confront pregnancy and death in an action resonant with complex, subtly rendered symbols. After they explore empty graves in an old country cemetery, Paul shoots and flays a rabbit, only to discover it was pregnant. Miranda, on the brink of adolescence, views the unborn baby rabbits with fascination and pity, meanwhile sensing the experience has helped to teach her about "the secret, formless intuitions in her own mind and body, which had been clearing up, taking form, so gradually and so steadily she had not realized that she was learning what she had to know."

"Old Mortality," which traces Miranda's life and that of her parents' and grandparents' generations from 1885 to 1912, initially returns Miranda to a childhood marked by family restraints and distinguished by family legends revolving around the girl's dead Aunt Amy, who, according to legend, had been beautiful, adored, and unhappy, and who had died young. Central to "Old Mortality" is the effect of the Amy story on Miranda and her older sister Maria, who gradually learn the discrepancies between the romantic vision of the past held by the older generation and the disturbing realities of the present conveyed through events that occur as they are growing up. In early adolescence, the sisters meet a major figure from the past, Amy's husband Gabriel Breaux, who lives on his sentimental memories of his dead wife and who is not the dashing figure of the legend but a sad, impecunious drunkard obsessed with horse racing. In late adolescence, newly and unhappily married, Miranda encounters her cousin Eva Parrington, an elderly, staunch, and forthright spinster, who tells Miranda that Amy had been less glamorous and desirable than indiscreet and flamboyant. She also implies that Amy's early death from an overdose of medicine may have been a willful suicide.

Porter uses the ambiguous circumstances of Amy's death to communicate the unhappiness of a lively, unconventional young woman made miserable by the constraints of late nineteenth-century provincial society, just as she uses the various versions of the Amy legend to propel Miranda toward a future marked by fewer and fewer traditional restraints. Hence at the end of the tale, Miranda—rejecting both the untrustworthy romanticized legend of Amy and Eva's equally untrustworthy debunking version—determines to leave her husband and confront the world alone, unencumbered by "the legend of the past, other people's memory of the past, at which she had spent her life peering in wonder like a child at a magic-lantern show."

"Pale Horse, Pale Rider," Porter's final tale about Miranda, shows the young woman at age twenty-four, unmarried and living in Denver, Colorado, where she works as a newspaper reporter. Drawing indirectly on her own experience, Porter uses the Great War and the influenza epidemic of 1918 as pervasive influences on the fortunes of Miranda and her suitor Adam Barclay. Resisting patriots who pressure her to buy war bonds and spout propaganda about "the **WAR** to end **WAR**," Miranda attends plays and frequents museums with Adam, meanwhile sensing that the conflict has precluded whatever future they might have had. Ironically, however, it is not war but influenza that brings the death alluded to by the title of the tale, a phrase drawn from the Book of Revelation as transmitted through a gospel melody. As Porter had done, Miranda falls victim to the flu; and like a young soldier in Denver, who had tended Porter and then died of the disease himself, Adam nurses Miranda, gets her to a hospital, develops flu, and dies. After nearly dying herself, Miranda regains consciousness only to learn of the armistice and Adam's death. At the end of the story, facing life in peacetime without Adam, the recuperating but bitterly disillusioned Miranda thinks: "No more war, no more plague, only the dazed silence that follows the ceasing of the heavy guns; noiseless houses with the shades drawn, empty streets, the dead cold light of tomorrow."

After the South and the efforts of south-ern women like Miranda to attain independence, Porter's other major subject in short fiction was Mexico, a country she portrayed through a subtle mixture of sympathetic understanding, irony, and criticism. In her tales about Mexico, she scrutinizes its native Indian peoples onto whom Christianity has been imperfectly grafted, its obtuse or hapless Americans who are in the country for sound or unsound purposes, and its unprincipled, opportunistic Mexicans attempting to manipulate the principles of the early twentieth-century revolution for personal gain. The remarkable early story "María Concepción" (1922) reveals Porter's balanced handling of violent material as well as her knowledge of the fundamental disjunctions between American and Mexican culture. It also shows her understanding of how Christianity both veils and fosters brutal indigenous Indian behavior. The tale, which involves three major characters—María Concepción, her husband Juan de Dios Villegas, and Juan's lover María Rosa—centers on the stalwart title figure who, married to Juan and expecting his child, discovers him making love to María Rosa. Juan and María Rosa leave the village with the army, an event that causes María Concepción to miscarry. A year or so later, Juan deserts the army and returns with a pregnant María Rosa. The indomitable María Concepción uses her long butchering knife to murder María Rosa, who has just given birth to a son. She then confronts and cows her husband, who helps her conceal the murder; frustrates the official police inquiry into the crime; and adopts María Rosa's infant. Near the end of the story, the major elements in her world having been set right, María

Concepción senses the night and the earth swell and recede "with a limitless, unhurried, benign breathing. She . . . closed her eyes, feeling the slow rise and fall within her own body. . . . Even as she was falling asleep, head bowed over the child, she was still aware of a strange, wakeful happiness."

An overview of Porter's short fiction suggests that the most important settings of her work were places and times she knew well: the South, especially Texas, of the late nineteenth and early twentieth centuries; Mexico at several points in its modern history; and Western civilization between the two world wars as depicted in *Ship of Fools*. Emerging from these settings, Porter's most memorable female characters are independent, resourceful women like Miranda Gay and María Concepción. Among her other notable characters are confused, directionless women such as Laura in "Flowering Judas"; distraught mothers, unhappy children, and manipulative servants in such stories as "The Downward Path to Wisdom," "Magic," and "He"; and inept, financially imprudent, unkind, or irresponsible male relatives, husbands, and suitors based variously on figures in her private life.

The central themes of Porter's short fiction reflect her keen mind, her wide experience, and her unflinching scrutiny of human nature and human life. In her tales, young women and men like Miranda and Paul learn that relatives and other adults, however well-meaning, rarely provide the unconditional, affectionate acceptance required for personal maturation ("The Circus"); that a family's collective version of its past may be merely romantic or vindictive fabrication ("Old Mortality"); that love of any kind ends in death ("The Fig Tree," "The Grave"); and that in order to survive, individuals must develop courage and integrity while cherishing whatever affection and certainty life offers ("Pale Horse, Pale Rider"). Described in this manner, Porter's tales present a bleak vision born in part of the extremely difficult circumstances over which the author had triumphed, often at great personal cost. But the obstacles that Miranda, María Concepción, and other Porter characters overcome indicate that it is not a vision entirely without hope.

During the twentieth century, Porter's literary standing, like that of other mid-century authors, fluctuated. Throughout much of her life, her writing was widely praised and highly regarded by fellow writers, reviewers, and readers in America and Europe. Since her death, her literary achievement has been temporarily eclipsed by scholarship about her contemporaries, particularly Welty and O'Connor; but with the publication of important biographical and critical studies in the 1980s and 1990s she is once again in the forefront of scholarly study. As a supreme artist, widely considered to be a "writer's writer," Katherine Anne Porter richly repays close analysis for her finely rendered vision of life and for the clarity and immense brilliance of her style.

Mary Ann Wimsatt

SELECTED BIBLIOGRAPHY

Works by Katherine Anne Porter

Flowering Judas. New York: Harcourt, Brace, 1930.

Flowering Judas and Other Stories. New York: Harcourt, Brace, 1935.

Pale Horse, Pale Rider: Three Short Novels. New York: Harcourt, Brace, 1939.

The Leaning Tower and Other Stories. New York: Harcourt, Brace, 1944.

The Old Order: Stories of the South. New York: Harcourt, Brace, 1955.

The Collected Stories of Katherine Anne Porter. New York: Harcourt, Brace, 1965.

Critical Studies

Givner, Joan. *Katherine Anne Porter: A Life.* New York: Simon & Schuster, 1982. Revised edition, Athens: University of Georgia Press, 1992.

Johnson, James William. "Another Look at Katherine Anne Porter." *Virginia Quarterly Review* 36 (fall 1960): 598–613.

Stout, Janis P. *Katherine Anne Porter: A Sense of the Times.* Charlottesville: University Press of Virginia, 1995.

Unrue, Darlene Harbour. *Truth and Vision in Katherine Anne Porter's Fiction.* Athens: University of Georgia Press, 1985.

WILLIAM SYDNEY PORTER (O. HENRY)
(1862 – 1910)

O. Henry is a byword for formulaic fiction with wide popular appeal, being a pen name associated with a story form marked by anecdotal variety, shrewd observation, deft handling of coincidence and ironical circumstance, and, most typical, the frequent use of an attention-grabbing surprise ending, qualities long since fallen from critical favor as being glib and superficial. Recent biographical studies suggest O. Henry's stories came by their devices honestly, being intimately connected to the personal history of the man behind the mask, William Sydney Porter. Though his pseudonym was associated with fiction having a humorous point of view and an upbeat, sentimental conclusion, Porter's posthumous fame was darkened by revelations about his tangled and shadowy personal life, which was given a tragic dimension by his early death at the height of his literary reputation.

Porter was born in Greensboro, North Carolina, during the second year of the Civil War, a regional calamity coupled to the harsh circumstances of his childhood. His mother died when he was three and his father drifted away from his profession as a physician into a hapless career as an "inventor," increasingly a fabrication to cover his avocation as an alcoholic. The boy was brought up by his grandmother, and his education ended when he turned fifteen and began an apprenticeship in his uncle's pharmacy. Although he became skilled at that trade, he was bored by it and in 1882 headed for Texas, then thought to be a southern region that, lying beyond the defeated Old South, held out hope and opportunity for the ambitious. More hopeful than ambitious, Porter did, however, demonstrate a talent for drawing that enhanced his other charming qualities—a lively sense of humor, a pleasant singing voice, and a penchant for practical jokes. Like his "last troubadour," he mostly worked at avoiding work and was fortunate in finding a hospitable roost in the ranch of a family friend in LaSalle County; here he spent the next two years learning Spanish and reading romantic fiction and poetry. Moving to Austin, he became convinced that regular employment would be necessary if he wished to enjoy the middle-class respectability to which he aspired. Working briefly as a pharmacist, he then became a bookkeeper, a draftsman, and eventually a bank teller.

In 1887 he married Athol Estes, but it was not a happy union, in part because of Porter's frequent absences in pursuit of the carefree male companionship he had earlier enjoyed. In the late 1880s, Porter submitted humorous sketches to newspapers and magazines and then undertook a venture fated to turn his life into a series of reverses. In early 1894, he bought a weekly paper and reshaped it into a vehicle for humorous sketches, mostly his own. *The Rolling Stone* lasted for about a year, and though the income from this venture was intended to supplement Porter's salary as bank teller, the reciprocity seems to have gone in the opposite direction. In the last months of 1894 irregularities in the accounting practices of the bank were discovered and explained at first by Porter's carelessness. Porter consistently protested his innocence, but it is undeniable that he resigned his position in the bank and that the persistence of a bank examiner led to his being charged with embezzlement.

He had meanwhile left for Houston to work as a columnist for the *Post*, writing sketches and stories that anticipated his later fascination with imposters and disguises as well as the overpowering presence of fated circumstances in the lives of his characters. Although Porter seems to have recovered his good spirits, his domestic situation became even more troubled when Athol developed tuberculosis. During this period, the charge of embezzlement, earlier dismissed by a grand jury, was renewed, and this time Porter was arrested and released on bond (the money provided by his in-laws). When he took the train for Austin to face trial, Porter disappeared, surfacing at first in New Orleans and then in Honduras. Forced to return to Texas by his wife's impending death, he was convicted on several counts of theft and sentenced to five years in prison.

Assigned to the pharmacy in the hospital of the Ohio State Penitentiary, Porter was saved from the rigors of prison life and began to write the stories soon to bring him popularity. Several were published before his sentence was reduced to three years for good behavior, most notably "Whistling Dick's Christmas Stocking," a Bret Harte-like tale about a hobo with a heart of gold that was given a contemporary relevance by the "tramp menace" then threatening the countryside. Another was "Money Maze," based on his sojourn in Honduras, which would provide the nucleus for his first book, *Cabbages and Kings* (1904), made up of previously published stories revised to promote a loose, novelistic continuity about shadowy doings of American expatriates in Central America.

Porter's prison experience not only provided the enforced leisure to allow him to become a skillful writer but also gave him material for many stories, especially those gathered in *The Gentle Grafter* (1908), about the adventures of Jeff Peters, a genial, self-defeating con man. It is "A Retrieved Reformation," however, about a noble-hearted safecracker, that is O. Henry's best-remembered tale about chivalric crooks, thanks in part to *Alias Jimmy Valentine,* the popular play and movie it inspired.

The prison experience had other effects as well. Soon after his release in 1901, the writer, now known simply as O. Henry, moved to New York, where his stories were appearing in popular periodicals and where he quickly settled into the anonymous, even fugitive existence that would characterize the rest of his short life. Overweight from the prison diet, increasingly dependent on alcohol, shy of appearing in public for fear of being recognized by a fellow inmate, Porter devoted most of his time to writing for the *New York Sunday World* and limited his acquaintance to editors and others associated with his newfound profession.

A second marriage in 1907, to a boyhood sweetheart, was no happier than the first, and he died three years later, though the gathering into collections of his stories, which numbered more than 250, continued until 1923. At the height of his brief but great fame, Porter turned out at least one story a week to meet the demands of editors and to support his daughter. Given the circumstances of their composition and his increasing ill health, the quality and variety of his fiction are amazing. Both fell off toward the end, and his correspondence with editors was reduced to begging letters in which he asked for advances against stories supposedly written but not even begun.

These facts enforce the conclusion that the interplay between circumstance and personal strength and weakness that characterizes so many of Porter's stories is clearly derived from his own experience, much as the local-color backdrop of his stories was derived from the places through which his life took him, from North Carolina to Texas to New Orleans to Honduras to Manhattan. "I am like Lord Jim," he remarked to a friend, "because we both made one fatal mistake at the supreme crisis of our lives, a mistake from which we could not recover." Though not even Porter's Central American stories suggest Conrad's influence, certainly the novel in question provided him with an apt analogy for his own sudden reversal of fortune, a coupling of circumstances and fatal weakness of character. His stories may have evinced the fund of good humor that made him so popular among his friends and associates, and his trick endings most certainly are not those cruel traps set for characters by Ambrose Bierce, but the sunny streets of his most famous New York stories are matched by those with dark shadows derived from his abiding sense of fatality.

Enormously popular in their day and still widely read, O. Henry's stories rely on mechanical contrivances for their effects that have alienated many literary critics who are unwilling to concede the sheer brilliance of the author's devices. Thus critical denigration started shortly after Porter's death, motivated largely by the then dominant vogue for grimly naturalistic fiction like that produced by Jack London, who was hardly innocent of using authorial traps for the unwary but seldom softened his endings with sentimental resolutions. Later, Cleanth Brooks and Robert Penn Warren dismissed his work in their influential book *Understanding Fiction* (1943); in the syllabus-framing *Literary History of the United States,* which appeared just after World War II, and in the *Columbia Literary History of the United States* (1988), O. Henry is mentioned only in passing. As early as the 1920s, the more sophisticated and realistic work of Hemingway, Anderson, and Fitzgerald, with their virtually plotless stories and often indeterminate endings, changed the tenor of the craft strategically and forever. H. L. Mencken, an arbiter of taste at that time, scorned O. Henry for his "smoking room smartness," but he ignored Porter's precedence in using the lingo of con men and cowboys for its latent humor, the qualities Ring Lardner exploited during the decade marking O. Henry's decline. Neglected too is the restless energy and slangy force in O. Henry's fables, inseparable from the rich texture of humanity that made them so engrossing in their day.

The gritty realism of American proletarian fiction in the 1930s also left little room for appreciation of O. Henry's sentimental formulas, despite his enduring (and paradoxical) popularity among readers in the Soviet Union during the same period. In 1953 there appeared on television a "round-up" of five O. Henry stories, including "The Cop and the Anthem," starring Charles Laughton as the hapless tramp, which, along with "The Gift of the Magi" and "The Ransom of Red Chief," continues to be anthologized in school textbooks.

Pegged from the beginning as the "Caliph of Baghdad on the Subway" in recognition of his allusive familiarity with *A Thousand and One Nights,* O. Henry has always been thought of as the quintessential New York writer at the turn of the century, an emphasis that ignores his western tales and his stories of Central America and the southern United States. At a time when regionalism was in flower, William Sydney Porter drew upon all these places, through which he at one time passed, and though he spent his last and most productive decade in Manhattan hotels, his formative years were spent in rural communities. Moreover, though he was born and raised to young manhood in North Carolina, Porter's literary career began in Texas, the setting for a considerable number of his finest tales, like "The Last of the Troubadours" and "The Ransom of Mack," which inspired an obvious but misleading comparison to Bret Harte.

There is a slangy realism in Porter's western stories and a general lack of sentimentality distinguishing them from the lachrymose, Dickens-derived fiction of Harte. His fiction with a southern setting, erroneously compared to the work of George W. Cable, whose social concerns were never O. Henry's, contributed to the ongoing myth of gallant southern colonels, loyal former slaves, and courageous (and aging) maidens that was the regional response to the humiliations of Reconstruction. Indeed, because of his fame as a sentimental chronicler of starving shop girls and counter-hopping clerks in New York, Porter's southern origins have been overlooked. He is truly a quintessential southern writer, for whom chivalry was not only not dead below the Mason-Dixon line but alive and well in Manhattan.

To the same cultural inheritance may be traced the dark dimension of so many of O. Henry's stories. Even the most famous tales, such as "The Gift of the Magi," are bent to a fatalistic curve, in which the best of intentions cancel out benevolent impulses, a plot line that is given a much crueler closure in "The Last of the Troubadours," when a well-meant action has an effect opposite to the one intended. In "The Cop and the Anthem," the tramp gets his long-sought jail sentence only after undergoing a religious conversion that promises to set him on a new path, an impulse lost when he is suddenly put behind bars. The tricks played by Fate, bringing unexpected misery and unforeseen blessings, are a constant theme in O. Henry's stories and are intrinsic to those often mechanical and contrived endings, with their sudden reversals and revelations; the sentimentalism of some of his best-known tales often introduces an element of optimism that mitigates the bleaker implications of the plot.

However, sentimental conclusions are not inevitable in O. Henry's fiction. As the frequently reprinted story "The Furnished Room" demonstrates, the author's abiding sense of fatality could at times prevail unrelieved by a silver lining. The story is set in the transient world of Manhattan's lower west side, where drab rooming houses are often occupied briefly by anonymous theater people, including young persons drawn to the city by a dream of success on the stage. A young man arrives at one such house, already exhausted from a five-month search for his hometown girlfriend, who has come to New York to pursue a singing career. The housekeeper claims not to recognize the girl's description, but when the young man moves into one of the rooms, he recognizes a faint scent of the perfume his sweetheart wore. Further frantic questions lead no-where, and in a profound depression, the man turns on the gas and lies down on the bed to await his death. In the conclusion of the story, we learn from a conversation that the girl the young man sought had killed herself in the very same room only a week before, information withheld by the housekeeper as harmful to the reputation of her house. The strained use of coincidence harms the story for anyone insisting on a realistic plot, but it is O. Henry's brilliant evocation of ghostly figures coming and going amid the menacing decay of urban rooming houses—a setting he knew so well—that enhances the eerie inevitability of the young man's quest and the double suicide with which the story ends. Closure comes with a sudden wrench of pathos, the potential sentimentality of which is blocked by having the final revelation delivered by the cold-hearted housekeeper over her evening glass of beer.

Even more bitter in its conclusion is O. Henry's undeservedly neglected story "The Moment of Victory," inspired by the Spanish-American War. Ignoring chivalric formulas, the narrative explains the reckless heroism of a young soldier in Cuba as a response to a casual remark by a female friend, who ridicules him for his attempts to "look fly," which is to say smart in dress and appearance. The "moment" in question does not occur in Cuba but after the young man has a chance to use his heroism (and uniform and medals) to put down the woman who had insulted him, a conclusion that underwrites recent psycho-historical "explanations" of the Spanish-American War as a validation of American manhood and gives a savage twist to a sentimental formula.

Such a dark finale contrasts with the sun-filled endings of O. Henry's best-known stories, like "The Gift of the Magi" and "The Last Leaf," which are sweetly sad yet positive in their inevitability, involving the sentimental postures that were anathema to a rising generation of realists. Yet these stories have become virtual folktales in our national anthology, again carrying forward the tradition of Washington Irving even while violating the strict verisimilitude young writers insisted on at the turn of the century. Thus another of O. Henry's western stories, "The Reformation of Calliope," may be compared to Stephen Crane's comically revisionist "The Bride Comes to Yellow Sky." In Porter's story, a standoff between a western marshal and a drunken gunman is given a maternal not a marital resolution, the author resorting to an undeniable sentimentalism entirely missing from Crane's story. Yet both authors reaffirm the contemporary wisdom that the Wild West did not end with the closing of the frontier but with the appearance of women as brides and mothers, advents that in both stories inspire the sudden transformation of hard-bitten western gunmen.

Ironically, O. Henry's skillful use of sentimentalism explains his contemporary and continuing popularity, even as it accounts for the subsequent decline of his reputation among literary critics. Because much has been made recently of the fact that sentimentality is a complex impulse, it is important to acknowledge that sentimentalism in O. Henry's stories inevitably sustains a chivalric burden, lending an idealistic and heroic impulse to the action, playing against the fated circumstances integral to his sense of plot. The facts of Porter's life connect to the substance of his art, the inherited chivalry of his southern origins coupled with the reversals he suffered during his youth and young manhood.

Ultimately, O. Henry remains a singular instance, an example of a unique if overworked talent perfectly suited to his age. It is ironic that the prestigious annual award created in 1918 for the best American short story still bears O. Henry's name, inasmuch as the direction of American short fiction has steadily moved from the tightly plotted, tricky, and sentimental mode in which he excelled toward the realistic, often skeptical constructs first devised by Hemingway and typified by the open endings and cool narrative detachment of so many contemporary short stories. Yet, despite his absence from authoritative literary histories and anthologies, O. Henry's entertaining tales are still read around the world. Ordinary readers, as Harold Bloom has recently observed, "find themselves in his stories, not more truly and more strange, but rather as they were and are."

John Seelye

SELECTED BIBLIOGRAPHY

Works by William Sydney Porter (O. Henry)

The Four Million. New York: Burt, 1904.

Heart of the West. New York: McClure, 1907.

The Trimmed Lamp. Garden City, N.Y.: Doubleday, 1907.

The Gentle Grafter. New York: McClure, 1908.

The Voice of the City. Garden City, N.Y.: Doubleday, 1908.

Options. New York: Harper, 1909.

Roads of Destiny. Garden City, N.Y.: Doubleday, 1909.

Strictly Business. Garden City, N.Y.: Doubleday, 1910.

Whirligigs. Garden City, N.Y.: Doubleday, 1910.

Sixes and Sevens. Garden City, N.Y.: Doubleday, 1911.

Best Short Stories of O. Henry. New York: Modern Library, 1994.

Critical Studies

Bloom, Harold, ed. *O. Henry.* New York: Chelsea House, 1999.

Current-Garcia, Eugene. *O. Henry: A Study of the Short Fiction.* New York: Twayne, 1993.

Eikhenbaum, Boris Mikhailovich. *O. Henry and the Theory of the Short Story.* Ann Arbor: University of Michigan Press, 1968.

Langford, Gerald. *Alias O. Henry.* New York: Macmillan, 1957.

ANNIE PROULX
(1935–)

In 1992, E. Annie Proulx published her first novel, *Postcards,* which won her immediate critical acclaim and the PEN/Faulkner Award for Fiction. In 1994, Proulx won the Pulitzer Prize for her best-known novel, *The Shipping News* (1993). The highly stylized tale of an awkward and tormented boy who grows into a cuck-olded and love-starved man sold over one million copies, and brought the author's darkly humorous and disturbing vision of isolation and everyday violence to a large audience. Proulx followed *The Shipping News* with the best-seller *Accordion Crimes* (1996), essentially a series of stories interwoven into a novel, united by the characters' possession of a green accordion.

For those who know Proulx primarily as a novelist, her first short story collection (and her first published volume) offers a rich introduction to the signature themes and often bitter wit of her novels. *Heart Songs and Other Stories,* published originally in 1988 (and reissued in 1995 with the addition of two distinctly darker and more pessimistic works), includes eleven stories, some written especially for the volume and others published from 1979 through 1994 in popular and literary magazines or sporting journals. Proulx was in her mid-fifties when the collection first appeared, her ability to produce serious fiction having likely been limited by her years as a single mother to three sons.

More than a decade after the publication of *Heart Songs and Other Stories,* Proulx's second short story collection, *Close Range* (1999), brought her renewed acclaim. Set in a landscape distinctly different from her previous New England and Canadian settings, the stories span more than a century in Wyoming's history in which the state at the beginning of the millennium is remarkably similar to the frontier West of the 1800s. Proulx's storytelling artistry has grown tremendously in this second collection, as she creates more sympathetic, multidimensional, and audience-pleasing characters, and incorporates both more humor and more horror. She experiments notably with form and genre and finds inspiration in local legends and foreign folktales. Stories may have the epic feel of compressed novels, or consist merely of series of job changes or two paragraphs. They may read like a traditional Western, suggest supernatural or horror writing, or interweave the genres. Appropriately, in a volume that carries the epitaph "Reality's never been of much use out here," Proulx tests the boundaries of reality.

Edna Annie Proulx was born in Connecticut in 1935 to a family whose frequent moves presaged her own well-known wanderlust and interest in rootless characters—travelers, settlers, and immigrants. Her father was a textile executive of French-Canadian extraction, her mother an artist whose New England roots reached back to the early 1600s. Proulx dropped out of Maine's Colby College in the 1950s, and earned her bachelor of arts degree over a decade later from the University of Vermont. In 1973 she completed a masters degree in history at Sir George Williams University in Montreal (now Concordia University), where she finished the coursework for a Ph.D. but never completed a dissertation. Before publishing *Heart Songs and Other Stories* Proulx wrote magazine articles and how-to books, worked as a medical writer, newspaper editor, and historian, embraced the back-to-the-land movement, and spent years in "boring jobs" and three marriages that she seldom discusses. Collecting her stories in a book was the suggestion of an editor at *Esquire,* which had published Proulx's stories over the years. The name she used was also suggested by an early men's-magazine editor, who felt

that he could not publish male-oriented "hook-and-bullet material" by a contributor named Annie. According to Proulx, he suggested something like "Joe or Zack," and she compromised with E.A. Proulx. The first initial stuck, and it was not until the 1997 original publication of her story "Brokeback Mountain" in *The New Yorker* that she dropped the initial and again became Annie Proulx.

Set in the fictional Chopping County or in other unnamed backwoods towns in Vermont, the stories of *Heart Songs and Other Stories* create a world of hunters and fisherman, of small-town inhabitants plagued by big-city vacationers and refugees, of dissatisfied urbanites seeking fulfillment in the country, of men and women unhappy and frustrated with each other. Proulx populates her New England towns with lonely and crotchety characters engaged in long-standing feuds. Her families range from wild, incestuous, and murderous to mystifyingly strange. Characters are often tragic or destined for tragedy. Far from the Norman Rockwell vision of the American small town, Proulx's lovely landscapes and quaint country stores do little to hide the inevitability of misunderstanding or threat of violence among three groups: long-time neighbors, natives and newcomers, and men and women.

While class conflict and ownership struggles divide the blue-collar inhabitants from the newly arrived or vacationing bourgeoisie, money and success prove equally divisive for those who have been living side by side for decades. In daily coexistence, neighbors become envious when their peers surpass them in wealth or status. They learn each other's weaknesses in ways that let them plan the most effective traps or cruelest possible acts of revenge.

Hawkheel and Stong in "On the Antler" are aging adversaries in Chopping County. "All through their lives there had been sparks and brushfires between the two," and from childhood on they had planned little acts of sabotage and trickery against each other. Hawkheel retreats into books, his worth meanwhile dwindling down to the "trailer, ten spongy acres of river bottom and his social security checks"; Stong revives his failing feed store by catering to the people who are "coming into the country, buying up the old farmhouses and fields and making the sugarhouses into guest cottages." Discovering that these prosperous arrivals want "canning jars, books, tools, and antiques," Stong puts price tags on all of the artifacts of his life to authenticate the rural existence of his urban customers. Hawkheel watches with contempt as Stong transforms himself into a lovable, colorful character for his customers by spinning tall tales about locals and by making humor out of his family's tragedy. For this metamorphosis and the myriad torments of the past, Hawkheel engages in subtle retaliatory theft. He buys books from Stong's store at far less than their value, and although it is a comparatively minor and not actual crime, he delights in his deception.

However, Stong has tricks up his sleeve. He offers Hawkheel a "poisoned brandy" to disable him during the start of hunting season and then trespasses on Hawkheel's private deer stand with a hunter derisively referred to as "Mr. Tennis Court," the two of them bagging the "biggest buck ever took in the county." Hawkheel's sad, ineffectual retaliation is an act of symbolic self-annihilation as much as one designed to hurt his enemy. He takes the boxes of books he has bought to Stong's drive and hurls them at the buck's carcass. Ripping the pages out, he destroys the words that have come to give his life its only meaning, thus showing the uselessness of books against bullets.

While Stong and Hawkheel have had a lifetime to plot against each other, "Bedrock" illustrates that much less time suffices for envious poor characters to weave a plan to advance at their rich neighbor's expense. The protagonist, Perley, is an aging widower with a comfortable farm and a new wife four years younger than his daughter. A year after his first wife's death, Maureen drives up to his home and, ignoring his protests of self-sufficiency, moves into his house and bed. Proulx quickly establishes Maureen as a strong and dangerous woman. In the first sentence of "Bedrock," she splits wood and is surrounded by a "circle of broken bark." Her blade "gleams" "like a sardonic smile in the air," and the wood she has struck "bursts into two pieces with a ringing beat as though she had struck the stone beneath the earth." Not surprisingly, Maureen becomes an abusive, controlling wife. By the conclusion of "Bedrock," Perley has come to see that his wife and her brother, who spends long periods of time with her, are out to steal his farm and that they are continuing a long, consensually incestuous relationship likely begun in childhood.

Incest appears in the collection's stories both literally and symbolically like an epidemic. In "Stone City" the local hunter, Banger, describes his terrible legendary neighbor Stone as "the worst of the whole goddamn tribe. Had kids that was his grandkids." Later, Noreen confesses that she has been with her brother, Raymond, but tries to mitigate the act by adding, "He ain't my full brother, see, he's only my half brother." In "Heart Songs" Snipe declares to the elder Eno, "I love your daughter!" only to discover that she is Eno's wife, and in "Bedrock," Perley's daughter rejects him because he has taken a wife whose proximity to her own age she finds disgusting. Proulx shatters the sanctity of family life with these frequent incestuous or pseudo-incestuous pairings, couplings that make sex, particularly women's sexuality, disturbing.

"On the Antler" and "Bedrock," stories that depict debilitated old men beaten emotionally or physically by neighbors, exemplify the thematic significance of names Proulx gives her characters. In "On the Antler," Hawkheel's name evokes both strength and weakness; he hunts animals and bargain books like a "hawk," but is hit in his emotional "Achilles' heel," his pride in his private "deer stand," and he is forced to heel by Stong's superior cunning. His rival's name suggests the word strong, but sounds also like the bitter sting he gives Hawkheel at the story's conclusion. Perley in "Bedrock" fares poorly, and his tormenting brother-in-law, Bobhot, is a sneaky bobcat whose eyes like that of a cat "shine in the dark," are "orange and inhuman," "scalding," and "hot and glaring." "The Wer-Trout" features neighbors called Sauvage and Rivers. Sauvage has a wife who drives and acts like a savage—wrecking property and devouring a mouse in a fit of madness.

"Electric Arrows," which has its suggestive names—Clew and Moon-Azures—illustrates another major conflict in Proulx's stories: that between long-standing homeowners and the well-to-do new people whose cash and patronage keep the inhabitants and their towns afloat. This conflict is thematic to "Heart Songs," "On the Antler," "The Unclouded Day" and "The Wer-Trout," stories in which Proulx explores a range of the emotions that the natives feel in dealing with the invasion of new people, emotions that range from amusement to outright contempt. As an avid outdoorswoman Proulx clearly identifies with the natives, her author biographies in her first short story collection and novels suggesting how her life resembles theirs: her "greatest pleasures" were "fishing, canoeing and partridge hunting, and she lived in "an unfinished house on a steep hill in Vershire, Vermont." While sympathetic to the locals, Proulx nevertheless describes their eccentricities. The musical Twilight family in "Heart Songs" represents hillbilly or redneck types, and they perform a concert each week for no audience but God. Still, Proulx portrays natives as destructive to their neighbors as the newcomers, like the Stones of "Stone City," who haunt their community with the memory of their senseless murders, madness, and lust.

A third significant battle waged in these rural hamlets is that between the sexes. The narrators and protagonists of all the stories of *Heart Songs* are male. Proulx is one of the few female writers notable for her focus on male heroes, machismo, and masculine pursuits. Her depictions of women in this volume are mostly negative: whiny, demanding wives and girlfriends dissatisfied with their mates; an unmaternal and unnurturing mother who harms her children; a white-trash welfare mother; a Medusa-haired madwoman; a seductress who leads a man to ruin. "On the Antler" subverts the image of mother as life-giver and nurturer dramatically. Bill Stong's mother is a "slovenly housekeeper" who serves the family a Sunday dinner pork roast from a pan unwashed even though it had contained strychnine; the result is the death of all of his immediate family. "In the Pit" has a maternal monster introduced unflatteringly as "looking like Charles Laughton," with "smoke curling out of her nose." Her wardrobe consists of "carnival tent clothes," and her shoes are "sprawled like dead fish." Her son's adult neuroses appear to spring from childhood neglect when the mother did not feed him. Though the son was crying and hungry, his mother preferred to remain with her husband to have sex so passionate that "the brown sofa creaked as though they were tearing it apart." As an adult, the appropriately named Blue is distressed by both his mother's bad housekeeping and her overt sexuality. The children of Albina Muth, the welfare mother of "Negatives," have "chapped smeared faces" and lice, and are periodically abandoned.

Having made it to adulthood, the collection's men embark on relationships with women fraught with disappointment, danger, and contempt. The men are frequently hunters, and the hunting analogy applies to the ways men and women stake each other out and set traps. Maureen in "Bedrock" traps her husband by first offering to help him around the farm after he is widowed, disguising her brutal strength in a show of "meek" sexuality. When Amando goes on a hunting trip in "A Run of Bad Luck," he is also set up to hunt his unfaithful wife. The story builds to its conclusion with Proulx's signature portents, but has a twist in store for the reader primed for bloodshed. For Amando tells his family that he already knew of his wife's infidelity, and he drives away from a scene of potential violence, leaving the reader feeling strangely cheated. In "Heart Songs," Snipe is caught in another trap when he is drawn to a quiet country singer who acquiesces to his love-making, thus endangering his life as the man Snipe believes is her father turns out to be her jealous husband.

Proulx's most hostile male-female relationship develops in "Negatives," one of the two stories added to *Heart Songs and Other Stories* in the 1995 reissue. Albina Muth, whose name suggests albino mutt, befitting her pallor and her bad breeding, is a member of the struggling working class—a welfare recipient, perpetrator of welfare fraud, and sometimes homeless person. Even more desperate than her financial and emotional states is her physical state. She has "stale breath," eyes surrounded by "bruised looking flesh," and a throat ringed with "grainy dirt." Albina becomes involved with Walter Welter, a photographer specializing in images of the "rural downtrodden," who exploits her as an artistic subject and sexual outlet. He takes Albina to a nearby poorhouse, where he compels her to take off her clothes, squat precariously on piles of glass, and crawl into an oven. Focused on the "tremendous image" rather than her safety, this session is as much an exercise in sadism as a duplicitous attempt to create a documentary or realistic portrait of the lives of poorhouse inhabitants. After Albina is both weeping and bleeding, having fallen into a rusty stove, Walter begins a coupling that is rapelike in its suddenness, mean-spiritedness, and violence. In "Negatives" Proulx uses the medium of photography to craft some of her most indelible images, and finishes her exploration of rural New England in a town truly without hope.

In 1919 Sherwood Anderson published *Winesburg, Ohio,* the story-cycle classic of disillusionment and loneliness in small-town America. Seventy years later, Proulx's *Heart Songs and Other Stories* recalls and updates Anderson's sad exploration of small-town life. Though her characters and stories are less tightly connected and the geographical location is not as clearly fixed on a single town, Proulx creates a similarly cohesive and full emotional portrait of the characters in her New England landscape. Anderson's midwesterners are "grotesques," desperately and futilely reaching out to one another. Proulx takes this grotesqueness further in her first collection. Her lonely, desperate characters live in a community with a wide class division, and they reach out for one another to advance themselves, trick, steal, harm, and kill.

The fact that *Close Range*'s disparate characters all live in Wyoming unites them emotionally. Proulx established full-time residence in Wyoming in the mid-1990s, and the collected stories she published in 1999 reflect her concern with how Wyoming's brutal weather, cowboy culture, history of frontier justice, and wide-open spaces shape the personalities and longings of the state's inhabitants. Her western natives are battered, bruised, and world weary, but also tough, independent, and resilient. In "Pair of Spurs," she notes that the "state's unwritten motto is take care

a your own damn self." In "A Lonely Coast," "Wyos" are described as "touchers, hot blooded and quick, and physically yearning." They also share unique forms of unhappiness and solitude. In "A Lonely Coast," women "need" to read the personal ads because "if you don't live here you can't imagine how lonesome it gets," and the frumpy heroine of "The Bunch-grass Edge of the World" feels she is "dissolving" because she lives "too far to anything." Artfully melding the young woman's intense appetite and her profound emotional distress, Proulx writes that she "had eaten from a plateful of misery since childhood."

For men, the legacy and hard, competitive day-to-day life of Wyoming manifests itself in their desire to assert their masculinity and physical prowess aggressively. In doing so, they may risk violent physical or psychological injury to themselves or others. Diamond Felts in "The Mud Below" is a twenty-three-year-old man whose small stature and teasing, emasculating mother lead him to embark on a dangerous career as a rodeo rider. The same sense of inadequacy leads him to rape the statuesque wife of one of his traveling partners. In "People in Hell Just Want a Drink of Water," the son of a rancher is maimed and mentally incapacitated by an auto accident but still feels strong erotic urges. Reunited with his childhood horse after a long absence, he rides to neighboring ranches and exposes himself to young women. Brutal retribution follows when his neighbors castrate him. Nowhere, however, is the linkage of sex and male violence clearer or more horrifying than in the strange, unsettling "55 Miles to the Gas Pump." This story, comprised of only two paragraphs, suggests the work of Edgar Allen Poe in its macabre resolution—a wife's discovery of the corpses of her rancher husband's "paramours" in their padlocked attic.

Although Proulx's primary focus in *Close Range* is on the men of Wyoming, there are also several sympathetic female characters that illustrate the difficulties of being a working-class woman in this part of the country. In "The Bunchgrass Edge of the World," the overweight young adult daughter, Ottaline, is the "family embarrassment." Desperate to get away from the ranch and "know something of the world," she believes her struggle may be "hopeless" because "there were no jobs" and her uncompassionate father fears that driving her into town might ruin "the springs on the passenger side." Proulx lyrically intertwines the descriptions of the wide-open spaces surrounding Ottaline with her feelings of isolation. She is left to "stare at the indigo slants of hail forty miles east" and "regard the tumbled clouds like mechanic rags." Ottaline's funk is interrupted by a character that is comic and chilling in equal measure—a lovesick, broken tractor that plots revenge against those who have contributed to his disrepair. While the tractor confesses to a murder during Ottaline's childhood and spews vituperation against her father, it is also full of entertaining stories. When Ottaline argues against their peculiar courtship, a romance she originally believes inspired by hallucinations or madness, the tractor offers a list of human-machine relationships. "There's girls fell in love with tractors all over this country," he says. "There is girls married tractors."

A more worldly female character is the middle-aged waitress/bartender narrator of "A Lonely Coast." The neglected wife of an unfaithful man, the narrator tells the story of Josanna, a sad but passionate woman (the husband's former mistress), Josanna's two female friends, and her reckless new lover. Josanna and her friends are drawn to "drinking men" with "hair-trigger tempers," and all three had been in "rough marriages full of fighting and black eyes and sobbing imprecation." They work at unfulfilling jobs, but though these women may not be able to better themselves economically and are subjected to physically abusive or degrading relationships, they fight back and will not allow themselves to be underappreciated or victimized for long. Josanna is rumored to have shot at her ex-husband during their breakup, and her friend profanely summarizes the women's cynical views of dating and marriage when she says, "Listen, if its got four wheels or a dick you're goin a have trouble with it."

"A Lonely Coast" is also one of several stories in *Close Range* where the female partner is the one to leave an unsatisfactory relationship. The narrator walks out on her husband after she catches him seducing a fifteen-year-old girl. In "People in Hell Just Want a Drink of Water," Naomi is a rancher's wife whose husband begets on her children "as fast as she could stand to make them." In 1913, "ridden hard and put away dirty," she is "looking for relief," and deserts her husband and brood of nine boys for another man. Alma Del Mar of "Brokeback Mountain" becomes disenchanted with her husband's inability to support their family and his lack of interest in their daughters and her, and thinks, "What am I doin hangin around with him?" She quickly betters her standard of living by divorcing him and marrying a successful grocer.

Proulx writes in the collection's preface, "The elements of unreality, the fantastic and improbable, color all of these stories as they color real life." Unreality, however, operates on several different levels. In some stories, characters foolishly or comically believe the unthinkable, and the reader knows they are misguided. In the frozen 1886 winter setting of "The Blood Bay," the frigid conditions lead a cowpuncher to cut off a corpse's feet for his warm boots, and the horrified old man who discovers the abandoned feet is convinced that his horse has eaten a man whole. In the magic realism of "The Bunchgrass Edge of the World," readers must believe that the heroine is not delusional, and that a tractor can talk and harbor homicidal and romantic sentiment. "The Half-Skinned Deer" depicts an elderly former Wyoming rancher who returns to the state for his brother's funeral, and faces his own death when his car breaks down in a snowdrift. His fate stalks him as a "half skinned" steer whose "red eye had been watching for him all this time." We do not know whether this vision of the ghastly animal is a dying delusion or the messenger of death in an environment where the landscape seems alive with destructive intent. Finally, Proulx asks readers to question whether we can believe the teller of tales or the narrator of a story, and whether they can separate the Wyoming of frontier legends from the facts of today. She concludes "People in Hell Just Want a Drink of Water" with the postscript that the story's action took place more than sixty years ago, and that the characters are dead and gone. Of the shocking violence that ends the story, she writes teasingly, "We are in a new millennium and such desperate things no longer happen. If you believe that you'll believe anything."

Proulx gained initial critical praise with her first short story collection, but it was not until her second novel, *The Shipping News,* that her work was embraced by a wide readership. In the story of a man whom she called "large, white, stumbling along, going nowhere," she forged an endearingly sweet love story between unlikely partners, and against a backdrop of sudden violent deaths, insanity, and incest. She refines this ability to mix a poignant and unexpected romance with her trademark rough-mannered characters and unglamorous settings in the best story of *Close Range,* the 1988 O. Henry Award-winning "Brokeback Mountain." In 1963, in rural Wyoming, where hypermasculinity is the expectation for men and open homosexuality may be punished with death, Jack Twist and Ennis Del Mar meet as poor teenage shepherds and begin a passionate affair. They part at the end of the summer, and both marry and start families soon thereafter, but over the next twenty years they rekindle their fierce erotic bond with increasing affection and emotional longing on infrequent "fishing trips." Filled with extremely frank and profane language and graphic sex, and featuring a particularly horrific incident of child abuse and a gay-bashing castration and murder, "Brokeback Mountain" nevertheless registers as a touching illumination of the sentimental and nostalgic sides of outwardly tough characters. It completes Proulx's emotional journey into the psyche of the macho Wyoming male by ripping away the masque of masculinity and revealing a sense of tenderness and longing to love that comes as a surprise even to the men who experience it.

Janet R. Raiffa

SELECTED BIBLIOGRAPHY

Works by Annie Proulx

Heart Songs and Other Stories. New York: Simon & Schuster, 1988.
The Shipping News. New York: Simon & Schuster, 1993.
Accordion Crimes. New York: Simon & Schuster, 1996.
Close Range. New York: Scribner, 1999.

Critical Studies

Bolick, Katie. "Imagination is Everything: A Conversation with E. Annie Proulx." *Atlantic Unbound,* November 12, 1997.
Rimer, Sara. "At Home With: E. Annie Proulx; At Midlife, A Novelist Is Born." *New York Times,* June 23, 1994.
Steinberg, Sybil. "E. Annie Proulx: An American Odyssey." *Publishers Weekly,* June 3, 1996.

THOMAS PYNCHON
(1937–)

Thomas Ruggles Pynchon was born May 8, 1937, in Oyster Bay, New York. After an initial period in the college of engineering at Cornell University and a two-year stint in the navy, he graduated from Cornell as an English major in 1959. There is little publicly available information about his life and background after this point. According to an essay by his close friend Richard Fariña, he went into hiding in 1963 after the publication of his first novel, *V.,* when reporters started chasing him, intrigued by the wild and esoteric quality of his fictional universes and hoping to uncover a personal life at least as printworthy. He is legendary for refusing to make public appearances. For instance, after the 1973 publication of *Gravity's Rainbow* he declined the Howells Medal from the National Institute of Arts and Letters. He sent a comedian to pick up his National Book Award. Perhaps anticipating a similar public humiliation, the Pulitzer editorial board overturned the prize committee's decision to give him the award for fiction, calling the novel "obscene and unreadable" and "turgid and overwritten." The enigma of this elusive character still piques the public imagination, as evidenced by the mid-1990s media excitement over a Pynchon "sighting" on Manhattan's Upper West Side. The writer's anonymity is not altogether perplexing, however. Pynchon is clearly a very private person who needs freedom from surveillance to live and work. Because of the passion his novels have excited, he has been forced to choose between an invasive celebrity and complete refusal to let the public into any aspect of his personal life. Presumably for the same sorts of reasons, he has offered few explanations for what or why he writes. The introduction to his one collection of short stories, published in 1983, is the main source of his own opinions of his own work.

Pynchon called this collection *Slow Learner*. The self-deprecating title refers to the status of the stories as juvenilia—writing by the artist as a young man, in fact as an undergraduate—and to the assessment of this writing presented in his introduction: "My first reaction, rereading these stories, was *oh my God,* accompanied by physical symptoms we shouldn't dwell on." Both the humility and the tongue-in-cheek overstatement are characteristic of the reclusive writer. The stories reveal that he was not a slow learner but a remarkably quick study, although what he was studying to be was a novelist. They show Pynchon sketching out the historically, philosophically, and politically detailed fictional universes that would be fully realized only in the novels he went on to write.

Four of the five pieces in *Slow Learner*—"The Small Rain" (1959), "Low-Lands" (1960), "Entropy" (1960), and "Under the Rose" (1961)—were composed when Pynchon was an undergraduate at Cornell. (A fifth story not included in the collection, perhaps the earliest of the published fiction, was "Mortality and Mercy in Vienna," written for a creative writing class that rose spontaneously to its feet and applauded.) The last of the *Slow Learner* stories, "The Secret Integration," appeared in 1964, after the publication of the novel *V.* and in many respects after Pynchon had ceased altogether to be a learner and had become the most original and startling of a new generation of fiction writers. Along with "Under the Rose," "The Secret Integration" is

the most developed and assured of the stories, in part because in neither of these relatively late works was Pynchon writing about anyone who could be a Cornell student (the writing workshop dictum "write about what you know" seems to have led him initially to dwell on party scenes, fraternity pranks, and allusions to "The Waste Land") and in part because in both stories Pynchon allowed himself the space and imaginative scope to invent the kinds of intricate fictional universes that are hallmarks of his great novels.

"The Secret Integration" is about a group of children headed by a "boy genius with flaws" named Grover Snodd. It is not, however, a children's story. In an exaggerated rendering of 1960s youth culture, the children are an organized and often effective counterculture in the heart of what Pynchon's most celebrated novel, *Gravity's Rainbow,* would call a They-System—here constituted of racist white adults. In the process of planning a part-playful, part-serious "slave" revolt against grownups, the members of Grover's gang encounter the real viciousness of their own parents, who are secretly working to force out the only black couple in town. The child's-eye view allows Pynchon to present key terms of contemporary civil rights conflicts with a particular kind of innocence, a sort of brilliant literal-mindedness. The kids understand "integration" as a mathematical function with metaphorical possibilities for liberation, while for them "color" is not a binary of black and white but a potentially infinite spectrum of possibilities. What lies in wait to dispel this innocence is not experience but ignorance. The parents' misguided attempts to preserve their own and their children's security throw the children into a double bind, in which they are forced to collude with racism in order that each can return "to his own house, hot shower, dry towel, before-bed television, good night kiss, and dreams that could never again be entirely safe."

Much of the appeal of this story comes from its virtuoso world-making. In his introduction to *Slow Learner,* Pynchon discloses that the basis for the fictional universe came from a 1930s Federal Writers Project guidebook to the Berkshires region of western Massachusetts, onto which he superimposed details of his own Long Island childhood. Out of these beginnings Pynchon imagined a richly detailed and historicized underworld in which the children's secret activities take place. The center is an abandoned Gilded Age mansion, architecturally distinguished by fairy-tale "turrets, crenellations, flying buttresses" and full of "a pressure, an odor, that resisted intrusions, that kept them conscious of itself until they left again." The children themselves seem of a piece with this extravagant playground, where the idea of an alternative world is seamlessly integrated into the central theme of racial pluralism as a miraculously enlarged spectrum of experience. More than in any other story, in "The Secret Integration" plot and theme motivate the exuberance of description and character.

"Under the Rose" is an earlier exercise in world-making, arguably a breakthrough for the author, whose stories up to that point had been set in a contemporary world and whose characters seemed at only a few removes from undergraduate life. The Alexandria, Cairo, and Luxor settings came from an old Baedeker guide to Egypt, while the two protagonists, veteran spies with the hyperbolically British surnames of Porpentine and Goodfellow, arose from Pynchon's reading of thrillers. The labyrinthine plot introduces the idea of a major change in Western civilization, heralding the end of what Pynchon portrays as a quasi-gentlemanly, individual, willed model of statecraft, including espionage and warfare.

The idea of this sort of ominous change is at the heart of *V.* and returns in the encyclopedic and apocalyptic *Gravity's Rainbow*. In fact, a version of "Under the Rose" itself recurs in *V.*—heavily revised, with a different climax and told from eight sequential points of view. But the earlier story is coherent in its own terms and fascinating in its own right. In the older spy, Porpentine (Elizabethan English for "porcupine"), Pynchon managed to create a three-dimensional, sympathetic protagonist out of materials far from his own surroundings: not only the guidebook and the novels but also film and radio stereotypes of British speech and behavior, popular histories of late Victorian imperial conflicts and World War I, and a section on the Surrealists in what Pynchon identified as "one of those elective courses in Modern Art." The success of this story belies the frequent warnings in the introduction to *Slow Learner* about the danger of looking to "sources" rather than experience for things to write about. Apparently, Pynchon managed to produce his first thoroughly effective character by turning completely away from his immediate milieu and writing not about what he knew firsthand but about what he had just learned.

The earlier stories tend to be shorter

and more schematic. "Entropy," the most anthologized of all Pynchon's writings, can serve as an example. Like most of the stories, "Entropy" turns on an opposition between two characters embodying two principles, in which one side is clearly intended to elicit approval and sympathy. The two characters are the youthful Meatball Mulligan, who is hosting a lease-breaking party in his Washington apartment, and a middle-aged man named Callisto, who is dictating memoirs upstairs in an apartment sealed off from the outside world. The metaphor of entropy, elaborated as both a thermodynamic and cybernetic principle, sets up a narrative that switches back and forth from the Prufrockian Callisto in his hothouse to the gregarious Mulligan at his bacchanalia. The narrative strategy thus emphasizes a contrast between, on one hand, a closed system, ironically doomed to the chaos of heat death precisely because of its success at shutting out the surrounding decadent culture; and on the other hand, a system that remains open to incursions of energy (in the form of people) from the outside, and deals locally with the resulting enclaves of chaos. Open systems win over closed, and a number of critics have written on the values of caring, responsibility, work, democracy, and hospitality that seem entailed by this outcome, which could never have been in doubt.

Indeed, all the stories use a conventional model of plotting in which an initial opposition is intensified and complicated until the protagonists arrive at a climactic experience or disclosure. "Lardass" Levine in "The Small Rain" has a life-changing experience when he has an unpleasantly literal whiff of mortality. Dennis Flange

in "Low-Lands" resolves his marital problems by joining the alternate universe of a child-gypsy. Porpentine in "Under the Rose" is killed, foreshadowing the larger catastrophe of the Great War. And even "The Secret Integration" offers a pat revelation to bring its events to a close. Pynchon needed a form that could accommodate the proliferating scenes and themes of his extraordinary imagination. His contemporaries Donald Barthelme, Grace Paley, Robert Coover, and John Barth were inventing new structures for the short story. But by the time he wrote "The Secret Integration," Thomas Pynchon had already, in *V.,* recast narrative time and narrative voice in a novel. His apprentice work led him out of the short story form entirely and into the embeddings, diversions, multiple chronologies, and mutating voices of his experimental long narratives.

Molly Hite

SELECTED BIBLIOGRAPHY

Works by Thomas Pynchon

"Mortality and Mercy in Vienna." *Epoch* 9 (1959): 195–213.
"Introduction." In Richard Fariña, *Been Down So Long It Looks Like Up to Me.* New York: Penguin, 1983.
Slow Learner: Early Stories. New York: Little, Brown, 1984.

Critical Studies

Barnett, Stuart. "Refused Readings: Narrative and History in 'The Secret Integration.'" *Pynchon Notes* 22—23 (1988): 79—85.

Fariña, Richard. "The Monterey Festival." *A Long Time Coming and a Long Time Gone: Essays by Richard Fariña.* New York: Random House, 1963.

Keesey, Douglas. "The Politics of Doubling in 'Mortality and Mercy in Vienna.'" *Pynchon Notes* 24—25 (1989): 5—19.

Larsson, Donald F. "From the Berkshires to the Brocken: Transformations of a Source in 'The Secret Integration' and *Gravity's Rainbow.*" *Pynchon Notes* 22—23 (1988): 87—98.

Slade, Joseph. *Thomas Pynchon.* New York: Warner, 1974.

Tanner, Tony. *Thomas Pynchon.* London and New York: Methuen, 1982.

MARJORIE KINNAN
RAWLINGS
(1896—1953)

Marjorie Kinnan Rawlings was born in Washington, D.C., on August 8, 1896, and died in Jacksonville, Florida, on December 14, 1953. She married Charles Rawlings in 1919, divorced him in 1933, and married Norton Baskin in 1941. Rawlings's literary life can be divided into three periods: her student days, her newspaper days, and her Florida days. While a high school student, Rawlings wrote stories and poems for the *Washington Post* and *McCall's*; and, while a student at the University of Wisconsin, where she

was graduated with honors in English in 1918, she wrote stories, poems, and essays for university publications. After graduation Rawlings tried unsuccessfully to find a publisher for her work. While sending out manuscripts she worked for the YWCA in New York in 1919 and as a feature writer for the *Louisville Courier-Journal* in 1920—1921 and the *Rochester Evening Journal* and *Sun American* in 1922. She did some freelance work, most notably for the short-lived Rochester society magazine *Five O'Clock* in 1924. Her first recognized success as a writer came with her column "Songs of a House Wife" for the *Rochester Times-Union.* From 1926 to 1928 she wrote nearly five hundred poems, syndicated throughout the United States, in championship of the housewife. In 1928, she moved to Cross Creek, a hamlet in remote central Florida, where she operated an orange grove and composed her most famous stories and novels. A favorite of her famed editor Maxwell Perkins of Scribners, Rawlings was awarded the Pulitzer Prize for *The Yearling* in 1939. Her books include *South Moon Under* (1933), *Golden Apples* (1935), *The Yearling* (1938), *When the Whippoorwill—* (1940), *Cross Creek* (1942), *Cross Creek Cookery* (1942), and *The Sojourner* (1953). Her children's book, *The Secret River,* was published posthumously in 1955.

During her lifetime, Rawlings was well known for her short fiction, which appeared in the best magazines of the day, including *Scribner's Magazine, Saturday Evening Post, Harper's,* and *The New Yorker.* Though at the time of her death in 1953 she had slipped from public view, in the fifteen years between 1932 and 1947 she enjoyed wide popularity among both edu-

MARJORIE KINNAN RAWLINGS [481]

cated and popular readers. Her early fiction was about the exploits of her new-found friends, the Crackers (poor whites in whom she found dignity and honor), who lived near her at Cross Creek. Rawlings experienced firsthand how the Crackers lived. She stayed with them, ate with them, and above all prized their unique life of noble subsistence. In turn, they accepted her and shared with her not only their lives but also their folk traditions. The Crackers came alive in her stories. Her first publication, a series of vignettes of Cracker life entitled "Cracker Chidlings" (1931), brought her to the attention of Perkins, who was able to channel her efforts with forthright guidance and careful editing. In the early Florida years, Scribners made only one mistake with her; they turned down her short story, "Gal Young 'Un" (1932), immediately picked up by *Harper's* and awarded the O. Henry Memorial Prize for the Best Short Story of 1932.

During the 1930s, Rawlings literally overwhelmed *Scribner's Magazine* with her talent, beginning with her novella "Jacob's Ladder" (1931), which immediately convinced Perkins that he had a first-rate writer to nourish for the Scribners empire. Stories flowed from her Royal typewriter into the pages of *Scribner's Magazine*: "A Plumb Clare Conscience" (1931), a story about the unusual survival methods of a moonshiner whose frontier morality triumphs over civil law; "A Crop of Beans" (1932), about how female ingenuity saves male pride from the potential disaster of a bank closing; "Benny and the Bird Dogs" (1933), about an ingenious Cracker entrepreneur who sells his trained bird dogs to Yankees, knowing that the dogs will

come home at the earliest opportunity; "The Pardon" (1934), about a compassionate misfit who upon his release from prison for a crime he did not commit comes home to find that his wife has remarried; and "Varmints" (1936), about two ingenious Crackers who artfully dodge culpability for a dead mule named Snort.

Rawlings also published widely in the *Saturday Evening Post*. "Alligators" (1933) gives a quasi-fictive account of her experiences on alligator hunts; and "Cocks Must Crow" (1939) introduced the ubiquitous Qunicey Dover, Rawlings's semi-autobiographical narrator, who learns painfully that a man must be given the freedom, or at least the illusion of freedom, to pontificate. In "The Enemy" (1940), Rawlings explored a classic confrontation between a dominant Cracker and an interloper Yankee over the fencing of cattle. "The Friendship" (1949), titled ironically, describes a boy's betraying his friends.

Some of Rawlings's very best short stories appeared in *The New Yorker*. Here she turned from her Florida subject matter and delved into the innermost psychology of human nature. "Jessamine Springs" (1941) considers the rejection of an itinerant preacher's unwanted advances by a polished businessman. "The Shell" (1944) is a sadly ironic, humanly pathetic account of a mentally retarded woman who because of the unkindness of others seeks her soldier husband by walking into the ocean, only to find death. In "Black Secret" (1945), another O. Henry Prize-winning story, the subject of racism is addressed when a white boy learns that his uncle fathered a child by a black woman. Also published in 1945, "Miriam's Houses" portrays an impoverished prostitute who moves her family from house to house to hide her shame. Rawlings called these *New Yorker* psychological explorations her "queer stories."

"In the Heart," published in *Collier's* in 1940, alters the usual white/black racist theme by exploring the racial bias of a black family toward a black gardener, while "The Provider" (1941) examines the meaning of charity from the giver's point of view when a railroad man provides sustenance for a poverty-stricken family that lives along the tracks. "Miss Moffatt Steps Out" (1946) shows a poor old-maid schoolteacher broken in spirit by an insulting waiter who claims her last coins. Rawlings's posthumously published stories "Lord Bill of the Suwannee" and "Fish Fry and Fire Fireworks" respectively chronicle the exploits of a white John Henry and satirize a character's misplacing a rattlesnake on a political stage.

Perhaps the most famous and certainly the most reprinted story by Rawlings is "A Mother in Mannville" (1936). Set in the mountains of North Carolina, this story is about an orphan boy named Jerry, a Wordsworthian innocent, who teaches a visiting writer (clearly Rawlings) about the meaning of loyalty through his devotion to her and to her dog, Pat. Hemingway-like in its simplicity and force, the story hinges upon a surprising revelation at the end, an ironic twist that leaves the reader suspended between joy and sorrow. Jerry gives the impression that he has a loving mother who is alive and well in nearby Mannville. Hurt that she cannot be a mother to Jerry, the writer then learns too late that Jerry's revelation is a fiction

the boy created to hide his embarrassment at being an orphan. The child the writer wanted, the child whom she would have adopted, is now lost to her. So popular was this story of personal loss that Rawlings, succumbing to the demands of Hollywood, rewrote the story for the movie *The Sun Comes Up,* although the movie version has little in common with the story, and she later expanded it into a novella titled *Mountain Prelude.*

"Gal Young 'Un" (1932) is undoubtedly Rawlings's most sophisticated story, showing Rawlings at her best and her most feminist as she traces the saga of Mattie, a woman who has done well for herself, until the entrance of the contemptible Trax, a drifter whom Mattie befriends and loves. From the outset, the reader knows what the lonely Mattie is unwilling to see: Trax is an odious male who acquires and then dismisses women as objects of utility. Trax seizes Mattie's wealth, turns it into a profitable moonshine business, and then has Mattie operate the still while he philanders, finally bringing into Mattie's home Elly, his "gal young 'un." Elly is the archetypical innocent who looks like and acts like a wounded doe. Rawlings is merciless as she bores in on the shallow dependence displayed by these two women, both competing for the same man because of their need to be desired, or more important, because of their fear of being alone. Trax, the utilitarian, sleeps with Elly while Mattie cooks his meals. In the end, however, Mattie comes to her senses and dispatches Trax in a scene of violent confrontation in which she simultaneously asserts her womanhood and takes Trax's manhood. Mattie then takes into her home the forlorn Elly, who would have otherwise been left to suffer the consequences of her own youthful weakness.

Another widely acclaimed story, "Jacob's Ladder" (1931), which had convinced Maxwell Perkins to groom Rawlings as a Scribners writer, concerns a Cracker girl named Florry whose sensitivity is squelched by her abusive father. Indeed, Florry's sensitivity is barely evident until she sets out on an epic quest with her lover, Mart. Both endure the many hardships of learning and living, but it is Florry who emerges as the emblem of strength. On their odyssey, they confront hurricanes, hunger, and maltreatment. Florry survives in a landscape of male figures and finally triumphs in a male-oriented culture. Her triumph of will was suggested by Perkins, who thought that Rawlings's original characterization of her was too bleak. Rawlings relented and wrote a romantic ending, even though she knew that such a triumph for most women was unlikely. The prototypes for Florry and Mart were former tenants on Rawlings's grove property, and their life is further described in *Cross Creek* in the chapter "Antses in Tim's Breakfast." The real Florry and Mart lived with their newborn baby in appalling squalor, refusing, out of pride, any help, even from Rawlings.

Why Rawlings's reputation as a writer is at present in eclipse, especially after the prominence she enjoyed in the 1930s and 1940s, is difficult to determine. She was, after all, one of Scribners' most celebrated writers, in the words of Margaret Mitchell a "born perfect storyteller." Perhaps when descriptive fiction once again enjoys prominence, Rawlings's name will resurface as one of the masters of the art.

Rodger L. Tarr

SELECTED BIBLIOGRAPHY

Works by Marjorie Kinnan Rawlings

Short Stories. Edited by Rodger L. Tarr. Gainesville: University Press of Florida, 1994.

Critical Studies

Bellman, Samuel I. *Marjorie Kinnan Rawlings*. New York: Twayne, 1974.

Silverthorne, Elizabeth. *Marjorie Kinnan Rawlings: Sojourner at Cross Creek*. Woodstock, N.Y.: Overlook Press, 1988.

Tarr, Rodger L. *Marjorie Kinnan Rawlings: A Descriptive Bibliography*. Pittsburgh: University of Pittsburgh Press, 1996.

Tarr, Rodger L. *Max and Marjorie: The Correspondence Between Maxwell E. Perkins and Marjorie Kinnan Rawlings*. Gainesville: University Press of Florida, 1999.

ALBERTO ALVARO RÍOS
(1952–   )

Alberto Alvaro Ríos was born in the border town of Nogales, Arizona, in 1952 to a Mexican father, Alvaro Alberto Ríos, and an English mother, Agnes Fogg. He grew up speaking Spanish and English. "As kids in school," he recalls, "you got swatted for speaking Spanish, so one of the first equations you formed was that Spanish must be bad." By the end of elementary school, the young Ríos was no longer willing to speak Spanish. Yet growing up bilingual created in him "a fusion of sensibilities and perspectives," says Ríos, along with the juxtaposition of two worlds that has become the basis for his work.

Ríos received a bachelor's degree in English and a master of fine arts degree in creative writing from the University of Arizona in 1974 and 1979. In 1980 he was awarded a poetry fellowship by the National Endowment for the Arts, and in 1984 his first short-story collection, *The Iguana Killer,* received the Western States Book Award for Fiction. He served from 1978 to 1983 as the Pinal County writer-in-residence, a position he developed with Arizona's Commission on the Arts to promote the craft and realm of writing. Ríos has remained an active proponent of writing on national and local levels. He is currently a regents' professor of English at Arizona State University, where he teaches literature and creative writing. He lives in Chandler, Arizona, with his wife, María Guadalupe, and a son, Joaquin.

Alberto Ríos's work is a study in the dynamic of life lived between two countries, Mexico and the United States. "They are stories from a time-between-times about people who inhabit what is a place-between-places, physically, emotionally and historically," he writes in his author's note to his third collection of stories, *The Curtain of Trees* (1999). Growing up on the border, one is neither one thing nor the other; the pull of each country on its neighbor creates a mini-universe, often bemusing, that cannot be seen as anything but itself.

The stories in *The Iguana Killer* are written more conventionally than those in Ríos's second and third collections. His characters are mainly children who live in the dual-culture province of the "borderland," and his themes are typically those of coming of age. Yet the clash of two cultures creates snapshots that are anything but typical, and Ríos, ever the observer, describes these with humor. The story of the iguana killer is that of eight-year-old Sapito, who opens a package from his grandmother in the United States and finds a baseball and a baseball bat. Knowing what a ball is, he smiles. But the bat puzzles him. Then the light dawns. It is an iguana killer, beautiful and perfect: "His grandmother always knew what he would like."

"The Child" is the most plot-driven of *The Iguana Killer*'s dozen stories. Mrs. Sandoval and Mrs. García are riding a bus from Guaymas to Nogales on their way to a funeral. "The two ladies shared a single face, held together by an invisible net, made evident by the marks it left on their skins. They wore black, more out of habit than out of mourning for their husbands, both of whom had been dead for more than ten years. Ten or eleven, it was difficult to say. Time was different now." The narrator's voice is the timeless voice of both Mrs. Sandoval and Mrs. García, who, knowing each other so well, have become the same person. "They complained to each other now . . . only with large sighs. No words. . . . The man across the aisle began to smoke. Mrs. García sighed, and Mrs. Sandoval understood." The smoker is accompanied by a sleeping boy. The curious Mrs. García learns from the man that the boy is sick; they are going to see a specialist in Nogales. When the bus makes a stop in Hermosillo, Mrs. García thoughtfully decides to bring the boy a glass of water from the restaurant.

What follows when she and Mrs. Sandoval draw back his blanket is a rude surprise. "'¡Dios mío! Jesus? Help, ah, this child is dead, he is dead!' screamed Mrs. Sandoval in much the same voice as Mrs. García had screamed." Detained by the police in Hermosillo to give the facts of her discovery, Mrs. García learns some even ruder facts about the dead boy, whose guardian by this time has disappeared. He has been "operated on," his insides replaced with bags of opium. "'Oh my God, Dios mío, Dios mío,'" is all Mrs. Sandoval can say when Mrs. García arrives in Nogales with this news. "Their heads moved from side to side, but not fast enough," is our last glimpse of the two women, shocked beyond speech by what modern times have shown them.

Growing up with his Spanish half in a self-imposed silence has made relating in and around language a theme of Ríos's work. Mrs. Sandoval and Mrs. García are past the need for language, in the same way that the young Ríos was when he ate at his grandmother's table: "She spoke only Spanish and I thought I spoke only English," he explains. "So we invented for ourselves a third language, one we both could understand and share. My grandmother would cook and I would eat. She gave me the realm of the senses—food, smells, tastes." And thus it is without speech that the grandmotherlike characters of Mrs. Sandoval and Mrs. García relate, both before and after their tragic discovery, for the world of emotion is far bigger and deeper than the limited world of language.

In Pig Cookies (1995) the stories rotate the reader, mindless of real time, through the past, present, and future (in the form of hopes and dreams) of a colorful Mexican town, peopled by the circus strongman Don Noé, who loses first his hand and then his life to the elephant Saturnino, and who at an earlier time in the story of this town was the local butcher with a penchant for clocks, and before that a young boy spying on a girl; Lázaro Luna, who as a young baker stirring cochito (pig-cookie) batter is afraid to approach the girl of his desire, but whose sex organ later in life becomes legendary; and the Chinese Mr. Lee, who finds space to live, for years, "between the bedsheets and in the bathroom" when the soldiers arrive to deport him. The style of Pig Cookies is known as magical realism, a term applied to Ríos's work and a subject he now teaches, for which there exists, he says, a multitude of definitions. "I hand my students three pages of definitions, but I think of magical realism as a kind of layering, and the sense of perspective and fusion—finding a border between poetry and prose."

Time works on a different principle in Ríos's second and third story collections. "It's much more slowed down," he says. "I think of these as books of very long poems, in that the movement, rather than being linear, from beginning to end, is lateral. It moves side to side." Pig Cookies shows us the lyric capacity of prose, with sentences that speak through rhythm and mood much more than the meaning of their words. Language in this collection is spare and lilting, riding on metaphor and making links beyond the reach of conventional prose.

The curandero (healer) in "Susto" ("The

Scare") has the young Mariquita standing beneath the night sky awaiting the light of the moon. "The moon appeared to her as if it were one more piece of cotton from the field. It looked as if it would . . . take in from her what was wrong, in the way that one dabs something from the skin. This was the simplest cure of things, just to wipe them away. Hers, she thought, was such a small event . . . but in need, the *curandero* said, of the entire moon for its cure. *The small things,* he said, *this is how they are.*" Characters in this story collection seem to move and breathe as similar parts of a whole, that whole suggesting Ríos himself, who omnisciently and lovingly skates through and upon the ice of their lives, in and out of their fears and their reflections. Irony, tragedy, and bliss all take on the hue of inevitability, which is born of the ebb and flow, the rhythm, of the everyday.

Ríos's third collection, *The Curtain of Trees* (1999), consists of what he terms stories of the moment. Again, time is transformed. "These stories look at the moment at least two minutes longer than what I would characterize as normal," he explains. In this volume, Ríos marries the informal presence of his early prose with the fecund metaphors of his second series, resulting in a voice that is both openly familiar and, because of its frankness, eerily prophetic. "Nine Quarter-Moons" personifies the wind, like a visiting cousin, as a bearer of change, news, and emergency. Drollness remains the author's trademark: "Inside itself the wind was full of newspapers and book leaves. People here enjoyed learning about family in distant towns and about what the government was

up to—up to yet again." Metaphor remains his signature: Once the wind has stopped, the dust that was part of the wind falls gently to the ground, covering the townspeople "in a clean, dry snow, a flour comprised of everything around them that had been ground by the wind into dust and lifted up. It was a flour of their lives, tinged a little with blue, and it made them look like they had gray hair and old milk on their upper lips."

The Curtain of Trees frames complex interrelationships (such as a boy's love for his father in "What I Heard from the Bear") with ephemeral moments (hearing the town crier announcing his father's funeral). The prose is devoid of a traditional beginning, middle, and end; it forms a network of impressions, connections, and images. The reader is taken to a "borderland" of fiction itself, where prose takes on the effect of poetry; point of view is dreamlike, quirky, indistinct; and story is secondary to language. "There is no real story, of course," writes Ríos as he opens "Salt Crosses in Doorways." "There never is. Everybody has a different story, so instead of a rose it's always a bouquet. This doesn't seem so bad unless you're a reporter or something and need to write the real story. You're in trouble then. You're not a reporter, are you?" With this question, Alberto Ríos challenges his reader to leave the convention of who/what/when/where/why and venture into a place where prose is set free to perform a panoply of bold and unexpected tricks, pushing the meaning of "story" into a new, different, and experimental dimension.

Sofia Shafquat

SELECTED BIBLIOGRAPHY

Works by Alberto Alvaro Ríos

The Iguana Killer: Twelve Stories of the Heart. Tucson, Ariz., and Lewiston, Idaho: Blue Moon and Confluence Press, 1984.
Pig Cookies and Other Stories. San Francisco: Chronicle Books, 1995.
The Curtain of Trees. Albuquerque: University of New Mexico Press, 1999.

Critical Studies

Shafquat, Sofia. Interviews with Alberto Ríos, 1999.
Wild, Peter. *Alberto Ríos.* Boise, Idaho: Boise State University, 1998.

PHILIP ROTH
(1933–)

Probably the most popular and influential of the Jewish American authors, and certainly the funniest, Philip Roth has (to date) published twenty-four novels, short story collections, and books of essays, plus numerous other occasional pieces of writing. Since his earliest fiction, Roth has been the ethnic construct Jewish American, which he tends to view with jaunty humor and cutting satire. Born in Newark, New Jersey, in 1933, to a family well aware of itself as Jewish but largely nonobservant in terms of religious practice, Roth received little formal education in Judaism or Jewish history. Like many Jewish Americans of his generation who were the children of immigrants or of first-generation Americans, he followed a typical path of assimilation into American life: He went to college, taking a bachelor of arts degree in English literature at Bucknell University in 1954 and a masters degree from University of Chicago in 1955. After serving in the army, he embarked on a career of teaching (primarily at University of Pennsylvania) and writing, winning many prestigious awards during the course of his career, including the National Book Award in 1960 and the National Book Critics Circle Award in 1987 and 1992. Roth's first wife, who died in an automobile accident and who served as a the prototype of the wife in the troubled marriages of several of his fictional protagonists, was Margaret Martinson. His second wife was the actress Claire Bloom.

In many ways, Roth resembles just those assimilated Jews who populate his fiction, in particular Nathan Zuckerman, who is the major protagonist in six of Roth's books: *The Ghost Writer* (1979), *Zuckerman Unbound* (1981), *The Anatomy Lesson* (1981), *The Counterlife* (1987), *The Facts: A Novelist's Autobiography* (1988), and, most recently, *American Pastoral* (1997). Much of the drama of the Zuckerman novels concerns, in transmuted and fictionalized form, the struggles that ensued between Roth and a vocal portion of this Jewish readership, including prominent Jewish rabbis and intellectuals, who felt that his satiric portraits of Jewish American life, in particular *Goodbye, Columbus* (1959) and *Portnoy's Complaint* (1969), constituted unseemly assaults against the Jewish American community. Roth himself recorded the controversy, much of which was conducted in the pages of *Commentary* magazine, and responded to it in a set of critical essays collected in *Reading Myself and Others* (1975).

Roth's first and only volume of short works, *Goodbye, Columbus and Five Short Stories,* was greeted with tremendous acclaim. In addition to the novella of the title, the collection contains Roth's major contribution to the field of short fiction: "The Conversion of the Jews," "Epstein," "You Can't Tell a Man by the Song He Sings," and the widely anthologized short stories "Eli, the Fanatic" and "Defender of the Faith." "Defender of the Faith" is a classic example of Roth's subject and manner of exposition. It also exhibits the aspects of Roth's fiction that provoked, simultaneously, great admiration and severe condemnation of his work. In the story, Nathan Marx, an American army sergeant, is rotated back from the European theater at the end of the fighting to an army base in the States. There he confronts three Jewish soldiers who appeal to his Jewishness, as one Jew to another, in order to secure for themselves certain rights, such as Friday night worship, but also privileges beyond what might be considered fair or appropriate. Even the plea for Friday night services turns out to be an excuse for the three to get out of cleaning their bunks. The major spokesperson for the three is the aggressive and self-serving Sheldon Grossbart, a stereotype of the Jewish wheeler-dealer. In an uproariously funny scene, reminiscent of the Marx Brothers in its irreverence and chaos, Grossbart pleads with Marx to grant the three soldiers leave for the Jewish holiday

of Passover, even though the holiday has already passed. Grossbart's aunt, Marx is told, has promised to make them a belated seder. To show their gratitude, the soldiers bring Marx a present of nonkosher egg rolls from the Chinese restaurant where they dine instead—the seder feast never having taken place. Grossbart finally manages to rearrange the soldiers' posting to the Pacific front so that he is not included among those shipped abroad. In the interests of serving his American as well as his Jewish identity, Marx intercepts the orders and changes them, so that, in the end, the three Jewish soldiers do find themselves on the way to active service. Though many readers, especially Jewish readers, chose to focus upon the critique of Jewish behavior implicit in the portrait of Grossbart, the hero of the story is Marx, whose behavior both explores and finally resolves the Jewish Americans' dual loyalties.

The other stories in the volume dwell less on the Jews' divided loyalties, a theme that returns in the Zuckerman novels, than on the loss of cultural richness and personal integrity that may have accompanied the assimilation of Jews into American life. "Goodbye, Columbus" sets a shallow, materialistic, upwardly mobile Jewish family against an equally assimilated but more sincere Jewish character, whose lower-class status makes him the object of the family's snobbishness. In the background of the story is an African American child, whom the protagonist Neil Klugman befriends, and who comes to represent a cultural authenticity that suburban Jewry may have forfeited in its ascent to the American middle class.

"Goodbye, Columbus" is a comic satire

of middle-class Jewish American life. Nonetheless, like "Defender of the Faith," it preserves behind the humor the serious question that Jewish assimilation raises: does assimilation signal the end of Jewish identity as such, or is the Jewish American, as embodied by Nathan Marx or Neil Klugman, the beginning of a new form of Jewish identity characterized by a secularizing Americanization of Judaism's commitment to ethics and communal activism? In raising the question, Roth might be said to shift the definition of Jews in America from that of the American Jew— the Jew who happens to live in America as opposed to some other country, including Israel—toward that of the Jewish American as an ethnic American, like Italian Americans or African Americans.

Whatever the balance between the Jewish and the American elements of their identities, Roth understood that sustaining dual identity was no simple matter. The anxiety of suburban Jews concerning their place in a dominantly non-Jewish world emerges as the focus of "Eli, the Fanatic." In this story, a Jewish community opposes the establishment in its midst of a yeshiva populated by religious European refugees because it will upset the precarious harmony between Jews and non-Jews in the neighborhood. That the refugees are both religious and immigrants seems to the residents of Woodenton to make these Jews too Jewish. What, then, makes the Jewish American Jewish at all? This question is raised also in "The Conversion of the Jews," which features some of the same forces of Jewish defensiveness against the imagined threat of the non-Jewish world, and the hypocrisy and paranoia it produces, particularly in "On the Air," a full-blown parody of the paranoid Jew. The story "Epstein" is less a story about Jews than a psychological exploration of human relationships in which the major figure happens to be Jewish. It elicited negative critiques from members of the Jewish community because, even here, where the issue of the story was not Jewish identity per se, it seemed to them that Roth chose to present Jews in the least favorable light. A less defensive reading of the story might interpret it as demonstrating that Jewish experience contains the general range of human emotions and behaviors, and that to write about Jews might be, finally, to write about humanity in general.

Philip Roth's achievement as a writer has been to help place the ethnic American at the center of the national literary tradition by depicting both the general American characterization of the ethnic experience and the unique tensions experienced by the non-WASP population. A gifted artist, Philip Roth is also a powerful commentator on contemporary American culture.

Emily Miller Budick

SELECTED BIBLIOGRAPHY

Works by Philip Roth

Goodbye, Columbus and Five Short Stories. London: Penguin, 1964.

"On the Air." *New American Review* 10 (1970): 7–49.

Reading Myself and Others. New York: Farrar, Straus & Giroux, 1975.

A Philip Roth Reader. New York: Farrar, Straus & Giroux, 1980.

Critical Studies

Milbauer, Asher Z., and Donald Watson, eds. *Reading Philip Roth.* New York: St. Martin's Press, 1988.

Pinsker, Sanford, ed. *Critical Essays on Philip Roth.* Boston: G. K. Hall, 1982.

DAMON RUNYON
(1880 – 1946)

Alfred Damon Runyan, later known as Damon Runyon, was born on October 8, 1880, in Manhattan, Kansas, where his father was editor of the *Manhattan Enterprise.* In 1887 the family moved to Pueblo, Colorado; as a teenager Runyon published his first two stories in one local newspaper (temporarily edited by his father) and in 1895 began his career as a reporter with another, the *Pueblo Evening Press.* During the Spanish-American War he enlisted and served in the Philippines (though his subsequent accounts embroidered several aspects of his record). After the war he reported on topics from crime to sports for several newspapers, including the *Rocky Mountain News* and *San Francisco Post.* Eventually he moved to New York, and in 1911 was a sports reporter for William Randolph Hearst's *New York American.* In the same year he married Ellen Egan, who had been society editor for the *Rocky Mountain News,* and he published a book of verses. Throughout his life Runyon continued to write features and columns for Hearst publications, but by 1929

he had embarked on the series of stories that would bring him his greatest recognition. After the death of his first wife, Runyon remarried in 1932, but was divorced in 1946. In 1944 his larynx was removed after a diagnosis of throat cancer; he died of cancer two years later.

The first of Runyon's Broadway stories, "Romance in the Roaring Forties" (that is, the forty-numbered cross-streets of Manhattan) was published in *Cosmopolitan Magazine.* The Broadway stories, written over the next fourteen years, were initially collected in *Guys and Dolls* (1931), *Blue Plate Special* (1934), *Money from Home* (1935), *Take It Easy* (1938) and *Runyon à la Carte* (1944); other collections mixed the stories in various combinations, and gathered his early sketches or newspaper columns. *My Wife Ethel* (1940), which comprised primarily populist editorials, had a minimally fictional frame as Joe Turp, an ordinary guy from Brooklyn, narrates incidents of his daily life and the conversations with his wife to which they lead.

According to Patricia Ward D'Itri, sixteen of Runyon's stories (and one play) were adapted for Hollywood films, including *Lady for a Day* (from "Madame La Gimp") and *Little Miss Marker* (starring Shirley Temple, the most famous child star of the day). Runyon himself did a brief stint as a Hollywood producer for *The Big Street,* based on "Little Pinks." Frank Loesser's musical *Guys and Dolls,* with a book by Jo Swerling and Abe Burrows, opened in 1950, appropriately enough, on Broadway, and may have done most to give Runyon's characters a continuing presence in popular culture. It borrows elements of plot from at least two of Runyon's stories, "The Idyll of Miss Sarah Brown" and "Pick the Winner," and draws widely on his writings for atmosphere and dramatis personae; more importantly, it accurately captures the flavor of Runyon's dialogue and foregrounds the loony, gangster-in-love romanticism that propels many of his plots.

While much has been written about Runyon's trajectory from one Manhattan to another, the importance of Manhattan, Kansas, was that, like the Colorado towns that influenced Runyon, it was part of the West. Runyon's fiction owes as much to Bret Harte and other lesser-known Western writers as to later, more urban influences. Among his earliest stories are the "sketches" eventually collected in *Runyon First and Last*. The section entitled "My Old Home Town" includes regionally inflected narratives like "The Wooing of Nosey Gillespie" and "The Strange Story of Tough-Guy Sammy Smith," which rely on the same kind of hearsay and anecdote that supplies the groundwork of all Runyon's plots. The outlaws in these early stories, dangerous but somehow ingenuous, clearly anticipate the gangland types of his Broadway stock company. (Such complementary images of America's violent innocence, on the frontier and in the eastern metropolis, may account for the enduring popularity of Runyon's stories in England.) Runyon's passage eastward seems echoed in the biography of The Sky in "The Idyll of Miss Sarah Brown": "His right name is Obadiah Masterson, and he is originally out of a little town in southern Colorado, where he learns to shoot craps, and play cards . . . and where his old man is a very well-known citizen and something of a sport himself." Along with prudent advice about

betting on sure things, the father tells The Sky that "going out into the wide, wide world" is a good thing "as there are no more opportunities for you in this burg."

What these early stories lack is the distinctive idiom that Runyon developed— "the patented Runyon brand of Times Square Swahili," as James Agee called it, "in which a worn-out race horse is 'practically mucilage,' and marriage is described as 'one room, two chins, three kids.'" The early stories also lack the vividly confidential voice of the first-person narrator whom Runyon created for his Manhattan melodramas. What this small-time grifter "does for a livelihood" (as he says about Nicely-Nicely Jones in "Lonely Heart") "is the best he can, which is an occupation that is greatly overcrowded at all times along Broadway." Mostly he gambles and drifts from New York to Baltimore to Miami, in the wake of losing racehorses and of more daring, if not necessarily more successful, entrepreneurs. He also appears to have the reporter's gift for being at the right place for either a bird's-eye view of the action or at least a first-hand account of some juicy incident, and he eagerly passes his insider's knowledge on to us. In "Dream Street Rose" he alone has heard the story that might unveil a respectable businessman's apparent suicide as homicide, the final act in a tragedy of abandonment that begins in Pueblo, Colorado; and in "The Bloodhounds of Broadway" he knows whom the bloodhounds Nip and Tuck— an improbable pair of imports from Georgia to Manhattan—were actually tracking in Miss Missouri Martin's nightclub and why. The last sentence of "Romance in the Roaring Forties" casually gives the key to its dénouement, the narrator's role as backstage Cupid: the softhearted mobster Dave the Dude has gallantly relinquished his claims to Miss Billy Perry and plans to subsidize her union with the impoverished newspaperman Waldo Winchester, but a well-timed telephone call from the narrator averts a bigamous marriage by summoning Lola Sapola to reclaim her errant husband, Winchester. After a chance meeting with "Mr. and Mrs. Dave the Dude" the narrator characteristically questions the happy ending he has enabled: "maybe I do not do Dave any too much of a favor, at that." The narrator's frequently belated revelations give the stories' endings a twist that underlines Runyon's indebtedness to O. Henry.

Whether the events are current or remembered, Runyon's Broadway narrator relays them in a perpetual storytelling present tense and a looping syntax that characteristically doubles back on itself. The opening of "Blood Pressure" catches his characteristic rhythms: "It is maybe eleven-thirty of a Wednesday night, and I am standing at the corner of Forty-eighth Street and Seventh Avenue, thinking about my blood pressure, which is a proposition I never before think much about." Runyon repudiated H. L. Mencken's description (in the first edition of *The American Language*) of him as a linguistic innovator, and asserted that he reported what he heard. Like Ring Lardner, Runyon is able to distill the rhythms and inventiveness of American speech and transplant the racy immediacy of journalistic writing into fiction.

The "citizens" who populate Runyon's tales are gamblers, bootleggers, thieves, mobsters, racetrack touts, "scribes" (newspapermen), and policemen—not to mention their respective "dolls." Despite occasional acts of homicide to protect their territorial prerogatives, the racketeers and petty criminals are on the whole loyal, upstanding fellows who discharge their obligations, even if honoring a gambling marker entails further felonies. Historically, the demise of Prohibition may have left many of Runyon's readers with a lingering good will toward extralegal activity. In "The Brakeman's Daughter," the narrator speaks sympathetically of "all the hardships and dangers that these [bootlegging] brewers face through the years to give the American people their beer"—Runyon's irony here seems mild. Moreover, these shady characters are conspicuously softhearted toward children, animals, and the down-and-out, and gallant toward vulnerable young "dolls," like the eloping teenager in "Hold 'em Yale" or the seduced and abandoned "Lily of St. Pierre." The redemptive qualities of a golden-haired child in "Little Miss Marker," for example, signal it as a variation on *Silas Marner* by way of Bret Harte. While the dotingly naive male characters are frequently suckered by their sweethearts and wives, who in the casually misogynistic view of Runyon's narrator are generally gold-diggers and more trouble than they are worth, their sentimental streak can be rewarded as well as exploited. In "The Brain Goes Home," "the biggest guy in gambling operations in the East" is stabbed at the behest of a disgruntled debtor. Having been turned away successively by the wife and three mistresses he has supported in high style, he is readily taken in by a "red-haired raggedy" apple seller, because his five-dollar tip has allowed her to buy medicine for her sick child. One major strain of the stories' humor derives from placing thugs in incongruously domestic circumstances. In "Butch Minds the Baby," a one-time safecracker is cowed by the thought of his wife's wrath if he leaves the baby for a moment but, cajoled out of retirement by such pals as Harry the Horse and Little Isadore, he discovers that babysitting is the perfect cover for a heist and even receives some helpful advice about teething from a police sergeant who pauses in his misdirected pursuit of the burglars. The narrator's inside information often supplies an ironic fillip to the story's finish, as when the narrator reveals that the mission worker Miss Sarah Brown "wins" the soul of The Sky with loaded dice — as The Sky well knows but Miss Sarah does not.

The mixture of cynicism and pathos or domestic comedy in these examples may suggest the qualities that allowed Runyon to achieve mainstream success and publish many of his stories in such periodicals as *Collier's* and the *Saturday Evening Post*. The romantic feelings and middle-class moralities that make his characters dupes or at least professionally inept criminals seem potential objects of satire, but Runyon's satirical impulse is muted. His transgressors may be saps, but by the same token they endearingly share the values of his more law-abiding readers. In "The Snatching of Bookie Bob," the prospective kidnappers are fastidious about their victims, "it being wicked to snatch dolls and little children . . . no guys who are on the snatch nowadays will ever think of such a thing." However, practical considerations — children are a nuisance — sometimes mingle with morality. Harry the Horse, Spanish

John, and Little Isadore play their gambling debts with such unflinching rectitude that they lose far more than they gain when they eventually kidnap a bookie. Like the criminal milieu of *The Beggar's Opera,* John Gay's "Newgate pastoral," Runyon's seedy underworld mirrors respectable society, but in a confirmatory rather than a subversive mode. His dialogue offers the pleasure of the wisecracking exchanges in *film noir* without the brooding vision of a world gone wrong.

Runyon's narrator, on the other hand, is often more resistant to sentiment than are the characters whose fortunes he records. Of Butch's baby he comments: "I judge the baby on this stoop comes of this marriage between Big Butch and Mary [Murphy] because I can see that it is a very homely baby, indeed. Still, I never see many babies that I consider rose geraniums for looks, anyway." Moreover, he seems bemused by his fellow citizens' enthusiasm for the opposite sex. While "scribes" such as his creator may fall for happy endings, he is the resolute enemy of illusion. "Lillian," the cat — and romantic surrogate — of a decayed vaudevillian, leads her owner into a burning hotel to rescue a trapped toddler. Though both become heroes, the narrator makes sure we know that Lillian, a souse like her master, has reentered the hotel in search of spilt Scotch rather than her three-year-old playmate, and unlike her master she is too confirmed an alcoholic to make her moment of glory a new beginning.

The reader may wonder whether the toughness of Damon Runyon's alter ego is more than a mask, whether the narrator's canniness and mockery of the sentimental allow him to traffic all the more shamelessly in the heartwarming anecdote. On the other hand, the indeterminacies of the narrator's attitude also engage us immediately in the activity of storytelling, as though he were still sorting things out as he confides in us. The details of plot and character in the Broadway stories fade quickly from a reader's memory; their vernacular energy—the inventive, improbable names and turns of phrase—linger far longer. So does the sense of an insider's access to an underworld that is finally more gaudy than threatening. Violence is vivid but intermittent; most of the time, the improvised moralities of this demimonde, the petty profits of its grifters, and the lavish expenditures of its more ambitious criminals are reassuringly familiar—if not as American as apple pie, at least as New York cheesecake.

Barry Weller

SELECTED BIBLIOGRAPHY

Works by Damon Runyon

Guys and Dolls. New York: Frederick A. Stokes, 1931.

Money from Home. New York: Frederick A. Stokes, 1935.

The Best of Damon Runyon. New York: Frederick A. Stokes, 1938.

Blue Plate Special. New York: Frederick A. Stokes, 1938.

Take It Easy. New York: Frederick A. Stokes, 1938.

More Guys and Dolls. Garden City: Sun Dial Press, 1939.

The Damon Runyon Omnibus. Garden City: Sun Dial Press, 1944.

Runyon à la Carte. Philadelphia: J. B. Lippincott, 1944.

Runyon First and Last. Philadelphia: J. B. Lippincott, 1949.

Critical Studies

Agee, James. Review of *The Big Street. Agee on Film* vol. 1, pp. 338–340. New York: Grosset & Dunlap, 1958.

D'Itri, Patricia Ward. *Damon Runyon.* Boston: Twayne, 1982.

J. D. SALINGER
(1919–   )

Given the singularity of his subject matter and the odd shape of his career, J. D. Salinger's fiction both benefits and suffers from a frozen-in-time quality. The stories on which his reputation is based were published over roughly eleven years, and they do not fall into early, middle, or late periods in which a style or worldview develops. Rather, they are products of the sensibility of the late 1940s and early 1950s, one that reflects the postwar concerns of anxious young people growing up in a world without clear guiding values. Most of the stories focus on the lives of a mere half-dozen members of the eccentric Glass family, and particularly on the mysterious suicide of Seymour, the revered oldest son. It is thirty-five years since Salinger published his last story, so the boundaries of his fiction remain clear and almost claustrophobic.

Jerome David Salinger was born in New York City on January 1, 1919, to a Jewish father, Sol, and an Irish Catholic mother, Miriam. He had one sister, Doris, and the prosperous family lived for most of his childhood on the Upper East Side of Manhattan. He attended McBurney School and then transferred to Valley Forge Military Academy in Pennsylvania. After graduating in 1936, he studied briefly at both New York University and Ursinus College, but did not earn a degree from either. Deciding to become a writer, he enrolled in a writing workshop taught by Whit Burnett at Columbia University, and his first short story, "The Young Folks," was published in Burnett's magazine *Story* in 1940. From 1940 to 1946 Salinger published roughly twenty short stories in "slicks" like *Saturday Evening Post* and *Collier's*.

Drafted into the army in 1942, he landed at Utah Beach as part of the D-Day invasion, and in July 1945 was hospitalized in Nuremberg and nearly given a psychiatric discharge. In September of that same year he married—for a short time—a French girl named Sylvia, about whom little is known.

By 1948, Salinger had a small reputation as a short story writer. His fame escalated with the appearance in 1951 of *Catcher in the Rye*. Its selection by the Book-of-the-Month Club made it newsworthy, and at least two hundred reviews appeared in the months following its publication. There is little in even the early positive reviews to indicate that the novel would have great staying power, but by

1955 it had gained a devoted readership and caught the notice of academics. By 1968 it ranked as one of America's twenty-five leading best-sellers of the century, and it continues to sell a quarter of a million copies a year worldwide. In 1953, *Nine Stories* received an unusual degree of attention, partly because *Catcher in the Rye* had come out in paperback the month before. Eudora Welty gave the collection a glowing review in the *New York Times,* and it remained on the *Times* best-seller list for three months.

In 1955, Salinger married Claire Douglas. A daughter, Margaret Ann, was born in 1955, a son, Matthew, in 1960. The couple divorced in 1967.

Between 1955 and 1959, Salinger published four long stories in *The New Yorker* that solidified his reputation. "Franny" and "Zooey" appeared in book form in 1961. "Raise High the Roof Beam, Carpenters" and "Seymour: An Introduction" were published in one volume in 1963. One more story, "Hapworth 16, 1924," followed in 1965. Since then, Salinger has published no fiction and lives as a recluse in Cornish, New Hampshire. In a 1974 telephone conversation with a reporter from the *New York Times,* Salinger said he was still writing busily, though not for publication: "There is a marvelous peace in not publishing. I love to write. But I write for myself and my own pleasure."

That same year, he denounced and successfully suppressed an unauthorized *Complete Uncollected Short Stories of J. D. Salinger,* and in 1986 he blocked the inclusion of personal material in Ian Hamilton's unauthorized biography. Salinger stunned involved parties by giving the required legal deposition in New York. Whatever hopes his starved reading public may have had for the contents of that deposition were unfulfilled, at least in the excerpt Hamilton reprinted. Salinger seems a somewhat sad, frustrating, polite man who feels put upon by questions, his biography, and the world, which he has been trying to escape for decades. In short, he seems like one of his own characters.

For American young people of the 1950s, Salinger was what Hemingway and Fitzgerald had been to those of the 1920s: millions of young Americans felt closer to him than to any other writer. At the core of this intimacy was their unshakeable sense that Salinger was speaking directly to them. As his biography makes clear, Salinger shares with his fiction a fixed-in-time quality. For this reason, readers tend to imagine a Salinger who went to his characters' private schools, who lived in their Upper East Side apartments, who struggled with the same phonies. In any list of traits that define his characters, a revulsion toward the world in which they find themselves would be near the top. His protagonists are continually sickened by the materialism and inhumanity surrounding them, and what they do, and what Salinger does through them, is endlessly search for moral and religious enlightenment and the possibility of love.

"A Perfect Day for Bananafish" is a useful starting point for understanding this search. It was the first major work that *The New Yorker* accepted; it is the opening piece in *Nine Stories*; it introduces the Glass family; and it is one of his best-known stories. "A Perfect Day for Bananafish" takes place in a Florida resort where Muriel and Seymour Glass are vacationing.

The first half concerns Muriel and her phone conversation with her mother. They chat about various things—Muriel's sunburn, a dress from Bonwit's, the hotel room—but mostly about Seymour, who has had some kind of unspecified breakdown. According to Muriel's mother, there is "a very *great* chance . . . that Seymour may comp*letely* lose control of himself. My word of honor."

Greater understanding of what actually ails Seymour is left incomplete, but after several pages of Muriel and her mother, the reasons why Seymour might choose to spend all day on the beach become clearer. Salinger offers no word of overt judgment; he describes, as in the story's opening paragraph as Muriel waits for her phone call to go through: "She used the time, though. She read an article in a women's pocket-size magazine, called 'Sex Is Fun—or Hell.' She washed her comb and brush. She took the spot out of the skirt of her beige suit. She moved the button on her Saks blouse. She tweezed out two freshly surfaced hairs in her mole. When the operator finally rang her room, she was sitting on the window seat and had almost finished putting lacquer on the nails of her left hand."

In the phrase, "She used the time, though," it is the "though" that stands out. By the paragraph's end that word is impossible to read as anything but ironically judgmental. And the repetitive simplicity of the syntax emphasizes the banality and emptiness of Muriel's activity. The repetition of "She" opening most of the sentences indicates that everything Muriel does has Muriel as its focus. From this scene, it might appear that people like Muriel and her mother are the problem for someone like Seymour, who is morally offended by banality and narcissism.

The second paragraph reads: "She was a girl who for a ringing phone dropped exactly nothing. She looked as if her phone had been ringing continually ever since she had reached puberty." The two sentences wryly underscore the sense of entitlement with which Muriel travels through life, but they also highlight another element of Salinger at his best: a certain level of tenderness for the "worst" of his characters. The slight preciousness of the rearranged syntax of the first sentence calls attention to this quality of Muriel's as something offensive but charmingly offensive, and therefore somewhat inoffensive, or even downright endearing. These two women, daughter and mother, may be ghastly, but Salinger treats them with enough regard to suggest to his readers that when Seymour appears in the story, the two women and what they represent cannot be all there is to his problem. They may be the salt in the wound, but not the wound itself.

The story's second half concerns Seymour—on the beach in his bathrobe—and Sybil Carpenter, his beach playmate. Sybil, about five years old, shows how wonderfully Salinger depicts small children, especially girls, mostly through his ability to capture their particular forms of speech and logical illogic. Above all, Salinger's children are access to new ways of seeing. Sybil plays a word game with Seymour's name. "See More Glass," she says to her mother; "Did you see more glass?" Her mother, who belongs to the same club as Muriel and *her* mother, has no patience for this kind of play, which reveals Sybil as someone special, as some-

one who pays attention to language and to the capacities of the world beyond nail polish and dresses.

Seymour has already recognized her specialness, and their scene explores some of Salinger's central concerns, which Eudora Welty described as "the crazy inability to make plain to others what is most transparent and plain to ourselves; the lack or loss of a way to offer our passionate feeling . . . the persistent longing to return to some state of purity and grace." Seymour embodies these problems, and Sybil, an innocent child, offers some glimpse of purity and grace. By both their accounts, he needs her to set him right and their conversation is a study in contrast with Muriel's conversation with her mother. Here, the two conversers finish their sentences, listen to each other, respond to each other. And their conversation is a serious parody of adult topics of discussion: kindness, jealousy, love. At one point, they spend several minutes on the virtues of wax and olives. In response to Sybil's queries as to whether Seymour likes them, he says, "'Olives—yes. Olives and wax. I never go anyplace without 'em.'" They do what Muriel and her mother cannot. And probably more significantly for Seymour, they do what Seymour and Muriel cannot.

But as Seymour's description of bananafish will make clear, despite this connection, there is nothing simple about experiencing the world. Seymour puts Sybil on a float and they head out into the ocean. He tells her to keep an eye out for bananafish. Sybil has no idea what bananafish are, but she is willing to trust him about their existence. He explains: "'They lead a very tragic life . . . they swim into a hole where there's a lot of bananas. They're very ordinary-looking fish when they swim *in*. But once they get in, they behave like pigs. Why, I've known some bananafish to swim into a banana hole and eat as many as seventy-eight bananas. . . . Naturally, after that they're so fat they can't get out of the hole again.'" After prodding from Sybil, Seymour reveals what happens to them: "'They die . . . they get banana fever. It's a terrible disease.'" Seymour's description is an elegant metaphor for the problem of living in the world. It is not just Muriel and her mother; experience in its entirety can result in banana fever. The banana hole is life in its entirety, and everything in it— positive and negative—can be our undoing.

What, then, is a person to do? One cannot avoid experience, but one can refrain from behaving like a pig. Behavior is key. Almost all of Salinger's subsequent fiction will struggle with the question of how to behave inside the banana hole of experience. Seymour believes in stripping down, refusing the material world, engaging in a spiritual fast. Sybil offers another answer. Unfazed by his dire description, she reports seeing a bananafish with six bananas in his mouth. The banana hole is not something to be avoided or feared. She treats it as a given, as desirable. It is significant that she sees a bananafish who is eating, not fasting. How can you experience something without partaking of it? But her bananafish has only six bananas in his mouth, not seventy-eight. Six, as we know from her earlier discussion of the tigers in "Little Black Sambo," is not a number to worry about. ("'There were only six,'" Sybil said. Seymour's response:

"'*Only* six! . . . Do you call that *only*?'") At Sybil's reminder of moderation, Seymour suddenly kisses her foot. She is surprised but not—as many readers and critics have been—offended. She understands it for what it is: a gesture of respect, tender regard, and gratitude. Their scene closes with her running "without regret" in the direction of the hotel.

At the close of the story, Seymour sits on the twin bed opposite the one on which Muriel is sleeping, puts a gun to his head and fires a bullet through his temple. The question that remains is not so much why he kills himself, but why Sybil's influence was not enough to keep him from doing so. The Glass family saga begins with Seymour's suicide, and Salinger spends much of his later career writing his way around and back—freezing himself—to that day in 1948 to show how Seymour failed, and how the rest of us can be influenced by the Sybils of the world.

The epigraph to *Nine Stories* is a Zen koan: "We know the sound of two hands clapping. But what is the sound of one hand clapping?" The enlightenment that would allow such a sound to be heard could reveal a world without distinctions, a world of unlimited freedom as unlike a banana hole as possible. In Salinger's fiction, its location is best indicated by children whose imaginations are not yet ruined by parents or other rationalizing and therefore deadly forces. In "Uncle Wiggily in Connecticut," "Down in the Dinghy," "The Laughing Man," and "Teddy" the adult world repeatedly infringes upon a Zen-like child's world, but "For Esmé— With Love and Squalor" highlights the ways in which the resilient world of children affects the world of adults, and returns to love as one answer to the questions raised in "Bananafish."

The story opens with the male narrator receiving an invitation to a wedding—an invitation he would like to accept, but which his "breathtakingly levelheaded" wife talks him out of. He decides to jot down a few notes about the bride, whom he knew briefly when stationed in Devon before the D-Day landings.

The narrator's world is the world of the banana hole. He is isolated from his fellow soldiers and his wife. Once, during the war, alone and wandering around a rain-soaked town, he had gone into a local church to listen to a children's choir practice: "Their voices were melodious and unsentimental, almost to the point where a somewhat more denominational man than myself might, without straining, have experienced levitation." The description applies to what Esmé, one of the girls in the choir, ends up doing to the narrator.

He notices her voice leading the rest, but at the same time she seems "slightly bored with her own singing ability." He goes to a tearoom, where he is soon joined by Esmé, her younger brother, and their governess. Like most Salinger children, Esmé is extraordinarily poised, thoughtful, straightforward, and verbally adept. At the same time, her hair is wet and plastered to her head and her nails are bitten to the quick. These are flaws she works hard to deemphasize. She wants to appear poised and proper, but part of what defines her, and part of her appeal, derives from her shortcomings. The title does, after all, contain both love and squalor; and this story works to explain how the two not only coexist but also require each other.

Their conversation reveals that Esmé's parents are dead, that she is trying hard to be more compassionate, and that coldness and a lack of a sense of humor are things that other people have listed as at least two of her flaws. She apes the adult tendency to spell out words she does not want her younger brother to understand. She learns that the narrator writes short stories and she asks him to write one for her, as she is "an avid reader." She suggests he make it extremely "squalid and moving," and asks if he is acquainted with squalor. He replies that he is getting better and better acquainted with it all the time, and she gallantly offers to write to him. When the children leave, the narrator describes it as "a strangely emotional moment," and when Esmé comes back to reiterate that she really would like him to write a story for her, he says that he has "never written a story *for* anybody, but that it seemed like exactly the right time to get down to it." To write a story for someone is an act of empathy, a gesture indicating faith in the possibility of communication and connection, areas in which the narrator needs faith.

The second half is the narrator's story, introduced as "the squalid, or moving, part." Squalid *and* moving. Weeks after V-E Day, Sergeant X, "a young man who had not come through the war with all his faculties intact," is recovering after a hospital stay for a nervous breakdown. He is in serious psychological and emotional trouble: his mind teeters "like insecure luggage on an overhead rack." In this state, he discovers a book by Goebbels called *The Time Without Example,* and inside someone has written, "Dear God, life is hell." Certainly this applies to the horrors of World War II, but also to the horrors of

Sergeant X's own particular existence. He confirms this by adding to the inscription: "Fathers and teachers, I ponder 'What is hell?' I maintain that it is the suffering of being unable to love." Hell is being unable to love, not the more familiar state of being unloved. Being able to love is a complicated endeavor, though one can go through the motions insincerely, as Sergeant X's friend, Clay, does with his fiancé at home. The fiancé writes Clay "fairly regularly, from a paradise of triple exclamation points and inaccurate observations." In contrast to her letters, Esmé's letter to Sergeant X expresses concern about his safety, asks after his wife, and hopes that D-Day will be an end to "a method of existence that is ridiculous to say the least." Even in this short note, she offers more than X has gotten anywhere else: genuine interest, concern, and communication, and acknowledgment of what he has earlier acknowledged to us: the ridiculousness of this sort of life. But she goes further. Enclosed is her father's watch. She lists its merits—waterproof, shockproof—and hopes he will accept it as "a lucky talisman" in "these difficult days." She stresses his acceptance as opposed to the gift itself. She understands that for it to work as a talisman, he must accept it as such. In the tea shop, X had noticed Esmé's watch, and now he remembers wanting it: "I remember wanting to do something about that enormous-faced wristwatch. . . . " In the story, it is Esmé who does something with it, lifting X from his squalor. X's reaction to the gift, and the ending of the story, is a feeling of ecstasy and sleep: "You take a really sleepy man, Esmé, and he always stands

a chance of again becoming a man with all his fac—with all his f-a-c-u-l-t-i-e-s intact."

While Esmé acts on her understanding, the narrator's responses to her are partial. He does write her the story; he does not go to her wedding, and the story ends without his achieving a complete or fully epiphanic understanding.

As the fiction following "Bananafish" indicates, Salinger seems to believe that finding a solution to the problem often involves revisiting the problem, which usually resides in the family. That is, after all, where one learns how to behave. So Salinger's later career is an exploration of the Glass family as an attempt to understand the Seymour of "Bananafish." The danger of this approach is that at their worst the stories read like the work of a family member convinced he knows better than others in the family. At their best, they read as compassionate testimony for the people and the place where suffering is most intense.

"Franny" and "Zooey," belong to the latter category. In these two stories about the youngest members of the Glass family, Salinger arrives at an understanding of how one can respond after confronting "a method of existence that is ridiculous to say the least." Franny is in the midst of a kind of spiritual breakdown, and after collapsing in a restaurant, she goes home to the Glass apartment in New York City to recover. Home is where one goes for help, even given the kind of help home can offer. As her brother Zooey puts it: "'*You came home.* You not only came *home* but you went into a goddam collapse. . . . By rights you're only entitled to the low-grade spiritual counsel we're able to give you around here, and no more.'" This low-grade spiritual help is what Franny needs and it comes by way of Seymour, who had offered his advice years ago. For years, the Glass children had performed on the radio show, "It's a Wise Child." Zooey recalls Seymour's request that he shine his shoes for the shows even though no one could see them: "He said to shine them for the Fat Lady." Zooey had no idea who she was, but a clear picture of her formed in his mind, and he complied. Franny received the same advice: Seymour once told her to be funny for the Fat Lady.

Zooey seems to be offering mainstream Christian ethics—"There isn't anyone out there who isn't Seymour's Fat Lady," and, *"don't you know who that Fat Lady really is? . . .* Ah, buddy. Ah, buddy. It's Christ Himself. Christ Himself, buddy"—but this is actually a shrunken version of what Seymour was after in "Bananafish." If Seymour's aspiration was to make the world a better place *and* achieve spiritual transcendence, Zooey's is only the former: *here's how you get through.* "The only thing you can do now, the only religious thing you can do, is act. Act for God, if you want to—be God's actress, if you want to. What could be prettier? You can at least try to, if you want to—there's nothing wrong in trying." *Acting* and *trying* are rather diminished versions of Seymour's metaphysic in "Bananafish." Perhaps above all, one should remember what Esmé tried to teach: that it is not enough to give, that you need a response for the gift to be truly valuable.

Karen Shepard

SELECTED BIBLIOGRAPHY

Works by J. D. Salinger

Nine Stories. Boston: Little, Brown, 1953.
Franny and Zooey. Boston: Little, Brown, 1961.
Raise High the Roof Beam, Carpenters and Seymour: An Introduction. Boston: Little, Brown, 1963.

Critical Studies

Bloom, Harold. *J. D. Salinger.* New York: Chelsea House, 1987.
French, Warren. *J. D. Salinger, Revisited.* New York: Twayne, 1988.
Wenke, John. *J. D. Salinger: A Study of the Short Fiction.* New York: Twayne, 1991.

BIENVENIDO N. SANTOS
(1911 – 1996)

Bienvenido N. Santos was born in the slums of Tondo, Manila, on March 22, 1911. His parents were illiterate peasants; his father, a laborer for the Bureau of Public Works, knew only two English words: "roads" and "bridges." Santos grew up in a household where no English was spoken and no reading materials were available. He started school when the Philippines was a colony of the United States and instruction was in English only. For the boy this turned out to be more of a blessing, "a tool for expressing our feelings," than a colonial imposition. As he read Whittier, Longfellow, and Tennyson, he fell in love with the sound of the English language and wrote mostly imitative musical poems. In his early attempts at creative writing, Santos learned to develop an ear for three kinds of communication: Pampango in the songs his mother sang at home; English in the poems and stories his teacher read at school; and Tagalog in the games he played or fights he survived as a child navigating the rowdy streets of his Tondo slums.

This multilingual background perhaps provides the answer to the question raised by Maxine Hong Kingston when years later she reviewed Santos's *Scent of Apples* (1980) for the *New York Times Book Review*. How is it possible, she asked, for Santos to write stories in English that so successfully echo a uniquely Filipino accent? Expressing admiration for Santos's handling of the dialogue of ethnic characters who do not speak English, Kingston wrote: "Mr. Santos is a master at giving the reader a sense of people speaking many languages and dialects. . . . All of us for whom English is a second language and all of us who write in English about people who are not speaking English must read him and try to figure out how he does it smoothly."

Santos left for America in September 1941 as a *pensionado* (scholar) of the Philippine Commonwealth government. Thirty years old and an established short story writer in English at home, he enrolled at the University of Illinois in the master of arts degree program in English. When war broke out in December, he found himself an exile in America, cut off from his homeland and the wife and three

daughters he left behind. The heartbreak of this separation during his first sojourn in America was crucial to Santos's development as a writer. Exile defined the central theme of his fiction from then on. In the summer of 1942, he studied at Columbia University with Whit Burnett, the founder of *Story* magazine, who published his first fiction in America. After studying Basic English with I. A. Richards at Harvard in 1946, Santos returned home to a country rebuilding from the ruins of war. With his wife and ten-year-old son, he came back to America in 1958 as a Rockefeller Foundation fellow at the University of Iowa Writer's Workshop, where he taught for five years. His first two novels, *Villa Magdalena* and *The Volcano,* written under a Rockefeller grant and a Guggenheim fellowship, were published in Manila in 1965, the year Santos won the Philippine Republic Cultural Heritage Award for Literature.

In 1972, Santos and his wife were on their way to the Philippines to "stay home for good," when news of the declaration of martial law reached them in San Francisco. The new regime banned *The Praying Man,* his novel about government corruption, and he and his wife decided to extend their exile and wait out the Marcos dictatorship. From 1973 to 1982, Santos was distinguished writer-in-residence at Wichita State University, and in 1976, after much soul-searching, he became a U.S. citizen. His short story, "Immigration Blues," won the best fiction award given by the *New Letters Journal* in 1977. In 1980, the University of Washington Press published *Scent of Apples,* his first and only book of short stories to appear in the United States. The next year it won the American

Book Award. Santos died at his home in Albay on January 7, 1996.

Santos's stories can be grouped into three literary periods that coincide with his comings and goings between his homeland and his adopted country. The stories of the first period, the prewar years in the Philippines (1930–1940) are set in the fictive Sulucan slums of his Tondo childhood and the rural towns and villages in the foothills of Mayon volcano in Albay, where Santos married his wife, started his family, and built his "forever" house. These stories are in the collections *Brother, My Brother* and *Dwell in the Wilderness*. Santos's exile in America during the war years produced stories set in Chicago, Washington, New York, and other cities, where he lectured extensively for the Philippine Commonwealth government in exile. *You, Lovely People, The Day the Dancers Came,* and *Scent of Apples* belong to this period. In the postwar years Santos set his stories in many different places as he commuted between the Philippines and America. These years mark a period of maturation and experimentation, and a shifting away from the short story to the novel form.

From 1970 to 1986, Santos experimented with a narrative form that "from all appearances is a novel but is actually far from novelistic." This loose and disjointed narrative cut out into segments that are like stories is the technique he used to tell the tale of the life and times of Filipino old-timers and the new breed of younger Filipinos in America. This experimentation with "stories within a novel" technique resulted in his novels *The Man Who (Thought He) Looked Like Robert Taylor* (1983) and *What the Hell for You Left Your Heart in San Francisco* (1987). From 1987 to his death in 1996, Santos worked on remembering his past and revisiting his beginnings, a journey of rediscovery that resulted in four books of personal history: *Memory's Fictions* (1993), *Postscript to a Saintly Life* (1994), *Letters, Book One* (1996), and *Letters, Book Two* (1998).

In the 1930s, before he left for America and learned from Whit Burnett and others the craft of fiction from a Western tradition, Santos had already written some of the memorable stories now considered classics of Philippine fiction in English. "And Men Decay," "End to Laughter," "Prologue," Theme: Courage," and "The House That I Built" show his gift as an intuitive writer. With sensitivity, compassion, and grace, he portrays fishermen and butchers, teachers and students, fathers and sons, wives and husbands, drawing from the wellsprings of memory and experience of people he lived with and knew so well. These God-fearing, simple dwellers in the wilderness "take us back to the rain forests of our forbears where human aspirations are deep and elemental." They are the precursors—kin in flesh and bone—of Santos's uprooted, hurt, and lost Filipino exiles in America.

If Santos's characters tug at the heart and rankle in memory long after they are set aside, that is because character and conflict are the primary elements in his fiction, not theme or message, which he said often led to preaching. Santos's use of irony achieves fictional distance and relieves tension in rendering human emotions in fiction.

He liked Hemingway's economy of style but favored even more Faulkner's ear for the lyrical, a language closer to his poet's sensibilities. Santos often used a first-person point of view "I" narrator named Ben, as in "Scent of Apples" and "Manila House," to narrate events as if they were the author's own remembered memories. This interplay between memory and invention, between fact and fiction, is a "magic trick" that allowed Santos "to make seem true even things that are not true." Asked which of his characters were real and which invented, Santos said: "I no longer know which of my characters really existed, whom I made up and whom I really knew, and I meet them everywhere."

His use of memory—or, rather, a fictionalized memory—evokes empathy for his characters. A variation of this technique is Santos's use of other "I" narrators, like the Pinoy old-timer Ambo, with the trembling hands ("The Door" and "The Faraway Summer"), or Tingting, the tennis player, in the San Francisco novel. But even with the voices of Ambo and Tingting, the stories are told from "within," as if Santos had crawled inside their souls and felt their hurting himself. This evocation of characters that are "real in the flesh" gives resonance to many of his stories. Like Faulkner, Bienvenido Santos believed it was important for a writer to feel compassion for his characters: "When you have created a story . . . you can take with you, and remember, then you have magic."

Leonor Aureus Briscoe

SELECTED BIBLIOGRAPHY

Works by Bienvenido N. Santos

You, Lovely People. Manila: Benipayo Press, 1955, 1966. Reprint, Manila: Bookmark, 1991.

Brother, My Brother. Manila: Benipayo Press, 1960; Reprint, Manila: Bookmark, 1991.
The Day the Dancers Came: Selected Prose Works. Manila: Bookmark, 1967, 1991.
Scent of Apples: A Collection of Stories. Seattle: University of Washington Press, 1979.
Dwell in the Wilderness. Quezon City: New Day Publishers, 1985.

Critical Studies

Alegre, Edilberto N. and Doreen G. Fernandez. "Bienvenido N. Santos." In *The Writer and His Milieu: An Oral History of First Generation Writers in English,* pp. 217–258. Manila: De La Salle University Press, 1984.
Cruz, Isagani, and David Jonathan Bayot, eds. *Reading Bienvenido N. Santos.* Manila: De La Salle University Press, 1994.
Santos, Tomas N. "The Filipino Writer in America—Old and New." *World Literature Written in English* (November 1976): 404–414.

WILLIAM SAROYAN
(1908–1981)

William Saroyan was born in Fresno, California, the only son of Armenak and Takoohi Saroyan, Armenian immigrants from Bitlis in eastern Anatolia. Armenak died in 1911, and Takoohi, unable to support her son and two daughters, sent them to the Fred Finch Orphanage in Oakland, California, where they remained until 1916.

Saroyan's work is largely autobiographical, but in print he never discussed his years in the orphanage until *The Bicycle Rider in Beverly Hills* (1952). In the early, popular stage of his career, he characteristically avoided discussing the unpleasant parts of his life—and of life generally. Critics coined the term *Saroyanesque* to describe his work and its genial tone, but they did not necessarily mean it in a complimentary way. On one hand, the word could be used to suggest a surface brilliance and a facility and deftness in creating characters and credible dialogue, but it could also mean "whimsical," "sentimental," and "shallow." Critics did not always recognize that the whimsy and humor were essentially antidotes to some tragic condition or recognition. For example, in the story that made Saroyan famous, "The Daring Young Man on the Flying Trapeze" (1933), a writer creates wonderful fantasies and visions, but he is also destitute; he has no money and no food, and dreams are all that keep him from despair.

In spite of his fame, Saroyan's private life was marked by repeated disappointments and tragedy including a failed marriage and consequent estrangement from his children. Gambling debts and difficulties with the Internal Revenue Service led to financial crises, and in the late 1940s and the 1950s he lost much of his popularity and was repeatedly assailed by critics for what they considered a superficial idealism and an abuse of literary conventions. Saroyan dealt with adversity by trying to remain untouched in his inner self—to be like his "daring young man," absorbed by private fantasies and visions.

In the 1930s and early 1940s, Saroyan was a celebrity; few writers have been as popular. His reputation was primarily the result of short stories collected in *The Daring Young Man on the Flying Trapeze and Other Stories* (1934), *Inhale and Exhale* (1936), *Three Times Three* (1936), *Little Children* (1937), *Love, Here Is My Hat* (1938), *Peace, It's Wonderful* (1939), and *My Name Is Aram* (1940). *The Time of Your Life* (1939) was one of the most popular plays ever written by an American, and *The Human Comedy* (1943)—published as a novel, although actually a series of interrelated stories—became a best-seller and has never gone out of print.

Saroyan's later work includes short stories, plays, a series of autobiographical novels, and memoirs, but none was as acclaimed as the early works. He had discovered a formula and an attitude that had great appeal during the Depression and the war years but that lost its resonance and audience with the return of prosperity. The stories he wrote in his last years about the fictional Bashmanian family—collected in *Madness in the Family* (1988)—re-created the tones and characterizations in the stories about the Garoghlanians in *My Name Is Aram,* and are among his most crafted works. Although esteemed by critics, *Madness in the Family* had only a modest reception by the public.

Saroyan's popularity began to fade in the late 1940s, but his work was important to fiction writers who flourished in the following two decades. His lineage as a writer can be traced to Gertrude Stein, for whom writing was, ideally, spontaneous and personal; an author was to be at the center of the work, his or her moods and observations being the root and justification for the writing. In his essay "American Qualities" (1940), Saroyan, following Stein's example, argued that "if a man says twenty words that are fresh and genuine, these words *are themselves form,*" a notion that much influenced Beat generation writers. In "Essentials of Spontaneous Prose" Jack Kerouac revealed his allegiance to Saroyan's aesthetic in the claim that good writing was like "[swimming] in sea of English with no discipline other than rhythms of exhalation and expostulated statement." Kerouac's disciples in turn carried Saroyan's aesthetic to the next generation.

Saroyan was fundamentally an expressionist in the Stein tradition, and within that aesthetic he mastered a number of different kinds of short stories. He excelled at stories that illustrated concisely and plainly a moral or facet of human nature—stories that found a ready audience through publication in the *Saturday Evening Post* and other mass-market magazines. These stories were whimsical and lighthearted—Saroyanesque—and required little intellectual or imaginative effort from readers. They were Saroyan's bread and butter. *The Human Comedy* is a collection of short pieces of this sort—sentimental, wistful, and occasionally sad, but never tragic.

Saroyan also wrote fables, drawing heavily on Armenian traditions, and a collection, *Saroyan's Fables* (1941), was among his most popular works. Perhaps his greatest stories are the more experimental works collected in *Three Times Three* and his stories dealing with Armenian life in the diaspora. The best known of the Armenian stories are those involving the Garoghlanian family, collected in *My Name*

Is Aram, but there are stories of this sort in almost all of Saroyan's books. These stories share with other popular Saroyanesque works a whimsical and lighthearted surface, but a closer reading reveals more complex emotional issues, often entailing a vision of character shaped by ethnic factors beyond a person's control. Armenians, in Saroyan's view, may have a superb sense of humor, but this barely covers a deep fatalism, resonant with memories of centuries of oppression and, finally, massacres under the Ottomans.

"The Beautiful White Horse," the opening story in *My Name Is Aram,* exhibits Saroyan's ability to cast almost anything in an amusing and jocular light. In this story, the narrator recalls that when he was nine years old, he was visited at four in the morning by his cousin Mourad, who rode a white horse that could not have been his own. A member of his family would never steal, says the narrator, but he reasons that "stealing a horse for a ride was not the same thing as stealing something else" and so is able to join his cousin with a clear conscience. Later, the narrator's uncle says, with Armenian humor, that the stolen horse must be returned "in six months at the latest," and when the owner, an Armenian neighbor, discovers the missing animal, he finds him "stronger than ever. Better tempered, too." The story can be seen as a study of Armenian characteristics and is deepened if one knows that under the Ottomans, Armenians were forbidden to have horses. Pleasures like that were available only when stolen—although, as good Christians, Armenians would presumably never steal.

Some experimental stories in *Three*

Times Three show Saroyan following his expressionist aesthetic to an extreme, writing in fact with little thought about a potential audience. They are very personal stories—"The Living and the Dead" being, for instance, a defense of Saroyan's anarchist beliefs against his grandmother's conservative politics—and in the most unusual story piece he ever published, "Quarter, Half, Three-Quarter, and Whole Notes," he comes very close to the kind of writing Gertrude Stein was at the time pursuing in such works as "Stanzas in Meditation," basically a transcription of the author's feelings and moods while writing. These are not described but represented or expressed in the rhythms and music of the words. The "Stanzas" would not be published for many years, and Saroyan's story is, therefore, no imitation but rather, like Stein's work, a logical extension of an aesthetic that saw personal, fluid, and spontaneous expression rather than the controlled development of character and plot as the more desirable object of writing.

The best-known story in *Three Times Three* is "The Man with the Heart in the Highlands," the basis for Saroyan's play *My Heart's in the Highlands* (1939). It was written one afternoon when Saroyan was sick and suffering extreme pain; writing the story was his remedy, a structure of words so pleasing that it would distract him from the suffering. The story is told by a resourceful boy named Johnny, whose eccentric family includes his father, a failed though cheerful poet, and his grandmother, who sings operas while cleaning her house. The family has no money, and Johnny must convince the grocer, who thinks everyone should work hard, to extend more credit. Johnny says there will be money for the food eventually, but the grocer knows that there won't. He is, however, charmed by Johnny's talk and explanations. A onetime actor, Jasper MacGregor, moves in with the family, and when all of the food is gone he gives a bugle concert that pleases the neighbors so much that they fill the family's larder.

The story is a Depression-era fable, and that may be one reason it had some success as a play. Saroyan suggests that those who can entertain, whether they be good talkers like Johnny or musicians like MacGregor, will always find ways out of difficulties. But it is important that Johnny and MacGregor be cheerful and light-hearted, as was Saroyan at his most "Saroyanesque." As he wrote in "The Declaration of War," collected in *Dear Baby,* writers have "little pride" because they know that life is transitory and everyone will eventually be forgotten. "Knowing all this," he wrote, "a writer is gentle and kindly where another man is severe and unkind." Doubtful as that usually may be, it was Saroyan's conviction, and he wrote throughout much of his career as if fiction were a means through which he could sustain his humor in spite of economic and personal threats.

Traditional distinctions between prose fiction and autobiography mean little in Saroyan's aesthetic, and episodes in his short stories occasionally appear in autobiographical works. Later books like *Letters from 74 rue Taitbout, or Don't Go, But If You Must, Say Hello to Everybody* are variously categorized as autobiography or short stories, depending on the critic. These books in effect call into question the very notion of the short story, for

Saroyan writes with the same versatile narrative ease that one finds in, say, *My Name Is Aram*. The only difference is that now the characters appear with their "real" names.

The true subject of all Saroyan's work is Saroyan himself. Whatever mastery of the conventions of fiction one finds in his work (and it is a considerable mastery), it exists not as an end in itself but as the means through which the author could find room for himself in the world. William Saroyan understood the power of being simply "Saroyan," for as long as he was the center of his fiction, he could overcome, at least in print, whatever threats the world brought to him.

Edward Halsey Foster

SELECTED BIBLIOGRAPHY

Works by William Saroyan

The Daring Young Man on the Flying Trapeze and Other Stories. New York: Random House, 1934.

Inhale and Exhale. New York: Random House, 1936.

Three Times Three. Los Angeles: Conference Press, 1936.

Little Children. New York: Harcourt, Brace, 1937.

Love, Here Is My Hat. New York: Modern Age Books, 1938.

The Trouble with Tigers. New York: Harcourt, Brace, 1938.

Peace, It's Wonderful. New York: Starling Press, 1939.

My Name Is Aram. New York: Harcourt, Brace: 1940.

Saroyan's Fables. New York: Harcourt, Brace, 1941.

The Human Comedy. New York: Harcourt, Brace, 1943.

Dear Baby. New York: Harcourt, Brace: 1944.

The Assyrian and Other Stories. New York: Harcourt, Brace, 1950.

The Whole Voyald and Other Stories. Boston: Little Brown, 1956.

My Kind of Crazy Wonderful People: Seventeen Stories and a Play. New York: Harcourt, Brace & World, 1966.

Letters from 74 rue Taitbout, or Don't Go, but If You Must, Say Hello to Everybody. New York: World, 1969.

Madness in the Family. New York: New Directions, 1988.

Critical Studies

Foster, Edward Halsey. *William Saroyan: A Study of the Short Fiction*. New York: Twayne, 1991.

Hamalian, Leo, ed. *William Saroyan: The Man and the Writer Remembered*. Rutherford, N.J.: Fairleigh Dickinson University Press, 1987.

Keyishian, Harry, ed. *Critical Essays on William Saroyan*. New York: G. K. Hall, 1995.

DELMORE SCHWARTZ
(1913 – 1966)

Born in 1913 in Brooklyn, New York, Delmore Schwartz was the son of middle-class, Eastern European Jewish immigrants. An emotionally damaging childhood was to haunt his personality, his literary art, and his professional career. As a young boy, Schwartz became a pawn in a doomed marriage that was a theater of open and bitter conflict. Tellingly, the Kafkaesque narrative frame of seminal short stories throughout his career—for example, "In Dreams Begin Responsibilities" (1935), "America! America!" (1948), and "The Track Meet" (1958)—involves a protagonist who anguishes helplessly about events that vitally concern him, but over which he has no control or influence.

An erratic if brilliant student, Schwartz attended the University of Wisconsin (1931–32) but returned to New York, where he earned a bachelor of arts degree in philosophy at New York University (1935). He went on to pursue graduate studies in philosophy at Harvard (1935–37), though literary ambitions and marriage plans prompted him to leave Cambridge without taking a degree.

The New York years from 1937 through 1940 saw Schwartz's precipitous rise to renown as an essayist, poet, and fiction writer. In Dreams Begin Responsibilities (1938), which appeared the year Schwartz married Gertrude Buckman, includes the title story, poetry, and a play. This first book earned its young author acclaim from the likes of Allen Tate, Wallace Stevens, and T. S. Eliot. During this period, Schwartz also gained wide respect as a critic of modern literary culture for essays on Eliot, Hemingway, Auden, Dos Passos, and other writers that appeared in major literary periodicals, most notably the Partisan Review. Schwartz's 1939 translation of Rimbaud's A Season in Hell, though badly requiring a corrected edition (1940), drew at least qualified praise from Eliot and Stevens.

In 1940, Schwartz began several years of teaching at Harvard (1940–45, 1946–47) and won a Guggenheim fellowship. Increasingly plagued, however, by insomnia, manic depression, and paranoid obsessions (fueled by heavy drinking and barbiturates), Schwartz alienated colleagues and caused his marriage to end in divorce (1944). Still, he wrote copiously—publishing a verse play, Shenandoah; or, The Naming of the Child (1941), and a book-length narrative poem, Genesis: Book One (1943)—and served as editor of the Partisan Review.

From 1947 to 1951, Schwartz, back in New York, continued to produce influential essays and reviews—becoming, in John Berryman's judgment, "the ablest critic of modern poetry." Additionally, although temperamentally ill suited for the lecture hall, he taught briefly at the New School (1949), Princeton (1949–50), Kenyon College (1950), and the Indiana School of Letters (1951). Schwartz's most successful book in the 1940s was The World Is a Wedding (1948), a volume of short fiction that has been hailed as "the definitive portrait of the Jewish middle class in New York during the Depression" (R. W. Flint). Vaudeville for a Princess and Other Poems, which appeared in 1950, drew decidedly mixed reviews.

Schwartz's dependency on alcohol and pills exacerbated his emotional instability and precipitated a twenty-year period of mental deterioration and artistic decline.

His unpredictable mood swings and paranoia led, in 1957, to the dissolution of his eight-year marriage to Elizabeth Pollet. Despite worsening personal difficulties, Schwartz, with the help of friends, managed to secure teaching positions at Princeton (1952–53), the University of Chicago (1954), the University of California at Los Angeles (1961), and Syracuse University (1962–65).

In 1959, *Summer Knowledge: New and Selected Poems, 1938–1958* confirmed Schwartz's stature as a major contemporary poet, as did his receipt that year of both the *Poetry* magazine prize and the Bollingen Prize for poetry. In 1960, he won the Shelley Memorial Prize. Before his final collapse in 1966 in a seedy New York City hotel, Schwartz lived to see one more book published, *Successful Love and Other Stories* (1961), a volume of short fiction that, except for "The Track Meet" (which was extensively edited by William Maxwell), falls considerably below the standard of his earlier work in the genre.

Schwartz's fiction is typically classified with that of Jerome Weidman, Tillie Olsen, Grace Paley, and other Jewish-American writers who, as cultural "regionalists" (in Irving Howe's words), depict "the force or fading" of shared ethnic values. The emphasis, as Mark I. Goldman observes, is on "the theme of alienation or separation, and a concomitant striving for oneness or identity." What distinguishes Schwartz is a highly individual narrative form characterized by "little visible plot but much entanglement of relationship among characters, stylized dialogue replacing action or drama, and a major dependence on passages of commentary, ironic tags, deflated epigrams,

and skittish ventures into moral rhetoric" (Howe).

In Dreams Begin Responsibilities and Other Stories (1978), edited by biographer James Atlas, features Schwartz's most original and successfully realized short fiction. Three of the pieces—"In Dreams Begin Responsibilities," "America! America!" and "New Year's Eve"—are Schwartz's best-known short stories and widely admired models of narrative form. Each of these stories vividly conveys the author's sardonic vision of the intergenerational conflicts and vain ambitions of second-generation Jewish intellectuals during the Depression. Like *The World Is a Wedding* and *The Child Is the Meaning of This Life* (the two signature novellas included in the Atlas volume), each of the stories characteristically reverses "the happy ending of the immigrant legend," by depicting how "instead of joining a transatlantic utopia, the eternal wanderers get lost in a deeper and darker wilderness" (Harry Levin). Of the three other short stories in the collection, "Screeno" and the terrifying dream-vision of "The Track Meet" are also, if on different counts, works of genuine power.

Schwartz's major short stories tend to be strongly autobiographical, none more dramatically so than his first. "In Dreams Begin Responsibilities," which he wrote at the age of twenty-one, is a six-part dream-vision narrative that many readers (including Vladimir Nabokov) have regarded as a masterpiece. The protagonist is an unnamed Schwartz persona in a darkened theater—Schwartz was an inveterate moviegoer—watching with mounting distress a silent film about his parents on the Sunday afternoon excursion, in

1909, when his father proposed. From the young couple's behavior on the screen, it becomes ominously clear that the marriage—like that of Harry Schwartz and Rose Nathanson—will prove a disaster. Both characters betray the "vanity and tenacious ambition" (Atlas) that tore apart the home life of Schwartz as a child. On their way to Coney Island, the couple strives more to impress each other than genuinely to communicate. At the seashore they proceed from the boardwalk—where, forebodingly, they seem oblivious to "the terrible sun which breaks up sight, and the fatal merciless, passionate ocean"—to the restaurant, the photo booth, and finally to the fortune-teller. All the while, their dreaming son, watching in the theater, weeps from time to time and grows increasingly hysterical. When at the restaurant his father proposes, Schwartz's protagonist leaps from his seat and cries despairingly, "Don't do it. . . . Nothing good will come of it, only remorse, hatred, scandal, and two children whose characters are monstrous." Dragged from the theater and scolded for his outbursts, the narrator suddenly wakens "into the bleak winter morning of my twenty-first birthday, the windowsill shining with its lips of snow. . . ." Structurally, the pathos of this earliest of Schwartz's mature short stories derives largely from the effective use of the dream-vision frame. The latter generates an intensifying sense of dramatic irony that culminates in the climactic wakeup that casts the nightmare as a devastating rite of passage.

The theme of Jewish immigrant experience, if tacit in "In Dreams," is explicit in "America! America!", a tale that focuses on the rising and then declining fortunes of the Baumanns. The focal narrative is dramatically refracted through the consciousness of a Schwartz persona, Shenandoah Fish, though here the protagonist's mother rather than a film is the depictive medium of "a revelation of waste and failure." Shenandoah is an artist, recently back from Paris, who finds himself depressed and disaffected at home in New York. He becomes deeply engrossed in the saga of his neighbors, the Baumanns, which his mother relates with ironic commentary: "Her words descended into the marine world of his mind and were transformed there, even as swimmers and deep-sea divers seen in a film, moving underwater through new pressures and compulsions. . . ." Similar to "In Dreams," the pathos in "America! America!" evolves with the persona's mounting anxiety as he gets passionately caught up in the fate of the others with whom he deeply identifies. The sense of irony and the contempt that Schwartz's protagonist feels intensify as he listens to the Baumanns' story. Profoundly disturbed, Shenandoah ultimately realizes, in a bleak epiphany, that what he feels about his neighbors is actually a disguised form of "self-contempt and ignorance" and that "his own life invited the same irony."

As opposed to concentrating on family and neighbors, "New Year's Eve" concerns the character, ideals, and frail alliances of Shenandoah Fish, a "youthful author of promise," and his circle of politically and socially alienated artists and intellectuals. Most at the New Year's party had been reluctant to attend, and only the continued drinking produces "a feeling of well-being and intimacy." The guests gossip "at the expense of those not present" and in the process display a vanity and excessive self-consciousness that undermines their relationships with each other. The various academic disputes and personal crises that flare up at the party ultimately betray an underlying sense of universal insecurity and despair: "everyone knew that soon there would be a new world war because only a few unimportant or powerless people believed in God or in the necessity of a just society sufficiently to be willing to give anything dear for it." Schwartz's theme of intergenerational conflict is played out in the subplot involving Wilhelmina Gold, a fictionalized version of Gertrude Buckman, who rejects "with violence and contempt the *mores* and ethos of her parents," and who declines Shenandoah's indirect offer of marriage as they leave the party in a mood of "emptiness and depression." As is often the case in Schwartz's fiction, the characters in "New Year's Eve" are "cut off from their parents, but lack inward direction," something that causes them to "devolve into a brittle cynicism and cliquishness that leaves them cut off from 'real life,' trapped in their own feelings of superiority" (Morris Dickstein). The author's larger point, however, is that the modern culture in which these young artists and intellectuals struggle for significance and self-realization (through the cultivation of sensibility) lacks the moral, political, and institutional authority that could afford them a basis for establishing meaningful lives.

Delmore Schwartz's contribution to the genre of the short story reflects a unique convergence of Jewish American writing and post—World War I literary modernism. Despite the laments over his unfulfilled potential and tragic decline, Schwartz did realize to an impressive degree his aim of crafting a literature that renders in vivid solution the "contemporary moral and social history" of his milieu.

Phillip Stambovsky

SELECTED BIBLIOGRAPHY

Works by Delmore Schwartz

The World Is a Wedding. Norfolk, Conn.: New Directions, 1948.
In Dreams Begin Responsibilities and Other Stories. Edited by James Atlas. New York: New Directions, 1978.
Successful Love and Other Stories. New York: Persea, 1985.

Critical Studies

Atlas, James. *Delmore Schwartz: The Life of an American Poet.* New York: Farrar, Straus & Giroux, 1977.
Goldman, Mark I. "Delmore Schwartz." *Dictionary of Literary Biography* vol. 28, pp. 285–291. Detroit: Gale Research, 1984.

LESLIE MARMON SILKO
(1948–)

"I grew up at Laguna Pueblo," wrote Leslie Silko in Kenneth Rosen's 1974 collection of contemporary American Indian short stories, *The Man to Send Rain Clouds,* where six of her early stories were published. "I am of mixed-breed ancestry, but what I know is Laguna. This place I am from is everything I am as a writer and a human being." She continued to pay tribute to the origins of her work in the dedication to her third book, *Storyteller* (1981): "to the storytellers as far back as memory goes and to the telling which continues and through which they all live and we with them." These comments announce key themes in her work: storytelling, memory, tradition, ceremony, place and landscape, and identity, both individual and communal.

Silko has published three novels, *Ceremony* (1977), *The Almanac of the Dead* (1991), and *Gardens in the Dunes* (1998); a collection of poetry, *Laguna Woman* (1974); a collection of essays, *Yellow Woman and a Beauty of the Spirit* (1996); and an autobiography, *Sacred Water* (1993). In 1981 she collected most of her short fiction in *Storyteller,* a genre-blurring work that defies categorization. In addition to eight stories—"Storyteller," "Lullaby," "Yellow Woman," "Tony's Story," "The Man to Send Rain Clouds," "Uncle Tony's Goat," "A Geronimo Story," and "Coyote Holds a Full House in His Hand"—the collection contains numerous poems (many of which can be read as stories), retellings of tales from the oral tradition, autobiographical fragments, excerpts from letters, and photographs, primarily by Silko's father, Lee Marmon. Within the text, Silko comments on the relationships among its various parts, sometimes obliquely, sometimes more directly: "The photographs are here because they are part of many of the stories and because many of the stories can be traced in the photographs," she says. The form of Silko's collection grows from oral storytelling in her cultural tradition: "within one story," she says, "there are many other stories together again. There is always, always, this dynamic of bringing things together, of interrelating things . . . . Through the narrative you can begin to see a family identity and an individual identity." In fact, *Storyteller* can be read as a kind of collective autobiography, establishing Silko's place within tribal culture and history.

In postmodern terms, we might call Silko's short stories "metastories," for they are indeed about the nature and implication of fiction itself. But like other American Indian writers, Silko sees her self-consciousness about storytelling as part of her cultural inheritance. With N. Scott Momaday and James Welch, Silko was one of the significant early writers in the "Native American Renaissance" of the 1970s and early 1980s. Momaday's much-quoted essay "Man Made of Words" (1979) expresses the writer's faith in the power of language to create identity. Man, he says, tells "stories in order to understand his experience . . . . Only when he is embodied in an idea, and the idea is realized in language, can man take possession of himself."

While Momaday's comment stresses the individual creative spirit and capacity for self-creation, Silko's many comments on storytelling emphasize her place in a community. "At Laguna," she says, "storytelling is a whole way of seeing yourself, the people around you . . . the place of your life . . . not just in terms of nature and location, but in terms of what has gone before, what's happened to other people. So it's a whole way of being."

In the opening poem of *Storyteller*, Silko establishes herself as the latest in a long line of many storytellers and accepts responsibility for passing on what she is able to remember of her Aunt Susie's tales. The oral tradition, she says, "depends upon each person/listening and remembering a portion." Only "remembering what we have heard together" can "create the whole story." Silko repeatedly asks her readers to consider the past's influence on the present and the present's connection to the past. "You should understand / the way it was / back then, / because it is the same / even now."

She develops this theme most strikingly in one of her best-known stories, "Yellow Woman," which she wrote for a creative writing class when she was twenty years old. "Yellow Woman" is a contemporary version of a whole cycle of Kochininako— Yellow Woman—stories that Silko's Aunt Alice seemed to enjoy a great deal. In *Storyteller*, Silko includes seven Yellow Woman stories, written in many voices, most in poetic form, some traditional, evoking oral storytelling, some contemporary and comic, such as the poem "Storytelling," where the Yellow Woman story is embellished with "a red '56 Ford," "wine bottles and / size 42 panties." Yellow Woman stories are about all sorts of adventures, but the ones Silko retells concern a young woman, married and often a mother, who wanders beyond the pueblo and has a sexual encounter with a spirit-man, a ka'tsina from the mountains. Sometimes she is abducted by him, sometimes she seeks him out. Sometimes she is killed by either her abductor or her

husband. Often she returns to her tribe with a gift—kidnapped by a buffalo-man, she brings the tribe buffalo meat—or with richer spiritual understanding.

In "Yellow Woman" Silko uses a first-person narrator to emphasize the ways the tribal stories influence a contemporary woman. The unnamed narrator, married with children, meets a mysterious man by the river; after a sexual encounter they ride to his cabin in the mountains. Sexually awakened, the young woman begins to wonder about her identity, if she is the Yellow Woman of her grandfather's favorite stories. "This is the way it happens in the stories, I was thinking, with no thought beyond the moment she meets the ka'tsina spirit and they go." But the stories, she thinks, "can't mean us . . . eventually I will see someone, and then I will be certain that he is only a man— some man from nearby—and I will be sure that I am not Yellow Woman. Because she is from out of time past and I live now. . . . " But she begins to think about the origins of stories, wondering if "Yellow Woman had known who she was—if she knew that she would become part of the stories. Maybe she'd had another name [too]," realizing that her own experience is the stuff of myths. Imagining the stories that will be told about her absence, she wishes her grandfather were still alive because "he would tell them what happened—he would laugh and say, 'Stolen by a ka'tsina, a mountain spirit. She'll come home—they usually do.'" Her grandfather, in fact, provides her with an end to her story, for she does decide to head home to the pueblo, to her husband Al, her baby, and her mother teaching her grandmother to make Jell-O. But she has acknowledged and acted out her sexual desires, encouraged by the stories she has heard about other women who wandered outside the confines of everyday life. And she returns to tell the tale. A story about a young woman's rebellious longings, "Yellow Woman" also stresses her place in her community. As Silko said to an interviewer, "That's how you know you belong, if the stories incorporate you into them. . . . In a sense, you are told who you are, or you know who you are by the stories that are told about you."

Although stories are embedded in all of her work, Silko has after the 1980s preferred long forms to short, and has written few individual stories. Yet two of her other early pieces, like "Yellow Woman," also told from the point of view of an Indian woman, have been widely anthologized and very influential. "Storyteller" explores the ways a young Eskimo woman uses inherited stories to retaliate for her parents' deaths at the hands of a white shopkeeper, to tell the story on her own terms, "without any lies." In "Lullaby," a Navajo woman attempts to make sense of the loss of her children, who have been taken from her by Bureau of Indian Affairs officials; in the story's painful and ironic end, she sings a lullaby she remembers from her past, a lullaby that promises that the family "will always be together." One or the other of these three stories has appeared in virtually every anthology of American Indian or multiethnic literature and in most recent anthologies of American literature. Silko's work has often been compared to Toni Morrison's and Maxine Hong Kingston's. Like them, she has become one of the most widely read and frequently quoted writers on the contemporary literary scene.

Melody Graulich

SELECTED BIBLIOGRAPHY:

Works by Leslie Marmon Silko

Storyteller. New York: Seaver Books, 1981.

Critical Studies

Graulich, Melody, ed. *"Yellow Woman": Texts and Contexts.* New Brunswick, N.J.: Rutgers University Press, 1993.
Jaskowski, Helen. *Leslie Marmon Silko: A Study of the Short Fiction.* New York: Twayne, 1998.
Salyer, Gregory. *Leslie Marmon Silko.* New York: Twayne, 1997.

JEAN STAFFORD
(1915–1979)

Jean Stafford produced a small but brilliant canon of short stories whose settings and themes echo her geographical rootlessness. She was born in Covina, California, in 1915, but when she was seven, her family moved to Colorado. All of her formative years were spent in the university town of Boulder, where her mother took in boarders to support the family while her father attempted to pursue a writing career. Stafford received her bachelor's and master's degrees in English from the University of Colorado at Boulder and subsequently studied philology at the University of Heidelberg, Germany, beginning her lifelong quest to shed what she saw as her provincial western roots. Each of her three marriages was to a writer: first to the poet Robert Lowell, then briefly to the *Life* magazine writer Oliver Jensen, and finally to the journalist A. J. Liebling. She died in 1979 and is buried beside Liebling in Greenriver Cemetery, East Hampton, Long Island.

During Stafford's distinguished career, she wrote three novels—*Boston Adventure* (1944), *The Mountain Lion* (1947), and *The Catherine Wheel* (1952)—and more than forty short stories. After brief stints as instructor at Stephens College in Columbia, Missouri, and as creative writing student at the University of Iowa in the late 1930s, Stafford decided against an academic career and turned her attention to writing. Her first marriage to poet Robert Lowell plunged her into the heady New Criticism world of Lowell's mentors John Crowe Ransom and Robert Penn Warren and made her aware of writing as a craft and a profession. After the publication of her first novel, Stafford received a Guggenheim fellowship and began short story writing in earnest. Her stories appeared in some of the most prestigious periodicals of the day: *The Southern Review, Partisan Review, Kenyon Review,* and *The New Yorker*. During a formative time in her career, Stafford developed a personal and professional relationship with *New Yorker* fiction editor Katharine White, which would help her to mature as a writer and shape the final form of some of her most significant short stories. She received the Pulitzer Prize in 1970 for her *Collected Stories,*

and most critics agree that these short stories represent her major achievement.

Jean Stafford's short stories deal almost exclusively with the lives of girls and women at all stages, from childhood to old age, charting the fears, anxieties, and compromises women often face. She wrote only nine stories with boys or men as central characters, and included only two of these, "A Summer Day" and "The Maiden," in her *Collected Stories*. Issues of female self-definition, marginality, and powerlessness surface in all of her stories, whether about a lonely young girl growing up in the rugged male West or an aging spinster who realizes that life has passed her by. Taking as her literary mentors Henry James and Mark Twain and appropriating some of their titles, Stafford echoes the sense of displacement both these writers evoked in their works but feminizes it by locating it within a distinctly female context.

Each of the four divisions of her 1969 *Collected Stories* bears a regional heading marking those places in Stafford's life that formed critical stages not only in her emotional and psychological development but also in the formation of the American psyche. "Innocents Abroad" contains stories of characters who are geographically transplanted and alienated from their environment; "The Bostonians and Other Manifestations of the American Scene" depicts and ironically critiques the cultured, sophisticated Eastern locale Stafford yearned for; "Cowboys and Indians, and Magic Mountains" treats the Western landscape of Stafford's youth as both nurturer and inhibitor of female development; and "Manhattan Island," as its title suggests, dramatizes in its stories the ur-

ban loneliness and anonymity character-
izing our modern era. But whatever its
setting, a Jean Stafford short story typically dramatizes the disparity between illusion and reality—American illusions
about Europe; poor, uncultured westerners' illusions about the elite East; naive
country girls' fantasies about New York
high society.

Stylistically, Stafford alternates between the colloquial, folksy diction of
Mark Twain and the elegant, refined prose
of Henry James, often mixing the two for
comic effect as in her 1954 story "Bad
Characters" when she contrasts Emily
Vanderpool's formal diction with the
western slang of her reprobate friend Lot-
tie Jump. Her early love affair with language resulted in the mature Stafford's
careful, precise, and nuanced style, her
ear for offbeat metaphors, and the sprinkling of archaic words one finds in her
works. Irony abounds in her tales of lost
loves, shattered dreams, and missed opportunities, and this characteristic detached authorial stance gives the author
the distance and objectivity she advised
young writers to adopt. Stafford's stories
are structured in a mode typical of the
modern short story since James Joyce
and Henry James. They usually end
with a painful or tragic moment of self-
awareness or "epiphany" for the central
character, which reinforces the ironic
point of view and the thematic focus on
loss or alienation.

Two of Jean Stafford's acknowledged
masterpieces in the short story genre are
"Children Are Bored on Sunday" (1948),
her first *New Yorker* story, and "A Country
Love Story" (1950), also appearing in *The
New Yorker*. Though they take place in two

radically different settings—the first in
the Metropolitan Museum of Art in New
York and the second in an isolated farmhouse in Maine—both share a common
theme of loneliness and disaffection and
a female protagonist who serves as the
center of consciousness.

"Children Are Bored on Sunday" concerns a chance encounter of Emma and a
past acquaintance, Alfred Eisenburg, who
meet in the Metropolitan one cold Sunday.
They know each other from the New York
social scene, though Emma is not a New
Yorker. Both she and Alfred have just been
through a nervous collapse, he from divorce, and she from some unnamed cause.
They take refuge in the museum—and
ultimately in drink—as the story ends
with them in a bar, two lonely souls in a
fleeting romantic moment. Emma's first
sight of Alfred evokes painful memories
of sophisticated cocktail parties where
pretentious, self-conscious intellectuals
drop learned allusions and where she remembers herself "moving, shaky with ap-
prehensions and martinis, and with the
belligerence of a child who feels himself
laughed at." Throughout the first part of
this three-part story, Stafford emphasizes
Emma's disenchantment with the elite
world she had once wanted so desperately
to be a part of, exposing its social rituals
as empty, vicious, and uncivilized. Emma
is a typical marginalized Stafford heroine
who feels a cultural defensiveness about
her provincial background and simultaneously judges herself by the standards of
the same world she rejects.

In the second section, Emma reflects
upon the young boys she sees wandering
through the museum; she wonders if Alfred had been such a boy, exposed early

to the rich intellectual and cultural world of New York but deprived of the rural joys that had marked her own childhood. She guiltily believes that "her own childhood . . . had not equipped her to read, or to see, or to listen. . . . She envied them [the boys] and despised them at the same time." Trapped between these two worlds, Emma nevertheless emerges as having her own genuine gifts of observation as she relates to the museum masterpieces aesthetically and personally rather than intellectually.

The last section of "Children Are Bored on Sunday" brings these two tortured souls—the "rube" and the intellectual—together in a brief moment of communion, "for they cunningly saw that they were children and . . . were free for the rest of this winter Sunday to play together . . . quite innocent." The story ends with Emma and Alfred fleeing the museum together to the illusory comfort of a whisky bottle.

"A Country Love Story" is a similarly bleak tale involving a young woman who finds herself in a disintegrating marriage with a man whose recent illness has left him withdrawn and unfeeling toward her. Its title underscores Stafford's defining irony, and its examination of marriage recalls the work of other women writers, such as Charlotte Perkins Gilman's "The Yellow Wallpaper" or Kate Chopin's *The Awakening*. May and Daniel in Stafford's story become increasingly estranged during the bitterly cold, isolating winter, so much so that in her craving for conversation, May is eventually driven to imagine a ghostly lover who appears to her sitting in the antique sleigh that adorns their wintry front yard. (Stafford and Robert Low-

ell bought a house in Damariscotta Mills, Maine, with the proceeds of her first book, and critics often point to this autobiographical connection.) Initially proud and awed by this, their first house, May gradually feels the house enveloping her, "as if it were their common enemy."

Besides the obvious disenchantment May feels about her marriage, the theme of her repressed desire also continues to surface—desire for companionship, for conversation, for useful work, for physical intimacy—until in a fit of paranoia, Daniel accuses her of going mad. The ghostly lover becomes her retaliation for this attack. He is confidant, friend, and lover, tempting May to lustful thoughts while she has tea with the neighborhood ladies, and consuming her waking and sleeping hours.

Seasonal references underscore the story's sexual subtext. May and Daniel move in during the summer, caught up in the beauty of the farmhouse and with each other in a "second honeymoon." But as winter sets in, May remembers the doctor's warning that long illness changes a man and makes life with him seem "like living with an exacting mistress." Winter repeatedly appears as yet another antagonist in this tale of a marriage gone awry. Cold settles into the drafty old house, snowdrifts accumulate against the antique sleigh's runners, spirea bushes droop with the weight of icy cobwebs, and May and Daniel lie stiffly in bed together at night as the snow ditcher flings the snow from the road and flashes its red and blue lights.

When early spring finally approaches, the chill of winter remains in the marriage as a penitent but ill and weak Daniel pleads with May not to leave him, and she loses her fantasy world. Realizing that nothing will ever change in this relationship, she resignedly admits to herself, "There was no place warm to go." The story ends with May's epiphany, her acknowledgment of being trapped and alone, "rapidly wondering over and over again how she would live the rest of her life." Both "Children Are Bored on Sunday" and "A Country Love Story" are vintage Jean Stafford in their focus on a trapped, alienated young heroine whose insecurities force her to desperate measures. In the first story, the protagonist's perceived intellectual inferiority plagues her and drives her to nervous exhaustion and drink; in the second, the professor/husband's retreat into his intellectual ivory tower causes May to turn inward and imagine another life. Both stories isolate a Jamesian center of consciousness—in each case, the woman—and end with ironic epiphanies. Typical of *New Yorker* short stories, these two Stafford works de-emphasize plot and concentrate instead on nuances of character and psychological insight.

Mary Ann Wilson

SELECTED BIBLIOGRAPHY

Works by Jean Stafford

Children Are Bored on Sunday. New York: Harcourt, Brace, 1953.

The Interior Castle. New York: Harcourt, Brace, 1953.

Stories. (With John Cheever, Daniel Fuchs, and William Maxwell.) New York: Farrar, Straus & Cudahy, 1956.

Bad Characters. New York: Farrar, Straus & Giroux, 1964.

Selected Stories of Jean Stafford. New York: New American Library, 1966.

The Collected Stories. New York: Farrar, Straus & Giroux, 1969.

Critical Studies

Ryan, Maureen. *Innocence and Estrangement in the Fiction of Jean Stafford.* Baton Rouge: Louisiana State University Press, 1987.

Walsh, Mary Ellen Williams. *Jean Stafford.* Boston: Twayne, 1985.

Wilson, Mary Ann. *Jean Stafford: A Study of the Short Fiction.* New York: Twayne, 1996.

WALLACE STEGNER
(1909 – 1993)

Wallace Stegner is best known for such novels as *Angle of Repose* (1971) and *The Spectator Bird* (1976)—the first awarded a Pulitzer Prize and the second a National Book Award. Early in his career, however, Stegner was hailed for his short stories. Between 1941 and 1955, his fiction was included in seven annual volumes of *Best American Short Stories* and four O. Henry Awards volumes, and he received first prize in the O. Henry competition in 1950 for "The Blue-Winged Teal." Born in Iowa in 1909 and raised in North Dakota, Washington, Saskatchewan, Montana, and Utah, Stegner was educated at the universities of Utah, California, and Iowa, where he completed a Ph.D. in English in 1935. He taught writing over the years at Augustana, Utah, Wisconsin, Harvard, and most notably at Stanford, where he directed the creative writing program from 1945 until his retirement in 1971. A gifted nature writer and natural historian, he served as assistant to the secretary of the interior in 1961 and of the National Parks Advisory Board from 1962 to 1966. Stegner was elected a fellow of the American Academy of Arts and Sciences in 1965. He died from injuries suffered in a car accident in Santa Fe, New Mexico, in 1993.

Stegner published virtually all of his short fiction between 1937 and 1958. "It seems to me a young writer's form, made for discoveries and nuances and epiphanies and superbly adapted for trial syntheses," as he explained in the foreword to his *Collected Stories*. Many of his tales began "without the intention of being anything but independent, tended to cluster, wanting to be part of something longer," he discovered, and so he wove six of them into the fabric of his early novel, *The Big Rock Candy Mountain* (1943) and cannibalized others in his novels *All the Little Live Things* (1967) and *Recapitulation* (1979). "I don't have any formula or theory of the short story," he remarked in 1990. "The only thing I do demand of a short story . . . is that it ought to close some sort of circuit." In all, Stegner's short stories are traditionally realistic in style, often nostalgic or even elegiac in tone, and usually devoted in theme to ideas of community or family in the sparsely settled regions of the American West.

Stegner's antimodern bias is evident, for example, in his series of Bruce Mason stories, which Joseph M. Flora has favorably compared to Hemingway's Nick Ad-

ams tales. "Both writers had to probe in fictional guise their own relationships with their fathers before they could treat their relationships with their own sons," Flora explains. George Stegner was, by all accounts, a stern patriarch and ne'er-do-well who sometimes skirted the law, and the father in the Bruce Mason stories is a struggling farmer and businessman who bends both nature and his family to his will. In "Goin' to Town," the father staggers his weeping son (who is called simply "the boy") with "a swift backhand blow," and in "Butcher Bird," the father callously kills a harmless sparrow over the protests of his wife and son.

Stegner explored the false and cruel masculine codes of western experience more fully in "The Colt." Set in rural Saskatchewan in spring, this story opens as Bruce Mason chases a pack of dogs away from the family mare, which has foaled. Before he arrives, however, the colt has broken its front legs while trying to escape the snarling pack. It walks "flat on its fetlocks, its hooves sticking out in front like a movie comedian's too-large shoes." Rather than allow the colt to be shot and skinned for his hide, however, Bruce persuades his parents to let him try to nurse him to health. All spring he tends "the hobbled, leg-ironed chestnut colt" he names Socks, whose legs fail to mend. Because the family spends its summers at a farm fifty miles distant, the boy faces a crisis. His father refuses to carry the colt to the farm and instead arranges to sell him for three dollars (that is, the equivalent of thirty dimes or thirty pieces of silver, the price of Christ's betrayal) to a neighbor who ostensibly will care for him over the summer. "Maybe when I come back he'll be all off his braces and running around like a house afire," Bruce hopes. Five days later, as they drive past the town dump on their way to the homestead, Bruce and his parents are struck by "a rotten, unbearable stench." Then they see "the bloated, skinned body of the colt, the chestnut hair left a little way above the hooves, the iron braces still on the broken frontlegs." The father had sold the colt for its hide, after all, an act of deceit he had hoped to conceal all summer. Rather than honorable farmers or ranchers who behave according to an unspoken "code of the West," the men in "The Colt" trade in lies. Rather than the virgin territory celebrated in myth, the western landscape foregrounded in this story is despoiled by a junkyard and subtle treachery.

In "The Blue-Winged Teal," the son and father are gradually and tentatively reconciled. This initiation story qualifies as a Bruce Mason tale if only because in the version of it reprinted in *Recapitulation* the son and father are named Bruce and George Mason. In the original magazine story, however, they are called Henry and John Lederer. The son is now twenty years old, his mother has died six weeks earlier, and within ten days of her death his father had bought a seedy pool hall with an illegal blackjack game. (Stegner's father had briefly invested in a Reno gambling hall.) While the son waits to return to school, he lives with his father, though they are estranged. "He did not forgive the father the poolhall, or forget the way the old man had sprung back into the old pattern, as if his wife had been a jailer and he was now released," and he "neither forgot nor forgave the red-haired woman" who sometimes waited "while the old man

closed up." The story opens on a Saturday night as Henry brings his father nine ducks—"offering or tribute or ransom or whatever they were"—he has killed while hunting that day. His eyes "bright with sentimental moisture," the old man compliments his son. "There ain't a prettier duck made than a blue-wing teal. You can have all your wood ducks and redheads, all the flashy ones," he says. Such a remark implicitly betrays his attitude about his affair with the redhead who wears "cheap musky perfume." With Max Schmeckebier, who runs the blackjack game, the father and son feast on roast duck the next day, a type of Communion Sunday. John Lederer has tacked the wings of the teal on the frame of the back bar mirror because, as it happens, his late wife had "thought a teal was about the prettiest little duck there was," and she had once painted blue duck wings on an entire set of white china. When the old man begins to cry at the memory of his late wife, young Henry realizes how profoundly he has misjudged his father. He will leave town the next day as he had planned, but without resentment, rather "with the feeling he might have had of letting go the hand of a friend" who is "too weak and too exhausted to cling any longer" to a spar of driftwood "in a wide cold sea." The old man, once robust, his face now drawn and sallow, is doomed. The son begins to forgive his father's many failures because at least they share a common grief. Without the wife and mother as their center, however, they remain forever a broken family.

Unlike the Bruce Mason tales, "The Traveler" (1951), the opening narrative in Stegner's *Collected Stories,* describes the epiphany of a middle-aged protagonist.

Like most of Stegner's fiction, "The Traveler" is vaguely autobiographical. One night during the winter of 1941, as the author recalled in a interview in 1990, with the temperature "about 20 below" zero and his entire family sick, "the car wouldn't start, and I had to walk about two miles to town . . . to get some help." In the story, a pharmaceutical salesman abandons his stalled car next to a snowdrift on a country road late at night to find help. Ironically, this "salesman of wonder cures" turns from seeking rescue to offering it to a young boy whose grandfather lies dying in the first farmhouse he comes to. He discovers in the "boy's thin anxious face" how "his own emergency had been swallowed up in this other one." As he leaves in a cutter for the next farm, two miles distant, where he can telephone for help, "he felt that some profound contact had unintentionally, almost casually, been made" with the boy, in whom "for one unmistakable instant [he] recognized himself." The story is reminiscent in some respects of John Steinbeck's *Grapes of Wrath,* with its depiction of an indifferent and even hostile nature, an archetypal journey, and even such specific incidents and characters as the breakdown of a car and the stricken grandfather. The final scene of Steinbeck's novel, in which a starving man receives succor at the urging of a boy, seems particularly apropos to the rescue theme in "The Traveler." Whereas Steinbeck's novel ends with the image of a comforting madonna, however, Stegner's story ends with the salesman's recognition of the common plight he shares with the young boy and the distance each of them must yet travel.

Formally, Stegner's short fiction is un-remarkable, neither avant-garde nor academically fashionable. Though he was a skilled and versatile writer, he did not experiment with the short story form. "The word 'artist' is not a word I like," he once ruminated. "It has been adopted by crackpots and abused by pretenders and debased by people with talent but no humility." However, he was both a critically and commercially successful writer. Most of his fifty published tales—of which only thirty-one are gathered in his *Collected Stories*—originally appeared in such popular and well-paying magazines as *Collier's, Harper's, Scribner's, McCall's, Redbook,* and the *Atlantic Monthly*. A versatile craftsman in the tradition of such mannered realists as Henry James, Hemingway, and John Cheever, Stegner rehearsed in his short fiction many of the same issues—for example, the hostility of the natural environment and the alienation of the pioneer—that he elaborated more fully in his late novels.

Gary Scharnhorst

SELECTED BIBLIOGRAPHY

Works by Wallace Stegner

The Women on the Wall. Boston: Houghton Mifflin, 1948.
The City of the Living. Boston: Houghton Mifflin, 1956.
Collected Stories of Wallace Stegner. New York: Random House, 1990.

Critical Studies

Ahearn, Kerry. "Stegner's Short Fiction." South Dakota Review 23 (winter 1985): 70–86.

Flora, Joseph M. "Stegner and Hemingway as Short Story Writers: Some Parallels and Contrasts in Two Masters." *South Dakota Review* 30 (spring 1992): 104–119.

Zahlan, Anne Ricketson. "Cities of the Living: Disease and the Traveler in the Collected Stories of Wallace Stegner." *Studies in Short Fiction* 29 (fall 1992): 509–515.

JOHN STEINBECK
(1902 – 1968)

John Steinbeck, who won a Nobel Prize for Literature in 1962, was born in 1902 in Salinas, California, where his father was a minor government official. He was educated in the local schools and attended Stanford University, although he failed to graduate. He spent the first half of his life in the Salinas-Monterey region of California, which provided a backdrop for most of his best fiction. In his later years, after two unsuccessful marriages, he settled in New York with his third wife, Elaine.

As a writer of short fiction, Steinbeck produced some of his finest works: a collection of linked stories called *The Pastures of Heaven* (1932) and *The Long Valley* (1938). Both collections contain some remarkable stories, and both anticipate the style and themes of his major novels of the Depression era, such as *Of Mice and Men* and *The Grapes of Wrath*, which continue to attract a wide audience.

The Pastures of Heaven has elements in common with *Winesburg, Ohio,* by Sherwood Anderson, who remarked that "the novel form does not fit an American writer." Anderson added, "in *Winesburg,* I have made my own form," one that possesses "a new looseness," a term that also describes Steinbeck's first collection. Its linked stories offer a portrait of a group of California farm people as a case study of human behavior in relation to a particular region. Steinbeck heard tales of this region from his mother and aunt, both of whom once lived in a mountainous valley called the Corral de Tierra: hence, the title. The gorgeous valley, which is cut off by its geographical terrain and its mentality from the rest of the world, becomes in Steinbeck a microcosm similar to Frost's region north of Boston, Joyce's Dublin, or Faulkner's mythical county in Mississippi. It is the country of Steinbeck's childhood, and he evokes it with lyrical detail.

The Monroe family lies at the center of these stories, which chart the disarray caused by an element that should not be there. The Monroes have about them "a flavor of evil" they seem incapable of overcoming. The evil that they bring to the valley is not all of their construction, it should be said; indeed, the origins of the problem seem inexplicable. These stories resemble what Thomas Hardy once called "satires of circumstance," and they are laden with ironies, as when the ancestral home of an elderly character called John Whiteside is destroyed by fire after Bert Monroe, wishing only to help, offers to burn the brush around the house.

The families living in this bucolic landscape are all descendants of the original immigrants who wrested the land from Native American people living there before them. This is a world founded on violence, and violence remains a natural part of its texture, as well as the underlying subject of many of the tales. But an immense beauty is present too. This beauty is enhanced by the work of human hands in the cultivation of fruit trees, beans, peas, and various root crops.

Like Hemingway, to whom he has often been compared, Steinbeck was attracted to the violence that had long been part of his world. But violence is not seen as a test for manhood; rather, it is random and pervasive. Violence itself becomes the subject of one story about a character named Raymond Banks, a "jolly" chicken farmer who is much admired for the quality of his poultry. He takes great trouble to slaughter his chickens with the least amount of pain. A few times a year he visits an old school friend, a warden in the federal penitentiary at San Quentin, where he serves as an official witness to public executions. Just as in the slaughtering of chickens, he is fascinated by "the killing time."

Bert Monroe, who likes to imagine scenes of execution, wants to go with Banks to see an actual hanging. Eerily, he seems to enjoy the shudder these mental images produce. Alas, when Monroe confesses to Banks about the images of slaughter he summons in his head, the chicken farmer is aghast. "If you think things like that you haven't any right to go up with me," Banks tells him bluntly. Steinbeck sides, implicitly, with Banks, who has what might be considered a normal or natural interest in the drama of death. Monroe's interest, on the other hand, is unnatural, even decadent.

The real heroes in The Pastures of Heaven are people like Junius Maltby, an educated man who has managed to resist the corruption of bourgeois life. Obsessed by his favorite authors, such as Robert Louis Stevenson, he fails to look after his farm in the fastidious way that Bert Monroe does. Instead, he cultivates his relations with his son: "They didn't make conversation; rather, they let a seedling of thought sprout by itself, and then watched with wonder while it sent out branching limbs. They were surprised at the strange fruit their conversation bore. . . ."

In conversation with T. B. Allen, another strong figure in the stories, Bert Monroe says rather mournfully: "I had a lot of bad luck." He recounts instances of this bad luck from his recent past. Allen responds: "Maybe your curse and the farm's curse have mated and gone into a gopher hole like a pair of rattlesnakes. Maybe they'll be a lot of baby curses crawling around the Pastures first thing we know." In the stories that follow, these baby curses multiply almost uncontrollably, bringing a plague of misfortune on this formerly peaceful valley. Each member of the hapless Monroe clan casts a dark shadow on someone outside of the family circle.

Jimmie Monroe, Bert's teenage son, plays a large part in the downfall of Edward "Shark" Wicks. Bert himself unwittingly becomes responsible for the institutionalizing of sweet but simple Tularecito— a simpleton not unlike Lennie in Steinbeck's Of Mice and Men. In another story, Bert's foolishness sets in motion a train of events that leads Helen Van Deventer to kill her mentally unstable daughter. Elsewhere, Mrs. Monroe sets out purposely to destroy the self-created paradise that Junius Maltby and his son enjoy on their unkempt farm. This cycle of destruction caused by one family culminates in the destruction of John Whiteside's house— a symbol for his soul.

The beautifully written and artfully related tales of *The Pastures of Heaven* constitute a quiet peak in the Steinbeck canon. *The Long Valley* is more uneven, but it contains some of this author's finest work, such as the opening story, "The Chrysanthemums," which follows a brief period in the life of Elisa Allen, a woman married to a well-intentioned but dull farmer. The story opens, typically for Steinbeck, with the evocation of a symbolic landscape: "The high grey-flannel fog of winter closed off the Salinas Valley from the sky and from all the rest of the world." Thus, the claustrophobic world of Elisa Allen is signaled by the oppressive weather.

This haunting story is partly about the way Elisa's dreams are manipulated by a passing rogue, a man who repairs household goods. The repairman plays upon Elisa's feelings in order to get her business, pretending to sympathize with her love of flowers, which is all-consuming. Her passion for chrysanthemums symbolizes her intimacy with the rhythms of the natural world and represents her most essential self.

Elissa is deeply hurt by the behavior of the traveling repairman, who violates her innermost feelings by his indifference, much as Mary Teller is hurt by her husband in "The White Quail." Mary, another gardener, has married Harry, a well-off man who allows her the complete freedom to make her garden into a prelapsarian paradise. She wants to keep out "the world that wants to get in, all rough and tangled and unkempt." She is unable to recognize that her efforts to create this artificial world are misguided, linked to a neurotic desire to control what cannot be controlled. Mary identifies with a white quail—a sign of purity—that lives in her garden. This totemic creature is more symbolic than real, and when it is threatened by a cat, she begs her husband to shoot the predator. Instead, he shoots the quail, murdering by proxy the wife who has gardened him out of her life. "Oh, Lord, I'm so lonely," she cries at the end.

In "The Murder," Jelka and Jim live together on their isolated farm without speaking or really communicating. Steinbeck vividly imagines the torture and indignity of Jelka's loneliness within marriage. Not surprisingly, Jelka takes a lover, whom Jim murders; then Jim beats Jelka, establishing a crude form of communication that the narrator seems almost to condone.

Steinbeck takes the measure of several couples in this collection, often adopting a bitterly sardonic tone, as in "The Harness," a story about a man who is quite literally "harnessed" by his wife, Emma. She forces him to wear a back brace, as if to stiffen his spirit and make a man out of him. Although he slips off to the brothels of San Francisco once a year, indulging his fantasies, he never shakes the harness his wife has put upon him. Unfortunately, he is aware of his own ridiculousness, and painfully so. "A man ought to stand up straight," he says. "I am a sloucher."

One associates the Steinbeck of the Depression era with realistic fiction about the displaced and the dispossessed. There is not much of this in *The Long Valley,* but "The Raid," a thrilling story, reads at times like discarded footage from *In Dubious Battle* (1936), Steinbeck's novel about strikes in California's apple-picking country. "The Raid" is covertly about the psychological consequences of violence, focused on two Communist Party political organizers, Dick and Root, who try to organize workers in a small California town. The narrative centers on Root's efforts to overcome his personal fear of being thrashed by the anticommunist mob. Dick, the older man, a seasoned veteran of the class war, says to Root: "If someone busts you, it isn't him that's doing it. It's the system. And it isn't you he's busting, it's the System." Steinbeck tells the story in a straightforward, realistic manner, not taking sides. As in his great novels of this era, he catches the mood of the 1930s with unerring accuracy.

André Gide once remarked that John Steinbeck never wrote anything "more perfect, more accomplished, than certain of his short stories." Certainly, the linked stories of *The Pastures of Heaven* and several tales in *The Long Valley* merit serious attention, and may well be among the best things this celebrated author ever wrote.

Jay Parini

SELECTED BIBLIOGRAPHY

Works by John Steinbeck

The Pastures of Heaven. New York: Brewer, Warren and Putman, 1932.
The Long Valley. New York: Viking, 1938.

Critical Studies

Lisca, Peter. *The Wide World of John Steinbeck.* New Brunswick, N.J.: Rutgers University Press, 1958.
McCarthy, Paul. *John Steinbeck.* New York: Unger, 1980.
Parini, Jay. *John Steinbeck.* New York: Holt, 1995.

ELIZABETH TALLENT
(1954–)

Though her first published book was a critical work titled *Married Men and Magic Tricks: John Updike's Erotic Heroes* (1982), Elizabeth Tallent is best known as a writer of short stories. She has published three collections of stories to date: *In Constant Flight* (1983), *Time with Children* (1987), and *Honey* (1993). The prose of all three collections can be broadly characterized as elegant, sensuous, devout in capturing the moment, the gesture, the high-wire tension of human exchanges. Tallent's ability to describe emotional complexity is almost scientifically careful and, arrestingly, both clinical and insinuatingly intimate at the same time.

Elizabeth Tallent was born in Washington, D.C., in 1954. Her father William was a research chemist with the United States Department of Agriculture, and her mother, Joy, was a speech therapist. Tallent has a degree in anthropology from Illinois State University. She was writer-in-residence at the University of Southern

Mississippi in 1983, in 1986 a visiting writer in the Programs in Writing at the University of California at Irvine, and a faculty member in the Department of English at the University of California at Davis. She is currently on the faculty of the Stanford Creative Writing Program.

For a time Elizabeth Tallent was a frequent contributor to *The New Yorker,* writing stories that earned her three inclusions in *Best American Short Stories* (1981, 1987, and 1990 for, respectively, "Ice," "Favor," and "Prowler"). In a short essay included in the contributors' notes to the *Best American Short Stories 1987,* Tallent describes the impetus for her short story "Favor": "Maybe the first detail that I had for 'Favor' was a smell, the faint, familiar, grassy dustiness of an old denim jacket my husband had almost worn to pieces, and the fact that he once left a spice jar out on the kitchen table, having rubbed his hunting gloves with cloves. Those details seemed to belong together, and . . . to provoke others to appear and fit into a kind of constellation that began to feel . . . storylike. . . . I sometimes imagine that writing a story is a way of setting up a field of details such that the feeling you are chasing can play over and through those details." Hortense Calisher, editor of *Best American Short Stories 1981,* distinguished Tallent's story "Ice" from the typical *New Yorker* story: "'Ice' is not one of them. Rather, it is made of shards stuck together like charms to keep down the violence, to close out the hidden knowledge." The story's narrator is a figure skater—much to the dismay of her mother, who can only find this profession tawdry—and she has recently allowed with little resistance, emotional or otherwise, her lover, the

Travelling Ice Adventures' photographer, to take another job far away in Los Angeles. Nightly she skates with a man who is gay and dressed in a bear costume, and though their performance is a set routine, the narrator has been varying her skating, angering their manager. Her hair has been dyed blonde because "the promoters of the show cannot envision a dark-haired woman dancing with a bear," and throughout the story the mother calls to report on her Abyssinian cat given to spontaneously aborting her litters. The "field of details" or shards of the story accrue, and without any overt or simplifying pattern, the reader understands that at stake is the narrator's heart, its ever-threatened ability to respond or flourish, an issue in any Tallent story. The story closes with the narrator waltzing on ice, weeping but suspended, skating with the bear, who tilts his head and whispers, "You know, don't you, that you are not yourself?" This question, really a statement, poses the possibility of choice rather than acceptance or inheritance. The narrator, though now skating within the prescribed routine, is nonetheless revealed by the bear as a character on the verge of becoming. Who precisely the narrator is is not as important as the manifestly pleasing sense that she will escape the forces working against her individual identity within the story. *Publishers Weekly* noted that "most of Tallent's endings [are] mesmerically right and satisfying." In a serious study of the short story, Elizabeth Tallent's endings would constitute and merit a chapter to themselves. The reader is at once taken off guard and assured of astute perfection.

In the story "Get It Back for Me," included in *Honey,* the "it" is a wedding ring, and though the bulk of the story is the tension of the ring's retrieval, once gotten the wife walks out the door to the back field and flings the ring as far as her pitching allows. The story ends with the parents making love, something the story's child narrator interprets as the perversity of the power her parents have over the lives of their children: "I think I hated them then because they could save us, or not save us: because it was in their hands." Just one striking dimension of this ending is that the reader understands the rightness of the parents making love, but the reader is not left easy in his or her confirmation of human nature but instead is brought to the recognition of the action's violence within the psyche of the child. It is not a child's story, but it reminds us of what children have always known best: the perversity of the adult world.

Tallent published a novel, *Museum Pieces* (1985), set in Santa Fe, New Mexico, the landscape within which many of her stories take place. In the contributors' notes to *Best American Short Stories 1987*, Tallent says of the New Mexico landscape that there are certain images she wishes to dwell on, and that "the country of northern New Mexico is very generous that way. Though famous, it's not exhausted. It's a landscape you can fall for and then find yourself wildly grateful to for years. Things aren't crowded together here. I find that visually and morally attractive," Tallent explained in 1985 to *Esquire* magazine.

Tallent's evocation of place is exceptional, whether it is Santa Fe or Española, New Mexico, Los Angeles, or London. Her use of topography, and of flora and fauna, to extend the implications of a story is striking, and in many cases, masterful. In the short story "Prowler," included in *Honey*, the character Dennis urinates around his ancient cottonwoods to establish his "proprietary interest" and to ward off the destructive beavers, called *castrados* in Spanish, "because after a fight the victorious male scythes off the scrotum of the loser." As details in the story accrue, the reader realizes how deeply the story develops issues of ownership and trespassing, of possession and of what is inherently sovereign. "Prowler" opens with Dennis's ex-wife unexpectedly returning from Europe and sitting in the living room wanting custody of their thirteen-year-old son for the summer. Dennis is loath to relinquish Andy, who he feels has been abandoned by his mother. Later in the story when Dennis confronts his son over a tattoo he has gotten without permission, Andy defends his actions by stating "it's my body." Though Dennis must come to understand his son as "someone strictly separate" from himself, the perfection of his son's body, which Dennis and his ex-wife have made and protected, is not something easily surrendered. Testament to Tallent's skill as a writer is the beautifully rendered paradox that the only other person who would truly mourn the loss of the perfection of Andy's body is Christie, Dennis's ex-wife, the person into whose care he resists giving the boy.

Tallent's critical appraisal of John Updike's male characters in *Married Men and Magic Tricks* is refreshing and brilliantly insightful, both for Tallent's intricate exploration of the calculus of Updike's couples and, just as important, for the gift of watching how a good writer, Tallent herself, reads and thinks while apprehending a genre in which she herself toils. Tallent says plainly in her preface that she read Updike "first for love, on buses, or when I had the flu. . . . I am reluctant to banish my first infatuation to the distinctly un-wistful tone of voice appropriate to criti-cism." It is this deep belief in the grounding of understanding, even truth, in emotion that undergirds any Elizabeth Tallent en-deavor.

Like Updike's, Tallent's subject matter is marriage, adultery, and the almost in-finite variations on the theme of family that widespread divorce has caused in America. In the story "The Minute I Saw You," collected in *Honey,* Kevin, a teen-ager, reminds his father, "Andrea is my stepcousin's name, remember?" To which his father replies, "Stepcousin. You have such an elaborate way of keeping track. I guess you need an elaborate way. God knows we've done enough to confuse you. Stepmother; new half sister; stepcousin, right, excuse me; *desaparecida* mom." In stories such as "Black Dress," "Honey," and "The Minute I Saw You," Tallent very con-certedly examines the elaborate way we keep track today; she charts just as dog-gedly the ways in which we do not. Dean Flower in the *Hudson Review* said of Tal-lent's characters: "These are not charac-ters who understand themselves. Tallent's purpose seems rather to trace their flick-ering tensions and recognitions, bursts of doubt and hope, without making any judg-ments. Her empathy is for the struggle to understand."

Readers of Tallent's work must not ig-nore the finely wrought emotional worlds of her characters, nor the intricate cir-cuitry of her characters' emotional ex-changes with the landscapes in which they live. In the contributors' notes to *Best American Short Stories 1987,* she writes, "I suppose that minor emotion connects to a theme of 'belonging' that I find in . . . stories I've written—especially those set in New Mexico—which seems to me to be about how land or a house belongs to someone, or how some*one* belongs to someone, and what two people, if they 'belong together,' must exclude; not only that, but how those two people interpret belonging, what responsibility it entails for them, and how it feels to them. That is the crux for me: how it feels to them."

Michelle Latiolais

SELECTED BIBLIOGRAPHY

Works by Elizabeth Tallent

Married Men and Magic Tricks: John Updike's Erotic Heroes. Berkeley: Creative Arts Book Company, 1982.

In Constant Flight. New York: Alfred A. Knopf, 1983.

Museum Pieces. New York: Alfred A. Knopf, 1985.

Time with Children. New York: Alfred A. Knopf, 1987.

Honey. New York: Alfred A. Knopf, 1993.

Critical Studies

Buffington, Robert. "Tolerating The Short Story." *Sewanee Review* 102 (fall 1994): 682–688.

Flower, Dean. "Impersonations." *Hudson Review* 47/3 (fall 1994): 495–502.

Fonseca, Isabel. "Defective Houses." *Times Literary Supplement,* July 1988.

Gorra, Michael. "American Selves." *Hudson Review* 41 / 2 (summer 1988): 401 – 408.

Smith, Starr E. "Honey." *Library Journal,* September 6, 1993.

PETER TAYLOR

(1917 – 1994)

Peter Taylor was born to a politically connected family in Trenton, Tennessee, and spent much of his early years in Nashville and St. Louis, where his father was a lawyer and businessman. Betrayed by a client, the financier Rogers Caldwell, whose corruptions figure in Taylor's novel *A Summons to Memphis* (1986), Taylor's father moved the family to Memphis in 1932 to rebuild his fortunes. Taylor's stories are keenly perceived and subtly presented examinations of upper-class life in these places, and frequently the stories turn on the fine differences among their cultures. Few authors can render a city or town, whether the real Pottsville of John O'Hara or the imagined Winesburg of Sherwood Anderson, with the eye for detail and with the sense of social distinctions that Taylor employs in his treatments of Nashville, Memphis, and Trenton. Taylor also has few rivals in the ironic yet sympathetic presentation of generational conflict (which he saw against the background of the major changes in southern culture in the middle decades of the last century); and in his stories of the emotionally complicated relationships between upper-class white southerners and their African American servants Taylor captures, with tact and insight, an intimate but neglected aspect of the racial mores of the South of his youth.

Taylor's much-interrupted and turbulent education included stints at Southwestern College in Memphis, Vanderbilt University, Kenyon College, and Louisiana State University. At Southwestern, his teacher, the poet Allen Tate, encouraged Taylor to study with John Crowe Ransom at Vanderbilt (and later at Kenyon). Taylor's decision to go to Vanderbilt, so important for his intellectual development as a writer, put him under the influence of the Agrarian circle, whose political ideas he never took seriously but whose aesthetic tutelage he always valued. He also met at Kenyon two lifelong friends and colleagues, Randall Jarrell and Robert Lowell. Frequently published in the quarterlies and in *The New Yorker,* Taylor was a sympathetic presence in the careers of many of the next generation of writers, with guest appointments to Kenyon, the University of Chicago, Ohio State, Harvard, and other universities, and long-term positions at the University of North Carolina at Greensboro (where he again had Jarrell as a colleague) and at the University of Virginia.

Schooled as he was by poets, Taylor always sought the concision and suggestiveness of poetry, and resisted (with some distaste) the comprehensive discursiveness of the novel. Indeed, it was his habit to draft his stories in verse (or in what he modestly called "broken-line prose"), recasting them in prose only at a late stage of composition. Toward the end of his career, he chose to keep certain stories in verse, stories with particularly startling subject matter and turns of plot, such as "The Hand of Emmagene" or "The Instruction of a Mistress." Taylor's thoughts about short fiction aligned it not only with narrative poetry but also with drama, which, like the short story, can allow itself only limited exposition and development, and must make its point in a key action concisely related. Only at the end of his life did Taylor write novels, finding the novel form surprisingly congenial after all, and winning a broader fame from his novels than he had enjoyed from his stories.

Taylor's first collection, *A Long Fourth and Other Stories* (1948), appeared with a foreword by Robert Penn Warren in which Warren defined Taylor's subject matter late and soon ("the contemporary, urban, middle-class world of the upper South") and Taylor's tone, which is critical and satirical but never so heavy-handed as to destroy his subjects ("an irony blended of comedy and sympathetic understanding"). The thematic center of the book is the slight air of disarray pervading the sexual lives of country people who have established themselves in the city. In the much anthologized "A Spinster's Tale," the young woman protagonist, terrified by and obsessed with the obscenely drunken Mr. Speed, who staggers by her house every day, calls the police in a panic when he stumbles up her porch to get out of the rain, and discovers in her own revulsion from the man, who passes out in the mud and probably never was any threat to her, an erotic cruelty of her own. In "The Fancy Woman," conceived as a kind of companion piece to "A Spinster's Tale" a vulgar kept woman radically miscon-

ceives the meaning of a poem her lover's rather innocent son recites for her. And in "Rain in the Heart," a newly married sergeant, hurrying home from a military base where his soldiers are preparing various kinds of debauchery for the weekend, has a disturbing encounter at a bus stop with a poor white servant woman who regales him with ugly and resentful racist remarks and anecdotes about attempts on her virtue by soldiers. She gives him a handful of sweet peas to take home to his wife, and contemplating it later that evening he wonders just how much he and his wife will be able to protect themselves from the ways of the world, until his musings on the subject subtly but inexorably come between them.

The title story, "A Long Fourth," also delicately suggests a state of sexual disarray. The parents upon whom this story centers represent an old order which Taylor does not sentimentalize. Harriet Wilson, for instance, is a condescending fussbudget much concerned with the bad smell of her African American houseboy, B.T. Her husband, who is only referred to as "Sweetheart," is ineffectual and uxorious. When the story opens, the crabby grown daughters of the family are preparing the house for the visit of "Son," who is visiting his home on the way to his army posting (the story is set during World War II), and his companion Miss Prewitt, a bohemian girl with whom he insists he is not in love. B.T. is also about to leave home, to do war work in an aircraft factory. When B.T.'s mother, Mattie, the family cook and in a way Harriet's confidante, ventures to observe that she and Harriet will share the grief of their children's departure, Harriet is offended and cruel, working herself up into a near nervous collapse over the slight she feels in the comparison of B.T. to her son. The story promises to turn on a dual conflict: first, a generational clash between the newly urbanized parents and their more sophisticated and worldly children, and second, a sectional conflict between the northern-educated Son (who has been publishing "disturbing articles" about the South) and Miss Prewitt (a northern-educated southerner, like Son, with equally progressive ideas and habits of life) on one hand, and the two unmarried sisters on the other, who are studying with "those reactionaries" at Vanderbilt, and who seem to be putting on an elaborate show of conservatism for the benefit of Miss Prewitt. But the key to the story turns out not to be these conflicts (which, however, are played out with rich ironies directed at both sides), but the disarray within each side. We learn, for instance, that Son has manipulatively brought out Miss Prewitt to shock his home folks, and in her drunken final speech we learn that his pretence of merely intellectual friendship for her has been his rather cold way of holding her unacknowledged love for him at a distance. We also see the disarray in the relationships among the Nashvillians, not only the bickering among the daughters, but also the increasingly unbridgeable distance between Harriet and Mattie, once her friend.

Most of the characters of Taylor's second volume of stories, *The Widows of Thornton* (1954), have pulled up stakes from that provincial town and resettled in Memphis, often bringing their African American servants with them. In various ways, the ties of culture and feeling that attach characters of this volume to the old order have come under strain, and frequently they are caught up in sentimental attachments that have turned false. The keynote of the volume is struck by "What Do You Hear from 'Em?" The title is the repeated question of Aunt Munsie, an elderly African American lady, a former nursemaid, who is taken by most who hear this question to be inquiring after the welfare of her long-grown white charges, Thad and Will Tolliver. In fact, she is not inquiring about their fortunes in the cities to which they have departed, but rather about when they plan to return to Thornton for good, for she believes their departure from the town to be a temporary thing. Her question is a way to bring to the fore the sentimental obligations of relationship that the young people, seeking success and urban life, have betrayed. Although they continue to keep up the fiction of intimacy with her by visiting and by sending her presents at Christmas, they have entered a modernity in which Aunt Munsie has no real place. The remaining Thornton women also seek to betray Aunt Munsie in the name of modernity, for they take exception to how she blocks traffic (or, they say, endangers herself in traffic) as she travels about town gathering slop for her hogs. But their plan to prevent her from keeping hogs within the town limits gets nowhere until Thad and Will, perhaps believing they act in her interest but in fact treating her as an old nuisance, secretly pressure the town authorities on the subject. Threatening her collie in a rage, Munsie says what she hadn't been able to say to Thad and Will: "Why don't I go down to Memphis or up to Nashville and see 'em sometime. . . . Because I ain't nothin' to 'em in Memphis, and they ain't nothing to me in Nashville. . . . A collie dog's a collie dog anywhar. But Aunt Munsie, she's just their Aunt Munsie here in Thornton. I got mind enough to see that."

These three groups of themes—generational conflict, the complicated relationship between white employer and black servant, and the intricacies of class in the upper South—play out in the volumes of Taylor's middle period, *Happy Families Are All Alike* (1959) and *Miss Leonora When Last Seen* (1964). Much of Taylor's early work was gathered in *The Collected Stories of Peter Taylor* (1969).

The most subtle, but also the strangest, story about class from this period is the much anthologized "Venus, Cupid, Folly and Time." In the Chatham (or Memphis) of this story, upper-class youth are initiated into social adulthood by a party at the house of an aging unmarried brother and sister, Alfred and Louisa Dorset. Survivors of a once numerous and wealthy family, the pair has been reduced to supporting themselves by selling paper flowers and the shriveled figs from their garden. There is something uncanny about their relationship, which, while not literally incestuous, has an incestuous flavor, and the vaguely perfumed aestheticism of their demeanor owes something to Tennessee Williams and to Poe. Despite their poverty and oddness, the Dorsets are the social arbiters of Chatham's youth, each of whom is compelled, at an important age, to attend their elaborately choreographed yearly party in their house full of erotically suggestive works of art such as an antique plaque of Leda and the Swan and a plaster replica of Rodin's "The Kiss." The strange

coming-of-age ritual is disrupted when an upper-class brother and sister, Emily and Ned Meriwether, contrive to have the paperboy, Tom Bascomb, admitted in Ned's place, with Ned sneaking in later. Tom and Emily are discovered necking (to Emily's evident excitement), and when Ned cries (about Tom and Emily, but evidently in a way also about the Dorsets) "Can't you tell? Can't you see who they are? They're brother and sister!" chaos breaks out. The Dorsets, believing they know quality when they see it, suppose that Ned, not Tom, is the interloper, and lock him in a disused bathroom. The discovery of which child is which evidently unnerves the Dorsets completely, and also puts an end to their yearly ritual.

Taylor's career had a remarkable late flowering, and the last years of his life not only were his most productive but also brought him his greatest fame. The late story "In the Miro District" (the title story of Taylor's 1977 collection) is perhaps Taylor's most mature and subtle treatment of generational conflict. In the background of the story is a low-level conflict between the protagonist's genteel but rather unperceptive parents and the protagonist's grandfather, Major Basil Manley (a resonant name from Taylor's own family history). The parents would like the grandfather to move into the city with them, not only so that they can better care for him and be closer to him, but also to keep him under their thumbs and to encourage him to play the role of decorative Confederate veteran in the social life of the city and in their son's education. The grandfather, scornful of the ritual promotions one receives as a Confederate veteran (he had been a major, but had, since his brush with the Klan, refused the paper promotions to Colonel and General that the veterans organizations vote for their members), and eager to preserve his independence from his children, deliberately does not dress the part (wearing only grubby gabardines), and remains on his rundown and rather unromantic farm in Hunt County.

The grandson seeks ever more powerful ways of discrediting himself, always accidentally-on-purpose, with his grandfather. Arriving unannounced while the grandson, his parents being away for the weekend, is engaged in a drinking spree with his prep-school friends, Manley rebukes the boy but sternly brushes aside his attempts to get his goat, refusing to dress him down fully. The grandson takes this refusal as a refusal of acknowledgment, as if Major Manley were too detached from him to quarrel with him. Major Manley is similarly gruff, but not mortally offended, when six weeks later he again walks in unannounced on his grandson and several of his friends in bed with girls "of the other sort." Finally, he stumbles upon the narrator just as he has been making love in the Major's own bed, not with a raffish girl of the underclass, but with a "nice" girl from Ward Belmont school. Instantly recognizing the nature of the transgression (and perhaps even recognizing the girl, when he discovers her huddled in his wardrobe), he says not a word and leaves the house. From this point on he attends Confederate veteran functions, regales people with Civil War anecdotes, moves in with his children, and in other ways plays the part his daughter and son-in-law have scripted for him.

Only his grandson knows how much he has been defeated.

Another high point of Taylor's late career is the long title story of his 1985 collection *The Old Forest and Other Stories*. As in "In the Miro District," the narrator is recollecting a sexually charged incident of many decades before. During his engagement, he had, like many upper-class youth of Memphis during the 1930s, dated many women of a different class. Although he refers to these women jocularly as being "of the demimonde," they are for the most part career women of the middle class, many of them educated and cultured, most of them in a way far more earnest about their lives than the society types of the narrator's own crowd. The week before his wedding, he was driving through Overton Park, a surviving stand of old-growth forest, with a young woman named Lee Ann Deehart, on his way to Southwestern College, where, in a somewhat pointless display of independence, he has been studying Latin poetry. Although many of the narrator's liaisons are not so innocent, this one apparently is little more than a study date. But the narrator has an automobile accident in the park, and in the aftermath of the accident Lee Ann disappears. During the search for Lee Ann, it is the narrator's fiancée, Caroline Braxley, who comes to the fore, and who, knowing that her marriage hangs on the outcome, shows herself a more formidable and more human person than one might have guessed from the role of Society Girl that has been chosen for her to play. Lee Ann turns out to have taken refuge with her mother, the proprietor of a speakeasy that the protagonist frequents, and she had, it turns out, gone into hiding so that her friends would not discover who her parents were.

Taylor's final volume of stories, *The Oracle at Stoneleigh Court* (1993), is bound together by a concern with the supernatural. Taylor had always admired the ability of drama to introduce supernatural figures with the brisk simplicity of "Enter Ghost," and noted that in the more circumstantial and more realistically constrained world of fiction it was difficult to do such a thing. In the title story, the "Oracle" is the widow of a Tennessee politician, Augusta St. John-Jones, who lived most of her life at the Stoneleigh Court apartments in Washington, D.C. (like a real relative of Taylor's). There she becomes a Catholic of a mystical kind, and dresses up and behaves like a gypsy fortune-teller. In some mysterious way, she breaks up the wartime romance of the narrator and Lila Montgomery, who had come to Washington to do war work and who stays on after the war as a professional woman. Dying and insane, Mrs. St. John-Jones is brought back to Memphis by Lila, who, decades after their failed romance, practically throws herself at the narrator, apparently compelled in some occult way by Augusta. In "The Witch of Owl Mountain Springs: An Account of Her Remarkable Powers" the other signal story from this volume, a young woman is betrayed by her lover and her best friend at the resort of the title, and remains on there as a recluse and eccentric. Many years later, the betraying couple, on their way to Owl Mountain Springs, are killed in a mysterious auto accident. As in "The Oracle at Stoneleigh Court" the occult aspects of the story

never explicitly surface, and the story presents itself as a socially realistic account of class and courtship such as occupied Taylor from *A Long Fourth* to *The Old Forest*. Taylor revisited many of the incidents from *The Oracle of Stoneleigh Court* in his last novel, *In the Tennessee Country*, published in the year of his death.

Peter Taylor brought to his depiction of the changes in the political, racial, and class structure of the upper South a unique gift, and he chronicles that change not with the tragic grandeur of Faulkner or the corrosive satire of Flannery O'Connor, but with the tender, clear-sighted irony of Chekhov and Turgenev.

John Burt

SELECTED BIBLIOGRAPHY

Works by Peter Taylor

A Long Fourth and Other Stories. New York: Harcourt, Brace, 1948.

The Widows of Thornton. New York: Harcourt, Brace, 1954.

Happy Families Are All Alike. New York: McDowell, Obolensky, 1959.

Miss Leonora When Last Seen and Fifteen Other Stories. New York: Ivan Obolensky, 1964.

The Collected Stories of Peter Taylor. New York: Farrar, Straus, & Giroux, 1969.

In the Miro District and Other Stories. New York: Carroll and Graf, 1977.

The Old Forest and Other Stories. Picador, 1985.

The Oracle at Stoneleigh Court. New York: Alfred A. Knopf, 1993.

Critical Studies

McAlexander, Hubert H., ed. *Conversations with Peter Taylor.* Jackson: University Press of Mississippi, 1987.

McAlexander, Hubert H., ed. *Critical Essays on Peter Taylor.* Boston: G. K. Hall, 1993.

Robinson, David M. *World of Relations: The Achievement of Peter Taylor.* Lexington: University Press of Kentucky, 1998.

Robinson, James Curry. *Peter Taylor: A Study of the Short Fiction.* Boston: Twayne, 1988.

Wright, Stuart. *Peter Taylor: A Descriptive Bibliography, 1934–1987.* Charlottesville: University Press of Virginia, 1988.

JAMES THURBER

(1894 – 1961)

The author of many witty, elegant sketches, memoirs, fables, parodies, and spoofs, James Thurber was perhaps America's preeminent twentieth-century humorist. Born in 1894 in Columbus, Ohio, the middle of three boys, he was the child of a civil servant and a playful, theatrical mother. When James was seven years old, he was blinded in his left eye in a bow-and-arrow accident. He attended Ohio State University where he began his career as a journalist. After a brief stint in France as a reporter for the *Chicago Tribune,* he settled in New York City and began writing for the fledgling *New Yorker* magazine. Thurber won renown as the quintessential *New Yorker* humorist, the heir of Robert Benchley and peer of E. B. White, with whom he collaborated on the 1929 best-seller *Is Sex Necessary?*, a satiric spoof of self-help manuals. Books such as *My Life and Hard Times* (1933) found a large, appreciative audience in America and England. His character Walter Mitty became an archetype of the yearning Romantic, henpecked husband and put-upon citizen. In 1945, his retrospective collection of humorous writings and drawings, *The Thurber Carnival*, solidified and expanded his reputation. He was married twice, to Althea Adams in 1922 and to Helen Wismer in 1935. Despite eye operations, near total blindness after 1941, heavy drinking, and increasing gloom about contemporary life, Thurber remained remarkably prolific and popular until his death in 1961.

Thurber's favorite subject was himself, his family history, and his travail, most gloriously exposed and celebrated in the 1933 collection *My Life and Hard Times,* which includes such comic masterpieces as "The Night the Bed Fell" and "The Day the Dam Broke." Recounting "those bewildering involvements for which my family had . . . a kind of unhappy genius" ("A Sequence of Servants"), Thurber depicts eccentricities, his own and those of his ludicrous relatives, with affection, amusement, clinical detachment, and understated irony. His spontaneous overflow of flustered feelings is recollected in tranquility: "Until a man can quit talking to himself in order to shout down the memories of blunderings and gropings," Thurber remarked in "A Note at the End" (*My Life and Hard Times*), "he is in no shape for the painstaking examination of distress and the careful ordering of events so necessary to a calm and balanced exposition of what, exactly, was the matter."

Thurber excelled at parody and satire, such as the demolition of psychology in *Is Sex Necessary?*, the meticulous impersonation of Southern Gothic in "Bateman Comes Home," and the wacky obsessions of a crime aficionado in "The Macbeth Murder Mystery." His two most memorable stories remain "The Catbird Seat" and "The Secret Life of Walter Mitty," in which Thurber views unexceptional characters from multiple angles, including affection, tenderness, and sympathy. Both stories demonstrate Thurber's mastery of competing styles, the inflated, clichéd idiom of fantasy, the ragged rhythms of everyday life, and holding it all together, the commanding poise of the narrator. At its best, James Thurber's writing rises from modest mirth to modern myth.

Walter Mitty is the epitome of a Thurber figure, whose inner world is as dramatic and heroic as his real life is mundane and pathetic. Bossed about by his overbearing wife, yelled at by parking-lot attendants, laughed at by passersby, aimless, timid Mitty imagines himself as a fearless naval commander, an ingenious surgeon, an intrepid fighter pilot. Like Joyce's Leopold Bloom, he is all too human, outwardly undistinguished but gifted and redeemed by his richly imaginative sensibility. As in Joyce, the clashes and incongruities between inner and outer worlds are painfully amusing. A leitmotif of Mitty's secret life, the "ta-pock-eta-pocketa-pocketa-pocketa-pocketa" of machines that ordinarily befuddle him but in fantasy he masters, became a popular slogan and tagline during World War II. Everybody, it seems, knew and was Walter Mitty. By the end of this brief, unforgettable story, the little man has in a way indeed become "Walter Mitty the Undefeated," a humorous hero "to the last," occupying a permanent place in both our imagination and the *Random House Dictionary of the English Language*.

A typical Thurber piece begins with something prosaic, such as a domestic spat, a pet's misbehavior, a maid's malapropism, or an aggravating colleague. Whatever produces "all the confusion which his disorderly mind so deplorably enjoyed," as he says of his character Bert Scursey in the story "Destructive Forces in Life," Thurber gleefully embroiders, exaggerates, and caricatures. Regularly professing simplicity, he cherishes perplexity: "Whereas we had been one remove from reality to begin with," he comments with evident satisfaction in "A Ride with Olympy," "we were now two, or perhaps three, removes." These "interesting transferences" ("The Cane in the Corridor"), or ascents from the mundane to the sublimely ridiculous, provide (as Thurber reflects in "What Do You Mean It *Was* Brillig?") "a form of escapism that is the most mystic and satisfying flight from actuality I have ever known. It may not always comfort me, but it never ceases to beguile me." Such leaps from the ordinary to the bizarre are provoked or enabled by "twitchiness," a perpetual discomfort or dread, contemplated with as much poise as Thurber (or his protagonists and various personae) can muster.

Thurber fears many persistent perils:

menacing machines, mortal frailty, the hullabaloo of misunderstandings, the pathetic timidity of men, and the threatening encroachments of women. Because of the incessant confusion between the inconsequential and the significant, and the tendency of minor muddles to catalyze chaos, the humorous writer "of light pieces," says Thurber, "talks largely about small matters and smally about great affairs" ("Preface to a Life" in *My Life and Hard Times*). Stressing his constant anxiety, Thurber adds that humorists generally "lead an existence of jumpiness and apprehension. They sit on the edge of the chair of Literature. In the house of Life they have the feeling that they have never taken off their overcoats." In a much-quoted formulation, Thurber said, "The little wheels of their invention are set in motion by the damp hand of melancholy."

A story titled "The Secret Life of James Thurber" shows how artful Thurber's humor can be. It begins: "I have only dipped here and there into Salvador Dali's 'The Secret Life of Salvador Dali' . . . because anyone afflicted with what my grandmother's sister Abigail called 'the permanent jumps' should do no more than skitter through such an autobiography, particularly in these melancholy times." Thurber establishes himself as a casual dipper into life's profound mysteries, not because he is unable to dive deeper but because he is precariously balanced. Typically, Thurber bestows a family idiom, the "permanent jumps," on what more solemn writers might term existential dread. Yet despite his uncertain equilibrium, Thurber's authority is enabled by his humorous state. He finds both refuge

and weapon in what he terms "my secret world of idiom," language uniformly lucid, precise, and poised. A word like "skitter" perfectly conveys how twitchiness is transformed into reflection: "One does not have to skitter far before one comes upon some vignette which gives the full shape and flavor of [Dali's] book." While mocking at Dali's absurd pretensions and bizarre idiosyncrasies, Thurber also implies a covert affinity with folly. Much of what Thurber observes he finds laughable and lovable, the object of mild humor rather than savage satire, because it reminds him of something in and of himself.

Thus, the apparent dichotomy between Thurber's plain common sense and Dali's fantastic nonsense becomes more interesting and complicated than first appears. Thurber's discourse, ostensibly about Dali, is flagrantly subjective, though he claims the opposite: "The trouble, quite simply, is that [in *My Life and Hard Times*] I told too much about what went on in the house I lived in and not enough about what went on inside myself." And while he acknowledges that Dali "has the jump on me from the beginning" in inner vision, reiterating the word "jump" links Dali to Thurber with his "permanent jumps."

The stuff of Thurber's memories is ordinary—his father's derby, the Ohio Anti-Saloon League, and William Howard Taft—as opposed to Dali's romantic and exotic materials. But the amusing discrepancies suggest deeper connections: "Salvador Dali's mind goes back to a childhood half imagined and half real, in which the edges of actuality were sometimes less sharp than the edges of dream." Precisely what one might say of Thurber's *My Life and Hard Times*. "Thus he was born halfway along the road to paranoia, the soft Poictesme of his prayers, the melting Oz of his oblations, the capitol, to put it so you can see what I am trying to say, of his heart's desire." Thurber, defining himself as a man of plain good sense, reveals himself to be as imaginative, fantastic, and visionary as Dali, though he displays his cursed gift without the famous artist's self-aggrandizing fanfare.

Gradually we perceive the link between the great, strange Dali and the simple, mundane Thurber, and value their follies, all that "impetus toward paranoia." When Thurber specifically mentions his "escape" and sanctuary, that "secret world of idiom," its value is undeniable and demonstrable. For Thurber revels in "the enchanted private world" into which he drifts, or which descends upon him, at the slightest provocation or nudge. No less than Salvador Dali, he wanders "in the secret, surrealist landscapes," a wonderful, frightening, and amazing place: "It was a world that, of necessity, one had to keep to oneself and brood over in silence, because it would fall to pieces at the touch of words." Like Wordsworth's poetic vision, it "gleams, flickers, and vanishes away," but may return or be recalled, with nervous jumps, imagination, and joy.

If James Thurber the man existed apprehensively in the house of Life, the author surely sits comfortably on the chair of Literature.

Robert H. Bell

SELECTED BIBLIOGRAPHY

Works by James Thurber

Is Sex Necessary? Or, Why You Feel the Way You Do. (With E. B. White.) New York: Harper & Brothers, 1929.

The Owl in the Attic and Other Perplexities. New York: Harper & Bros., 1931.

The Seal in the Bedroom and Other Predicaments. New York: Harper & Bros., 1932.

My Life and Hard Times. New York: Harper & Bros., 1933.

The Middle-Aged Man on the Flying Trapeze. New York: Harper & Bros., 1935.

Let Your Mind Alone! And Other More or Less Inspirational Pieces. New York: Harper & Bros., 1937

The Last Flower: A Parable in Pictures. New York: Harper & Bros., 1939.

Fables for Our Time and Famous Poems Illustrated. New York: Harper & Bros., 1940.

My World—And Welcome to It! New York: Harcourt, Brace and Company, 1942.

Men, Women and Dogs: A Book of Drawings. New York: Harcourt, Brace, 1943.

The Thurber Carnival. New York: Harper & Bros., 1945.

The Beast in Me and Other Animals: A New Collection of Pieces and Drawings About Human Beings and Less Alarming Creatures. New York: Harcourt, Brace, 1948.

The Thirteen Clocks. New York: Simon and Schuster, 1950.

The Thurber Album: A New Collection of Pieces About People. New York: Simon and Schuster, 1952

Thurber Country: A New Collection of Pieces About Males and Females, Mainly of Our Own Species. New York: Simon and Schuster, 1953.

Thurber's Dogs: A Collection of the Master's Dogs, Written and Drawn, Real and Imaginary, Living and Long Ago. New York: Simon and Schuster, 1955.

Further Fables for Our Time. New York: Simon and Schuster, 1956.

Alarms and Diversions. New York: Harper & Bros., 1957.

The Years with Ross. Boston: Little, Brown, 1959.

Lanterns and Lances. New York: Harper & Bros., 1961.

Credos and Curios. New York: Harper & Row, 1962.

Thurber and Company. New York: Harper & Row, 1966.

Selected Letters of James Thurber. Edited by Helen Thurber and Edward Weeks. Boston: Little, Brown, 1981.

Thurber: Writings and Drawings. Selected by Garrison Keillor. New York: Library of America, 1996.

Critical Studies

Bernstein, Burton. *Thurber: A Biography.* New York: Dodd, Mead, 1975.

Bowden, Edwin T. *James Thurber: A Bibliography.* Columbus: Ohio State University Press, 1968.

Grauer, Neil A. *Remember Laughter: A Life of James Thurber.* Lincoln: University of Nebraska Press, 1994.

Holmes, Charles S. *The Clocks of Columbus: The Literary Career of James Thurber.* New York: Atheneum, 1972.

Holmes, Charles S., ed. *Thurber: A Collection of Critical Essays.* Englewood Cliffs, N.J.: Prentice-Hall, 1974.

Kinney, Harrison. *James Thurber: His Life and Times.* New York: Henry Holt, 1995.

JOHN UPDIKE
(1932–   )

One of the most prolific, versatile, and widely read of late twentieth-century writers, John Updike was born in 1932, in Shillington, Pennsylvania, the only child of Wesley R. Updike, a high school mathematics teacher, and Linda Grace Hoyer, an aspiring writer. After graduating summa cum laude from Harvard in 1954, he studied for a year at the Ruskin School of Drawing and Fine Art in Oxford, and on returning to America, joined the staff of *The New Yorker,* the magazine where he has since published much of his short fiction, poetry, light verse, parodies, essays, and book reviews.

Since 1957, Updike has lived north of Boston, mainly in Ipswich and Georgetown, where, "equipped with pencils, paper [and computers]" he has practiced his "solitary trade as methodically as the dentist practiced his." That singular pursuit has produced more than fifty books, among them twenty novels, six volumes of poetry, six of book reviews and essays, a memoir, a play, four books for children, and nine collections of short stories. Two other volumes of short fiction, *Olinger Stories* (1964) and *Too Far to Go* (1979), bring together mostly reprinted pieces. The first explores growing up in an imagined version of Shillington; the second portrays the marriage of the recurring characters, Joan and Richard Maples, in the suburbs around Boston. Updike's work has been honored with the Pulitzer Prize, National Book Award, American Book Award, National Book Critics Circle Award, Howells

Medal of the American Academy of Arts and Letters, and National Medal of Arts. More than twenty of his short stories have been selected for the prestigious annual volumes *Best American Short Stories* and *Prize Stories: The O. Henry Awards.*

"I want stories to startle and engage within the first few sentences," Updike has said, "and in their middle to widen or deepen or sharpen my knowledge of human activity, and to end by giving me a sensation of completed statement." In more than two hundred works of short fiction written over five decades, he has admirably fulfilled his own wishes, and produced a body of work that (along with the Rabbit tetralogy of novels) is often considered his major contribution to American literature. Four groupings have achieved particular renown: the dozen-or-so Olinger stories, eighteen pieces about the Maples, some twenty narratives featuring the novelist Henry Bech, and the thematically connected tales of late middle age ("the other side of the slope") that appear mostly in *Trust Me* and *The Afterlife.*

"If I had to give anybody one book of me it would be the Vintage *Olinger Stories,*" Updike has remarked. "They are dear to me." Readers and critics have shared the author's affection; "Pigeon Feathers," "Flight," "The Persistence of Desire," and "The Happiest I've Been" remain among his most admired, frequently anthologized works. The area of human action explored is boyhood and adolescence, and the title's punning invitation to stay a while is irresistible. Set in rural Pennsylvania (just west of Philadelphia and south of the coal-mining country), the stories depict and ponder the experiences of a gifted local boy (variously named), who is keenly self-conscious of the weight of the past and the pull of the future in every moment of an intensely felt present. Although he longs to escape the confinements of provincial life, he is aware of the nourishing connections to the people and places of his youth—the silken ties that he will guiltily yet necessarily sever.

The structural principle in each of these stories (whether in third or retrospective first person) is a fine counterpoint between the mature reflections of the older writer and the bright-eyed impressions of the young protagonist. "Flight," for instance, opens: "At the age of seventeen I was poorly dressed and funny-looking, and went around thinking about myself in the third person. 'Allen Dow strode down the street and home.' 'Allen Dow smiled a thin sardonic smile.' Consciousness of a special destiny made me arrogant and shy." After this fondly satiric opening, the older Allen moves immediately to a sharp memory of a time in boyhood when he and his mother hiked up a hill overlooking Olinger, and she surprisingly announced: "There we all are, and there we'll all be forever. . . . Except you, Allen. You're going to fly." Back home, though, she treats him as ordinary as ever and makes him feel "captive to a hope she had tossed off and forgotten."

But before the adult narrator goes on to develop this fundamental tension of early adolescence, he recalls the family history in resuscitating detail, creating in a few paragraphs a mini-saga that not only fleshes out the Dow parents and grandparents but conveys the allure and limits of small-town life and of the unknown, beckoning world beyond. Returning to develop the conflict between mother and son, Allen recalls how on a school trip in his senior year, he became romantically involved with Mollie Bingham, of whom his mother strongly disapproved. In the triangle that followed, the boy ricocheted between girl and mother, angrily capitulating at the end to his mother's fervent yet reluctant desire for him to escape from Olinger.

The distinction of "Flight" (and of many of the other Olinger stories) rests in Updike's gift for capturing, in an iridescent yet meticulously precise prose, the vibrancies and unresolved tensions of adolescent life: the avidity, self-display and warm-heartedness of youth; a boy's desire to leave and to stay, to be ordinary and extraordinary, realist and dreamer, tied to others yet also free. Despite his apprehension of limits, however, the protagonist is (as Updike himself insisted) "rewarded unexpectedly." The bitter quarrel with his mother points toward liberation, and toward a deepening understanding of flight itself as a contradictory fact in human life.

If the Olinger stories record the enchantments and disillusionments of adolescence, the Maples stories constitute a rueful, yet oddly invigorating chronicle about marriage, separation, and divorce. Through eighteen intimate yet deliberately distanced vignettes, we follow husband and wife from Greenwich Village in the mid-fifties to Tarbox (a fictional suburb of Boston) in the early nineties. We observe them embracing and quarreling, raising children, keeping house, committing adultery, coming back together, splitting, agreeing to get one of the first "no fault" divorces in the Commonwealth of Massachusetts, and finally, married to different spouses, meeting again at the birth of one of their grandchildren, where they surprisingly find that they have more in common with each other than with their new partners.

Updike once spoke of "the Maples duet," and these stories of misalliance do have a distinctive music all their own. The surface sound is light, sophisticated, seductive: the Maples talk wittily, racily, insightfully, about every aspect of their private lives; but their conversation becomes "increasingly ambivalent and ruthless as accusation, retraction, blow, and caress alternated and canceled," and they are knit "ever tighter together in a painful, helpless, degrading intimacy." And yet despite their failures and transgressions, they share many heartening moments. As their creator put it, "That a marriage ends is less than ideal; but all things end under heaven, and if temporality is held to be invalidating, then nothing real succeeds. The moral of these stories is that all blessings are mixed."

One work in which the Maples music is plangently yet pleasingly heard is "Separating," which opens on a brilliant June day that mocks marital misery with "golden shafts and cascades of green." Richard had wanted to leave at Easter, but Joan insisted he stay until the four children were finished with exams and home from school, so they could have summer ahead to console them. Waiting for the end, he had involved himself with domestic repairs, "battening the house against his absence . . . a Houdini making things snug before his escape." But he was haunted by his secret and an image of each child as a knife-sharp wall "with a sheer blind drop on the other side."

Now, with everyone home, Richard wants to minimize fallout by announcing the separation at dinner. Joan argues for telling the children one by one: "they're individuals, you know, not just some corporate obstacle to your freedom." However, at the dinner table, before anyone has been told, Joan blurts out the truth. Surprise, pain, and confusion turn swiftly into lacerating domestic farce. Trying to strike a mature pose, the eldest daughter, Judith, dismisses as silly the plan for a trial separation; the young son John accuses his parents of not caring about him and the others, and clownishly lights matches, chews cigarettes, and pops a salad-filled napkin into his mouth. Later that night, the older son Richard, Jr., kisses his father passionately on the mouth and moans "the crucial, intelligent word: '*Why?*'" The story ends: "*Why*. It was a whistle of wind in a crack, a knife thrust, a window thrown open on emptiness. The white face was gone, the darkness was featureless. Richard had forgotten why."

Much of the impact of "Separating" comes from the accuracy with which Updike detects all the pressure points in the now-familiar modern ritual of breaking bad news to the kids: the guilt-ridden embarrassment of the parents; the alarm, fright, and dodginess of the children; the unnerving echo of "why?" The mix of exquisite delicacy in the telling and the awkwardness of what is being told is the indelible Updike signature.

Updike puts his virtuoso prose and his perception of life as forked, unwieldy, and encumbered to different use in a third story sequence: the scenes from the life of Henry Bech, a prominent but now unproductive, unmarried Jewish novelist, nine years older than his creator, "an alterego not myself." As a mouthpiece with a difference, Bech is a sly creation, for through him the much-acclaimed Updike is able to create a satiric yet not unsympathetic picture of the writing life in America without seeming ungrateful or narcissistic. Having scrutinized the country in Olinger and the suburbs in Tarbox, he turns to Manhattan to probe another part of his own life experience: his having been a shy, small-town Christian prodigy in a cosmopolitan environment dominated by enormously talented, self-fashioning Jews such as Norman Mailer, Saul Bellow, and Philip Roth.

As Bech himself puts it in a foxy "Dear John" letter addressed to his creator: "my childhood seems out of Alex Portnoy and my ancestral past out of I. B. Singer. I get a whiff of Malamud in your city breezes, and am I paranoid to feel my 'block' an ignoble version of the more or less noble renunciations of H. Roth, D. Fuchs, and J. Salinger? Withal, something Waspish, theological, scared, and insulatingly ironical that derives, my wild surmise is, from you."

By presenting his protagonist in episodic short stories, Updike is able to reflect on a variety of bookish activities, locales, and predicaments without feeling obliged to develop in depth any one character or theme. The result is a gallery of snapshots which taken together provide a vivid impressionistic view of important aspects of contemporary literary life. We hear of New York writers having trouble with work, women, and fame, who write novels about writers who live in New York and have trouble with work, women, and fame. Bech too has trouble with all three, but unable to write, he restlessly pursues romantic entanglements and accepts invitations to serve as cultural emissary in, among other places, Moscow, Nairobi, Sydney, Bucharest, Toronto, and Seoul.

Many of the Bech vignettes are very funny, laced with acerbic, on-the-mark jokes about the ironies of Bech's situation (the sought-after writer who can't write), the vagaries of reputation, the trendiness and commercialism of current book publishing, and the cultural misunderstandings that often occur when West meets East. The eminent blocked novelist receives the Melville Medal, awarded every five years to the American writer "who has maintained the most meaningful silence"; he squirms to our amusement when Africans and Asians press him about "the political role of the novelist"; and at the close of the first volume, Updike playfully provides a fake Bech bibliography in which he works off various grudges, settling scores with critics who have unfavorably reviewed his own work.

These are among Updike's edgiest stories. The novelist's fame and his inability "to do his thing"—to write—is at the heart of his uncomfortable relations with women, editors, publishers, and literati around the globe, as well as a central source of Updike's astringent comedy. From the start, Bech is compromised by his own shortcomings and his awareness of "the silken mechanism" by which America "reduces her writers to imbecility and cozenage." After much disappointment, he gets unblocked and writes *Think Big,* a best-seller about media figures who grease the country's celebrity machine. But this unadventurous and cozy book betrays the values his work used to embody, and in which Bech still believes, and he sinks further into disillusionment, self-doubt, and—most likely—the pit of greater celebrity.

Returning sixteen years later in *Bech at Bay: A Quasi-Novel* (1998), the seventy-four-year-old writer had taken quite literally to settling some of his accounts by murdering reviewers who had dismissed his earlier work: pushing one off a subway platform, mailing another cyanide-laced stationery, and driving a third to suicide by feeding him subliminal messages on the Internet.

At bottom, the Bech stories are as much about a condition as a character—the condition of a writer compromised first by his inability to write and then by his writing a book shaped in large part by the celebrity role he has assumed. The so-called downhill slope stories, the fourth notable Updike grouping, are also studies of a condition: that of "living in death's immediate neighborhood . . . in a universe without a supernatural." The characters tend to be men around sixty with names like Morison, Fulham, Fogel, and Fanshawe. Having become increasingly aware of diminishment—of time passing, of the body's accumulating failures, of a loss of interest in the weighty world—they feel more and more as if they are acting in a stale play at the end of its run. Yet despite the keenness with which Updike registers the increments of their feelings about dwindling (from crabbiness to self-pity, fuming, hostility, panic, and despair) the mood is rarely gloomy. Not only does he give his aging figures an arsenal of wryly witty responses to their own decline, but he also records epiphany moments in which they unexpectedly discover a bearable lightness of being as the end nears. Prosaic events such as the delay of a check, the loss of a wallet, the arrival of Daylight Savings Time, even a mild earthquake become objective correlatives for sharpening one's senses, accepting the slipping away of life, and recognizing that "dying is the last favor we do to the world" and to ourselves.

These autumnal pieces include "Short Easter," "Deaths of Distant Friends," "Conjunction," "Slippage," "The Wallet," and "Playing with Dynamite," but the most densely textured and resonant of all is "The Afterlife." In this story, a prim, too-comfortably settled, late-middle-aged lawyer, Carter Billings, and his wife Jane decide to visit their friends, Frank and Lucy Eggleston, now settled in England. Arriving in Norfolk, the Billingses are startled to find the transplanted couple living energetic, fruitful lives: Frank devoted to painting and Lucy to birdwatching and local charity work. Each speaks blissfully of living a long-deferred dream. Despite plentiful food and drink, the cordial reunion evening is disconcerting. The Egglestons are bored by gossip from America; the Billingses do not quite know what to make of their friends' equanimity; and all four are aware of not having rekindled the old connection. Before retiring, they agree on the next day's plans: Lucy will drive them to the sea while Frank rides in the local hunt.

In the middle of the night, Carter goes to the bathroom, takes a wrong step on the dark, unfamiliar landing, and tumbles down the stairs. The fall, bruisingly real, is also strangely surreal, perceived in a dreamy slow motion in which he imagines someone has hit him hard in the center

of his chest, and yet is composed enough to feel pangs of guilt at disturbing his hosts.

At breakfast, the Egglestons jokingly thank him for not "popping off on us," and Carter says, "It happens. More and more, you see your contemporaries in the *Globe* obituaries. The Big Guy is getting our range." Unembarrassed by this "outburst of theology," he begins the day feeling serene; and from then on, everything falls on his "revitalized senses with novel force." As he, Jane, and Lucy go off to tour the splendid countryside, he feels increasingly weightless, "as if, in that moment of flight headlong down the stairs, he had put on wings." The nocturnal adventure continues to have startling, almost magical consequences, and a quiet realistic tale evolves into an exhilarating redemptive fable. The day turns stormy. Violent winds and rains uproot trees and down power lines, but Carter is captivated by birds, animals, and a sparkling landscape in constant motion. "A miraculous lacquer lay upon everything, beading each roadside twig, each reed of thatch in the cottage roofs, each tiny daisy trembling in the grass by the lichen-stained field walls." The old lawyer's earlier intimation of mortality has been transformed into an exquisite appreciation of Nature's (and God's) grandeur. The fall becomes— amazingly but credibly—a Fortunate Fall, an event orchestrated by the Big Guy to quicken Carter's sense of life's wonder, at the same time that it heightens his awareness of the brevity and precariousness of his life.

When the trio returns from their outing, Frank berates them for having driven about in cyclonic weather: the hunt had been called off and the broadcasters were warning people to stay off the roads.

"In this bit of a breeze?" Lucy cooed.

Jane said, "Why Frank, darling, how nice of you to be worried."

And Carter, too, was surprised and amused that Frank didn't know they were beyond all that now.

The originality and beauty of "The Afterlife" comes from Updike's marvelous tonal control: his ability to mix droll domestic comedy, breathtaking descriptions of nature, and the oscillating feelings about death and life in the ignited mind of an ordinary man. Here, as in the best of the other stories of aging, afterlife is the time before death, an interval which—in the hands of an Updike—turns out to have potent mixed blessings and unexpected rewards of its own.

The four groups described earlier constitute the core of Updike's achievement as a short story writer, but he has written many other memorable pieces that exist outside these categories. Among them are "A&P," the brash, self-exposing monologue of a teenage supermarket clerk (a great favorite on school syllabi); "The Christian Roommates," a riveting account of a clash of faiths in a Harvard dormitory; "The Other," a realistic fable about a man obsessed with his marriage to a twin; "The Music School," a densely woven meditation about transubstantiation; and "The City," the tale of a stricken businessman who unexpectedly finds compassionate care in a large urban hospital. Other readers might expand the choice of favorites by choosing "Should Wizard Hit Mommy,"

"The Hermit," "Harv Is Plowing Now," "The Lifeguard," "The Gun Shop," "Trust Me," or "Leaf Season." And everyone is likely to agree on the splendid "A Sandstone Farmhouse," the aging writer's return to Olinger that won the O. Henry Prize for the best story of 1991. Whatever the final list, though, the large number of first-rate works ensures Updike's permanent reputation as a master of the short story genre.

Lawrence Graver

SELECTED BIBLIOGRAPHY

Works by John Updike

The Same Door. New York: Alfred A. Knopf, 1959.

Pigeon Feathers. New York: Alfred A. Knopf, 1962.

Olinger Stories. New York: Alfred A. Knopf, 1964.

The Music School. New York: Alfred A. Knopf, 1966.

Bech: A Book. New York: Alfred A. Knopf, 1970.

Museums and Women. New York: Alfred A. Knopf, 1972.

Problems. New York: Alfred A. Knopf, 1979.

Too Far to Go. New York: Alfred A. Knopf, 1979.

Bech Is Back. New York: Alfred A. Knopf, 1982.

Trust Me. New York: Alfred A. Knopf, 1987.

The Afterlife. New York: Alfred A. Knopf, 1994.

Bech at Bay. New York: Alfred A. Knopf, 1998.

Critical Studies

Greiner, Donald J. *The Other John Updike: Poems, Short Stories, Prose, Play.* Athens: Ohio University Press, 1981.

Luscher, Robert M. *John Updike: A Study of the Short Fiction.* New York: Twayne, 1993.

Plath, James M., ed. *Conversations with John Updike.* Jackson: University of Mississippi Press, 1994.

HELENA MARÍA

VIRAMONTES

(1954–)

Helena María Viramontes was born in East Los Angeles in 1954. She has a bachelor's degree in English literature from Immaculate Heart College and a master of fine arts degree from the University of California at Irvine. Coordinator of the Los Angeles Latino Writers Association, literary editor of *XismeArte Magazine* and *201: Homenaje a la Ciudad de Los Angeles,* coeditor with María Herrera-Sobek of *Chicana Creativity and Criticism: Charting New Frontiers in American Literature,* she is the winner of several literary awards, including the University of California Irvine Chicano Literary Contest. She has made her name as one of the most prominent Latina writers with a slim collection, *The Moths and Other Stories* (1985), and a novel, *Under the Feet of Jesus* (1995). Her

reflections on the writer's craft are gathered in a moving testimonial essay, "'Nopalitos': The Making of Fiction" in *Breaking Boundaries: Latina Writings and Critical Readings* (1989).

Her terse, lyrical writing is concerned with the lives of Latin American women, children, migrant workers, and illegal immigrants. Experimental and innovative, her stories oscillate between different characters' points of view and follow a nonlinear narrative sequence. She writes predominantly in English interspersed with familial and affective Spanish terms. As a child Viramontes spoke Spanish, but it was "stolen" from her by what she calls the "lingual censorship" of the public school system. Her extreme care in the use of language strips words down until they shine with their own luminosity and may be attributed to the fact that she feels uncomfortable writing in English about a world that she lived and experienced in Spanish.

Viramontes's stories are so intricately woven that they lend themselves to innumerable readings. For example, "The Moths"—a work that along with "The Cariboo Cafe" is most often anthologized—is a story about the desire for immanence and wholeness of a young girl alienated by her father's tyrannical and patriarchal nature. She finds comfort and a church of sorts at her dying grandmother's house. This very simple plot moves forward by means of the girl's reminiscences and by Viramontes's poetic deployment of two organizing metaphors. The first is the girl's "bull hands" (so called because she refuses to perform any "feminine" tasks like embroidering), hands that are transformed into "liar's hands" by suddenly growing disproportionately, like Pinocchio's nose, when she questions her grandmother's healing ability and calls her a liar in her mind. The second is that of "the moths" out of which her grandmother makes a healing salve to shrink the girl's hands back to normal size. Viramontes here transposes a creative fairy tale from a European cultural context onto a Mexican American one in which, as critic Juan Bruce-Novoa has pointed out, the hands become a privileged signifier related to the manual labor performed by the Mexican American working class.

The moths reappear at the end of the story as the creatures that come out of her grandmother's body after her death. "The Moths" couples Viramontes's critique of patriarchy with a critique of the church as the instrument used by men, in this case the girl's father, to "feminize" her. Just before her grandmother's death, the young girl enters a church, apparently to look for candles. While there she experiences the coolness of the church as distance, lack of caring, and coldness. She feels alone amid the frozen statues with blank eyes when only moments before at Abuelita's she had felt "safe and guarded and not alone. Like God was supposed to make you feel." Her feelings of isolation while in church remind her of the brutal way her father orders her to attend mass saying that he will "kick the holy shit out of [her]." The blasphemous phrasing of his order belies his Christian intent and unveils his desire that by veiling his daughter she will finally be frozen: feminized and passive. Instead, the daughter takes her veil and pretends to go to church only to escape to Abuelita's house, which proves

to be her true church and where she learns about life, plants, the cycles of nature, and ways of healing. Upon entering the house, she smells chiles being toasted and starts to cry, "the tears dropping on the table like candle wax." Poetically coming full circle, church in "The Moths" is for the girl her grandmother's home, and her live tears parallel the tears of wax that frozen statues in churches shed when submissive women light candles at their feet.

Abuelita is an archetype of Mexican American literature, for grandmother figures are invariably seen as a connection to the past (the culture being left behind yet being held on to), the land, animism, and an indigenous tradition of healing. Like Rudolfo Anaya's archetypal grandmother, Ultima, Abuelita is mythical both while alive and in death. As the young girl takes a bath with her dead grandmother in one last purifying moment of desire when she tries to re-create the wholeness she had felt with the old woman, small, gray moths come from Abuelita's soul "fluttering to light." They literalize Abuelita's belief that moths lie within the soul and "slowly eat the spirit up."

Like her use of the Pinocchio tale in another form and context, in "The Cariboo Cafe" Viramontes transposes the myth of La Llorona from a Mexican context (arising out of Malinche's loss of her children to conquering Spain in some versions, and in others out of the Medea myth translated to the Rio Grande) into a myth joining the Americas. The washerwoman María loses her son in an unspecified Central American civil war. After years of futile search, sometimes amid hallucinatory Dumpsters of body parts and children searching for their dismembered parents, she crosses many borders and ends up in Los Angeles fleeing from a United States –funded war at home. There she finds two little latchkey children, son and daughter of illegal immigrants, wandering lost in the city and in her madness believes she has finally found her long-lost son. In fact, three different sets of people are searching for their children: María the washerwoman/Llorona whose search for her son spans the Americas, the parents of the boy and girl lost in the city, and the Cariboo Cafe's owner, a racist figure who despises his clients (illegal immigrants, whores, drug addicts), unaware that he, like them, is a second-class citizen since he has lost his son JoJo in Vietnam. In "The Cariboo Café," unlike "The Moths," moths stand for Latin American illegal immigrants who come to the United States crossing multiple borders, fleeing tragic wars at home. Attracted to the "light," the promise of a better future, they arrive in the States only to get "burned" here by racism, discrimination, and economic exploitation.

With her stories, Helena María Viramontes has emerged as an accomplished and promising American short story writer.

Silvia Spitta

SELECTED BIBLIOGRAPHY

Alarcón, Norma. "Making 'Familia' From Scratch: Split Subjectivities in the Work of Helena María Viramontes and Cherríe Moraga." In María Herrera-Sobek and Helena María Viramontes, eds., *Chicana Creativity and Criticism: Charting New Frontiers in American Literature,* pp. 147–159. Houston: Arte Público Press, 1988.

Saldívar-Hull, Sonia. "Feminism on the Border: From Gender and Politics to Geopolitics." In José David Saldívar, ed., *Criticism in the Borderlands: Studies in Chicano Literature, Culture, and Ideology,* pp. 203–220. Durham: Duke University Press, 1991.

Yarbo-Bejarano, Yvonne. "Introduction." In Helena María Viramontes, *The Moths and Other Stories.* Houston: Arte Público Press, 1988.

ANNA LEE WALTERS
(1946–)

The short stories of Anna Lee Walters, written primarily for other American Indians, affirm a respect for customs and the land that is of absolute necessity to tribal peoples. Her book *The Sun Is Not Merciful: Short Stories* won the American Book Award in 1986. This collection of eight stories illustrates the continuing importance to tribal peoples of stories that link them to the cosmic forces, shaping their identity and commitment to the natural world and to their culture. Her experience of Pawnee, Otoe-Missouri, and Navajo cultures has shaped Walters's vision as a writer.

In an autobiographical preface to her short story "Buffalo Wallow Woman," Walters wrote, "I was born into two modern cultures of non-writers and these are the communities to which I best relate.

In these communities, unwritten philosophies, ethics, values and premises are at work for who I am, what I do." These communities, the Pawnee and the Otoe-Missouri, were removed to Indian Territory on adjoining tracts of land in the late nineteenth century. Born in Pawnee, Oklahoma, on September 9, 1946, Anna Lee Walters is the daughter of Luther McGlaslin, an Otoe-Missouri, and Juanita M. (Taylor) McGlaslin, a Pawnee. For several years, before she entered school, Walters was raised by her paternal grandparents at their home near Black Bear and Red Rock creeks in Oklahoma. She then lived with her parents until her mother was hospitalized with tuberculosis, and she and her younger sister were placed in a Pawnee boarding school, where they spent two years. Thereafter, Anna returned to live with her parents and attended public schools from the fifth through the eleventh grades. At sixteen, she left Oklahoma to study painting at the Institute of American Indian Arts in Santa Fe, New Mexico. During this period she began to write. She attended the College of Santa Fe (1972–74) and worked as a library technician for the Institute of American Indian Arts, Santa Fe, New Mexico (1968–74). She was a technical writer for Dineh Cooperatives, Chinle, Arizona (1975) and for curriculum development for Navajo Community College, Tsaile, Arizona (1976–84). She has also served for a number years as director of Navajo Community College Press. She is married to Harry Walters, a Navajo museum curator. They have two sons. Walters holds a bachelor of arts degree (1989) and a master of fine arts in creative writing degree from Goddard College.

In her preface to "Buffalo Wallow Woman," Walters said she does "a lot of unwriterly things" every day, such as caring for "little housebirds" and communicating with them, and "walking in deep coppery canyons as a way of leaving writing behind and going forward into something else that is quite separate from everything as we know it in our modern everyday world."

Such experiences connect characters with a large and enduring reality in Walters's short fiction. Her story "Chapter 1," which appeared in Kenneth Rosen's collection The Man to Send Rain Clouds (1974), is an imaginative account of Dineh (Navajo) life in Canyon de Chelly in 1863. For the first time in many years the drought has broken, and the people are enjoying the bounty of a good harvest. But the feast day that opens the story turns into a horrendous slaughter when U.S. soldiers invade the village. The story is told from the limited third-person perspective of Natanii, a Dineh boy, injured in the attack, who finds shelter among the junipers as he waits for darkness and a chance to escape. This story foreshadows the "Preface" narrative of Walters's novel, Ghost Singer (1988), in which a Dineh family camped in the mountains falls victim to slave catchers in June 1830. Walters's essay "The Navajos" in Talking Indian: Reflections on Survival and Writing (1992) provides a historical context for these stories.

Stories told by Walters's mother inspired her to write "The Resurrection of John Stink," originally published in Frontiers: A Journal of Women Studies (1981) and later included in Walters's collection The Sun Is Not Merciful. Set in Oklahoma in the 1920s, "The Resurrection of John Stink" is based on legends told of a man descended from tribes removed to Indian Territory in the late nineteenth century. Because he has seizures, John is an outcast. But a young woman, Effie, falls in love with John after she goes to his house to care for him in his old age. Effie decides to move into his house because she is afraid to leave John alone when his seizures get worse. After a particularly hard seizure, the doctor pronounces him dead, and John is buried on the tribal burial grounds. Soon John's dogs alert Effie that something is wrong. They lead her to the grave, and she hears noises coming from it. She then realizes that John has been buried alive and she helps him out of the grave. After that, people in the community treat the man even worse and start calling him "John Stink." But Effie always stays with him, and he teaches her "there is no death, only a change of worlds"—a perception John has experienced through his seizures many times during his life.

"The Warriors," also set in Oklahoma but during the 1950s, and first published in Simon Ortiz's anthology *Earth Power Coming* (1983), is the first story in *The Sun Is Not Merciful*. The warrior, Uncle Ralph, is a Korean War veteran who teaches his nieces what it means to be Pawnee. The younger niece narrates the story. Though Ralph later becomes an alcoholic and eventually dies, his knowledge and understanding of the Pawnee language, his stories of the Evening Star and the Morning Star as their progenitors, and his philosophy, passed on to the girls, remain as his legacy. As the traditional Pawnee warrior provides food for his family, Uncle Ralph provided not only groceries when he came to visit, but food for the spirit:

"For beauty is why we live," he told his nieces.

Also emerging from Walters's childhood in Oklahoma is her title story, "The Sun Is Not Merciful," which ends the collection. At the center of the story set in 1980 are two Otoe sisters, Lydia and Bertha. Both are nearly seventy years old. As they sit fishing, a ranger drives up and tells them he will have to fine them unless they promise not to fish there anymore. Lydia tells the ranger, whom they know as Hollis, that they cannot do as he asks because they have always gone there to fish. Within this story is embedded an older story, one Old Man told the women when they were girls: "'Fact is, alla us came outta water. Happened up north, round Canada somewhere. Well, girls, we found ourselves on the shore of this wide lake. We came outta it, see? Weren't no other people then— just us back then. And that's why we're fishermen from way back, fore time even began.'" When Lydia had asked Old Man how they got to the place where they were then living, he told her they walked four weeks, and he was age seven at the time.

The more modern story occurs during a severe drought, when the Otoe-Missouri people are being pressured to sell their land so it can be flooded to make a reservoir. Though along with several of their neighbors, the sisters resist, they are eventually forced to sell. At the end of the story the creek has been dammed, the women's original home is under water, and they have been moved to a different cabin. Nevertheless, they are again sitting on the bank fishing when Hollis drives up again and angrily says he is going to fine them. But he decides not to do that when he notices that Lydia is now missing a leg, lost to gangrene. The women tell him about their origins as people who "'Fished since time began,'" and Hollis decides to stop harassing them, though the women agree that "'he don't really understand at all.'" These women are true survivors who have been taught to stand the heat and to know that "the sun is not merciful."

Sun is a character in "Going Home," one of a number of stories in *The Sun Is Not Merciful* set in the Navajo homelands of New Mexico and Arizona. Commenting on aging, sexuality, marriage, and the destructive potential of anger, the contemporary characters take on mythic qualities: "Sun had no woman until he met Nita. It was with her that all this began. She came into his life like a storm blown from the flat prairie land in the east. He found her in the desert, a flower which he picked for himself and carried home."

But Sun and Nita have grown old. Sun notices his wrinkles and those of his wife and decides he needs a younger woman. When Nita confronts Sun about his affair and threatens to leave, he tells her, "'Go on home if you want to go. . . . The old folks were right. You don't belong here anyway. You never did!'" He goes so far as to say, "'I'd shoot myself first before I'd ask you to stay.'"

Nita tells him, "'Sun, when you come back again, I'll not be here anymore.'" As she leaves, Nita sees an elderly woman walking and offers her a ride home. The woman asks Nita how long she has lived in the community, and when Nita says she has lived there twenty years, the elderly woman says it is now Nita's home. She also reminds Nita that Sun is "nothing more or less than a man."

Nita drives on to Albuquerque, where she reconsiders and decides to drive back to her home with Sun. About the same time Sun decides to go home too. He has been drinking and is driving on the wrong side of the road. His truck hits an approaching car on the driver's side, and the collision knocks the vehicle over the edge of an embankment, into the darkness. Sun cannot see the wreckage, and he drives away until he finds a turnoff a few miles away and stops. In the morning, with his head aching, he remembers the accident as if it had been a dream and drives back to the scene. Fear begins to grip him before he finds Nita's car and Nita, dead. He sings a song of "deep hurt and suffering." And after the song ends, so does the story: "He wrapped the gun in his bearlike hand."

Thus, the grim harvest from the mixing of anger, alcohol, automobiles, and a gun is told. The plot could be critiqued as too coincidental to be believable; yet, real life sometimes results in such coincidences, and it is the truth of life that Walters's story is telling.

Sometimes this truth seems too ugly—some would say raw—for telling. But it should be told. "Apparitions," also from *The Sun Is Not Merciful,* features Marie Horses and her daughter Wanda, who have gone shopping. Both are wearing cotton print dresses. Wanda's mother wears braids and moccasins. Wanda wears faded blue tennis shoes. They look very different from the fashionable mannequins in the store windows and the fashionably dressed customers and salespeople. When Marie and her daughter go into a store to purchase an item held for them on layaway, the store clerk is rude. But Marie patiently answers the clerk and pays for the item. Then she takes Wanda to try on some shoes, which she plans to put on layaway. The shoe salesman, who is also rude to them, sends Marie back to talk to the clerk because he says he wants to make sure she will approve the layaway. In fact, he wants to get rid of Marie, so he will be free to molest her daughter. While the mother is gone, he gropes Wanda's legs and feels inside her underwear. At the end of the story, after they have left the store, Marie asks her daughter if she likes going to town, and Wanda emphatically says "'No!'"

The story ends, "'Me neither,' Marie Horses said, and they walked on in silence." Though Wanda has not told her mother what the salesman has done, the two have at least communicated to one another their dislike of their demeaning treatment. The story relates the kind of incident that is too much a part of life for adolescent girls and Native women.

Increasingly, Walters's fiction has centered on the female consciousness. This is true of her story, "Buffalo Wallow Woman," which is included along with two other short stories, "Che" and "The Web," in *Talking Indian.* The modern Buffalo Wallow Woman lives on the sixth floor of "the white man's hospital in the mental ward." This woman, whose moccasins and other clothing have been taken from her, wanders the halls of the institution wearing a wrinkled gown. Having become a "bag of bones and white hair," she feels she is a ghost and longs to escape. Her salvation occurs when she tells an Indian nurse, Tina, the story of Buffalo Wallow Woman, who would have died had she not reached the water of a buffalo wallow and been given new life.

People in the modern world who live as visionaries are often viewed as crazy. But the old woman in the mental ward completely understands and accepts her visions. She tells Tina, "'I structure my life around the visions and voices because it pleases me to honor them this way. I am never alone because of this. It is my inheritance from Buffalo Wallow Woman, from my own flesh and blood, from the visions I have received, and from my identity as this kind of person.'" Tina helps her to escape, and Buffalo Wallow Woman becomes all spirit at the end of the story, floating out through the bars.

Norma C. Wilson

SELECTED BIBLIOGRAPHY

Works by Anna Lee Walters

"Chapter 1." In Kenneth Rosen, ed. *The Man to Send Rain Clouds,* pp. 82–92. New York: Viking, 1974.

"The Resurrection of John Stink." *Frontiers: A Journal of Women Studies* 6/3 (1981): 68–72.

"The Warriors." In Simon J. Ortiz, ed., *Earth Power Coming: Short Fiction in Native American Literature,* pp. 37–50. Tsaile, Ariz.: Navajo Community College Press, 1983.

The Sun Is Not Merciful: Short Stories. Ithaca, N.Y.: Firebrand Books, 1985.

Ghost Singer. Flagstaff, Ariz.: Northland, 1988.

"Bicenti." In Craig Lesley, ed., *Talking Leaves: Contemporary Native American Short Stories,* pp. 304–318. New York: Dell, 1991.

*Talking Indian: Reflections on Survival and Writ-
ing.* Ithaca, N.Y.: Firebrand Books, 1992.
Preface to "Buffalo Wallow Woman." In Joy
Harjo and Gloria Bird, eds., *Reinventing
the Enemy's Language: Contemporary Native
Women's Writings of North America*, pp.
532–549. New York: W. W. Norton,
1997.

Critical Studies

Lisa, Laurie. "Walters, Anna Lee." In
Gretchen Bataille, ed., *Native American
Women: A Biographical Dictionary*. New
York: Garland, 1993.
Ruppert, James. "Anna Lee Walters." In
Andrew Wiget, ed., *Handbook of Native
American Literature*. New York: Garland,
1996.

ROBERT PENN WARREN
(1905–1989)

Robert Penn Warren was born in
Guthrie, Kentucky, in 1905, and died
in 1989. Educated at Vanderbilt University and Oxford, he taught for many years
at Yale, where he was associated with a
group of literary scholars often referred
to as the New Critics. He is best known
as a poet and novelist, the author of such
major works as *All the King's Men* (1946),
a novel about Willie Stark, a corrupt but
charismatic southern state governor based
on Louisiana's Huey Long, and *Brother to
Dragons* (1953), a book-length poetic
drama. Warren won the Pulitzer Prize for
poetry twice, and once for *All the King's
Men*. He was also a prominent critic who,
with Cleanth Brooks, wrote a major textbook, *Understanding Poetry*.

Warren's earliest success, however,
came in the realm of short fiction, with
"Prime Leaf," a long story written while
the author was a graduate student at Oxford. Its subject was the tobacco wars
fought by local planters during Warren's
childhood in Kentucky. These planters
were protesting against powerful tobacco
trusts from outside the region that had
been arbitrarily fixing prices on the chief
product of this state, the source of their
economic stability. The violence that occurred led to the imposition of martial
law in Kentucky, and one of Warren's first
memories was that of an encampment of
state guards outside his boyhood town of
Guthrie. He grew up hearing about the
"night riders" who sought to break the
backs of the trusts, and these stories provided the material for "Prime Leaf" as well
as for Warren's first novel, *Night Rider*
(1939).

"Prime Leaf" is the central story in *The
Circus in the Attic* (1947), Warren's only
volume of short fiction. It revolves around
a quarrel between an impulsive man and
his father, and the impact of this quarrel
on the man's young son. The man has
become involved in a scheme to shoot one
of the "night riders," whom he despises;
he is finally ambushed and killed—a
deeply ironic outcome that calls into question the whole enterprise of opposing the
protest movement. The story is, for the
most part, a meditation on the old conflict
of ends and means, as the young boy in
the story wonders whether his father's
impetuous actions were even remotely

justified. Set in the lush country of Warren's boyhood, the story conjures the
small towns and farms of the Deep South
with a peculiar freshness.

Warren drew heavily here, as in most
of his work, on reservoirs of memory, and
his recollections have an almost hallucinatory clarity in "Prime Leaf," which anticipates the major themes of his later fiction: the impact of violence on daily life,
the consequences of choosing one path of
action over another, and the inevitable
clashes that occur between fathers and
sons. As always, Warren was concerned
with the burden of guilt, often traced to
family histories and the larger conflicts of
the South, especially the Civil War, which
he viewed as a family conflict writ large.

"Blackberry Winter," perhaps his best
story, is suffused with a tone of deep nostalgia for a world long gone. The tale opens
with the narrator-hero, Seth, remembering a day from his boyhood some thirty-
five years before. The action of the story
consists of one morning on a tobacco farm
in Tennessee. The story's best moments
are those of deep recollection, as when
Seth remembers a time when he stood "in
the stillness of woods," a place where "you
feel your very feet sinking into and clutching the earth like roots and your body
breathing slow through its pores like the
leaves."

The boy's impressionable mind registers each passing moment with incredible
vividness as the June morning comes up
cool and damp. This season is traditionally
called "blackberry winter" because it
seems a throwback to the previous season
and to a previous time when a storm or
"gully washer" had flooded the nearby
stream, ruining crops and wreaking havoc

on the local village. As a boy, Seth had
wandered into the village to see what had
happened and encountered a scene of destruction that surprised and shocked him.
First, he sees the "stringy and limp" bodies
of chicks drowned in the overflow; their
eyes have "that bluish membrane over
them which makes you think of a very old
man who is sick about to die." He stands
shoulder to shoulder with a crowd watching a dead cow float down the stream. He
listens to a Civil War veteran reflect on
devastation. Then he visits a black family
of his acquaintance. Their normally tidy
cabin is a mess; trash has washed out from
under the cabin, and the couple is fighting.
The father, suffering from "woman mizry,"
slaps his son hard for being too noisy. Seth
becomes disoriented.

In the culminating scene, the boy encounters a tramp, who wields a knife. This
man has also been washed out by the
storm—like the trash from under the
black family's cabin. Seth follows him, out
of morbid curiosity and some inner compulsion; suddenly, the tramp turns on
him, saying: "You don't stop following me
and I cut yore throat, you little son-of-a-
bitch." "But I did follow him," the narrator
confesses, "all the years."

In a single morning, the child has gone
from innocence to experience, discovering the "jags and injustices" of the adult
world. Human nature and the natural
world itself are hauntingly interlocked in
this tale, as the "gully wash" becomes a
force of human history. As always in his
work, Warren dwells on contrasts: farm
versus town, white versus black people,
the timeless world of the child against the
time-haunted world of adults. This vivid
morning, which once baffled the child, no

longer puzzles the adult; rather, he regards this "blackberry winter" as emblematic. It represents life, and the way things are.

While none of the other stories in this collection quite matches "Blackberry Winter" or "Prime Leaf," there are striking scenes in "The Circus in the Attic" (which chronicles the life of Bolton Lovehart in a manner that anticipates Warren's fine last novel, *A Place to Come To*), "Christmas Gift," and "When the Light Gets Green." As a writer of prose and poetry, Robert Penn Warren was never less than interesting, and often inspired. His gift for anecdote, witnessed most obviously in his long narrative poems, serves him well as a writer of short stories, even though he worked only occasionally in this genre. With William Faulkner, Flannery O'Connor, and others, he remains a central writer of the American South in this century.

Jay Parini

SELECTED BIBLIOGRAPHY

Works by Robert Penn Warren

The Circus in the Attic. New York: Harcourt Brace, 1947.

Critical Studies

Boner, Charles H. *Robert Penn Warren.* New York: Twayne, 1964.

Burt, John. *Robert Penn Warren and American Idealism.* New Haven: Yale University Press, 1988.

Gray, Richard, ed. *Robert Penn Warren.* Englewood Cliffs, N.J.: Prentice-Hall, 1980.

Justice, James H. *The Achievement of Robert Penn Warren.* Baton Rouge: Louisiana State University Press, 1981.

SYLVIA A. WATANABE
(1 9 5 3 –   )

Sylvia A. Watanabe is a third-generation Japanese American, born in Hawaii on the island of Maui, and it is this birthplace that has inspired her stories. She is the recipient of a Japanese American Citizens League National Literary Award and a creative writing fellowship from the National Endowment for the Arts. Her stories have appeared in literary journals and anthologies such as *The Best of Bamboo Ridge* (1986), *Passages to the Dream Shore: Short Stories of Contemporary Hawaii* (1987), and *Home to Stay: Asian American Women's Fiction* (1990). *Talking to the Dead* (1992) is Watanabe's first collection of short stories about the life and people of a multicultural and multiethnic community on the Lahaina coast of Hawaii.

In addition to the unique locale of her birth, the stories her father told while she was growing up have had a profound impact on Watanabe's fiction. "Even now when we go for walks," says Watanabe, "[Father] tells me names of things—of plants, and birds, and trees. He tells me where to hunt guavas and when to go down to the beach to harvest seaweed." According to Watanabe, her title story, "Talking to the Dead," grew out of "these naming walks I take with my father." However, in this and most of the stories in her collection, the harmony of local Hawaiians' lives with the rhythms of nature is disrupted by the penetration of commercialism, while new constructions and businesses are mushrooming on the islands, threatening to destroy not only the ecosystem but also the old values systems that regulate people's relationships.

Like many stories by other Hawaiian writers, Watanabe's narratives show the hardships, griefs, and poverty in local Hawaiians' lives beneath the idyllic surface of the islands. Watanabe portrays these lives with great compassion, humor, and ambivalence, which helps her in capturing the complexity of the historical changes Hawaii is undergoing and their impact on individuals' lives in various ways. The drama and tension of her stories are often created by a clash between traditional beliefs and new attitudes. In fact, the conflicts among the contending forces in the lives of those who struggle to maintain old traditions, and those who seek to thrive with new ideas and opportunities, are the major thematic concerns of *Talking to the Dead,* which provide a cohesiveness to this collection.

The stories are linked not simply by common themes, but more explicitly through recurring characters and development of events, though each story is a separate narrative with a distinct plot, voices, and different protagonists, and stands on its own as an independent story. This relationship among the stories, at once individual and interconnected, is characteristic of the genre of story cycles, which has been developed and transformed by contemporary Asian American writers such as Maxine Hong Kingston in

The Woman Warrior, Amy Tan in *The Joy Luck Club,* and Lois Ann Yamanaka in *Wild Meat and the Bully Burgers,* in their respective search for a form to realize the dynamics between individuals and communities. Like these story cycles, Watanabe's *Talking to the Dead* displays a double tendency to assert the individuality of each story and to highlight the bonds of unity that make the separate narratives into a single whole. Although Watanabe's collection shares some formal similarities with these other story cycles, it remains distinct from them.

For instance, while Kingston's and Tan's narratives shift between China and the United States, portraying the immigrants' and their children's in-between-worlds experiences, the settings in Yamanaka's and Watanabe's stories are rooted in their respective locales of Hawaii. But Watanabe's story cycle further differs from Yamanaka's, partly in thematic concerns and mostly in narrative perspectives. The series of stories in Yamanaka's book is told from the perspective of the same child narrator with a concentration on her childhood in Hawaii, whereas Watanabe's stories give equal weight to the lives of various protagonists, and are told from different perspectives. Moreover, Watanabe links these lives through such intricate relationships among the characters that she succeeds in creating a live multiethnic community within which to "explore the forces which bring individual human beings of different cultures together, and to imagine the private struggles which arise from such meetings."

Watanabe is especially skillful at interweaving themes and characters in her narratives. For instance, in connection to the story, theme, and major characters of the opening story "Anchorage," Hana, Little Grandma, and Aunt Pearlie, Watanabe introduces a number of minor characters that are to become major characters in the following stories. Emiko McAllister, a Japanese Hawaiian who comes to visit Hana, in the next story, "Emiko's Garden," deals with her Caucasian husband Dr. McAllister's love affair with apparently typical Japanese women's silence and submission, which turn out to be winning tactics when we find out indirectly through the major characters' conversation in the fourth story, "Certainty," that Dr. McAllister will not divorce his wife for the much younger woman, Lulu. Lulu injured herself after hearing the news about the death of her lover, Jimmy, a Japanese Hawaiian, who is a major character in the third story, "The Cave of Okinawa." Jimmy's father, Henry, tries to save his life by helping him and Lulu to elope to Canada when he is home on leave from the army, but his plan fails because of the intervention of his wife Haru, who is jealous of his son's love for Lulu. We later learn in "Certainty" that Haru's intervention has actually led to her son's death in Vietnam. Haru appears briefly in "Emiko's Garden" in association with Dr. McAllister's conversation with Freddy Woo, who is the husband of Aunt Pearlie. In turn, Little Grandma and Emiko McAllister, among others, reappear in the last story, "The Prayer Lady," about a Japanese Buddhist head priest, who is mentioned in the first story.

With interlocking characters and stories such as these, Watanabe establishes a living community with a wide range of characters to explore her thematic concerns from different perspectives, while maintaining a dynamic relation between plurality and unity in both the structure and theme of her story cycle. The interconnectedness among the stories also enables Watanabe to develop and reinforce her themes through multiple perspectives. Such narrative strategies and their effects are especially explicit in the link between the opening story, "Anchorage," and the two closing stories, "Talking to the Dead" and "The Prayer Lady." In these stories, personal conflicts are all intertwined with the changing environment of Hawaii and local people's values.

Watanabe is equally skillful at making the most of the materials within a single story to enhance the dramatic effect and thematic concerns. In "Anchorage," for instance, she deftly deploys the narrator Hana's situation to serve several functions. Hana returns home for a short visit after graduating from college and before leaving for Anchorage to take up her job as an art teacher in a public high school. Her long absence from home has kept her in the dark about the conflict between Aunt Pearlie and Little Grandma over Hana's father, who apparently has been suffering from Alzheimer's disease. Hana's ignorance of what has been going on at home enables Watanabe to create dramatic tension and build up suspense, thus keeping readers curious, then surprising them with unexpected turns of narrative development. Hana's absence from home also enables Watanabe to reveal to the reader the changes on the islands through her observation:

Down the hill, the cloud shadows drifted over the sugar fields. The shifting green and yellow of the cane, the red furrows of earth, and the blue curve of the water joined into a patchwork of shapes and colors. On the opposite shore of the bay, the skyline bristled with the metal and glass towers of the fast-spreading resort town, where there had been miles of empty beach and some of the best net fishing on the island just ten years before.

The juxtaposition of the images on the hillside and the opposite shore of the bay takes on a symbolic meaning as the story unfolds. A way of life on the islands is in danger of disappearing. The forces that give rise to the "fast-spreading resort town" also drive Aunt Pearlie to threaten to hand her brother (Hana's father) over to the law on charges of laundry theft if Hana and Little Grandma do not agree to put him into a nursing home, under the pretext that Grandma is unable to take care of her son, but with the motive of urging Grandma to sell her place to the Canadian investment company that built the new hotels across the bay.

Furthermore, in association with Hana's artistic talent, Watanabe weaves into the narrative both the father's and Grandma's struggles in resisting the infiltrating forces of commercialism, and their efforts to capture and record the disappearing beautiful sights of Hawaii and village life, through their respective artistic works. The father used to make paintings and sketches of the coastal scenes before being disabled by his disease; Little Grandma has been making a huge quilt

with pieces of stolen materials from the laundromat—a collage depicting places and people in the life of the village, including a scene of the Japanese festival for the dead with the old head priest leading a procession of lights to the sea. These images, juxtaposed with the sights of the Laniloa Geriatric Care Facility and a vacant lot for sale, possibly to be bought by a fried chicken operation from Texas, reinforce the theme of the story dramatized in the conflict between Little Grandma and Aunt Pearlie.

The theme of individuals' struggles against historical forces in order to preserve a sensibility, a particular view of the world, and traditional values is further explored and developed in "Talking to the Dead" and "The Prayer Lady." The major characters and their actions in these two stories offer a sense of healing and triumph. In the former, Aunty Talking to the Dead refuses to give up her practice of a Hawaiian tradition of preparing the dead body for burial, even though her son owns a successful modernized funeral home. Her healing chants put "the stones, and trees, and stars back into their rightful places." Her singing makes "whole what had been broken." In the closing story, "The Prayer Lady," the bedridden retired head priest of the Buddhist temple decides to end his life, feeling defeated by changes such as the loss of worshippers at his temple and the new head priest's inviting a rock star from Japan to the *bon* festival (Japanese festival for the dead). Eventually the retired head priest is healed physically and spiritually by the Prayer Lady through her advice: "Neither of us could have held back what is happening." While struggling to preserve a traditional way of life, Watanabe's stories suggest, people must recognize the historical forces and adapt to the changes by renewal of the old through transformation. Cultures and traditions are not static; they are constantly reinvented. Yet this implication is countered by the destructive aspects of "progress" and the failures in many characters' efforts to make a better life. The interlocking possibilities of the story cycle offer Watanabe more space than a single story would allow to explore the complexity of her thematic concerns.

Sylvia Watanabe refashions the short story cycle—a genre that can be traced to Homer's *Odyssey,* Ovid's *Metamorphoses,* Boccaccio's *Decameron,* and Chaucer's *Canterbury Tales,* and to the Indian *Panchatantra* and the Arabian *A Thousand and One Nights*—into a fitting form for the particular concerns of her time and place. Both the theme and structure of *Talking to the Dead* have profound implications for our understanding of tradition, culture, and progress, for the transformation of genres such as the short story cycle, and especially for the relation between form and content of literary texts.

Zhou Xiaojing

SELECTED BIBLIOGRAPHY

Works by Sylvia A. Watanabe

Talking to the Dead and Other Stories. New York: Anchor Books, 1992.
Home to Stay: Asian American Women's Fiction. (With Carol Bruchac.) Greenfield Center, Vt.: Greenfield Review Press, 1990.

Critical Studies

Davis, Rocio G. "Identity in Community in Chinese American Short Story Cycles: Sigrid Naunez's *A Feather on the Breath of God.*" *Hitting Critical Mass: A Journal of Asian American Cultural Criticism* 3/2 (spring 1996): 115–133.
Seaman, Donna. Review. *Talking to the Dead. Booklist* 88 (August 1992): 1996.

EUDORA WELTY
(1909–)

The last of a great generation of southern writers that includes Robert Penn Warren, Caroline Gordon, Carson McCullers, Katherine Anne Porter, and Flannery O'Connor, Eudora Welty was born in Jackson, Mississippi, in 1909. She was educated at Mississippi State College for Women and at the University of Wisconsin, where she developed a passion for photography, and where she studied Woolf, Yeats, Chekhov, and Turgenev, who indeed are imaginatively closer to her than Faulkner, Warren, or O'Connor. After a year spent studying advertising at the Columbia University Business School, she returned to Jackson in 1931, and has lived in her family's home since. Through her long career she has won a great deal of recognition, from a Guggenheim fellowship in 1942 to the Pulitzer Prize (for *The Optimist's Daughter*) in 1972, the National Medal for Literature in 1979, the Medal of Freedom in 1980, and the National Book Critics Circle award in 1984. In 1996 she was inducted into France's Legion d'Honneur. Welty also has a distinguished career as a novelist and essayist.

Thoreau said that he had "travelled a great deal in Concord." Welty may be said to have traveled a great deal in Jackson, for before fully establishing herself as a fiction writer, she worked as a correspondent and radio news editor, and developed a considerable reputation as a photographer, traveling throughout the state during the Depression as a publicity agent for the Works Progress Administration. Welty's photographs have been collected and republished in *Eudora Welty Photographs* (1989), with a preface by the novelist Reynolds Price.

These photographs illuminate many of the features of Welty's stories. Coming to them from the photographs Walker Evans made for *Let Us Now Praise Famous Men*, one is struck by how little Welty is invested in making grand claims about the Depression or about her region, and how much she is invested in the individual emotional lives of her sitters, and in the intimate back-and-forth between sitter and photographer. "Every feeling waits upon its gesture," Welty said of her photographs. "Then when it does come, how unpredictable it turns out to be, after all." Her continuing project in both of her arts, she says, "would be not to point the finger in judgment but to part a curtain, that invisible shadow that falls between people, the veil of indifference to each other's presence, each other's wonder, each other's human plight."

Welty's stories have often been criti-

cized (famously by Diana Trilling) for their indifference to the subjects northern readers think ought to be the overriding concerns of southern writers, which is to say, racial inequality, economic squalor, and a historical burden of tragedy and shame. The criticism is as misplaced as similar complaints about the fiction of Jane Austen, whose comic generosity, punctuated by lightning insights into the limitations and complexities of live human beings entangled with each other, is recognizably akin to Welty's. Welty does indeed sometimes explicitly treat politically charged subjects. The civil rights struggle, for instance, is the subject of two late stories, "Where Is the Voice Coming From," a chilling dramatic monologue in the voice of the murderer of Medgar Evers, and "The Demonstrators," in which the newspaper accounts of the domestic-abuse murder of an African American woman dwell all too defensively on the fact that it has no racial overtones. But she more often treats these themes, and themes of gender conflict, in implicit ways. Welty's stories, like her photographs, are intimate. In remaining at the personal scale, Welty steers clear of what she calls "generalities that clank when wielded," and serves that value which is central to politics but so often missing from explicitly political writing, the mutual acknowledgment of person and person.

Welty's fiction is famous for its lyricism. Welty particularly admires Virginia Woolf's ability to indirectly register unrepresentable powers that lurk behind the surface of narration by attending to the way they permeate and burn through an intensely perceived universe of sensations, and Welty's own lyricism shares this quality with Woolf's. Welty's prose is often shadowed with a rich but completely implicit presence that words suggest but do not constrain. Welty's modernist indirection is very different from Faulkner's (although both occasionally seduce the reader into making wrong guesses about what is actually happening in the story) in that it is less magisterial, less grand in scale, but more suggestive and delicate. Like Woolf's, Welty's is a sublimity of local illuminations, of a sudden insight into a vitality as radiant as a freshly plucked leaf, rather than a sublimity of global sweep and dark omnipresences.

Welty's stories often turn on moments of suspension of time, such as the famous climax of "A Still Moment," in which the three protagonists breathlessly behold a white heron, each finding in it a charged bearer of private meanings. These moments of epiphany are recognizably high modernist in character, and they are also, for Welty, the hallmark of the short story as a genre, and one of the features that distinguishes the short story from the novel, which, by contrast, extends a series of actions through time.

Welty's first collection, *A Curtain of Green* (1941), was wide-ranging and won her fame for its rich vein of ironic comedy. In "A Piece of News," a rather simple country woman named Ruby Fisher, reading a newspaper spread out on her floor, spells out the sentence "Mrs. Ruby Fisher had the misfortune to be shot in the leg by her husband this week." This rather puzzles her, since "it was unlike Clyde to take up a gun and shoot her." Ruby is as strange as she is simple, and it is her habit,

whenever Clyde makes her blue, to flag down a stranger on the highway and sleep with him. (The newspaper in which she reads about the shooting had been left behind by one of these strangers, as Clyde later seems to guess.) Although there is an air of repressed violence in her relationship with Clyde (who is described as "slapping at her"), there is also a strong erotic electricity, of which the violence seems to be somehow a part. After reading the newspaper, Ruby constructs a story in which this erotic quality is made comically present. Clyde's imagined shooting of her becomes elaborated, in her fantasy, into a dark sexual dream, in which she visualizes Clyde's remorse as he weeps over her dying body, and sees herself lying there, in a new nightgown, with a bullet in her heart, "composing her face into a look which would be beautiful, desirable, and dead."

When Ruby actually confronts the gruff and sour Clyde with the newspaper story, he replies, "It's a lie" (as if she ever really believed that he had shot her). But in a moment they are both swept up into the tale and possessed by its dark, romantic possibilities: "Slowly they both flushed, as though with a double shame and a double pleasure. It was as though Clyde might really have killed Ruby, and as though Ruby might really have been dead at his hand." Ultimately Clyde breaks the spell, pointing out that the Ruby Fisher of the story was a different Ruby Fisher, from Tennessee. Yet the story ends with a playfulness and an erotic renewal that would not have been possible without the dark fantasy.

One of the more startling aspects of

Welty's writing is her completely un-shocked openness to some of the seamier aspects of sexual life, of the kinship of desire and destruction. Odd glimpses of this, in the midst of basically comic nar-ratives, are features of *The Robber Bride-groom* (1942) and *Delta Wedding* (1946) as well as of her stories. What is startling is not the fact that Welty recognizes the dark sides of erotic feeling, but that, as Joyce Carol Oates noticed in a perceptive re-view, she does so in so offhand a way, treating that recognition as if it were merely one fact among many, rather than playing it up luridly or seeing it as a great forbidden discovery, as Faulkner or Carson McCullers (or Oates herself) might have done.

"A Curtain of Green" is a good example of the odd way violent events surface in Welty stories that seem to be running in another direction. The protagonist, Mrs. Larkin, obsessively keeps a garden whose unruly profusion seems somehow an em-blem of her unresolved mourning for her husband, killed randomly by a falling tree in front of their home. She plants her gar-den more and more thickly, with no regard for design or order, as if the hyperbolic fecundity of the soil measured both the intensity of the grief she feels and the im-possibility of expressing it or working it through. In a rage of frustration with life (and with the inability of her love to save the life of her husband), and feeling the first stirring of what seems to be a heart attack, she sneaks up behind Jamey, the African American boy who helps her tend her garden, and raises her hoe, preparing to strike his head off. The randomness of the intended act of violence seems to be a kind of striking back at the random vi-olence of nature, as if by killing inten-tionally she can gain control of a world in which people are subject to random, un-intentional death. The thwarted intensity of her temptation is another version of the thwarted intensity of her garden, and she holds the hoe in the air for a very long moment. But suddenly it begins to rain, and Mrs. Larkin's sudden rage dissolves into an equally inexplicable tenderness. The very richness and haunted beauty of Welty's description of the rainy garden, as Mrs. Larkin stands, frozen, still holding her hoe, seems charged with that beauty of the perfect otherness of nature, death-dealing but deathless: "In the light from the rain, different from sunlight, every-thing appeared to gleam unreflecting from within itself in its quiet arcade of identity. The green of the small zinnia shoots was very pure, almost burning. One by one, as the rain reached them, all the individual little plants shone out, and then the branching vines. The pear tree gave a soft rushing noise, like the wings of a bird alighting. She could sense behind her . . . lighted in the night, the signal-like white-ness of the house."

Welty's lyricism here marks the place where language is deformed by the pres-sure of something at once ineffable and unbearable, a powerful feeling powerfully thwarted, a force which may move one to destroy the world or to throw one's self on the ground in baffled praise of it. When the moment passes, and Mrs. Lar-kin sinks down dead, it is as if in the shad-ows that feeling was hidden while some-thing fatal but great blew by.

The most memorable story of the volume is "Powerhouse," which was inspired by a performance by the jazz pianist Fats Waller. Powerhouse's *unheimlich* quality, as disturbing and hard to pin down as it is charismatic and fascinating, presses through even the racist preconceptions of the collective narrator. The explicit plot of the story is quite simple—Powerhouse and his sidemen perform at a white dance, repair to a black bar during the intermission, and return to the dance. Welty articulates the wordless themes of the instrumental solos of the performance as a conversation among the performers. To represent how the melody is passed from soloist to soloist, Welty imagines a story that they pass from teller to teller, unfolding it as they go. This improvised narration, which continues explicitly, in words—in the conversation among the players during the intermission—develops a strange, dark story concerning a telegram Powerhouse has received from one Uranus Knockwood, telling him that his wife, Gypsy, is dead. As the story proceeds, Powerhouse embroiders the tale much as one embroiders a riff in a jazz improvisation, describing in exquisite detail how Gypsy jumped out the window to her death in front of him, and then how she was discovered by Uranus Knockwood on the ground. Then he imagines Uranus Knockwood sneaking into his house and making off with Gypsy (and with the wives of his sidemen). None of these contradictory but eerily similar stories is true, Powerhouse admits to a curious onlooker during the intermission, adding "Truth is something worse, I ain't said what, yet. It's something hasn't come to me, but I ain't saying it won't. And when it does, then want me to tell you?"

"Powerhouse" captures the otherworldly quality of both Powerhouse himself and of his music. The story Powerhouse improvises variations upon is recognizably a version of the story of Orpheus and Eurydice, and in the telling it changes restlessly and unpredictably, combining love and death, joy and pain, in the way that jazz is famous for doing. The power and inventiveness and darkness of Powerhouse's elaborations, so fascinating and horrifying (and at the same time unsettlingly comic), are the work of a kind of Orphic poet whose genius burns away not only time and place, race, and caste, but whatever it is that separates life and death. Powerhouse's story, both the one he tells and the one he lives, is, like Orpheus's story, a parable about the power and limitations of art; through it he finds a kind of aesthetic immortality, finding it, as Orpheus himself did, not through a repudiation of mortality but through an experience which at once undergoes and transcends it.

When *The Wide Net* came out in 1943, Robert Penn Warren noted that it was narrower in scope but more intense in focus than Welty's first volume. All of the stories are tied together by oblique references to the Natchez Trace, the footpath that linked Nashville and Natchez in frontier days. The keynote of the volume, and indeed of much of Welty's thought about love, is struck in its most famous story, "A Still Moment." It is the nature of human beings to seek intense and transforming experiences that put us into contact with the deepest things. Love is one such experience, and so is religious faith; various other kinds of extremity also provide similar experiences. But these experiences bring with them their own opposites, since in Welty's view love not only unites with but also annihilates the object of love, and the redemption of the world is also its destruction.

In the story, the early nineteenth-century evangelist Lorenzo Dow (a real person, as are the other characters of this story) is riding up the Natchez Trace in the grip of his obsession to save all souls and searching, with increasing despera-tion, for signs of God's approval of his vocation. Evading an Indian ambush as well as more metaphysical obstacles, he falls in with the bandit James Murrell, whose proud sense of his own evil matches Dow's God-hunger. Murrell is planning to lead a slave insurrection (another his-torically accurate detail), but robbing and murdering Dow and revealing himself to him to be the Devil are his more imme-diate aims. Murrell is a philosophical killer (like his literary descendent, the Misfit of Flannery O'Connor's "A Good Man is Hard to Find"), who "in laying hold of a man meant to solve his mystery of being."

Before Murrell can act, however, they are joined by Audubon, who also is in the grip of a great passion, the passion to know all things: "If my origin is withheld from me, is my end to be unknown too? Is the radiance I see closed into an interval be-tween two darks, or can it not illuminate them both and discover at last, though it cannot be spoken, what was thought hid-den and lost?" At this moment a white heron alights in the marsh in front of the three men, and each sees it as a triumphant sign of his own vocation. Audubon dispels the moment by shooting the heron, and the three men disperse. Like Murrell, he cannot know without killing, but like Lor-

enzo Dow he seeks the kind of knowledge that is also praise. That knowledge, how-ever, can only disclose itself fleetingly, and all three, even as they experience this mo-ment of knowledge, also know that it will leave them behind. The lesson of the mo-ment is Lorenzo's: "Suddenly it seemed to him that God Himself, just now, thought of the Idea of Separateness. . . . He could understand God's giving Sepa-rateness first and then giving Love to fol-low and heal in its wonder; but God had reversed this, and given Love first and then Separateness, as though it did not matter to Him which came first. . . . How to explain Time and Separateness back to God. . . . Who could let the whole world come to grief in a scattering moment?"

The lesson of a similar difficult and fleeting insight into the heart of things is the subject of "The Winds." The protag-onist, Josie, is a little girl who is awakened in the middle of the night by her parents to be led to the basement for shelter from a powerful equinoctial storm. The storm is obviously dangerous, but it also seems to her to be "a chorus of wildness and delight." In the child's mind, the danger and thrill of the storm are linked somehow with the thought of Cornella, the mag-netic daughter of the tenant in the run-down house next door, as if they both somehow partook of vitalizing danger. In the child's reverie, the thought of Cor-nella is also tangled with a memory of hearing a female trio play at a Chautauqua. The moment (which Josie remembers sharing with Cornella) when the female cornet player begins her solo is clearly a moment of artistic and erotic awakening: "If morning-glories had come out of the horn instead of those sounds, Josie would not have felt a more astonished delight. She was pierced with pleasure. The sounds . . . from the striving of the lips were welcome and sweet to her. . . . Josie listened in mounting care and suspense, as if the performance led in some direction away—as if a destination were being shown her."

The cornet solo, like the equinoctial storm, is a summons to beauty and danger, a challenge such as when "the beauty of the world had come with its sign and stridden through their town," offering an opportunity that must be grasped or lost forever. The morning after the storm, searching for the signs of the metamorphosis of the world, Josie finds a storm-blown bit of paper, a note from Cornella to an unknown lover: "O my darling I have waited so long when are you coming for me? Never a day or a night goes by that I do not ask When? When? When?"

The interdependence of artistic and sexual awakening, and the constraints put upon both by small-town life, the subjects of "The Winds," are also the central concerns of Welty's third and most important volume of stories, *The Golden Apples* (1949). The stories of *The Golden Apples* are linked, sharing a setting (the fictional town of Morgana, Mississippi, a name meant to suggest at once the fata morgana and Morgan le Fay), overlapping sets of characters (whose careers they follow over about thirty years), and an intricate network of allusions to Greek mythology and to the poetry of Yeats (from whose "The Song of Wandering Aengus" the title is drawn). Two characters in particular, King MacLain and Virgie Rainey, tie together the various stories through their adventures and transgressions.

King MacLain, like Zeus a sexual aggressor and like Aengus a wanderer, haunts the outskirts of many stories. In the opening story, "Shower of Gold," which retells the story of the impregnation of Danae, King MacLain periodically slips away from his albino wife, Miss Snowdie, once even leaving his hat on the bank of the Big Black River to persuade her that he has drowned himself. On one of his returns he arranged a mysterious assignation in the woods with his wife, who returned looking as if "a shower of something had struck her, like she'd been caught out in something bright," and pregnant with the twins Ran and Eugene MacLain. The key event of the story concerns another of King's failed visits home. It is Halloween, and his twins, gruesomely disguised, descend upon him on roller skates, neither recognizing the other (since King does not yet know that he even has children, and the children have never before seen their father); the twins drive him comically away. King MacLain lurks in the shadows of many of the stories, a kind of magic figure, someone outside of the constraints of town life, a figure of lawless freedom and wonder. He is seen indirectly, through the eyes of more or less repressed townspeople, who see in him the freedom they both repudiate and long for. As Katey Rainey, the gossipy narrator of "Shower of Gold," explains, "With men like King, your thoughts are bottomless."

The other figure whose story unfolds in *The Golden Apples* is a young woman, a talented pianist and sexual rebel, named

Virgie Rainey. In "June Recital" she appears as the star student of Miss Eckhart, the town piano teacher. The piano teacher, as a German (during World War I), a northerner, and a single woman, was an outsider to Morgana from the beginning. But it is not her cultural difference that marks her as an outsider so much as her intense passion for music; music has to carry the burden of all of her otherwise strongly repressed feelings, and it also represents her access to a world not only beyond the confines of Morgana but beyond the confines of mortality. Miss Eckhart herself, for all her longing, lacks the genius to enter that world, although she recognizes that genius in Virgie, through whom she seeks the vicarious experience of greatness.

Miss Eckhart is a trapped figure, of a kind made famous in the stories of Sherwood Anderson, a character made desperate both by internal and external limitations. She befriends a shoe salesman, who plays the cello at the local movie theater. Nothing comes of the relationship, but when the shoe salesman dies suddenly, Miss Eckhart makes a spectacle of herself at his funeral by throwing herself into his grave. Her students torment her with indirect allusions to the event ever after. Then she is sexually assaulted by a mentally disturbed black man, which does not earn her the town's sympathy (because she refuses to play the victim), but makes her instead into a figure at once disreputable and horrifying, causing her to lose all her students and to leave town.

Until her final fall from grace, however, Miss Eckhart has, because of her talent, the youth of Morgana under her power.

She treats her students dictatorially and with an edge of cruelty, organizing the yearly recital with painstaking detail and tyrannical force of character. Virgie Rainey is Miss Eckhart's star student, and because Miss Eckhart recognizes genius in her student, she is vulnerable to her. Virgie perceives this vulnerability and never misses an opportunity to make Miss Eckhart feel her contempt for her. She resolutely will not make use of her talent (the closest she comes is to replace the shoe salesman as the accompanist at the movie theater), and in doing this she somehow asserts her freedom both from Morgana and from Miss Eckhart. Later on, Miss Eckhart returns to the now decrepit MacLain house, with the intent of burning it down (and presumably, of dying in its flames). At the same time, perhaps unknown to her, Virgie Rainey and her sailor boyfriend are using the bedroom upstairs. Two yokels happen to break in just as Miss Eckhart ignites the broken-down piano, and with Keystone Kops clumsiness (as King MacLain mysteriously arrives and departs again) they manage to subdue her. As they are bundling Miss Eckhart off to the lunatic asylum in Jackson, Virgie Rainey walks past her, and their eyes meet in a mutual withholding of acknowledgment. Virgie's refusal of Miss Eckhart, both when Miss Eckhart means her well and when Miss Eckhart needs her sympathy, is an assertion of a transgressive if rather cruel freedom. Welty's portrait of Virgie Rainey is as dark a portrait of the artist as any in the canon.

King MacLain and Virgie Rainey's stories converge in "The Wanderers," the final story of *The Golden Apples*. Virgie Rainey, now in early middle age, is leading a life at loose ends, working in an office and leading an illicit but not very secret sexual life. During her mother's funeral, she catches the eye of King MacLain, old and broken and returned home now, but still with his characteristic fierceness unchecked. Virgie recognizes him as a kindred spirit, someone who even in the grip of death retains a rebellious vitality. Having packed off her surviving relatives, closed up her mother's house, and given all her livestock away, Virgie pauses in the neighboring town of MacLain on her way out into the big world. There she notices the grave of Miss Eckhart and discovers that, deep down, she had not really hated her one-time teacher. Indeed, thinking about old King MacLain, and reflecting upon the picture of Perseus and Medusa that used to hang above Miss Eckhart's piano, Virgie comes to understand the aesthetic heroism—the search for an aesthetic truth that demands transgression, loneliness, and wandering—that Miss Eckhart had tried to pass on to her. As she sits upon a stile in the rain in silent communion with a mysterious elderly African American woman, Virgie reflects once more upon the dark face King MacLain had made at her mother's funeral, and she hears, undefeated, the possibilities of transgressive vitality with new freshness: "They heard through falling rain the running of the horse and bear, the stroke of the leopard, the dragon's crusty slither, and the glimmer and the trumpet of the swan."

The most important stories in Welty's last collection, *The Bride of the Innisfallen* (1955) share a concern with wandering and with cross purposes in love. "No Place

for You, My Love," strikes the keynote of the volume. The protagonists are two northerners, strangers to each other, who meet at a luncheon in New Orleans and decide to drive together down to the delta south of that city. Each is in some way bound up in a romantic failure, the man in a marriage that seems to have faded, the woman in an impossible relationship of some kind that both obsesses and entraps her. The power of the story is in the ever-present but ever-evaded possibility of a romantic relationship between them, a relationship that might have freed them from their lives up North. The protagonists' conversations are minimal, but the wild and heat-saturated landscape through which they travel seems to express the fraughtness and thwartedness of their emotional lives: the landscape has the passion of the relationship lack, but it also suffocates and intimidates them into withdrawal, having a flamboyant expressiveness before which they draw back. The erotic possibilities between them never materialize: he raises his hand to shush her when she asks about his wife, and when, dancing with her, he notices a bruise on her temple, he knows that he has something to do with the erotic entanglement she has not told him about but whose existence he has somehow divined. On the way home, he suddenly kisses her and as suddenly draws away, leaving her in her hotel lobby, where he notices that a man has been waiting for her. This haunting and haunted nonaffair is Welty's most sophisticated and most understated version of the tension between Love and Separateness, between the presence of meaning and its ineffability, that has haunted Welty's fiction since *The Wide Net*.

Eudora Welty is a practitioner of the arts of subtlety and indirection, opening out the inner lives of her characters with perfect judiciousness and impartiality into radiance, but always by means of restraint. Welty says of Henry Green that his indirect writing does not represent life but presents it. The same can be said of her own writing.

John Burt

SELECTED BIBLIOGRAPHY

Works by Eudora Welty

A Curtain of Green and Other Stories. New York: Doubleday, 1941.

The Wide Net, and Other Stories. New York: Harcourt Brace, 1943.

The Golden Apples. New York: Harcourt Brace, 1946.

The Bride of the Innisfallen, and Other Stories. New York: Harcourt Brace, 1955.

Critical Studies

Evans, Elizabeth. Eudora Welty. New York: Ungar, 1981.

Johnston, Carol Ann. Eudora Welty: A Study of the Short Fiction. New York: Twayne, 1997.

Schmidt, Peter. The Heart of the Story: Eudora Welty's Short Fiction. Jackson: University Press of Mississippi, 1991.

Turner, Craig W., and Lee Emling Harding. Critical Essays on Eudora Welty. Boston: G. K. Hall, 1989.

Vande Kieft, Ruth M. Eudora Welty. Boston: Twayne, 1962.

EDITH WHARTON
(1862 – 1937)

Edith Wharton, whose career spanned five decades, has long been considered one of America's best female novelists. Famous for such novels as The House of Mirth (1905) and the Pulitzer Prize-winning The Age of Innocence (1920), she is known also for her many finely crafted short stories—eighty-five in all. Among her twelve collections of stories are, notably, The Greater Inclination (1899), Human Nature (1933), The World Over (1936), and the posthumous volume Ghosts (1937). Though Henry James was seen as Wharton's precursor, his influence has been exaggerated. Neither he nor Edgar Allan Poe, Nathaniel Hawthorne, Sarah Orne Jewett, nor Mary Wilkens Freeman count very highly as literary forebears. Wharton was convinced, as she contended in The Writing of Fiction (1925), that she had to ignore predecessors and audience, editors and publishers, in order to please herself, her muse, and her most exacting of critics.

Wharton was born Edith Newbold Jones into an "old New York" family that was embarrassed by her writing. As Wharton wrote in her 1934 autobiography, A Backward Glance, she "had to fight [her] way to expression through a thick fog of indifference" at a time when women claiming self-expression, let alone sex-expression, was an act of resistance. Married at twenty-three to Edward "Teddy" Wharton, she was never happy with him, although the marriage lasted for twenty-eight years, until their divorce in 1913.

Wharton turned to cultural and intellectual pursuits in order to stave off the despair of her marital life; in 1902, she published a book about domestic arts with Ogden Codman. entitled *The Decoration of Houses*. Once she won fame for her 1905 novel, *The House of Mirth,* she wrote at an ever-increasing pace. Meanwhile, she started another great affair in her life, her erotic friendship with the bisexual and rakish Morton Fullerton, who taught her "what happy women" feel. Starting in 1907, Wharton lived in France and befriended such intellectuals and writers as James, the art critic Bernard Berenson, and Walter Berry. She died in 1937, before the publication of the last of her novels, *The Buccaneers*.

Wharton's stories revolve around such themes as love and its failure, society and its victims. Her first short story, "Mrs. Manstey's View" (1891), tells of a failed and frustrated woman artist. The question motivating one of Wharton's final short stories sustains that investigation by asking, as all her most memorable fiction asks, what are the rules and rituals of "polite" society, and what disciplines the appetites and desires submerged in this "ethnography of manners," Nancy Bentley's apt phrase. In her book-length meditation on her craft, *The Writing of Fiction,* Wharton explains—in the chapter "Telling a Short Story"—that the first obligation of a tale "is to give the reader an immediate sense of security. Every phrase should be a signpost, and never (unless intentionally) a misleading one: the reader must feel that he can trust to [the writers'] guidance." For Wharton, the short story's economy made it the most cogent genre—one in which she could strive for the unities of time and single perspective, and the one in which she self-consciously and continually explored her most trenchant views.

Wharton wrote many of her tales as "magazine fiction," even if she generally distrusted the conventions of formula fiction with its "standardized" plots and characters. Nevertheless, she wrote pointedly for a genteel audience in magazines like *Scribner's* and *Century Magazine,* as well as for an explicitly female one in publications like *Pictorial Review*. Most critics hail her satirical works as her best, although others make cases for her ghost stories or her artist tales, her metacommentaries on the state of being an author in the light of the growing mass culture industry of the early twentieth century. In "The Other Two" (1904), for example, Wharton shows how readily these types of stories overlap in her satire on the way that wives become commodities. Alice Haskett Varick Waythorn moves through a succession of husbands to become as "worn as an old shoe." Her third husband adjusts to the situation, which he had first taken to be tragic but now appreciates for its irony, since he is the husband who benefits from his predecessors' "breaking in" of his wife. Thus he complies with his wife's adopting of the "custom of the American country"— divorcing to solve the problems of intimate and financial life, moving up the social ladder by changing spouses, as Undine Spragg does in *The Custom of the Country* (1913). Told from the third husband's perspective (the "male reflector" as Barbara White calls him), the story ironically documents *his* sense of loss of innocence. Again, in "Autres Temps" (1911), Wharton codifies the morality of such social contingencies: Mrs. Lidcote's divorce causes scandal; her daughter's, barely a whiff. Signpost by signpost, the writer adumbrates the changes in social values, especially between the generations, and leads us to see through the eyes of the outsider.

In "Xingu" (1911), one of her funniest satires, Wharton attacks the pretensions of an elite audience in claiming high culture as cultural capital. In that story, she parodies the Lunch Club's attempt to master various philosophical issues often considered no-man's land for women. In their meetings, these women try to come to terms with "ideas" that they would be reluctant to explore by themselves. As Wharton states it, these "ladies . . . pursue Culture in bands, as though it were dangerous to meet alone." Indeed, it is dangerous for them to meet culture alone, for their practices turn them into "huntresses of erudition." The hunt for the distinction conferred by the right literary reference, the prestigious cultural signifier, is itself a violent pursuit, given the hierarchy the ladies hope to reinforce between high culture and low, between those with privilege and those without. Wharton's story thus unfolds as a revenge comedy that comes back to haunt and humiliate the victims of Wharton's intense satire. The ladies of the club are shocked by the doubts that Mrs. Roby, their scapegoat, advances about the way they use the occasion of discussing fine literature to reaffirm their pretensions. The women agree among themselves that "as a member of the Lunch Club, Mrs. Roby was a failure." In turn, Mrs. Roby questions the value of their sense of culture by challenging the context in which such knowledge gains value. The Lunch Club values

culture only insofar as the ladies can mystify it, for they characteristically confuse cultural, social, and economic capital as one. "'Nothing would induce me, now, to put aside a book,' Mrs. Plinth argues, 'before I'd finished it, just because I can buy as many more as I want.'" Wharton's ideal of the disinterested intellectual disappears in the face of these women's interests in proving their social superiority and their "private property" of reading. Such tales about the cultural value of literature were also balanced by stories about the challenges facing an artist. As "The Muse's Tragedy" (1899) and "The Pot-Boiler" (1904) typify, these fictions combine Wharton's interests in art, female authorship, and metacommentary about the mass public.

Wharton experimented with ghost stories as variations of the female gothic, alternating them with tales of the vaguely fantastic—all emphasizing the liminal experience of the realist encounter with the supernatural. Her first was "The Lady's Maid's Bell" (*Scribner's*, 1902), which creates a supernatural analogue to the prisonhouse of marriage. Other ghost fictions include "Afterward" (1910), "The Eyes" (1910), "The Triumph of the Night" (1914), "Kerfol" (1916), "Bewitched" (1925), "Miss Mary Pask" (1925), "A Bottle of Perrier" (1926), "Mr. Jones" (1928), and "All Souls'" (1937), a drama of social class as well as a lament about women's losses. Like "Pomegranate Seed" (1936), one of her most analyzed stories, these mystery tales explore the frustration in relationships—sometimes the impossibility of true intimacy or the tyranny of that same intimacy—that remain even after death. The ghost story allowed Wharton to exploit the ambiguity of the genre, while interweaving her other most crucial interests: art, love, grief, and the secrets of female sexuality (especially in a story such as "Miss Mary Pask"). "All Souls,'" for example, is overlaid with ambiguity about sexual repression. For in Wharton's ghost fictions, the prevailing social structures contain within them skeletons and secrets: of taboos transgressed and secrets repressed until finally revealed past the pain of death.

Wharton's most memorable short stories, like "Roman Fever," encapsulate and surpass any of the categories into which her tales might be said to fit. They bring to the foreground such issues as social rivalry, patriarchal power, writing and language, the effects of the new modernity (especially illegitimacy). In his biography of Wharton, R. W. B. Lewis describes "Roman Fever" as a masterpiece of "rhetorical coherence," and indeed this oft-anthologized story has been widely hailed as one of Wharton's best. Written in 1934 and published as part of the collection *The World Over,* "Roman Fever" is set against Roman ruins, an appropriate site of battle between two women locked in nasty contest over their past as well as their daughters' futures. The story highlights the historical trajectory stemming from the Roman past of violence and ruin to the present destruction that Wharton saw Mussolini enacting in her beloved Italy.

In the story, two middle-aged women meet accidentally in Rome and spend their afternoon recounting their shared pasts as girls in Rome and their daughters' ramblings there. They contemplate the ironies of the present that includes their daughters' rivalries for the same Italian aviator, just as the mothers had competed as teenagers for the same suitor, Delphin Slade. Alida Slade envies Grace Ansley's daughter Barbara for her exuberance, while Jenny Slade "made youth and prettiness seem as safe as their absence." Pained as she is by the comparison between the daughters, Alida Slade admits that, twenty-five years before, she had forged a letter to Grace Ansley in the name of Alida's future husband, Delphin Slade. Knowing that Grace was also in love with Alida's fiancé, she meant to trick Grace by exposing her to Roman fever, or malaria (a fleeting reference to James's *Daisy Miller* [1878]). The letter was supposed to fabricate a rendezvous between Grace and Delphin in the Colosseum, which Delphin would not know about, but, unbeknownst to Alida, Grace communicates to Delphin her willingness to meet him (Alida forged the letter in his name). In a tense moment—precisely when Alida thinks she must now after all these years have the upper hand—Grace confesses, out of anger and pique, that Barbara is, after all, Delphin's illegitimate child. This comeback is the last line of Wharton's tale of bittersweet revenge, a story that is also about how the present negotiates the past, and how the prevailing terms of social success lead to a distortion of our humanity.

Recent scholarship has uncovered Wharton's World War I short fiction, along with her charity work with refugees, and its relation to the conflict over German aggression. Wharton spent considerable time on the front in heroic war relief efforts, and three short stories from 1915 to 1919 were shaped by her experiences: "Coming Home," "The Refugees," and "Writing a War Story" (1919). She also wrote several nonfiction pieces about France and war's havoc, the devastating consequences it had on a way of life she had treasured.

Not surprisingly, in the last fifteen years of her career, she turned more and more to America as her subject, teasing out the meanings of the past and the seeming arbitrariness of the present's new freedoms. In her short fiction, Wharton chronicles the move to modernity and new, postwar morals over which she expresses considerable ambivalence. While modernity ushered in a relaxation of forms, Wharton saw that the emancipation of the spirit came at the expense of a new vulgarity and a standardization of culture, every bit as stultifying as the past but with none of its comforting assurances. In this light, Edith Wharton records her social scene, a writer who would attempt to interpret "the hieroglyphic world"—a phrase from *The Age of Innocence*—of the past for the new generation of Americans coming into their maturity past the Victorian age.

Dale M. Bauer

SELECTED BIBLIOGRAPHY

Works by Edith Wharton

The Greater Inclination. New York: Scribner's, 1899.
Crucial Instances. New York: Scribner's, 1901.
The Descent of Man and Other Stories. New York: Scribner's, 1904.
Hermit and the Wild Woman, and Other Stories. New York: Scribner's, 1908.
Madame de Treymes. New York: Scribner's, 1907.
Tales of Men and Ghosts. New York: Scribner's, 1910.
Xingu and Other Stories. New York: Scribner's, 1916.
Here and Beyond. New York: Appleton, 1926.
Certain People. New York: Appleton, 1930.
Human Nature. New York: Appleton, 1933.
The World Over. New York: Appleton, 1936.
Ghosts. New York: Appleton, 1937.

Critical Studies

Beer, Janet. *Kate Chopin, Edith Wharton and Charlotte Perkins Gilman: Studies in Short Fiction*. New York: St. Martin's, 1998.
Lewis, R. W. B. *The Collected Short Stories of Edith Wharton*. New York: Scribner's, 1968.
Price, Alan. *The End of the Age of Innocence*. New York: St. Martin's, 1998.
White, Barbara. *Edith Wharton: A Study of the Short Fiction*. New York: Twayne, 1991.

JOY WILLIAMS
(1944–   )

Joy Williams was born in 1944 in Chelmsford, Massachusetts, and grew up in Cape Elizabeth, Maine. Both her father and grandfather were Congregational ministers, and her most influential reading, she said, was the Bible: "The Bible influenced me because all those wonderful stories—about snakes and serpents and mysterious seeds and trees—didn't mean what they seemed. They meant some other thing . . . that began my preoccupation with what a story can do . . . the literal surface is not important." While a student at Marietta College in Ohio, she began writing and publishing fiction. She sharpened her skills at the University of Iowa, where she received her master of fine arts degree in 1965. Williams has written three novels, two collections of stories, and a guidebook to the Florida Keys. She has received several awards for her work, including a National Endowment for the Arts Grant and a Guggenheim Fellowship. Williams has contributed regularly to *Esquire* magazine and has taught creative writing at the University of Houston, the University of Florida, the University of California at Irvine, and the University of Iowa. She currently teaches one semester annually at the University of Arizona in Tucson. Married to writer and editor Rust Hills, she has a daughter, Caitlin, and homes in Florida and Arizona.

Joy Williams admits that while writing her first novel in a trailer in central Florida, she was miserable. But, she states, "it was all very good for my writing. . . . It's good to be miserable and a little off balance. . . . Life isn't the point really. . . . It's that teeming, chaotic underside." Williams's interest in the "chaotic underside" is dramatized through her characters, who spend most of their time wrestling with

inscrutable conflicts while trying to figure out what to do with their lives. Her plots are character-driven, focusing on the portrayal of subjective realities. And yet she has said, "I'm not much interested in people. . . . I guess that's why the short story is my favorite form. Novels have to have more characters in them. They depend on people, but the ever-approaching nothing interests me more than society."

Like the author, Williams's characters have an obsession with an "ever-approaching nothing." The adults are usually divorced or widowed, the children often abandoned. With their families disjointed, characters are plagued by a sense of absence that generates a steady anxiety. Their lives are fueled by fear. In "The Lover," the protagonist's fear of losing lovers drives a steady supply of them away. In "The Excursion," a little girl "fears that birds will fly out of the toilet bowl." Drawing on sometimes mundane, sometimes surreal images, Williams evokes a visceral fear of chaos as she tells secular tales of spiritual crisis. Usually recovering from the random and often freakish deaths of loved ones—death by ant bites, bat bites, pieces of bread—her characters have given up trying to make meaning of life. Instead, they try to live with meaninglessness and to distract themselves from sorrow.

In "The Lover," the opening story of *Taking Care*, the main character is like many of Williams's protagonists: in her mid-twenties, divorced, and working on a new relationship. Williams chooses to refer to the woman as "the girl," and "the girl" has a child, referred to only as "the child." The lack of names in the story suggests that roles are more significant in the dynamics of relationships than individual identities. The narrative voice is simultaneously detached and attentive: "The girl wants to be in love. . . . It is so difficult! Love is a concentration, she feels, but she can remember nothing."

The girl cannot even remember her ex-husband, recalling only trivial things like his sunglasses and the fact that he "loved kidneys for a weekend lunch." She likes to imagine that his kisses had "the faint odor of urine." With these observations Williams establishes an issue that she will depict repeatedly in her stories: the frustrated attempts of characters, who barely engage with lovers, or children, or themselves, to connect with their own lives. Finding the emptiness at heart too painful to bear, characters often focus on trivia. The girl is addicted to talk-show radio programs where an "answer man" responds to phoned-in questions about trivial topics such as why lemon meringues are runny. The girl "thinks this man can help her." He keeps her comforted during her insomniac nights. He often confirms her bleak sense of reality, observing, "Our homes suffer from female sadness, embarrassment and confusion. Absence, sterility, mourning, privation and separation abound through the land."

The girl embodies this curse. She is incapable of pleasure: "When lovemaking, she feels she is behaving reasonably well," though her feelings of passion come sporadically and give more pain than joy. For the girl, love is an annihilation of self, irresistible and terrifying: "Death is not so far, she thinks. Love is further than death." By the end of the story her anxiety alienates her lover, who is on his way to her past of other vaguely recollected lovers. The only solid relationship in the story seems to be the girl's involvement with the "answer man," his grim philosophy seeming to speak for the detached narrator when he observes that "each piece of earth is bad for something. . . . The land itself is no longer safe. . . . Nothing is compatible with living in the long run."

In spite of Williams's statement that she likes the Puritans and that the Bible was a strong influence on her literary sensibility, she portrays souls adrift in a godless world, finding messages not in divine doves, burning bushes, or Jesus, but in the answer man. In "Breakfast," a depressed wife, her alcoholic friend, and an abused boy hope for inspiration from brief biblical blurbs engraved in the bottom of the Mennonite restaurant's pie tins. Phrases such as "Be zealous and repent!" ring grimly comic in her secular world of shattered lives.

"Shepherd" dramatizes more directly Williams's concern with the loss of faith. The protagonist is another "girl" unable to love her boyfriend. Incapable of love, she focuses exaggerated love on a dog referred to simply as "the shepherd," the name suggesting its role as potential protector. However, this shepherd has abandoned the protagonist by running off to drown in the Gulf of Mexico. The story opens with "the girl" staring out at the water, recalling how she bought the dog from a breeder who had once been a priest. While making the girl spend careful time with each puppy, the former priest suddenly announces: "We are all asleep and dreaming, you know. If we could ever comprehend our true position, we would not be able to bear it." Williams frequently juxtaposes dark philosophy with bits of trivial detail from the mundane world; the effect flattens intensity of emotion and evokes the character's state of ennui. The girl responds to the former priest's grim declaration by sipping her Pepsi, picking up her dog, and saying, "We all dream each other." Then she goes.

The girl alienates herself from her lover by sinking into memories of the dog once trained to leap in her arms with frenzied adoration whenever she asked: "Do you love me?" The girl clings to memory, holding on to an illusion that "once the world had been promising." The girl's boyfriend points out that "a little realism is in order here" and reminds the girl that she often screamed at the dog; when, trying to escape, the dog tore the screen, she swore she would kill him. But the girl chooses not to respond to his dose of reality. She lapses into reverie of her shepherd, and asks, "I did love you, didn't I? . . . And didn't you love me?"—questions that hang unanswered.

However, in the final story, "Taking Care," Williams depicts the process of living one's faith from the point of view of an expert, a minister. Unlike the Williams women who cannot seem to concentrate enough to be in love, Jones "has been in love all his life" but is baffled "because as far as he can see, it has never helped anyone." Williams suggests that love is a freakish vulnerability when she compares the minister to "an animal in a traveling show . . . that wears a vital organ outside the skin, awkward and unfortunate." Jones's wife is dying of cancer, and his vast capacity for love cannot help. But Williams steers the story away from pathos with the appearance of his granddaughter, left in his care by a mother who has gone to Mexico,

where "she will have a nervous breakdown."

Faced with the task of caring for his dying wife and his vulnerable yet budding-with-life granddaughter, Jones maintains without complaint, though even for an expert, the struggle to live one's faith is an exhausting process. Jones is "gaunt with belief." However, he never prays; instead, he acts with his strength coming not from God but from love of his wife and granddaughter. He buys roses for his wife and a baptismal dress for his granddaughter. He carefully launders the baby's clothes, and feeds her "a bottle of milk, eight ounces, and a portion of strained vegetables." Jones is a man of God who does not think about God because he is preoccupied with taking care of life. Rather than sustain himself with thoughts of eternal reward in the hereafter, he comforts himself with good memories of his past. When he goes to bring his dying wife home from the hospital, he sees her brought out to the car in a wheelchair, and, he notes, "She is thin and beautiful. Jones is grateful and confused. . . . Have so many years really passed? Is this not his wife, his love, fresh from giving birth?" The delusion empowers him, and redeems him if not from death, at least from pain.

In Williams's second collection, *Escapes*, self-absorption continues as the predominate spiritual handicap, but, like Jones in "Taking Care," characters are capable of gaining a little insight that helps them grow out of the past to define themselves in a present and a future. The title story is a first-person recollection in which the narrator, a girl, describes happy family vacations at a resort where there was a nightclub with a "twenty-foot-tall champagne glass on the roof." Williams immediately establishes a theme of the desire to escape the confines of the mundane world when the protagonist recalls, "At night someone would pull a switch and neon bubbles would spring out from the lit glass into the black air. I very much wanted such a glass on the roof of our own house and I wanted to be the one who, every night, would turn on the switch." The image illustrates Williams's technique of using precise concrete description to evoke a character's internal world. Of course, the girl never gets a giant champagne glass; what she gets is a family broken apart by an alcoholic mom. The crux of the story lies in the daughter's relationship with her mother, a woman who spends her time drinking and recalling her own childhood, when she was still capable of believing in the magic tricks of Houdini.

Caught in a habit of escaping her life with drinking, the mother becomes a dangerous role model for her daughter. The narrator recalls imitating her mother's way of holding a glass: "I had the gestures down. I sat opposite her, very still and quiet, pretending." There seems nothing solid in this girl's world; but Williams suggests the girl will escape her mother's habit when she has the narrator reflect on the smell of booze, which reminds her "of daring and deception, hopes and little lies." Grown, the narrator realizes that the habit of drinking is far from glamorous; rather, it is a brief and sordid sidestep from pain.

In Williams's world, children are extremely vulnerable to the self-absorbed actions of adults as well as the random strokes of death—often the result of car wrecks. In "The Blue Men," a boy abandoned by his father's death and his mother's retreat to California is raised by his widowed grandmother. At the end of the story, when the usually fatal car wreck ends well, Williams gives shaky hope in survival. Just as death is random and strange in her world, so is survival: "The car flipped over twice, miraculously righted itself, and skidded back onto the road, the roof and fenders crushed." Their salvation is as random as the many deaths in Williams's stories, and the damage done renders the characters' lives more intense. The boy and his grandmother "seemed more visible than ever after that, for they drove the car in that damaged way until winter came." People do a lot of driving and living in a "damaged way" in Williams's stories, with physical actions becoming a metaphor for psychological states.

But the title story gives hope not in the flukes of fate, but in human resiliency. The girl in "Escapes" goes on a perilous ride with her mother, figuratively in a life shaped by her mother's habits, and literally in her mother's drunken car journey to see a magician. They arrive late to the show in a run-down theater where a second-rate magician tells bad jokes and does cheap tricks. The show is, as the drunk mother says, "a far, far cry from the great Houdini." She slips out of the theater for a drink and then suddenly emerges on the stage, babbling incoherently and demanding that she replace the magician's assistant, who is about to be sawed in half. They are quickly escorted out of the theater by an usher dressed in a tawdry uniform with cardboard shoulders and cheap gold braid. The narrator recalls hating him and his overly large ears and the "bump on his neck above the collar of his shirt." But she is more repulsed by his connection with her mom. A recovered alcoholic himself, he gently urges the drunken mother to "pull herself together," and, the protagonist reflects, "His kindness made me feel he had tied us up with rope." Her choice of imagery evokes the physical sensations that accompany emotional states, and it simultaneously provides a metaphor for a human need to escape life's restraints.

Throughout the collection, Williams's characters are in transit, struggling to escape an old life as well as their future, which will inevitably culminate in death. Constantly on the move, either physically or emotionally, they try to ease pain with imagination. In "The Skater," the teenaged Molly invents a friend for her dead sister: a boy whose parents endowed the local high school with a skating rink in his memory. Molly's imagination stretches the grim reality of death into a fantasy happy ending where in death the dead might be friends. In "Health," adolescent Pammy, infected with tuberculosis, routinely goes to a tanning salon, where she feels like Snow White "lying in her glass coffin." But no prince awakens this girl. Instead, a strange man steps in the room, stares at her nakedness, and disappears, leaving Pammy with a recognition of her vulnerability in an adult world. The stranger becomes a menacing symbol of the frightening realities she will soon face in a grown-up life, realities that include predatory men as well as the ultimate predator, death.

Although Joy Williams tells stories of eccentric characters gripped by unique fears, the "ever-approaching nothing" is the looming central antagonist, silently taking center stage while the comparatively small protagonists struggle for sanity, sobriety, and love in a doomed world. They can escape pain with tricks of the mind comparable to the sleight of hand of magicians. Like the great Houdini, they can escape many things, but never death. Williams's stories refuse to try posing meanings in a world made meaningless by mortality; rather, Williams depicts how characters try and most often fail to cope. Occasionally they discover love can ease the burden of the exhausting task of life.

Jane Bradley

SELECTED BIBLIOGRAPHY

Works by Joy Williams

State of Grace. New York: Doubleday, 1973.
The Changeling. New York: Doubleday, 1978.
Taking Care. New York: Random House, 1982.
The Florida Keys: A History and Guide. New York: Random House, 1986.
Breaking and Entering. New York: Random House, 1988.
Escapes. New York: Atlantic Monthly Press, 1990.

Critical Studies

Cooper, Rand Richards. "The Dark at the End of the Tunnel." *New York Times Book Review,* January 21, 1990.
Kakutani, Michiko. "Books of the Times: Taking to the Highway, Fleeing the In-

escapable." *New York Times,* January 5, 1990.

McQuade, Molly. "Joy Williams." *Publishers Weekly,* January 26, 1990.

Stine, Jean C. and Daniel G. Marowski. "Joy Williams." *Contemporary Literary Criticism,* pp. 461–465. Detroit: Gale Research, 1985.

TENNESSEE WILLIAMS
(1911 – 1983)

Overshadowed by his celebrated work as a playwright, Tennessee Williams's warmly evocative short stories have been unjustly neglected. A number of them were published in obscure or popular magazines, sometimes long after they were first written, or collected in limited editions because of their frank treatment of sadomasochism or homosexuality. A few, such as "Desire and the Black Masseur" (1946), achieved minor notoriety without ever being widely read. Several were seen as little more than source material for his plays. It was not until they were brought together posthumously in his *Collected Stories* (1985), with an incisive introduction by Gore Vidal, that Williams's gift for prose fiction could be fully appreciated.

Williams's best stories were written between the mid-1940s and the early 1950s, at the peak of his powers as a dramatist. This was the heyday of the well-made story, carefully plotted, oblique, often ironic. The lyrical flow of Williams's sto-

ries made them seem like formless effusions—shapeless memories or fantasies charged with strong feelings. Inspired by Chekhov and D. H. Lawrence, these stories were keenly attuned to sensuous detail, to the fine vibrations of feelings and human attachments. Having grown up as the unhappy child of mismatched parents, uncertain about his sexual orientation and oppressed by the conventions of bourgeois propriety, Williams always shows an astonishing tenderness toward losers and outcasts, whose lives he evokes without judgment or condescension.

Williams was an autobiographical writer but also a mesmerizing storyteller, constantly rearranging his recollections to search out their emotional truth and inner meaning. In "Three Players of a Summer Game," he writes, in a typical discursive aside: "It would be absurd to pretend that this is altogether the way it was, and yet it may be closer than a literal history could be to the hidden truth of it." With a remarkable if narrow passion, Williams always circled back to the handful of people and experiences that had formed his mind, for they offered a key to the enigma of who he was. As Gore Vidal put it, he spent "a lifetime playing with the same vivid, ambiguous cards that life dealt him."

Thomas Lanier Williams was born in Columbus, Mississippi, in 1911. He was a sickly, dreamy, unhappy child whose father, Cornelius, worked as a traveling salesman for a shoe company, which kept him away from home for long periods. When Cornelius was reassigned to the main office, the family moved to St. Louis. He grew increasingly alcoholic, quarrelsome at home and at work, and boorishly harsh toward his genteel wife and seemingly effeminate son. The enmity and in-comprehension of his father strengthened young Williams's bonds with the women in his life, including his mother Edwina, whom he would portray memorably as Amanda in his first successful play, *The Glass Menagerie* (1944); his increasingly disturbed older sister Rose, whose mind would one day be destroyed by a pre-frontal lobotomy; and his maternal grand-mother, Rose Dakin, whose life and death he would describe indelibly in such sketches as "The Man in the Overstuffed Chair" (1960) and "'Grand'" (1964), both included in the *Collected Stories*.

Williams flunked out of the University of Missouri in 1931 and worked for several years in the warehouse of his father's shoe company, spending his evenings and week-ends trying to write. Following a break-down in 1935, he lived for a year with his grandparents in Memphis before enrolling in Washington University. He earned his undergraduate degree from the Univer-sity of Iowa in 1938 and spent time in New Orleans, New York, and Hollywood in the early 1940s, exploring the byways of the homosexual demimonde. After writ-ing several unproduced or unsuccessful plays, Williams gained fame when *The Glass Menagerie* conquered Broadway in 1945, soon followed by *A Streetcar Named Desire* in 1947.

Williams often used fiction to reshape memories that would later become the basis for his plays. Thus "Portrait of a Girl in Glass" (1943) developed *The Glass Me-nagerie*, "Three Plays of a Summer Game" (1952) was transformed into *Cat on a Hot Tin Roof* (1955), and "The Night of the Iguana" (1948) provided material for the

1961 play of the same name. Williams endlessly revisited the memories that haunted him and the ways he had already written about them. Yet the stories un-derlying the stage versions have an integ-rity and power all their own. "Three Play-ers of a Summer Game" is altogether nostalgic and understated, a fine fragment of social history; in the play, however, the same material becomes shocking, lurid, and violent. The central character in both is Brick Pollitt, once handsome, athletic, and self-possessed, now alcoholic and in-creasingly emasculated by his mannish, domineering wife (in the story), or by fears of his own repressed homosexuality (in the play).

But where the stage version is charged with animal energy, with explosive force at once intimate and public, the original story is wistfully internalized and retro-spective. It gives us a summer idyll dis-tantly remembered, in which Brick, in the absence of his wife, regains his confidence through an affair with a recently widowed young woman, only to lose it again when his wife returns to take charge of his life. This is observed through the eyes of two children who understand very little about such troubles, children to whom the sum-mer seems like a golden moment. Like many of Williams's best stories, "Three Players of a Summer Game" is about grow-ing up, about negotiating the delicate boundaries between childhood and adult-hood, which takes place as the youngsters witness the complications of other peo-ple's lives.

Some of Williams's best coming-of-age stories focus on his sister, two years older, whose passage through adolescence brings traumatic emotional conflicts. "Portrait of a Girl in Glass" and a later story, "Completed" (1973), are only sketches of his sister's strange behavior, but "The Resemblance Between a Violin Case and a Coffin" (1949) describes its impact on the narrator as he becomes aware of his nascent sexuality. His sister, long his closest companion, has moved into the "country of mysterious differences where children grow up," and this separates them as she is separated not only from her childhood but also from her sanity.

While his sister's musical performances with her male partner are disrupted by her inner turmoil, the narrator, disturbingly attracted to this young man, finds himself on the unexplored ground of his own sexual feelings. "For the first time, prematurely," he says, "I was aware of skin as an attraction. A thing that might be desirable to touch." Fleeing the young man's outstretched hand, he recalls, "I could never afterwards be near him without a blistering sense of shame."

The narrator and his sister have gone through an upheaval that their family cannot understand, and it has left them isolated, awkward, and unhappy. She will take refuge in madness, as he will in writing and in a Laurentian affirmation of the carnal power of blood and desire. Williams would become a poet of the incongruities of desire, the irresistible need for love, with its tragic and comic effects on people's lives. He shows dispassionate empathy for the good burgher who seeks forbidden love in the balcony of an old movie theater in the "Mysteries of the Joy Rio" (1941) and "Hard Candy" (1953); for the white-collar clerk who seeks pain, atone-

ment, and eventually death at the hands of a sadist in "Desire and the Black Masseur"; and for the brooding, self-tormenting writer, not so different from Williams himself, whose blocked sexuality is released by a Mexican girl he mistreats and neglects in "Rubio y Morena" (1948).

These stories are completely unforced in their treatment of the search of sex and its unpredictable consequences. Sometimes they grow more garish than realistic as they descend into the dark side of the psyche, with its self-destructive conflicts and guilt feelings. Moreover, Williams has a way of losing interest in his stories before he fully rounds them off. But "Two on a Party" (1951–52) is different, a wonderful sketch of the hustling life ("the party") that teams a gay man and a woman of easy virtue in a touching partnership that keeps loneliness at bay and becomes the closest thing to love they will ever know. Cruising together, remarkably tender toward each other, they find "spiritual comforts as well as material advantages in their double arrangement." Sometimes beaten up, often abused or disappointed by the men they pick up, chronically in need of money, they know they do not have much of a future, certainly not together. But they are willing to live for the moment, for luck and kicks, as long as the party lasts.

Without reaching for portentous significance, Williams has a warm feeling for these bruised and vulnerable lives. His characters, toughened by insecurity, mock the normal patterns of the straight world. Tennessee Williams's more lurid stories, taking flight into the grotesque, remind us of the often gauche symbolic intensities of the plays, but "Two on a

Party" offers another kind of poetry, full of wry and affecting details, and lit up by Williams's amused tolerance of these quirky but altogether human relationships.

Morris Dickstein

SELECTED BIBLIOGRAPHY

Works by Tennessee Williams

Memoirs. New York: Doubleday, 1975.
Collected Stories. New York: New Directions, 1985.

Critical and Biographical Studies

Leverich, Lyle. *Tom: The Unknown Tennessee Williams.* New York: Crown, 1995.
Stanton, Stephen S., ed. *Tennessee William: A Collection of Critical Essays.* Englewood Cliffs, N.J.: Prentice-Hall, 1977.
Williams, Dakin, and Shepherd Mead. *Tennessee Williams: An Intimate Biography.* New York: Crown, 1983.

WILLIAM CARLOS
WILLIAMS
(1883 – 1963)

Born on September 17, 1883, in Rutherford, New Jersey, William Carlos Williams was the oldest son of William and Raquel Hélène Rose Hoheb Williams.

Growing up in then rural northern New Jersey, Williams developed a profound sense of place, a knowledge of the spirit, the colors, sights, sounds, and smells of his home turf. His passion for literature was instilled in him early by his father's frequent reading, especially of Shakespeare, to William and his brothers. Williams's formal schooling involved a year in Europe with stints in a school in Geneva, Switzerland, and extensive travel in France, before he graduated without distinction from Horace Mann School in New York City. There, his teacher, "Uncle Billy Abbott," introduced Williams to the formal study of literature, and the aspiring writer balanced a high school career characterized by sports, literature, and ungratified lust. As Williams recounted his career decision in his *Autobiography,* "Words offered themselves, and I jumped at them. To write, like Shakespeare! And besides I wanted to tell people, to tell 'em off, plenty." Williams enrolled in the School of Dentistry, but quickly switched to the School of Medicine at the University of Pennsylvania, from which he graduated in 1906. During his years at Penn, he met and soon became friends with Ezra Pound, Hilda Doolittle, and other luminaries of high modernism. As Williams put it in his *Autobiography,* "I enjoyed the study of medicine, but found it impossible to confine myself to it. No sooner did I begin my studies than I wanted to quit them and devote myself to writing." Williams interned at French Hospital and at Child's Hospital, both in New York, before studying pediatrics in Leipzig. Spending the bulk of his life practicing medicine and writing poetry and fiction in Rutherford,

New Jersey, Williams died there on March 4, 1963.

Best known for his poetry, Williams produced also an important corpus of drama, nonfiction, and fiction, including his novelistic trilogy *White Mule, In the Money,* and *The Build-Up.* He wrote more than fifty short stories, mostly during the 1920s and 1930s, usually for little magazines such as *Blast* and the *Little Review.* Williams's stories are, in most respects, a fictional elaboration of the vision and the values around which his poetic work revolves. Above all, it is the shrewd, incisive, and gutsy perspective of Williams the physician that illuminates the work of his short fiction, much as it enlivens the magic moments of his verse. Courage, honesty, heart, stubborn self-sufficiency, fierce self-protection, openness to the worlds of wonder definitive of even the most impoverished economic circumstances: these constitute the world of Williams's short fiction, just as they are definitive of his characters' lives and ideals. As his narrator remarks of a sickly infant in "A Face of Stone," "he had a perfectly happy, fresh mug on him that amused me in spite of myself." Elsewhere, in "The Girl with a Pimply Face," he praises a young girl in charge of a house because "nobody was putting anything over on her if she knew it, yet the real thing about her was the complete lack of the rotten smell of a liar. She wasn't in the least presumptive. Just straight." The same could be said of virtually every praiseworthy character in the Williams canon. As in his poetry, Williams infuses his characters and his narratives with his own personal experiences, priorities, and values. His own "fresh mug," his "complete lack of the rotten smell of a liar" are the figures that form his signature on his short fiction, as on all his literary work.

Like William James in psychology, Williams struggles to recognize and incorporate the margins and the extremes of contemporary experience into the mainstream of American short fiction. And like William James, but like Sherwood Anderson and Ernest Hemingway too, Williams the doctor, the lover, the fully functioning human being is rarely very far from the characters, settings, and tensions of his fiction. According to J. E. Slate, Williams "was an esthetic revolutionary who never stopped thinking of himself as a dangerous outsider or—at the very least—a subversive agent. He usually wrote to attack academic assumptions about the short story and continually questioned the premises of successful fiction."

The range of Williams's short fiction will not surprise anyone familiar with his poetry or with his other prose works, such as *In the American Grain* and *A Voyage to Pagany.* Williams writes proletarian stories (both overtly and subliminally political), doctor stories, love stories (heterosexual and homosexual), biographies, portraits, conversations, stories about drug and alcohol addicts, about alternative sexual lifestyles, about children, about the aged and infirm, about the strong and the weak, the privileged and the oppressed. His stories are regional, to be sure, and most communicate the area around Rutherford, New Jersey in a nearly "local color" fashion, but they are also experimental in tone and style. Williams writes dialogue without the usual quotation markers and, at times, verges on the "free indirect discourse" characteristic of much modernist fictional experimentation. Williams's sense of an ending too partakes fully of modernist openness, often leading the reader up to an epiphany but stopping short of any full, closural containment of his narratives and their gritty details. In fact, Williams's reluctance to provide full coherence through his conclusions often mitigates the sentimentalism that some critics have located throughout his literary works.

Another facet of Williams's scope lies in his responsiveness to the racial and ethnic diversity of his characters. Not surprisingly, either for the poet who refused barriers or for the aspiring writer who wanted to "tell people off," Williams's stories are populated by a vast array of early twentieth-century figures. Polish immigrants struggle with English-language people in "Four Bottles of Beer." Two men discuss Native American construction workers and their high-altitude laboring virtuosity in "Above the River." Italian American parents struggling through the night delivery of their ninth child are the focus of "A Night in June." And the main players of "The Colored Girls of Passenack—Old and New" are announced unambiguously in that piece's title. "The Zoo" (1950) depicts a stocky young Finnish nanny, Elsa, wandering through the hideous spectacles of a zoo, while her young charge seems blithely content and unafraid of the threatening glares of the big cats. Williams's representation of various racial, ethnic, and immigrant peoples might not conform to the tastes and values

of contemporary readers, and his stories might strike some as still biased, even condescending, in their treatments of people of color and minority characters. However, Williams's own brand of political progressivism and his openness to the lives, the needs, the desires, and the importance of his ethnic and racial characters were certainly bold and daring for his own time. Careful, appreciative, and loving representations of immigrant and minority characters might not recognize the full dignity of their lives, but they surely broke with the exoticizing of racial and minority types that constituted much of what most other early twentieth-century writers had to offer.

From the beginning to the end of his short story writing career, Williams imagined the form in terms of conversation. In fact, when asked if he wrote "short stories on a different 'level' than the poems—as a kind of interlude to them," Williams responded: "No, as an alternative. They were written in the form of a conversation which I was partaking in." His dialogue is remarkable—full of the cadences, color, and often stuttering honesty of actual conversation. In one characteristic instance, "The Burden of Loveliness," an autobiographical sounding "Doc" has the following exchange with a gas station attendant:

Dance much, Sonny?
What's that, sir?
Do you take the girls out much to dances these fine October days?
No, *sir*. Not me, . . .
Why not?
Costs too much money.

Lots of pretty girls around nowadays would count it a treat to get their fingers in that curly hair of yours.

Perhaps because of his interest in the lives of those living on the margins of "proper" American society, Williams also wrote convincingly in their dialects. The substandard English spoken by his immigrant characters may not reach the heights of great dialogue writing, but their clipped, often ungrammatical utterances do convey much about their stations in and their struggles with life. It might be fair to say that Williams imagined the entire form of the short story to be a conversation, between the writer and his genre, his style, his character, or his scene, just as much as between one character and another.

"The Use of Force" (1938) is the most frequently anthologized of Williams's short works. One of his "doctor stories," this brief, unforgettable account of a little girl's refusal to open her mouth to a probing physician and thus to protect the secret of her diphtheria encapsulates many of Williams's themes, a strong and willful person defending the sanctity of her being against those who would intrude (even to help her), the weakness and sentimentality of the girl's parents, and the dogged determination of the physician, who knows that babying the child, giving in to her rage, might well cost her her life. After the child's mother chides her for not cooperating, Williams's doctor reflects that he "had already fallen in love with the savage brat, the parents were contemptible to me. In the ensuing struggle they grew more and more abject, crushed, exhausted while she surely rose to magnifi-

cent heights of insane fury of effort bred of her terror of me." In all such battles of Williamsian will, "force" must battle force, but when a life is on the line, nobody can afford to play games.

"The Sailor's Son" (1932) is one of Williams's most interesting early stories. "The Kid," Williams's "rebel without a cause" protagonist, spends most of his time leading a gang of urban motorcycle outlaws on their assaults on their city. The twist in this story, and one of the signs of Williams's aggressive acceptance and virtual endorsement of unconventional lives, so long as they are lived with gusto, is that "the Kid" punctuates his urban outlawry with occasional visits to his homosexual lover, Manuel, a laborer on a nearby farm. The outraged employer, Mrs. Cuthbertson, forbids the liaison but is shocked when Manuel's fiancée, Margy, arrives and explains that her lover's conduct neither bothers her nor jeopardizes her engagement with him. As in most of his short stories and all of the historical sketches that make up In the American Grain, Williams sides with force, energy, libido, rebellion, and human spirit, however bizarre and unconventional they may strike others.

Perhaps Williams was strongly motivated by his desire to "tell people off," but his resistant attitude was never divorced from compassion and honesty, albeit the compassion and honesty of a cultural and aesthetic iconoclast. The commitment Williams brings to his short fiction, like that which he brought to every dimension of his literary career, results in stories often as packed and allusive as his poems. As he put it in A Beginning on the Short Story (his only theoretical and practical discussion of short fiction), "the principal feature re. the short story is that it is short—and so must pack in what it has to say." As terse as Ernest Hemingway's and as fresh as Gertrude Stein's, William Carlos Williams's stories recapitulate much of the history of modernist prose fiction in the United States, and it is likely that his stature as a writer of short fiction will continue to grow.

Russell Reising

SELECTED BIBLIOGRAPHY

Works by William Carlos Williams

The Knife of the Times and Other Stories. Ithaca, N.Y.: Dragon Press, 1932.
Life Along the Passaic River. Norfolk, Conn.: New Directions, 1938.
Make Light of It: Collected Stories of William Carlos Williams. New York: Random House, 1950.
The Farmers' Daughters: The Collected Stories of William Carlos Williams. New York: New Directions, 1961.
A Beginning on the Short Story (Notes). Yonkers, N.Y.: The Alicat Bookshop Press, 1950.
The Doctor Stories. Compiled by Robert Coles. New York: New Directions, 1984.

Critical Studies

Derounian, Kathryn Zabelle. "William Carlos Williams." In Frank Magill, ed., *Critical Survey of Short Fiction,* vol. 6, pp. 2486–2491. Englewood Cliffs, N.J.: Salem Press, 1993.

Gish, Robert F. *William Carlos Williams: A Study of the Short Fiction.* Boston: Twayne, 1989.
Perloff, Marjorie. "The Man Who Loved Women: The Medical Fictions of William Carlos Williams." *Georgia Review* 4 (1980): 840–853.
Slate, J. E. "William Carlos Williams and the Modern Short Story." *Southern Review* 4 (1968): 647–664.

TOBIAS WOLFF
(1945–)

Tobias Jonathan Ansell Wolff was born on June 19, 1945, to Rosemary Loftus and Arthur Saunders "Duke" Wolff in Birmingham, Alabama. In 1949, Wolff's parents separated and Tobias moved with his mother to Washington State. Wolff began prep school at The Hill School in Pottstown, Pennsylvania, in 1961 but was expelled in 1963. Trained as a Green Beret and conversant in Vietnamese, Wolff served four years in the U.S. Army. In 1972, Wolff received a bachelor of arts degree from Oxford University in English language and literature.

Wolff married Catherine Dolores Spohn in 1975. Also that year, he took his master of arts degree from Oxford, and his first work of fiction, his only novel, *Ugly Rumours,* was published in England. For a brief time, Wolff served as a reporter for the *Washington Post.* Wolff received a Wallace Stegner Fellowship at Stanford University, where he met the short story writer Raymond Carver, with whom he would remain close friends until Carver's death. Wolff took a second masters degree from Stanford.

Wolff's first short story, "Smokers," was published in 1976 in the *Atlantic Monthly* magazine. In 1980, Wolff began teaching creative writing at Syracuse University, where he remained until 1997. A slow and methodical writer who admits to being his own harshest critic, Wolff's first short story collection appeared in 1981. *In the Garden of the North American Martyrs* met with widespread critical success. A novella, *The Barracks Thief,* appeared in 1984 and won the PEN/Faulkner Award. In 1985, Wolff published his second collection, *Back in the World.* A collection more pessimistic in tone and more oracular and parabolic in style, it met with less success than the first. Wolff published *This Boy's Life* in 1989. The protagonist serves as a thinly veiled study of Wolff's own childhood with his mother and step-father.

In 1994 Wolff continued his autobiography with *In Pharaoh's Army: Memories of the Lost War.* In this volume, the reader gains further insight into the fiction writer. *The Night in Question,* the third collection of short fiction, appeared in 1996 and is a continuation of many of the themes Wolff has explored in both his fiction and nonfiction. Wolff now teaches fiction writing at Stanford University.

Wolff's literary output has been recognized in many ways. Besides the PEN/Faulkner Award, he has won the Mary Roberts Rinehart Award, two National Endowment for the Arts Fellowships, a Guggenheim Fellowship, and a Whiting Foundation Writer's Award. Numerous

individual stories have appeared as prize-winners in various anthologies, *The O. Henry Awards, Best American Short Stories,* and *Pushcart Prize* among them. Wolff has edited *The Vintage Book of Contemporary American Short Stories, Matters of Life and Death: New American Short Stories, A Doctor's Visit: Short Stories by Anton Chekhov,* and a volume in the *Best American Short Stories* series.

Wolff is a modernist writer who eschews plot in favor of emphasis on character undergoing change. Along with the great figures of twentieth-century modernism—Joyce, Anderson, and Hemingway—Wolff has been influenced by Chekhov, widely regarded as the "Father of the Modern Short Story." Like Chekhov and other modernists, Wolff writes "middle-grounded" stories that eliminate the expansive exposition and definite closure of earlier and more traditional stories. Obeying the maxim of "show, don't tell," Wolff leaves much of the story for the reader's intuition.

Wolff belongs to the modern renaissance of the American short story, which began in the 1970s and continues today. This resurgence—which includes such short story writers as Raymond Carver, Ann Beattie, Andre Dubus, and Jayne Anne Phillips—rose to meet what they perceived as a challenge by postmoderns to the modernist rendering of story through mimetic, lifelike stories set in the real world and peopled by characters the readers would perceive as like themselves. Wolff has been further defined by some critics as a member of the "dirty realism" school, which includes Richard Ford, Raymond Carver, and others. Such writers often focus on blue-collar workers, criminals, alcoholics, or others on the fringes of society. Wolff has likened post-modern writers (Donald Barthelme, Robert Coover, and John Barth might serve as examples) to experimenters interested more in the experiment than in the fashioning of a readily comprehensible story.

Wolff's fiction is primarily realistic, engaged by the psychological dimensions of a protagonist's dilemmas, and concentrated upon small, individualistic moments of character change and development. Often understated, Wolff's narratives force the reader to become engaged in the collection of strands that will result in the full comprehension of a story. Besides the literary influences upon his work—the stories of Chekhov, Hemingway, and Cheever, for instance—there are other personal forces at work in Wolff's short fiction. Documented in his two autobiographical volumes, Wolff's fragmented childhood and his relationship with his father provided him with the desire to use his fiction to explore alienation, the nature of lying and make-believe, and the essential foundations of relationships: sons with fathers, husbands with wives, brothers with brothers (Geoffrey Wolff wrote of their father in *The Duke of Deception*). Wolff's Catholicism is another source that informs much of his work. Sometimes his seemingly mimetic stories become parablelike in nature—jeremiads that warn the audience of the corrosive tendencies of egotism, which fails to take into account our essential responsibilities and duties toward others weaker, more vulnerable in a materialistic and mean-spirited world. At these times, Wolff's simple, lucid prose takes on the voice of the oracle, of a biblical prophet attempting to forewarn the reader of worldly dangers. For Wolff, fiction becomes didactic, a teaching medium. Wolff believes that people can triumph over their situations through transformation. If the short story is, as some have maintained, a perfect form to explain the modern world through the illumination of a single character's predicament, then Wolff believes that such moments can redeem the wayward protagonist if only he or she can recognize the need to somehow destroy alienation through a renewed connection with others.

Finally, Wolff has been influenced by his service in Vietnam. Several stories—among them "Wingfield," "Soldier's Joy," and "Casualty"—focus on soldiers before, during, and after the Vietnam War. Some of the soldiers have given up their humanity for the security of the army, which supplies them with a simple, straightforward task—to kill the enemy, to obey the order—but has left them bereft of humanity. Others have sought to hide, maintaining their alienation from others. In these stories, Wolff deals with issues of community and conscience, with the rites of passage of the innocent, and with the corrosiveness of self-betrayal.

In "The Liar," the last story in *In the Garden of the North American Martyrs,* the protagonist is James, a first-person narrator who achieves an epiphany with delayed consequences. James's mother and father are antithetical in character. The father is much admired by the boy because of his witty cynicism, which, the reader understands, is actually masking fear of commitment. The father encourages his children's witty conversation at the dinner table. By contrast, the mother is at a loss during the tableside witticisms. A devout Catholic, she enjoys her faith through ritual observance and rote devotion. She does not consider cleverness a virtue, and she remains happily passive and contrite.

After the death of James's father, the boy develops into an habitual liar whose lies are filled with death and disease. The mother, who once tried to get her husband to forsake his egotism and put his energy into causes and activist groups, now tries to attract James to the same activities. Before she has envisioned her son singing in harmony in a choir—as someone who is part of something larger than himself. She thinks that such service to others would alleviate the withdrawn cynicism he has taken from his father.

The epiphany occurs when James considers his mother's attitude toward Francis, a woman at church who is always seeking his mother out to listen to her endless complaints. James has thought her paranoid, but he realizes that his mother, in listening to the woman, has shown more imagination than he. He understands that his mother can see things "coming together, not falling apart." For the moment, this epiphany remains an intellectual one, not from the heart. But when the bus that is taking him to visit his older brother breaks down, James's epiphany comes to emotional fruition. Asked by the passengers about himself, James begins by lying. However, the lies are not morbid. Instead, they tell of his service to foreigners lost and alone in this country. This cleverness seems born from those dinner-table competitions. But when asked to sing in a language he supposedly knows, James begins to sing to the audience in "tongues" foreign to them all but comprehensible and soothing to their hearts. The bus becomes a cathedral, and though James is singing solo and not harmony, the service done for others lifts him above self and cynicism.

"The Rich Brother," a much anthologized story, contains one of Wolff's most recurrent themes, the obligations of people to one another. By updating the biblical Cain and Abel parable, Wolff emphasizes the dictum that one is indeed his brother's keeper. Peter is the rich, successful brother, a California realtor whose materialism reflects his self-satisfaction. Donald, on the other hand, is a lost soul thrashing around in the spiritual milieu of the times. Whereas Pete is worldly-wise, Donald is inept. He reminds one, in some ways, of Prince Myshkin in Dostoyevsky's *The Idiot*.

The story begins with Pete once again traveling to rescue Donald. Uncomfortable in the splendor of Pete's new Mercedes—in which Donald has already spilled an orange soda—Donald, his hooded jogging suit fashioning him into a monk, admits his failure. As they talk of their past, Pete gradually reveals his long-held jealousy of the sickly brother who must have received much of their parents' attention. As in the parable, there seems to be a long-standing uneasiness between the two, which results from their inherently different character and habits. Pete feels that his sacrifices for Donald have gone unnoticed, while Donald, the more foolish and less adept, is somehow more blessed. Donald's life seems to adhere to some sort of natural rhythm. This harmony angers Peter, who sees himself as the constant mediator between the crass world and the naive Donald.

The story is complicated when the two pick up a hitchhiker who turns out to be a loquacious confidence man who fleeces Donald of the $100 Pete had given him earlier. When Pete awakes to find the man and the money gone, he explodes in fury, and Donald slowly comes to see how he has been taken advantage of. Suddenly, through this incident, Pete becomes aware of the irony in their relationship. He understands that if there is a blessing to be had then Donald, not he, would be the beneficiary. He is stung by the realization that his own skill within the world would somehow obviate his receiving such grace while Donald's very innocence would make him eligible.

Pete feels "a shadow move upon him, darkening his thoughts." But he does not yet reach for the stone; instead, he tells himself that his role is that of Donald's keeper. But when Pete tells Donald what he is thinking, Donald grows angry and asks to be let off. Pete angrily agrees but warns that this is the end of them.

Out by the car on the shoulder of the road, Pete is further enraged by Donald's saying that Pete is not to blame. And when Donald offers Pete his blessing, the brother drops on one knee, his hands seeking the murderous rock. But Donald's touch on the shoulder forces Pete to drive away without having hurled the stone. Pete tells himself that he is at liberty, free finally of Donald's presence. He plays a tape. He rehearses what he will tell his wife, when, like God in Genesis, she

asks the whereabouts of his brother. But Pete is not Cain; he has failed to murder, and now he cannot even maroon. Mumbling and still angry, almost without knowing it, he has begun to slow the car, looking for a place to turn around. He understands both the injustices in the world and his burdensome obligation. He is his brother's keeper.

Tobias Wolff has fashioned for himself a unique place in contemporary American fiction. His modernist tendencies are fused with an older, more oracular voice that travels beyond the description of a dilemma to the prescription for an ameliorative change. At those times, Wolff's suggested salvation is almost always the need to reconnect one human with others. In Wolff's fiction, to be human is to be humane.

James Hannah

SELECTED BIBLIOGRAPHY

Works by Tobias Wolff

In the Garden of the North American Martyrs. New York: Ecco Press, 1981.
Back in the World. Boston: Houghton Mifflin, 1985.
The Night in Question. New York: Alfred A. Knopf, 1996.

Critical Studies

Bailey, Peter J. "'Why Not Tell The Truth?': The Autobiographies of Three Fiction Writers." *Critique: Studies in Contemporary Fiction* 32/4 (summer 1991): 211–223.
Desmond, John F. "Catholicism in Contem-

porary American Fiction." *America,* May
14, 1994: 7–11.

Hannah, James. *Tobias Wolff: A Study of the
Short Fiction.* New York: Macmillan,
1996.

RICHARD WRIGHT
(1908–1960)

The publication of *Uncle Tom's Children*
in 1938 announced the advent of a
radical new voice in American literature.
Born in 1908 in Mississippi, Richard
Wright exemplified the militant spirit of
the African American left in the 1930s.
Wright explicitly acknowledged his own
combative spirit in his autobiography,
Black Boy (1945), which praises H. L.
Mencken for "fighting with words."
Richard Wright himself aspired to be
just such a literary warrior. He made this
intent apparent in the blunt, pugnacious
stories of *Uncle Tom's Children.* In ensuing
years, Wright's literary and intellectual
ambitions broadened, reflecting his serious engagement with works of modern
philosophy and literature. This growing
sophistication is clearly manifested in
Wright's short stories.

Due to his family's poverty and his
mother's chronic health problems, Richard's early life was marked by moves from
one relative's household to another. After
graduating from ninth grade in 1925,
Wright moved to Memphis and worked
there for two years, and in 1927 he moved
north to Chicago. There he became in-

volved with the John Reed Club, a cultural
organization associated with the Communist Party. This became a crucial experience for his literary development,
brining him into contact with many aspiring and established writers. He read
voraciously, honed his writing skills, and
began to publish in a number of periodicals
associated with the left. He soon joined
the Communist Party. He wrote his first
novel, *Lawd Today,* during this time, but it
was not published until 1963, after his
death. His first collection of stories, *Uncle
Tom's Children* (1938), was very successful,
and his novel *Native Son* (1940) made him
an international celebrity. In 1947,
Wright moved to Paris, where he was
quickly embraced by Jean-Paul Sartre,
André Malraux, and other writers associated with existentialism. During the
1950s Wright published an overtly philosophical novel, *The Outsider* (1953), that
clearly reflected the style and themes of
existentialism. Subsequently, he published a series of nonfiction books such as
White Man, Listen! that attack racism and
colonialism. He died suddenly in 1960.
Wright became the most famous and influential black fiction writer of his time.

The stories in *Uncle Tom's Children* depict black southerners struggling against
natural forces and the racist attitudes and
acts pervading their social environment.
These stories are cast in a naturalist mode,
strongly reminiscent of Theodore Dreiser's work. The lives of Wright's characters seem wholly determined by natural
and social forces, and a heavy sense of fate
hangs over the stories, moving the characters inexorably toward confrontations
that in most cases eventually destroy them.
Often at issue in these stories too is the

question of black manhood, a concept that seems to be an oxymoron in the violently white supremacist world that Wright describes. In his essay "The Ethics of Living Jim Crow," Wright refers to his various shocking encounters with aggressive racial bigotry as installments in "my Jim Crow education." The central lesson of that education is that he must defer to white people, accept his emasculating position as an inferior, and be glad that whites have only abused rather than killed him.

Despite their harshness, these stories attracted much acclaim when they were published. They were positively reviewed by magazines such as *The Nation,* and even Eleanor Roosevelt praised the collection in her newspaper column. *Uncle Tom's Children* became a book club selection, and it led to Wright's winning a Guggenheim fellowship in 1939. The original 1938 edition consisted of four stories: "Big Boy Leaves Home," "Down by the Riverside," "Long Black Song," and "Fire and Cloud." When Harper & Brothers decided to publish a hardcover edition of this collection in 1940, Wright added "The Ethics of Living Jim Crow" as an introduction and a fifth story, "Bright and Morning Star." *Uncle Tom's Children* is best known in this expanded configuration.

"Big Boy Leaves Home" became the most notorious of Wright's stories. It begins with a group of four black Mississippi boys, rowdy but innocent, skinny-dipping on the property of a white neighbor. A young white woman stumbles upon them and screams in alarm. As the boys try to flee, the woman's fiancé dashes up with a gun to her "rescue." He shoots two of the boys and takes aim at a third, Bobo, who

pleads for his life. At this point Big Boy, the most robust of the group, tussles with the man and wrests the gun from him. When the man ignores Big Boy's warning and attempts to seize the gun, Big Boy shoots him and flees with Bobo. The boys' parents understand immediately that a lynch mob will soon follow, and they arrange for the two boys to meet a truck bound for Chicago the following morning. Meanwhile, the boys must hide. In the course of the night, the mob captures Bobo, but Big Boy, after killing a huge rattlesnake and strangling a hound with his bare hands, manages to elude them. He meets the truck, and the story ends with him falling asleep inside its dark trailer.

Sleep carries a strong symbolic charge in Wright's work, and it might be debated whether Big Boy's concluding slumber represents the gestation of manhood, the death of childhood, or more simply, a well-earned unsymbolic rest after heroic labors. Wright continued more systematically to explore the symbolic resonances of sleep in his novel *Native Son,* published in the same year as the expanded edition of *Uncle Tom's Children.* Many of the themes introduced in "Big Boy Leaves Home" are repeated and elaborated in the four subsequent stories. All of them deal with the struggle against racism as a matter of life and death, and most of them consider gender conflict or the taboo against interracial sexual attraction. All of them depict characters trapped in highly deterministic circumstances, struggling to survive against overwhelming odds. Big Boy is quite unusual in his success against the odds.

In the second story, "Down by the Riverside," the protagonist Mann faces the rising floodwaters of the Mississippi and his wife in labor. He steals a boat from some white neighbors in order to escape the flood and find medical help for his wife, but his wife dies and he cannot escape the vengeful white people who are determined to punish his theft. He kills a white man and is eventually shot in the back by soldiers. The story concludes with his corpse's being shoved into a ravine. "It rolled heavily down the wet slope and stopped about a foot from the water's edge; one black sprawled limply outward and upward, trailing in the brown current. . . . " Social and natural forces have combined to ensure Mann's destruction.

"Long Black Song" has a female protagonist, Sarah. Like Wright's male protagonists, she is a victim of forces beyond her control, and in addition, she is afflicted with isolation and loneliness. Her memories of a departed suitor arouse the sadness of missed opportunity, and Silas, the man she married, pays her little attention as he labors obsessively at farm work to earn a scant living for the two of them. A white traveling salesman, taking advantage of her isolation and naïveté, rapes her; and when Silas learns what has happened, he kills the man. The inevitable lynch mob soon arrives, and Sarah escapes with her daughter as Silas barricades himself for a futile showdown against them. Fatalistically, Silas tries to kill as many of his assailants as possible before he perishes in the house, which they have set afire. For the black woman as well as the black man, defeat and destruction are unavoidable.

"Fire and Cloud" is the most optimistic of these stories, and it is also the most nuanced. The protagonist, Reverend Taylor, is, like Wright's other protagonists, a man trapped in the middle. Unlike most of Wright's other protagonists, however, Taylor faces a dilemma of choice and not an absence of choices. He is caught in a public role in the midst of political struggle, not isolated in a personal battle for survival. The crisis of "Fire and Cloud" reflects directly the hardships of the Depression era. Crops have failed, there are no jobs, and people are desperate. The black community wants Taylor to lead a protest and the white politicians want him to squelch it. Communist organizers prod him to take a radical stance, and a reactionary faction among his board of deacons conspires to betray him to the white people as a Communist sympathizer if he decides to take action on behalf of his people. Marxist social analysis competes with his religious beliefs as he struggles to decide what to do. In the end, Taylor decides that militancy is the true path of social conscience, and he leads a march. Though the ultimate result is left unresolved—an atypical ambiguity for Wright—there is a powerful sense of moral resolution at the conclusion: "A baptism of clean joy swept over Taylor. He kept his eyes on the sea of black and white faces. The song swelled louder and vibrated through him. This is the way! he thought. Gawd ain no lie! He ain no lie! His eyes grew wet with tears, blurring his vision: the sky trembled; the buildings wavered as if about to toppled; and the earth shook. . . . He mumbled out loud, exultingly: '*Freedom belongs to the strong!*'"

The story, the original conclusion of

the collection, reveals a growth of sophistication in Wright as a fiction writer. In it, he explores a situation defined by multiple determinants but does not reduce it to a predictable and mechanical determinism. By leaving room for Taylor to make real choices, Wright allows the story to have greater moral complexity.

Moral complexity was not a priority for Wright's Communist Party comrades. Though pleased to have a black comrade gain such a high profile, they were certainly not pleased by this conclusion to the book, with a preacher as protagonist, an apparent affirmation of religious faith, and a less than flattering depiction of the Communist organizers. Wright's differences with the party would soon result in his exit. At this moment, however, he did incorporate a new story to end the collection, a story that adheres more closely to the party's views of working-class heroism. "Bright and Morning Star" has a female protagonist, an older woman of exemplary courage who stands up to a racist sheriff and his posse, killing one of them before she herself is gunned down. The story combines elements of "Long Black Song" and "Fire and Cloud." Indeed, its conclusion appears to be a less explicitly religious rewrite of the previous story's conclusion: "Focused and pointed she was, buried in the depths of her star, swallowed in its peace and strength; and not feeling her flesh growing cold, cold as the rain that fell from the invisible sky upon the doomed living and the dead that never dies." "Bright and Morning Star" is more flattering to Communists, but it is not so sophisticated and compelling as "Fire and Cloud."

While *Uncle Tom's Children* is, appropriately, an acknowledged classic of American literature, Wright's second collection of stories, *Eight Men,* is virtually unknown. Since its publication in 1961 it has been out of print more often than not. Admittedly, the stories of *Eight Men* are not so closely unified in style and theme as the stories of *Uncle Tom's Children*. In fact, the transparent attempt to link them by using the word "man" in each of the eight titles accentuates the discontinuities it intends to elide. *Eight Men* is more properly understood as a miscellaneous collection of stories written over the course of more than twenty years. They vary in style and substance, not having been written for a single book. Nevertheless, *Eight Men* contains some of Wright's finest writing.

Eight Men is also very revealing about Wright's development as a literary artist. Some of the stories represent alternative versions of episodes or ideas that appear in his other works. For example, "The Man Who Saw the Flood" is an earlier and much less complicated story based on the same flood and situation examined in "Down by the Riverside." "The Man Who Killed a Shadow" closely resembles the killing of Mary Dalton in *Native Son*. In both cases, comparing the two stories allows an insight into the author's procedures and decisions as a literary craftsman that most often can only be gleaned from the study of manuscripts. By contrast, "The Man Who Went to Chicago" is a finished version of material that appears essentially unchanged in Wright's *American Hunger,* the second volume of his autobiography.

More important, the stories in *Eight*

Men reveal aspects of Wright's art that are not readily apparent in his better-known works, such as *Native Son, Uncle Tom's Children,* and *Black Boy.* In particular, several of these stories exhibit humor, nuance, and lightness of touch that most readers would not associate with Richard Wright. The opening story, "The Man Who Was Almost a Man," is an example. It begins by introducing Dave, the seventeen-year-old protagonist, who has become obsessed with the notion that owning a gun would bring him manhood that he has failed to achieve on his own merits. He thinks, after a day of plowing, "Shucks, a man oughta have a little gun aftah he done worked hard all day." Dave soon buys an old revolver for two dollars; then, on his first shot, he kills his employer's mule. To escape the whipping his father promises him, Dave hops a train for Chicago, "where he could be a man." A comic version of "Big Boy Leaves Home," this story mocks Dave's immaturity. The interactions between the white and black characters do not suggest racism, and except for the shooting of the mule, the story avoids both violence and the tense, desperate atmosphere that dominates much of Wright's fiction.

"The Man Who Lived Underground" is arguably Wright's finest short story. Given its length, fifty-two pages of the text, it might more properly be described as a novella. First published in 1944, this story gestures explicitly toward Dostoevsky's *Notes from Underground,* and it also indicates Wright's growing engagement with existentialist philosophy. His next novel, *The Outsider* (1953), manifests that development fully. Unlike this heavy, gray, and pedantic novel, its precursor, "The Man Who Lived Underground" is playful and inventive, despite its somber themes. Though the story explores Wright's familiar preoccupations—murder, racism, persecution, and violence—it also unfolds in a spirit of wonderment. The unnamed protagonist, fleeing police, drops through a manhole and enters a dark subterranean labyrinth that allows him to view the outside world unobserved. Through his eyes, our familiar world, represented in various buildings he enters, appears surreal. This story is pivotal in Wright's literary evolution, and it is an obvious precursor to Ralph Ellison's *Invisible Man* as well.

Perhaps most surprising of all is "Big Black Good Man," a story set in a Danish hotel with its night manager, Olaf, as its protagonist. Olaf is a nondescript, middle-aged fellow who suddenly encounters a huge, loud, insistent black American demanding a room. Olaf is instantly overwhelmed by fear, which manifests itself as racism. Over the course of the story, he fluctuates between chagrin and terror, dismayed by his bigoted reaction yet viscerally awed by the intimidating black giant. Published in 1957, this late story indicates how Wright might have evolved had he not died prematurely three years later. The black man turns out to be a gentle giant, and, despite some misleading hints, the story never erupts into the violence one expects from Wright's fiction. Most surprising of all, Wright handles Olaf with restraint, subtlety, and a touch of humor. It is a remarkable story, but so different from readers' expectations of Wright that it may never gain the wide audience it deserves.

Richard Wright's primary reputation is appropriately as a novelist. Nonetheless, his best short stories are classics of the genre, and several of his finest stories have yet to gain the audience they deserve. Wright became furious as the articulate voice of African American anger, protesting the racist strictures that truncate the options and the lives of black people. It is profoundly ironic, then, that so many readers have ignored his many works that move beyond the narrow limits of racial anger and racial conflict. His short stories offer a broad representation of Wright's multifaceted art.

David Lionel Smith

SELECTED BIBLIOGRAPHY

Works by Richard Wright

Uncle Tom's Children. New York: Harper & Bros., 1938. Reprint, New York: Harper Perennial, 1993.
Eight Men. Cleveland: World Publishing, 1961.

Critical Studies

Fabre, Michel. The Unfinished Quest of Richard Wright. Urbana: University of Illinois Press, 1973.
Gibson, Donald B. The Politics of Literary Expression: Essays on Major Black Writers. Westport, Conn.: Greenwood, 1981.
Hakutani, Yoshinobu. Critical Essays on Richard Wright. Boston: G. K. Hall, 1982.
Kinnamon, Keneth. The Emergence of Richard Wright: A Study in Literature and Society. Urbana: University of Illinois Press, 1972.

HISAYE YAMAMOTO
(1921–)

Hisaye Yamamoto, along with Toshio Mori, was one of the first Japanese American writers to gain national recognition after World War II. Her stories, some of which were included in Martha Foley's Best American Short Stories of 1949, 1951, 1952, and 1960, delineate with great sensitivity and complexity a variety of Japanese American experiences before and after the war, often from a woman's perspective. In 1988 they were collected in a single volume, Seventeen Syllables and Other Stories.

Hisaye Yamamoto was born in Redondo Beach, California, in 1921. She began to write as a teenager, receiving her first rejection slip at age fourteen and her first acceptance by a literary magazine at age twenty-seven. During World War II, she was interned at the relocation camp in Poston, Arizona, where she wrote for the camp newspaper, the Poston Chronicle, and befriended Wakako Yamauchi, a painter and writer of short fiction and drama. From 1945 to 1948 Yamamoto worked for the Los Angeles Tribune, a weekly newspaper. In 1950, a John Hay Whitney Foundation Fellowship enabled her to write full-time for a year. From 1953 to 1955, she lived and worked with her adopted son Paul in a Catholic Worker rehabilitation farm on Staten Island. She is now married and lives in Los Angeles. The author of short stories considered classics of Asian American literature, Yamamoto now lists her occupation as "housewife."

Many stories in her collection *Seventeen Syllables and Other Stories* are characterized by irony, emotional restraint, unreliable narrators, and narrative indirection. Often the narration proceeds along one line that seems central but is actually tangential, while a seemingly tangential story line is the narrative's real emotional center. Readers thus have the sense of viewing a subject askance, as though that subject were too emotionally charged to be looked at directly. The result is a heightened effect of tragedy, chaos, and disorder, all while the narration proceeds along ordinary, mundane lines. The tension between the explicit and implicit narratives creates work of extraordinary complexity, depth, and power. "Seventeen Syllables," "Yoneko's Earthquake," and "The Legend of Miss Sasagawara" are examples of this narrative technique.

In "Seventeen Syllables," while the adolescent narrator, Rosie Hayashi, is preoccupied with her own growing discovery of sexuality, the story's emotional power lies in the tension between her mother's preoccupation with writing haiku and her father's brutal repression of his wife's artistic strivings. Each member of this small family is on a different trajectory in life. Rosie, a high school sophomore, has just discovered "the helplessness delectable beyond speech" when she receives her first kiss, to which she can only think to say "yes and no and oh." Rosie's mother begs her daughter to promise never to marry, for she wants to protect her child against the smothering of spirit she had experienced. Having been deceived in love and settling for an arranged marriage instead of committing suicide, she has had her artistic dreams and impulses brutally shat-

tered by her husband. Rosie's father, driven by the demands of ripe tomatoes and the necessity of making a living for the family, and seeing the haiku as a wedge between himself and his wife, takes action in the first way that occurs to him, to protect and claim what is his. Yamamoto has compassion for them all; it is no one's fault that their separate trajectories led them to conflict. Each person's motives are understandable; no one is unreasonably cruel, and yet they intersect only to cause each other pain.

In "Yoneko's Earthquake," another unreliable narrator, a ten-year-old girl, tells of her loss of faith in God when, frightened by an earthquake, she prays God to stop it, but her prayers are not answered and she concludes that God does not exist. Again, the emotional heart of the narrative—the real earthquake—lies in the relationships among the adults: Yoneko's mother and father, and Marpo, the Filipino hired hand and a man of many talents. The three adults are involved in a tragic adulterous triangle which the child Yoneko cannot understand, but about which she provides hints for the careful reader.

"The Legend of Miss Sasagawara" is also narrated by a peripheral character, a kind of Greek chorus commenting on and speculating about the central character, the beautiful, sensitive, and mysterious Miss Sasagawara, whom we see only in bits and pieces as though through tiny holes in a heavy curtain. The dramatic conflicts and tension of the story occur offstage, as it were, within the psyche of the former ballet dancer, to which we are not privy. While Kiku's narrative makes the incarceration of fifteen thousand Japanese

Americans in Poston, Arizona, seem an ordinary, everyday fact of life, Miss Sasagawara's behavior reveals that imprisonment and isolation are horrors. The story questions the very notion of madness. Who is madder? Those, like Kiku and Elsie, who take the incarceration in stride, who accept imprisonment because of their race, who gratefully work full-time for $19 a month; or Miss Sasagawara, who cannot reconcile herself to this humiliation? Because Miss Sasagawara refuses to conform to life in the camps, because she is starved for love, she is institutionalized as insane.

As Dorothy Ritsuko McDonald and Katharine Newman have astutely observed, "All those who seek but lose are of interest to Yamamoto." This interest in conventionally defined "losers" appears particularly in the stories that make up the last third of *Seventeen Syllables*. In "Epithalamium," a plain but respectable Japanese American woman, Yuki Tsumagari, falls in love with an alcoholic Italian American. Yuki feels her "bowels as molten wax" at the "mere thought of Marco," and he, "the type . . . who should have been driving a Cadillac convertible . . . [with] some golden-haired goddess by his side," feels that she had "a rope tied around [his] neck that won't let go." They meet in a kind of halfway house, where she is a volunteer and he is one of the loser types who "came because they had nowhere else to go— the alcoholics, the laicized priests, the mentally disturbed, the physically handicapped, the unwed mothers, the rejected Trappists, the senile, the offscouring of the world." With this marriage, is Yuki willingly entering martyrdom or sainthood? Another woman who married an alcoholic from this community, now mother of his seven children and the sole support of the family, asks plaintively, "If I don't love him, who will?" The question seems also to be Yuki's. "Epithalamium" is thus an ironic title, for the story is not a hymn in celebration of marriage but an exploration of the inexplicability of love.

"The Brown House" tells of a long-suffering wife, but the blame for the family's poverty and the father's gambling addiction seems to fall on circumstances rather than on the individual. In "Las Vegas Charley," Yamamoto focuses on the failed man, presenting his life in sympathetic detail, fully believing Charley, a dishwasher, broke and out of work, to be deserving of interest and compassion. Three other stories in the last third of the collection, "The Eskimo Connection," "Underground Lady," and "Reading and Writing," bring together unlikely pairings between the narrators and different "offscouring of the world." In "The Eskimo Connection," a grandmotherly Japanese American woman writer receives a fan letter from a reader and admirer of her poetry, a twenty-three-year-old Eskimo in prison. She is quiet, retiring, modest, self-effacing, yet highly skilled in writing. He is outgoing, religious, bold, determined, energetic, exuberant, and ambitious; what his writing lacks in discipline he makes up for in enthusiasm. They are an odd pairing, and yet a relationship develops between them. In "Underground Lady," the middle-class Japanese American narrator, waiting for her husband to pick her up from the grocery store, strikes up an amiable conversation with a Caucasian bag lady, homeless among her Japanese former neighbors. The "bag lady's" lack of rancor and bitterness soon creates a sense of guilt in the narrator for having too much: a full grocery cart, an intact home, even cigarettes and a lighter.

In "Reading and Writing," an unlikely friendship develops between a writer and an illiterate. The writer has a "passion for Scrabble and addiction to word puzzles," while the illiterate must use different-colored caps to identify her medicines and vitamins. In this story, Yamamoto surprises the reader by inverting the usual power differential between racial minority immigrant and dominant WASP, for the writer is Kazuko, the daughter of Japanese immigrants, while the illiterate is Hallie, a beautiful, thrice-married Caucasian woman, whose ancestors arrived soon after the Mayflower.

"Life Among the Oil Fields: A Memoir" is Yamamoto's most explicit protest against a careless kind of racism linked with class callousness. In this memoir, Yamamoto has fond childhood memories of a home in the midst of oil rigs, which, with adult hindsight, she realizes was hardly a desirable location. When a rich couple runs down her little brother and refuses any responsibility, her parents are angry but powerless. The Japanese lawyer they hire is totally ineffectual, so that "the helpless anger of my father and my mother is my inheritance." Yamamoto contrasts two ways of dealing with the world, two personality types: the selfishly aggressive and the meekly unassertive. The narrator clearly belongs in the latter group. In seeing this arrogant couple as "young and beautiful . . . their open roadster as definitely and stunningly red . . . their tinkling laughter, like a long silken scarf . . . borne back by the wind," Yamamoto admits to

a double consciousness about them. Through her mainstream education, the author has been taught to admire this type, reminiscent of F. Scott Fitzgerald, whom she quotes in the epigraph, as glamorous personifications of an age, the epitome of the beautiful, the talented, rich, and famous, as stars in the firmament to be envied by the ordinary person on the street. Perhaps those who have been trampled by the wayside, like poor Myrtle, the mistress in The Great Gatsby, were trashy and inferior to begin with: lower-class and therefore expendable. However, the little brother who was run over without a twinge was innocent. In an unusually pointed sentence, its anger softened only slightly by its interrogation point, Yamamoto asks, "Were we Japanese in a category with animals then, to be run over and left beside the road to die?"

The World War II–era incarceration of 110,000 people of Japanese ancestry, most of whom were American citizens, in makeshift camps in desert locations, is the central trauma of Japanese American history. Because none of the incarcerated people were ever found guilty of sabotage, Yamamoto's question, "Were we Japanese in a category with animals then," alludes obliquely to the injustice and inhumanity of this incarceration. Because of her own trauma of imprisonment as an adolescent, Yamamoto takes a particularly sympathetic stance toward others whom society has cast aside as "undesirables." With her keen, nonjudgmental eye and her large compassion for all of human variety, Yamamoto forces her reader to reconsider such categories as sanity and insanity, good and evil, weakness and strength, value and worthlessness. She shines her light on the underdog, the powerless, and finds them beautiful and courageous in their ability to endure. Her stories ask us to stop judging such people negatively, and to extend to them our sympathy, patience, and understanding. Using understatement, emotional restraint, condensation, and indirection, Yamamoto's stories show us the arbitrariness of racial, sexual, and class divisions and hierarchies, and challenge us to expand our capacity for love.

Amy Ling

SELECTED BIBLIOGRAPHY

Works by Hisaye Yamamoto

Seventeen Syllables and Other Stories. Berkeley: Women of Color Press, 1988.

Critical Studies

Cheung, King-Kok. *Articulate Silences: Hisaye Yamamoto, Joy Kogawa, Maxine Hong Kingston.* Ithaca, N.Y.: Cornell University Press, 1993.

McDonald, Dorothy Ritsuko and Katharine Newman. "Relocation and Dislocation: The Writings of Hisaye Yamamoto and Wakako Yamauchi." *MELUS* 7/3 (1980): 21–38.

Sugiyama, Naoko. "Issei Mothers' Silence, Nisei Daughters' Stories: The Short Fiction of Hisaye Yamamoto." *Comparative Literature Studies* 33/1 (1996): 1–14.

Yogi, Stan. "Rebels and Heroines: Subversive Narratives in the Stories of Wakako Yamauchi and Hisaye Yamamoto." In Shirley Geok-lin Lim and Amy Ling, eds., *Reading the Literature of Asian America,* pp. 137–163. Philadelphia: Temple University Press, 1992.

ANZIA YEZIERSKA
(1881 – 1970)

As a child of perhaps eight or nine, Anzia Yezierska joined the throng of Jewish emigrants fleeing religious persecution in Eastern Europe. With her family, she left the small shtetl of Plinsk, arriving in New York probably around 1890. The difficult early years, the smells and sounds of the Lower East Side where she lived, poverty and its lasting effects on family relationships and friendships—these became the enduring topics of Anzia Yezierska's work. But its themes were much broader, touching on such huge issues as the meaning of America, the democracy it promised, and the terrible loneliness awaiting those who tried to achieve the American dream.

Yezierska replayed her biography many times over, selecting aspects of it to illuminate in her stories and novels. She was born of a poor family, driven out of Polish Russia when the tiny religious school operated by her schoolteacher father was destroyed by Cossacks. Her parents, six of their seven children in tow, arrived in Castle Garden, where they were met by the oldest son, who had preceded them. Like generations of Jewish immigrants who would follow, the teenage children worked in the sweatshops of the garment industry, attended school whenever they could, and earned their educations while contributing to their family's support. Anzia was no exception. As a young teenager, she worked at the sewing machine, then in laundries, and as a janitress, struggling to earn enough to support herself while she made her way through high school to a degree in home economics at Columbia University Teachers' College. She was probably twenty-four when she earned the degree in 1904. But she had only contempt for her field and disliked the teaching career that then opened to her. Still, she worked at it sporadically, married briefly, then divorced and married again. In 1912 she gave birth to her only child, Louise. Three years later, she separated from her second husband. The child would grow up with her father and grandmother.

By the time Louise was born, Yezierska had set her heart on becoming a writer and had already begun a lifelong struggle to produce the stories that would become the hallmark of her success. It was the second decade of the century, and while she did not participate in the growing campaign for women's suffrage, Yezierska was fully aware of the new lifestyles rapidly opening to women. Like other brave women of her generation, Yezierska rejected a conventional marriage and a traditional role to follow her own path. She benefited as well from her immigrant community's approaching maturity. Influenced by socialist friends and a rich cultural milieu, she vigorously refused to succumb to the meanness of poverty. At the same time, she believed that material success could numb the soul. Yezierska thought she could avoid that pitfall by writing fiction that, in her words, gave

"something back to America." In her mind and in her stories, immigrants were "the promise of the centuries to come . . . the heart, the creative pulse of America to be." She would be their voice.

Yezierska published her first story in 1915. Others followed with anguished slowness. In 1919 she won the coveted Edward J. O'Brien award for the best short story of the year. The following year her most popular collection of stories, *Hungry Hearts,* appeared, and after that the books came in quick succession: four novels and one more collection of stories, all published before 1932. Thereafter, she turned to reviews and stories, struggling to alter her themes and without great success.

At the core of Yezierska's work lies the continuing drama of the immigrant experience, especially for Jews and for women. Written in a deliberately adopted and powerfully rendered Yiddish idiom, the stories skillfully capture the sordid poverty of immigrant life even as they magically evoke the warm generosity that sustains community. Critics have described the language as crude, the spirit as overwrought, and the themes as sentimental. But the stories also capture the human spirit's unquenchable search for beauty, for poetry, and for creativity.

Three large themes dominate in Yezierska's work. The first is the play of a mythological America against the debilitating poverty with which immigrants struggled. "How I Found America," for example, begins with a letter from a recent immigrant sent to his wife in the old country. There, Gedalyah Mindel fosters dreams of emigration by announcing that in America even poor people have doors they can close, and each man who becomes a citizen "will have as much to say who shall be the next President in America as Mr. Rockefeller, the greatest millionaire." Inspired, the family of the nameless narrator sells its possessions to scrape together the money for passage, only to arrive in the promised land to face the specter of making a living. Her father retreats into prayer as the teenaged narrator becomes the family breadwinner. She loses one factory job and then another for daring to believe that even a poor worker can tell a boss that he is committing an injustice. As she tumbles into illness and despair, our protagonist recalls the promise of America and determines that her American dream will not be undermined by a hungry stomach. She enrolls in night school, finds a sympathetic teacher to lead her through the maze, and eventually reaps the rich rewards of believing that she is released from class barriers. She leaves the classroom filled with hope that through her "inarticulate groping and reaching out I had found the soul—the spirit—of America."

Embedded in the story are several challenges to America's image of itself. Yezierska repudiates wage labor as the path to the American dream—defining it in far broader terms than the economic security for which most people settle. In a theme that repeats itself in much of her fiction, she offers a radical critique of class privilege, suggesting that by stifling the souls of the poor, the trappings of class inhibit their dreams and therefore act as barriers to democracy. Yet Yezierska is convinced that ultimately, the human spirit and democracy will prevail.

A second theme blends the flowering of freedom and opportunity for women in the 1920s with the opening of immigrant life. Sophie Sapinsky, protagonist of "To the Stars," wants to be a writer. Seeking help from a venerable academic institution, she is abruptly turned away: she lacks the credentials for admission and the appearance and clothes as well. In the face of closed doors, a kind look from the college's distinguished president emboldens her to keep struggling. Fiercely, she determines to follow what she thinks of as the dicta of Emerson. "Trust yourself. Hold on to the thoughts that fly through your head, and the world has got to listen to you even if you're a nobody." She quits her job as a cook, and, hoarding her last few dollars, devotes herself to writing what is in her heart. When she wins a prestigious short story competition, she is vindicated—those who had refused her help now flock to her side.

As in many of Yezierska's stories, success is crafted from a combination of faith in oneself and luck, which often adopts the guise of a handsome and sympathetic American-born male. At first bewildered by becoming a heroine, Sophie soon finds that her own dream draws sustenance from such a man, and simultaneously inspires others. She is the new immigrant woman at her best: assertive and self-directed. But the immigrant fears the lure of material rewards aware that they might stifle her; and the woman resists the comforts of family life that threaten to deprive her of precious time she will require to achieve her goals. Sophie escapes unscathed, but, typically, Yezierska's aspiring woman writer pays heavily for her efforts, the price ranging from loss of family in "Children of Loneliness" to isolation in "Soap and Water"—and, in "Wild Winter Love," to suicide.

Inevitably the search for identity lies at the core of women's goals, measured in Yezierska's stories by a continuing struggle to determine where the immigrant belongs. "Children of Loneliness" offers the most direct statement of this theme. Ruth, the child of immigrants, graduates from college and returns to live with her parents on the Lower East Side. But the warmth and love that had nurtured her as a child now smother her. She finds her father's religious exercise primitive, her parents' manners uncouth, their food foul-smelling. Angrily, Ruth rejects their comforts for a room of her own. But the new world is cold and unwelcoming. When she turns to a college friend for solace, she is astonished to discover his romantic vision of "her people." Torn between two worlds and unable to live in either, Ruth painfully submits to the marginal sphere that she expects will be her lot in life.

Here, as in other stories, Yezierska provides her protagonist with the satisfaction of achieving the upward mobility to which she aspires. Her heroines (and an occasional hero) graduate from college and become well-known songwriters or achieve financial heights undreamed of in the ghetto. But success turns to dust and ashes as the immigrant loses contact with the energy and life that gave her breath, and she discovers that she can neither return to the past nor construct a future that is free of it. Yezierska offers no answer to this dilemma. Rather, her stories elucidate the pain of a shared process, providing balm for the continuing predicament of every immigrant child. In "'The Tax of the Land,'" Hannah Breineh is a long-suffering mother who curses her fate at not being able to fill her small children's hungry stomachs; but later on, she cannot abide the opulent sterility in which, once they are grown, her children want to ensconce her. In "Brothers," Moishe, a hard-working tailor, sacrifices body and soul to bring his family from the old country only to discover that they betray him willingly to the dream of wealth. A dozen Sophies who aspire to beauty people Yezierska's tales. Each finds spiritual awakening in the poverty she wants to reject and is ultimately destined to write about ("Wings," "Hunger").

Toward the end of the author's life, these themes and characters altered a bit. Yezierska's later female protagonists are older, their memories of immigrant life more romantic, and their struggle for prosperity sometimes achieved. But for those who chased the almighty dollar, as in "A Chair in Heaven," satisfaction remains elusive. And for those who pursued their poetic dreams, as in "One Thousand Pages of Research," the price of alienation still remained to be paid. In her old age Anzia Yezierska continued to deplore the spiritual emptiness of comfortable rooms compared to the richness of the soul that accompanied poverty ("The Open Cage"). If her forceful convictions limited her range as a writer and account for her evanescent popularity, they also provided her with exactly what she wanted: to speak clearly and powerfully on behalf of the immigrant community with which she was never reconciled.

Alice Kessler-Harris

SELECTED BIBLIOGRAPHY

Works by Anzia Yezierska

Hungry Hearts. Boston: Houghton Mifflin, 1920. Reprint, with an introduction by Blanche H. Gelfant, New York: Penguin, 1995.

Children of Loneliness: Stories of Immigrant Life in America. New York: Funk and Wagnalls, 1923.

Bread Givers. Introduction by Alice Kessler-Harris. New York: Persea, 1975.

How I Found America. New York: Persea, 1991.

Critical Studies

Gelfant, Blanche H. "The Jewish Landlady in Anzia Yezierska's Unwritten Novel." In Ben Siegel and Jay Halio, eds., *American Literary Dimensions: Poems and Essays in Honor of Melvin J. Friedman,* pp. 39–64. Newark: University of Delaware Press, 1999.

Golub, Ellen. "Eat Your Heart Out: The Fiction of Anzia Yezierska." *Studies in American Jewish Literature* (1983): 51–61.

Kamel, Rose. "'Anzia Yezierska, Get out of Your Own Way': Selfhood and Otherness in the Autobiographical Fiction of Anzia Yezierska." *Studies in American Jewish Literature* (1983): 40–50.

INDEX